# 2021
# PUSHCART PRIZE XLV
# BEST OF THE
# SMALL PRESSES

## EDITED BY BILL HENDERSON
### WITH THE PUSHCART PRIZE EDITORS

Note: nominations for this series are invited from any small, independent, literary book press or magazine in the world, print or online. Up to six nominations—tear sheets or copies, selected from work published, or about to be published, in the calendar year—are accepted by our December 1 deadline each year. Write to Pushcart Fellowships, P.O. Box 380, Wainscott, N.Y. 11975 for more information or consult our website www.pushcartprize.com.

*Acknowledgments*
Selections for The Pushcart Prize are reprinted with the permission of authors and presses cited. Copyright reverts to authors and presses immediately after publication.

*Distributed by W. W. Norton & Co.*
*500 Fifth Ave., New York, N.Y. 10110*

Library of Congress Card Number: 76-58675
ISBN (hardcover): 978-09600977-0-8
ISBN (paperback): 978-09600977-1-5
ISSN: 0149-7863

*For*
*Our Contributing Editors*
*over the decades*

**From the Directors of the Pushcart Prize Fellowships**

We are pleased to announce that Pushcart Prize publisher Bill Henderson has been awarded the 2020 Distinguished Service To The Arts citation by The American Academy of Arts and Letters.

The Academy stated:

> Editor and visionary publisher Bill Henderson began Pushcart Press 50 years ago to celebrate under-celebrated writers. Devoted to publishing literature that is deserving and noncommercial, Pushcart Prize started with founding editors Joyce Carol Oates, Paul Bowles, Ralph Ellison and others, and continues today as the publisher of the prestigious Pushcart Prize anthology, revered among writers. . . .

Members of the Board congratulate Bill and note his insistence that "this award is not for me alone. It belongs to the thousands of small press editors and writers who have supported the Pushcart Prize through the decades."

# INTRODUCTION

"We have all known the long loneliness and we have learned that the only solution is love and that love comes from community."

Dorothy Day

Almost from the first Pushcart Prize edition the editors of this series have been recognized with awards. I always remind myself that none of these notices are for Pushcart, they are for you - the writer, the editor, the reader.

The Pushcart Prize exists because of the spirit of our little tribe of word nuts. We know what we write, edit or read will often have little effect on what is happening to our planet, our species, or the other animals that share our round neighborhood.

But we persist We endure even as we battle yet another pandemic - a viral one - on top of the continuing pandemics of global climate change, persistent nationalism, and fraudulent, power-crazed politicians.

So dear writer, dear editor, dear reader thank you. You *have* made a difference in these forty-five years. As the energy of these stories, essays, memoirs and poems indicates, we will all survive, indeed we will triumph because of our empathy, our joy and our sense of the sacred.

❀   ❀   ❀

My thanks this year to our guest editors: Cally Fiedorek, Rebecca Mc-Clanahan, Ben Shattuck (prose editors), and Grace Schulman, Kaveh

Akbar, Stephen Corey (poetry editors), and to our legion of Contributing Editors. A special thanks to W. W. Norton Co., our distributor, and to the donors to our Pushcart Prize Fellowships who make it possible for us to publish the Prize each year. And to Ruth Wittman, our Managing Editor, who does all the detailed labor from her home in Berkeley, CA.

❀   ❀   ❀

No pandemics will keep us down. Many more will be on the horizon. If you have doubts about our future, banish them. Be inspired. Be comforted. Read on.

Bill Henderson, Publisher

# THE PEOPLE WHO HELPED

FOUNDING EDITORS—Anaïs Nin (1903–1977), Buckminster Fuller (1895–1983), Charles Newman (1938–2006), Daniel Halpern, Gordon Lish, Harry Smith (1936–2012), Hugh Fox (1932–2011), Ishmael Reed, Joyce Carol Oates, Len Fulton (1934–2011), Leonard Randolph (1926–1993), Leslie Fiedler (1917–2003), Nona Balakian (1918–1991), Paul Bowles (1910–1999), Paul Engle (1908–1991), Ralph Ellison (1913–1994), Reynolds Price (1933–2011), Rhoda Schwartz (1931–2013), Richard Morris (1936–2003), Ted Wilentz (1915–2001), Tom Montag, William Phillips (1907–2002). Poetry editor: H. L. Van Brunt

CONTRIBUTING EDITORS FOR THIS EDITION—Steve Adams, Dan Albergotti, John Allman, Idris Anderson, Tony Ardizzone, David Baker, Mary Jo Bang, Kim Barnes, Graham Barnhart, Catherine Barnett, Eli Barrett, Ellen Bass, Rick Bass, Claire Bateman, Bruce Beasley, Lisa Bellamy, Molly Bendall, Karen Bender, Pinckney Benedict, Bruce Bennett, Marie-Helene Bertino, Linda Bierds, Marianne Boruch, Michael Bowden, Fleda Brown, Rosellen Brown, Michael Dennis Browne, Ayse Papatya Bucak, Christopher Buckley, E. S. Bumas, Bonnie Jo Campbell, Richard Cecil, Jung Hae Chae, Ethan Chatagnier, Kim Chinquee, Jane Ciabattari, Christopher Citro, Suzanne Cleary, Bruce Cohen, Michael Collier, Martha Collins, Lydia Conklin, Stephen Corey, Lisa Couturier, Paul Crenshaw, Claire Davis, Oliver de la Paz, Chard deNiord, Jaquira Diaz, Jack Driscoll, John Drury, Emma Duffy-Comparone, Camille Dungy, Karl Elder, Angie Estes, Nausheen Eusuf, Kathy Fagan, Ed Falco, Beth Ann Fennelly, Gary Fincke, Maribeth Fischer, April L. Ford, Robert Long Foreman, Ben Fountain, H. E. Francis, Alice Friman, John Fulton, Frank X. Gaspar, Christine Gelineau, David Gessner, Nancy Geyer, Gary Gildner,

Elton Glaser, Mark Halliday, Jeffrey Hammond, Becky Hagenston, Jeffrey Harrison, Timothy Hedges, Daniel Henry, DeWitt Henry, David Hernandez, Edward Hirsch, Jane Hirshfield, Andrea Hollander, Chloe Honum, Christopher Howell, Maria Hummel, Joe Hurka, Allegra Hyde, Mark Irwin, David Jauss, Ha Jin, Leslie Johnson, Bret Anthony Johnston, Jeff P. Jones, David Kirby, John Kistner, Ron Koertge, Keetje Kuipers, Peter LaBerge, Don Lee, Fred Leebron, Sandra Leong, Sandra Lessley, Margaret Luongo, Hugh Martin, Matt Mason, Dan Masterson, Alice Mattison, Tracy Mayor, Robert McBrearty, Nancy McCabe, Davis McCombs, Erin McGraw, Elizabeth McKenzie, Edward McPherson, David Meischen, Douglas W. Milliken, Nancy Mitchell, Jim Moore, Joan Murray, David Naimon, Michael Newirth, Aimee Nezhukumatathil, Nick Norwood, D. Nurske, Joyce Carol Oates, Dzvinia Orlowsky, Tom Paine, Alan Michael Parker, Dominica Phetteplace, Catherine Pierce, Leslie Pietrzyk, Mark Jude Poirier, Dan Pope, Andrew Porter, C. E. Poverman, D. A. Powell, Melissa Pritchard, Kevin Prufer, Lia Purpura, Anne Ray, Nancy Richard, Laura Rodley, Jessica Roeder, Dana Roeser, Jay Rogoff, Mary Ruefle, Maxine Scates, Grace Schulman, Philip Schultz, Lloyd Schwartz, Maureen Seaton, Asako Serizawa, Anis Shivani, Robert Anthony Siegel, Tom Sleigh, Suzanne Farrell Smith, Justin St. Germain, Maura Stanton, Maureen Stanton, Pamela Stewart, Ron Stottlemyer, Ben Stroud, Barrett Swanson, Mary Szybist, Nancy Takacs, Ron Tanner, Katherine Taylor, Richard Tayson, Elaine Terranova, Susan Terris, Joni Tevis, Robert Thomas, Jean Thompson, Melanie Rae Thon, William Trowbridge, Lee Upton, G. C. Waldrep, BJ Ward, Michael Waters, LaToya Watkins, Charles Harper Webb, Roger Weingarten, William Wenthe, Allison Benis White, Philip White, Diane Williams, Joy Williams, Eleanor Wilner, Eric Wilson, Sandi Wisenberg, Mark Wisnieski, David Wojahn, Pui Ying Wong, Shelley Wong, Angela Woodward, Carolyne Wright, Nam Ye, Christina Zawadinsky

PAST POETRY EDITORS—H.L. Van Brunt, Naomi Lazard, Lynne Spaulding, Herb Leibowitz, Jon Galassi, Grace Schulman, Carolyn Forché, Gerald Stern, Stanley Plumly, William Stafford, Philip Levine, David Wojahn, Jorie Graham, Robert Hass, Philip Booth, Jay Meek, Sandra McPherson, Laura Jensen, William Heyen, Elizabeth Spires, Marvin Bell, Carolyn Kizer, Christopher Buckley, Chase Twichell, Richard Jackson, Susan Mitchell, Lynn Emanuel, David St. John, Carol Muske, Dennis Schmitz, William Matthews, Patricia Strachan, Heather McHugh, Molly Bendall, Marilyn Chin, Kimiko Hahn, Michael Dennis Browne, Billy Collins, Joan Murray, Sherod Santos, Judith Kitchen, Pattiann Rogers, Carl Phillips, Martha Collins, Carol Frost, Jane Hirshfield, Dorianne Laux, David Baker, Linda Gregerson, Eleanor Wilner, Linda Bierds, Ray Gonzalez, Philip Schultz, Phillis Levin, Tom Lux, Wesley McNair, Rosanna Warren, Julie Sheehan, Tom Sleigh, Laura Kasischke, Michael Waters, Bob Hicok, Maxine Kumin, Patricia Smith, Arthur Sze, Claudia Rankine, Eduardo C. Corral, Kim Addonizio, David Bottoms, Stephen Dunn, Sally Wen Mao, Robert Wrigley, Dorothea Lasky, Kevin Prufer, Chloe Honum, Rebecca Hazelton, Christopher Kempf, Keith Ratzlaff, Jane Mead, Victoria Chang, Michael Collier

ESSAYS EDITOR EMERITUS—Anthony Brandt

SPECIAL EVENTS EDITORS—Cedering Fox, Philip Schultz

ROVING EDITORS—Lily Frances Henderson, Genie Chipps

EUROPEAN EDITORS—Liz and Kirby Williams

CEO—Alex Henderson

CFO—Ashley Williams

ART DIRECTOR—Mary Kornblum

MANAGING EDITOR—Ruth Wittman

GUEST PROSE EDITORS—Cally Fiedorek, Rebecca McClanahan, Ben Shattuck

GUEST POETRY EDITORS—Stephen Corey, Kaveh Akbar, Grace Schulman

EDITOR AND PUBLISHER—Bill Henderson

# CONTENTS

# PUSHCART PRIZE XLV

# IN THE EVENT

fiction by MENG JIN

from THE THREEPENNY REVIEW

In the event of an earthquake, I texted Tony, we'll meet at the corner of Chinaman's Vista, across from the café with the rainbow flag.

Jen had asked about our earthquake plan. We didn't have one. We were new to the city, if it could be called that. Tony described it to friends back home as a huge village. But very densely populated, I added, and not very agrarian. We had come here escaping separate failures on the opposite coast. Already the escape was working. In this huge urban village, under the dry bright sky, we were beginning to regard our former ambitions as varieties of regional disease, belonging to different climates, different times.

"Firstly," Jen said, "you need a predetermined meeting point. In case you're not together and cell service is clogged. Which it's likely to be. Because, you know, disasters."

Jen was the kind of person who said things like *firstly* and *because*, *disasters*. She was a local local, born and raised and stayed. Tony had met Jen a few years ago at an electronic music festival back east and introduced us, thinking we'd get along. She had been traveling for work. Somehow we stayed in touch. We shared interests: she worked as a tech consultant but composed music as a hobby; I made electronic folk songs with acoustic sounds.

"The ideal meeting place," Jen explained, "is outside, walkable from both your workplaces, and likely free of obstacles."

"Obstacles?"

"Collapsed buildings, downed power lines, blah blah hazmat, you know."

17

Chinaman's Vista was the first meeting place that came to mind. It was a big grassy field far from the water, on high ground. Cypress trees lined its edges. In their shade, you could sit and watch the well-behaved dogs of well-behaved owners let loose to run around. We had walked past it a number of times on our way from this place or that—the grocery store, the pharmacy, the taquería—and commented on its charm with surprise, forgetting we'd come across it before. In the event of a significant earthquake, and the aftershocks that typically follow significant earthquakes, I imagined we would be safe there—from falling debris at least—as we searched through the faces of worried strangers for each other.

Other forces could separate or kill us: landslides, tsunamis, nuclear war. I was aware that we lived on the side of a sparsely vegetated hill, that we were four miles from the ocean, a mile from the bay. To my alarmed texts Tony responded that if North Korea was going to bomb us, this region would be a good target: reachable by missile, home to the richest and fastest-growing industry in the world. Probably they would go for one of the cities south of us, he typed, where the headquarters of the big tech companies were based.

nuclear blast wind can travel at > 300 m/s, Tony wrote. Tony knew things' like this.

He clarified: meters per second

which gives us

I watched Tony's avatar think.

approx 3 mins to find shelter after detonation

More likely we'd get some kind of warning x hours before the bomb struck. Jen had a car. She could pick us up, we'd drive north as fast as we could. Jen's aunt who lived an hour over the bridge had a legit basement, concrete reinforced during the Cold War.

I thought about the active volcano one state away, which, if it erupted, could cover the city in ash. One very large state away, Tony reminded me. But the ash that remained in the air might be so thick it obscured the sun, plunging this usually temperate coast into winter. I thought about the rising ocean, the expanding downtown at sea-level, built on landfill. Tony worked in the expanding downtown. Was Tony a strong swimmer? I asked with two question marks. His response:

don't worry 'lil chenchen
if i die i'll die


I was listening to an audiobook, on 1.65x speed, about a techno-dystopic future Earth under threat of annihilation from alien attack. The question was whether humans would kill each other first or survive long enough to be shredded in the fast-approaching weaponized supermassive black hole. Another question was whether humans would abandon life on Earth and attempt to continue civilization on spacecraft. Of course there were not enough spacecraft for everyone.

When I started listening, it was at normal 1.0 speed. Each time I returned I switched the speed dial up by 0.05x. It was a gripping book, full of devices for sustaining mystery despite the obvious conclusion. I couldn't wait for the world to end.


Tony and I were fundamentally different. What I mean is we sat in the world differently—he settling into the back cushions, noting with objective precision the grime or glamour of his surroundings, while I hovered, nervous, at the edge of my seat. Often, I felt—more often now—I couldn't even make it to the edge. Instead I flitted from one space to another, calculating if I would fit, considering the cosmic feeling of unwelcome that emanated from wherever I chose to go.

On the surface Tony and I looked very much the same. We were more or less the same percentile in height and weight, and we both had thin, blank faces, their resting expressions betraying slight confusion and surprise. Our bodies were constructed narrowly of long brittle bones, and our skin, pale in previous gray winters, now tanned easily to the same dusty brown. We weren't only both Chinese; our families came from the same rural-industrial province south of Shanghai, recently known for small-goods manufacturing. But in a long reversal of fortunes, his family, business people who had fled to Hong Kong and then South Carolina, were now lower-middle-class second-generation immigrants, while my parents, born from starving peasant stock, had stayed in China through its boom and immigrated much later to the States as members of the highly educated elite.

Tony's family was huge. I guess mine was too, but I didn't know any of them. In this hemisphere I had my parents, and that was it.

A couple years ago I did Thanksgiving with Tony's family. It was my first time visiting the house where he'd grown up. It was also the first time I had left my parents to celebrate a holiday alone. I tried not to guess what they were eating—Chinese takeout or leftover Chinese takeout. Even when I was around, my parents spent most of their time sitting in separate rooms, working.

"Chenchen!" his mother had cried as she embraced me, "We're so happy you could join us."

My arms rose belatedly, swiping the sides of her shoulders as she pulled away.

She said my name like an American. The rest of the family did too—in fact every member of Tony's family spoke with varied degrees of Southern drawl. It was very disorienting. In normal circumstances Tony's English was incredibly bland, neutered of history like my own, but now I heard in it long-drawn diphthongs, wholesome curls of twang. Both his sisters had come. As had his three uncles and two aunts with their families, and two full sets of grandparents, his mom's mom recently remarried after his grandpa's death. I had never been in a room with so many Chinese people at once, but if I closed my eyes and just listened to the chatter, my brain populated the scene with white people wearing bandanas and jeans.

Which was accurate, except for the white people part.

The turkey had been deep fried in an enormous vat of oil. We had stuffing and cranberry sauce and ranch-flavored mashed potatoes (a Zhang family tradition), pecan and sweet potato and ginger pie. We drank beer cocktails (Bud Light and lemonade). No one regretted the lack of rice or soy sauce, or said with a disappointed sigh that we should have just ordered roast duck from Hunan Garden. It was loud. I shouted small talk and halfway introduced myself to various relatives, as bursts of yelling and laughter erupted throughout the room. Jokes were told—jokes! I had never heard people who looked like my parents making so many jokes—plates clinked, drinks sloshed, moving chairs and shoes scuffed the floor with a pleasing busy beat.

In the middle of all this I was struck suddenly by a wave of mourning, though I wasn't sure for what. The sounds of a childhood I'd never had, the large family I'd never really know? Perhaps it was the drink—I think the beer-ade was spiked with vodka—but I felt somehow that I was losing Tony then, that by letting myself know him in this way I had opened a door through which he might one day slip away.

20

In the corner of the living room, the pitch of the conversation changed. Tony's teenage cousin Harriet was yelling at her mother while Tony's mom sat at her side loudly shaking her head. Slowly the other voices in the room quieted until the tacit attention of every person was focused on this exchange. Others began to participate, some angry—"Don't you dare speak to your mother like this"—some conciliatory—"How about some pecan pie?"—some anxious—Harriet's little sister tugging on her skirt. Harriet pushed her chair back angrily from the table. A vase fell over, dumping flowers and gray water into the stuffing. Harriet stormed from the room.

For a moment it was quiet. In my pocket my phone buzzed. By the time I took it out the air had turned loud and festive again. this happens every year, Tony had texted. I looked at him, he shrugged with resigned amusement. Around me I heard casual remarks of a similar nature: comments on Harriet's personality and love life—apparently she had just broken up with a boyfriend—and nostalgic reminiscences of the year Tofu the dog had peed under the table in fright. It was like a switch had been flipped. In an instant the tension was diffused, injury and grievance transformed into commotion and fond collective memory.

I saw then how Tony's upbringing had prepared him for reality in a way that mine had not. His big family was a tiny world. It reflected the real world with uncanny accuracy—its little charms and injustices, its pettinesses and usefulnesses—and so, real-worldly forces struck him with less intensity, without the paralyzing urgency of assault. He did not need to survive living like I did, he could simply live.


I woke up to Tony's phone in my face.

r u OK? his mom had texted. Followed by:

R U OK????

pls respond my dear son

call ASAP love mom (followed by heart emojis and, inexplicably, an ice cream cone)

His father and siblings and aunts and cousins and childhood friends had flooded his phone with similar messages. He scrolled through the unending ribbon of notifications sprinkled with news alerts. I turned on my phone. It gave a weak buzz. Jen had texted us at 4:08 A.M:

did you guys feel the earthquake? i ran outside and left the door open and now i cant find prick

*pickle

21

Pickle was Jen's cat.

A lamp had fallen over in the living room. We had gotten it at a garage sale and put it on a stool to simulate a tall floor lamp. Now it was splayed across the floor, shade bent, glass bulb dangling but miraculously still intact. When we lifted it we saw a dent in the floorboards. The crooked metal frame of the lamp could no longer support itself and so we laid it on its side like a reclining nude. There were other reclining forms too. Tony had put toy action figures amongst my plants and books; all but Wolverine had fallen on their faces or backs. He sent a photo of a downed Obi-Wan Kenobi to his best nerd friends back home.

He seemed strangely elated. That he would be able to say, Look, this happened to us too, and without any real cost.

Later, while Tony was at work, I pored over earthquake preparedness maps on the internet. Tony's office was in a converted warehouse with large glass windows on the edge of the expanding downtown. On the map, this area was marked in red, which meant it was a liquefaction zone. I didn't know what liquefaction meant but it didn't sound good. Around lunchtime Tony sent me a YouTube video showing a tray of vibrating sand, on which a rubber ball bobbed in and out as if through waves in a sea. He'd forgotten about the earthquake already, his caption said: SO COOL. I messaged back: when the big one hits, you're the rubber ball.

That afternoon, I couldn't stop seeing his human body, tossed in and out through the rubble of skyscrapers. I reminded myself that Tony had a stable psyche. He was the kind of person you could trust not to lose his mind, not in a disruptive way, at least. But I didn't know if he had a strong enough instinct for self-preservation. Clearly, he didn't have a good memory for danger. And he wasn't resourceful, at least not with physical things like food and shelter. His imagination was better for fantasy than for worst case scenarios.

I messaged:

if you feel shaking, move away from the windows. get under a sturdy desk and hold onto a leg. if there is no desk or table nearby crouch by an interior wall. whatever you do, cover your neck and head AT ALL TIMES

He sent me a sideways heart. I watched his avatar think and type for many moments.

I'm SERIOUS, I wrote.

Finally he wrote back:

umm what if my desk is by the window

. . .

should I get under the desk or go to an interior wall

I typed: get under your desk and push it to an interior wall while covering your head and neck. I imagined the rubber ball. I imagined the floor undulating, dissolving into sand. I typed: hold onto any solid thing you can.

I couldn't focus on work. I had recorded myself singing a series of slow glissandos in E minor, which I was trying to distort over a cello droning C. It was supposed to be the spooky intro before the drop of an irregular beat. The song was about failure's various forms, the wild floating quality of it. I wanted to show Tony I understood what he had gone through back east, at least in its primal movement and shape, that despite the insane specificity of his suffering he was not alone.

Now all I could hear were the vibrations of sand, the movements of people and buildings falling.

I went to the hardware store. I bought earthquake-proof cabinet latches and L-bars to bolt our furniture to the walls. According to a YouTube video called "Seeing with earthquake eyes," it was best to keep the bed at least fifteen feet from a window or glass or mirror—anything that could shatter into sharp shards over your soft sleeping neck. Our bed was directly beneath the largest window in the apartment, which looked out into a dark shaft between buildings. The room was small; I drew many diagrams but could not find a way to rearrange the furniture. Fifteen feet from the window would put our bed in the unit next door. I bought no-shatter seals to tape over the windows. I assembled the necessary things for an emergency earthquake kit: bottled water, instant ramen, gummy vitamins. Flashlight, batteries, wrench, and a cheap backpack to hold everything. I copied our most important contacts from my phone and laminated two wallet-sized emergency contact cards in case cell service or electricity went down.

I bought a whistle for Tony. It blew at high C, a pitch of urgency and alarm. I knew he would never wear it. I'd make him tie the whistle to the leg of his desk. If the sand-and-ball video was accurate, and a big earthquake struck during business hours, there was a chance Tony would end up buried in a pile of rubble. I imagined him alive, curled under the frame of his desk. In this scenario, the desk would have absorbed most of the impact and created a small space for him to breathe and crouch. He would be thirsty, hungry, afraid. I imagined his dry lips around the whistle, and the dispirited emergency crews layers of rubble above him, leaping up, shouting, "Someone's down there! Someone's down there!"

Suddenly I remembered I had forgotten to text Jen back.

did u look in the dryer? or that box in the garage?

everything ok over here thanks just one broken lamp

It'd taken me five hours to text Jen yet now I was worried about her lack of instant response.

did u find pickel? let me know i can come over and helpyou look

maybe she's stuck in a tree??

tony can print out some flyers at his office let me know!!!

I was halfway through enlarging a photo of Pickle I'd dug up from Google photos when my phone buzzed.

found pickle this morning in bed almost sat on her she was under the covers barely made a bump

She sent me a photo. Pickle was sitting on a pillow, fur fluffed, looking like a super grouch.

My office had no windows. It was partially underground, the garage-adjacent storage room that came with our apartment. We had discarded everything when we moved so we had nothing to store. The room had one outlet and was just big enough for my recording equipment and a piano. It was soundproof and the internet signal was weak. The recordings I made in there had a muffled amplified quality, like listening to a loud fight through a door.

The building where Tony and I rented was old, built in the late nineteenth century, a dozen years before the big earthquake of 1904. It had survived that one, but still by modern building codes it was what city regulators called a soft story property. According to records at City Hall, it had been seismically retrofitted by mandate five years ago. I saw evidence of these precautions in the garage: extra beams and girding along the foundations, the boilers and water tanks bolted to the walls. I couldn't find my storage/work room on any of the blueprints. Tony thought I was hypocritical to keep working there, given my new preoccupation with safety. I liked the idea of making music in a place that didn't technically exist, even if it wasn't up to code.

Or maybe it was. I imagined, in fact, that the storage rooms had been secret bunkers—why else was there a power outlet. I felt at once safe and sober inside it, this womb of concrete, accompanied by the energies of another age of panic. Now I filled the remaining space with ten gallons of water—enough for two people for five days—boxes of Shin noodles and canned vegetable soup, saltine crackers, tins of spam, canned tuna for Tony (who no longer ate land animals), a small camping stove I found on sale. I moved our sleeping bags and our winter coats down.

My office, my bunker. More and more it seemed like a good place to sit out a disaster. If we ran out of bottled water, the most vital resource, there stood the bolted water heaters, just a few steps away.


"Holy shit," Tony said when he came home from work. "Have you seen the news?"

I pursed my lips. I didn't read the news anymore. The sight of the new president's face made me physically ill. Instead I buried myself in old librettos and scores, spent whole days listening to the kind of music that made every feeling cell in my brain vibrate with forgetting: the Ring Cycle, Queen's albums in chronological order, Glenn Gould huffing and purring through the Goldberg Variations.

Tony did the opposite. Once upon a time he had been a consumer of all those nonfiction tomes vying for the Pulitzer Prize, big books about social and historical issues. He used to send me articles that took multiple hours to read—I'd wondered when he ever did work. Now he only sent me tweets.

He waved his phone in my face.

Taking up the entire screen was a photograph of what appeared to be hell. Hell, as it appeared in medieval paintings and Hollywood films. Hills and trees burning so red they appeared liquid, the sky pulsing with black smoke. A highway cut through the center of this scene, and on the highway, impossibly, were cars, fleeing and entering the inferno at top speed.

"This is Loma," Tony said.

"Loma?"

"It's an hour from here? We were there last month?"

"We were?"

"That brewery with the chocolate? Jen drove?"

"Oh. Yeah. Wow."

According to the photograph's caption, the whole state was on fire. Tony's voice was incredulous, alarmed.

"Have you gone outside today?"

I hadn't.

We walked to Chinaman's Vista, where there was a view of the city. Tony held my hand and I was grateful for it. The air was smoky; it smelled like everyone was having a barbecue. If I closed my eyes I could imagine I was in my grandmother's village in Zhejiang, those hours before dinner when families started firing up their wood-burning stoves.

"People are wearing those masks," Tony said. "Look—like we're in fucking Beijing."

Tony had never been to Beijing. I had. The smog wasn't half as bad as this.

We sat on a bench in Chinaman's Vista and looked at the sky. The sun was setting. Behind the gauze of smoke it was a brilliant salmon orange, its light so diffused you could stare straight at it without hurting your eyes. The sky was pink and purple, textured with plumes of color. It was the most beautiful sunset I had ever seen. Around us the light cast upon the trees and grass and purple bougainvillea an otherworldly yellow glow, more nostalgic than any Instagram filter. I looked at Tony, whose face had relaxed in the strange beauty of the scene, and it was like stumbling upon a memory of him—his warm dry hand clasping mine, the two of us looking and seeing the same thing.


Tony's failure had to do with the new president. He had been working on the opposing candidate's campaign, building what was to be a revolutionary technology for civic engagement. They weren't only supposed to win. *They* were the ones who were supposed to go down in history for changing the way politics used the internet.

My failure had to do with Tony. I had failed to save him, after.

Tony had quit his lucrative job to work seven days a week for fifteen months and a quarter of the pay. The week leading up to the election, he had slept ten hours total, five of them at headquarters, face-down on his desk. He didn't sleep for a month after, though not for lack of time. If there was ever a time for Tony to go insane, that would have been it.

Instead he shut down. His engines cooled, his fans stopped whirring, his lights blinked off. He completed the motions of living but his gestures were vacant, his eyes hollow. It was like all the emotions insisting and contradicting inside him had short-circuited some processing mechanism. In happier times, Tony had joked about his desire to become an android. "Aren't we already androids?" I asked, indicating the eponymous smartphone attached to his hand. Tony shook his head in exasperation. "Cyborgs," he said. "You're thinking of cyborgs." He explained that cyborgs were living organisms with robotic enhancements. Whereas androids were robots made to be indistinguishable from the alive. Tony had always believed computers superior to humans—they didn't need to feel.

In this time I learned many things about Tony and myself, two people I thought I already knew very well. At our weakest, I realized, humans have no recourse against our basest desires. For some this might have meant gorging in sex and drink, or worse—inflicting violence upon others or themselves. For Tony it meant becoming a machine.

Because of the wildfire smoke, we were warned to go outside as little as possible. This turned out to be a boon for my productivity. I shut myself in my bunker and worked.

I woke to orange-hued cityscapes. In the mornings I drank tea and listened to my audiobook. Earth was being shredded, infinitely, as it entered the supermassive black hole, while what remained of humanity sped away on a light-speed ship. "It's strangely beautiful," one character said as she looked back at the scene from space. "No, it's terrible," another said. The first replied: "Maybe beauty is terrible." I thought the author didn't really understand beauty or humans, but he did understand terror and time, and maybe that was enough. I imagined how music might sound on other planets, where the sky wasn't blue and grass wasn't green and water didn't reflect when it was clear. I descended to my bunker and worked for the rest of the day. I stopped going upstairs for lunch, not wanting to interrupt my flow. I ate dry packets of ramen, crumbling noodle squares and picking out the pieces like potato chips. When I forgot to bring down a thermos of tea I drank the bottled water.

Fires were closing in on the city from all directions; fire would eat these provisions up. The city was surrounded on three sides by water—that still left one entry by land. It was dry and getting hotter by the day. I thought the city should keep a ship with emergency provisions anchored in the bay. I thought that if a real disaster struck, I could find it in myself to loot the grocery store a few blocks away.

In the evenings, Tony took me upstairs and asked about my work day. In the past he had wanted to hear bits of what I was working on; now he nodded and said, "That sounds nice." I didn't mind. I didn't want to share this new project with him—with anyone—until it was done. We sat on the couch and he showed me pictures of the devastation laying waste to the land. I saw sooty silhouettes of firefighters and drones panning gridwork streets of ash. I saw a woman in a charred doorway, an apparition of color in the black and gray remains of her home.

Once Jen came over to make margaritas. She put on one of Tony's Spotify playlists. "I'm sorry," she said, "I really need to unwind." She knew I didn't like listening to music while other noises were happening. My brain processed the various sounds into separate channels, pulling my consciousness into multiple tracks and dividing my present self. For Jen, overstimulation was a path to relaxation. She crushed ice and talked about the hurricanes ravaging the other coast, the floods and landslides in Asia and South America, the islands in the Pacific already swallowed by the rising sea.

Jen's speech, though impassioned, had an automatic quality to it, an unloading with a mechanical beat. I sipped my margarita and tried to converge her rant with the deep house throbbing from the Sonos: it sounded like a robot throwing up. Tony came home from work and took my margarita. Together they moved from climate change to the other human horrors I'd neglected from the news—ethnic cleansings, mass shootings, trucks mowing down pedestrians. They listed the newest obscenities of the new president, their voices growing louder and faster as they volleyed headlines and tweets. In the far corner of the couch, I hugged my knees. More and more it seemed to me that the world Jen and Tony lived in was one hysterical work of poorly written fiction—a bad doomsday novel—and that what was really real was the world of my music. More and more I could only trust those daytime hours when my presence coincided completely with every sound I made and heard.

I was making a new album. I was making it for me but also for Tony, to show him it was still possible, in these times, to maintain a sense of self.

My last album had come out a year earlier. I had been on tour in Europe promoting it when the election came and went. At the time I had justified the scheduling: Tony would want to celebrate with his team anyways, I would just get in the way. Perhaps I had been grateful for an excuse. On the campaign, Tony had been lit with a blind passion I'd never been able to summon for tangible things. I'd understood it—how else could you will yourself to work that much?—I'd even lauded it, I'd wanted his candidate to win too. Still, the pettiest part of me couldn't help resenting his work like a mistress resents a wife. I imagined the election night victory party as the climax of a fever dream, after which Tony would step out, cleansed, and be returned to me.

Of course nothing turned out how I'd imagined.

My own show had to go on.

I remember calling Tony over Google Voice backstage between shows, at coffee shops, in the bathroom of the hotel room I shared with Amy the percussionist—wherever I had wifi. I remember doing mental math whenever I looked at a clock—what time was it in America, was Tony awake? The answer, I learned, was yes. Tony was always awake. Often he was drunk. He picked up the phone but did not have much to say. I pressed my ear against the screen and listened to him breathe.

I remember Amy turning her phone to me: "Isn't this your boyfriend?" We were on a train from Brussels to Amsterdam. I saw Tony's weeping face, beside another weeping face I knew: Jen's. I zoomed out. Jen's arms were wrapped around Tony's waist; Tony's arm hugged her shoulder. The photograph was in a listicle published by a major American daily showing the losing candidate's supporters on election night, watching the results come in. I remembered that Jen had flown in to join Tony at the victory arena, in order to be "a witness to history." The photo-list showed the diversity of the supporters: women in head-scarves, disabled people, gay couples. Tony and Jen killed two birds in one stone: Asian America, and an ostensibly mixed-race couple. Jen was half-Chinese but she looked exotic-white—Italian, or Greek.

That night I'd called Tony. "How are you?" I'd asked as usual, and then: "I was thinking maybe I should just come back. Should I come back? I hate this tour." There was a long silence. Finally Tony said, "Why?" In his voice a mutter of cosmic emptiness.

I have one memory of sobbing under bright white lights, some terrible noise cracking into speakers turned too high. This might have been a dream.

For a long time after, I was estranged from music. What feelings normally mediated themselves in soundscapes, a well I could plumb for composition, hit me with their full blunt force.

Now I was trying to re-enter music by making it in a new way, the way I imagined a sculptor makes a sculpture, to work with sound as if it were a physical material. Music was undoubtedly my medium: I had perfect pitch, a nice singing voice, and I liked the monasticism and repetition of practice. According to my grandmother, I had sung the melodies of nursery songs a whole year before I learned to speak. But I had the temperament of a conceptual artist, not a musician. Specifically, I was not a performer. I hated every aspect of performing: the lights, the stage, the singular attention. Most of all I could not square with the irreproducibility of performance—you had one chance, and then the work disappeared—which, to be successful, required a kind of faith. The greatest performers practiced and practiced, controlling themselves with utmost discipline, and when they stepped onto the stage, gave themselves over to time.

This was also why I couldn't just compose. I wanted to control every aspect of a piece, from its conception to realization: I did not like giving up the interpretation of my notes and rests to a conductor and other musicians.

I wanted to resolve this contradiction by making music in a way that folded performance theoretically into composition. Every sound and silence in this album would be a performance. I would compose a work and perform it for myself, just once. From this material I would build my songs. If the recording didn't turn out, I abandoned the mistakes or used them. I didn't think about who the music was for. Certainly not for a group of people to enjoy with dance, as my previous album had been—I, too, had been preparing for celebration. My new listener sat in an ambient room, alone, shed of distractions, and simply let the sounds come in.


In the morning, Tony showed me a video of three husky puppies doing something adorable. "Look," he said, pointing up and out the window. From the skywell we could see a sliver of blue.

We got up and confirmed that the smoke had lifted. Tony reported from Twitter that the nearest fire had indeed been tamed. "Huzzah!" I said. I walked outside to wait with him for his Uberpool to work. The sun was shining, the air was fresh, the colors of this relentlessly cheerful coast restored. I kissed him on the cheek goodbye.

I watched his car drive away and couldn't bear the thought of going back inside. My legs itched. I wanted—theoretically—to run. I put in earbuds and turned on my audiobook. I walked around the neighborhood, looking happily at the bright houses and healthy people and energetic pooping dogs.

In the audiobook, things had also taken a happy turn. The *lady* protagonist, who had escaped Earth on a light-speed ship, found herself reunited in a distant galaxy with the man who'd proved his unfailing love by secretly gifting her an actual star. This reunion despite the fact that eight hundred years had passed (hibernation now allowed humans to jump centuries of time) and that when they had last seen each other, the man's brain was being extracted from his body in order to be launched into outer space (it was later intercepted by aliens who reconstructed his body from the genetic material). She bad discovered his love in that final moment, when it was too late to stop the surgery—aside from then the two had barely spoken. Now he was finally to be rewarded for his devotion and patience. I thought the author had an exciting imagination when it came to technology but a shitty imagination for love. Somehow I found the endurance of this love story more unbelievable than the leaps in space and time.

That afternoon I tried to work but didn't get very much done. dinner out? I texted Tony. For the first time in a long time I wanted to feel like I lived in a city. I wanted to shower and put on mascara and pants that had a zipper.

Tony had a work event. I texted Jen. sry have a date! she wrote back, followed by a winking emoji that somehow seemed to say: *ooh-la-la*.

I decided to go out to dinner alone. I listened to my audiobook over a plate of fancy pizza, shoveling down the hot dough as I turned up the speed on my book. By the time I finished the panna cotta, the universe was imploding, every living and non-living thing barreling towards the end of its existence. I looked at my empty plate as the closing credits came on to a string cadenza in D-minor. I took out my earbuds and looked around the restaurant, at the redwood bar where I was sitting, the wait-staff in black aprons, the patrons in wool sneakers and thin down vests, the Sputnik lamps hanging above us all. Would I miss any of this? Yes, I thought, and then, just as fervently—I don't know.

Outside, the sky was fading to pale navy, a tint of yellow on the horizon where the sun had set. A cloudless, unspectacular dusk. I walked to dissipate the unknowing feeling and found myself at Chinaman's Vista, which was louder than I had ever heard it, everyone taking advantage of the newly particulate-free outdoors. I weaved through the clumps of people, looking at and through them, separate and invisible,

31

like a visitor at a museum. That was when I saw, under a cypress tree, a woman who looked exactly like Jen, wearing Jen's gold loafers and pink bomber jacket. Jen was with a man. She was kissing the man. The man looked exactly like Tony.

I was breathing quickly. Staring. I wanted to run away but my feet were as glued as my eyes. Tony kissed Jen differently than he kissed me. He grabbed her lower back with two hands and seemed to lift her up slightly, while curling his neck to her upwardly lifted face. Because Jen was shorter than him. This made sense. I, on the other hand, was just about Tony's height.

I blinked and shook my head. Jen wasn't shorter than Tony. She was taller than us both. Jen and Tony stopped kissing and started to walk towards me, and I saw that it wasn't Tony, it was some other Asian guy who only kind of looked like Tony, but really not at all. Horrified, I turned and walked with intentionality to a plaque ahead on the path. I stared intently at the words and thought how the guy wasn't Tony and the girl probably wasn't even Jen, how messed up that I saw a white-ish girl with an East Asian guy and immediately thought Jen and Tony.

"Chenchen!"

It *was* Jen. I looked up with relief and dread. Jen stood on the other side of the plaque with her date, waving energetically.

"This is Kevin," she said. She turned to Kevin. "Chenchen's the friend I was telling you about, the composer-musician-*artiste*. She just moved to the city."

"Hey," I said. I looked at the plaque. "Did you know," I said, "China-man's Vista used to be a mining camp? For, uh, Chinese miners. They lived in these barrack-like houses. Then they were killed in some riots and maybe buried here, because, you know, this place has good fengshui." I paused. I'd made up the part about fengshui. The words on the plaque said *mass graves*. "This was back in the—1800s."

"Oh, like the Gold Rush?" Kevin said. His voice was deep, hovering around a low F. Tony spoke in the vicinity of B-flat. I looked up at him. He was much taller than Tony.

"Yeah," I said.

I stood there for a long time after they left, reading and re-reading the historical landmark plaque, wishing I could forget what it said. Chinaman's Vista, I thought, was a misleading name. The view was of cascading expensive houses, pruned and prim. The historic Chinese population, preferring squalor and cheap rents, had long relocated to

32

the other side of town. Besides me and probably Kevin and half of Jen, there weren't many living Chinese people here.

What was wrong with me? Why didn't I want to be a witness to history, to any kind of time passing?

The temperature skyrocketed. Tony and I kicked off our blankets in sleep. We opened the windows and the air outside was hot too. Heat radiated from the highway below in waves. The cars trailed plumes of scorching dust.

Tony texted me halfway through the day to say it was literally the hottest it had ever been. I clicked the link he sent and saw a heat map of the city. It was 105 degrees in our neighborhood, 101 at Tony's work. We didn't have an air conditioner. We didn't, after all my disaster prep, even have a fan. Tony's work didn't have AC either. Nobody in the city did, I realized when I left the house, searching for a cool café. Every business had its doors wide open. Puny ceiling fans spun as fast as they could but only pushed around hot air. It was usually so fucking temperate here, the weather so predictably perfect. I walked past melting incredulous faces: women in leather boots, tech bros carrying Patagonia sweaters with dismay.

My phone buzzed. Jen had sent a photo of what looked like an empty grocery store shelf. It buzzed again.

the fan aisle at Target!!

just saw a lady attacking another lady for the last $200 tower fan #endofdays?

That weekend, I took Tony to the mall. Tony had been sleeping poorly, exasperated by my body heat. He was sweaty and irritable and I felt somehow responsible. I felt, I think, guilty. Since the incident at Chinaman's Vista I'd been extra nice to Tony.

The AC in the mall wasn't cold enough. A lot of people had had the same idea. "Still better than being outside," I said hopefully as we stepped onto the crowded escalator. Tony grunted his assent. We walked around Bloomingdale's. I pointed at the mannequins wearing wool peacoats and knitted vests and laughed. Summer in the city was supposed to be cold, because of the ocean fog. Tony said, "Ha-ha."

We got ice cream. We got iced tea. We got texts from PG&E saying that power was out on our block due to the grid overheating, would be fixed by 8 P.M. We weren't planning to be back until after sunset anyways, I said. I looked over Tony's shoulder at his phone. He was scrolling through Instagram, wistfully it seemed, through photographs of Jen and other girls in bikinis—they had gone to the beach. "But you don't like the beach," I said. Tony shrugged. "I don't like the mall either." I asked if he wanted to go to the beach. He said no.

We ate salads for dinner and charged our phones. This, at last, seemed to make Tony happy. "In case the power is still out later," he said. We sat in the food court and charged our phones until the mall closed.

The apartment was a cacophony of red blinking eyes. The appliances had all restarted when the power came back on. Now they beeped and hummed and buzzed, imploring us to reset their times. Outside the wide-open windows, cars honked and revved their engines. So many sounds not meant to be simultaneous pressed simultaneously onto me. In an instant the cheerfulness I'd mustered for our wretched day deflated. I found myself breathing fast and loud, tears welling against my will. Tony sat me down and put his noise-canceling headphones over my ears. "I can still hear everything!" I shouted. I could hear, I wanted to say, the staticky G-sharp hiss of the headset's noise-canceling mechanism. Tony was suddenly contrite. He handed me a glass of ice water and shushed me tenderly. He walked around the apartment, resetting all our machines.

We took a cold shower. Tony looked as exhausted as I felt. We kept the lights off and went directly to bed. Traffic on the highway had slowed to a rhythmic whoosh. I wanted to hug Tony but it was too hot. I took his hand and released it. Our palms were sweaty and gross.

I was just falling asleep when I heard a faint beep.

I nudged Tony. "What was that?" He rolled away from me. I turned over and closed my eyes.

It beeped again, then after some moments again.

It was a high C, a note of shrill finality. I counted the beats between: about 20 at 60 bpm. I counted to twenty, hoping to lull myself to sleep. But the anticipation of the coming beep was too much. My heart rate rose, I counted faster, unable to maintain a consistent rhythm, so now it was 22 beats, then 25, then 27.

Finally I sat up, said loudly: "Tony, Tony, do you hear the beeping?"

"Huh?" He rubbed his eyes. It beeped again, louder, as if to back me up. Tony got up and poked at the alarm clock, which he hadn't reset because it ran on batteries. He pulled the batteries out and threw them to the floor. He lay down, I thanked him, and then—*beep*.

I sat on the bed, clamping my pillow over my ears, and watched Tony lumber about the dark bedroom, drunk with exhaustion, finding every hidden gadget and extracting its batteries, taking down even the smoke detector. Each time it seemed he had finally identified the source there sounded another beep. It was a short sound, it insisted then disappeared: even my impeccable hearing could not locate from where exactly it came. It sounded as if from all around us, from the air. Tony fell on the bed defeated. He said, "Can we just try to sleep?" We clamped our eyes shut, forced ourselves to breathe deeply, but the air was agitated and awake. My mind drifted and ebbed, imitating the movements of sleep while bringing nothing like rest. I couldn't help thinking that the source of the sound was neither human nor human-made. I couldn't help imagining the aliens in my audiobook preparing to annihilate our world. "Doomsday clock," I said, half-aloud. I was thinking or dreaming of setting up my equipment to record the beeps. I was thinking or dreaming of unrolling the sleeping bags in my bunker, where it'd be silent and I could sleep. "Counting down."

"I'm sorry," Tony said.

"It's okay," I said, but it wasn't, not really, and Tony knew it. He grabbed my hand and squeezed it hard. Between the cosmic beeps his lips smacked open as if to speak, as if searching for the right words to fix me. Finally he said, "I kissed Jen," and I said, "I know."

Then, "What?"

Then, "When?"

My eyes were wide open.

"Last November."

High C sounded, followed by ten silent beats.

"You were in Germany."

Another high C. Twenty beats. Another high C.

"I'm sorry," Tony said again. "Say something, please?" He tightened his hand. I tried to squeeze back to say I'd heard, I was awake. I failed. I listened to the pulses of silence, the inevitable mechanical beeps.

"Tell me what you're thinking?"

I was thinking we would need a new disaster meet-up spot. I was wondering if there was any place in this city, this world, where we'd be safe.

*Nominated by The Threepenny Review*

# THE MASTER'S CASTLE

fiction by ANTHONY DOERR

from TIN HOUSE

Basil Bebbington from Bakersfield isn't good at basketball, wood-shop, or talking to girls, but he's fair at physics, and guts his way through technical college, and lands a job grinding lenses for Bakersfield Optometry, and his parents move to Tampa, and Hurricane Andrew floods their basement, and by age twenty-two Basil begins to worry that he's missing out on things—women, joy, et cetera—so on a whim he applies for a job as an optics technician at an observatory on the summit of Mauna Kea on the island of Hawaii.

The interviews take place at sea level, with a rotating slew of astronomers in flip-flops who warn him that the job involves heavy-duty solitude, weeklong shifts alone atop the volcano, "like being a lighthouse keeper on Mars," one says, but Basil is eager to adjust the trajectory of his life, so he signs the papers, completes the training, leases a Jeep, and on the day of his first shift, drives from sea level to fourteen thousand feet in two hours. By the time he gets out of the truck, the wind is throwing snow across the summit, and his skull feels as if a hatchet has been dropped through it.

A tiny flame-haired woman opens the observatory door, seizes him by the collar, and hauls him inside.

"Ow, what wa . . ." Basil stops midsentence.

"Get in here, Mr. Basil Bebbington from Bakersfield." She force-feeds him four aspirin and twelve ounces of Fresca, and shows him the composting toilet and the telescope—which is not the big Copernicus-type cylinder-with-eyepiece you might expect, but a three-hundred-ton compound mirror thirty-three feet across that adjusts its position twice per second—and she apologizes for the absence of the microwave, which, she explains, made spooky noises at night, so she dragged it to the edge of the road and pitched it off. Her name is Muriel MacDonald, and she's his age, and looks like a woodland elf but moves like a caffeinated jaguar. Before she leaves, she pours him a bowl of Raisin Bran, hands him a Stevie Wonder CD, and says, "When you get lonesome, put 'Higher Ground' on repeat."

By the time Muriel drags her duffel to her Dodge, orange hair blowing everywhere, yelling, "See you in a week!" Basil is ninety-six percent in love.

All that first night he listens to the wind crash against the walls. Fourteen thousand feet below, waves explode onto reefs and tourists gobble deep-fried prawns, but up here it feels to Basil as though life is finally beginning.

He measures wind speeds, radios reports to the astronomers in Waimea, analyzes Muriel's handwriting in the log. At night he puts on "Higher Ground"—

*People keep on learnin'*
*Soldiers keep on warrin'*
*World keep on turnin'*

—and dances idiotically in the mirror barn beneath the burly arm of the Milky Way, and when Sunday finally arrives, and Muriel churns back up the summit road to relieve him, his heart kicks against his sternum like a frog. He makes her coffee, tells her he saw fifty-six meteorites; her green eyes turn like whirlpools; she tells him she believes most stars in the universe support solar systems. "What if," she says, "*every* star has planets circling around it? What if there are hundreds of billions of Earths? Earths where you can high-jump eighty feet! Earths where little turtle-people build little turtle-people cities!"

All week in Hilo, flush with oxygen, Basil dreams of her, brushing her copper hair, flinging appliances off the summit. Cumulonimbi gather along the flanks of the volcano like battleships, and Basil watches them flicker with lightning: blue ignitions, as if Muriel were a god, incinerating things up there.

One hour each Sunday: that's all the time he ever sees her, sixty minutes on the boundaries of their respective shifts. Yet on the calendar of his life, what hours have shone more brightly? Muriel never touches him, or asks about his week, or notices his haircuts, but neither does she mention a boyfriend, and she always meets him at the door looking woozy and grateful, and ensures the cot in the control room has clean sheets, and one wondrous Sunday, after they have traded shifts for five months, she pokes him on the shoulder and says, "I always say, Basil, if you want something, you need to just go for it."

How many times during the next week, alone on the volcano, does Basil parse the possible implications of that sentence? Did she mean "you" as in the impersonal *you*, or did she mean "you" as in Basil, and "something" as in *her*? And could she have meant "it" as in *doodle-bopping*, as in *jingle-jangling*, as in *sexual relations*, and has she been waiting all these weeks for him to "just go for it"?

## AROUND THIS TIME OTIS STARTS WEARING AN OFF-BRAND BLACK SUPERHERO CAPE DAY AND NIGHT.

The next Sunday, after seven straight nights at fourteen thousand feet, Basil cuts fifty paper hearts from the pages of a protocol manual, writes a different simile on each—*I love you like a fish loves water, I love you like we're eggs and bacon*—and stashes the hearts all over the observatory: behind doors, rolled up inside the toilet paper, taped to the back of her Raisin Bran. Muriel comes up and Basil heads down, and all that week he imagines her discovering his valentines. She'll be euphoric, flattered, at least amused, but the following weekend, as he is packing for his next shift, the supervisor calls from Waimea to say that Basil has been reported for making inappropriate advances, that a lawyer is involved, that they are going to have to let him go.

✿　✿　✿

He finds a job at an ophthalmologist's in Eugene, then a LensCrafters in Pocatello, the ninth happiest city in Idaho, hoping that an increase in distance will correspond with a decrease in heartbreak, but every few nights he dreams of volcanoes and flame-haired goddesses and humiliation. *I love you like the sky loves blue. I love you like putting up the Christmas tree.* What happens to all the one-sided desire in the world? Does it dissipate into the air, or does it flit around from soul to soul, anxious, haunted, looking for a place to land?

The '90s turn into the 2000s. One Thursday at a foosball tournament, eleven years after leaving Hawaii, Basil is handcuffed by a drunken English department secretary named Mags Futrell who makes fun of his name for half an hour, then kisses him right on the mouth.

38

Mags drives a Ford Ranger, has eyes like holes burnt into a blanket, prefers Def Leppard to silence, and wears a T-shirt to sleep that says, *Lips that touch liquor touch other lips quicker.* She and Basil have a backyard wedding, and mortgage a two-bedroom rancher on Clark Street across from Al's Comix Warehouse, and Mags stays mostly sober through a pregnancy, and produces a bug-eyed infant named Otis, and during Otis's first year on Earth, Basil pushes his stroller up every hill in Pocatello, shedding pounds like he's shedding insecurities, and on his best nights he stops brooding over what life could have been and starts appreciating it for what it is.

But when Otis turns five, Basil catches Mags mixing Jack Daniel's into her morning Pepsi, and discovers a fifth in her glove compartment and a pint in her snow boots, and when he confronts her, she says, "Sure, Basil, I'll cut down on my drinking, how about I only drink on days that end with Y." Then she books a room at the Ramada and does not come home for four nights.

Around this time Otis starts wearing an off-brand black superhero cape day and night, every hour of every day—to kindergarten, to dinner, to sleep. Dr. O'Keefe says the boy is responding to "an atmosphere of stress" in his home environment, that he'll outgrow it, but soon Otis is six, then eight, and Mags is regularly heading to the guest room at bedtime with a Solo cup full of enough Wild Turkey to tranquilize a zebra, and Otis won't take off his cape even to shower, and for Basil, driving home from Lens-Crafters every evening has started to feel like a prison sentence.

In October Al's Comix Warehouse goes out of business, and a portly, white-bearded contractor named Nicholas starts putting crews to work on the building, erecting drum towers on the facade, and hanging a portcullis above the entrance, and in March a sign goes up that says, THE MASTER'S CASTLE COMING SOON, flanked by two aluminum skulls on posts with spotlights shooting out of their heads.

Nicholas assures Basil that it's all family-friendly, zoned for "entertainment"—"just keeping it secret to generate interest," he says, and winks over his bifocals, and tries to high-five Otis, who wants nothing to do with high-fives from strangers—and although Nicholas has a kind face and even resembles a sawdust-covered, dentally challenged Saint Nick, it's hard not to worry that the Master's Castle is going to be some kind of S&M dungeon, that soon Clark Street will be clogged with perverts in hot pants, that Basil's already battered home value will sink to zero, that his wife needs the kind of help he can't give, that his son might be damaged in some fundamental way, and that his life has descended to a nadir only a few, very particularly sorry lives reach.

Today though, the first of April, Mags wakes before Basil and scrambles a dozen eggs, and announces she's going to clamber back on top of the heap, vacuum the truck, get an oil change, and promises Basil she'll drive Otis to his appointment with Dr. O'Keefe after school, and Basil leaves LensCrafters at 4:00 PM feeling buoyant, and he empties the house of alcohol—pouring out the cooking sherry, the mouthwash, even the vanilla extract—and prepares a mushroom casserole, and preheats the broiler, and watches an internet video of a cat doing yoga, and another about a dolphin who turns pink when he's sad, then clicks a link to a story about a new best-selling book called *Memoirs of a Planet Hunter* and Basil's heart catapults into his mouth because the face that blooms across his iPad belongs to Muriel MacDonald.

Same green eyes, same narrow nose, slim, dignified, posed against a pillar in a lab coat, an orange-haired Joan Didion for the telescope set. Even now, after twenty years, to see the pale knobs of her collarbone floods Basil with a longing that threatens to capsize the kitchen.

The article describes how Muriel leads a NASA astronomical team that has discovered 540 extrasolar planets, including a sister Earth sixty light-years away, a rocky world only slightly smaller than ours, with life-friendly temperatures, and now she is slated to win a National Academy of Sciences medal, appear on *The Today Show*, and eat lamb shanks with Queen Elizabeth.

He downloads *Memoirs of a Planet Hunter*. Chapter one opens with seven-year-old Muriel building cardboard rockets. Chapter two covers high school. By page forty she's in Hawaii, interviewing with the observatory.

"Okay," Basil says to the empty kitchen. "Okay, okay, okay."

Out the window Nicholas exits the Master's Castle carrying plywood. The sky is purple. Somehow it has become 6:15 PM, and shouldn't Mags have had Otis home by 5:00? Basil slides his casserole onto the center rack, and sits at the table beneath a waterfall of memory.

The way the observatory loomed in the dusk, its dome pale against the sky. The way he'd have to rest his hands on his knees when he'd get out of the Jeep just to catch his breath, heart thudding, dust blowing across the summit. He brought Muriel his grandmother's macaroni and cheese; he bought her a Michael Bolton CD because the guy at the record shop in Hilo said Bolton was the white Stevie Wonder.

*I love you like Saturday mornings when you wake up and realize you don't have school.*

*I love you like the wind loves kites.*

Maybe he came on a little strong, maybe he was a little naive, but at least what he offered was pure, wasn't it?

On page forty-eight, he reads:

> *Every seven days the other optics technician, a man—they were always men—would roll back up, blinking and slow from the altitude, and I'd be blinking and slow from seven days of thin air and sleep deprivation.*
>
> *I was learning things in the cold nights, in the silence, in the spray of stars that would show when the big door rolled back and they poured their ancient light onto the mirror. I was learning how to see.*
>
> *When the other optics tech came up, I didn't ever want to go.*

Then it's chapter three, and Muriel is off to Caltech, the Kepler program, a photoshoot with Annie Leibovitz, et cetera, and is it possible that in the 460-page story of Muriel's life, Basil didn't warrant a single sentence?

## "OKAY," BASIL SAYS TO THE EMPTY KITCHEN. "OKAY, OKAY, OKAY."

He scrolls ahead, scans for his name, uses the search tool—*no results found.* The clock reads 7:15 PM, Clark Street is dark, everything smells like a forest fire—the kitchen, his life—and the smoke detector screeches, and Basil opens the oven door to a rolling wave of smoke and hurries his smoldering casserole out the door and flings the pan into the front yard. At 7:20 he's standing on a kitchen chair, yanking the smoke detector off the ceiling, when Mags's Ford Ranger rolls over the curb and skids past the casserole and comes to a stop with its front bumper inside the hedges.

Otis sprints through the front door sobbing, making for his bedroom—no cape flying behind him—and Mags leaves the truck lights on and the driver's door open and comes seesawing through the door with her giant handbag.

"Reeks like fuck-all in here."

"What happened to Otis?"

Mags paws through cabinets.

"Where were you? Where is Otis's cape?"

A half-dozen bottles roll across the floor. "I took it."

"Dr. O'Keefe said to confiscate his cape?"

"Not Dr. O'-Flipping-Keefe, me, me, me. I took him to O'Keefe's and then we stopped at the Ramada and everyone agreed that third grade is too old to wear a cape, that all the kids who don't think he's a freak already will think so soon, so I took it."

"You brought our son to a bar?"

"I took him to see people. *Sane* people!" and she slides to the floor, and Basil drops the smoke detector in the sink and puts a frozen pizza in the oven and goes out the front door and backs the still-running, still un-vacuumed Ranger off the lawn and parks in the driveway and sits a moment behind the wheel wondering about distance and the other world Muriel found sixty light-years away.

## ACROSS THE STREET, THE TWIN SPOTLIGHTS OF THE MASTER'S CASTLE RISE INTO THE SKY.

When he goes back inside, Mags is slumped against the dishwasher. "April," she says, "the month to throw yourself off things." Basil can just see the hem of Otis's cape sticking out of her handbag, so he balls it up in his back pocket and slides the half-cooked pizza from the oven and hacks it into slices and carries two plates and a glass of milk into Otis's room and shuts the door and the two of them sit on the carpet, and Otis sips his milk, and Basil ties the cape around his son's neck, over his parka the way he likes it, and Otis brings its hem to his face and wipes his eyes. They eat their pizza, and the house is quiet, and after a while Otis runs Lego cars over the carpet. Basil imagines driving Otis straight to the Pocatello airport and flying all night and queuing up outside *The Today Show* just as Muriel begins her appearance. She'll see him pressed against the studio window and cock her head in amazement; she'll tell Al Roker—right in the middle of *Today's Take*—that she is realizing only now that she made a mistake, that you never lose by loving, you only lose by holding back, and at her insistence security will escort Basil and Otis onto the set, and Al Roker's producer will whisper into Al's flesh-colored earpiece, *Twitter is going bananas, keep this rolling*, and Muriel will throw her arms wide and say, "Get in here, Mr. Basil Bebbington from Bakersfield," and Basil will look thin on TV, and Al Roker will don a cape in honor of Otis, and by nightfall half of America will be wearing capes, everyone superhero-ing everything, and Al will invite them to spend the weekend in his brownstone, and Basil will cook his mushroom casserole, and Basil and Otis will monitor storms on Al's rooftop X-band Doppler radar, and Al will poke his head through the hatch onto his roof deck and say, "Basil, that was the best goddamn casserole I've tasted in my life," and Basil will say, "Thank you, Al, but please don't swear in front of my son."

Lego men colonize Basil's ankles. He retrieves the carbonized casserole from the yard and scrapes the remains into the garbage can in the garage. Across the street, the twin spotlights of the Masters Castle rise into the sky. He says, "We could go to Florida. Stay with my parents."

Back inside, Mags snores against the dishwasher. He places a pillow under her head, and hand-washes the dishes, and the boiler in the basement exhales its ancient, burnt-hair smell, and when Basil next looks out the window, he sees Nicholas the contractor set something on the front step. The old man gives a wave, and his truck drives off, and Basil is still a moment, then opens the door and there on the front step are two head lamps and an envelope that says, *Seems like you and the kid could use a night out.*

Inside: a skull key chain bearing a single key.

Basil looks at the iPad still on the table, the shape of Mags on the floor, the key in his hand. Then he walks into Otis's room and stretches the band of a head lamp around his son's head.

He leads Otis out the back door so he doesn't see his mother, and they switch on their head lamps and cross Clark Street and stand in front of the Master's Castle. In the strange, purple light it looks large and frightening, a temple risen from some Mephistophelean underworld.

"We're going *in* there?" asks Otis. Basil turns the key, imagining ball gags and pommel horses, middle-aged men in latex trussed up in clotheslines, but in the beam of his head lamp, maybe twenty feet away, he sees what looks like a ten-foot-tall toy castle complete with battlements and turrets and pennants. Spiraling around it are pastures and villages, populated with waist-high windmills and stables, and what appears to be an actual flowing river, and everywhere five-foot-tall miniature oaks hold up thousands of real-looking leaves, and three-inch woodcutters stand beside wagons, the whole thing meticulous and miraculous in the strange light, and Basil blinks on the threshold, confused, overwhelmed, until Otis says, "Dad, it's Putt-Putt!"

To their left, down a cobbled path, stands a sign saying, *Hole #1*, with two putters and two golf balls and a little scorecard waiting on an apron of real-looking grass. Otis, in his big blue coat with his cape trailing off the back and the little cyclopic light of the head lamp glowing in the center of his head, looks up at his father and says, "Ready?"

They pick up the putters, one long-handled, one short, and set their balls in the little dots, and begin.

They play over ramps, through tunnels, under staircases, little wooden ponies drowsing in little wooden stables, mini blacksmiths frozen beside mini anvils, tiny swallows nesting under the eaves of the tiny cottages, everything detailed down to the tongs in the blacksmiths' hands. With each hole they wind closer to the great castle at the center, and Otis keeps score, and they roll their balls over moats, and Basil watches his sweet, mysterious son bend over each stroke, concentrating hard. And so what if he's not a shadow in Muriel's memory? She dreamed her dream after all, found her other Earth, just like Nicholas found his, and sometimes people just love who they love and what can you do about that? There are advantages in not getting what you want. Basil starts computing the realities of moving to Florida—plane tickets, separation from Mags, custody, schools, the size of his parents' condo in Tampa—but rather than feel overwhelmed, he feels light, even dizzy, as if he has rapidly ascended from sea level to fourteen thousand feet and can see the vast glimmering platter of the Pacific stretched out below.

They reach the eighteenth hole, Otis up by twenty, and the castle walls loom in the beams of their head lamps, little wooden guards in guard-houses peering down at them and little archers in archer loops and little golden chains holding up the drawbridge. Otis places his ball on the tee and looks at his father and says, "I'm not ready to give up my cape."

"I know, kid."

"I just need it a little longer."

"You take your time."

Otis sets his feet and whacks his ball straight up a ramp, and it flies right into a hole in the center of the drawbridge, a one-in-a-thousand shot, and some kind of machinery inside the castle comes to life. The three-inch guards lower their four-inch halberds, and the archers on the battlements lower their bows, and lights glow in the windows of the keep and in the towers and in the miniature oaks, and what looks like real smoke rises from chimneys, and the drawbridge comes down like the maw of a terrible beast, and a royal guard of bannermen marches out from the castle and stands to each side, and between them a harp-ist slides out, moving on some kind of indiscernible track, and begins to pluck her tiny instrument, and though it might be his imagination, Basil hears the tune of Stevie Wonder's "Higher Ground" . . .

*No one's gonna bring me down*
*Oh no*
*Till I reach my highest ground*

. . . and the harpist plays and the castle glows, and when the song ends she turns, and slides back into the castle, and the royal guard retreats, and the drawbridge rises, and the lights in the windows wink out one by one, and the warehouse goes dark again.

Otis waves the scorecard and says, "I wrecked you, Dad." They lock the door behind them and stop on the edge of Clark Street and switch off their head lamps. Above them a few stars burn above clouds. A jet glides past, flashing its wing lights.

*Nominated by Tin House, Elizabeth McKenzie*

# BLAKE GRIFFIN DUNKS OVER A CAR

by MATTHEW OLZMANN

from FOUR WAY REVIEW

with a full gospel choir crooning behind him,
with twenty thousand spectators surging to their feet,
with an arena of flashbulbs flashing its approval,
and I'm spellbound, thinking it's all so spectacular, until

the broadcast team weighs in,
and Charles Barkley says, "That *wasn't* the greatest dunk,"
and Marv Albert says, "But the presentation was pretty fun,"
and I'm made to revisit what I thought I saw
as one question replaces all others—

Was it *truly* extraordinary? Or, by the paragon
of unimpeachable aesthetic standards by which
the annual NBA Slam Dunk Competition is adjudicated,
was it actually pedestrian, mortal, a somewhat *meh* occurrence
made mythic only through gimmicks and frills?

Like those little fish that eat bits of plastic
in the Pacific because they believe bits of plastic
look like microscopic food particles,
I too can be charmed by any well-made illusion.

Copperfield makes the Statue of Liberty disappear.
Penn and Teller catch bullets between their knowing teeth.

Smelling like a new vacuum cleaner, the conman in my heart
successfully hawks all his useless trinkets
to the hopeful stooge who stumbles through my brain.
Snake oil and radium ore. The furcula of a partridge.
The foot of a rabbit. I want to believe
in the marvelous, not because it feels authentic,
but because the alternative

is a world where no one dons a cape to leap over buildings.
No one turns lead to kindness.
No one sings the kraken to sleep.

In a kingdom that insists on repudiating all enchantments,
I feel catastrophic and alone. I watch the trees get older.
I watch the ice form on their branches. Last winter,

I sat in an emergency room
after my wife collapsed at work.
Her doctors asked questions but provided no answers.
They sent us home not knowing
why, or what, or if it would happen again.

You can look for an explanation, but sometimes
there's no wand to wave, no sorcery to make anything okay.
There's just doubt, and it rocks us toward
whatever trick of light we'll reach for next.

I will cling to any rationale offered.
I might pray or go to a church where a priest
tells a story about transubstantiation,
hands me a chalice filled with possibility.

And I know there's no blood in there.
I know the wine will taste like wine. Still—
I *lift* the cup.

*Nominated by Four Way Review, Paul Crenshaw, Nausheen Eusuf*

# MILK

## by JANE HIRSHFIELD

from PIRENE'S FOUNTAIN CULINARY POEMS

From time to time the placid
shrugs its shoulders—
earthquakes, for instance—

but still the world
depends
on placid things' resistance.

The fire requires
its trees,
the sea its hem of boulders,

the wind
without its halls
would howl in silence;

for everything that
flares up, something lowers itself,
digs in

for an existence
in the long haul, slows.
It may well be the placid knows

its worth. The cow whose
calf was taken
eats again—but do not guess

too quickly at the meaning
in the red hips' unbent squareness,
the large-jawed head

half-buried in the grass:
with each fly's weightless
bite, the thick skin shivers.

The placid, unlike us,
lives in the moment.
Something must;

like chairs,
or painted dressers,
on an earth where loss

is so all present
that we drink it without thinking,
blue-white in its early morning glass.

*Nominated by Pirene's Fountain, Alice Mattison, Joyce Carol Oates*

# TOUCH

by POPPY SEBAG-MONTEFIORE

from GRANTA

Between 1999 and 2007, I lived in China on and off. I worked as a journalist at the BBC bureau in Beijing for some of that time. I wasn't there for the job; I was there, and the job helped me stay longer. The first story I covered was the launch of China's first manned spacecraft. We broadcast astronaut Yang Liwei's message that crackled and fizzed back to Earth: 'All's well,' he said, as he orbited our planet alone. The good lines may have already been taken, but it was 2003 and China was transforming from a socialist into a market economy, from a developing country into a global superpower. Our news cycle turned between the thrills and promises of development and the fallout from such rapid modernisation: pollution; unequal rights for migrant workers in the cities; people beaten when they petitioned the state for compensation over land illegally confiscated and sold off by local officials. It was an epic story, but the lows were distressing. By the end of my time there, I'd interviewed so many people who were in such a state of fear that I began to catch it, and after being detained a couple of times, I was paranoid. I'd check behind my curtains when I got home.

Before reaching that point, I was having my own passionate relationship with China. Just to be awake was to absorb—the language, ways to live—like a baby learns the world. Every day I was touched. Many times, by friends, by strangers, by the lady who swept the street by the courtyard where I lived. By the water sellers, the restaurateurs, by old men playing chess, by people I didn't know. Most I would never meet again. I was handled, pushed, pulled, leaned upon, stroked, my hand was held. And it was through these small, intimate, gestural moments that I began to get a hold on how macro changes imprinted themselves onto people's relationships and inner lives.

Touch had its own language, and the rules were the opposite of the ones I knew at home. Beijing's streets were scenes of countless gestures of touch. If people bumped or rubbed arms as they passed in the street there was no need for an apology, not even a flinch. Strangers would lean their whole body weight against one another in a queue. Everyone seemed to have a certain kind of access to anyone else's body. Shoppers and stallholders would hold on to each other's arms as they negotiated with one another. People would pack in together around a neighbour-hood card game. In the evening, women would hold each other in ball-room embraces as groups waltzed on street corners.

Touch in public, among strangers, had a whole range of tones that were neither sexual nor violent. But it wasn't neutral either. At times, yes, you'd be leaned on indiscriminately because of lack of space, or to help take some weight off someone's feet. Yet other times you'd choose people you wanted to cling on to, or you'd be chosen. You'd get a sense of someone while haggling over the price of their garlic bulbs and you'd just grab on to each other's forearms as you spoke or before you went on your way. Touch was a precise tool for communication, to express your appreciation for someone's way of being, the brightness in their eyes as they smiled, their straightforwardness in a negotiation, a kindness they'd shown.

I felt buoyed and buffeted by this touch. I sometimes felt like I was bouncing or bounding from one person to the next like a pinball, pushed and levered around the city from arm to arm. If the state was like an overly strict patriarch, then the nation, society or the people on the streets were the becalming matriarch. This way of handling each other felt like a gentle, restorative cradle at times. At other times all the hands on you could be another kind of oppressive smothering. But usually touch was like a lubricant that eased the day-to-day goings-on and in-teractions in the city, and made people feel at home.

I wanted to document this unselfconscious touch. To keep hold of it. I could tell that this ease between the bodies of strangers might not sur-vive rapid urbanisation. This touch was so visual, so visible. I freed my camera from the head-and-shoulders interview shot and took it out to the streets.


A few weeks ago I found a tape of video footage that I'd labelled TOUCH I and shot in Beijing sometime between 2005 and 2006. Low sunshine

51

glows pink-gold on people's faces. An open-fronted clothes shop blasts a techno beat out onto a giant pedestrian street near the centre of the city. There's a long queue of customers waiting to go inside. My camera is on the closeness between the people standing in this line.

I focus on two men in particular. One is older, perhaps in his sixties. He's wearing an army-style jacket and grey woolly hat. In front of him is a man probably in his forties; he's wearing a mauve jacket, spattered with tiny flecks of yellow paint. These two men are leaning against one another. Neither notices particularly. The man in khaki now bashes into the man in mauve several times as he turns to look at how the queue has grown behind him.

They get closer to the front of the queue. I move with them and the music booms louder, a heart pumping, like a soundtrack from the inside of the body amplified onto the street. The man in mauve starts to bop. B-boom, B-boom goes the music, left-to-right goes the man in mauve. Each time he steps to the beat—he's dancing, he's keeping warm; he's standing sideways in the queue—his right arm bumps into the man in khaki's belly, repeatedly, rhythmically, again and again. The man in khaki doesn't flinch, he's welcoming it as much as he doesn't acknowledge it at all. He's comfortable. Watching, it now seems to me that it's impossible that these two men don't know each other, in fact they must really be quite close: friends, workmates, family even. Most likely they are father and son. Just as I'm about to fast-forward the tape to skip to the next vignette—the two men get larger—I'm approaching them with my camera—their faces fill the frame, and I hear myself ask: 'Where are you from?'

'Hebei,' says the man in mauve.

'Hubei,' says the man in khaki.

Hebei means north of the river, and Hubei means north of the lake. These are provinces about six hundred miles apart.

'How do you know each other?' I ask.

Their voices overlap:

'We don't know each other,' says the man in khaki.

'We don't,' says the man in mauve.


Up a dingy staircase, above the Lucky House Mini Market on Shaftesbury Avenue in London, there is a traditional Chinese medicine clinic. Dr Fan is in his sixties, he left China about thirty years ago and tells me, when I'm back in London, that this touch I'm describing is a rural way of being together: the touch of peasants. I've struggled to find people in Beijing to think about this touch with because it's so obvious to them they can hardly see it. But Dr Fan tells me, as he pummels the sole of my foot with his knuckles, that intellectuals and the ruling classes have always kept a respectful distance from each other, have always been more self-contained. During the period I lived in China—that time of mass migration and urbanisation—Beijing was a city of villages piled on top of and around each other. Dr Fan said it was true that under Mao everybody did come physically closer to one another. Especially within the sexes, men with men, women with women. Mao sent people from the cities, the 'educated youth', down to the countryside to learn from the peasants. Maybe all hands that know each other's work, know each other.

Touch is an important part of China's traditional medical practice. Doctors feel their patients' wrists for six different pulse lines to make a diagnosis. Massage is used for preventative health and as a cure. Pressure points on the skin relate to specific internal organs and touching them releases toxins and reduces inflammation. Once I had stomach cramps on an eleven-hour boat journey from Shanghai to an island in the East China Sea. A lady on the next bunk, whom I'd never met before, took my hand and found the acupressure point that corresponds to the uterus and began to press it for me. Gradually the pain dulled away.

*Yang sheng* 养生 means 'nourishing life'. It's an active pursuit of health through the medical arts—massage, exercise, food. Think wellness—if wellness was less about gym memberships and spirulina shots, and more about a set of ancient ideas for how to cultivate your body's energy to improve your health and sense of well-being. It's combined with a fear for your life because of the lack of health-care welfare, and the necessity not to be too much of a financial burden on your one child in your old age. When I lived in Beijing, *yang sheng* wasn't so commercially inflected among the older, urban generation. It was a bodily intellect, a tuning-in to the needs of the body: at times carefully considered, at times instinctive and ingrained. It's what brought people together for ballroom dancing in the evening, and exercising in the park together in the morning.

In many ways this kind of coming together on the streets to attend to the needs of the body felt like a form of resistance to the state, a complicity among people. Although this kind of solidarity may in some ways have been made possible and encouraged by socialism, taken into people's own hands, it felt like a form of personal autonomy. In a place heavy with censorship, where published and broadcasted words can't necessarily be trusted, this was a public sphere of the senses, a way to feel one another out. Being together like this was also a way to derive pleasure and vitality from each other, without asking or taking anything from anybody. Instead, it's a reciprocity, an openness, an attention to a personal need.

I remember the first time my boundaries dissolved to accept the confident, unselfconscious touch of a stranger. I was standing in the audience at a Tibetan Buddhist festival at Labrang monastery in the yellow-grey mountains of China's north-western Gansu province, and a man, probably in his eighties, came up behind me and wrapped his arms around my waist. I turned round affronted at first, then bemused. He didn't even look at me but craned his neck over my shoulder towards the show. I saw that his grip around me meant nothing to him but to be able to stand and see without toppling over. He was using my body as if it was part of his. Once I'd checked out whether there might be anything sordid going on, and realised there wasn't, I remember I couldn't help but feel delighted by having this man hang on to me. I was a bit ecstatic about it. An elderly man could use my body to help him stand and see. And it was lovely. I made my friend take a photo of us from behind and from the front. My face is beaming. It could be compared to the invigoration you get from standing in front of a painting that you love. But this touch is more powerful: it can happen at any time, often when least expected, and it's personal—the medium is another living being. It gives you something of Freud's 'oceanic feeling'—when the baby doesn't know the contours of its own body, before the ego, when it's one with everything else.

I sometimes wonder if there's a shadow side to this touch. If the accessibility of everyone's bodies can be mistaken by those with power as a right to them. Could it be partly why local officials can be quick to hire thugs to beat petitioners as a way to deter them from complaining to the 'higher-ups'? Does the easiness and informality between people encourage corruptibility among officials, leaning on other leaders to sway them?

At that time, touch in China between friends and peers of the opposite sex, of all ages, was restrained, almost taboo. If I tried to hug or kiss my male friends as we parted, they'd be embarrassed and squirm away. But within the sexes, friends and colleagues, especially younger ones, would lounge all over each other. Women would often walk with their arms linked. Guys would walk with their arms across each other's shoulders. Men on construction sites would sit on one another's laps.

Platonic touch had its own erotics. It imbued you with a direct hit of the love, energy and camaraderie that you get from friendship. Perhaps touch between friends was partly set free, and came to the fore, because sexual touch was prohibited by the Communist Party under Mao. Sex was confined to marriage, and even then wasn't supposed to distract from the love for the revolution.

Among the older generation, who grew up under these ideas, couples are fairly formal with each other physically in public. When I spoke to older people sitting by Beijing's Back Lake about the kinds of touch they shared with their spouses in their homes they were matter-of-fact. Sex was sex, one lady told me, it never involved kissing. An elderly man told me of his relationship with his wife: 'I rub her back, she rubs mine.'

In a bestselling Chinese short story of the late 1990s, 'I Love Dollars' by Zhu Wen, the narrator, also a writer called Zhu Wen, decides the best thing he could do for his father, who is visiting him in the big city, would be to help him get laid. Zhu Wen muses: 'Thinking about it, I realised Father was a person with quite a libido, just that he was born a bit before his time. In his day, libido wasn't called libido, it was called idealism.'

The sense I had was that the mainstay of physical, intimate life for the older generation in Beijing was felt on the streets.

After I moved back to London, I would return to Beijing for a couple of weeks each year. In 2008, I went back during the summer Olympics. I'd been there in 2001, the night Beijing won the bid. A spontaneous street party sprang up. People abandoned their cars in the middle of the road. They were euphoric. They'd been accepted by the world. Now, seven years later, Beijingers seemed to be putting up with the Games with muted acquiescence. Much of the Beijing of 2001 had been bull-dozed. A modern city had replaced it. And in elaborate preparations for the Olympics, Beijing had been cleaned up. In the immediate run-up to the Games, anybody vaguely questionable had been removed. The city's Spiritual Civilisation Committee had banned certain behaviours: spitting, disorderly queueing, the indiscretions of the body. Volunteer elders were given official red armbands and a phone number to ring if there was trouble. They'd sit on stools on the pavement with a good view of their patch. The city was straitjacketed. I didn't go to the Games, but I did get out my camera to record the ways that people would touch one another. It was hard to find instances of the old touch. Now along the boulevards my viewfinder filled with the clasped hands and interlinked arms of young couples and lovers.

Touch was relocating from the street to the home, from public to private life. It was becoming privatised and sexualised. The younger generation now performed a newly liberated sexuality on the streets. They offered each other different kinds of tenderness, attention and care, sometimes with gestures that resembled the globalised, romantic Hollywood way. In 'I Love Dollars', the father reads some of Zhu Wen's writing and complains that it's all about sex: 'A writer ought to offer people something positive, something to look up to, ideals, aspirations, democracy, freedom, stuff like that.' Zhu Wen responds: 'Dad, I'm telling you, all that stuff, it's all there in sex.' Where for his father's generation there was a forced sublimation of sexuality into idealism, for Zhu Wen the new and potentially difficult ideals are sublimated into sex.

The city had sped up. People couldn't shuffle past each other in the same old ways. The new middle class had places to be. Supermarkets were taking over from street markets, where there's no bartering, or need for much communication at all, in fact customers were often on the phone to someone else. Migrant workers now lived in the city in large numbers but were usually sequestered away. They slept in dorms on their construction sites and didn't have the same rights as urban residents. Where previously I'd barely been able to distinguish between rural migrants and urbanites, now the differences between people who'd arrived from the countryside and the city residents were striking, visible in fashions, faces, how beleaguered they were. Now urbanites kept their distance. There was a growing fear of migrants, that they might want what urbanites had. People began to talk about migrant workers as dirty, dangerous, people to stay clear of. They were untouchable.

Somehow the bland, fatigued Soviet-style rooms—a portrait of a leader on a white chalky wall, paint that brushed off on your clothes—had been a background for people to have a certain social command over their bodies. But the architecture, infrastructure and public spaces of late capitalism—sparkling malls, privately owned and patrolled, steel towers, underground trains—were all spaces that encouraged more public formality, better behaviour, more self-consciousness, wider gaps between strangers.

I went for reflexology in a clinic I used to go to in Beijing, an offshoot of a large traditional Chinese medicine hospital, and for the first time the masseur wore plastic, scratchy gloves. It's for hygiene purposes, he told me, there are so many people in the city now.

Suddenly massage and acupuncture weren't the only therapies. Psychotherapy talk shows were appearing on television. Rather than healing through touch, people were now interested in sitting in a room with a therapist with strict boundaries against physical contact. As this was a brand-new profession, in the absence of a psychotherapist whose experience people could trust—some who felt they needed to understand more about their inner lives began to train to be therapists and analysts. Over the next few years, 400,000 psychological counsellors would qualify in China's main cities.

When I moved back to London in 2007—I missed that public sense of touch. I continued to bump into people on the street. Friends walking beside me would be embarrassed and apologise on my behalf as the people I'd pushed into would be annoyed and I wouldn't notice. But soon I readapted to London streets and grew as irritable about the clamour and crush of strangers as the next person. And then I did what everyone with a sensory project did at the beginning of the twenty-first century. I went to talk to a neuroscientist.

Francis McGlone's work centres around nerve receptors in our skin called C-tactile afferents. They've only been recently discovered in humans. They lie within our hairy skin, and are particularly concentrated in our back, trunk, scalp, face and forearms. They respond to slow and light stroking. None are found in the genitals. When stimulated, through stroking, the C-tactile afferents produce pleasure. It's not a sexual pleasure, but the kind of feeling brought about by the touch between a mother and baby. Neuroscientists call this 'social touch'.

These nerve fibres are ancient, they existed early in the life of the species, long before language, and even before the receptors that tell us to move our hand away from pain. This is a sign that they're vital for the protection of life and health. In early times we needed people nearby throughout our lives to help us groom and to clear us of parasites. The reward for sticking together was pleasure.

McGlone is interested in moments when modernity overrides what he sees as evolutionary processes. He believes that we need C-tactile stimulation from birth for the social brain to develop. When I told him about what I noticed in Beijing, he said that it might be that poorer people gather together more than richer people because they rely on each other more for survival. He describes his world of science where everybody tinkers away alone to get their work done. Social distance, he says, has its uses—it allows the brain to get on with other things.

But Francis McGlone does bring people together. He runs the Somatosensory & Affective Neuroscience Group at Liverpool John Moores University for scientists and psychologists working on the relationships between C-tactile afferents and our emotional lives. He invited me to present my anecdotal observations from Beijing to the group. Jayne Morton, a massage therapist and occupational therapist for the Cheshire police force, said that my descriptions reminded her of where she grew up in the Wirral in the 1970s. Her parents ran the social club. Men would be in one room lounging on one another, and women in another room, arms linked, sitting squashed together. The men had finished National Service and needed a closeness with people who'd gone through similar things. The women, used to the men being away, spent time with friends who were also home with their children.

When the church closed down in the early 1980s, so did the school and the club. Everyone dispersed. People spent the evenings with their families. Then the Wirral became more diverse and multicultural, but without a big hub for meeting. In the 1980s, Jayne said that organising events for parents at the school had become more difficult because of higher divorce rates—step-parents and parents often wouldn't be in a room together.

This made me wonder if, when communities break apart, the relationship between the couple becomes overdetermined. Does the pressure for all the different kinds of erotics that I found on the streets of Beijing fall on just one other person? In the group, perhaps we are able to replay some of the intimacy of our infancy, the gentle touch of our mothers, that kind of care we must still long for. It makes us feel good, part of the world around us and with people we trust—even if that trust is calculated in an instant.

Francis and I shake hands as we part. We didn't touch when we met or when we said goodbye after dinner the night before. We'd spoken for hours, straight-faced, professional. But as he guided me down the purpose-built university corridor he did pat me on the back of the shoulder blade. The pat gave me the impression that he thought I was all right. It was nice.

The shock of the UK's Brexit referendum result when it happened caused intellectuals and cosmopolitans to reflect on how 'out of touch' they are. Academics called themselves out of touch, a presenter admitted that the BBC was out of touch. London was declared way out of touch. And now words are barely trusted. We're post-touch, post-truth. How will society communicate now?

Could it be that anxieties and fears are stoked when people are so far out of reach from each other—not only from establishment elites, but from the rest of the majority of the population too. Church halls, community centres have been closing down; work places with zero-hour contracts offer limited opportunities for socialising. There are few spaces where people can jostle together, to share and make the world with our hands.

Perhaps this atomisation means that some people feel threatened by the idea that immigrant groups seem, at least, to have something that the majority population don't have: functioning 'communities'. New migrants often do create expat networks for work, spaces to gather for faith, to eat, to speak native languages, live close to each other. They need each other to survive. The thing about touch is that it's visual, visible. And if there isn't enough integration then people who already feel isolated will feel excluded from the perceived closeness of immigrant communities, and then too from those bonds that enable us to come together and help one another thrive.

The most acute moments of life—birth and mourning—require us to live at increasing distance from those we are closest to. The distances and proximities at which we live from our loved ones, and everybody else, are also modulated by macro forces: economy, ideology, identity. The metropolis imprints itself onto the intimate details of our lives. Wherever that leaves us, my experiment (sample size: one) says—we aren't stuck like this. It takes just a few months in a different world of ideas and our bodies respond, adapt, and the space between us can change again.

*Nominated by Granta*

# UPRIGHT AT THYATIRA

fiction by DARRELL KINSEY

from NOON

Long ago in my reading, I came across a term, a single word, used to describe the phenomenal blending of voices that can occur when close blood relatives sing together. I have forgotten the term and have not run across it since, nor have I had any success in looking it up, but one of my fondest memories from going to church, long before becoming a minister, involves singing with my father and my little brother, who both had bright, clear tenor voices. Without discussing it, one of them would choose the harmony, the other the melody, and though my voice was always much weaker than theirs, they would carry me through the hymns, and I could feel my voice transforming in my throat as it strove to match theirs in power and tone. The effect was so noticeable, so startling and disruptive, that we would glance up from the hymnals at each other to acknowledge that our three voices had melded into a single instrument.

No one sings very well at Thyatira. The problem, I think, is with the piano. The piano does not encourage the congregation as it should. Though Nancy Rankin plays as someone whose fingers cannot bend, and though she does not mind stopping midway through a verse and starting over, I assign much of the fault to the upright itself. Nancy has no piano at her house but comes to the church Friday evenings to practice the hymns for Sunday. From the porch of the manse, I can see the stained-glass windows lit and hear her playing.

When I walk over and sit in the sanctuary listening, she finishes the hymn and turns to speak to me. "That's one of my favorites," she says. "That's a pretty, pretty hymn."

"Something's wrong, though, isn't it?" I ask.

"What?"

"I think we need to get the piano tuned."

We are a poor congregation, and when I call the church secretary the following morning, I learn there are no funds available for hiring a professional tuner. Thinking I might be able to handle the task myself, I begin researching the process, and in so doing, Eli Eason comes to mind. Eli and I once waited tables together. He majored in piano performance and often carries, as a talisman in his back pocket, a tuning fork. Whenever he has an anxious moment, he brings it out and slaps its tines on his thigh to get it droning an eerie tone. No one ever needed a tuning fork less than Eli, who has perfect pitch. If a stool leg screeches across the floor, he names the note it has played. On the back counters of the restaurant, he used to set up several goblets with varying levels of water to have the waitstaff run our dipped fingers over the rims, creating in the ringing the most portentous minor ninths.

I call Eli, and though he has never tuned a piano himself, he claims familiarity with the process, and he knows someone from his days at the music school from whom he can borrow the required tools. He comes over on a Sunday morning at eight, not very aware that it is Sunday or that the service will need to begin just three hours later. When I remind him, he hangs his fingers from his empty belt loops, tugging his pants into place, and says he thinks he can do it in time.

I pace the aisles while he works. When the first members arrive to take their places in the pews, the lid is still off the upright, exposing the soundboard and the harpish set of strings. Several elders of the church ask what is happening. I come up with the idea in the moment to have a less formal service featuring Eli on the piano. When one of the more venerated gentlemen of the church learns I will not be delivering a homily, he says, "So you won't be earning your keep today?" He grins and adds that it might be nice to take a break from the sermon. When Nancy Rankin arrives and I tell her we will not be needing her services this morning, she is very polite, almost glad, I think, saying this will give her the opportunity to visit her grandchildren over in Maxeys. She and her husband decide not to stay but get back in their vehicle and leave.

While I deliver the opening prayer and announcements, Eli still tinkers with individual notes, playing them over and over again to get them right. Then he closes the lid and takes to the bench to play, as a test, a scale and an etude. Already the congregation is impressed. The rest of the hour, with the hammer and forks and pins and mutes still scattered across the sanguine carpet, Eli seduces us with the most beautiful pieces. The bass notes rumble like the voice of the mountains while the treble notes flirt and fly with impishness. No one can understand how only two hands and ten fingers are capable of all the notes we hear. He plays one of his own little sylvan masterpieces, followed by a highly technical sonata composed by one of the greats. The sound waves are almost visible to me. The melodies flow among the people and gather about them, vivid and full of static. These are rustic country people who do not often get to hear live performances of such sophisticated music, and it is a privilege to sit watching them as the pieces reach their emotions. Then Eli asks for requests, any of their favorite hymns, and one old man, rather than calling out a title, simply belts out the first verse, and Eli is able to pick it up with him, playing in whatever chance key the old man's vocal cords have chosen.

At the end of the hour, when Eli stands up from the bench, his response to the applause is a nod and more of a stoop than a bow. He and I head next door to the manse, where I fix him a tomato sandwich. We drink beer and eat lunch on the front porch. When I thank him and tell him his talents should be put to the service of the Lord every day of the week, he makes it clear through his response that he still does not believe. Though I have suspected this as the case, I have just witnessed the Holy Spirit flow through his fingers, and I am particularly hurt by his blunt affirmation of denial.

"Why then," I ask, "would you give up your Sunday morning to come tune the piano for a church worshipping a god you don't believe in?"

"Because you asked me to," he says.

Adding to my sorrow is a feeling of powerlessness. I have been through all this with him before. Many a late night, we stood on the curb outside the restaurant with the topic of faith preventing us both from heading home. From having grown up in the church, he knows the gospel well, just as he remembers all the hymns, and he thoroughly and wholeheartedly rejects the message. I can feel him becoming agitated in his chair, and I have little else to say, because I have become sad and confused. I know he is a wonderful person who regularly performs acts of charity and kindness, and in many ways, I know him to be more Christ-like in his daily activities than a number of others whose readings of the Sermon on the Mount number in the dozens. We know nothing else to do but to stand in silence on the porch. We hug goodbye in the driveway, and maybe both of us are parting with the feeling of having failed each other.

The manse landline is ringing. No one ever calls the manse landline except when one of the church members deems something an emergency. The crisis surrounds Nancy Rankin, who has called in tears, wondering if she has been permanently replaced as the church pianist. I try to explain over the phone but decide I need to visit her in person. I immediately drive to her house, a brick ranch in the southern reaches of the county. I meet her at the storm door. She carries her pocketbook in the crook of her arm, acting like she is on her way out for errands and will have no time to speak with me. I nearly push her back inside and make her sit still in her recliner. She acts flustered when I tell her she is the church pianist and always will be, as far as I am concerned. "I know I'm not musically gifted, but I try so hard," she says, and her voice becomes rough and glottal. She starts to weep. I get to my knees in front of her recliner and embrace her and speak into her ear. I tell her she is a great service to the church, and as I am hugging her, my arm is brushed by something on her garment. I back away and see a tag hanging from her blouse. Noticing how the seams stand and how the floral print is somewhat dull, I feel obligated to tell her that she is wearing her blouse inside out.

*Nominated by Noon*

# LATE RUMSPRINGA

## fiction by AUSTIN SMITH

from NARRATIVE

One Morning, after chores were done, chores his boys used to do, Abraham Zimmerman told his wife through the door of their bedroom that he was going to town. He waited a moment to see if she would ask what the job was, prepared to tell her that he was helping a crew that had gotten behind on roofing work, but she said nothing and he was relieved that he didn't have to lie.

The dogs tried to follow him down the lane. They were confused about where Abraham's two sons had gone and so were cloying and needy. He had to yell and throw a few rocks to get them to stay.

It was a good two-mile walk to reach the county highway along the network of gravel roads that linked the community together. He knew that any interaction had the power to make him change his mind. If someone asked him to lend a hand with something, he wouldn't be able to refuse. But he met no one.

He hadn't been up Cording Road since the evening of the accident, but because the accident had everything to do with his decision this day, it seemed necessary to pass the spot where his boys died. There was no visible sign, and he resisted wading into the ditch grass to search for one. And then he saw, on the fence, the remnants of a bouquet someone had tied there with twine. Anyone who didn't know about the accident would assume it was just a tangle of wildflowers blown off a windrow after haying.

At the top of the hill the land leveled out, and he could see, in the distance, the glare of cars and trucks headed toward town. He stood at the intersection, in the oblong, octagonal shadow of the stop sign. He didn't bother putting his thumb out. There was no reason to. Everyone driving past could see, from his clothes, why he needed a ride. It wasn't long before a pickup stopped, raising dust off the gravel shoulder. There were bales in the bed, stacked higher than the cab. He could never keep the names of the retired farmers straight, but he recognized the man from past rides. The windows were down, the radio blaring, and it was too loud to have to try to talk.

It wasn't until the outskirts of town where the speed limit dropped that it became quiet enough in the cab for the farmer, whose name, he remembered now, was Keiser, to say, "The son-in-law wants straw for his berries but he doesn't have the decency to come out and pick the bales up himself. Says he doesn't want to get his car all chaffy. I pre'near popped a hernia loading these up this morning. But between the wife and the daughter, I'd never hear the end of it if I'd refused to deliver them."

They pulled into the lot of the Oasis, the farmers' diner at the edge of town, marked by a fake palm tree. The trunk was a telephone pole painted grayish, the fronds pieces of green plastic. Two testicular coconuts hung high up there by twine, and sometimes someone would get drunk and try to climb the trunk to get them, only to lose heart and have to slide back down.

The lot was full, and Abraham Zimmerman knew that every stool would be occupied by various versions of Keiser.

"Buy you a coffee?" this particular Keiser said.

Abraham Zimmerman shook his head.

"Roofing work?"

Abraham Zimmerman nodded.

"I don't blame you for trying to get it done sooner rather than later. It's gonna be hotter than hell up there this afternoon."

And then, remembering his own tribulations and the suffering his son-in-law was putting him through, he winced and put his hand on his lower back and waddled toward the door of the diner.


When Abraham Zimmerman walked into Nelson Julius's barbershop, everyone turned and stared. He was younger than most of them but seemed older, what with his long chin beard just beginning to gray, his old-fashioned clothes, his straw hat and suspenders. The men waiting for haircuts held the pages of the *Pearl City Standard* in the air, losing their places in the black columns of news. Two of the three swivel chairs were occupied by a father and son, and they stared too, only their heads visible above the paper collars (the one around the boy's neck was too tight) and black capes. Staring, Jack let the buzzer delve too high up the boy's scalp, but managed to rein it in, then fixed the nick as well as he could. Only the boy's mother would notice, and soon the mistake would be lost under a football helmet and fresh hair. They all knew who this man was, if they didn't know his name. His teenage sons had been killed earlier that summer when a car hit the buggy they were riding in out on Cording Road.

Nelson Julius himself was at the father's head with clippers that whisked and snapped like a scolding redwing blackbird even as Abraham Zimmerman shuffled in across the hair-strewn floor. He remembered the days after the accident, how his customers had talked of what a tragedy it was, then proceeded to offer their opinions, which, aside from slight differences in tone, were more or less the same: if the Amish insisted on driving buggies on county roads, they'd better be prepared for the occasional accident. The men didn't say that that's what you got when you tried to live in a dead world in the midst of this living one, but that's what they were all thinking.

Nelson Julius respected the Amish, even admired them. They seemed not only of another time but of another dimension. That a car could have hit that buggy at all seemed impossible, as if it ought to have passed straight through the bodies of those two boys and those two horses, causing them to flicker briefly and take on, for a moment, the forms of the world their people had refused. One world had met another on that road, and Nelson Julius was of the world that had triumphed, and that made him feel guilty. He felt he was as much to blame as the woman who was driving, and he'd even imagined apologizing to Abraham Zimmerman if he ever had the opportunity.

Everyone watched Abraham Zimmerman try to hang his straw hat on the hat rack with the seed company caps, but it wouldn't hang, so he reached up and hung it on the antlers of a six-point buck that Nelson Julius had shot in northern Wisconsin a decade earlier. The canted hat made the buck look rakish and sly. Then Abraham Zimmerman sat down in the only available chair and took up the top magazine from the pile on the coffee table. It was an old issue of *Field and Stream*. On the cover a grinning man crouched on one knee, wrenching a dead buck's head toward the camera.

It was August. An oscillating floor fan stood in the corner, shaking its head as if in disapproval, raising dandruff that the men breathed in, making their lungs tickle. The men sitting on either side of Abraham

Zimmerman could smell him, though it wasn't an unpleasant smell. It reminded them of how their grandfathers smelled when they came in from the barn, back when they still farmed with horses. His hair was longer than any of the men in that shop would have let their hair grow before getting it cut, long enough to curl. The men didn't envy the barber who drew him, for either Jack or Nelson Julius would have to get right down into the lanolin-like odor of that hair and keep a straight face while cutting it.

Jack and Nelson Julius had been cutting hair together for so long that each could sense what the other was thinking. Nelson Julius sensed that Jack really didn't want to cut Abraham Zimmerman's hair, and Jack sensed that Nelson Julius, as the owner of the shop and the kinder of the two brothers, would volunteer to do it. As always, they had timed it so that father and son were finished at the same instant and neither would have to wait for the other, spinning them around and unknotting their paper collars and shaking their capes out. Nelson met them at the register. The boy kept rubbing his buzzed head in amazement while his father paid.

"Football starting up soon, then?" Nelson asked the boy, who was wearing paint-stained mesh athletic shorts and a Stockton Blackhawks T-shirt.

"Practice starts Monday, doesn't it, bud?" his father answered for him. Had it not been for his father, the boy wouldn't have played. He would have preferred to get off the school bus at Matt's farm so they could walk along the river, reaching down into the cold water so that the surface encircled their wrists with the thinnest bracelets, pocketing stones that lost their luster once they dried. At some point Matt would turn back and Brian would continue on alone, crossing back and forth over the river, coming up to his house from below, his pockets full of unremarkable stones.

Nelson would have asked the boy about football and the boy's father would have answered for him had Abraham Zimmerman not been there, but everyone who spoke was conscious of the fact that Abraham Zimmerman was listening, even if he seemed preoccupied with flipping through the glossy pages of *Field and Stream*.

Somehow Nelson managed to invite Abraham Zimmerman up to his chair without embarrassing him, knowing that the men who were waiting their turn wouldn't mind. They wanted to watch Abraham Zimmerman have his hair cut anyway. Jack was relieved for two reasons. First, that Nelson had taken the initiative and, second, that there was something else to stare at for once that wasn't the tumor in his back. It had appeared twenty years before as a hard knot under his left shoulder blade, and had grown, in the years since, to such a size that it was visible to folks when he was facing them, rising up over his shoulder. Even men whose hair he'd cut since they were boys couldn't help but let their eyes settle upon it. And one day he had arrived at work to find "Jack the Hunchback" spray-painted on the side of the shop.

Usually Nelson's was loud with talk, but the shop had become very quiet. The only sound was the golf tournament on the dusty television that, if anyone would have thought to wipe its screen of a decade of male duff, would have brightened to a degree that would have astonished the barbers. Anticipatory silence, the slicing sound of the club through air and the hollow thwack of the ball, then either groans or polite applause and the voices of the commentators.

Abraham Zimmerman sat down in Nelson's chair.

"Who's next?" Jack said.

"You go ahead," said the man who'd been sitting on Abraham Zimmerman's left. "I'm in no big rush."

"No, no, you were here first," said the man who'd been sitting on Abraham Zimmerman's right, "if I remember right."

The first man rose reluctantly. He wouldn't have as good a view now, but Jack obligingly spun his chair in such a way that he'd be able to watch in the mirror. Jack had to ask his customer twice how he wanted his hair cut before he answered, but he was just making conversation. Jack knew how the man liked it. It wasn't a style he would have recommended, but he was a barber, not a stylist.

The other men, some of whom had already had their hair cut earlier and were just hanging around because they were lonely, and now were hanging around to see what Abraham Zimmerman would look like with a haircut, had taken up their newspapers and pretended to have found their places, but the eyes hovering over the newsprint betrayed them. Aware that he was being observed more closely than usual, with a flick of his wrists Nelson made the black cape billow out. It seemed to hang in the air forever before settling beautifully down upon Abraham Zimmerman's body. It covered his white dress shirt that was slightly yellowed at the armpits, his blue suspenders, his woolen black pants. Only his boots, with real nails in the soles, showed. Out of habit Nelson prepared the paper collar to tie around Abraham Zimmerman's neck, but promptly gave up on the idea when he realized that the neck was too thickly bearded.

Coming around to face the man, Nelson Julius crossed his arms and said, "Well, how would you like your hair cut?"

"Short," Abraham Zimmerman said. His voice was surprisingly high.

"And what are we doing with the beard?"

"Shaving it off," Abraham Zimmerman said.

It was hard to detect any accent in these few words, but there was something, a singsongy quality to how he said, "Shaving it off." He accented the first and last syllables ("SHAVing it OFF") so that the phrase started high and fell and rose again, as if he'd said, "LA-dee-dee-DA."

If the onlookers had been interested before, they were fascinated now and gave up all pretense of reading the paper. Not only were they going to see Abraham Zimmerman get his hair cut: they were going to see his face.

Nelson Julius had gazed down upon countless heads in his career. He knew cowlicks and thinning patterns the way a weatherman knows high and low pressure and warm and cold fronts. But Nelson was no mere barber. He also considered the minds beneath hair, scalp, skull. The reason he was so beloved a barber was not because he was excellent at cutting hair (though he was that) but because, aside from certain bartenders and the priest, he was the only man many men would confide in. In fact, unlike the bartenders, whose advice was doled out with intoxicants that led to that advice being forgotten, and the priest, whose office was a little too close to God's, there was nothing preventing his customers from being honest with him. He liked to think that by cutting their hair he was also cutting their worries, if only by listening to them. He would have liked to do the same for the man sitting in his chair now. Had they been alone, he might have tried. But with the shop full, and everyone watching, it was impossible.

He started in. The man had beautiful hair, beginning to gray in places, but still mostly black. It was the beard that made Abraham Zimmerman seem older. Looking down at the thick, rich hair, Nelson realized how young Abraham Zimmerman was, and the tragedy of the deaths of his boys struck Nelson anew. It was a shame to cut this hair, but he had no choice but to give the man what he was paying for. The black, oily ringlets fell on the black cape in a pretty way, like maple seeds whirling down upon still water, and they were the prettiest shape, full circles, like lorgnettes.

"Not so hot today, is it?" Nelson said quietly, weather being his go to topic of conversation. He couldn't exactly ask Abraham Zimmerman what he thought of the Packers' playoff chances, or if he'd seen the great upset at the tractor pull the week before at the fair, and he certainly couldn't ask him if his boys were ready to go back to school, not only because they had been homeschooled, but because they were dead. But Abraham Zimmerman seemed to have taken Nelson's question for a statement and didn't see any reason to respond.

When Nelson was done cutting Abraham Zimmerman's hair, he spun him around in the chair so he was facing the mirror. He looked odd, with his long beard and short hair. He didn't smile, but there was a softness in his face that encouraged Nelson to make the joke he'd been considering making the whole time.

"Well, we can give you a discount on the shave since we're not having to shave any mustache."

The joke was worth the risk of making it. Abraham Zimmerman smiled, and everyone else laughed, and the man in Jack's chair, who was balding, said, "Does that mean I get a discount for the top of my head, Jack?" to which Jack replied, "If we gave discounts for thinning hair we'd go out of business."

There was more laughter and chatter. A tension that had been in the air since Abraham Zimmerman walked in had been released. But now Nelson was focused on the problem of Abraham Zimmerman's neck beard. And it was a problem. He'd never dealt with anything of its like. It was impossible to discern where the beard ended and the neck began. But slowly, like someone wading a fast-moving river by feeling their way along the gravel bottom, he entered in. The beard hair, surprisingly soft, almost silken, fell away from his clippers. Gradually, the face revealed itself, the jutting chin, the sallow cheeks.

"Where would you like your sideburns to end?" Nelson asked quietly. Abraham Zimmerman had closed his eyes. Without opening them he brought a hand up from under the cape and touched his earlobe. Nelson Julius cut there with the electric razor, but when Abraham Zimmerman flinched he realized he'd likely never heard a sound like that before, so close to his ear, and put the electric razor away. Then he opened a drawer he rarely opened anymore. The old shaving kit had been his old man's, as had the shop. He remembered, when he was a boy, how men would come by every morning for a shave. His father had a policy that if he drew blood, the shave was free. The very look of the box, the embossed initials on the lid, the snugness with which all the pieces fit into the maroon velvet compartments, made him miss his father with such intensity he nearly doubled over. He took his belt off and stropped the straightedge. Everyone was watching, even Jack, who kept clipping fruitlessly at the air above his customer's thinning hair.

Working the warm lather into Abraham Zimmerman's face and neck, Nelson was afraid he would cut his throat. But when it came time to shave him, his hand was as steady as a surgeon's. The shop fell away, the golf tournament, the red-and-white pillar swiveling upward infinitely outside the door, the eyes of the others. It was just Nelson and the problem of Abraham Zimmerman's neck beard. The blade was so sharp it made no sound and met no resistance. The wake it cut through the lather was beautiful. Even without running his fingertips over it he knew it was as smooth as baby flesh. Little did Abraham Zimmerman know that the problem of his neck beard would lead to men asking Nelson for a straightedge shave again, like their fathers used to.

When he was finished, Nelson put a towel under hot water in the sink and said, "Be right back." In the back room, among the clutter of hair-care products, broken electric razors, scissors that had rusted closed, he found what he was looking for: a tiny, unlabeled, faceted glass vial. He dabbed some on his wrist, smelled it. Rosewater.

He tipped the vial upside down into the steaming towel and rubbed Abraham Zimmerman's face and neck so vigorously that someone looking in the window might have thought he was trying to smother him. Then he spun him toward the mirror for the second time and the men who'd been watching saw the man see himself. They were all waiting for some kind of affirmation, but he merely nodded. The cape came off, his beautiful hair shaken to the floor. In his white dress shirt and blue suspenders and black wool pants, he looked somewhat like himself again. But if his intention in getting his hair cut and his beard shaved off had been to see what it was like to live in the world that had killed his boys, he had succeeded.

To pay Nelson, Abraham Zimmerman pulled out the biggest wad of cash the barber had ever seen. He had counted the money before leaving home. Three thousand four hundred and forty-three dollars. Because most of the bills had circulated within the community, they featured the old designs, so that there was something old-fashioned about them. One of the men waiting to get his hair cut, a young kid Nelson had never seen before, whistled when he saw the wad, but Abraham Zimmerman didn't seem to notice.

"How much?"

"Twelve for the cut, five for the shave."

He gave Nelson a twenty, then reached up and took his old straw hat off the buck's antlers and put it on his new head. It sat a little loosely, slightly awry. He said, "Much appreciated" to the whole shop and walked out, the summer air cool on his neck.

He walked downtown, keeping to the shade of the storefronts. From time to time he touched his new face. It was surprising to reach his bare neck. He thought he must look strange, though no one would have thought twice about his face, only his clothes, inherited ones, made before he was born and mended so well that they'd improved in quality as time went on.

Now when he saw clothes hanging in the window of a store, he went in. The conditioned air wicked the sweat right off his skin. It was a Goodwill, a name that gave him confidence he might have lacked had it been a Dollar General.

The store smelled of old lives, a laundry-like and slightly sour odor, clean and unclean at once. The woman behind the counter, wearing a blue vest too big for her shoulders, was preoccupied with hangers. Her greeting was to raise one into the air. After he walked past, she glanced up and stared.

There were a few other shoppers, women all. They had either just been or were about to go to the city pool. Their shoulders were bare and oily looking, like buttered rolls. Their flesh troubled him. It amplified the discomfort he felt at being clean-shaven.

He spent some time considering pants before realizing that he was in the women's section. Intimidated by clothes now, he walked over to the power tools and kitchen appliances, their cords taped up, stuck with pieces of paper that read, simply, "Works." It was amusing to try to divine what each was for. The egg beater resembled a wire whisk, the flashlights suggested lanterns, and so on. He felt a sudden longing to be back home, but it had grown unbearable to be there, in that empty house with the sounds of ticking clocks and the sweep of his wife's dress on the floor.

He found the men's section. He was interested in a pair of jeans but had no idea what size he wore. The numbers, beginning at 28, ending at 44, meant nothing to him. He chose a pair he figured should fit and moved on to the T-shirts. Most were sports-related, donated by empty nesters in epic bouts of spring cleaning. Then there were the funny ones, their humor lost on him, featuring popular cartoons and their common one-liners, or jokes with the punchline on the back.

A green shirt that said "Irish Yoga" featured a drunk man in three positions of blackout. Another said "Exercise? I thought you said 'Extra fries.'" Another showed two ears of corn lying side by side on beach towels. One of the ears was exploding into popcorn. The other ear said: "I told you to wear sunscreen!"

In the end, he chose a shirt that said "Muck Fichigan" because he liked the color, a familiar blue. It resembled the gingham shirts still hanging in his sons' closets. From the shoe rack he chose a pair of white Converse sneakers.

In the changing room, blocked from the browsing women by a mere curtain, he put on his new clothes. The jeans were too big. He tried clipping his suspenders to them, but they hung too wide around his waist. He would need a belt. The shirt was fine, as were the sneakers. He thought he looked strange, but he couldn't tell if he looked strange only to himself or if he would look strange out in the world. Carrying his old clothes in his arms, he emerged. The women turned their heads at the sound of the metal rings sliding on the curtain rod but promptly resumed shopping, which assured him that he looked more or less normal. He took a belt from the rack, passed it through the loops, cinched it tight, and went up to the counter.

"Wearing it right out of the store, are we?" the woman said, not unkindly. "Well, what do we have here? Jeans, shirt and shoes, is it?"

"And belt."

"And belt."

"Seventeen dollars and fourteen cents."

When he pulled out the wad of cash, she said, "Sure you don't want to buy a wallet to keep all that cash in? We've got a few down here in the case. I'll throw it in if you just give me one of those twenties."

And so he bought a wallet too.

"Want me to cut those tags off for you?"

She came around the counter and for the second time that day someone was at him with a pair of scissors. The belt presented an issue. The tag was around the buckle. Sensing his unease, she said, "Here, I'll let you get that one."

He took the scissors and cut it.

"How about a bag for your old clothes?" she said. She took them from him, folded them with care, and slid them into a plastic grocery bag.

73

As soon as he took the bag by the handles, they lost the form she had given them.

As he walked down the street, his jeans kept dragging under the heels of his shoes. He stopped to roll them up.

On the next block a man was smoking an e-cigarette and looking at his phone, leaning against a van that said "Schultz's Heating and Cooling" on the side.

"Do you know where the nearest used-car dealership is?" Abraham Zimmerman asked. He'd been rehearsing the sentence in his head.

"Break down, did you?" the man asked, glancing at the bag of clothes.

"No."

"Just in the market for a beater then, are you? Well I think the nearest would be Barker's, but it's a ways." The man paused, seeming to consider what sort of day he was having and whether he was in the mood to indulge his inherent tendency to be kind. "I could run you out there, I suppose."

When they got in the van the man held out his hand and said, "Eric."

"Abraham."

"Abraham. Well, okay."

On the way, Abraham Zimmerman observed Eric's driving so carefully that Eric worried he was about to get carjacked. Abraham Zimmerman had been in many trucks in his life, but he had never paid much attention to how one went about driving one.

After deciding he wasn't in danger of getting carjacked, Eric said, "Now, you're gonna wanna be careful with these guys. The kid's all right but the old man is a crook. Careful he doesn't sell you a lemon."

Abraham Zimmerman nodded, imagining an old man holding out a yellow lemon and taking all his cash.

Stopped at a light, Eric turned to face him and said, "Mind if I ask you a question?"

Abraham Zimmerman looked at him with a look of such pure innocence that Eric took it as a yes.

"What do you have against Michigan?"

Abraham Zimmerman said nothing. He kept staring at him just as he had been staring at him before.

"Your shirt?"

Abraham Zimmerman looked down, then back up.

"That personal, huh?" Eric said, raising his hands off the steering wheel. "I understand."

The light turned green. They were through the intersection before Eric let his hands fall back on the wheel.

When they pulled into the used-car lot, Abraham Zimmerman peeled a twenty off the roll.

"No, no, no, I don't need that," Eric said, which was a lie. But when Abraham Zimmerman didn't put the bill away, he said, "Oh, all right. Maybe I'll swing by the Dairy Queen and order a blizzard."

This sentence made as little sense to Abraham Zimmerman as the sentences about the lemon and about Michigan. He imagined a beautiful woman, the queen of the cows, from who one could request snow, even in August.

Eric wished him good luck and drove off. Of course the kid wasn't at work that day. It was the old man who came out of the store, still chewing his ham and cheese sandwich, not having expected any customers in this heat.

"What can I do you for?"

"I need a car."

Barker swallowed.

"Need a car, do you? Why, we've got a few of those."

Barker considered himself a genius when it came to character types. After discerning what sort of person he was dealing with, he could change, chameleon-like, to become the sort of man they trusted. With the elderly he was hokey and sanctimonious. With a man who seemed to know cars, he was profane and shoptalky. With a woman, who was usually with a kid or two, he was mellifluent and compassionate. There were as many Jim Barkers as there were customers. And for this reason he bristled whenever anyone suggested that all used-car salesmen were crooks. Sometimes he was a crook, sure, but other times he wasn't. It depended on the situation.

Even so, to reverse the prejudice, which seemed broadly held, that he was a liar and a thief, Barker worked hard to polish his public image. He was active in the church, where he stuffed the collection envelope with another envelope so it would feel more substantial as it was passed down the pew. He'd helped carry more coffins than any man in Pearl County, quick to volunteer if the funeral home was in need of pallbearers for a man who'd alienated his family and whose funeral was a mere formality. It stood him in good stead with the church ladies who made a point of attending these funerals out of respect for the dead. If a customer came back to the dealership, on foot or in a cab, and demanded a refund, he was quick to give it to them, all handshakes and apologies. Then the car would go back to his partners, a self-described hack mechanic out near Lanark and a demolition derby kid who was an expert at bodywork and detailing. Once they'd put the minimum amount of money into it, it would be back on the lot, for sale again.

It bothered Barker that he'd gone and had such a morally upstanding son. Jim Jr. was easily talked down and practically had Tourettes's when it came to blurting out what might be wrong with a car. Barker had always figured he would be retired by now, spending all his time on the river, where he had a little hunting and fishing cottage, but instead he felt inclined to stay close to the lot, lest his fortune slip through his son's loose hands.

As good as he was at figuring a customer out, this man stumped him. The plastic bag of clothes suggested hard times. He had the look of a man whose wife had left him for another, taking the car with her. What had that van he arrived in said? "Heating and Cooling." That must be it. He'd gotten off a shift fixing burnt-out air conditioners and his partner had run him over. Well, not run him over literally. That would be mean. But he looked about like he had been. Run over, that is. Barker laughed at his own wit and decided to try the marital trouble angle in order to shake things up a bit.

"Let me guess, the old lady drove off with the car, but not before filling her up with everything she could fit in her?"

The man looked at him blankly.

"Okay, tell you what. Let's start here. What's your price range?"

Abraham Zimmerman approximated what he had left in his pocket, after the haircut and the wardrobe.

"Three thousand."

Barker whistled.

"You can get a nice car for that. Hell, you can get a pretty damn decent car here for *two* and walk off with an extra thousand to thumb through. Tell you what. I don't show this one to many folks because to be honest I've been thinking of driving her home myself, but I can see you in this car, sir, I can see you in this car as clear as if you'd just pulled up in her."

Barker led him to a blue Cadillac he'd been trying to get rid of for months. It was one of those cars that's striking at first glance but that, upon closer inspection, suggests all sorts of problems. It was a money pit, this one. It had been left in a weedy, appliance-strewn yard for years and, though his mechanic and touch-up guy had done wonders with it, it had just barely been salvaged from the salvage yard. The seats were covered in mismatched upholstery where they'd been torn open and tenanted by mice, and, running, the car made a low rattling sound that was concerning but that his mechanic had chosen to interpret optimistically, saying, when they'd taken it for a drive, "Would you listen to that purr?"

The price had been extravagantly slashed from an absurd price to a lower but still absurd price to a final price that, while still absurd, suggested one was getting a great deal. Barker looked at Abraham Zimmerman looking at the car. He wasn't inspecting it. He was simply looking at it, the way certain high school kids, suddenly flush with cash after summer work putting up grain bins or detasseling corn, just looked. Had their fathers come with them, the salient questions would be asked, the hood raised, but their fathers were always absent, so that they saw the surface only, and only considered how the car would look in the lot of the McDonald's, where they gathered before football games. Color and style were more important to them than whether the car could be trusted to start in winter, which was why Barker invested more in the detailing than he did in the engine.

But this man was many years out of high school and, based on what he was wearing, didn't seem terribly concerned about appearances.

"Go ahead," Barker said. "Sit behind the wheel there, see how she feels."

When Abraham Zimmerman climbed into the driver's seat, it wasn't for the first time. When he was a boy he used to go walking through the woods in winter, when there was less work to do, to a gully of wrecked cars. They'd been there so long that good-sized trees had torqued up through the chassis. Sitting in this blue Cadillac in the lot at Barker's, he remembered sitting in a junked car as snow settled down upon the cracked windshield, making the light within strange and holy seeming, and afterward he'd walked back through the woods to feed and curry horses.

Around this time, a cousin had left the community. Most who went through Rumspringa promptly came back, but this cousin hadn't. The world had gotten ahold of him like a river you try to cross, underestimating its current, that bears you away. The elders never spoke his name, as if, by entering the world, he was dead to them. But Abraham Zimmerman regarded this vanished cousin with awe. His leaving the community had opened a door that he hadn't even know was there.

Maybe this was why, when it came time for his own Rumspringa, Abraham Zimmerman had declined to take it. He was afraid he would be sucked into the world like this cousin had. Remembering how he had felt when he heard that his cousin wasn't coming back, and how he had felt sitting in those junked cars, he hadn't been confident that he was strong enough to resist the temptations of the world.

Abraham Zimmerman counted out the cash and handed it to Barker through the window.

"Sure you don't wanna take her for a spin first?" Barker asked, suddenly suspicious of the ease of the sale. For all his brashness, he was at heart a petty and insecure man, and he wondered whether this man didn't know something about this car that he and his mechanic and his touch-up guy somehow didn't. But the feel of the cash in his hand comforted him.

"Trust me then, do ya? Well, you might be the first," he said, pocketing the money.

Abraham Zimmerman managed to drive off more or less smoothly, leaving Barker standing there thinking of the gambling boats on the river near Dubuque. His favorite was called the *Mississippi Belle.* He would take one of the nicer cars from the lot, leave his wedding ring in the glovebox, lay his smallish, ringless hands on the green felt tables. He always met a woman, and even if nothing ended up happening it was still fun to make her laugh, using the indomitable dealer as a common point of contact, saying things like, "You folks would be a hell of a lot more trustworthy if you dealt cards in T-shirts." His neck reddened at the thought of it. He took the money out and, licking his finger, which tasted vaguely of the cheddar-and-sour-cream Ruffles he'd been eating when the heating and cooling van pulled in, he counted the money again. Three thousand on the dot. Why, wasn't that something. Hadn't he told him he could buy a perfectly good car for two?

When Abraham Zimmerman walked into the Schapville Tap, only one man recognized him. The summer before, John Williams had hired an Amish crew to put a new roof on the barn after an F3 tornado lifted the old roof off, scattering the shingles in the woods, to be discovered and wondered at years later by as-yet-unborn boys. But Williams recognized Abraham Zimmerman only because everyone had just been talking about how an Amish guy had walked into Nelson Julius's barbershop and had his hair cut and his beard shaved off.

Now Williams remembered the day the Amish roofing crew came down his lane not in a horse and buggy, as one might expect, but in a brand-new F-150, pulling a flatbed trailer of hand tools and wooden ladders. There were four men squeezed into the cab: Abraham Zimmerman, two other Amish men, and the driver. The latter was an odd guy, a historian of sorts, who got off on all things Amish and enjoyed driving them around.

Williams remembered them as silent and unsmiling. Not unfriendly but, rather, turned toward one another, as if the world could offer them nothing that they couldn't provide themselves. Despite the heat, they wore woolen pants that looked itchy and long-sleeved white shirts that seemed composed of too substantial a material to be cool. He showed them the barn, open to the sky, covered here and there with blue tarps. The fresh black shingles were piled up on the grassy earthen ramp that horses would have climbed once upon a time, pulling the rickety ricks of loose hay. He wondered at how that time was theirs still. Seeing that they had all they needed, he commented on the heat and pointed out the hydrant, a few mason jars lying wide-mouthed in the grass.

Feeling awkward, he said, "Well, I'll leave you to it then."

Williams had watched them throughout the day, black silhouettes against the white July sky. There was no noise of power tools, nor did they seem to call to one another, as most work crews would. In mid-afternoon, when the sun was most brutal, they took their lunch in the shade of an oak tree. Williams just so happened to be replacing a broken float in a water tank nearby. He watched this same man, bearded then, snap a quilt out in the dead air and lay it down over the grass. They sat casually, with one knee drawn up, one elbow on the ground. He wondered what they were eating. He supposed they had pie. Weren't the Amish famous for that? He had half a mind to walk over there and join them but didn't want to impose, and anyway, they had lain down and placed their straw hats over their faces, the sunlight dappling their cheeks through the hexes of straw.

They finished in two days what would have taken professional roofers a week. Near the end, Abraham Zimmerman's boys had come along to help, riding in the bed among the tools. He assumed they were his boys anyway, by the way they followed him, their thumbs tucked under their suspenders.

Paying the men in cash, as they'd requested, he expected a moment of connection, a smile and a handshake, but they hardly looked at him.

"Were they not friendly then?" his wife asked that evening as they sat on the porch, where he'd situated himself in order to think back upon the experience of hiring the Amish to put a new roof on the barn.

"It wasn't that," Williams said. "It was like they were of another world."

"Well, naturally," his wife said, turning the pages of *Home and Garden*. He knew that she believed they were foolish for living the way they did, as if it were a choice and not their identity. She longed for more modern everything: a more modern dishwasher, a more modern microwave, a more modern vacuum cleaner. He gave up trying to explain.

When he heard about the accident, he wanted to send a note of sympathy but didn't know where to send it to and, even if he had, he couldn't have thought what to say. He remembered the boys, how they had followed their father as closely as his shadow. But he couldn't tell whether the news of the accident had affected him so much because this man and his sons had worked on his barn, or because of an experience of his own.

A few years before, Williams had been responsible for an accident that had broken a hired hand's back. Williams had thought the man yelled "Go!" when he actually yelled "Ho!" The hired hand was paralyzed from the waist down. The hand, who was deeply religious, had forgiven Williams long ago, but Williams still went out of his way to avoid running into the injured man.

Williams figured that whoever hit the buggy and killed those Amish boys was feeling even worse. He'd heard it was a group of four women from Chicago, two pairs of sisters. They'd driven out to Galena to shop for antiques. They had gone too fast over the hill, and the driver, distracted by an antique the other three were studying, panicked and stamped the accelerator instead of the brake. It wasn't her car. She'd just offered to drive because her sister was feeling sleepy from the wine they'd had at lunch.

And now here was this man come beardless into the Schapville Tap on a Friday afternoon, wearing a T-shirt that said "Muck Fichigan," oversize jeans, and white sneakers. He sat down to Williams's right, a stool between them, with such nonchalance that Williams began to doubt whether this really was the man. But then he ordered.

"What'll it be?" Jim asked.

"Whisky."

"Okay, you're gonna have to help me out a little. What kind of whisky?"

Williams winced. Jim could be a bit of a jerk. Williams tried to catch Jim's gaze to convey, somehow, that he should be gentle with this man. But Jim didn't glance toward him, and when Abraham Zimmerman still hadn't answered Williams took it upon himself to say, "Two Wild Turkeys."

"Pair of gobblers, okay," Jim said, turning away.

"Ice?" Jim asked over his shoulder.

"Ice?" Williams asked Abraham Zimmerman.

"No," Abraham Zimmerman said.

"No ice," Jim said to himself.

"This one's on me," Williams said to Abraham Zimmerman, who made no sign of having heard him.

Their drinks came. Abraham Zimmerman threw the shot back like it was some kind of herbal tincture that would clear up an infection. Williams thought about leaving the man alone. He seemed to want that. But he couldn't go without saying something.

"Excuse me, but I think you might have done some work for me last summer?"

Abraham Zimmerman turned toward him.

"John Williams. Out Highway 53 there. You put a new roof on the barn. We had a tornado tore through two, was it three years ago? I don't know that there's a tighter roof in Pearl County what than the one you folks put on there. I go up the silo from time to time just to admire it."

The look on Abraham Zimmerman's face said neither no nor yes.

"Well, in any case, I was sorry to hear about your boys," Williams said. He had to say it.

"Another pair of gobblers?" Jim asked.

"Not for me," Williams said, feeling uneasy. He placed a ten on the bar, stood up, and left.

It was dark by the time Abraham Zimmerman stumbled out of the Schapville Tap. Drinking had been easy. Every time his glass was empty, he simply slid it toward the bartender, who'd fill it to the brim and break whatever bill was on the bar and give him the change. There were bills riding up out of his jeans pockets, bills under his chair.

Drinking had been easy but walking was harder. He couldn't seem to make it through the front door. First his left shoulder, then his right, hit the doorframe. Then there were hands on both shoulders, guiding him outside and across the parking lot. He was appreciative until the hands spun him around and a voice said, "Give me that cash you had today in the barbershop."

He tried to say that he'd spent it all on the car, but his tongue wouldn't work. The same hands that had seemed so kind before were in his pants now, pulling loose bills out. Then the hands reached around, grabbing his backside, feeling for the wallet. He opened it, took out the last of the bills, and said, "Where's the rest?"

When he didn't answer, one of the hands punched him in the jaw and Abraham Zimmerman fell on his knees to the ground, feeling the sharpness of the gravel pressing into his knees. And the kid, who, like him, had gotten his hair cut that day by Nelson Julius, walked away.

The punch sobered him up a little. For a while he looked for his car, and when he found it, he struggled to get into it and then to start it. When he finally managed to, he thought better of trying to drive it. What if he killed someone? He shut it off.

He started walking. The ground slanted, first this way, then that. He careened from one side of the sidewalk to the other. At some point he had to stop and be sick in some bushes, after which he felt better, sturdier. The ground didn't slant so, as if whatever fulcrum it had been tottering on had lost its fine point. Such were his thoughts as he walked.

Outside town and its miasma of artificial light, the stars came back. He followed the north star north. The houses were sparser. Dark ranch-styles, half garage. He was spooked by a garden gnome. He thought it was a pale child, beseeching him for help. From time to time a car would come, first the swishing sound of tires on pavement, then the false dawn of its lights. He imagined what his sons had heard.

Another car was coming. Instead of walking down into the ditch, Abraham Zimmerman stepped out into the middle of the road. The driver saw him at the last moment, swerved as if he were a deer, and barely avoided hitting him. The driver was a man who had taken his wife, who was in the early stages of dementia, out for fish for the first time all summer. He had never bothered locking his doors at home, but he did that night. Watching him do so, his wife thought he was locking her in. They lay awake a long time, afraid without reason, isolate in their mistakenness.

Getting to his feet, Abraham Zimmerman realized he was desperate to get home. His desire was akin to thirst. He started running down the road until he came to a sign he recognized. It was a yellow caution sign, warning cars that they were in Amish county. The sign held a black silhouette of an Amish horse-drawn buggy. Someone had shot up the sign but not hit the image of the buggy. Beneath the yellow caution sign another sign read "Next 18 Miles." But he had only a few to go.

He came to the bridge his father had always called the Bluff Bridge because from it, if you were going slow enough, you could watch the swallows flitting in and out of their nests along the bluffs of the Apple River. Just past the bridge was the intersection with Cording Road.

As if to avoid it, he sidestepped down the steep bank to where the river slowed amid the buttresses that held the bridge aloft. He washed his face in a pool. It had been years since he had felt water on his face like this. He remembered waiting his turn at the basin his mother kept on the bureau, the drying cloth hanging from a hook on the wall. The river was low from the heat. He walked along its margin for so long that he began to worry he'd gone the wrong way from the bridge, but eventually he came to the old mill. He knew where he was now. He scrambled up the bank on all fours. The road he came out on was gravel.

It was only another mile or so, though he had never measured it that way. There was the oak that the road seemed to bend around, and the old house they had harvested stones for fences from, though not so many that it wouldn't be able to stand, and the farm where his cousin Aaron lived with his wife Hannah and their sons, Jacob and Daniel and Moses, and their daughters, Mary and Rebecca. He passed their house, candlelight dancing in the windows, and the thought of those children, which had pained him before, made him so glad that he started running, his jeans slipping down his waist.

He wondered what Rachael would say when he came to the door beardless, in a T-shirt and jeans and Converse sneakers, smelling of whiskey. But it didn't matter what she thought when she saw him. When he saw her he would tell her everything.

He was close now. The land to his left was his. He and his sons had built the fence that separated him from the horses that came galloping up to him in the dark, whinnying and tossing their heads. And as Abraham Zimmerman ran alongside them, he became aware of a strange sensation. He was weeping, but there was no beard to catch his tears. They were running down his neck, over his Adam's apple, which Nelson Julius had shaved so carefully, without nicking it, without drawing even a single drop of blood.

*Nominated by Narrative*

# THE RED ONE WHO ROCKS

fiction by AAMINA AHMAD

from ONE STORY

Humair first saw the girl, brittle and angular as a kite, from the window of the train. She stood near the tracks looking up at the sky, her arms in the air, ready to catch something, whatever it might be, in her hands. He had laughed when the pilgrims talked of roadside djinns but he thought of them now, lying in wait for souls to steal. His mother-in-law, Rashda, was sitting next to him. She had fallen asleep, and her head bobbed against his shoulder. Last night, he'd woken whenever the train stopped, which was often, and each time he'd found her awake, staring out the window. Now that she had finally dozed off, her dupatta had slipped from her head and he could feel the sweat pooled around her hairline, damp against his shirt. He shifted, but shamefully; he knew he should sit still, that since Saima's death the old woman slept little and poorly, and that was his doing.

The train jerked to a halt. The pilgrims stood and looked out of the open windows. Humair craned his neck. Before them was a bridge standing precariously on a line of stilts over the Indus lapping below. "God is Great," a pilgrim shouted as if to encourage the train. "Ya Ali, Ya Ali," a few others chimed in, but they sounded tired; they had been traveling for hours, they had smoked their charas, consumed the last of their food, and they were still miles from Lal's shrine. Rashda murmured in her sleep. *Please*, Humair willed the train, *please*; the sooner they got there, the sooner this would all be done with. The train began to roll forward, lurching from side to side. Humair felt someone walk past him, brush his arm, and he looked up. It was *her*—the girl he'd seen by the tracks.

She was puffing; she must have clambered aboard when the train idled at the bridge. She wasn't much more than a child, fifteen, maybe sixteen. She was thin and her hair hung loose around her. As she moved through the car, dirt spilled from her chappals, from the seams of her fitted kurta. The careless way she walked and the absence of a male chaperone attracted, briefly, the interest of the other passengers. She tucked herself into the corner of the car. She stared at them, the pilgrims, her eyes shadowed by dark circles, with the bored gaze of the faithless. An unbeliever. Humair feared she might glimpse in him something she recognized, so he looked down and played with the slip of red material one of the old men had tied around his wrist, gifted to him because he was the only one among them not wearing anything red in the saint's honor.

"Kotri station! Five minutes!" the rail attendant hollered, banging on the carriage wall. Rashda opened her eyes at the sound, blinking at the sunlight.

"Sorry, son," she said, straightening up, shrinking from him in embarrassment. Humair avoided her eyes. He didn't want to make her more uncomfortable.

"Tea?" he said, offering her the small flask. She shook her head and looked out the window. The earth here was dry, cracked, empty of people and animals. She seemed troubled by it. He wanted to tell her he found this place desolate, that he felt as though he were passing through another country, one he didn't recognize, and that it made him feel anxious and alone, but he didn't. He excused himself, saying he needed some air.

At the back of the car, the rail attendant stood by the open door. "Bismillah," he said as the train juddered, "if your Amm-iji needs more room, you tell her to come up here. I'll move these boys so she can sit here." Humair nodded. He felt a twitch of discomfort every time people referred to Rashda as his mother, but neither of them had corrected any of the strangers who assumed they were mother and son. It was easier and less painful to let them think that than to explain that Saima, his wife, had been dead almost a year and he'd brought his mother-in-law to visit Lal's shrine for the three-day Urs because there was no one else to bring her. "The woman is too much," Humair's mother had said, exasperated. The Urs was for the desperate, for the sick and the dying in search of miracles. "And why ask you," his mother exclaimed; the old woman should ask anyone else to take her to Sehwan, anyone but *him*. But he had to go when Rashda asked him. He had to do anything she asked because last year, on a clear day near Shimla Pahari, he took a turn too quickly on his motorcycle and crashed into an oncoming car, killing Saima, who was riding side saddle. Saima, her only child.

He didn't remember much about it now, the accident that had so quickly snapped the life from her. When he told his family he'd seen Saima lying in the road, they said it was impossible, he hadn't woken till the following day in hospital, but he didn't believe them.

He knew he had stood over her as she lay there smashed, so tiny he could have lifted her in the palm of his hand. They had been married only three months and he peered at her as she lay on the road, staring at her as he did most mornings when he woke, trying, while she slept, to work out who she was.

"I'll pray for you, brother."

He turned. It was the girl. She had walked across the carriage to come and stand by him. She looked out at the hills from the open door. "For your soul, brother," she said. "Your soul is black, brother."

"What?" he said.

"For good luck," she said. "For protection from the evil eye. I'll pray for you."

"Can you move aside," he said.

"For whatever you want, brother. I'll pray for it," she persisted. He looked around, troubled by the intensity of her gaze. He tried to squeeze past her but she blocked him.

"Brother, brother," she said. He felt her eyes looking for his as he tried to look past her. Then she held out her hand. Money. She wanted money. That's all. That's all this is, he thought. What else would it be? There were dozens of them, beggars, wanderers, junkies, all heading to the shrine for the saint's Urs, ready to swindle, to pilfer whatever they could get from the pilgrims. Rashda was looking around the carriage for him. Her hand lay flat on his empty place, holding it for him.

"I can pray for your Ammah, too," she said, glancing at Rashda. "Is something wrong with her? She looks ill."

The train was swaying. Or perhaps he was shaking. It had to be the train—rocking as it lumbered towards a red mountain range that looked aflame from where he stood.

"Do you have a ticket?" he said.

The girl blinked, suprised.

"I don't think she has a ticket," he announced to the carriage. He was louder than he meant to be, and pilgrims nearby turned to look. He pointed her out to the rail attendant and repeated his accusation.

For a moment he felt ashamed as the girl's eyes darted around the car, startled by the attention. The rail man nodded, but he looked at Humair with disappointment. There it was again: the generosity of the faithful. Humair was tired of the sharing of food, of blessings, the forgiveness of every transgression, as if nothing really mattered anymore. He headed back toward Rashda, leaving the girl in the rail man's hands.

When he glanced back, he was surprised; the girl had vanished. Perhaps the attendant had sent her to another car, or perhaps she'd climbed up to the roof. He was discomfited by the thought of her scrambling around for a safe perch somewhere up there, alone among the crowd of men. But he swallowed his unease. She didn't have a ticket, she was a beggar. It was only fair.

"We're close now, so close. I feel it," Rashda said as he sat down next to her. She held her prayer beads close to her chest as she looked out into the rocky landscape. "God is Great," she said, squinting as if she could see something out there. He followed her gaze, searching the dusty hills but seeing nothing and feeling just then the emptiness into which they were traveling opening inside him.


A jigsaw of mud houses, their walls smooth, stood in the middle of the desert like a series of disorderly battlements. Along the town's edge where the houses disappeared into a dirt track, the tents of a traveling circus ballooned and men scaled a lopsided big wheel, readying it for tonight's revelry. Humair blinked as the lights on the structure flashed on and off in the distance, the men testing the power of their generator. Sehwan's narrow roads were chaotic with parties of pilgrims traipsing in and out of doorways. The shops and tea houses in the main bazaar brimmed; young and old, tens of thousands of them, swarmed the streets. Humair tried to push forward but was weighed down by their bags, their bedding, and the swell of the crowd in the bazaar was too great. The scent of henna, of charas, of urine was strong, but above it rose the foul smell of flesh turning in the heat. At the mouth of a narrow street, a teenage boy held up the legs of a dead goat coated in thick, white fat while a man in a red headdress skinned it, chanting as he worked. The carcass, sacrificed in Lal's name, lay in the dust like an open wound, leaking. When Humair looked down, he saw that he was crossing rivulets of blood running through the streets, slowly and gently towards the shrine.

Rashda wasn't far behind him. Heavy and languid, she moved awkwardly. A boy wearing a red bandanna pushed past her. "We're coming, we're coming," he said, and Humair wasn't sure if he was calling out to a friend in the crowd or to the saint himself.

"Humair, Humair, where are you?" Rashda said, her voice rising.

"Here, here." He struggled to free a hand and held it out to her; she took it. Her palm felt hot and sweaty and rough. He pulled her along, but they were shoved from all sides, the sound of drums, the braying of camels close. He needed to get out, he needed air. Another push from behind and he felt her hand slip from his. When he turned back to look for her, to reach for her, she was gone.

He forced his way to a far wall and stood there, searching the crowd for her. People streamed past him toward the gold dome in the distance, but he couldn't see Rashda. He thought of her lying trampled somewhere, and he felt helpless and afraid and yet—strangely—relieved, too, at the thought of being alone, of being free of her.

For the last year, she had regularly visited the house he shared with his mother and sister, the house in which Saima had lived during the three months of their marriage. He would find Rashda there almost every day when he came back tired and depressed from his work at a government school. She sat in the small living room, her eyes drifting across the crumbling paintwork, as though Saima might have left some trace of herself there. She would press her lips to her tea cup in a kiss, and occasionally she flicked through the stack of old magazines left in the rack by the table, and he knew she was thinking: *Saima drank from this cup, Saima's fingers ran along these pages.* He knew it because that's what he thought as he watched her.

His mother and sister had been dutifully kind at first, but after a time he had noticed an impatience in his mother's manner: she sighed often, offered tea halfheartedly, and had even started to leave the television on during visits. Eventually Rashda stopped coming. While he had dreaded the evenings in her company, her smallest gestures had absorbed him: the constant twisting of the rings on her fingers, her sharp squeak of a sneeze, the way she slurped her tea, all of which reminded him of Saima. And then occasionally he would glimpse Saima in her face, in her long nose, in the lines around her mouth. In her thickening jowls he knew what Saima would have looked like had she lived another twenty years. "Thank God," his mother said, when Rashda hadn't come for almost a week. He knew his mother meant it was time for everyone to move on, and by this what she *really* meant was that it was time for him to re-marry. All this, his mother gestured at the air, would be over if he married, and the truth was he longed for nothing more. He might even yet have the life he was supposed to have—children, a family, the company of a woman, the shape of her next to him as he slept, the things that made a man normal instead of the wretched thing he had become.

A couple of months passed before Rashda finally called on them again. When she did, she asked him to take her to Sehwan Sharif so she could visit Lal's shrine, Jhule Lal, The Red One Who Rocks. That weekend Humair was supposed to be visiting a possible bride with his mother. A girl with great potential. "You can't take that woman to Sehwan instead of going to see this girl," his mother said. "The family'll be insulted, think of the lost opportunity, good matches are hard to find especially for a widower." He thought of the new life he had imagined for himself, one he wanted but didn't deserve. "Yes," he said to Rashda, "of course I will take you."

He had now spent almost an hour in the heat on the edge of the crowd, trying to spot her. They hadn't arranged a meeting place or decided where to stay, thinking they would rent a couple of rope beds some-where outside, so he had no idea where to look for her. She must have gone on to the shrine. He took in a breath and re-joined the crowds, letting them carry him along. And then, there it was. Just a few hun-dred yards from him: the mausoleum. He couldn't see the tip of the dome or the minarets, just the walls lined with thousands of blue tiles, the color of the mid-morning sky. Saima hadn't seen this, she would never see this. The crowd seemed to quiet. Then, near him, a man be-gan to sing. Others laughed, some nervously, they were so close now to Lal. Lal who could turn himself into a falcon, Lal who had brought back the dead, Lal who was so beloved by God that any prayer he whispered into God's ear from a pilgrim devoted to him would be granted. The man in the crowd was still singing and others joined him: *O Laal meri pat rakhiyo bhala Jhule laalan.*

Up ahead, the crowd had come to a standstill as pilgrims moved into the courtyard. The people behind him extended beyond his sightline; there was no way to move back or even to the side now. He would have to go in. He closed his eyes. He thought of school, of the empty corri-dors, of the heads of his students curled over their workbooks. And then Saima: eating with her hands, the gravy running down her forearms, Saima kneading dough, beads of sweat on her upper lip, and Saima lying in the road bloodied and almost unrecognizable, her arms stretched out by her sides as though she were trying to reach something just beyond her fingertips. He opened his eyes. He was moving again, being buoyed forward.

Inside the courtyard just before the room where the saint's body lay, women and men danced the dhamaal to the pounding of drums. A group of prostitutes whirled, their clothes tight against their bodies, their hair swinging around them, their bodies shaking. He had never seen women dance like this, and he was stilled by the sight. Occasionally, one of them would pause and scour the crowd, holding for a moment too long the gaze of an interested man. He felt blood pounding in his ears as one of them locked eyes with him. He blinked.

It was the girl from the train.

She stared at him, dispassionate, apart from the intensity of the devotees around them, apart from everything.

A group of young men pushed in front of him, and he stumbled. He straightened. The girl was talking to an older woman now, and as the woman leaned toward the girl he realized it was Rashda. And as the girl talked to Rashda, Rashda reached out and touched her face and the girl didn't recoil as he expected a hard-faced creature like her to do but instead sank into Rashda's touch. The crowd was pushing him further on to the small room where the saint lay. He called out to Rashda, but he couldn't hear himself above the drums. He looked behind him but couldn't see Rashda. Just the girl's black hair fluttering in the wind.

A moment later and the saint lay only a few feet from him in a tall silver cage, his tomb covered with velvet shrouds and rose petals, thousands of them. But he couldn't smell the flowers. The air was heavy with the scent of all the unwashed men and women who had passed through the room, their stale sweat. The whole world was here: the dying, the filthy, and the hated. Hindu men and women stood on one side of the tomb and didn't flinch when the Shias standing next to them cried, "Ya Hussain, Ya Hussain! Ya Ali, Ya Ali! God is Great!" and beat their own bare chests with their hands as hard as they could. And the Hindus didn't even cry out when some of the Shia men hit their own scarred backs, covered in purple welts, with chains. Perhaps they were unafraid because they had seen it all before. Or perhaps it was because they loved Jhule Lal like the men thrashing themselves, but as Humair stood in the sight of Lal, as close to God as he thought he would ever come, he knew he didn't feel anything. It was only when he looked down and saw he was standing in the splattered blood of the Shia men that he felt something like recognition.

It was hours before he found her. Before he found them. And when he did, he realized Rashda had not been looking for him, that she had forgotten him entirely, and he felt, to his surprise, bereft. He had roamed Sehwan and then walked into the desert back towards the station. There, he found a crowded camp of makeshift tents and plastic ground sheets for those too late or too poor to find housing closer to the shrine. Rashda sat on the ground beneath a canvas awning and the girl squatted beside her, hungrily eating a piece of blackened chicken. The girl seemed even younger than he had first thought, and perhaps sick too, her skin yellowing, jaundiced. Rashda didn't seem at all troubled by being in such close quarters with so many pilgrims or by the ragged surroundings. He hovered, uncomfortable, waiting for her to notice him. When she finally did he sensed a glimmer of a smile about her mouth and he was struck by the strangeness of it.

"There you are. Come, come, son. These kind people said we could share their shelter," Rashda said, gesturing to an elderly couple sitting behind her.

The girl brought her plate closer to her chest, as if she feared he might snatch it from her. He thought of the train and stiffened. He had walked the circumference of the town, hundreds of faces passing him in the camps. He had worried he might never find Rashda, that he'd have to return home without her, but he couldn't say that in front of a stranger, and now that he had found her he was worried that perhaps he wasn't welcome anymore.

"There's room for you there," Rashda said. She pointed to a space on the plastic sheet a few feet away.

"Imli will sleep with me," she said as though he already knew everything he needed to know about the girl. He wondered if she had told Rashda about the train, or if Rashda planned to explain any of this to him. He sat down. The girl's narrow back was to him now, her thick, black hair hanging loose all around her. Then she turned, staring him straight in the eyes, chewing slowly, and he felt the color rising in his cheeks.

"Go and get a drink for yourself, child," Rashda said to the girl, handing her a twenty rupee note. Imli stood up and stretched, her back arching, her long arms reaching into the night around her with the grace of a dancer, and then she wiped her greasy mouth with the back of her hand. She sauntered off, disappearing into the darkness.

Humair and Rashda sat in silence. A firework blew up in the sky, the sparks trailing down to the ground like tears.

"Did I tell you I came here years ago?" she said.

The shrine was illuminated now by hundreds of tiny colored lights hanging across the building like garlands of flowers. The pilgrims were getting ready to mark Lal's Urs, the anniversary of Lal's death—his wedding night—the night he would be united again with his one true love: God.

"I never told Saima," she said. She brought her hand up to her mouth as though she was trying to hold in Saima's name, as though every time it slipped from her lips, she lost her again somehow. He hadn't mentioned Saima's name in front of Rashda since her death—*your daughter*, he had said, *my wife*, he had said, never *Saima*, never that.

"Qaiser and I were married and after four years I still hadn't had a baby, so he brought me here and we prayed for a son. We went to the shrine on the night of the Urs and I promised Lal that if God gave me a child, I would come the following year and bring a sacrifice."

He could hear the drums still beating, faster and faster as men and women danced the dhamaal at the shrine.

"But I never came back with a gift. I kept thinking, next year, next year, and then after a while, I just forgot. My prayers were answered but I didn't come. If I had come back, if I had brought a gift for him, perhaps—" There was another whistle and then another explosion in the sky. She was quiet. Then she said: "Sometimes, sometimes, I feel like something is happening to me, here." She placed her hand against her chest and looked at him as if to ask him if he understood. He wanted to say: *Yes, I know, I feel it too*, but he knew he could never understand what she felt. He knew he ought to tell her that her mistake was nothing like his, that God would never punish her for so minor a transgression. But he didn't know, he didn't understand God's rules. What was *his* mistake that day? He was going too fast, distracted, showing off perhaps, because after three months of marriage all he really knew of his wife was that she seemed entirely unimpressed by him, by her new life with him.

"God is Great, God is master of all," Rashda said, apologetic, as though wary of offending God further.

*God is our Master.* All his life he had heard it, that and countless other words of devotion: *God willing, Praise God, Thank God, God is*

*Great,* phrases woven so deeply into daily conversation they had become almost invisible, meaningless.

"Who knows who our master is," he said, tired of all of it just now.

She froze. "Don't say things like that," she said, scanning the lines of tents for pilgrims or perhaps even angels who might report them to God Himself, her fearful eyes saying there was no more punishment she could bear, however else they might offend God, this was enough.

Every living moment of this last year he had breathed *his* punishment from God, its horror, and he still wanted to say, *Maybe it's all just bad luck, maybe that's all it is.* But he couldn't because God had saved him, he knew that. He wasn't thinking of the day of the accident but all the days after when Rashda said to him, this was God's will, and God is our Master, surely from God we come and to Him we must return, absolving him, forgiving him. And yet even mercy was hard to live with. There were the black days when he went to school barely able to teach the one class they'd given him in compassion for his loss, the violence that sometimes overwhelmed him when his sister said something disparaging about his dead wife, and the nights he listlessly walked around the house looking at the ceiling fan wondering if he could hang himself from it, shamed not by the sinfulness of the thought, but by the truth that he still wanted to live.

"You should pray," she said, "it helps."

The girl was stalking the edge of the camp, watching them.

"Nothing can help this," he said, "it will never go away."

Rashda's eyes filled and then she turned from him and lay down, her back to him, and he wished he had said other things, things that helped, that didn't hurt her.


He walked up the dunes close to the campsite and stood in the sand. It felt different from anything he had ever known, as if he were being sucked into the ground, disappearing into the earth like the dead. He wondered if the dead were here, in each grain, traces of the millions of humans who had lived before them, their cells, their blood. He yanked his legs from the sand, resisting its pull. He was tired. He wanted to sleep. But the girl had returned. She sat by Rashda, now asleep. He thought he'd go back to the shrine, or to the bazaar; he couldn't bear to go and lie down by them. But then the girl got up again and walked away from Rashda, picking her way through the campsite, and he found himself following her as she headed to where the circus grounds began.

At the gate, stages were set up where dancers performed, most of them transvestites, calling out to male passersby, trying to entice them inside. The girl walked straight in—she knew where she was going and he had to jog to keep up with her, past a handful of fairground rides around which groups of young men had gathered, their faces illuminated by the colored lights that shone from the tall structures. She stopped. She looked up; the Well of Death—a huge barrel built from planks of wood, inside which he could hear the roar of motorcycles and cars as they drove around the vertical walls. There was no one at the ticket booth and she climbed up a set of stairs to stand on the platform built around the giant well. He wanted to leave, the pounding of the women's feet at the shrine was better than the thundering of the bikes, but he didn't. He kept going up the stairs. He couldn't see her on the dark, crowded platform; all that was before him was the Well of Death.

Drivers were speeding along the ten-foot high walls, and he felt the planks jitter with the vibration of the bikes, the most skilled of the riders climbing higher and higher, so that they traveled round on an almost horizontal axis. The spectators were loud, some of them screaming. The riders whirled past and his eyes couldn't focus. The thought came, as it did to him sometimes: what did Saima see, just before? He felt dizzy. He stepped back.

"I've ridden one of those cycles," the girl said. She was next to him. "Do you want to try it? You pay and they let you try it."

He turned to walk away from her, desperate to escape this place.

"Are you scared?" she said as she followed him down the steps.

He stopped.

Her hair flying around her made her look tinier. She said, "You followed me here. I thought you wanted to try it."

He didn't say anything, but the night air quivered around him, pulsing with the pressure of the engines, the wheels. "You just have to line up and you can have a turn," she said.

"What do you want? Why did you bring me here?" he said, challenging her to say it.

"I didn't bring you."

Of course she had brought him here. She meant for him to see this. He was certain of it, and he struggled to catch his breath. "Why are you bothering me and my mother-in-law?"

"She's not your mother-in-law now," she said.

"What do you *want*?"

"What do *you* want?" she said, staring at him in a way that no respectable woman would. He knew what she meant. But he didn't say anything.

"No?" she said. She cocked her head to one side but seemed neither flirtatious nor offended, just tired. She moved closer. Her kameez was tight against her belly, and it was then he realized she was pregnant. This confused and alarmed him. He turned and walked back toward the camp. He could feel her behind him.

"She says I can come home with you to Lahore," said the girl.

He stopped. "What?"

"She saw, when I was at the shrine," she said. She touched her belly and looked gentle, just then. "Do you think I should come with you?" she said and he realized she was trying to appraise him, them, and most of all she was trying not to look scared.

"Is she all right?" the girl tapped her head. "Up here?" He could tell from the rise of her chest that she was breathing quickly.

Was Rashda all right? Sane? She woke each day and washed and dressed, cooked meals, cleaned her home, but he didn't know, not really. The girl blinked, waiting. What for? A verdict? Advice? Did she want his approval, his permission perhaps? Or was she wondering if she was expected to service him as part of this proposal? He shuddered. She wrapped her arms around her slight figure. A girl her age with no people—she probably moved from one shrine to another, dancing in the day, looking for trade among the crowd when darkness fell. It was a hard life. He wondered what Rashda had said—that she would look after her, after the baby? It must have sounded tempting. But this girl didn't know anything about them. Rashda could have lied. For all the girl knew, he and Rashda might be nabbing girls or babies to sell, to use as slaves, to ruin. Or *she* could be a thief snaking her way into Rashda's life to pave the way for her gang to come in and steal everything an unsuspecting lonely old woman possessed, to throw her out and take over her home, and he thought of Saima, what Saima, so protective of her mother, so suspicious and ungenerous, would say. He pictured her scolding the beggar children, her hands on her hips, her eyes narrowing, telling them they should be working, not insulting God by begging, that they were little more than thieves stealing from those who worked hard. "Stay away from her," he said. "I know what you're up to. I know you're trying to take advantage of her. You're no better than a beggar, a thief."

The girl folded her arms across her chest and stood up straight, her eyes flashing like the torches behind them, and he thought she might

95

reach for the dirt on the ground and throw it at his face, but she didn't. Her breathing slowed, her shoulders slumped, and she looked past him to the shrine. Then she walked on wearily, and a moment later the desert and darkness had swallowed her whole. He tried to hold onto the sense he'd had of Saima next to him, her arm grazing his, the thrumming he'd felt in his body for a second, but it was gone now leaving him with just the hollow blackness that followed him everywhere. And he thought of the girl and her baby wandering the crowded roads of Sehwan, her dancing the dhamaal day and night, the baby kicking in her belly as the drums beat.

He woke the next morning, the morning of Lal's Urs, bad-tempered because all night he had dreamt of Saima. He didn't see her much in his waking life except in fragments. But at night she stood vividly before him, difficult and argumentative, moody, funny, as she was when she was alive. He turned to his side and closed his eyes, fearful that she would disappear again. There she was: standing in the kitchen, entertaining them all with imitations of the neighbors, and then he saw her through the crack in the door to the living room, sitting with Rashda, making her laugh as she did an impression of his mother, an impression that made his mother seem meaner and more ridiculous than she was. He had caught her eye that day and she wasn't embarrassed or sorry; instead she smiled. "She's a witch," his sister had said. And he had stood by, bewildered, as Saima and his sister fought, arguing over the loan of a shawl or was it over the housework? He didn't remember now. "If I'd known," his mother said, meaning she would never have married him to this thin, bony, and yet fearsome girl who had disrupted their peaceful household. Then, all of a sudden, they were released from it. She was gone and their home was quiet again, and the only thing that remained was this feeling, black and thick, locking itself to him.

He felt a blow on the side of his head. He put his fingers up to his face, shocked. Rashda stood above him, her cheeks marked with tears. "What did you say to her?" She was breathing heavily.

"Nothing." He sat up. He looked around panicked but they were alone in the tent.

Her lips were pursed with fury.

"She told me you were going to bring her back with us," he said. "I don't think we should pick people up here. We don't know anything about her, she could be a thief, a con artist. She could be anyone."

96

Rashda stared into the desert. She looked much older than she had when he had married Saima.

"It would be madness to take her with us. Imagine what everyone would say, Saima would—" He froze, startled by the sound of it, by the ease with which it had tumbled from his lips. Rashda turned to look at him, as if she too were apalled by his lapse; Saima might have been his wife, but Rashda's expression said her daughter was really a stranger to him. He wanted to look away but couldn't.

"I don't remember any of last year," she said, "I don't remember any of it. I thought if I kept going, it would get better, that with time it would change, but nothing's better. I'm still here and my child's still gone. And I don't know what I did to deserve this. What did I do?"

His mouth was dry. He followed her gaze as she looked at a group of pilgrims praying together. "God forgive me," she said. "I've tried to understand. I've tried to understand this was *God's* will. But why would He want *this* for her." She stood. She stared at him, her face hard now. "Saima said you used to drive too fast, that you scared her on that bike. She told me." The drums were already playing. She held his gaze a moment and then she turned and trudged towards the shrine. He stood, his legs buckling, but as he opened his mouth to call out to her, he stopped; he had waited so long for her to say it, and now that she finally had, there was nothing else left to say.

He sat just outside the tent, the skin on the back of his neck singed by the midday sun. Rashda's bag was still there where she had left it. Humair looked at it. Perhaps Rashda would come back. Perhaps, like the fakirs, she would stay here forever; what was there to go home to, after all? He knew it was his duty to make sure she got back safely, but when she still hadn't returned as the afternoon light softened, he left, putting her things in the care of the pilgrims who'd housed them. Perhaps she hadn't returned because she thought he was still here waiting for her. Leaving, then, was the least he could do. He ought to head to the station, to start for home, but he didn't. He walked up to Bodla Bahar's shrine north of Lal's mausoleum. Bodla, Lal's most devoted disciple, had been cut into pieces and Lal had brought him back to life; it seemed the most obvious place to pray for the restoration of those lost to you. But in the small courtyard where the drummers beat their instruments relentlessly and the pilgrims danced—all manner of them: fakirs, prostitutes, transvestites—he wished he could believe, as they did, that what you'd lost might be yours again. Women he presumed were housewives or aging mothers also danced. They let down their hair and stomped, working themselves into a trance for Lal. He guessed they were praying for children, or praying for children to return. The men shook their heads as they smoked their charas, losing themselves in their trance. He wondered if they really felt it, Lal's spirit. He wondered if it really filled them.

When he got to the train station, it was dark and the platform was crowded with sleeping pilgrims. The train, decorated with red flags and bunting, stood on the tracks, its carriages dark. It wouldn't be ready to leave for a few hours. He picked his way through the sleeping bodies and the pilgrims still smoking and singing, in search of a seat, when he spotted Rashda. She sat cross-legged in a corner of the platform, her back against a wall, her eyes closed. The girl, Imli, lay next to Rashda, her head in the older woman's lap, but her eyes were open. The two women had found each other. He froze for a moment, not sure if the girl had seen him.

Imli lifted her head carefully, cat-like, and stared at him as if to say *she* would make sure Rashda got home safely—the one thing, the only thing he could still have done for his former mother-in-law. A moment later, she lay her head back down again in Rashda's lap and closed her eyes, the gentlest of smiles about her lips. He stood there, conscious of the relief with which Imli relaxed into Rashda, of the ease with which Rashda's arm fell across her, and to his surprise, he felt his eyes filling with tears.

He left before Rashda could catch sight of him. He walked towards the camp, but then with the sound of firecrackers close around him, he stopped, turned, and headed back towards the circus grounds. The lights on the rides glimmered hazily. The big wheel turned slowly and the young men sitting on it shouted down to their friends. Children bought bags of popcorn from hawkers. The dancers sat on their podiums, smoking now. Ahead of him, the crowd screamed down into the Well of Death, louder than they'd been the night before. "Takbir," a voice crackled into a microphone from inside the drum. "Ya Ali," the crowd on the platform answered. The torches hanging on the walls flickered against the planks, lighting up the cracks. The body of the Well shook and Humair remembered: the juddering of the bike beneath him, the speed of it, the stink of diesel and fumes. He remembered the press of her thin arms, her gold bangles against his waist. He remembered, also, though he did not want to, that when he'd looked down at her as she lay lifeless in the street, he'd felt lucky to find himself still here, alive; *blessed*. God forgive him, he had felt blessed. The drums at the shrine sounded in the distance, still playing, always playing. The crowd chanted into the darkness: "Ya Ali, God is Great. God is Great." He climbed the steps to the platform, and squeezed through the crowd to the front. He looked down.

*Nominated by One Story*

# FALL RIVER WIFE

fiction by PETER ORNER

from THE SOUTHERN REVIEW

It's said that after Delmore Schwartz went bonkers, the aged wunder-kind's poems began to sag like his once lean body. Poetry no longer paid. I mention this because an uncle of mine had a brief connection to Schwartz during those final batty years. He wasn't my uncle. Uncle Monroe wasn't anybody's direct uncle. He was an uncle in the way that every man of a certain age is an uncle. Technically, he was an uncle's brother, Uncle Horace's. Monroe wasn't his real name, either. He'd been born Morton. Everyone in Fall River called him Mort. At some point, in the '50s, just as he and Horace were beginning to make it as investment bankers, Mort changed his name to Monroe. At first, people laughed. "What, now your father sailed the Mayflower? The man arrived cargo from Danzig in 1919." Soon enough the brothers were so rich, nobody thought Monroe's new name was so funny.

James Joyce says there's one tony relative in every family. In my mother's, there were two. The Sarkansky brothers made good. Made very good. Eventually: outlandishly good. Turned out they were only moving money around—first piles, then hills, then small mountains. The old con: Rob Peter to pay Paul and around and around and around. A happy circle until Paul stops getting paid because Peter, for whatever reason, starts sniffing around and asks one too many questions. When that happened, in the mid-'60s, Uncle Monroe shot himself, leaving Uncle Horace holding an empty bag with a fat hole in it. By then, the Sarkansky brothers were in hock to the tune of millions. Only the major investors got anything back.

Family and friends ate the losses whole.

But for that good while, nearly two and half decades, things were flush, and the two brothers were the highest of fliers. They called themselves industrialists. What exactly was meant by this, nobody knew, but a title like that seduces. And who wouldn't have been sweet-talked by Monroe Sarkansky? His Manhattan office address? An apartment on East Seventy-Seventh? The pied-à-terre in Nassau? (Before I was born, my parents once stayed in this pied-à-terre.) Uncle Monroe played a good tycoon. Flamboyance and conspicuous spending were part of his act. So were the bolero worn aslant and the fake English accent. My grandfather said he sounded less British than constipated. As if Mort had been stuffing all his dough up his you know what.

People should have known a dependable 8, 9, even sometimes 10 percent per quarter return on their investment was too good to be true. But whoever puts the kibosh on what's too good to be true? Start making money like that, people begin to think they deserve it.

Adding to his mystique was the fact that Monroe "maintained" a wife back home in Fall River. Monroe had, long ago, left domestic life behind, but he would never, gallant that he was, divorce his Fall River wife. Occasionally, he'd breeze into town and visit the old homestead on Locust Street before screeching back to Manhattan in his limousine. On one of these conjugal visits, a child was conceived. The '50s were contradictory. Ike and picket fences. But if you had enough money and panache, you could get away with murder. Even Fall River couldn't help going a little nutty over a native with a chauffeur. He was always in the paper. A throwback to the heyday when Spindle City reigned supreme as the undisputed textile capital of the planet, when, it used to be said, Fall River produced enough cloth per year to wrap around the world fifty-seven times and still have enough left over to make a suit for William Howard Taft.

For years, I never even knew Monroe's wife's name. But I heard things. "Brilliant" was one.

"Troubled" was another. My mother once let slip that she'd been "disturbed."

Uncle Horace was more the modest of the two brothers, less the conquering hero. He was quiet, diligent, bespectacled. And in his respectable way, Horace collected the life savings of family and friends—except, it is always noted, Irv Pincus. Irv, being a crook himself, knew a swindle when he saw one. But whoever listened to Irv Pincus? Sure, Uncle Horace had a palatial house up in the Highlands and a summer place at Mattapoisett known as "The Shambles," but his role was to project sobriety and prudence. If any investor had doubts about the one brother, they could be reassured by the other, depending on their taste.

In '64, when a couple of shell companies went under unexpectedly, the brothers found themselves without enough cash flow to pay out that quarter's interest. The sudden announcement of losses tipped off some of the bigger fish that something stank. These investors called in their principals. The beauty of it had always been the utter simplicity. Money in, money out, easy as breathing. They didn't make anything, sell anything, or even, the amazing thing, invest in anything. When it collapsed, it all went poof, there being nothing there in the first place. (Aside, of course, from the millions they'd skimmed and spent.) The story goes that at a dinner party in Montauk attended by Sammy Davis Jr., Carol Channing, and a couple of sheiks from Arabia, Monroe excused himself, saying, "Wouldn't it be jolly to have a look at the moon?"

He used a pearl-handled pistol.

Monroe's corny last line brings me backward to Delmore Schwartz. At the apex of his wealth, the early '60s, Uncle Monroe began to pursue in earnest what was, apparently, his only true passion. He loved money, who doesn't, but more than anything else, Monroe Sarkansky wanted to be a poet. *A published poet.* He found it no more difficult than hustling relatives. He hosted a few bohemian gatherings. He provided oceans of premium-grade hooch. The doors of the New York literary citadel flung open. One drunk writer led to another. It was the critic Anatole Broyard, knowing his old friend was hard up and possibly losing his senses, who suggested that Monroe pay Delmore Schwartz for poetry lessons. "Pay him enough and he won't say no," Broyard told Monroe. Or, is said to have said. And Schwartz, though he may well have hated himself for it, agreed to give poetry lessons in his Greenwich Village apartment to a grossly wealthy man with airy dreams. Schwartz only demanded that Monroe order his driver to park the limo around the corner. He didn't want to see it when he looked out the window.

Now: there is no evidence, judging from the three volumes of poetry Monroe Sarkansky published in quick succession (one posthumously) with the Dial Press from 1962 through 1965, that he learned a single thing from Delmore Schwartz. At least not the Schwartz who wrote:

Oh Nicholas! Alas! Alas!
My father coughed in your army,

Hid in a wine-stinking barrel,
For three days in Bucharest

Then left for America
To become a king himself.


Monroe would have understood the hunger to become a king of America. But no, zero, not a line of Monroe's poetry sings. I'm hard on the man out of loyalty to my people, especially my dead-broke dead grandfather who died before I had a chance to know him much, but even now I can't force myself to quote even one line, not even to make fun of it, which would be too easy—though I've got all three of Monroe Sarkansky's books right here with me. *Gardenias and Salamanders. The Golden Afternoon. A Mother's Love and Other Poems.* It is telling though, isn't it, that after all their losses, my grandfather, and after his death my grandmother, held on to the books. The fake name on these spines is the only thing he left of his fake fortune.

I can't help wondering about those poetry lessons. For six months, Monroe spent Thursday afternoons in Delmore Schwartz's apartment on Charles Street in the West Village. Most of Schwartz's friends had begun to distance themselves. (They'd wait until he was dead to write about him. Who from that time, from his set, didn't take a crack at Delmore Schwartz after they found him alone, crazy, and very dead in a Times Square hotel in 1966? His fall into madness was just too delicious.) So, it's possible that a dapper wannabe in an exquisitely tailored suit and a bolero was harmless enough company enough for forty-five minutes. And at $150 per session, cash, it beat what a lot of the magazines paid for poems. Schwartz must have known the man was beyond hope. You might make a poet out of someone who's never written a poem. But give a fraud of an investment banker eyes to see? Even so, it stands to reason that the two of them, the poet and the eager student, must have settled into their afternoons together. Delmore Schwartz might have sat in a chair and recited a few lines as Monroe stood by, hoping that mere proximity to poetry might do the trick.

Schwartz may have even told Monroe one of his darlings. "You know, don't you, that Wallace Stevens was a lousy lawyer? They only kept him around the insurance company because he was such a wonderful poet!" When Schwartz laughed, he hooted.

And maybe after discoursing for a while, Schwartz would doze off and Monroe would stand there and wait.

A half hour later, Schwartz opens his eyes and says, "You're still here? Did you pay me?"

"We still have eight minutes left on the lesson."

"By whose authority? The New York Stock Exchange?"

And I also wonder if there came a moment when Schwartz, more paranoid by the day but still, deep down, the street-smart kid from Brooklyn, let his obedient pupil know that he saw through it, the elegant suit, the bolero, the accent—

Schwartz makes a paper airplane out one of Monroe's verses and launches it out the window. "What kind of kike uses the word *bough* for branch?"

"*Branch* doesn't rhyme with *frau*," Monroe says.

Schwartz smiles. You can't argue with that. And it's been days (weeks?) since he's smiled. Not since he wrote a ditty commemorating the death of Robert Frost, that frosty-haired toad.

"Anatole tells me you've got a loony wife home in Holyoke," Schwartz says.

"Fall River."

"Ah, our dead mill towns are romantic, aren't they?"

"They are?" Monroe says. "I never—"

Schwartz clasps his hands together like he's begun to pray. "So, this wife moldering away? Now there's a subject we can work with. How about a few lines about Miss Havisham? How many poems can one man write about mist?"

Maybe the pupil answered. Maybe he didn't. Probably he was just flattered that Schwartz took any interest in him at all. Still, he might have said, one man can write innumerable poems about mist, Professor Schwartz.

And it may have been Broyard (or Saul Bellow or Dwight Macdonald or Alfred Kazin) who recounts it, but eventually Schwartz tossed Monroe out on his ear. So long Mister Millionaire, I got vendettas to dream up, up, up.


If Monroe wasn't officially family, his wife was even less so. After all those losses, financial and otherwise—the amount of the losses always grew in the telling, year after year—who in the family wanted to be reminded of Mort Sarkansky or whatever the hell his name was? Or his wife? But even back in the '50s and '60s, in its brief peak, Jewish Fall River was still a postage stamp. A few blocks in the Flint. A few German

104

Jews and upstarts scattered across the Highlands. In an ancient cabinet at the Temple Beth El office (a kind of card catalog of the dead) I found her name: Adelaide (Addy). Maiden name: Weissman. Her father was a partner in a large Fall River hat factory, Marshall Hat, the company that made, among other things, Monroe's boleros.

My mother and I were in the kitchen. This was about a decade ago now. My mother, keeper of our family secrets. All information is on a need to know basis, and the basis is you don't need to know.

"Why'd they sock her away?" I asked.

"Sock who?"

"Monroe's wife."

"Monroe?"

"Mort!"

"Oh, Mort. You know your father and I once stayed at his pied-à-terre in Saint Thomas."

"Nassau."

"Was it in Nassau? Your father thought he died and went to heaven. I should have left him there. The place came with a butler. I wish I could remember his name. Marcel? I'd step out of the pool and this beautiful man would be standing there with a robe, the softest—"

"But what about her?"

"Let the dead bury their dead, isn't that what people say?"

"Not Jews," I said.

My stepfather, Herb, calls from the next room where he's watching the Blackhawks on mute. "He's right," Herb said. "Jews don't say let the dead bury their dead. We say, 'Call Pizer's and let's get this done as soon as possible.'"

"Why'd they put her away?" I said.

My mother took a sip of her martini and shrugged. Maybe she was calculating the statute of limitations on material intelligence of nonfamily members and figured what the hell. How many people alive even remember these people?

"Mort had a stroke."

"What? What about the pearl-handled pistol? What about Sammy Davis?"

"Sammy Davis was there, I think, so was Carol Channing. Mort and Carol Channing may have had a thing. But it was a stroke. My father made that up about the gun."

"Why?"

"I don't know. Poetic justice?"

My mother cackles, remembering her father, a melancholic who spent much of his life laughing because, as he said, what other choice have I got?

"Mom."

"You know my father never liked Mort. He'd have forgiven him the money. What he couldn't stomach was anybody thought they were superior. And Mort always had to be the cock of the walk. So, my father did him in with a pearl-handled pistol, so what? This is all water under a bridge that doesn't even exist anymore."

"I'm just asking—"

My mother sipped her martini. She ran her tongue across her teeth to make it go down slower.

"My God, it was so long ago. I remember she'd never quite look at you. Like she always found a spot on your ear to look at. Pretty, one of those oval faces. Always wore her hair short. And very bright. She spoke several languages, which for a Fall River girl was quite—"

"Mom."

"They must have sent her to a boarding school. For a while, Marshall Hat was one of the largest manufacturers of hats in the country."

"Mom."

"She and Mort had a few good years together. They'd come around to the family. Then the business began to take off and Mort started to stay in New York for long stretches. After a while, he stopped coming home at all. With Mort gone most of the time, we stopped seeing her. She just sort of vanished though she only lived over on Locust Street. We'd see her through the windows. And people started to say she was a little cuckoo, sure, but harmless. Then, almost out of nowhere, came the baby. And she refused any help. Any help at all. Of course, this alarmed all the aunties. Refuse help with the baby? Raise it herself? And then—darling, what's the score?"

"Predators up by one," Herb said.

"Predators?" she said.

"And then?" I said.

"Expansion team," Herb said. "Nashville."

My mother doodled on the telephone memo pad. "Nashville has a hockey team?"

"And then?" I said.

"She lit the crib on fire," my mother said.

"Huh?"

"It was the '60s," my mother said. "All kinds of wild things were happening. Setting a bed on fire was nothing. Anyway, the boy wasn't hurt. She dropped her cigarette by accident, that's what I've always believed. I never thought she was crazy."

"And then?"

"They sent her to Menningers." My mother called to my stepfather. "Herb, where's Menningers? Nebraska?"

"Kansas," Herb said. "Topeka."

"Kansas, that's right—"

"Why?" I said.

"Because she was crazy, she tried to burn the house—"

"But you just said she wasn't."

"Maybe she was, maybe she wasn't."

"And the boy?" I said. "What happened—"

"He went to Kansas, too. They had some sort of school for the children of patients. You know Menningers was *the* place when you lost your mind. They sent Gene Tierney there. There must have been some money left over from the hat factory. Either that or Mort had managed to squirrel some money away for her that the creditors couldn't attach. That's what my father always thought. Not that he begrudged it, he just assumed that Mort had outfoxed—out-squirreled? Can we talk about something else? How's your divorce going?"

"Who's Gene Tierney?" I said.

"He wants to know who's Gene Tierney?" Herb said.

"My God, Gene Tierney's cheekbones," my mother said.

"And then?" I said. "She couldn't have stayed in Kansas forever."

"Why not?" my mother said. "People don't live in Kansas forever? Listen, these people, they weren't family—Horace may have been a thief, but he was our thief, but Mort and Addy—She's dead. Is that what you're asking? Of course, Addy's dead by now."

"And the boy? Monroe's—Mort's—son?"

My mother. I have this picture of her and her father on a bike. I'm staring at it right now. It's on the wall above my desk. My grandfather has a cigarette hanging out his mouth and my mother is holding on to his waist, and her long blond hair is streaming in the wind behind her. My grandfather doesn't look like a rich guy or anybody who even wants to be a rich guy. He looks like a furniture salesman from Fall River,

107

Massachusetts, riding his kid on the back of his bike. My mother is right. These people with serious (stolen) money and private psychiatric hospitals. They weren't family.

"The boy?" my mother said. "The boy grew up. That's what boys do. But Mort didn't have a son. Coming into town every six months? That's not having a son. What is it about Mort? You've been snooping around him—"

"I guess I feel a kinship," I say. "Remember in college when I changed my name to Max to sound more Jewish?"

"You changed your name?"

"I lasted two weeks. For two weeks, I corrected people. 'The name is Max.' I admire a guy who can sustain that kind of bullshit for years, though I guess he wanted to sound less Jewish while for some reason I wanted to be—"

"You're Jewish enough."

"Not even that. I think I just wanted to be someone else."

"You're doing wonderfully, honey. Isn't he doing wonderfully, Herb? You're still sending your resume around, right? Life takes turns, it—"

"Wonderfully," Herb says. "He's doing wonderfully. He dinged my car, Allstate wants to raise my rates he's doing so—"

"Also," I said, "I turned my back on a wife after she went nuts."

"That's not how anybody sees it. Your wife has mental health issues."

"I didn't help," I said. "I tried to force a kind of normalcy—"

"Oh, please! You tried, period. You tried harder than most people would have ever tried. Do you hear this Herb? Now he turned his back—"

"I heard, I heard."

"Didn't he try, Herb? Didn't he try? For years—"

"Woo-hoo," Herb shouted. "Hawks just tied it up."


In the few pictures I found on microfilm at the Fall River Public Library, Monroe Sarkansky has dark, sleek, Sephardic features. Nothing at all like the saggy jowls of Horace. They don't look like brothers. And Monroe wears a moustache that somehow doesn't make him look ridiculous. And always that hat at an angle. Like an old-time private eye. I think the man was hiding out. He hid in Manhattan, on Long Island, in Nassau, but he also hid in the books that are sitting right here in a stack. And, so yeah, I feel a kinship. I'm only a poor relation who's not a relation, but I'm sure as hell hiding. I wonder if you reach a point when you don't even know who, or what, you're hiding from.

And though he may well have squirreled away some money for her, there's no evidence in any of the hundreds—Jesus, thousands—of lines of poetry he left behind that he ever thought much about the wife back home in Fall River. It was all clouds, and balloons, and his mother.

Addy has never taken shape for me, either. Of her, I've never even found any photographs. I do know that at some point she returned to Fall River from Kansas because she died in the city. The death certificate on file at Government Center lists Adelaide Sarkansky's cause of death as drinking paregoric. My mother knew, of course. Why dredge it up out of the darkness, out of the years? For what? Still, imagination fails. A faker, a scam artist, sure, him I get, though I'll never reach Monroe's highs or lows. At best, I'm a midlevel operator.

Once, a few years ago, I peeped into a back window of the house on Locust Street. I must have thought I might be able to conjure a vision of Addy's oval face by looking into what she had looked out of. All I saw was someone else's life. A pair of glasses on a kitchen table, some car keys.

*Nominated by The Southern Review, Pat Strachan, Andrew Porter, Katherine Taylor*

# ENTREATY

## by CATHERINE PIERCE

from COPPER NICKEL

Dear spring, commit. Burst
your bee-and-bloom, your blaze
of blue, get heady, get frocked,
get spun. Enough with your tentative
little breaths, your one-day-daffodils/
one-day-dewfrost. Honeysuckle us
right to our knees. Wake us
with your all-night mockingbirds,
your rowdy tree frogs. Gust
and dust us. Pollen-bomb the Hondas
and front halls, but please, no more
of this considering. This delicate-
tendrilling. Your pale green
worries me. Your barely-tuliped
branches, your slim shoots
any sideways look could doom.
The truth is I don't want to think
about fragility anymore. I can't
handle a blown-glass season,
every grass blade and dogwood
so wreckable. I'm trying hard
to teach the infallibility
of nightlights, to ignore the revving
of my own fallible heart. Spring,
you're not helping. Go all in.

Throw your white blossoms
into my gutters. Flood
my garage, mud my suede shoes,
leave me afternoon-streaked
and sweating. Vine yourself
around me. Hold me
to you. Tighter.

*Nominated by Copper Nickel, Gary Fincke, Nausheen Eusuf*

# A TOWN SOMEWHERE

## by TED KOOSER

from RATTLE

I'd like to find it for you but I can't. You might not
like it anyway. It's quaint and pretty in an old,
worn way, quite near to me at times. But then it's
gone, impossible to find. I've been there always
but I haven't been, if you can understand. It's a town
that I remember in sweet detail that was never.

It would be simple to find someone to love,
it's so open there. Whenever there's a fence around
a stand of flowers—bachelor's buttons—there's a gate
with a hook-and-eye latch that a finger can lift,
and whenever you see shutters framing windows,
they're decorations only, for they shut out nothing.

Those windows are Windex clean, too, sprayed
and wiped with wads of inessential news.
If you peer deep into the liquid shadows, careful
to avoid stirring the surface, you might see a figure
rising, as if to take a breath of what's beyond,
looking out at you above a sill of potted violets.

Was she the person you might love? She's gone.
And even as I call up the town for you I feel it
darken. Sundown. A dog is in the distance barking

and barking, as if aware that we'd been there
just passing through, leaving no more than a scent
on the wind, where no one was, or seemed to be.

*Nominated by Maura Stanton*

# TEAMWORK

fiction by SHAWN VESTAL

from THE SEWANEE REVIEW

Coach says we are the sorriest bunch of lazy-ass mother-flippers he's ever seen in shoulder pads. If we don't start acting like we want to win, he doesn't know what's going to happen. Coach says we must be *a team*— twenty-six boys, all on the same page. Coach says we have to *execute*. If every one of us would just *execute*, there's no reason on the gol-dang planet every play shouldn't go for a touchdown. But no. We don't execute. Not us.

It's halftime at the Declo game. We are in the locker room. We are five points down.

He says, "Maybe some of you guys don't need to be out there anymore." He says, "Maybe some of you prima donnas need some time on the bench." He says, "Try me. Just try me." Red in the face, he waves his arms around like he's being attacked by bees. He says, "You gotta get out there and fuck-dang *hit* somebody!"

He throws his clipboard against the wall and stomps out.

Everyone relaxes. Charles Qualls III hands out speeders—tiny white pills he orders from a magazine. Everyone treats them like they're cocaine or something, like it's *doing drugs*, like Charles is a *drug dealer*, but they're just caffeine.

Still, they get you up.

Cleats clapping on the concrete, Charles mutters, "Speeder? Speeder, dude?" as he walks past each of us. Our quarterback, Jason Ashman, is sitting on the bench and praying. He doesn't look up. He doesn't take a speeder. He leans forward, elbows on knees, hands clasped, head bowed between his hulking shoulders, asking God to help us win.

*　*　*

With 3:42 left, Charles Qualls III takes a swing pass from Jason Ashman out in the flat, stops in his tracks as the cornerback flies past, and runs twenty-four yards into the end zone, right onto those big orange Declo letters—HORNETS. The little bank of home-team bleachers goes quiet, while the even smaller bank of visiting-team bleachers sends up its puny cries of elation into the night, drifting into the atmosphere of cow shit and cut hay.

We hold them on their next possession and win; and thus we, the 1983 Gooding Senators, the pride of Idaho's Magic Valley Conference, the smallest eleven-man farm-town league in the state, take our record to 1–2. Afterwards, in the celebration huddle, Coach says we should thank our lucky stars Declo is so terrible, because the way we're playing right now we couldn't beat a team of fourth-grade girls, for cripes' sake. He looms over us, a Senators cap on his head and a whistle around his neck, taut globe of belly swelling against his shirt. We better decide that we want to be here or we're not going to be here anymore, Coach says. Our problem, Coach says, is we have too much wanna and not enough hafta. He nods as he says this, as though he's finally landed on it, as though after all this time trying to diagnose just what in the Sam damn hell is wrong with this team, he has seized on it at long last. Too much wanna, not enough hafta.

"OK!" he says. "Touch somebody."

This is his signal to pray.

*　*　*

Later that night, at the bonfire in the desert, we drink warmish beer from a keg and celebrate our victory. We talk about the good plays. We complain about Coach, who we love. We pair off with girls and try to guide them toward the outskirts of the fire, toward the back seats of cars, toward the dark, lonely night.

Charles Qualls III breaks out some weed he got from his uncle in Boise, and we smoke it from an old Meerschaum pipe he stole from his grandfather, a pipe without a screen. We inhale the embers straight into our healthy pink throats and lungs, and we cough and laugh and spit, and what are we in this glorious night but young princes, risen by lineage, coronated by merit?

Who are we but the elect?

Coach says drugs are for losers and queers. We don't want to be losers and queers, do we? We have to decide what kind of people we are going to be. We have to decide that *right fucking now.* We can be lazy, we can be quitters, we can be losers, we can be druggies, we can be gol-dang queers. Coach don't care, it's perfectly fucking fine with Coach if we do that. "Just don't come around looking to be on one of my teams," he says.

This makes the drugs—the whole idea of them—even better.

* * *

Monday, Coach starts focusing on the hafta. He has us run four sets of KYAs—Kick Your Asses—after practice. As punishment, he says. For not showing enough heart. A KYA goes like this: bear walk from goal line to goal line. Crab walk back. Army crawl one hundred yards. Sprint one hundred yards. Heart is the most important thing, Coach says. Heart and wanting. Heart and wanting and teamwork. And execution. But mostly heart. Which makes us wonder if hafta is just another way of saying *heart*, another way of saying *wanting*. Which makes us won-der: if wanting is the most important thing, then why would too much wanna be a problem?

We know better than to ask Coach about these things.

Four KYAs produce a festival of vomiting. Coach screams at us as we retch, shouts that maybe now we'll learn to show some fucking heart, that if we don't toughen up our candy asses we'll find ourselves losing more games this year. Is that what we want, *to accept the tragedy of losing*? Because Glenns Ferry, Coach says, is not going to be the cake-walk that Declo was. Glenns Ferry is *not* a pack of disgusting fucking pussies, and we can't take no candy-ass bull crap to Glenns Ferry and expect to win, and is that what we want, to be losers our whole god-damned lousy terrible lives?

* * *

After practice, Coach tells us we have to go to the nursing home on the edge of town and dance with the old ladies for the Harvest Festival in a couple weeks. Coach will make us wear ties, and give corsages to the old ladies, and dance with them to horrible organ music in the cafeteria, where everything will smell like pee and VapoRub and hamburger.

Coach says we are leaders, and leaders owe it to be fucking decent and whatnot to people in the community who are not. Like old people or math kids. He makes us wear ties on game days because we're supposed to be people the other kids look up to. We're *setting an example*. If we don't fucking like it, we can take our lousy ungrateful behinds right off this team and hang out with the rest of the losers and queers, out in the parking lot with the druggies and smokers who will never do a decent thing in their lives. But if we want to stay on the team with the gol-dang leaders and the winners, then we'll by God put on a mother-flipping tie and dance with those nice old ladies and not complain about it one bit.

✸　✸　✸

Glenns Ferry has this running back, Rodriguez, who drags half our defense downfield on every play. Jason Ashman throws two interceptions. Charles Qualls III can't make it past the line of scrimmage. At halftime, we're down 21-0, and Coach doesn't yell *at* us, but he's yelling in a certain way, in spirit, or he's past yelling, maybe, so gravely have we let him down. He's telling us he's never been as motherflipping disgusted with a group of kids as he is with us now, and we feel his disgust so sharply and personally—we feel Coach actually does not approve of us as human beings.

He says if we don't figure out a way to man up and stop that wetback—this is what he calls Rodriguez, although sometimes he calls him a spic or a beaner—then we might as well just lie down on the field and give each other pedicures and blowjobs. Once, when he calls Rodriguez a beaner, he looks over at Jesse Contreras, our huge right tackle, and says, "No offense, kid," and Jesse says, "No," and we think maybe Jesse is saying, *'No offense' doesn't cut it*, maybe he's saying, *There very much is offense, please don't say that*, or maybe he's saying, *Fuck that, Coach*, but then it doesn't seem like it, because Coach always talks like that, calls Jesse a beaner and a wetback all the time, just like he calls our terrible punter, Dana Sazue, who is Northern Shoshone, chief and shee-peater in that same almost sort-of friendly way. He does it, we mean, like he *likes* Jesse, like he's saying, *You're one of the good ones, kid*, and Jesse always acts like it's okay, like he's abashed at the affection he's being shown, so we always think that it's okay, too; we think that Coach's heart is in the right place, just like all of our hearts—our big farm-boy hearts—are in the right place, too.

But when Jesse gives Coach that look, we sometimes wonder.

Coach leaves, and Charles trawls the locker room, handing out speeders. Most of us double up, except for Jason and a couple of the underclassmen who go to his church, who're praying together while we wash down our pills, which honestly makes it better for the rest of us that the churchy kids don't join. We go out and do better in the second half, we score a couple times and hold them to three-and-out on a few possessions, but in the end we lose 34-13, and Coach tells us he's never been so appalled by a group of so-called football players in his everloving life.

✲   ✲   ✲

Next it's Buhl at home, and Buhl murders us. Charles Qualls III barely ever makes it out of the backfield, and Jason Ashman gets sacked eleven times.

Coach loses his voice at halftime—we hear it go, hear his scream break into a screech, like radio feedback squealing out of his purple, rage-darkened face. Then it falls into a rasp, an impotent whisper that's almost funny. He is whispering that, given the miserable, cocksucking way we're playing, given how the line can't make a block to save its life and how the defense is just going up to the Buhl players and giving them little hugs, he can't tell if any of us even want to *be* there anymore. And if we don't, then could we just go ahead and take off our pads and, by *God*, sit in the stands with the rest of the losers? Didn't we want to *hit* somebody? Can't he find just one kid—just one gol-dang little fucker— who *wants* to *hit* some—

And after that, his voice is all the way gone.

Never mind the score.

✲   ✲   ✲

Charles Qualls III gets some mushrooms before the old ladies' dance. He gets these hallucinogens from his uncle in Boise who's spent time in prison, who knows all kinds of things, things he's taught Charles, and which Charles has since taught us. How to hot-wire a car. How to shotgun a beer. How to hold the pot smoke in your lungs a long time so it makes you high.

He was right about the speeders, they really did provide a jolt, and he was also right about the marijuana, the dusty, green-brown weed he brought around in plastic sandwich baggies, weed that was full of little stems and purplish seeds that popped and crackled as they burned in the bowl of his grandfather's pipe and got us so baked it was all we could

118

do not to lie down on the ground. And so between that and the speeders and the beer, we keep this secret from the world—from our parents and our teachers, from the upstanding kids in school, from Jason Ashman and his freshman disciples, and from Coach, especially from Coach, this secret we share, that we carry apart from the ordinary others, and so what the heck, we—the elect—said we'd give the mushrooms a try, too.

But first, before the old ladies' dance, we're scheduled to play Wood River at home. Wood River is out of our conference, the worst of the bigger schools in the area. Game night arrives, and they come onto the field in their all-black uniforms, helmets flashing in the field lights. It's the first cool night of the season, the first time you can smell winter coming. Someone is burning ditch moss nearby, so there's a note of scorched material in the chill, a real football night, and our parents are all in the stands, most of them anyway, and the other kids from school, and the cheerleaders, and the pep band playing the theme song from *Hawaii Five-O*. Wood River has no kind of defensive line, and so for the first time in weeks, Jason Ashman has time to pass, and Charles Qualls III is hitting holes off tackle and turning the corners, and it's just like Coach said: if we each do our job, if we each just *execute*, they can't keep up with us.

We execute our asses off. We go up 17-0 by halftime and end up winning by way more, and Coach tells us he's proud, for the first time all year he's seen something in us, a spark, a flame, some God-sakes fucking heart, dang it, and maybe we're gonna be all right, he says, maybe we can get this season on track after all; and we wonder, *On track to what?*, but who cares, it's nice to see him happy, and it feels good to win, maybe not as good as it seems to feel for Coach, but good still, and later that evening when we gather in the desert, we feel like winners, we drink beer and woo-hoo and try to get girls to let us take their pants off.

The next Monday is the old ladies' dance.

Seven of us take mushrooms beforehand. Charles Qualls III doles them out in the parking lot after practice, all of us half-damp and sour-smelling from the locker room, and we chew them down. He says they'll be kicking in by the time we arrive at Frahm Senior Center. The mushrooms taste awful, like nuggets of dried cow turd that Charles has slipped us as a joke. We think surely once we swallow them Charles will start laughing at us, preparing the story for everyone else, but he doesn't, and when Brent Grogan makes a gagging sound and spits his

119

half-chewed mushrooms in his palm, Charles freaks out and shouts, "Don't waste them, dipshit!" Little brown bits decorate the sagging column of saliva between Brent's mouth and his open hand. Charles gathers up the spitty pieces, dries them on his shirtsleeve, and eats them himself.

Only three of the seven of us who take shrooms know before-hand what Charles Qualls III is planning to do at the dance. None of the rest of us do.

❄   ❄   ❄

What's weird is the way the world seems to breathe with us, in time with our own breathing. As if the walls of the nursing home cafeteria are gently and sustainingly expanding and contracting, like a bellows, like lungs. The quality of the light is pure and sweet, a magisterial, divine brightness emanating from tubes overhead, and some of us begin to stare up at these, which are also pulsing like living portals in the flesh of the world, and we cannot take our eyes off the light. We stand in the middle of the cafeteria—on the "dance floor"—looking up in amazement for a very long time until Coach comes stomping over, head way out over of his feet, asking what in the gol-dang everloving *hell* is wrong with us, and peering angrily into our faces.

"Your eyes are not right," he hisses. "I don't know what you little bastards have been up to, but right now I want you to get over there and ask those ladies to God-sakes *dance*."

❄   ❄   ❄

What happened was, after we got into the dance, Charles Qualls III put some liquid acid he'd gotten from his uncle into a few cups of punch. His uncle had taught him how to make blotter tabs out of it, thinking Charles could help expand his sales to Gooding, that Charles could be, like, his drug-dealing *franchisee* or something, and our town's young people, and the mighty 1983 Gooding Senators especially, would be his *clientele*. Charles's uncle had dreams of empire.

But nobody around here does acid, not that we know of anyway, not at the high school—maybe kids are doing acid in Boise or Twin Falls, but not out here in the sticks—and Charles hadn't gotten around to dosing out the blotters and trying to sell them or anything, and then he got this funny idea about the old ladies' dance and putting drops into the cups of punch sitting there on the table.

Five drops, five cups.

One of the things about what happens is how fast it goes. About as fast as a single play in football. One pass. One run. Fast the way life concentrates its energy and potency and importance into spasms that leap without warning, brief fits in the long flat line of hours. By the time you realize what's going on, it's already raced past you; the whistle is blown, and you're looking back on it, gazing at the irrevocable statistics.

In the cafeteria, the long tables have been folded up and rolled against the walls, along with the stacks of chairs. This leaves half the room for dancing. The fluorescent lights cast luscious buttery ovals on the linoleum. A Mentholatum-smelling man in suspenders and a bristling flannel shirt—one that seems to be alive, fibers waving in a gentle wind—plays songs at the organ that are unexpectedly, exceedingly beautiful. *Painfully* beautiful. The women are in polyester and rayon, in hairspray and flats. They tremble while we dance. We think they might be forced to be here just as we are, dancing with us only because to refuse to dance with us would be unkind. Coach is dancing with a tall, thin lady with large glasses and a bouffant. His belly rests between them like a stone they are hauling.

Those of us who ate the mushrooms are not doing a good job of dancing. Some of us forget to move, rapt at the gorgeous music, tears spilling down our cheeks. The old ladies, their hands light as Styrofoam in ours as we dance, find this confusing. Coach sidles up to us and intently considers our weeping faces, and we dance away from him as though he is a burning flame.

It is terrifying, the intensity and strangeness of our minds.

✿ ✿ ✿

One of the women sitting in a folding chair starts screeching and waving her clenched fists in front of her face. She screams louder and louder, though the screams are not very loud, and then freezes. As we turn to see what's happening, the woman dancing with Jason Ashman slumps right onto to the floor. Just *plop.* Her slipper comes off, and her pale, liver-spotted foot, with a big toe as crooked as a bone break, lies on the linoleum like a fish. Another woman, sitting by her walker in a housedress, puts her face into her hands and sobs.

Attendants rush to the women. The sober stand baffled. The Mentholatum-smelling man in the bristling shirt starts to pound the organ keys with his fists, and then leans on the entire board with his forearms like he's holding down a calf for branding. The woman dancing with Brent Grogan gets down onto her hands and knees and crawls, slowly, arthritically, under the punch table.

Coach releases the lady he's dancing with and looks around. He's acting like he acts during a close game, his focus is that intense, his face darting from one person in distress to the next.

What this feels like is: Coach is called upon to understand the moment and he cannot.

Or: Coach feels responsible for the event going well, and he cannot figure out why it isn't.

Or: Coach feels a crumbling loss of control, just as he does when we are behind, a slipping-away, a falling, a loss.

✻   ✻   ✻

Two of the women die. Their hearts couldn't bear the stress and amazement. In the first of a million newspaper stories, the local weekly, the *Gooding County Leader*, reports that the women suffered "heart attacks brought on by the presence of a hallucinogenic drug that police believe was introduced into food or drink at an event being held at the facility." Two others—one man and one woman—suffer heart attacks and are hospitalized, but survive. Several others are "traumatized and terrorized" by the experience, a staff nurse tells the newspaper.

The story doesn't mention the fact that the 1983 Gooding Senators football team had been present at the event. But the second, third, fourth, and fifth stories—the ones that run on the front pages of the daily newspapers in Twin Falls, Boise, Denver, and Salt Lake—mention it in the first paragraph.

Before long, reporters from everywhere in the country show up. We can spot them by their rental cars, their city clothes, their brusque manners. They go around town interviewing everyone about "the players," asking what kinds of kids we are, if anyone is surprised that this happened—and they approach us, too, saying they're trying to get our side of it, that they just want to make sure we know we can tell our stories if we want to, saying they want to be fair to us, but none of us talk to them.

Some of the people tell them we're good kids from good families in a good town, but others say we're trouble, have always been trouble, and everyone knows it. If we'd been a better football team, more people would probably have supported us.

The headlines are screamers.

TWO DIE IN ONE-WAY TRIP
DID FOOTBALL PLAYERS SPIKE PUNCH?
THEY CAME TO DANCE, BUT DID THEY DEAL OUT DEATH
INSTEAD?

Coach is quoted saying he doesn't believe his boys had anything to do with it, but if they did he will "gol-dang well find out."

\* \* \*

Nobody does. At least, not for sure. The police interview each of us individually, and we all say the same thing: we have no idea what happened. We were just as surprised as everyone else. We are sure, *sure*, that neither we nor any of our teammates were responsible. None of us even know what LSD really *is*. We were there to be nice to those old people, not to kill them.

It's pretty spectacular when you think about it. Twenty-six boys, all on the same page. Of course, lots of us actually *don't* know what happened. Most of us, in fact. We were coming apart way before the dance, we mighty Senators, back in the locker rooms when some of us took speeders and some prayed, back on the Friday nights when some of us drank at the desert keggers and some of us stayed at home. But most of us who don't know can guess. We can see it right on the face of Charles Qualls III, whose entire demeanor changed after the dance, taking on the pale blush of one who hides, a secret-keeper, guilty. But none of us rats. Not even Jason Ashman.

The school cancels the rest of the season anyway. It's too suspicious. Too distracting. The newspapers would have been at every game, for heaven's sake—those ferrety city men and women with their notebooks, nodding as they scribble. We forfeit to Wendell, Mountain Home, Filer, Valley, and Jerome.

Every single day in school, forever after, someone makes a joke about it, asks if we put anything in their milk at lunch, if we know where the punch bowl is, if they can have this dance. It's funny—sometimes funny ha-ha and sometimes funny weird and usually both—but it turns out it's not embarrassing. Not with the other kids. The other kids seem to kind of . . . approve of it? Or something?

Though it's hard not to think of Coach, to think of him telling us that the season has been canceled, like a man confessing a crime to his victims. We are sitting on the bleachers in the gym after school, the doors shut against a scrum of reporters outside. Coach pulls up a chair and sits before us, seemingly drained of blood.

123

He wants to believe the best of his boys, he says, and he is trying to believe the best of us. This is hard, a bitter disappointment, but that's one of the things we might as well learn about life, Coach says, how sometimes it's just one motherflipping loss after another. Sometimes, Coach says, we will find ourselves facing the fucking gol-dang true facts about life—sometime later, he means, when we are grown, when we have gathered up the disappointments that will come our way, deaths and heartbreaks and the dissolutions of football teams, the inevitable failures of the world to live up to our hopes—and we will have to learn to *keep living,* to *keep going,* to *persevere.*

It's the *only fucking way,* Coach says. The *only fucking way* to live is to keep going when you think you can't keep going. When people take away the things that are yours. When life gives you the royal gol-dang screw job. Head down, stick it out.

His voice falls quieter. He stares at the floor. We can see dandruff clinging to his neatly combed rows of dark gray hair, and his bright red scalp beneath.

He wanted to protect us from this, he says. He tried to get the school board to listen. To tell them we were good boys. That we don't deserve this. That our lives would be forever altered, worsened, ruined. *Ruined,* he says. A season, cut short.

He stops. Stares into the gym's floor. We think he's just paused, gathering his thoughts. We wait, not feeling ruined at all—just feeling that we are coming apart, we are separating, we are a team no longer, and that's fine—until we realize he has nothing more to say.

*Nominated by Mark Jude Poirier*

# IOWA

## by T. R. HUMMER

from AMERICAN JOURNAL OF POETRY

Somewhere east of Ames, in the blizzard
   of history, my people are taking off
Their white German skins and riding in blunt wagons
   pulled by blunt oxen, playing checkers and freezing
Bone-naked in the naked climate of this continent.
   Winter cloudbanks make the impersonal easier
To repair with nothing but pulp, and your own
   saliva, and a certain taste for metallic residues.
I don't know what we are looking for
   in the prairie between the South Skunk River
And heinous Squaw Creek. Look at us there
   in the 19th century, robbing beehives to make
Our old familiar mead in small casks, sipping it
   delicately between double jumps at checkers,
Growing unconscious now of the old country,
   dropping our tattered Franco-Prussian uniforms
On the bones of the Meskwaki Nation, driving
   home from a football game on the icy bypass,
Silhouetted at sundown in old Volkswagens, jubilant
   at one more victory, spattered with nameless blood.

*Nominated by David Baker*

# THE SAMPLES

## fiction by KRISTOPHER JANSMA

from THE SUN

It is a quarter past five on Tuesday morning as Sasha Trzynski treks down the snow-scraped sidewalks of 59th Street in Manhattan. Even for her it is unusually early. She's already taken her son, Peter, to Mrs. Russo's house and ridden an empty 4 train down from Mount Eden Avenue in the Bronx. As she passes the Christmas displays at Bloomingdale's, she wonders what to buy her sister this year. A vendor rolls the guard up on his newsstand with a screech of metal, and she watches him beckon to the delivery truck easing backward down the quiet street. A man in a hazard-orange vest bends down from the truck with a fattened square of newspapers between his gloved hands and passes it to the vendor like a sacrament on Sunday, both routine and delicate. The two men, hands almost touching, talk with their fingertips. *You got it?* Great ghosts of exhaust steam up between them from the tailpipe of the truck. *Yeah. I got it.*

Sasha lets herself into Dr. Von Hatter's office at Park Avenue Pathology. Before even turning on the fluorescent overhead lights, she crosses the room to boot up her decrepit computer. The monitor glows. Blue light shines through the burnt-in image of a patient record accidentally left on the screen over a long weekend ten years ago: Mr. Abraham Clemente. Dead six years now from the very prostate cancer the record indicates. Sasha hits the lights, hangs up her coat, and yanks off her salt-whitened boots before slipping into the sneakers from her bag. She makes the coffee, turns on the radio, and scrubs her hands with antibacterial soap. Snapping on a pair of white latex gloves, she opens the drawer containing the samples.

126

There are twenty-two today. Last week doctors all around the city delicately removed these slices of cyst and marrow and muscle. They bit away tiny segments of freckles, moles, and lymph nodes. Each half centimeter contains a thousand or so microscopic cells: a honeycomb of membranes that were once lungs, liver, or skin. The samples look innocuous enough, ordered in rows, already fixed by the weekend technician in 10 percent neutral buffered formalin, dehydrated in a series of concentrated ethanol baths, cleared with xylene, and finally infiltrated with paraffin and sliced so thin that light can pass through.

Twenty-two futures. Some are death sentences; others, full pardons. Some dictate life in a prison of chronic illness; others allow the possibility of parole. There are no minors in this court; all are tried as adults. For this last reason, mostly, Sasha does not often think about what the samples really are.

She submerges the slices in distilled water and stains them with hematoxylin. Then she has four minutes to kill, so she calls the doctor's nighttime answering service to get his messages. The computer grunts suddenly, and the noise makes her heart squeeze for one quick extra beat. The thing always takes so long to boot up that she forgets she's started it. Finished with the messages, she picks at a scab that she got on her knee while chasing Peter at Chuck E. Cheese's last week. Sasha has to take Peter back there for another birthday party tonight, after work. Dr. Von Hatter has promised she can slip out early if she takes care of all the reports before he arrives at eight, which is why her morning has begun unusually early.

The four minutes now up, she runs the stained cells under tap water. Then a splash of 0.3 percent acid alcohol, more water, another wash in the bluing solution, followed by a final splash of water. All that remains is to add a few drops of eosin and sit back for two more minutes. A far-off crossing guard's whistle signals to the Park Avenue parents bringing their children to the front doors of the Egan School across the street. They have before-school activities starting at 6 AM. Dr. Von Hatter said the Egan students have to keep up with the kids in Shanghai if they want to have a prayer of competing. Peter is too young still, but Sasha wants him to go to the Egan School and become a doctor someday. He could have his own office, even nicer than this one, and a beautiful wife, and then Sasha will be a grandmother and spend all day watching his children while Peter is at work, just like Mrs. Russo does for Sasha now.

Suddenly Sasha realizes more than two minutes have passed. The samples will be overexposed. She rushes across the room to wash away the eosin. If she messes up the slides, Dr. Von Hatter will make her redo them, all the way back to the formalin and the ethanol baths. She'll have to stay late, and Peter will miss the birthday party. She squeezes her eyes shut and prays as the water flows over the samples. Why is life like this? So mindless, until one tiny lapse in attention ruins everything.

The samples are all right. Relieved, she begins pressing each one onto a slide for Dr. Von Hatter to analyze when he gets in. She works busily, thinking how close she came to ruining Peter's evening. When she comes to the last sample, she lifts it up to the window. The sun is just beginning to come up behind the buildings to the east, and its pale rays shine through the tiny smear of blue and pink. Sasha reads the name on the coded strip at the end of the slide. This thousand-cell slice, this square half centimeter, is from a twenty-five-year-old named Irene Richmond.

Sasha has never met Irene Richmond. She does not know what this woman's slide contains. That's for Dr. Von Hatter to determine. Her only concern is that the slide has not been ruined, and so her day has not been ruined, and Peter will go to Chuck E. Cheese's, and his face will light up like he's at the pearly gates of heaven, though Peter doesn't know about heaven yet, because Peter doesn't know about Death yet, because Peter is just a little boy.

She returns to the sink and washes the blue dye off her latex gloves. It swirls into the basin, inky dark at first and then in lighter cerulean bands. Outside, the city is finally awake. Parents leave the Egan School and head to their offices or back to their apartments. The man on the corner is selling the newspapers from that morning's bundles. Their pages are full of stories about politicians and criminals and movie stars and ballplayers. Someone died in a fire. Someone won the Powerball. Someone is being sued or heading to jail. None of these stories are about Irene Richmond, and none of them are about Sasha Trzynski. In all of the stories in all of the newspapers in the entire knotted, tragic, waking city, none are about anyone either of them has ever known.


Irene Richmond's alarm goes off at eight, and she hits SNOOZE to buy herself another ten minutes, though this small movement immediately nixes any possibility of a real return to sleep. Resenting the yesterday self who set the alarm ten minutes earlier than was truly necessary, she sticks one foot out from under her blankets to confirm that, yes, it is still cold out there. Gathering the blanket around her, she rushes to the bathroom with her eyes closed and sets the shower as hot as it will go.

128

Will they call today? The doctor said middle of next week, and it is only Tuesday. Probably they meant Wednesday or even Thursday, or else they'd have said, "We'll call first thing," or, "We'll call Tuesday." So it's tomorrow's problem. If that, even. Today's problem is whether there will be time to stop for coffee on the way to the art gallery. Sometimes there is coffee there, but when there isn't, Irene's morning is a horror show. Really she should have green tea instead. Antioxidants are better for you. But no. Today she needs more than better. She needs caffeine.

The issue with stopping for coffee is that she'll have to carry the hot cup in one hand, and she'll also have to carry the large portfolio folder that is currently on the bookshelf—*You must not forget the folder on the bookshelf,* she reminds herself—which contains the contracts Abeba needs for the commission.

Leaving the shower, Irene begins to make plans for the day. Once her hair is mostly dry and her clothes are on, she moves to the window, where she keeps her jewelry box inside a large brass birdcage hanging by a chain from the ceiling. It is the only decorative item she owns— she doesn't count her own paintings, which stand facing the wall, like children who've been bad. The birdcage was left behind by the previous tenant. When the broker told her it came with the crumbling, fifth-floor walk-up, Irene signed the lease immediately.

She looks at her watch—her extra ten minutes have been squandered somewhere along the way, and now she has to hurry. If she gets to the studio late, she'll have to have lunch late, which will mean being late to meet her friend, which will mean not having time to pick up the last few Christmas gifts she still needs to buy.

*Don't forget the folder,* she reminds herself. *Don't forget it, don't forget it, don't forget it.* She turns the command around in her head, like a sentence in a foreign-language lesson: *By whom will the folder not be forgotten?* The folder will not be forgotten by me. *What is the thing which will not be forgotten by me?* The thing which will not be forgotten by me is the folder. *What will I not do to the folder?* What I will not do to the folder is forget it.

Abeba is already upset with Irene about losing the Levy donation, which wasn't Irene's fault. Irene thinks Abeba is really angry because there's going to be a feature about the gallery on the news—not the real news, but the news on those credit-card screens inside of cabs—and on the day the video producer came to shoot the gallery, Irene had, with Abeba's complete permission, been storing one of her own paintings in the back room. And somehow the producer saw it and included it in the video, and now it turns out that the interview with Abeba has been trimmed to one banal line—"It's an exciting time to be a young artist in New York City!"—lasting just four seconds, followed by a rather loving shot of Irene's painting, which will be getting *seven* seconds of screen time. Tiny, cab-screen time. It is such bullshit, really, but Irene knows all it takes is one wrong step and Abeba will fire her, and it will be good-bye, salary and good-bye, benefits and good-bye, cramped, cold apartment. Irene doesn't even take cabs usually.

Opening the tiny door to the birdcage, Irene rummages through the jewelry box until she locates two matching earrings. Then she holds her hair back with one hand and with the other pushes in the first earring while holding its mate in her clenched front teeth. She watches her mirror-self aim the slim metal post through the tiny hole, punched through her flesh by a Korean woman fifteen years ago (*Christ!*) during a back-to-school trip to the mall. Irene was ten. She remembers the way the dark-eyed woman rubbed her earlobe with a cold, wet cotton ball and how she pressed the piercing gun to the side of Irene's head. There was a stabbing sensation, along with a sudden loneliness as the million other mall-goers instantly vanished and were replaced by blank and blinding pain—and then there was this dark-eyed Korean woman saying, "Shush." Not making a shushing noise, but actually saying, "Shush." The strangeness of this brought the whole world rushing back again.

Irene caps the first earring, holds back the hair on the opposite side of her head, and carefully moves the second earring from her teeth to her free hand, using her lips. As she does, she thinks about what might happen if, for some reason—an inopportune sneeze, a mouse running by, a car backfiring on Avenue A—she opened her mouth at that moment and the second earring tumbled back over her tongue and down into her esophagus.

Shit, she's so late now. She closes the jewelry box and shuts the bird-cage door too quickly; it swings wildly on its chain as she dashes out, nearly tripping over the most recent canvas she's been working on (which already isn't coming out the way she hoped). The birdcage is still swaying as she heads to the door—late, hair damp, and without coffee. At the last second she remembers and runs back for the folder on the bookshelf.

On his lunch break Dr. Von Hatter rockets around the bend at the bottom of Central Park on his Orbea Orca Aero M30 road bike, tucking his Giro-helmeted head to minimize air resistance. Not happy, he fights his way up Center Drive. This is his third lap around the park, and his pace is terrible. At 6.1 miles a lap, he is averaging a pathetic nineteen miles per hour. The speedometer indicates he is barely hitting thirty-five on the downhill stretches. His bicycle is top-of-the-line, weighing only seventeen pounds; Peter, his lab assistant's eight-year-old, can lift it. Dr. Von Hatter's racing suit is a scientifically designed, sweat-wicking blend of polyester and Lycra. He has been training for six weeks. And yet he still cannot keep up with the other racers in his 7 AM practice team. *You'll be in the C Group forever,* his demons whisper over the radio in his earbuds. *They're a bunch of twenty- and thirty-year-olds!* his wife's scolding voice reminds him. *You just turned sixty!*

*Don't listen to her,* he tells himself. *You're in the best shape of your life. You're just getting started. Sixty isn't what it used to be. People are already living to be a hundred, and in forty more years who knows what we'll know?* Dr. Von Hatter has always taken precautions. He eats well, filters his water, and uses an air purifier. He has never once held a cellular telephone up against either of his temporal lobes. His blood pressure is 100 over 70, and his resting heart rate is 62 bpm. He has always exercised: boxing in college, swimming with the kids when they were young, running when the weather was nice, walking with Alice after dinner to aid digestion. Now he sees that he's wasted the better part of his six decades on earth rarely knowing the kind of adrenaline highs he experiences on a daily basis while cycling—the thudding of heart muscle against its cage of ribs, the sting of frigid air against the deepest bronchioles of his lungs, the springing throb of his abdominal muscles, which he feels protecting his organs as if surrounding them in iron.

Flying past the carousel, with the Sheep Meadow just ahead, Dr. Von Hatter thinks back on Mr. Kisor, a seventy-five-year-old patient who ran the New York City Marathon every year. Mr. Kisor had dared the doctor to run his first. Neither of them really expected Dr. Von Hatter to make it even halfway. In his practice runs he hardly ever got more than thirteen miles before throwing in the towel. But when the day of the race came, there in a crowd of thousands, the doctor found himself imbued with the resolve and resilience of a man half his age.

Already marathons are beneath him. There are only six months left before the triathlon: a one-mile swim down the Hudson River, a twenty-five-mile bike ride around the park (on this very route), and then a six-mile run back up the East Side to the starting line. He has to get his sorry ass out of the C Group if he wants to qualify. Alice is sure he is going to kill himself, but he is sure of just the opposite. *This*, he breathes, turning up toward the icy reservoir, *this is how I'll survive.*

And it isn't like he doesn't know Death. He isn't some fool teenager thinking he'll live forever. He's been a pathologist for thirty-five years: at Mount Sinai Hospital for a long time and now in private practice. No patients anymore, just a microscope. Staring into slides of blue-and-pink-stained universes—urine, blood, tissue. Flexible hours and a salary that allows for $3,100 racing bicycles and an apartment in Trump Place.

It sounds cold. He knows that. Most people don't understand. Most people have never told twenty patients in a single day that they are going to die. That's an honor pretty much reserved for wartime generals and pathologists. Most people will never see firsthand how a mother, spouse, or sibling reacts to such news. Helplessness makes monsters of people. He's seen chairs thrown, exam tables kicked. The rooms pathologists speak to patients in now have everything bolted down. Even the patients who ought to expect the bad news can be dangerous. Once, he watched a woman who had survived fifty-seven years of alcoholism rip out a chunk of her own hair in fury when he told her she had liver cancer. A colleague of his, Dr. Matthews, got twelve stitches in his forehead after giving a diagnosis of leukemia. *Leukemia!* And not even in the incurable stage.

Still, it was the zen masters who spooked him the most: The mother of five young children who took the news of a certainly fatal pancreatic cancer without even a deep breath. The grizzled union man with mesothelioma so bad that his heart was practically encased in asbestos. The man who had masterfully ignored his steadily encroaching death for eight months before finally seeing a doctor, then just laughed and said, "You know, I always meant to take a hot-air balloon ride just once." By that point the guy would have been lucky to ascend a stepladder.

Dr. Von Hatter pounds his $250 pedals past the silent boathouse and along a steady incline toward the rear of the Metropolitan Museum. A rainbow of Tiffany stained glass glints in the dull winter-noon light. *I paid $3,100 for a bicycle*, he likes to tell people at dinner parties, *and the pedals were extra! They had another pair of pedals for $350, but I thought,* That's *just ridiculous!* It never fails to get a chuckle out of the old guys, the best of whom are already in terrible shape: Creaking hips and murmuring hearts. Hair gone gray or just gone. Teeth yellow from a half century of coffee. Nostrils brimming with coarse hairs. Dr. Von Hatter grits his teeth, breathes deeper, tries to keep his speedometer above ten as he goes up and up and up.

People. All around the park, he buzzes by them: Young and old, fat and thin, boy and girl. Women drinking coffee. Children sledding, cutting great muddy swaths deep into the white landscape. Some geek with snowshoes on. Grown men building an obscene snow woman. Girls with apple-red cheeks catching snowflakes on crimson tongues. The doctor sees blurry coronas of light around them as he speeds by, like a comet passing loafing stars.

He pedals up the East Drive, past a yellow truck selling Belgian waffles and hot chocolate, the sweet scent of which follows him around the partly frozen disk of the reservoir, within sight of the solemn cement twist of the Guggenheim. He rides down into a long valley, reaching a top speed of thirty-eight miles per hour, and his sixty-year-old heart sings. He loves the valleys more than he hates the hills, and he supposes this is what it means to be happy. Uphill or down, the hours he spends on the bike are the happiest of his week—though he can't admit that to Alice, or to Sasha at the office. He has to pretend not to be thinking about cycling as he studies the slides she's prepared. She had a whole pile ready for him this morning when he came in, still reeling from his morning ride. *Depressing!* he says to himself as he coasts down a small hill. Once, he felt a certain joy in seeing the clean samples—knowing these were lives extended, right there in front of him. But these days he only takes note of the young patients, the cases beyond help, the disturbing mutations.

Today he left the lab for lunch after just a few hours, thinking only of his proximity to cell towers, of the air quality, of broken microwaves emitting radiation, of preservatives even in his supposedly organic food. Sasha was now sending out the reports for the day's samples: little verdicts transmitted in ones and zeros through the ether to his colleagues citywide. He took off before she even opened the first report. Because standing still is dying—of that much he is sure. Standing still is waiting for the end. But when up on his bicycle, flying across the pavement, he feels untouchable: Faster than the UV rays that the stratosphere doesn't block. Stronger than the heavy metals in his drinking water. Younger than he was in his youth.

He knows Death, knows His smell and His chill and His last gasping. Many times they have seen each other. He will never stop for Death. If Death wants him, He'll have to come fast or take him in his sleep. *B Group, here I come*, he thinks as he huffs past the baseball diamonds, their lines and bases and mounds lost under the snow. He puffs past Mount Sinai, the hospital where he spent more hours of his life than he has in any apartment. He looks up at the wide white sky, and for a

133

second he thinks he sees a red hot-air balloon way off over the Bronx. But it is just a child's mylar balloon, right there in the park—helium filled, nonbiodegradable, soon to be choked on by dolphins out in the churning black Atlantic. *Halfway around*, he thinks. *Just one last lap.*

In her office at Mount Sinai Hospital, Dr. Zarrani leafs through a report that was sent over from Park Avenue Pathology a few hours earlier. Another jagged, illegible signature: "Dr. Von Hatter." It's no stereotype that doctors have bad handwriting. She believes it stems from an innate unwillingness to take responsibility for anything, each stormy jot a last-ditch defense against a malpractice suit—as if, in a courtroom somewhere, some panel of experts might someday study the signature and conclude that they can't definitively say it belongs to the accused doctor. Beneath Von Hatter's scrawl is the loopy script of the histotechnician, Sasha Trzynski: carefree and cloud fluffy, not important enough to ever get in serious trouble. Lifting a pen to the opposing line, Dr. Zarrani adds her own stark signature, a sort of italicized printing in all capitals: DR. ATOOSA ZARRANI.

She takes the file with her down the hallway and into a little room with all the furniture bolted down, where Irene Richmond has been waiting for fifteen minutes. Irene turns out to be a young blond woman reading an old paperback. At her feet are several bags filled with, Dr. Zarrani guesses, Christmas gifts. She smells faintly like a pet shop. It's lucky she was able to come in so quickly after they called.

"Richmond? Irene?"

They shake hands. Dr. Zarrani pretends to study the file another moment, though actually she is glancing discreetly at the young woman, who has eyes the black-blue of the ocean and keeps one finger in the book of fairy tales to save her place. She is alone. Usually people bring a friend, a family member, *some*body.

"You came by yourself?"

The girl—it is hard not to think of her as a girl—looks around as if to check and, finding no one, shrugs.

"Usually people bring a friend or a family member." Fearing the girl is becoming uncomfortable, Dr. Zarrani laughs stiffly. "This morning a woman brought her doorman—a little Hungarian gentleman with red epaulets and a hat."

This makes them both smile. Once that is done, Dr. Zarrani clears her throat.

"Ms. Richmond, you have cancer."

The young woman looks down quietly as she digests this news. She sets the book on the table, leaving it open, and reaches to adjust the sleeve of her dress.

"Well, shit," she says finally.

Dr. Zarrani continues in her practiced, even tone, explaining to Ms. Richmond that she has a malignant osteosarcoma in the bone of her left eye socket. Dr. Zarrani watches as the patient slowly absorbs this information. She prefers the ones who don't cry—not because there is anything wrong with crying at this kind of news, and not because it makes the conversation easier for her (though it does), but because it is a sign of how things tend to go. Crying wastes time, and people who waste time, who wallow, are less prepared, less capable. It's that simple. In 1978, when supporters of the Ayatollah killed Dr. Zarrani's father and her older brother, she didn't cry. Instead she grabbed her little brother, Mehdi, by the wrist and pulled him down into a ditch behind the house, where they lay in the mud until the coast was clear. Those who do not cry survive more often. This she believes.

But even as they discuss things further, getting into the usual questions like causes (none known) and survival rates (around 68 percent), this girl—this young woman—remains eerily calm. Dr. Zarrani gives her a recommendation of chemotherapy followed by radiation, which doesn't go over well. The girl is a painter and more worried about losing her vision as a side effect of treatment than she is about staying alive, which is frustrating, though pretty typical with younger patients—actually, with patients of any age, which is why it can be helpful to have someone else there to provide perspective. In any event, the girl says it is nonnegotiable, and Dr. Zarrani resists the urge to remind her that having cancer is not a negotiation. They make small talk. The doctor wants to give her time to absorb the news. Eventually Dr. Zarrani ventures to ask why no one came with her.

Irene laughs and says, "Don't worry. I can handle this on my own."

Dr. Zarrani just shakes her head. "I'm sorry, Ms. Richmond, but I've seen Navy SEALS who couldn't handle this on their own. You're going to have to have some help. You'll need people to get you to treatments and take you back home again. You're going to feel sick all the time. Someone's got to make you eat, because you won't want to. You're going to need prescriptions filled and insurance claims filed. Listen to me when I say this: You are about to go to war with your own body. That's the best way to describe it."

For the first time Irene Richmond looks genuinely scared.

"If you don't have friends you can trust with something like this, we can arrange—"

"No, it's not that. It's . . . you know, my friends are great. . . ."

Dr. Zarrani is silent a moment. And then she understands.

"Ms. Richmond, you can't protect them from this. I'm sorry."

And this is when the girl begins to cry.

Dr. Zarrani reaches across the table and takes her hand. She wants to tell her how she pried open barbed-wire fences and stole pomegranates from guarded compounds just to feed her brother, while she went to sleep hungry. She wants to tell this girl how, after all that, they arrived at a boat heading for Italy, the lone survivors of the Zarrani family—but at least they survived. Then, two days after arriving in Rome, her brother came down with malaria. A thirsty mosquito had bitten Mehdi's neck during their escape, drunk his blood, and paid for the meal with a single parasitic cell, a *Plasmodium malariae* protist. One single cell. She hadn't understood that then, of course—on some level she hardly understood it now. She has seen the photos in medical books, taken with high-powered microscopes, of a little oblong creature, stained blue and purple on the slides, but it still makes no sense to her: That it, too, lives. That its only function is to feast upon blood cells, to survive, to multiply. That, in doing so, this thing kills the body it lives in—a universe so vast it can't ever know its borders—and so finally kills itself. What is the point?

Mehdi made it onto the boat bound for America. She'd hidden his vomiting, headaches, and fevers from authorities. But halfway across the ocean, his list of symptoms grew to include convulsions and partial blindness. The sailors forced them both to stay in quarantine. When Mehdi finally died, they tossed his body overboard—unsure what he had and not wanting anyone else to get sick. Grief-stricken, she jumped into the water after his blue body, but one of the sailors pulled her back out.

She remained in quarantine the rest of the journey, just in case. She arrived in America with nothing and went to stay with friends of a third cousin on Staten Island. They raised her like their own child. They put her in school. She learned English; she learned biology; she went to Westchester Community College; she went to City University; she went to Albert Einstein College of Medicine. Then she came to do her residency at Mount Sinai and never left.

Here she is. Watching Irene Richmond weep and holding her hand. She does this almost every single day. She pulls them from the shock of the cold water. With her touch she tries to express to them what she eventually came to understand after the sailor rescued her from the water: that just because it is all so very, very unfair does not mean there is not still great hope in the world.

*Nominated by The Sun*

# THE RULES

## by LEILA CHATTI

from POEM-A-DAY

There will be no stars—the poem has had enough of them. I think
    we can agree
we no longer believe there is anyone in any poem who is just
    now realizing

they are dead, so let's stop talking about it. The skies of this poem
are teeming with winged things, and not a single innominate bird.

You're welcome. Here, no monarchs, no moths, no cicadas doing
    whatever
they do in the trees. If this poem is in summer, punctuating the
    blue—forgive me,

I forgot, there is no blue in this poem—you'll find the occasional
pelecinid wasp, proposals vaporized and exorbitant, angels looking

as they should. If winter, unsentimental sleet. This poem does not
    take place
at dawn or dusk or noon or the witching hour or the crescendoing
    moment

of our own remarkable birth, it is 2:53 in this poem, a Tuesday, and
    everyone in it is still
at work. This poem has no children; it is trying

to be taken seriously. This poem has no shards, no kittens, no myths
    or fairy tales,
no pomegranates or rainbows, no ex-boyfriends or manifest lovers,
    no mothers—God,

no mothers—no God, about which the poem must admit
it's relieved, there is no heart in this poem, no bodily secretions,
    no body

referred to as *the body*, no one
dies or is dead in this poem, everyone in this poem is alive and
    pretty

okay with it. This poem will not use the word *beautiful* for it resists
calling a thing what it is. So what

if I'd like to tell you how I walked last night, glad, truly glad, for the
    first time
in a year, to be breathing, in the cold dark, to see them. The stars,
    I mean. Oh hell, before

something stops me—I nearly wept on the sidewalk at the sight of
    them all.

*Nominated by Chloe Honum*

# POST-NICU VILLANELLE

## by JOYELLE MCSWEENEY

from THE IOWA REVIEW

Eveningwear, the heron
unfolds like a glove in the sky
because it's Spring

peels back to expose
the cool wrist of evening
where

the hero peels off his armor
and walks around the bedroom flayed
because it's Spring. It's Spring,

the vets go down to the park on bikes
with their bedrolls, their desert camo
eveningwear, even to sleep

on the breast
of the lawn
in Spring.

Sweet rain, with your radioactive
pearl seeding, the eyelet ribbon in your braid,
this evening, wear

as lightly as you can upon her grave
but do not actually erase yourself from the scene.
You make the Spring come

& I consider that one a god
who sits by your cribside and watches your monitor
as evening wears on

your green cursor blinks
your high alarm rises, a detonator's depressed
then released and some fate arrives like Spring

in "cardiac collapse"
but before that: your unfocused newborn's eyes
peer up from your elsewhere

at the camera's eye, the heat lamp,
your nurse, your father, & me. We for once
align. O my sore eyes in Spring

as flower peers into flower
and flowers, that odor unfolds, a cotton diaper
newer than a newborn: not even once worn.

the no-scent of soap or air or air
I almost wrote "hope," but no, no-hope
and every no-evening, infant, know-nothing Spring,

you collapse and collapse. Some flower
lays its cool clean hand
across my eyes and, blind, I inhale you everywhere

nearby and leaving like Spring

*Nominated by The Iowa Review*

# HOWL PALACE

## fiction by LEIGH NEWMAN

from THE PARIS REVIEW

Last week, I finally had to put Howl Palace up for sale. Years of poor financial planning had led to this decision, and I tried to take some comfort in my agent's belief in a buyer who might show up with an all-cash offer. My agent is a highly organized, sensible woman who grew up in Alaska—I checked—but when she advertised the listing, she failed to mention her description on the internet. "Attractively priced tear-down with plane dock and amazing lake views," she wrote under the photo. "Investment potential."

I am still puzzled as to why the word *tear-down* upset me. Anybody who buys a house on Diamond Lake brings in a backhoe and razes the place to rubble. The mud along the shoreline wreaks havoc with foundations, and the original homes, like mine, were built in the sixties before the pipeline, back when licensed contractors had no reason to move to Anchorage. If you wanted a house, you either built it yourself, or you hung out in the parking lot of Spenard Builders Supply handing out six-packs to every guy with a table saw in the back of his vehicle until one got broke enough or bored enough to consider your blueprints. Which is why the walls in Howl Palace meet the ceiling at such unconventional angles. Our guy liked to eyeball instead of using a level.

To the families on the lake, my home is a bit of an institution. And not just for the wolf room, which my agent suggested we leave off the list of amenities, as most people wouldn't understand what we meant. About the snow-machine shed and clamshell grotto, I was less flexible.

Nobody likes a yard strewn with snow machines and three-wheelers, one or two of which will always be busted and covered in blue tarp. Ours is just not that kind of neighborhood. The clamshell grotto, on the other hand, might fail to fulfill your basic home-owning needs, but it is a show-stopper. My fourth husband, Lon, built it for me in the basement as a surprise for my fifty-third birthday. He had a romantic nature, when he hadn't had too much to drink. Embedded in the coral and shells are more than a few freshwater pearls that a future owner might consider tempting enough to jackhammer out of the cement.

My agent is named Silver. She brought me a box of Girl Scout cookies to discuss these matters, and so I tried my hardest to trust the rest of her advice. When she said not to bother with pulling out the chick-weed or flattening the rusted remnants of the dog runs, I left both as is. But then I started thinking about what people say about baking blue-berry muffins and burning vanilla candles. Buyers needed to feel the atmosphere of the place, the homeyness. Fred Meyer had some plug-in tropical air fresheners on sale. I bought a few. I shoved them into the outlets. Within minutes, the entire downstairs smelled like a burning car wreck in Hawaii.

Silver scheduled the open house for Saturday. "Noon," she said. "Before families have put the kids down for a nap." The night before, I lay back in my recliner and thought how every good thing that had ever happened to me had happened in Howl Palace. And every bad thing, too. Forty-three years. Five husbands. Two floatplanes. A lifetime. It felt as if I should honor my home, that strangers shouldn't come around poking through the kitchen or kicking the baseboards, seeing only the mold in the hot tub and the gnaw marks on the cabinets from the dogs I'd had over the years, maybe even laughing at the name. "Howl Palace" was coined by Danny Bob Donovan's littlest girl during a New Year's Eve party in 1977. She said it with awe, standing in the middle of the wolf room with a half-eaten candy cane.

"Mrs. Dutch," she said, "this is so beautiful, I think I need to howl a little." And howl she did, cupping her hands around her mouth and letting loose a wild, lonely cry that endeared her to me for forever.

Howl Palace was still beautiful, in my mind. And could be to other people, given the right welcome. Silver had said to just relax, to let her finesse the details, but I went to the locker freezer and pulled out fifty pounds of caribou burger, plus four dozen moose dogs. All we needed now were a few side dishes. And buns.

The next morning was bust a hump. The menu for the cookout had expanded to include green bean casserole, macaroni salad, guacamole, and trout almondine. Trout almondine requires cream for the cream sauce, which I forgot on my eight-thirty run to Costco, leading me to substitute powdered milk mixed with a few cans of cream of mushroom soup. My fifth husband, Skip, used to call me the John Wayne of the Home Range, not in the nicest way, until he got dementia and forgot who I was or that he had to follow me around explaining how I'd organized the produce drawer wrong or let too much hair fall off my head in the shower or failed to remove every single bone from his halibut steak because I didn't fucking ever *think*. Shipping him off to a facility in Washington near his daughter wasn't exactly something I struggled with.

The pool table, where I planned to lay out the buffet, was coated with so much dust it looked as though the velvet had sprouted a fine, silver fungus. I dragged an old quarter sheet of plywood from the snow-machine shed and heaved it on top. If you are looking for a reason to split five cords of wood by hand each year for forty-odd years, consider my biceps at age sixty-seven.

The plywood I covered with a flowery top sheet from a long-gone water-bed. Out went the side dishes, the salads, the condiments. On went the grill, the meat at the ready. All that was left was the guacamole. Which was when Carl's pickup pulled into the driveway.

Carl wasn't my husband. Carl was the beautiful, bedeviling heartbreak of my life. His hair had thinned, but not so you saw his scalp, and age spots mottled his arms. His smell was the same as ever: WD-40, line-dried shirt, the peppermint soap he uses to cut through fish slime. For one heady second, I believed he had come back to say in some soft, regretful voice: Remember when we ran into each other at Sportsman's Warehouse? It got me thinking, well, maybe we should give it another try.

As Carl told me long ago, "Inside you hides a soft, secret pink balloon of dreams." He wasn't incorrect, but the balloon has withered a little over the years. And it was not an reassuring sign that Carl had a dog in the back of his vehicle.

"I thought you might need a new Lab," he said. "She's pedigree, real obedient." I had some idea what he meant: she jumped ducks before he got off a shot and went after half-dead birds in the rapids despite the rocks he threw at her backside, trying to save her from injury. Once, she had eaten a healthy portion of his dishwasher.

Over my years at Howl Palace, I'd had a lot of dogs, all of them black Labs with papers proving their champion, field-and-trial bloodlines. I loved every one of them and loved hunting with them, but no matter how you deal with these animals at home—stick or carrot—they just can't deviate from the agenda panting through their minds, an agenda born of instinct and inbreeding, neither of which suggests that they sit there wagging their tails when a bumblebee flies through a yard. Or a bottle rocket zooms by.

I have seen my share of classic family retrievers on this lake—black or yellow Labs, dumb, drooling goldens, the occasional hefty Chessie—who live only to snuggle up with the kids at picnics and ignore the smoked salmon you are about to insert into your mouth. But I have never had one in my kennel or my house. My last dog, Babs, was a hunt nut, willful, with a hole in her emotional reasoning where somebody yanked out her uterus without a fully approved vet's license. I picked her up for free from an ad in the *Pennysaver*, and maybe that had something to do with it. She drowned after jumping out of a charter boat to retrieve halibut that I had on the line, unaware of the tide about to suck her into the Gulf of Alaska.

Still, I enjoyed her company more than Skip's and Lon's combined. Babs slept not just in my bed but under the covers, where we struggled over the one soft pillow. When she died, I was ready to retire from a lifetime of animal management. I was sixty-three years old and single, and I vowed to myself: no more Labs, no more husbands, no more ex-husbands, either.

The kennel in the bed of Carl's truck only confirmed the wisdom of my decision. The whole thing lay flipped on its side, jumping and heaving from the campaign being waged against the door. Nuthatches flickered through the trees, made frantic by the sound of claws against metal. Squirrels fled for other yards. "Carl," I said. "I'm about to have an open house. I can't take your dog."

He looked over at the woodpile, where the remains of the chain-link runs sagged along the ground. "You could put her in the basement. In the clamshell grotto," he said. Then laughed. He has a wonderful laugh, the kind that tickles through you, slowly, inch by inch, brain cell by brain cell until you are mentally unfit to resist him.

"No, Carl," I said—not even talking about the animal.

"She can drink out of the fountain."

"No," I said. "N. O."

"I'm not a dog," he said, his voice quiet.

Wind riffled through the birches, exposing the silverish underside of the leaves. A plane buzzed by overhead. Carl jammed his hands in his pockets. "Besides," he said, "you can't sell Howl Palace."

I looked at him, daring him to tell me that he and I needed to live here. Together. The way I had always wanted. He had a suitcase in the back of the cab.

Carl looked back at me—as if about to say all this. Then he said, "It's your home, Dutch. You love it." He smiled, the way he always smiled. Time drained away for a few moments and we were back in the trophy room at Danny Boy's, thirty-five and tipsy, his finger laced through the loop of my jeans. The Eagles skipped on the turntable and my second husband, Wallace, ceased to exist. Tiny dry snowflakes clung to the edges of window like miniature paper stars. Carl kissed me and a dark glittery hole opened up and I fell through, all the way to the bottom.

"I hate you, Carl," I said, but as so often happens around me, it came out sounding backward, fraught with tenderness.

The kennel creaked all of a sudden. We both looked over and, blam, the door snapped off. Seventy pounds of black thundering muscle shot out of the truck and into the alders.

"Oh boy," he said. "Not good."

"Hand me the zapper."

"She doesn't have a shock collar."

I tried a two-fingered whistle. Nothing. Not a snapped twig.

"I hate to say it," he said. "But there's this appointment—"

"Carl, I've got an open house."

He toed something, a weed. "It's a flight," he said. "To Texas. I'm fishing down in Galveston for a few weeks."

All the dewy romance inside me turned to gravel as I watched him move toward his vehicle. When he bent down to pick up the door to the kennel, his shirt twisted. It was a fly-fishing shirt, with a mesh panel for hot Texas days, through which I caught a glimpse of the pager-looking box strapped to his side. It was beige. A green battery light blinked on top.

Everybody our age knew what that box was. Carl was not here in my driveway to romance me all over again. Or even to piss me off. Carl needed someone to dog-sit while he went off to get fancy, last-ditch chemo down in the Lower 48. In Houston, probably.

146

I took a minute just to organize my face. "Get your animal," I said. "Get her back in the goddamn kennel and take her with you."

"Or what?" he said. "You'll hang her on a wolf peg?"

The cheapness of his comment released us both. I turned and went inside to not watch his truck peel down the driveway. Carl and I had always disagreed about the wolf room, which was the only thing that he, Lon, Skip, and my third husband, RT, might have ever had in common. None of them liked it, and I respected that. But it didn't mean I had to rip it out. I was proud of it. It was beautiful. It was mine.

Back in the kitchen, forty-five avocados sat on the counter, waiting. People wail about chain stores ruining the views in Anchorage, but if you lived through any part of the twentieth century up here, when avocados arrived off the barge, hard as the pit at their center, you relish each trip to the vast cinder-block box of dreams known as Costco. Every avocado I scooped out was packed with meat. Out it popped, one after another, like a creamy green baby butt headed to the bottom of the salad bowl.

Next mayonnaise, then mashing. I didn't hurry. Carl's dog needed to run off her panic and aggression. And I needed not to envision a wonderful, loving couple arriving for the open house—the husband in dungarees from the office, the wife in beat-up XtraTufs because she wanted to wade around and check out the dock for rot. Across the lawn they went, admiring the amazing lake views, telling Silver that the place was underpriced, actually, and sending their polite, unspoiled toddler to go catch minnows in the shallows. At which point Carl's dog charged in, fixated on a dragonfly she believed might be a mallard, knocking over the toddler and grinding him into the gravel beach.

I also needed not to think about Carl being sick, Carl not getting better, Carl having left, how I acted on the steps. He didn't have the money for a kennel, I suspected. Or for cancer. Mashing avocados helped. I mashed away, thinking how RT—a man I yelled at daily for three years just because he wasn't Carl—once said, "Maybe the reason you shout so much, Dutch, is that you really long to whisper."

RT was an orthodontist, a World War II model airplane builder, and an observant man. But all I thought at the time was that if Carl had realized about the shouting instead of RT, he and I might still be together.

Luckily, I had moose ribs in the freezer. Labs are not spaniels or pointers, they don't have the upland sense of smell, and Carl's was deep

147

in the alders. I couldn't call her over to my hand and grab her collar. She didn't know my voice, and I didn't know her name, and even if I had, a few hours in a kennel had no doubt left her suspicious of my motives. A rib tossed in the bushes and dragged in front of her nose, however, might kindle some interest.

My neighbor, Candace Goddard, was at home; I sighted her with the scope I kept in the kitchen. Candace's decor scheme is heavy on the chandeliers. Every room features at least one upside-down wedding cake made of cut-lead glass, and this was generally how I found her when I needed her. Where the crystals wink.

It was eleven, two hours before the open house, and she was still in her nightgown, bumping into furniture. By the time I got over there, she was playing acoustic guitar. The guitar was supposed to help with her anxiety when her husband, Rodge, flew off to go sheep hunting and forgot to check in by sat phone every three hours. Stopping to call home, while halfway up a shale-covered peak under a sky so blue you taste the color in your lungs, pretty much ruins the moment. Not surprisingly, Rodge often forgot.

Candace was fiddling around on the guitar, picking out some prelude number by Johann Sebastian Bach. Like more and more of the younger wives on the lake, she had dealt with turning forty by investing in injections that left her with a stunned, rubberized expression. Her hair is many, many shades of high-voltage blond. Her guitar playing, however, tells a different story. Listening to her is like listening to butterflies trip over each other's wings. You want them to flit around inside you for forever. This is one of the many reasons why we get along, and drive to book club together.

That day, unfortunately, the anxiety had gotten the upper hand. Her eyes were two dazzles of pupil. "Pills?" she said in her floaty voice. "What kind?"

"The sleepy kind," I said. "Enough for a seventy-pound—well—female."

"I think it's going to be fine, flying through the pass," she said. "What do you think?"

What I thought was that Rodge didn't put in enough flight hours, but he had a great touch with short landings, and the odds of him smashing his Cub into the side of a mountain were the same as anybody's: a matter of skill, luck, and weather.

It wasn't as if her concerns were that far-fetched. Flying in the wilderness, all your everyday, ordinary bullshit—being tired, being lazy, trusting the clouds instead of your instruments, losing your prescription sunglasses, forgetting to check your fuel lines—can kill you. And if it doesn't, a door can still blow off your plane and hit the tail or your kid can run between a brownie and her cub or your husband can slip on wet, frozen shale and fall a few thousand feet down a mountain, lose the pack and sat phone, break a leg, and that is that. Which is what you've got to live with, chandeliers or no chandeliers.

"I made him a checklist," she said as I rummaged through the bottles at the bottom of her Yves Saint Somebody purse. "Mixture. Prop. Master switch. Fuel pump. Throttle."

By the time she got to cowl flaps, I had long stopped listening. One of the biggest shames about Candace is that she still has a pilot's license. Her not flying, she said, started with kids, strapping them into their little car seats in back and realizing there was nothing—*nothing*—underneath them.

Sometimes I wish I had known her before that idea took hold.

"Play me a song, Candace," I said. "It'll make you feel better."

"You know what Rodge doesn't like?" she said.

"Natives," I said, because he doesn't. He got held up for a "travel tax" by one random Athabascan—on Athabascan land—and now he is one of those cocktail-party racists who like to pretend to talk politics just so they can slip in how the Natives and the Park Service have taken over the state. He and I nod to each other at homeowners association meetings and leave it that.

"Anal sex," she said, her voice as light as chickweed pollen. "He won't even try it."

"Look," I said, holding up a pill bottle. "How many of these things did you take?"

"I could live without him," she said. "I know how to waitress. I could get the kids and me one of those cute little houses off O'Malley."

I had some idea of what she was doing, only because I had done it myself, which was leaving her husband in her mind, in case he did die out in Brooks Range—which he wasn't going to—so that, hopefully, she'd fall apart a little less. But the thing about having gotten divorced four times and widowed once is that people forget you also got married each time. You and your soft, secret pink balloon of dreams.

"If you want anal sex, Candace," I said, "just drive yourself down to the Las Margaritas, pick some guy on his third tequila, and go for it. Just don't lose your house in the divorce like every other woman on this lake. Buy *him* out. Send him to some reasonably priced, brand-new shit-box in a subdivision. Keep your property."

Beneath her bronzer, Candace looked a little taken aback. "Gosh, Dutch," she said. "I didn't mean to make you upset."

I shook a bunch of bottles at her. "Which are the sleepiest?"

She pointed to a fat one with a tricky-looking cap. "Was it Benny?" she said. "Was it because I brought up crashing in the pass?"

"I'm having a bad day," I said, but only because there was no way to explain how I felt about Benny, my first husband, crashing his Super Cub, or about the search to find the wreckage, that smoking black hole in the trees. Even now, forty-one years later. The loneliness. The lost-ness. Not to mention what it had been like, being the first and only female homeowner on Diamond Lake.

If I had been cute and skinny and agreeable like Candace, it might have been easier. But I was me. The rolled eyes during votes, the snickers when I tried to advocate for trash removal or speed bumps, the hands, the lesbo jokes, the cigars handed to me in tampon wrappers—which I laughed about, seething, but smoked—I got through it all. What hurt the worst were the wives, all of them women I had known for years, who dropped me off their Fur Rondy gala list every time I was single. And stuck me back on when I wasn't.

Benny was a world-class outdoorsman and an old-school shotgunner who did not believe in pretending that everybody got to make it to old age. On trips he took without me, he always said, "Dutch, if I don't come back, hold tight to Howl Palace."

Four-plus decades later, I still had my property, and it had come at a sizable cost. Wallace put me through a court battle after I left him for Carl. RT needed an all-cash payment to make him run away to Florida. Add to that Lon's rehab and Skip's long-term care. The Cub and the 185 were gone, all the life insurance money, the IRA. Howl Palace was all I had left. And now I had to sell it in order not to die in a state nursing home, sharing a room with some old biddy who liked to flip through scrapbooks and watch the boob tube with the volume cranked up high. You can't cry about these things. But you can't sit around and contemplate them either.

Luckily, Candace's youngest boy, Donald, turned up at the top of the stairs. His electronic slab was tucked under his arm. "Where's the charger, Mom?" he said.

"Donald," I said. "Let's go fish for a dog."

"Donald has asthma," said Candace. "He can't handle a lot of dander."

"Get your boots on, Don," I said. "You, too, Candace."

"Really?" she said. "I get to come? Do I get to see the wolf room, too?"

For all the obvious reasons, I don't like people on drugs in the wolf room. Or people with drinks, food, or mental issues. "If you help me with these safety caps," I said. "And fine-tune the dosage."

Donald was a little wheezy fellow, with glasses attached to a sporty wraparound strap that kept them stuck to his face. He knew how to hustle, though, and stuck to my side as I laid out the plan. Your mom's job, I said, is to crush up some medicine and roll the moose rib in it. Your job is take the spin rod I give you and cast the moose rib at the end of the line into the bushes. Then slowly, *slowly* reel it in. The minute the dog bites on the rib, you sit tight, play her a little. We'll have only a few seconds for me to grab her by her collar. Then we'll stick her in the kennel with the rib. Nighty-night.

A few feet from the house, I got a feeling. It was a sucker-punch feeling—the grill. I started running. Donald ran, too, the way kids will, without asking questions, as if there might be matches and boxes of free Roman candles at end of it.

"Hey guys?" said Candace. "Wait up." In her peaceful, freewheeling frame of mind, she had put on Rodge's size 12 boots.

The last few feet of the path, I kept telling myself that I would not have taken the meat out and left it by the grill, that I would have not put the dishcloth over it to keep the flies off, that I could have, for some reason, left the meat in the fridge, even though everyone knows that meat can't be slapped cold on a hot fire, it needs to mellow out at room temperature. Except that I knew exactly what I had done and why I had done it—believing, at the time, I didn't own a dog.

I also knew what I was going to find, even as I ran through the backyard finding it: bits of gnawed plastic and butcher paper pinwheeling all over the grass. Here a chunk of hot dog casing, there a lump of caribou burger. Blood juice dripped down the steps. The grill lay on its side, propane flames still burning blue.

I knelt down and turned off the valve. The birches were in their last, tattered days of September green. A leaf whirled down and landed by my foot. It was small, the yellow so fresh and bright it belonged on a bird.

"Dutch," said Donald. "I saw her! She ran right by me."

"Don't chase her," I said. "She'll think it's a game." I stayed down there with the leaf, just for a few minutes. Hiding. The leaf had the tiniest edge of dead brown.

151

Footsteps thunked across the deck. Carl's footsteps. Carl's boots. He had not taken off and left me with the dog apocalypse. This was so unlike him, it took me a little longer than it should have to understand. "Your animal," I said, "ate sixty pounds of meat."

"Most of it, she threw up," he said. "By the looks of the grass."

"I have an open house, Carl." The flies were moving in—a throbbing blanket of vicious, busy bottle green. With the sun out, the smell would be next.

"I could always run to Costco. Pick us up some steaks."

He said this kindly, but steaks were not what I wanted. And there was no way to explain what I wanted, which was everything the way it was before, years before. Neighbors in the backyard. Charcoal smoke. Bug dope. A watermelon. People showing up with a casserole, leaving with their laughter and wet hair after a dip in the hot tub. Whatever my private upheavals, there was always that, at least.

A duck paddled past my dock, blown over by the current that was ruffling the surface. I missed wind socks. Everybody on Diamond Lake used to have a rainbow wind sock tied to their deck. It added a cheerful note to the shoreline.

"I had her by the woodpile," said Carl. "But she gave me the slip."

"I think you should go," I said. "Just go get your flight."

He shrugged, scratched a bit of dry skin on his neck. "I can get another."

"Right," I said. "The fishing trip to Houston."

He looked at me, as if ashamed, and I felt a little badly about calling him on his lie. As far he, I, and everyone we knew understood Houston, it wasn't even a city, just a mythical, cutting-edge treatment center, the Shangri-la of last-hope clinical trials. You went there to get a few more months to not die.

"Well," he said. "You got me, Dutch." He laughed. I didn't. Another leaf blazed down toward us. Fall lasts for weeks now—which, despite my best efforts, still befuddles me. All my life, fall took about three days in August, the leaves dropping almost overnight, followed by a licorice snow taste in the wind. Global warming, the papers say, though almost all the articles talk about are the dying caribou and the starving puffins, never the less obvious, alarming changes of every day—and the guilt about living in an oil state that goes along with it. As if the rest of the country, sucking up all that oil and burning all that coal, isn't also to blame.

Donald ran by us, headed for the water with a moose rib in his fist. Candace followed with my snow shovel and a garbage bag. She was still in her nightgown. Watching her try to scoop raw-meat dog vomit off the grass while wearing a gauzy orgasm of white chiffon was one of the more moving experiences of my life. She really did want to help.

I sat down on the steps. Carl sat next to me, close, then an inch closer. "Dutch," he said. "What a fucking corner we have found ourselves in."

I smiled. It felt like a small, broken snowflake in the middle of my face. There was a list of questions I was supposed to ask: what kind, what stage, what organ, herbal teas, protein smoothies? Instead an image floated through my mind. His trailer. His kitchen. The byzantine mobile-home cabinetry. For each of the six days that we lived together, I lay there in bed every morning, watching Carl make coffee, memorizing where he had stuck the cups, the creamer, the filters, so that I could make the coffee for us one day—an idea that made me so happy I had to shut my eyes and pretend to be asleep.

It was September then, too. Mushrooms bloomed in the corners of the walls. Carl scraped them down with a pocketknife he wiped clean with a chamois. We made spaghetti and played gin rummy and dragged ourselves out of bed only for glasses of cold well water. I was careful where I left my clothes, though, careful not to leave them on the floor where they would take up room. I had left Wallace. And the dog. And even Howl Palace.

On the morning of the seventh day, Carl sat me down and said, in the stiff, unsettled way he had adopted the minute I arrived, "It's just that I didn't know it'd be so close."

"Me neither," I said, still thinking he was talking about square footage.

How lonely it had to be, to realize that the only resource he had left— besides his trailer and a few truly world-class stuffed rainbows—was me. Maybe getting sick had made Carl softer. Maybe this was why he had shown up. Maybe this was why he had not left, despite my need for him, as fresh and pathetic as ever. The idea broke my heart, and into that jagged, bleak crevasse, all my fears rushed to fill the gap.

"I'm out of money," I said. "Just so you know. In terms of helping you with your deductibles."

He looked at me—puzzled, or maybe stunned.

"Out-of-network is expensive," I said. "That's how it is, I hear, down in Houston."

"Dutch," he said. "And you wonder why we always go to shit." He stood up. He started walking down the backyard toward the dock, where Donald was standing with the rib tied to a length of frayed plastic rope he had found in the snow-machine shed.

153

"Wait," I said, standing up. "I'll keep your stupid dog."

"I don't want your money," he said. "And you don't even like her."

"Sure I do," I said. "She's kind of spirited, that's all."

"What's her name?" he said, not stopping, not slowing down in the least.

"Rita," I said. All his dogs were named Rita, one after another.

He stopped to scrape some dog puke off the bottom of his boot. But he waved. "I call her Pinkie," he said. "After your secret balloon of dreams."

That was how I knew it was the last time we would see each other. Carl always liked to leave me a little more in love with him than ever.


Even before the open house was officially open, people were pulling into the driveway, clutching phones. Silver had hosed down the backyard and sprinkled baking soda all over the grass. There was nothing left to do, she said, but hope for the best. One of her ways of hoping was to stick Donald down on the dock with his rib and his rope, where he would look like an imaginative, playful boy. Calling to his dog. Possibly home-schooled.

Candace was subject to a similar redecoration. Silver laid her in a deck lounger under a blanket, so it would look like she was just dozing, enjoying the sun. I sat beside her for a while, wishing she could get herself upright enough to come up to the wolf room with me, the way she had always wanted and the way I was finally ready to let her—high or sober or even just a little brain-dead from the chemicals. Carl was gone. I had no one. All over again.

I did consider pouring water on her face. But she was curled up on her side, her hands tucked under her cheek—not because her high had brought out the child in her, I saw only at that moment, but because the child kept surfacing despite the pills she took to keep it asleep.

There was nothing to do but tuck her in under the blanket and take the back stairs, which are the only stairs up to the wolf room. The air in there is climate-controlled and smells just faintly of cedar from the paneling. I sat down in the middle of the skins, tried to look dignified, and waited.

A young couple with matching glasses stopped in the doorway, looked in—politely, alarmed—and wandered off. Over and over, this happened for the next few hours. A couple with fake tans. A couple with a baby. A couple with man buns, both of them. Single people and old people, apparently, do not buy houses at my price point. Every time another couple turned up, I told myself to smile. Or invite them inside. Or leave so they could marvel at it openly. Or disparage it. Or discuss their plans to replace it with a master bath.

Silver had told me that it was better for the closing price if the owner went out for lunch at a nice, expensive restaurant with a friend. Now I knew why. Nobody was being unkind, but you couldn't tell, just by looking at it, that the wolf room used to be a nursery. That's what it said on the plans that Benny and I ordered from Sears. The baby for the nursery didn't work out, the way it doesn't for some people. And so Benny and I did other things. He was tight with the Natives, as we called every tribe back then, as if they were all one big happy family or we just couldn't bother to learn the phonetics. He had grown up in the village of Kotzebue, the son of the Methodist missionaries who had tried to convert Inupiat and gotten confused about their life's agenda. The Arctic Circle is not the place to go if you have even the slightest existential question.

That was something Benny always said. He knew Alaska better than me, mostly because I showed up on a ferry at age five, with a baby-blue Samsonite and a piece of cardboard hanging from my neck: FLIGHT TRANSFER TO ANCHORAGE, DELIVER TO MRS. AURORA KING. My parents had died in a head-on crash outside Spokane. Aunt Aurora was my nearest relative.

Aunt Aurora was a second-grade teacher in the downtown school district. She was deeply into young girls being educated in the ways of our Lord, and I met Benny at yet another Sunday at United Methodist. I was seventeen. He grabbed me the last shortbread cookie at coffee hour and spilled tea on his flannel shirt so we would have matching stains.

A week later he took me to the Garden of Eatin', which was located in a Quonset hut in a part of Anchorage I had never been to. It was the fanciest place I had ever eaten in my life. Tablecloths on every table. Real napkins. We ate Salisbury steak and vanilla ice cream and I was careful not to lick my plate. Two months later we were married.

Benny loved me, but he also loved men. He was not that different from a lot of guides and hunters at that time. They wanted to be out in the wilderness with another man without anybody seeing. For weeks. For whole summers. He never lied about it and I never asked beyond the minimum and we never discussed it. We understood what marriage was—the ability to hold hands and not try to forgive the other person, not try to understand them, just hold hands.

155

After my fifth miscarriage, they removed my entire reproductive system while I was asleep and couldn't stop them. As soon as I was well enough to sit up, Benny dumped his shotgun buddy—a guy he had been affectionate with, in secret, since high school—and took me up to the snowfields to go after wolves.

"You have to have a taste for it," he said my first time. How else could he explain why you would shove your gun out of the open window of a single-prop plane drilling hell for the horizon, your face a mask of eyes and ice, your hands so cold that when you aimed for the animal fleeing across the white, your fingers did not move the way they were supposed to. Or mine didn't. The first time, I cut my finger on the window latch and had to pull back on the trigger still slick with my own blood.

It was warm blood, at least. And I was alive. Despite any wish I might have had to be otherwise. Which was maybe what Benny was trying to show me.

Most of this is to say that despite the local gossip, the wolf room was probably smaller than anybody at my open house expected. There are no windows. There is no furniture save 387 individually whittled pegs. On each peg hangs a pelt, most of them silver, black-tipped fur. Others reddish brown. The ones staple-gunned to the ceiling are all albino white. The ones laid down on the floor are all females, with tails that can trip you if you don't watch out, though no one watches out. Walking into the wolf room is like walking into a forest of fur. Or a feathery winter silence that lets your brain finally go quiet.

"You'll never trust anyone like you trust your shotgun buddy," Benny told me the night before my first hunt. Though he did not say it, he was speaking about his shotgun buddy and how much he missed him and who I had to be for Benny from there on out.

Our fire was huge and fantastical in the flat, white dark. I was afraid of the morning and what might happen, and I wasn't wrong to be afraid. Shotgunning, as shooter, you have to aim into the wind and snow behind you—the plane going faster than the racing pack—while compensating for the dive of the plane, at the same time, so that you not only don't miss the wolf but also don't get disoriented and shoot the propeller. And kill you both. Up front, the pilot has to get so low to the ground and swoop at such radical angles to keep up with the pack—who keep spreading out over the snow like dots of quicksilver from a broken thermometer—but not stall and crash. And kill you both.

"Think about it this way," said Benny. "We live or die together." I was nineteen by then and he was the age I am now—sixty-seven. I held on to his words as though they were special to our situation, not an agreement you enter into with every person you ever care about. Even just in passing.

Thousands of feet above Howl Palace, Carl was on his way to Seattle, where, changing planes for Houston, he bought a balloon for a girl in a gift shop who was being rude to her mother. Downstairs, Candace was stumbling through some demonstration of my dimmers in the dining room, while her future next-door neighbor—Californian, all-cash, above asking—was pretending concern about "the whole hot tub, mold problem." A poorly constructed staircase below, Silver was sitting in the clamshell grotto, dipping her toes in the fountain, surrendering to what she felt, at that moment, was a lost commission.

Outside, at the far end of the dock, Donald went on tossing out his rope, calling out across the water, "Here, Pinkie. Here, Pinkie," his voice squeaky with anticipation, his casts surprisingly surehanded.

Pinkie, I almost told him, was long past coming to anybody. Pinkie was charging down the shoreline, trampling kiddie pools and sprinklers, digging into professional-grade landscaping while mothers chased after her with shovels and fathers contemplated lawsuits and the implications of lawsuits at the homeowners association meeting—all of which they could avoid if they just jumped in the plane and took off for a few hours to remember why they had moved to Alaska in the first place.

The wind died down. Rainbows slicked along the shallows, bright with the smell of avgas and algae. Donald hardly noticed when I sidled up beside him, so intent was he on his task. He tossed out another cast—a perfect one, ending in a satisfying thunk as the rib hit the surface of water. He cast again. And cast again. "Pinkie!" he said, unable even now to give up.

*Nominated by The Paris Review, Ethan Chatagnier, Sandra Leong*

# VOWS

## fiction by DAVID MEANS

from GRANTA

I never caught exactly what was said about us and could only imagine the vicious forms the rumor took as it started at the church and jumped from house to house along the river, somehow making the two-mile leap over Tallman Mountain State Park as it headed to the town of Piermont where the Dickersons lived, and then from Jenny Dickerson's mouth up the river several blocks, skipping the Morrison house (she was rarely home), most likely to Sue Carson, and then from her mouth to Andrew Jensen, the rector at St Anne's, who, I still liked to imagine, spiced the rumor with some biblical flavor, somehow couching his comments in theological terms, mentioning the fall and temptation and the sins of adultery and so on and so on as he passed it to Gracie Gray, who tasted all the possible ramifications, twisted it even more to make me into a villainous antihero, unaware that both of us, Sharon and I, had betrayed each other, and then held the story in her mouth for several weeks, where it sat until I turned from the window at our annual holiday cocktail party to find her looking at me.

In a teal dress, tailored square to her shoulders, cut low in a rectangle, framing pale flesh and her pearls, which swayed as she moved gently to the music, Gracie winked at me and then turned away coyly, rotating at the waist and letting her legs—I swear I remember this!—swing around in an afterthought, as if she were resisting a magnetic pull. Then, in exactly the same way, she slowly turned back and reconnected with my gaze and, while the midnight cold from the window behind me brushed my neck, we seemed at that instant to share an exchange.

Her side of the exchange seemed to be saying: *in your public retaking of vows a few months ago, you and Sharon exposed a crack in the facade—the happy couple! Ha! The perfectly wonderful family!—and although that crack has been sealed in a ceremony with new vows, it remains a crack.*

While my part of the exchange went: *I understand that you think the seal might still be weak, Gracie, but it's not, not anymore.*

Then she squinted her eyes at me and gave me a look that seemed to say: *don't flatter yourself, jerk. You're a creep. I'm simply offering you a little holiday gesture of flirtatious cheer to warm your lonely, pathetic soul, and, anyway, after hearing the rumor, and then passing it on to Stacy Sutton, telling her how you betrayed Sharon, I'll be the first one to pry you two apart, to weaken the seal. On the other hand—*she widened her eyes and then winked—*perhaps sometime in the future on a night like this—crisp and clear outside, with an almost artificial-looking rime of frost in the corners of each windowpane—with all of this good fortune in the air, well, who knows? Is there anything more dangerous than a full-blown sense of good fortune?*


Looking back, I think that we might've had a similar exchange—if you want to call it that—at the church, after Sharon and I kissed, as I swept the sanctuary from pew to pew to make sure everyone got a chance to witness the frankness in my face, because after we sealed our new commitment with a kiss I got a sense in the late-day light trying to come through the stained glass overhead, in the big brass cross behind me, in the way it felt to stand on the altar, that Sharon and I were being held up to a judgment that hadn't existed before the ceremony.

Before the renewal ceremony began there had been a new sense of mission between us, an eagerness that had disappeared as soon as we started reciting our vows. When we turned to each other, with Reverend Woo between us, and began speaking, it was in the subdued, somewhat feverous voices of two people who had reconciled after one final, devastating argument that had lasted several months, beginning one day at the beach in Mystic, Connecticut, with the Thompsons, who were down near the water when I turned to Sharon and said, All this pain will pass. We really can work this out.

And she said, I no longer care what Dr Haywood says. The middle ground doesn't seem to be available for us.

And I said, quoting Dr Haywood again, Gunner must be kept front and center. It's our duty to him to do everything we can to build a new life out of the ruins.

Down the sand, Gunner yelled, What did you say about me? Hey, hey, you guys, what are you talking about?

Sharon's face was soft, lovely, tan. Her eyes were pooling a sadness that I found attractive. Near the water, Carol Thompson, who at that time didn't have the slightest idea what was going on, was lifting her son up by the hands, swaying him over the water and dipping his toes into the surf.

Her husband, Ron, was a few yards down the beach, holding himself at a remove, shielding his brow as he serenely scanned the water. For a few seconds there was a shift in the air, Sharon was gazing out at the water and we both felt a stasis, a place where we could rebuild our marriage, and then the feeling disappeared—and Gunner called again, waving his blue shovel—and she leaned in and whispered, Fuck you, and I whispered, No, fuck *you*, and then I lay on my side and watched out of the corner of my eye as Carol lifted her son up and down (she had strong shoulders and long, elegant arms, and I felt, watching her, with the sand against my legs, the soft seep of ardor coming again).

Ardor was a word I used a lot back then when I talked to myself. Ardor's taking over, I said. The air is loaded with ardor this afternoon, I said to Gunner as I watched him, day after day, in the backyard. Ardor's radiating from those trees, I said in a mock-British accent, pointing at the pines along the edge of the yard. Then he scrunched his face and gave me a look that said: *You're strange and silly, Dad. Whatever you're saying, it's dubious.*

His look seemed judgmental in the purest sense, as if he knew somehow that his mother and father had betrayed each other, parted ways, heading off into distant blissful worlds.


On the beach that day in Mystic I rolled over and kept my face down and admitted to myself, as I do now, that it had been in the end inevitable, considering the amount of ardor—or ardor-related gestures generated—that the lust, or whatever, would congeal, or perhaps the word is incarnate, into an act of adultery on my part and, at almost the same time, on Sharon's part.

Sharon had confessed to me about her lover, the Banker, and I had confessed to her about Marie, whom she called the Teacher, and in those

160

confessions we had each allowed carefully curated details in—the Standard Hotel on Washington Street, a few drinks after a long session briefing a client, a clandestine meeting in Piermont on a lonely, sad day in the fall when she was out in Los Angeles, time zones away. A Lorca poem memorized in Spanish. Funds transferred into an account managed by the Banker. The rest was left up to our horrific imaginations. I imagined her eating lunch with him, down the stairs, in one of those older Upper East Side establishments, with ivory-white tablecloths and candles flickering in the middle of the day. Outside the windows, I imagined the legs and high heels and shoes of those walking past while they whispered sweet nothings to each other, and felt the beautiful, clandestine joy of holding a secret together in Manhattan. What she imagined I can only imagine, but I'm sure she built images of me with Marie, images of her face drawn from parent–teacher conferences: the two of us leaning back on a blanket somewhere deep in the state park, looking up at the sky, smiling in postcoital quiet, watching the clouds meander over the river. I imagined that she imagined—as I did—lips hovering, dappled with sweat, just before a kiss. The faint, citrusy smell of her neck. The sweet moments between touch—a finger hovering just over the flesh. Exquisite pain, of course, came from these imagined moments because they were pure, clear, drawn from the mind's own unique desires.

At the beach that day in Mystic, with my cheek against the sand, I felt a keen injustice in the clichéd nature of our situation, that thinking it was a cliché was also a cliché, or maybe bringing it up as a cliché is even more of a cliché, and even more of a cliché to bring up the fact that a cliché is a cliché.

What are clichés but the reduction of experience into manageable patterns, Dr Haywood told us a few weeks later, during a counseling session. You call it a cliché, but the brain can only process so much.

That day in her office—on the ground floor of an apartment building on 96th Street, not far from the park—Dr Haywood explained that the brain's attention can only be drawn precisely to one thing at a time, and only those things the brain deems worthy. You catch a flick of movement in the grass, near the water's edge, and then you draw your attention to it if you deem it worthy, or else you let it float away and think: *that's just a bird alighting, or flying off, and I'm going to keep my attention on that boat, the leader of a regatta, tacking around a buoy, catching the wind in the belly of a sail.* Cliché, she explained, is the brain's way of speeding up cognitive analysis.

I lifted myself up and brushed the sand from my arms and leaned towards Sharon and said, Well, Sharon, we need to go back to our original vows and start from scratch, and she said, Honestly, I'm sorry to say but in retrospect the original vows didn't cut it in the first place. The original vows were obviously batshit silly.

She kept talking until Gunner came up along the sand, walking with his side-to-side sway, looking suspicious. For several days he'd been listening carefully as we spoke in a weird manner, keeping everything—as far as we could—cryptic.

Betrayal doesn't go away, Sharon said.

I'd like to find a firm footing. Something we can stand on.

What are you talkin' about? Gunner said. What about my foot?

Mom and Daddy are talking adult-talk. Sometimes adults have to talk adult-talk, Sharon said.

Then he began to pressure and pry and make us both deeply uncomfortable but also—it seems to me now, sitting here alone with my drink, watching the water—even more eager to find a language that might, without exposing our plight, also prove magically useful. We had to blur the details and speak in code and we ended up speaking in a kind of neo-biblical lingo.

I'm not sure we can make it up this hill.

The hill is made of your frickin' ardor.

No, no, the hill is a big-shot banker in Manhattan. We both climbed hills. We're both equally guilty.

What hill can't be climbed? I want to climb the hill with you, Gunner said, and in-between our words there would appear a hint of solace, of the reconciliation that would arrive if we simply continued speaking in code for the rest of our lives with our son between us, asking suspicious questions, redirecting our pain into his pale blue eyes, his tiny ears.

Anthony's Nose, one of us said, referring to the beautiful mountain north of the Bear Mountain Bridge. We're talking about taking a climb up Anthony's Nose.

I wanna climb the nose, Gunner said. His eyes were wide and resolute and sparked—it seemed—with a keen knowingness, a sense of playful desperation.


That afternoon with the Thompsons on the beach in Mystic, we began an argument that continued into fall, taking any number of forms: me in support of the original vows; Sharon against; vows dead and dried up and scattered forever in the dusty winds of our infidelity. Vows broken to begin with, tried, simplistic and never powerful enough to determine our future; vows subsumed to the weight of dead traditions, symbolic claptrap uttered from youthful throats that had been eager, ready to say anything (any fucking thing, Sharon cried) in order to instill a sense of permanency in the world. We fought and eventually—in that strange way that one argument can lead to another and then to something that resembles silence—we reached the endpoint, at which point action is the only recourse.

But before we got to that point we had to go through a fight that night, after our trip to the beach, with our skin still salty and taut and Gunner asleep in front of the television set. While I argued in support of our original vows, taken years ago on a crisp, clear fall afternoon in the city, Sharon made the case—her voice deepening, shifting into her attorney mode—that those vows were dead and gone, used up, depleted, scattered forever on the cold wind of our infidelity.

A week later, at the top of Anthony's Nose, keeping Gunner close at hand, standing there with her hands on her hips and her chin up as if speaking to the sky, she explained that she thought our commitment had been flawed anyway, silly and traditional. We were just kids. We didn't know what we were doing.

On Anthony's Nose we were rehashing previous fights, looking down at the river where it went north past West Point, buried in the haze.

Sharon pointed out, her voice getting soft and gentle, that we had never really discussed ('had a sit-down' was the phrase she used) the wording of those original vows and had instead entrusted their composition to Reverend Moody (Judson Church in Washington Square), the same man who had married her parents back in Cleveland. We had seen him as a kind of good-luck token, because his words had sealed the covenant—I remember she argued that that was a much better word—that had led to *her* conception and then her existence and, via her existence, to our meeting by pure chance that day in the Boston Common, sitting on the same bench and reading the same book (*Pale Fire* by Vladimir Nabokov).

We bickered and fought and then finally renewed our vows at the little Presbyterian church in Snedens Landing, New York, about twenty miles north of Manhattan, on the west side of the river, tucked amid expensive estates—Baryshnikov lived back there, along with Bill Murray.

The Reverend Woo presided, leaning forward in her vestments, quoting Merton on humility (my contribution) and Robert Frost on roads not taken (Sharon's contribution), while Gracie Gray, John and Sue Carson, Joanna and Bill and Jenny Dickerson, Bill and Liz Wall, Karen Drake and Janet Smith, Jillian and Ted Wilson-Rothchild, and Sharon's mother Anna Rose, who had flown over from Tralee, Ireland, looked on as I repeated Woo's words back to Sharon—*for eternity, ever after, we renew these vows in the great spiral of time itself, the dark matter of our particular, unique love, tucked in the folds of the universe, marking our small minutia of time here out of the random chaos, uniting our love to a semblance of form, tightening ourselves against the timescape of our lives*—until it was my turn to listen to Woo speak Sharon's part of the vows and I tried to stay focused as she recited her part back to me, something about *the renewal of the original impulse of our love, returning to the original pulse of desire that is on this day consecrated* (I'm pretty sure she spoke both those phrases: *the original impulse* and then *on this day consecrated*).

Her side mentioned Gunner—something along the lines of *between us, shared, our devout love of our son, Gunner, stands.*

She listened to Woo speak a few words and then to me as I repeated those words, and then I listened to Woo speak and then to Sharon again and then we kissed each other with honest eagerness and stood arm in arm while out in the pews, next to Sharon's mother, who was dressed in a lime-green blouse and a pleated herringbone skirt, looking weary and jet-lagged after her flight across the Atlantic, Gunner stared at me with blunt blue eyes that seemed to say: *you have betrayed me, father, insofar as you had a part in my creation.*


Please don't think I'm trying to say, as I sit here alone enjoying the warm summer evening, alone in the house, and once again, for perhaps the thousandth time, studying the Hudson River, that we didn't renew our commitment with the most devout sincerity, or that retaking our vows wasn't the right thing to do at the time, or that it wasn't a pleasure to leave Gunner with Sharon's mother and drive away from the front of the church, in the verdant spring air, trailing a ridiculous string of rattling cans all the way through Queens to the long-term parking at JFK. But the look my son gave me, or at least the look I imagined he gave me, seemed to reveal that even *he* was aware that the renewal ceremony revealed, or rather exposed, a rending to our friends, to the public, to the world at large.

Please, will you stop about the look Gunner gave you, Sharon said that night in Dublin. You're being ridiculous. He has no idea. If anything, he's happy for us.

She was at the window of our room in the Gresham Hotel, her back turned to me, looking down at O'Connell Street. It was a lovely evening with a breeze blowing through the window, brushing her hair around her shoulders. (Oh God, Sharon had the most beautiful auburn hair with natural highlights! And, oh, and those eyes, mercurial, quicksilver eyes that shifted with mood and light! Even now I can recall the look she gave me earlier that day in Dublin as we stood on a bridge and looked down at the Liffey—solemn and dark water below, which seemed to hold centuries of stonework and old barges and history going back to the Vikings, coming back up into her eyes as she gave me one of her sidelong glances, flirtatious and judgmental at the same time, and then she gave me her wonderful smile.)

At the window with her hands on her hips she was swaying gently, shifting her weight from one foot to the other. Come to bed, I said. I won't ever say that word again. It doesn't need to be said. I promise.

What word?

Vows, I said.

Oh, honestly, I said I don't want to hear that word ever again.

I stayed silent as we lay together in bed. We had walked aimlessly to stay awake, to fight off the jet lag, drinking coffee, surprised at the clean modernity of the city, arm in arm as we stood at Trinity Gate, which was closed, and then strolled down Grafton Street—like any other mall in America, we agreed—to St Stephen's Green, where we found a bench and sat for a while and held hands like proper newlyweds. Then, as we meandered back in the direction of the hotel, we lucked upon Oscar Wilde's house, or at least I insisted, before we crossed the street, that it was Wilde's house. In reality it was his father's house. The confusion sparked a short, brisk argument—the first of our renewed marriage!—as we waited for the light to change. Sharon's voice had tightened and became litigious, resolute and pristine in a way I admired and loved. The argument began on one side of the street and ended when we got close enough to read the round plaque that described an eye surgeon and folklore expert, Wilde's father.

You were right, I told Sharon, feeling incredibly happy.

Then we had made our way back down O'Connell Street, stopping here and there to look at the shops, laughing and teasing each other about Oscar Wilde, and we ended up at the bar in the touristy pub next to the hotel, sitting shoulder to shoulder, still weary from jet lag, leaning like regulars into our pints and sipping together in unison, sharing for the first time a mutual loneliness (a kind of blissful isolation, a sense that we were united in our new bonds) that would—I now see—last for years, until we held hands in the hospital room and prayed softly together while outside the sky over the river charged up with particles and produced, somewhere over New Jersey, a bright flash of lightning.

Was it a cliché to have a second honeymoon in Ireland? Sure. Is it a cliché to link that one drink together in the pub, after our first fight at Oscar Wilde's father's house, with our relationship after our renewal ceremony? Is it a cliché to make the leap from that moment—when we were first feeling the deep unity between us that would last for years and years—to that final night in the hospital along the upper western edge of Manhattan, when I held her hand and felt the faint bud of pulse in her wrist and then pulled her hand to my mouth and began to weep?

Yes, perhaps. But what Haywood said to us that day in therapy stuck. To push further, as I sit here today I am sure that in the hospital—with blue sawhorses in the street set up by the police, and a summer thunderstorm brewing over Jersey—with our hands cupped gently, we both felt the beauty of our commitment to time itself, to something vast and eternal and, above all, secretive. It was ours and ours alone. Whatever rumors and hearsay and conjecture floated around our story, whatever people made of it from gathered fragments, could only intensify what we had together.

On a family trip out west years after the ceremony, watching the road taper into the horizon outside of Bismarck, North Dakota, I began to wonder if we had completely nullified each other's vows by renewing them. I theorized that Sharon's vows had simply canceled mine out, creating a different kind of void. Gunner was sixteen at the time, lurking in the back seat with his headphones on, and the sight of his bobbing head, with a halo of hair puffing around his headphone band in the rearview mirror, had been disconcerting. Looking drunk back there, with his eyes loose and formless, lost in his music, he could've been anywhere.

Next to me, Sharon slept with her head back and her mouth open. That's what I recall from our Grand Canyon trip. Sharon sleeping and my son, with his adult bones eagerly hardening beneath his muscles and his muscles pushing against the fabric of his sleeves, in the back seat, lost in his beloved death metal. Even at the rim of the canyon, looking down, taking in the vast expanse, all he did was nod his head slightly to the music in his headphones and casually brush off the sublime vista.

On the way home, I think, this theory of a complete nullification of vows came to mind.

As I drove, I balled the thought up—the theory of complete nullification—and threw it out the window. That's a meditation technique I was using at the time: take a thought, write it down on some mental paper, hold it, turn it around in the mind, center on it and then ball it up and throw it away.

Somewhere along a road in North Dakota, I tossed that thought out the window.

Now, sitting here, I imagine it's still out there, curled in the scrub and dust, waiting to be discovered and unfolded.


One night, standing over my son as he slept, while the snow swirled around outside, it struck me that if we ever had another renewal ceremony, a kind of third-time-is-a-charm deal, we'd have to simply act as our own authority before God and avoid all the formal trappings. (Those are the fun parts, Sharon said, her voice light and happy, when we were planning the second ceremony. The trappings are the part you're required to forget the first time you get married. We were too young, and uptight, and we forgot them. The point of a renewal ceremony is to have a deeper awareness and enjoyment and focus so you actually experience the trappings, she said. I said, I don't like the trappings, but you might be right. You've got to have some kind of sacred space overhead, some sense that the vows are being taken in a holy environment. Even if you get married on the beach, there has to be a consecrated vibe in the air, and she said, Yeah, right, with an edge to her voice, not bitter but not sweet.)


Sharon and I are still uncomfortable with each other, I told my friend Ted one afternoon, before the renewal ceremony. We were out on the back patio, smoking cigars, facing the river. As the sun came in and out of clouds, the trees blazed with color and faded and blazed.

We're like a couple of crooks locked in a cell with a warden who looms over us to make sure we get along for eternity. We're both in for the death penalty, I said.

You're in for death, and so am I. Each meal is a last supper, he said, and we laughed. He and his wife Jennifer were astonishingly good cooks, master chefs, and their dinner parties were legendary. They weren't foodies. Their respect for food went beyond trends or fads. They cooked simple, elegant meals and knew how to set up a perfect party. Brisk fall nights with a hint of woodsmoke and harvest in the air. The windows of their house above the road, tucked in a notch in the palisade, flickering candlelight. Silver on white linen. Always perfectly balanced company, a few light-hearted guests, a sullen guest (Hal Jacobson, whose wife had jumped from the bridge), a blend of intellect, jest and despair brought together, drawn around a sense that the next dish would top the last, bringing all attention to the mouth and tongue.

No matter what was being said, no matter how happy the talk, no matter what grievances were exposed, the next dish brought the conversation to a satisfying lull.

Before the dish arrived, we'd be complaining about the town's new sidewalk design, or someone would bring up the so-called nunnery that was, at that time, proposed for the empty meadow lot up near Hook Mountain. (I would keep quiet about the fact that I owned the small parcel that was necessary for an easement. It would come out soon enough. One way or another, if the proposal moved forward and went through the planning-board review process, the need for an easement would come to light and, with it, the fact that I owned the land. Then the fact that the New York diocese was negotiating with me to purchase it would come out, too.)

I'm only kidding about prison, I said to Ted, who looked at me, took a deep draw, and released a cloud of smoke.

Ted was a federal judge and played the role even when he was off the bench, relaxing with a cigar in hand. He was the type who prepared his cigar in an old style, popping a nub out of the end of the cigar with his thumbnail, rejecting my clippers and then my expensive butane lighter—the flame powerful and invisible until it hit the tobacco and bloomed like a blue orchid—in favor of kitchen matches. Even when he was relaxed, he seemed to have the straight-backed reserve of a man who was withholding judgment, sticking with procedure. He took another draw on his cigar, kept his lips lightly around the wrapper leaf and spoke with firm authority, You're not in prison. If you'd rode the blue bus and then

168

went through the security check at Rikers Island, you'd understand what it means to be in prison. But I get your point, he said.

Well, you should, I said. I knew he had gone through some serious marital problems of his own. On the porch—this was late fall, a cold wind coming from the north, hunched in our coats with our collars up, enjoying the feeling of smoking outside, as if we were in the Klondike, two rugged explorers stopping for a smoke, he knew and I knew at that instant, sitting there, that the next thing out of his mouth—or mine— would be a comment about the quality of the cigars, and then one of us would say something about the quality of the Cubans, and then one of us would tell a smuggling story. His that day was about how he once hid cigars—purchased in Europe—in his wife's tampon box to get them through customs, and I told him about replacing the bands, turning Montecristos into Dunhills, something like that, and then we settled into a deep ritual that betrayed time itself, turning the moment into something utterly simple and meaningless.

Years later, at his funeral, up on the hill across from the hospital, with the river broken gray slates through the trees, I'd remember that moment on the back patio and how he drew the attention away from my failure and allowed us to go back to the ordained pattern of our friendship, which had started with our weekly tennis matches. You want to play with a judge? I know this judge, and he's pretty good, someone told me. He's federal so he pretty much sets his own hours and can play with you in the afternoon, someone said.

In the years after the renewal ceremony the judge came to know the full story of my marital problems with Sharon. His son was at West Point for a few years, and I remember that he talked often of him, saying things like—*my son is a plebe, and right now, as we play tennis, he is, most certainly, being tortured into adulthood.* His son would become a captain and die in his second tour in Iraq, killed by an IED, but of course we didn't know that at the time.


On the night of the party, months after the ceremony, Ted's loss of his son in Iraq was five years away, still up in the vapors, and he had no idea that it was ahead of him, and I had no idea that someday I'd look back and see both of us as we'd be years later and filter our friendship through that particular moment. Dare I say that as I turned and had that exchange with Gracie, and the judge glanced at me, we both sensed that in the future we'd look back at that moment? Ted's face as he held the cocktail shaker in his hands, had the placid look of authority, a look I had seen after one of his fantastic tennis serves, standing with his legs apart and his racket at his side, gazing over the net with honest humility. The ball had zipped past. The air was brighter, cooler on his side of the net and duller on my side. All of his efforts—the toss-up, perfectly placed, his racket going back to touch the crook of his massive back, his swing down to meet the ball, were gone, lost, and the serve manifested itself in the tink of the ball against the chain-link behind me and then disappeared into silence as it sat alone in the corner, nestled in leaves. That was the look he had when he turned to see me at the window, at our annual party, years ago.

Then he came over to where I was standing by the window and asked if I was okay. He had his hand on his shoulder and was leaning forward and his face seemed to be saying: *Yes, I'm holding you in judgment, old friend. I'll give you my verdict in a few years.*

True love is, when seen from afar, a big fat cliché. It is a glance from the side while looking down at deep water. A fight on a beach. A sweaty brow covered with sand. Lips between kisses. Betrayal eased into grace.

(Let it go, Sharon said. You theorize too much about these things. How many times have I heard a witness claim that they told themselves to remember what they were seeing when the truth is they were too freaked out, or too scared, or even, in some cases, unaware that a crime was even transpiring.)

All I can say now is that I stuck to my word. I don't think we ever discussed our vows again. We settled into life. We shared everything together. After that night in the Gresham Hotel we went on finding places, situations, where we could simply sit side by side, shoulder to shoulder, lifting a glass in unison.

One evening, years later, we walked up Lexington Avenue after dinner with Gunner and his fiancée, through a hazy, dusky midsummer evening at the end of a preposterously hot day. The streets baking with heat. A giant sinkhole had opened in Queens. An unbearable glaze hung over everything. Cars dragging themselves through the glaze of Park Avenue. With sunset, a breeze had arrived, fragrant with the smell of hot pavement and something that smelled like cotton candy. We were walking hand in hand, sauntering, and after the dinner—the cute formality of Gunner across from the love of his life—we were relishing a sensation of success. We had raised a gentle soul, a man who tended to his lover's needs and had found someone who would tend to his, and that fact alone seemed sufficient.

Before meeting Gunner and Quinn at the restaurant, Sharon and I had gone to a museum, stood before a Picasso painting of a lobster fighting a cat, and then moved on to examine a Franz Kline, a few wonderful thick blue brushstokes splayed in cross-hatch, and then, downstairs in the cool lower level, a Van Gogh, a small, secret scene of a shadowy figure of a lonely woman, or a man, passing out of (or into) a pedestrian tunnel in the glow of dusk.

As we walked south that evening at a leisurely pace towards Grand Central, we were feeling a contentment that came from the fact that we had passed from the cool, secretive moment together before some of the finest works of civilization, out into the blazing heat, and then into a restaurant on Lexington, and then, two hours later, back out into a cooler dusk alone together.

Years after the fact, I can still feel the vivid sensation of seeing my own situation within the one that Van Gogh had selected for his painting, out of an infinite set of possibilities, and the feeling would linger with me for the rest of my life.

That night, somewhere in the sixties, or perhaps farther south in the fifties, we glanced to the right and saw what remained of the sunset, framed by the length of the street all the way to the Hudson, a slab of pure lavender light, gloriously perfect, combining with the cold, concrete edges.

That's as beautiful as anything Rothko painted, I said to Sharon.

(Oh dear, wonderful Sharon. Oh Sharon, love of my life. Oh beloved sharer of a million eternal moments. Oh secret lover of secret situations. Oh you who day by day shared a million intricate conversations.)

That vision has stayed with me. It illustrates how the window looks right now as I sit here with my drink, with the hazy deep blue light edged with the serene, pure black of the window frame, as I sit alone in a room, a year after that night in the hospital, thinking about my wife, about our life together while the river out beyond the window quivers and shakes with the last sunlight of the day. I have come to believe, in this time of mourning, that only in such moments, purely quiet, subsumed in the cusp of daily life, can one—in the terrible incivility of our times—begin to locate a semblance of complete, honest, pure grace.

In an average life lived by a relatively average soul, what else remains but singular moments of astonishingly framed light?

*Nominated by Granta, Joan Murray*

# COMPOSED

## by BRIAN SWANN

from HUDSON REVIEW

Inside for days, gales whipping about,
TV with awnings torn from buildings,

cornices ripped from facades, pileups
on the throughway, downed power lines

catching fire with worse to come. Who'd
go out in that? Not me. With the world

rearing up like Hebridean seas and no
lighthouse in sight, I'm best off where I am,

my wife reading Virginia Woolf, telling me
she's "amazed" by the word *composed*

to describe the small house seen from the
rough waves: "the composed look of something

receding in which one no longer has any part."
She says the word reminds her somehow

of years ago returning late, climbing the steep
driveway, turning the bend and seeing rise out

of the trees under Bearpen our small house
as if lit from within by last sun, the garage door

opening as we entered slowly as into the
composed calm of a completed thought.

*Nominated by John Allman, Richard Cecil, Jeffrey Hammond, Maura Stanton*

# THE GOLDEN AGE OF TELEVISION

fiction by KARL TARO GEENFELD

from ZYZZYVA

First we called him Jared, then he was Rob Lowe, as we imagined that's who he would resemble, then he was just Rob, then he was Emilio, then Rob again, then he was Doug, and for just a day, he was Patrick Stewart, when we thought he might be a more overtly sinister villain, but he reverted to Rob and then Doug, Jared and Doug. At any time of any day in any pitch he could be any of those and all of us would understand who we were talking about.

When The Show Runner was present, we were quiet, our body language attentive. If we had possessed the feline attribute of turning our ears toward the source of our interest, we would have utilized that, as we wished to show that we were listening, that we were thinking, that we were positing his ideas and preparing to regurgitate them with Doug or Rob or Patrick Stewart in different variations, some with Doug or Rob Lowe ending up dead, others with Rob or Jared turning out not to be the villain at all, and every permutation in between. Our job as writers on this sixth-season show was to build another level upon the sixty-episode edifice already erected on which to scratch an original, or at least not totally clichéd, sentiment.

Save for The Show Runner, I was the oldest writer in the room, which itself made me an example of our diversity, discrimination against older writers being the subject of occasional Writers Guild of America emails urging show runners to consider scribblers over forty. There was no one type in our room but instead an array of the intelligent and insecure: the talented actress slightly too unattractive to have a career in front of the camera, the Oxford graduate English lad gone prematurely bald with face perpetually reddened in the California sun, the Show Me State native from Kansas City who spoke in the same comforting, broadly masculine affect as Vin Scully yet was vigorously homosexual, the wealthy African American who had grown up in Beverly Hills, attended Harvard-Westlake, and then Harvard itself, before winning a Rhodes Scholarship. And then there was me, slightly too old to still be trying to harmonize in the sextet of a TV drama room. Surely, my peers thought to themselves, by their mid-forties they would be show runners themselves. In this frequently alleged era of peak TV, we accredited television writers were pigs in shit. What was my excuse for not having my own drama on one of the premium cables or a subscription service? Not even an original pilot on my IMDB page.

My detour as a novelist was no justification. No one had heard of any of my three books, and none had been made into films. All they knew of me was my two seasons on a police drama, set in Atlanta, of no particular distinction or impressive viewership. But scripted dramas were proliferating, dozens staffing every year, and amiable writers who could convincingly hide their egregious egomania or addictions were in demand. So every morning I took my place at the oval, mid-century-modern table—a prop commandeered from another now-cancelled series—across from The Show Runner, next to the English lad (whose credits, by the way, comprised a bunch of British shows none of us had seen) and furrowed my brow and prepared to care about Jared or Rob Lowe or Doug or whatever he was called this morning.

Our show, The Show Runner reminded us often, was at a crucial inflection point. We had already exploited all the natural arcs, family members separating and reuniting, spouses cheating, second-tier characters dying, revenge sought, murders, murders covered up, long-lost family members appearing, those family members murdered, spouses cheating again, more murders, etcetera. He had done four season-sixes, The Show Runner warned knowingly of the perils ahead. And we would try to figure out what shows he could possibly be talking about, because his last show had lasted four seasons and the one before that just two. Nonetheless, he claimed for himself expertise at having confronted the thorny and particularly fraught issues of the sixth season and our success or failure hinged on Rob or Doug or Emilio, or whatever his name was, because we were only as good as our villain.

The problems with seasons three through five, The Show Runner observed, were our villains, an array of biker gangs, drug cartels, Russian mobsters, and Mongolians. By the end of each season, the writers—only two of whom were still in this room—had so tired of the villains they were no longer writing for them, so that the season wrap-ups felt sudden and contrived. With a great villain, with a Jared or Rob or Doug, played by a great actor, the writers would tear each other apart to write scenes for him.

How about, the English lad said, Doug pretends to kill himself to cast attention away from him, but he isn't really dead.

We did that, said Allison, the girl who typed up the notes of our ramblings. Season two.

Bollocks.

Long since divorced, with my son living with his mother, Marta, in Mar Vista, I shared an apartment with Dr. Marshall Bick, or The Bick as he insisted he be called. The Bick had been the owner of a chain of pain management clinics that were shut down in the opioid crackdowns of 2014—it turned out peak TV was coinciding with peak opioid abuse— as well as several apartment buildings, which he had been selling off gradually to pay for his own stupendous opioid and gambling addictions, any one of which would have long ago wiped out most mortals, but The Bick was possessed of superior financial and tachyphylactic powers that allowed him to survive toxic doses of oxycodone and hydromorphone as well as weekends in which he lost sixteen out of seventeen college games, thirteen out of fifteen NBA games and eight ill-conceived, multi-game parlays. Habits like that can eat up millions, and they did, forcing The Bick to consider a roommate in his spacious three-bedroom Pacific Palisades condominium. I moved in, and on weekends my son took the spare bedroom.

If at one point I had imagined I would be a steadying influence on The Bick, it quickly became clear that instead of being rescued by the life preserver thrown by me into his vortex, he would pull me down with him. The first weekend we were roommates, I brought in a three-team parlay—Creighton straight up, Oregon laying six, and Michigan laying one on the road—that I had no business making but that paid $2,550 on a $100 bet. That kind of good fortune, as the Wolverines were up four and Walton was making his foul shots to ice the game, simulates the sizzle in the mind of a brilliant idea borne out, similar to the feeling I got when I landed a pitch in the room, one The Show Runner bit down on, as if it was not chance but actual wisdom that had been at work when I chose those three teams. The joy and exhilaration hit me deep and hard and even jolted me awake that night as I was about to nod off. But it was fleeting and I woke up the next morning looking for another hit. I continued betting, professionals, collegians and even high school. Yes, The Bick had a service that would take high school action, but only the big schools, Mater Dei, Crenshaw, Long Beach Poly, Chino Hills. Hell, those players were already committed to colleges anyway.

The Bick was well into his mid '70s but had somehow aged out of any identifiable demographic, having squirted enough product into his hair so that it was perpetually upstanding in a kind of '50s teen idol pompadour of a luminescent rouge-tinted brown. As soon as he was up in the morning, sliding a 30-milligram oxycodone beneath his tongue, which he dissolved with his morning coffee, his hair was already at attention and saluting the new day. He was ectomorphic, wiry, still retaining the appearance of quickness and speed that had made him a three-year starter at Holy Trinity High School in Hicksville, Long Island. After three such mornings of watching his routine of caffeine and hard drugs, I gave up and took one of his proffered blue pills, crushed it up and insufflated it, feeling an immediate sense of belonging, as if The Bick and I were an amazing pair, each of us bringing to this endeavor an admixture of betting on basketball and abusing opioids, a particular and vital talent. And with this warm glow I departed for work, drove the twenty minutes to Sony in my battered, ten-year-old Porsche that my ex-wife was pressuring me to sell and that The Bick had already appraised at $33,000, having sold one himself just a few months prior. Perhaps, being in the business of symbols and archetypes, I should have read that as a portentous indicator, same car, same bad habits, same downhill trajectory. Well, I missed it, completely.

That morning, in my pleasant narcotic haze and possessed of unbounded warm feeling toward my comrades, I was glib in my pitches in precisely the manner that pleased The Show Runner. My ideas about Jared or Rob Lowe or, for some reason, today he was also being called Bartkowski, after a 1970s quarterback The Show Runner recalled, were landing and accreting into the sediment of our season. Characteristics I was proposing—Bartkowski having an affect more uncouth than couth, so that he had a winning up-from-the-bootstraps quality that would make the eventual reveal as a villain that much more of a betrayal, for he was seeking to repudiate, somehow, his own working class roots—were received with warm expressions and open, receptive gazes. I referenced the *Count of Monte Cristo*, *Julius Caesar*, The Molotov-Ribbentrop Pact and the Patrick Swayze picture *Road House*, unsure of my references in each case but my cadence and tenor were so confident and propulsive that my colleagues didn't dare correct me. I was moving the story forward bullet point by bullet point, each typed up by Allison, the assistant, on the vomitron, as we called the big screen at the front of the room on which we sometimes puked up our ideas.

I was on fire today, was the consensus of my peers, every pitch landing, The Show Runner giddy and nodding his head and saying that's interesting, as he did when he liked what he heard. We had gone, in just one day, from being behind the pace set last year, breaking episode three when we should already have been breaking five, to pulling even. And that was because of me, and my nimble mindset made possible in part by the 30 milligrams of powdered narcotic I had sniffed.

The Show Runner pointed to me and said, you're my favorite. He did this infrequently, and it was shameful how much it hurt me when he did it to one of my peers. Yet I couldn't help but feel a surge of vanity now that I was singled out as the special one. We lived like houseplants in desperate need of the sunshine of his praise. Otherwise we withered. Beneath the joviality, the witticisms, the laughter, was seething competition and bitter resentment of the smallest success of one of our peers. Today, I was the object of such jealousy, and it felt wonderful.

My son Caspar enjoyed the company of The Bick, in part because The Bick was indiscrete in discussing his experiences with prostitutes and gambling, recounting in detail in my son's presence the considerable effort it took to achieve ejaculation after he had consumed 90 or so milligrams of oxycodone and taken a 250-milligram Viagra. The effort, he related, felt like going a dozen rounds with a prizefighter, only the prizefighter was a Venezuelen prostitute's vagina. The Bick talked of tip sheets that he subscribed to, at a cost of several hundred to several thousand dollars a year, websites where you bought the passwords and then were given access to supposed expertise about which teams would cover and which games would go over or under. But The Bick's success seemed in no way enhanced by his expensive touts, a fact which I proved by my own smaller scale betting which achieved roughly similar results in that we were both losers, just of a different magnitude because The Bick was laying a dime on every game, while I was laying a dollar. (A dime being a thousand dollars, a dollar being a hundred.) My son, a precocious sixteen-year-old, glimpsed in The Bick's life of hookers and gambling what we all saw, even those of us in our forties: the fully realized life of an adult unlike other adults, a man unconstrained by a job or a marriage or sobriety or any of the usual ropes that bound us would-be raging bulls. I saw The Bick through Caspar, and I occasionally had to qualify for Caspar The Bick's ridiculous pronouncements and proclamations. But The Bick was funny. He was unique. He was wealthy, or he had been, and he still had the vestiges of that wealth, accounts scattered around the banks of Pacific Palisades containing hundreds of thousands of dollars. And he didn't get up in the morning and drive to a studio where he sat hoping a cruel and sarcastic man, The Show Runner, would glance his way and approve of his verbiage. He didn't give half his weekly check to an ex-wife. The Bick was free; I was a prisoner. And Caspar, my son, he was smart enough to clock this for what it was. If you could be either of us, The Bick or me, you'd be an idiot to choose me.

The Show Runner threw a holiday party at his spacious Brentwood mansion, home of his longtime wife and his three children, all enrolled in Los Angeles private schools, the tuition of the combined trio roughly equivalent to my season's salary. (Any script fees would put me over the top, but still.) The format of the party was that a half-dozen food trucks had been hired by The Show Runner, or maybe the network, and would be parked on his vast circular driveway and once we had gathered our drinks we could go out and wait in line for tacos or grilled cheese or lobster rolls only we would not have to pay, because this was The Show Runner's party. I had no date to bring for the occasion, as having my ex accompany me would be the worst combination of embarrassing and sad, or it could even have prompted speculation among my writer peers that we were somehow reuniting, which was utterly impossible. So I brought Caspar, who had been dropped at our apartment that morning, and The Bick, who, when I argued that my Porsche could only comfortably seat two, said he would drive us in his BMW 7 series. I worried what an uncensored and unsupervised Bick might do or say in front of my colleagues.

Instead, amid a show business party of producers, actors, writers and even a network head or two, The Bick looked around with an air of boredom and disappointment, plucked the olive from his martini, and commented that he had thought there would be more talent at a Hollywood party, and by talent he meant fuckable ass. I reminded him it was a holiday party, a family sort of affair, with a long table of desserts brought by guests, and a bouncy castle in the vast backyard, to which The Bick responded, What a bunch of losers.

My goal at the outset was to prevent a colliding of my two worlds, my drug and gambling addictions, represented by The Bick, and my television writing career, such as it was, but still lucrative, and totally at the whim of The Show Runner. I believed that each would see in the other the essential failings of my character and there would be a perfectly correlating decline of my status in the esteem of both men. I relied on each not knowing the other.

But when The Show Runner approached me, club soda in his hand, while The Bick stood on the other side of Caspar, I had no choice but to introduce the two men, whereupon The Show Runner and The Bick became locked into the exact conversation I had wanted to forestall, one in which the main zone of mutuality was me and the ensuing logical discussion of my many fuck-ups, both in the writers' room and in life, as The Bick was much better versed in the latter.

I separated them as quickly as I could, pulling The Bick away with an explanation that Caspar was due at his mother's, which Caspar immediately repudiated as he too was enjoying the recounting of my fecklessness. I prevailed, and when The Show Runner shook my hand, I suspected I felt in his grip a certain looseness, a decreased interest in me and my ideas based on his having now met the source of many of my observations about life, The Bick. Or was it all in my imagination, had The Bick and The Show Runner simply had a casual holiday exchange?

The Bick drove Caspar to his mother's house in Mar Vista and then took us both to a massage parlor on Wilshire across from an Italian restaurant where he paid for dual full services. I finished twenty minutes before him and sat in the waiting room, looking at my phone. I received a text message from my ex: Why are you exposing Caspar to that degenerate roommate? I responded: I'm the novelist and TV writer. I drive an old Porsche. I'm the cool dad, remember?

Then she asked: Where the fuck is the child support, cool dad?

When The Show Runner was absent, in a budget meeting or talking to network executives or assuaging the considerable ego of our leading man, the room degenerated into a state of chaos reminiscent of an unchaperoned fourth grade classroom. We had farting noise competitions. We recounted to each other embarrassing sexual stories. We had contests to see who could draw the most accurate looking penis on the whiteboard. We wrote fake cards to put up on the board indicating the most boring scenes possible—*Rob Lowe takes a nap. Rob Lowe eats lunch*—in the hopes The Show Runner would not notice them for several days, by which point we could honestly say, Oh, that's been there forever.

We checked constantly to see if lunch had arrived. We practiced fake Australian, Irish, and Scottish accents. We spent an entire half hour talking in awful and racist Mexican accents. We had contests to see who could throw the rubber coasters we were supposed to use to protect the table from drink circles into the tightest area, a writer's room version of horseshoes. We found out who could flare their nostrils, roll his tongue, or was double jointed at the fingers, wrists, and elbows. We knew one another's family histories, going back several generations. And we told touching stories about our childhoods, some of them—most of them, actually—lies, but they passed the time and deepened our knowledge of one another's ideas of ourselves.

When The Show Runner eventually joined the room, in his fake jovial manner, saying good morning you sexy sons of bitches, it was as if the headmaster had appeared in a class of unruly school kids. The British lad and I would say the rehearsed lines we prepared to pretend that we had been hard at it during The Show Runner's whole absence. The Brit would say, I think that should be the bottom of five. I would disagree, top of six. So it would sound as if we had been discussing matters crucial to episodes five and six. Such prevarication was actually unnecessary, as The Show Runner was uninterested in anything we discussed when he was not present, that being a particular egocentric trait of his, so that any good idea that was arrived at in his absence may as well have never uttered at all, or, a few us had learned, could be recycled later when The Show Runner was present and in a receptive mood. For after the first month in the room, there weren't really new ideas, but rather old ideas pitched at precisely the moment when The Show Runner was able to hear them. Rob Lowe as this manipulative Roy Cohntype had been offered by each of us at different points over the past few weeks, but it was the failed actress dropping it at a moment when The Show Runner was up for spending some serious budget on whoever this actor would be—and it was another morning I was blitzed out of my mind—that prompted a, That's interesting, from The Show Runner and gave the failed actress credit for an idea that we had all had. And nobody bitched or moaned that it was unfair. Or that we'd said that yesterday, last week, last month, we just realized that she'd had the good luck of spitting it out at the right moment.

That was the room, this ongoing verbal puzzle that circled around and around the same topics, the same characters, the same stories, The Show Runner repeating them with different verbiage, at one point calling our season a genre, at another a convention, or a myth, and at another a fable, but it was all the same story, just retold and repackaged in different words, and it was our job to somehow add to this ongoing, ever changing verbal carousel in a manner that was either funny, which scored the joke teller a point or two, introduced a new plot element, also worth a point, or, ideally, both funny and additive of new story, for that meant the carousel had a new prancing pony or elaborate princely sleigh we could all hop on for a few minutes or an hour or two and that might yield a scene or two that could make it up onto the vomitron and eventually the board and eventually be written into an outline and script, shot and probably cut by The Show Runner in editing.

It wasn't writing, not in any sense of typing words onto a page, yet The Show Runner would sit in his seat and while we were talking through the same storyline and making painful, trench-warfare-like progress through the season, he would say, God, I hate writing. I would think, this isn't writing, this is sitting in a room talking, and it was so much easier than actually writing that I could show up on increasingly intoxicating doses of hairy-chested analgesic opioids and be a functional "writer." Try writing a novel stoned on oxy.

I'm doing it right now. So, draw your own conclusions.

But the morn following the holiday soiree, The Show Runner came in and was excited by his conversation with The Bick. It had been, the Show Runner informed us, the highlight of his holiday party, this very strange and powerful and Dionysian figure who had appeared and made him rethink the entire Jared or Bartkowski character and that perhaps he could be, in his way, a Dorian Gray figure for the entire diseased culture of Hollywood. This degenerated Fabian of a man who still drugged, fucked, and gambled like the great moguls of old, amid all the veganism and iboga and kettlebell and yoga, this man was a vestige of a more muscular and brutal past, a Sam Pelicano combined with Sam Spade and Bill Holden in *Sunset Boulevard*, only instead of being at the bottom of a swimming pool he was encased in his own excesses, he would never die but instead serve as a kind of witness to all our sins. He began to call this character Bick, and Bick replaced Bartkoswki and Rob Lowe in our pitches, so that I was pitching storylines for a character named after my roommate, which wasn't unusual, as real life relatives and friends and acquaintances had often turned up in our pitches and for a few weeks been used as placeholder names.

But as The Show Runner expanded on his theories of The Bick and his possible permutations, I began to feel a certain possessiveness, as if The Bick was my intellectual property. I had found him. Had moved in with him. Had co-opted aspects of his life. Had developed an opioid addiction and lost thousands of dollars gambling in the thrall of The Bick, so shouldn't I be entitled to credit for this creation?

Of course not. That's not how television writing works. It's not who has the ideas, as I said, it's when you decide to repeat the ideas other people have had, not only in the room, but in the entire universe of the hundreds of scripted shows that have been made and are being made, hundreds of pods like this, each operating by this same principle, or lack of principles. I acquiesced. I surrendered The Bick, for, I had to admit, it was not me who had realized he was a living, walking TV character, but The Show Runner, and perhaps in that power of recognition lay his genius, or at least his ability to make seven figures a year writing and producing a solidly second-tier television show.

But The Bick was proving to be less durable than his own pompadour, and one evening, as we were in the bar of a local Chinese restaurant, drinking vodka sodas and letting 30-milligram oxycodones dissolve under our tongues, watching Oklahoma City take a shit in Houston and leave us both out of the money midway through the third quarter, The Bick confessed to me that he would soon be going under the knife. A routine MRI (which he had undergone so that a half-scrupulous physician would continue to write him scripts for powerful narcotics) had detected a series of irregular growths snaking around his spine. They were tumors, particularly unpropitious in appearance, and had prompted blood tests that had confirmed the most likely origin was uncontrolled and irregular cellular growth of the type most indicative of cancer.

The biopsy, The Bick explained, would be the surgery. They would go in, and, as delicately as they could, seek to unravel from his spine the intrusive matter. The risks were numerous and horrifying: possible piercing of the spinal column, resulting in debilitating fluid leakage, possible severing of spinal nerves, resulting in lower or upper body extremity paralyses, possible severing of the spine itself, resulting in total paralysis. And there was another possibility, that the croakers opened him up, took a look, and then just sewed him shut because there was nothing to be done about a man with cancer so far advanced he had just a few weeks to live.

The Bick had children, at least a half dozen, but he'd never married and beyond a financial obligation to a few of them, there was no emotional bond to speak of. The Bick would get himself to the hospital, he told me, but he would need to be collected after the surgery, after three or so days of what was optimistically being described as recovery. I of course told him I would visit and gather him when called. In our altered states we, or at least I, somehow kept an emotional distance from the true implications of what The Bick had just confided.

In the harsh morning, as I snorted my morning oxycodone and drank my coffee, I realized that another way of describing what The Bick had was a snake of cancer wrapping up his spine, and that was the best case scenario. The worst: it had already metastasized through the proximate organs, and The Bick was riddled.

We never talked about the impending surgery, save for The Bick, a physician himself, explaining that surgeons were now well acquainted with the high tolerance of certain patients to opioids, that being the one advantage of being well into our second decade of this epidemic.

In the room, The Bick's character was looming, growing, taking up more and more dramatic space as our villain finally achieved something like the characteristics and biography that could thrust him into scenes with our regular cast and perhaps even earn that rarest of goals of any guest star in a long-running series, objective scenes, these being the fruits The Show Runner could dangle to lure a famous or at least notorious actor.

It's remarkable how much talent is out there on the market, and periodically, when casting would show up in the room and put up on the vomitron images of the actors available, we would gasp in surprise that this Oscar-winner or that former *Star Wars* leading man or one or the other of the former James Bonds or a former beloved sitcom regular reputed to have made hundreds of millions from his decade-long run were eager to take a season-long arc on our show. None of them, as I saw it, were The Bick. But The Bick of our room had long since decoupled from The Bick of the world, and perhaps only I saw the irony of casting these variations of masculine standards of attractiveness versus the man I knew would soon be hospitalized, only I could appreciate the perfection of the incongruity.

We hadn't broken the whole season yet, but no matter: scripts had to be written because at some point, production had to begin. There was in the room a steady but never stated tension among the writers as to who would be assigned which of the dozen scripts to write. The season premiers and finales would be written by The Show Runner, some episodes would be cowritten with The Show Runner, some written individually by individual writers, some cowritten by pairs of writers. Some of us had in our contracts minimums of one, two, or three for the season, with the attendant script and production fees that could in a good year double our income. I had a guarantee for only one, which was fine, as I didn't actually want to write any and certainly didn't want to write the second episode, as I was aware that my own drug intake, while it made the room bearable and frequently pleasant, could cloud the judgment required to manufacture interesting scenes out of, say, our leading man speaking to his wife about an impending visit by an electrician. I was dreading having to write any scenes, and as if sensing my reluctance and hesitance, and with his unerring instinct as to who wanted something the least, The Show Runner assigned to me episode 2, the one where The Bick would be developed and firmly introduced as this season's villain.

But The Bick was dying. Indeed they had opened him up and, as if returning an ill-fitting pair of shoes to Zappos, they closed him and sent him to do whatever the opposite of recovering was in a hospital room he shared with an Asian man who never spoke and who was also plainly waiting to die. He was, in his way, a role model for how to die, as he did so with a gasping dignity.

The extent of the metastasis, The Bick told me, was such that there was almost more tumor than there was Bick. His excessive use of narcotic painkillers, it had turned out, had been driven by genuine pain. He'd truly been self-medicating, and now, on a fentanyl drip, he didn't feel any intoxication at all, but just a mild suppression of his considerable discomfort. The drugs, they don't actually numb the pain, The Bick advised, they just allow you to sort of walk around it in your thoughts and keep moving past it. But it's there, it's always there.

The Bick could cut through the Hippocratic euphemism if he had wanted too, but instead, he empathized with his own doctors' plight at having to state the obvious: there was no prognosis beyond the one we all share, only The Bick was dying much faster than the rest of us. How long? Would he make it to the end of the college basketball season? The end of the NBA regular season? The first round of the playoffs? The Finals, apparently, were out of the question.

Without his hair product, his dyed brown hair fell into a moptop descending from a bald pate, a patch of shiny scalp reflecting the fluorescent institutional light. Caspar, when I brought him to see The Bick, was most affected by the sight of The Bick's follicles flagging and drooping, like a pennant in dead calm. Like most teenagers in our modern era, Caspar had no experience with death beyond attending the funeral of my ex-wife's mother, a ceremony in a Brooklyn synagogue, his grandmother embalmed and encased in a pine box. Death transformed into a sort of giant wooden lozenge. But here was The Bick, reeking of it, his piss beside him gathered in the white plastic hand-held urinal, a vaguely fecal scent emanating from his body.

185

But The Bick wasn't dying fast enough, or at least not fast enough for his insurance company to keep paying and so, in the kind of perfectly ironic gesture at which unfeeling bureaucracies excel, he was moved to a rehabilitation center where, in theory, he could work on recovering some of the range of motion he had lost in his weeks of hospitalization. The assignment was the result of a practical need to send The Bick somewhere, and home hospice was out of the question as there was no one to manage his care. I was his roommate and required to be at my employment most of the day.

So he would die in a facility in theory dedicated to reinvigoration, where nurses were accredited to push the huge doses of pain medication The Bick required but which were never enough to really dull the pain, especially as the large tumors were deemed to be spreading to his brain, causing a rapid onset hydrocephalus, cerebrospinal fluid gathering in the fissures between skull and brain, causing unremitting pain, and a steady decline in verbal and motor function. The vibrant, vivacious Bick was reduced to mouthing his words like a wino three bottles in, and we all knew The Bick could hold his liquor almost as well as his opioids.

And so to me fell the onerous task. The Bick, always so verbally adroit and quantitatively facile—able to calculate the precise sum that could be taken off the table on a dime bet after two wins of a three-team parlay with the third team an eight-point dog or a +220 on the moneyline—was losing both his speech and his hearing. And soon, he would lose his eyesight, and this was just the beginning of how bad the ending would be.

He told me where the drugs were, the 750 milligrams of liquid hydromorphone that would propel him straight through tachyphylaxis and raise his blood serum opioid levels, when combined with the narcotics the nurses were dispensing, to a fatal dose. All I had to do, The Bick explained, was bring in the liquid and the syringe. He had both. I was to open the valve on his catheter line, and push the whole barrel full, reload, and push again. He'd feel his lethal dose first as a sparkle and crackle in the back of his neck, and then, nothing.

The Bick was surprisingly generous to Caspar in his will, though upon his passing, a number of putative descendants of The Bick emerged to challenge his testament. I left the battle to my ex-wife, as I was busy looking for somewhere to live, and all I really cared about were his narcotics, the pharmaceutical bottles of pain killers that I cleaned out as soon as I got back to the apartment. For a while, I lived in a hotel in Santa Monica, and then I moved to a cheaper one in Culver City, closer to the studio. After work, I supplemented the oxycodone and hydromorphone with hotel bar rye whiskeys. My lifestyle was cutting into my gambling, and despite it being the middle of the NBA playoffs, I could barely muster the interest to even study the lines.

If there is any small poetry to television writing, I believe it comes in the first draft, when the writer retires to wherever he or she does the dark work and expands an outline into full scenes, imagines the actual words that will be spoken to advance the story, and perhaps, in that small space in which to be creative, something totally new and original might be invented. It happens, not as often as it should but more often than one might imagine in the regimented and highly collaborative world of scripted television. Then, it is the job of the other writers in the room to rip it apart, and The Show Runner to angrily question every single decision the writer made while he or she was in solitude facing blank pages.

But, as I said, that is just my belief. I wouldn't know as I myself have never produced anything that might be close to poetry when writing for television—or any medium.

I wrote episode 2, and The Show Runner found it notably lacking. He said my depictions of The Bick were soft, melodramatic, that the villain of season six shouldn't be a kindly old man with a sparkle in his eye but a ruthless and manipulative corporate titan, a cunt who would, in the course of the year, murder his rivals to win control of the criminal enterprise. What I gave him, The Show Runner told me in several closed-door meetings in which he systematically and zealously, scene by scene, deconstructed my failure, was shit. I understood The Show Runner's plight. I actually empathized. Because in the end, whatever wound up on the screen, it was either his fault or his glory. The rest of us, the writers in the room, we were only valuable in so far as we made possible the latter. But when we fucked up, as I clearly had, it was no different from a stunt coordinator miscalculating the physics on a car crash or a sound editor getting the audio levels wrong on the one good take of a climactic scene, the resulting fix, the CGI wreck or the over-dubbed actors' voices, would never be quite as good as nailing it the first time. As I said, if there was any poetry to making a television show, fucking up a script so profoundly and totally as I had, and forcing The Show Runner to do a total rewrite, well, I had killed that and was leaving us with just another episode of just another season of just another television show.

To sum up: I am not making any moral stand about our portrayal of The Bick. I had just fucked up.

And The Show Runner went off and rewrote my every word. He was remarkably generous in giving me half a credit.

Oh, and he changed The Bick to a woman. We cast an Oscar-winning actress in her sixties.

I finished the season in a kind of stupor, and then, with the room broken after we'd table-read episode 12, I flew myself up to a rehab center near Bend, Oregon, where I detoxed in a room next to a guy in a wheelchair who had to ring an attendant to come and wipe him whenever he took a shit.

I cleaned up, spent a day in a Twelve Step meeting and thought, Fuck this, this was worse than being in a room of TV writers. But addiction technology had evolved in the decades since my more youthful drug escapades. There were new drugs marketed by the big pharmaceutical companies that took you down gently, Suboxone and that whole family of opioid blockers than in themselves provided a mushy high, a medically approved addiction to replace the illegal one. Who was I to reject the soft option? My WGA health insurance plan provided generous coverage for all forms of addiction recovery.

Three months later, just as staffing season was upon us, I made an informed and educated decision to quit the Suboxone, waited a harrowing forty-eight hours and then was back on the hard stuff. I joined a different show, this one on a subscription service, at a higher title for even more money, and I took my place in the room with a different show runner and different writers and played the game again, with similar desperation to please this new show runner and familiar panicked insecurity about the entire process.

So I went nowhere, gained nothing, didn't change or improve my being or consciousness in any way, and certainly didn't learn a damn thing from The Bick's dying. Caspar ended up with an eighth of the proceeds of the sale of a six-unit apartment building in Palms, after back taxes and estate taxes, enough for a couple of years of college. I'll pay the rest.

It's the least I can do. I haven't seen him in nine months. His mother believes the hotel I'm living in near MacArthur Park, closer to the sources of my synthetic opioids, is not a good environment for a growing boy. But he's almost eighteen, I reason, he's gotten what I have to offer, which isn't shit. As for you, I don't have any wisdom to impart. And with so many great shows on TV, why are you even reading this?

*Nominated by Zyzzyva, Ethan Chatagneir, H. E. Francis, Sandra Leong*

# A SEASON IN HELL WITH RIMBAUD

## by DUSTIN PEARSON

from FJORDS REVIEW

I dreamt I was showing my brother around in Hell.
We started inside the house.
Everything was brown besides the white sheets
in the bedrooms. I let him look
outside the windows, told him it was hottest there,
where the flames rolled against the glass,
as if a giant mouth were blowing them,
as if there were thousands caught in the storm,
pushing it onward with mindless running,
save a desperation for something else.
How had there been a house in Hell
and we invited with time to spend? Why was it
I hadn't questioned how I got there? My brother
growing so tired from the heat, the sweating?
*Surely we could open the door*, he said. *Surely there'll be
a breeze.* Even seeing already, even burning himself
on the doorknob. His eyes turned back in his head
working his way to the bedrooms, staining
the sheets with his blistered hands, and though I knew the beds
weren't for the rest of any body, I sat by and let him sleep.

*Nominated by Fjords Review, Christopher Citro*

# THE LONELY RURALIST

## by JANISSE RAY

from THE GEORGIA REVIEW

*Reinhabitation was my dream. But in rural America there's a chasm between what is real and what is myth.*

I lived my entire life to arrive on the farm. Ten years ago this quiet, quiet place had everything I wanted. I loved the heartpine house so much I would kiss its walls, as if it were a shrine, and blurt out loud, *I love you, house.* I was smitten with farming and the idea of farming, using the old way and the new way, neither of which is the corporate way. The climate was unraveling, and to be able to provide basic needs seemed smart. We could grow food, build soil, learn essential skills, capture carbon, and maybe help restore a landscape.

It was all a dream until it wasn't.

The farm was situated on a dirt road in what had once been a thriving community. Altamaha, Georgia, had a river landing and a sawmill, a post office and a school. It had a church built in 1868, during the evangelistic fervor that followed the Civil War. A few homes are left, five or six in a square mile, depending on how you draw the square, and the church still stands, with four members and services the first Sunday afternoon of the month. There's nothing else in Altamaha.

In our county Archives downtown, I found a 1916 picture of Altamaha School, now vanished: about forty children were lined up in the yard to have their photograph taken.

The rural emptied out, fell apart.

When people departed Altamaha, they took the quilting bees, barn-raisings, hay-mowings, syrup-makings, and peanut-boilings of rural

Georgia society in the early- to mid-twentieth century. They took the lowing and bleating of farm life, the beating of hooves on red clay. They took the fiddles and mouth harps. My neighbors, the last of the old guard, spool out their lives in these home-places, too old to square-dance or raise beams. In our ten years here Ben died, Leta Mac died, Howard died, Lynease died, Bill died, John had a stroke.

Almost every day on our farm, therefore, is a day with three people in it—myself, my husband, and our teenage daughter. I have seen days in which no car passed.


"May I talk to you a minute?" I ask my husband.

He takes off headphones. "What?"

"Are you at a stopping point? I'm wondering if I can talk to you?"

"Sure." He lays down the headphones and shuts the computer, completely present. His eyes are green like chlorophyll. Is this what I am craving, this being-seen-ness?

"I just find myself so lonely," I say. "I feel it almost all the time."

My husband glances back at his computer.

"I don't know what to do about it," I say. I start to cry.

He steps toward me and puts two muscled, working, handsome arms around me. He doesn't say anything. I want him to say something.

"I'm just lonesome. I spend most of my time alone. In truth, I feel like the most lonesome woman in the world. I'm sorry," I say. "I try to be self-contained."

I remember the loneliest morning one spring—oxymoron though that concept may be: a morning in spring should never be lonely. The mockingbirds were not lonely; they had each other, as did the rain crows, which had returned to find the tree leaves a tender green and the redbuds blooming.

I stood at the kitchen sink, glancing up from the day's dishes now and then to gaze into the pecan orchard. Any sort of movement attracted me—a bird, a leaf, a limb. I was reminded of a line in a poem by Patricia Waters, about farm people "driven by loneliness to see the one moving thing on their horizon." Out the window that particular morning the last of the white camellias offered no solace. Beyond them I could see the grove of large pecans, a congregation of live oaks across the pasture, and marching along the ancient, empty road some myrtle and haw and wild persimmon. Each tree was mute, silent, and possibly feeling its own form of loneliness. My loneliness went on and on like a fog.

191

We judge our aliveness by our relationships with others, I thought, in that we may experience a kind of death, a mini-death, unless we can see and be seen by others. If we are lonely we may as well be dead.


Attaching is one of the things we humans do extraordinarily well. We learn it early—in the womb, actually. We are attached to our mothers. Then we begin to attach to others, throwing out strings here and there like spiders. The incessant need to attach comes so naturally to humans that the only way it can be destroyed is if we have it scared out of us or beaten out of us.

I was born enmeshed in a wide net. I had a good mother and father and three siblings with whom I spent day and night. I lived in a town where seven generations of my family had lived. My white family attended a black church. I was taught to help relieve the suffering of others, to think of others, to share with others. Being from the rural South and of a certain age, I was taught to have manners—and manners meant you had to affiliate with people. The population of my hometown was 3,500, and a trip to the post office meant I'd see multiple people I recognized. I was expected not simply to *recognize* them, but to *know* things about them—their names, their histories, their jobs, their children, their sorrows. I was expected to remember what I learned.

In return, I was known by them.

After I grew up, I lived in towns and cities where the unremitting business of my life was connecting. In Brattleboro, Vermont, my husband and son made a game of guessing at the front door of the food co-op how many people inside I would know. I couldn't run in and grab a loaf of bread.

During the time I was away from the rural, we humans reached a landmark: for the first time in history, over half of the people in the world lived in cities. In the United States, the demography was even more marked—over 80 percent were city dwellers.

Then I moved back to rural America.


My loneliness is nothing new, I told myself. Plenty of people live far from community. They find animals. They find libraries and books on tape, radio and the internet. They find religion. They find all the things that make a person more resilient. They find themselves.

Remember, I told myself, human community is being battered in many ways. There's a father's mind pocked with holes, a brother's alcoholism, a neighbor's trauma, a buddy's opioid addiction, a friend's illness, a town's racism, a region's storm, a landscape's industrialization, a climate's coming undone. Most of us have erected glass walls around ourselves as we hide behind our technological devices, so much so that social scientists say we're in an "epidemic of loneliness." Plus, a part of loneliness is universal, existential, irreparable.

Think about cities, where people can be found. They have their drugs, their diseases, their violence, their rat races, their homeless and downtrodden, their anonymities. People have forever experienced a tension between city and country, and many can't live long in either. Look at E. B. White, Marjorie Rawlings, George Sand. Look at Thoreau, who couldn't stay out with the wild ducks forever.

Community means relationships, the people you know. Community is like an atom. In its nucleus are beloved kinfolk and dear friends. Beyond that are loops strung with people, loops for church, clubs, school, jobs. "In my circle of friends," we say, or "part of my sphere." The circles are not concentric, but elliptic, meaning their orbits cross, collide, tangle.

Of course, these rings depend on geography—people have to live within a certain distance, because too far and they're not your community. And the rings depend on shared interests. In the rural, as we replaced small farms with large farms, we took away the jobs. We took away the people. The people who were left were more dispersed in terms of geography and like interests. So if the people who are beekeepers or krautmakers or brewers live at such distance that seeing them more than once or twice a year is difficult, then do they exist? If they live online, do they exist?

After I'd lived at the farm about six years, I found myself traveling in rural Ohio. One afternoon I stopped at an Amish farm for apples. What I was looking for was an answer to a question that hounds me, which is how to live well in rural America.

Because it was late winter, nothing stirred in the modest farmyard or at the windows of the white clapboard farmhouse, although some distance away horses in a sere field cropped sprigs of dry grass. The silence was dense, almost impenetrable, and very familiar.

When I eased open a barn door marked "Store," a young man about twenty-eight or thirty looked up. He wore simple dark clothes and a black felt hat with a brim. He carefully bent, laid down some mechanism, and smiled. His eyes were clear as green marbles.

"I saw your sign for apples," I said.

"What we have left are there." He nodded toward a raised bin. "Plus vinegar." His voice sounded creaky.

Light streamed into the barn from a brace of windows, through which I could see the horses intent on the meager February meadow. I could see that this man had a beautiful life, a life I wanted—a life I *had*. How did he manage it?

"Looks like we'll get some snow," he said, pleasantly.

"I've heard it's a blizzard."

"Well," he said. The thing the man had been working on was spread out around a pot-bellied stove, which was not lit, and he seemed in no hurry to return to tinkering. In fact, he seemed to need something from me, too. Maybe it was my money—but I thought not. I rested my hand lightly on a spill of apples. One bin said McIntosh and the other Golden Delicious.

"What are you working on there, if you don't mind me asking?"

"It's a sheep-shearer," he said. "I'm trying to get ready for shearing."

"Your own sheep?"

"Yes. And I shear for the neighbors."

I hoisted a paper bag of McIntosh. "The horses?" I said.

One was a mare his father gave him when he turned sixteen. He had ridden her too hard, racing other boys. Now she was lame but he couldn't bear turning her over to the meat buyers.

I chose a gallon of vinegar and brought my items to the counter. The man totted up slowly. I told him I lived on a farm in southern Georgia, a long way from Ada, Ohio.

"What do you grow?" he asked.

"Mostly for ourselves," I said, and I listed some things. I told him we had acquired a couple of horses, that I was new to them.

"I've been around them all my life," he said. For ten minutes we stood talking about horses.

"What's your name?" I asked. "If you don't mind me asking."

"I don't mind." There was that smile again. "I'm Amos."

As Amos spoke, and as I spoke, our words in the vast silence of the hushed landscape wove something. They were like tendrils of mycelium, a delicate fiber, lacing together to make sentences, looping into an invisible network that began to fill the unlit barn. Our small and amiable conversation was a loom that, if we kept talking, seemed as though

194

it could produce enough loose webbing to engulf the whole of that countryside.

The rural problem isn't only that the people have vanished. The pastoral is often beautiful and nostalgic, but that's not the only truth about it. It is also depopulated, made depauperate, debased, destroyed, and, most tragically of all, dulled and dimmed. As the body seeks companionship, so does the mind.

A town twenty miles from our farm holds an annual Sweet Onion Festival with a Saturday morning parade. The three of us went. Shriners came through in go-carts, dressed like hillbillies, spitting tobacco juice on the fly. The high-school marching band moved languidly past, their missed notes flying off like startled sparrows. The mayor pasted a little sign on the side of his car and rode by, waving. A bunch of churches filled hay trailers with kids.

Later, at home, I tried to remember one cultured, far-thinking, progressive part of the parade: What had we learned? What had spoken to our values? What had made us proud?

"We should have entered a library float," my husband said.

"Anything," I said. "Even a sign that said, READ A BOOK, IT MAKES YOU SMARTER."

A hundred years ago, when the educated class was better educated and when more of us stayed where we were born, a person in the countryside could experience erudition: scholars of arts and letters, imagination and idea; talented people engaging in culture and civilization. Rural intellectualism was alive and well—admittedly among the white male elite for the most part, but not exclusively. We had black intellectualism, female intellectualism, poor intellectualism, even uneducated intellectualism.

Where I live, most people now have one foot firmly planted in the Baptist church and the other in the Tea Party, which usually means that they have found everything they need. They get what news they obtain from the most conservative sources. Most don't have a college education, often not even a high-school diploma.

We have been replacing real, live, interesting, and clever people with ghosts.

Too often I get the heart-flopping news that another friend is leaving the hinterlands, and by this I mean anywhere within an hour's drive of our farm. Larry and Cindy are filing for divorce and selling their permaculture fruit-tree haven. Phyllis is buying a place outside Athens, three hours to the north. John and Giana are talking about Asheville, North Carolina. Other friends leave for Savannah. Or Floyd. Or Amherst. Or Boulder, where they will smoke pot without going to jail, where plenty of hip people are starting nonprofits, doing yoga, practicing their art, and having meaningful conversations about subjects that matter.

One day I found myself in Eastpoint, an Atlanta neighborhood, to record an audiobook. As I was leaving the studio I noticed signs for a farmers market. When I reached it, vendors lined either side of a crowded greenspace selling not just milk, bread, and meat but mulberry sodas, chestnuts, morels, and fresh vegetables. A New Age bluegrass band honked and jammed down by the street. My old pal Robby Astrove recognized me. He was one of the market organizers and after a big hug he asked if I wanted a tour of all the cool stuff they were doing. "Back there's the community garden," he said. "We're planting a community orchard here—fig, persimmon. We're trying to plant native fruits too. This is serviceberry. Here is an edible hedge of blueberry, sumac, and elderberry. Those herb beds are open to the neighborhood."

Kids dashed around among the trees and beds, playing.

"Isn't this kid-tastic?" Robby said, grinning.

The whole enterprise seemed imminently civilized, progressive, intellectual, colorful, open-minded. Who wouldn't want to live among that beautiful circus? Later someone would remind me that Eastpoint had been 80 percent African American in 2000, before gentrification, reminding me that demography is fluid and that most of us seek some kind of community where we feel at home, where we are home, a fact that does not diminish the anguish any one of us may feel over losing our place.

Back home, I watched the cows in the pasture. Emma, our oldest, was an orphan and my husband and I raised her from a calf. Her own calf, Zinn, was born without trouble, and now Zinn is grown and has birthed a tiny, brown, doe-eyed grand-calf. My daughter and I discovered the newborn not even two hours old, a mound on the ground. To use the word "tan" would not do justice to the shining sepia-hued velvet of this baby. Her lashes were long and fluttery as black butterflies.

"Let's let them be," I said. As we went about our afternoon, we kept an eye on the cows. When Zinn felt strong enough to rejoin the herd, she presented her tan calf first to her mother. That was Emma, the grandmother. Emma touched Zinn's nose with her own and commenced to licking the beautiful calf. The calf stood trembly-legged. Over the next few hours Zinn slowly introduced her calf to the other fifteen cows in the herd. I felt grateful to witness that.

Cow society or not, Facebook or not, I needed people. To that end, therefore, at least part of my daily life became an engagement with creating community. I organized countless events, from full-moon potlucks to organic conferences to clothing exchanges to cheese-making workshops, from readings to concerts to harvest festivals.

People came—usually from Savannah, the closest city—nostalgic and hungry for a country life.

And then they went—back to their homes far from mine.

One night I dreamed an amazing dream.

Altamaha, Georgia, was thriving again. It had a tavern in John Sanders's useless barn. People gathered every Thursday evening to make wood-fired-oven pizza, and this was my first night going. I was trying to get my bicycle down to my neighbor Leta Mac's house, to return something, and after many thwarted attempts I arrived at the tavern. I was surprised at the number of interesting, colorful people, not a crowd by any means but a strong gathering of folks who looked like me: down-to-earth, free-thinking, outside-the-box people with long hair, long skirts, and denim jeans, sitting among the potted flowers and herbs. Fire burned in the clay oven, pizza coming out.

Across the road from the tavern was a large meadow, and the man who kept it mowed and looking beautiful had invited a choir to sing, a youth choir from a church. Metal folding chairs were faced so that people could look at the meadow while they listened to the children. The choir was dressed in emerald robes, brighter than the green grass.

In the dream I was deliriously happy. For days to come the memory of it would bring tears to my eyes as I, alone, planted running butter-beans in the warming ground.

Weeks and months and years passed on our farm in Altamaha, Georgia, which had been a ghost-community before we arrived and which will probably stay dead forever. Gradually something changed. More

197

and more the memories of and the desires for the trappings of society fell away—and by "trappings" I mean the sidewalks, the telephones, the holidays, the expectations, the schools, the fashions, the newspapers, the advertisements, the readings, the parties, the window-shopping. I sank, as so many others in the empty corners of the earth have done, into seasons, weather, birdlife and animal society, breath, my own company.

Rural people can self-actualize, even in the vacancy and the vacuum, and this sense of self-actualization derives from the relationships we *do* have in the rural, relationships with ourselves, with our beloveds, with our places, with art and ideas, with our sense of what some might experience as the divine and others might experience as the essential. After a while, anything that was not this quiet, deliberate, even transcendental consciousness felt dead to me.

Community is attachment. Much of what people suffer is caused by disattachment. In hollowed-out places, disattachment looks different than it does in populated places. Rural loneliness can look impenetrable, dark, roadless, like a thicket. It can look like a wall. So the attachment must look different, too, maybe something like a meadow or a gate. A bell, a nest, a wood.


Any night now, lying in bed, I see the gray shadows of the camellias outside the open window hanging with clumps of wispy moss in the moonlight. A night bird makes a sudden call. It sounds like a wren, or maybe it is a mockingbird mimicking a wren.

This could be community enough.

The facts have not changed: We need each other. We live longer and are healthier in community. Ultimately our evolution is communal whether we like it or not—friend and foreigner, comrade and foe. I would still choose to stand in an apple barn with a friendly stranger, creating a temporary, fragile, amorphous connection, something that bound his existence to mine, and I would hesitate to break that web. I would hear the threads popping behind me as I left, and I would carry the memory of the stranger with me.

But something did change, with the transformation taking years: where I was, and *that* I was, became enough, I think. Owls screeching, crows cawing, mare in heat whinnying her displeasure. Strip of pink sunrise across the sepia orchard with its pecans bare-limbed, line of seven deer running across the pasture as if it's the Serengeti. Golden webs of orb weavers, last bloom of the Prosperity rose, rickrack of a snake's passage basted in the sand of the road.

To all of that I am deeply attached.

Maybe some of my story is a map, some a warning, some an invitation. Maybe some is breath, me breathing as wind flutters strands of Spanish moss hanging from crepe myrtle: *I am. This is me.*

I have learned at least this much: in the twenty-first century, as human beings face the growing necessity for sustainable living, rural life is a challenge. If a person wants to live far from the madding crowds, with roosters crowing and hawks overhead, with forests and meadows and rivers, helping to create a more ecologically oriented and thus more sane society, she or he will have to reckon with what life is *really* like in the country.

One morning my daughter and I walked to the barn to get horse leads. Skye noticed that Sojourner, our oldest ewe, was missing from the flock. Sojourner was pregnant and had not lambed with the other five ewes, whose singles and twins bounced around the pasture. When we checked, we found Sojourner ensconced in a stall, bedded down with two newborns, their umbilical cords dangling wet and bloody.

We brought feed and sat in the hay near Sojourner. I leaned against the old gray planks of the stall, picked up her smaller lamb, an umber girl with a white face and a snow-tipped tail, and I cradled her in my arms. Tired from her first hour, the lamb relaxed, her head falling against my chest; I've known loaves of bread that weighed more than she did.

I breathed in the smell of hay, of sheep droppings, of lanolin, of birth, of old wood. Through the bars of the stall the other sheep watched me, their eyes level.

I could hear them breathing.

*Nominated by The Georgia Review, Camille Dungy*

# CHARLIE

## fiction by COLLEEN O'BRIEN

from THE GETTYSBURG REVIEW

I'm a little mystified when I hear about people who are friends with their college professors. They exist, these people, who correspond regularly with scholars decades older than they are, some famous in their fields. As students, they celebrated Thanksgiving at these professors' houses, house-sat for them whole summers, took care of their pets, their lawns, their kids. Years after graduation they invite them to their weddings.

How did these friendships form, I want to know. In college, as soon as class ended, I stuffed my books in my bag and got out of the lecture hall as fast as I could, assuming everyone else was doing the same. I never once went to office hours. People who loved office hours either had parents who were professors or were anxious about grades and wanted to ingratiate themselves, a personality type that disgusts me.

I was tipsily monologuing on this once, when a friend interrupted to say she'd always gone to office hours because she paid for her own college and wanted to get everything she could out of it. She wasn't trying to shame me, I don't think, but she did want me to shut the fuck up. My parents paid for my college, and I should be ashamed because I treated this like it meant nothing.

I treated my body this way also, if that matters. I was the girl with puke down her dress the guy would send his buddy in to see after he'd had his turn. Back then it was important to me to show the world—a world certainly not paying attention—that I didn't give a fuck. This friend, the one who called me out, understood that enough to pity me, not hate me completely. But we haven't stayed close.

200

I'd been a precocious kid, queen of standardized tests. I ripped through elementary and high school hungry and angry, like, Is that all you got? Private school, Chicago. My parents and stepparents—all divorced by the day I graduated high school—were a doctor, two lawyers, and a management consultant. All four spoke constantly of scarcity, of stock market and real estate losses, precarity of bonuses, malpractice insurance. Tuition, Jesus Christ, the tuition. Once, checking out of a ski lodge in Steamboat, Colorado, my father turned to me and said, "You think it's nothing, don't you? Like everyone gets this, it's a God-given right. Look at this. Look."

He showed me the printed hotel bill, dot matrix strips down two sides of the paper. I was ten. The hotel had cost four thousand dollars for the week.

"That's just the rooms," he said. "Not the food, not the car. Not the thousand other things."

"Thank you," I said.

"You don't mean that," he said. "You're not grateful."

He was right.

The way envy works—I read this in *Scientific American Mind* at the orthodontist's office in eighth grade, and it stuck with me always—the way envy works, you want as much of the envied thing as you can get, and whatever you can't get, you want to ruin. My mother and stepmother envied me for being a kid, no wrinkles, no cellulite, so they fixated on my prominent canine teeth, my acne, my eyebrows that grew together in the middle. No wonder I didn't have a boyfriend, they said. Most of the time I spent with them was at a salon or specialist, having hair ripped out or ironed flat, pimples injected with cortisone. We met once with a plastic surgeon I now see as one of the most responsible adults in my life, who told my stepmother my nose was still growing, it'd be a waste of money to do it now.

He looked at me with an expression I couldn't name. A combination of sadness and hope, telegraphing that the world was huge, life was long, that someday I'd be far away from these people.

Or I pretended he did. Sometimes I laugh at this fantasy and think this man probably had a daughter who disgusted him as much as I disgusted my parents.

So I'm a type, you know the type. You know the fun part: These parents of the violent caste are rarely around. From their unmonitored wallets I could steal a hundred dollars at a time. In their large, empty houses I could drink to blackout, have sex or masturbate for hours, cry at myself in the mirror. An older boy from another high school came over once and opened a package of prosciutto from my mother's fridge. He dangled a pink fatty piece in the air over his open mouth, but then changed his mind and draped it on my bare shoulder, beside the strap of my tank top.

"Ha, ha," I said. The meat was cold.

He peeled off a second piece and placed it on my other shoulder.

I'm thirty-eight now, married, have a kid, and I still masturbate thinking about this scene. In the fantasy, he pulls the straps of my tank top down over my arms, making sure the prosciutto doesn't fall off, pulls the tank top down and leaves it bunched around my waist. Then he pulls down my strapless bra and looks greedily at my nipples, which back then were soft and undefined. He puts a slice of prosciutto on one breast, then the other, and I loop the scene in my head—shoulder, shoulder, breast, breast—until I come.

In real life, he didn't pull down my tank top. Instead he opened the fridge again, and I remember clearly the contained smile that crossed his face when he got his next idea. He took out a pint of half and half.

"Can I pour this over your head?" he asked.

"Sure," I said.

I remember thinking he wouldn't really do it and also knowing for sure he would. He folded back the wings of the paper spout.


There was one professor I stayed in touch with after college. My last quarter of senior year, I did an independent study because my friend who paid for her own college said I'd be stupid not to, it was the only way to get a letter. Until she said it, I had no notion of needing letters and at first thought "get a letter" was a Briticism for "get a good grade"— this friend had studied abroad and come back full of Briticisms. She marveled at rich kids, how we never thought ahead.

"My parents aren't rich," I said, because if there was one idea they'd beat into me it was that.

"How much do they make?" she asked.

"I don't know."

"Uh huh," she said.

She was right, of course, that I never thought ahead. That past summer, I'd blacked out and fucked some guy who somehow found my email address and wrote to tell me he had HIV. I deleted his email, blocked him, and spent the rest of the day researching suicide methods, then cleared the cache on my mother's computer, which she yelled at me for later because it deleted all her passwords.

I got tested and was negative, but the nurse at Planned Parenthood said I had to retest in three months. For three months, I spent most of my time immersed in suicide fantasies. I had a summer job making copies for an estate planner my mom knew from law school, and on breaks, I'd walk to Walgreens and stand in the pest control section, reading the copy on packages of rat poison, calculating how much larger a human was than a rat, how many poisoned biscuits I could ingest before vomiting. In three months, I tested negative again and wondered if the guy who emailed me had done it as a prank.

Anyway, my last quarter of college, in a late-breaking surge of entitlement, I emailed a creative writing professor and asked if she'd do an independent study with me. She said no, she was too busy, but then wrote again saying she'd found someone who would.

His name was Charlie. For ten weeks we met alone in his office, the door partly open. He read my short stories, full of long passages of dialogue between people screaming at each other about child support. In ballpoint in the margins, he wrote questions I knew were meant to be neutral but felt deeply personal—"What's the narrator's reaction here?"; "Should we have more of the daughter's presence?" Reading his questions moved me, which I knew was out of proportion, and I was often afraid to speak because I might start crying.

Who Charlie was, I barely noticed. He was on a one-year fellowship at the college, not technically a professor. He emailed me once to reschedule our meeting so he could fly to Nevada for a job interview, adding that he'd sure never pictured himself in Nevada. I asked no questions about this, including how it went or whether he got the job.

Based on a few things he mentioned, I calculated he was the same age as my father. I deemed it preferable to be my father—clean fingernails, good posture, the slightly starved look of a dedicated runner. Charlie was heavier, shaggier, much less carefully dressed. He had knee problems I had no idea what to say about, which he often brought up at the start of our meetings. At least twice he confused me with another student, who was apparently very into *The Sopranos*, then explained what was happening with the show's plot, apologizing but insisting it was important stuff for a writer to know. I waited, shy, almost mute, till it was time to talk about my writing.

Shortly before graduation, I ran into my worst ex at a bar off campus. I said hi, he said I looked like a whore, and I threw a drink in his face.

Back in my room that night, quite drunk, I composed an email to Charlie describing the scene: Rum and Coke dripping down my ex's nose and chin, the little chip of ice that stuck in the neck of his T-shirt. His pathetic outrage, his friends dragging him away. "You need to leave," one of them said to me, and I just stared at him, thinking how much I wanted to try the palm strike I'd learned in women's self-defense, a hard jab up from below that would supposedly break his nose. But all I did was stare, I said in my email to Charlie, and he backed the fuck off. I didn't leave. I ordered another drink, and the bartender said if those guys bothered me again let him know, and furthermore, I did not fuck the bartender. I hadn't fucked anyone in months.

Even drunk, I didn't send the email. I signed off, "Going insane but feeling incredible," then cut and pasted it into a Word doc and deleted it from my email account.

A year or so later, I asked Charlie for a letter of recommendation for grad school. This was back when schools required paper letters, with signatures across the envelopes' seals, and as requested, Charlie sent me three. His return address was in Nevada.

I was living in San Francisco with Craigslist roommates, one who'd talked to me for hours in the kitchen one night after she had an abortion, who then moved out and I never saw again. My job was tutoring at a for-profit center for rich kids with learning disabilities. The kids criticized my accent and complexion, and spelled out *cock* and *cunt* with the alphabet tiles, openly curious what it would take to make me tattle. I didn't drink on the job but had an airplane bottle of vodka in my backpack for the bus ride home each night, a small funnel to refill it. Charlie's signature on the letters made me sentimental. It felt like a long time since I'd seen that handwriting.

I'd abandoned the idea of applying to grad school, so I slid my finger under the flap of one of the envelopes. The letter was nice. Between its lines I read true things: that I was talented but a little lost, that just a small amount of support would benefit me greatly. No one wanted to deal with someone like that, I knew. But Charlie meant well, and I wasn't offended.

A few weeks later, I stopped in a bookstore on my way home from work. I hadn't been inside a bookstore in a long time. Fifty milliliters of vodka wasn't much—most nights riding the bus I barely noticed a buzz—but walking into the store I felt it. The lights were too bright, and I seemed to be moving faster than intended, gliding instead of taking individual steps. Impulses to do destructive things, like bite the books' smooth covers and leave teeth marks, kept floating up, delighting me and filling me with paranoia.

I found a rack of literary magazines and selected one to browse, laughing at myself for trying to pass as a casual reader of literary magazines. There, in the table of contents, I saw Charlie's name.

I read his story ready to be disappointed, to find him a boring, vain, middle-aged man. That was not what I found. I read the whole thing standing there, leaning on the magazine rack.

It was good. I don't want to summarize it. I was an idiot back then but was capable of real feelings. I don't have to prove that to anyone.

✻   ✻   ✻

A couple years later, Charlie emailed to say he'd be in San Francisco for a few days and wondered if he could buy me a beer.

I was living with a man named Todd. He'd grown up in Alabama and saw this as something we had in common, both refugees from the Great Flyover. Chicago wasn't much like Alabama, I told him earnestly, and he laughed and said no, of course. He was ten years older—I was twenty-five, he was thirty-five—and understood the world much better. His mother had died when he was in college, and the grandmother who'd helped raise him had died more recently, leaving him a small trust. It wasn't enough to live on forever, he said, but for now it kept him out of a cubicle.

His father, who'd evaded child support when Todd was a kid, was well-off now, remarried with two stepdaughters. They lived in the suburbs of Atlanta and were—Todd glanced theatrically from side to side, then lowered his voice to say the word—"Republicans." Once a year his dad flew them all, including Todd, to Grand Cayman for a week, to pet stingrays and eat rum cake and avoid talking politics. "You might get to go too," Todd said to me. "If you're good."

Not long after we started dating, I said some insecure thing about how he'd probably decide I was frivolous and vapid, and he said the problem with women his age was they were mostly really bitter about men. Hearing this made me giddy with relief. It wasn't the compliment I'd been fishing for, of course. It was misogynist, and it made me feel less guilty about the two times I'd blacked out and had sex with other people. But it suggested my value was higher than I'd known, that he might not just be using me to kill time between real relationships.

I needed him badly. Even before I moved in, I slept at his apartment every night. The rare nights we spent apart I felt like I was going crazy, and to tamp down the craziness, I got drunk. Twice, I left mortifying messages on his answering machine. After that, any time I planned to drink alone, I hid my phone in an old purse on a high shelf in my closet.

All of this probably sounds horrible, but Todd was mostly very good to me, good for me. We went on hikes. We read *Harper's* in bed and saw arthouse movies and had a lot of sex, both of us always into it. When I got Charlie's email, I was using Todd's computer, sitting cross-legged at his desk in just my underpants while he made morning coffee.

"Aw," I said, as he set a cup in front of me. "My old professor."

He leaned over and kissed each of my breasts. "You look so sexy like that," he said.

"He's going to be in town," I continued.

Todd turned the swivel chair so I was facing him and got on his knees so he could kiss my belly, slide my underwear down, give me head. Then he stood me up, bent me over his desk, and fucked me from behind. I stared into the multicolored fractals of his screensaver, the outline of my reflection in the black behind it.

"He's a really good writer," I said later, clothed, drinking coffee at the tiny folding table in the corner of his studio.

"You're going to hang out?"

"Yeah, it'll be fun. I haven't seen him in so long."

Todd moved around the kitchenette, just out of view from where I sat. I could hear him pour cereal into a bowl, open and close the refrigerator twice to take out and replace the milk. Then he came around the narrow wall that separated the kitchenette from the rest of the room and set the cereal in front of me.

"That's great," he said.

He was never jealous. At the beginning of our relationship, I worried he would be and overexplained every male or lesbian friend. I told him how my college ex had read my diary and broken into my email, waited for me outside classrooms so he could scream at me about imaginary cheating. Real cheating also, but I didn't say that to Todd.

"Sugar," Todd had said, "I'm a grownup."

My mother had been a year younger than Todd, I calculated, when she and my stepfather screamed at each other the entire two-hour drive from Inverness to some medieval Scottish castle about a restaurant receipt, a comment his sister-in-law had made, accusations about their architect—a blond woman named Karen who'd come to dinner several times—and counteraccusations about my mother's divorce lawyer,

Marty, whose voice I knew from answering the house phone. I rode in back of the rental car, staring out the window at green hills, stone fences, sheep. ". . . would spread your legs anywhere," my stepfather said, and my mother lunged at him, and he shoved her against the passenger-side window, splitting her lip so that when she faced him again, her teeth and chin were smeared with blood. These details were still bright in my memory. It was the day after my eleventh birthday.

"Do you want to meet him?" I asked Todd. He'd joined me at the table, with his own coffee mug and cereal bowl. The table was so small two cups and bowls were all that fit.

"Maybe," he said, taking a bite of cereal.

"I don't really know him."

"But you like his work?"

"This one piece."

It was the loneliness in that story, the vivid, articulate loneliness, I'd been so moved by. I couldn't say that without sounding like a naive kid, romanticizing the loneliness of a self-absorbed academic. But I wasn't. There are a few things in my life I don't have to laugh at scornfully, and this is one. Anyway, the story wasn't about Charlie.

"What's it about?" Todd asked.

At some point, I'd made the mistake of trying to describe the story to a different guy, a friend's boyfriend who was in a PhD program, at some party. "See, the problem with American fiction," he'd said and then talked for a long time. "Is that fair?" he asked when he was done.

Right then I remembered I'd once thrown a drink in someone's face, and the memory made me burst out laughing.

"What?" the guy asked.

I couldn't stop. My nose started running, and I cried, "Holy shit," and wiped my nose with my wrist, my eyes with my fingers.

"You're really drunk," he said.

"It's hard to explain," I said to Todd now.

"Give me the basic plot."

He leaned over his bowl to take another bite of cereal. His hair, dirty blond and fine, stuck up in cowlicks all over his head, reminding me of a little kid. He had crow's feet, and his lower teeth slumped to one side, so many years past being straightened. But bent over his bowl, in T-shirt and undies, he was like a large eight-year-old.

"What?" he asked, looking up.

"You're cute," I said.

207

He smiled. The crow's feet, the teeth. Patchy blond stubble on cheeks that were slightly deflated. You don't even have a job, I felt like saying, in a sweet voice, like the sweet girlfriend I was supposed to be.

"Thanks, sugar," he said.

✻   ✻   ✻

Charlie suggested a bar in North Beach, down an alley across from City Lights. It was a classic, he said, which Todd always said about places in San Francisco too.

Before I left work, I stopped in the bathroom to drink my tiny amount of vodka, brush my teeth, curl my eyelashes. I put my hair up, then took it down, put it up, took it down. I wanted to seem healthy, like I was doing well. Up, my hair looked a little greasy, holding the grooves where I combed it with my fingers, but down it was ratty, needed a trim.

It took me a minute to find the bar, its door shadowed by a fire escape directly above. Inside it was dim and nostalgic, plain wood tables, kitschy seafaring decor. Charlie was sitting at a table by the wall, a full pint of beer in front of him.

"Long time, no see," he said when I sat down.

His hair, which was still mostly black, had a little more white than I remembered, or maybe the white was easier to see because his hair was cut much shorter. He seemed to have lost weight too, and it occurred to me he cared more what the world thought of him than I'd always assumed. His voice was the same, though. Hearing it made me happy. It was weird, and good, to see him.

He got up to get me a beer—I said I'd have whatever he was having—and when he left the table, my excitement started to veer toward panic, as I realized I had no idea what to say to him. He hobbled a little walking to the bar, and I remembered his knee problems, but then thought it'd be awkward to ask about that. As he walked back, carrying my beer, I stared at the brick wall by our table, which was dense with framed photos, news clippings, display cases full of ephemera. We could talk about anything. The main thing was not to get too drunk.

He set the pint glass in front of me. "So how's writing?" he asked.

I blushed, then sat through the anxious aftermath of blushing, struggling, as blood drained out of my head, to be able to speak. He looked away for a second, as if something in the bar had caught his attention, and this left me with no doubt he'd seen me blush. I must have seemed young, ingenuous, possibly cutesy, none of which I wanted to seem.

"It's okay," I said over the alarm-like monotone sounding in my ears.

No one at that time in my life asked about my writing. I'd mentioned it to Todd when we first started dating, but now if he brought it up, I felt like he was mocking me. But when Charlie asked, it was like he was giving me a compliment, and with my embarrassment I felt an outsized, soaring happiness that embarrassed me also.

"Good," he said, turning back to me like nothing had happened. "That means you're doing it."

"Well, sort of," I said.

"Right," he said. "I know all about sort of."

Then he talked for a while, like he used to in his office, about self-doubt and patience, how it was fine to be neurotic as long as it didn't stop you from working. His first year in Nevada, he didn't write at all, he said, but it felt good. It was the first time in his life he hadn't beat him himself up every day.

"I'm not kidding about every day," he said, looking directly at me.

"I know," I said.

"Every fucking day," he said. "No one should do that to themselves. Not even for art."

The last part seemed to be a joke, so I laughed, then drank what I was surprised to see was the last of my beer.

"But what if you feel terrible either way?" I asked. "Terrible but at least you're writing, or terrible and you're not even doing that."

"Right, it's a dilemma." He finished his beer quickly, seeing mine was empty. "You want another?"

I said I'd get the next round, but he wouldn't let me. He got up, and I sat alone again, staring at the framed things on the wall. A restored photo of longshoremen on strike, stern faced, wearing hats and smoking pipes. An old ad for women's face cream with the slogan "Unite against a common enemy," a beautiful young woman squaring off against a haggard one. I felt wonderful. The beer had calmed me down but hadn't made me drunk, and I loved what Charlie was saying and that he was saying it to me.

"I read a story of yours," I said halfway through the second beer.

"Uh oh," he said. "Which one?"

I told him the title, said how it was the first time I'd ever picked up a literary magazine. "I loved it," I said and then had to look down.

"I'm glad," he said.

I gathered myself to look up again, and when I did, Charlie looked down, and I could see I'd made him happy.

"That character," I said.

209

"That poor guy," he said. "I didn't have to make him such a creep."

"No, he's perfect," I said, and I must have been starting to get drunk because I added, "It's exactly what loneliness does to you."

"Sure. To some people."

"Sorry, that sounds weird."

"Don't be sorry," he said. "But I do want to say—that character." He scooted his chair a little closer to the table. "I mean, he isn't me."

"Oh, no, I know," I said.

"I mean, I didn't—" He shook his head, his face serious. "I didn't rape anyone."

"No, of course."

"Always a great day when you have to say that, right?"

I smiled. "I knew he wasn't you."

"Okay, phew."

He drank to the bottom of his beer, then pointed at mine, which had only an inch left. "Are we having one more? Or calling it a night?"

"One more," I said. "I'll let my boyfriend know I'll be late."

I'd gotten rid of my cell phone when I moved in with Todd, paranoid that having one aligned me with the rich tech people he hated who were driving up rents, ruining the city. There was a pay phone back by the bathrooms, and when I picked up the heavy black receiver, I saw there was a condom stretched over the speaking end. It was unused, an anonymous joke I felt obliged to laugh at. I rolled the condom off the phone and carried it between my thumb and finger to the women's bathroom, where I dropped it in the trash and washed my hands. Then I needed to pee, and as I squatted above the toilet, the condom having made me germophobic, I thought about Charlie's story.

The character right away is bitter and defensive, addressing the world as if he knows its tricks and won't be taken in. He deals with loneliness and social awkwardness by trying to sanctify his solitude, like some kind of monk, when really he's a guy with a cube job, a crush on a coworker, who watches a ton of TV. He knows this too—the cube, the crush, the TV embarrass him, as do his fantasies about solitude, which, when he comes out of them, he calls pathetic.

Reading it had felt like reading about myself. The anger, which had no end, and the worthless ways I tried to give it dignity.

I wiped and flushed and thought of Charlie telling me he hadn't raped anyone. I washed my hands again. In the mirror I was much prettier now than before the beer.

I promised myself I wouldn't say anything else about the story. The woman the character rapes is someone who likes him, who thinks he's just shy and that she can coax him out of his shell. They go on a date and afterward, back at her place, she wants to have sex with him. But it's pity, and when he turns violent, it's like he's saying, Here's what I think of your pity.

I put quarters in the pay phone. The receiver smelled like latex—so stupid—and I was careful to hold it away from my mouth.

"Hey, sugar," I said when Todd answered.

"There was a condom on the pay phone," I said to Charlie, back at the table.

"Whoa," he said.

"Would it be okay," I asked, when the third and fourth beers were empty, "if I kissed you?"

Besides the bed, desk, and table in Todd's apartment, there was a futon folded into a couch. When I got home that night, I flung myself onto it, fully clothed, and passed out. I woke before dawn, rigid with panic, and got in the shower to stop my heart from racing. When I got out, Todd was up making coffee.

"Rough night?" he asked.

I left for work early and on my way to the bus stopped at a pay phone so I could call Charlie's hotel. He answered on the first ring and quickly apologized for keeping me out so late. I asked him if anything had happened.

"Oh," he said. "You don't remember."

We'd made out in front of the bar, then went to another bar, bummed cigarettes from these goth kids, a detail that allowed him to chuckle, though I could tell he was nervous. Anyway, then he put me in a cab. "You got home okay?" he asked, and I said yes. I didn't ask what "made out" meant—probably it was minor, and anyway I couldn't change it now. I said I should really quit drinking. He said he should too.

A few days later, I got on the computer in the break room at work and looked up Greyhound schedules to Nevada. The ride was ten hours. There'd be desert billboards, rest stop vending machines—for ten hours, loneliness would feel romantic. But I knew I wouldn't go. At best, I'd be an interesting nuisance, interrupting his work, running up his phone bill. We'd go out to eat and people would think he was my father, inverting what happened sometimes when I was with my real father and people thought I was his girlfriend. After a while, it'd feel textbook and embarrassing, and I'd lash out at him because of that. At worst, he'd say he didn't mind.

I told Todd I was thinking of moving out. He said he understood—I was young, in a different place in life. He said I could take my time, look for a place, assess how I felt at the end of the month. I didn't mean we had to break up, I said, though that was what I'd meant originally. He shocked me by starting to cry, and I hugged him and said I still loved him. I thought about his dead mom, how he never talked about her, and said I wanted to quit drinking. He said he'd help me. Then, a few weeks later, I went out for a coworker's birthday and didn't come home at all.

After that, Todd cut me out completely. I had panic attacks for a few months, but gradually they stopped.

At some point during those months, Charlie sent me a long email. He said he was thinking about me and hoped I was doing well. Writing was going slowly, as always, but he was doing it. He hoped I was too.

Then he said he realized I didn't know much about him, and if it was okay, he wanted to fill me in a little. He used to be a really shy person, afraid to open up to people, and he was trying to do that more, open up.

His dad had walked out when he was three. His mom was a great person—he was amazed sometimes, thinking how hard she'd worked, holding down two jobs and taking care of him and his older brother, who weren't easy kids. His brother especially. Most of the email was about his brother, who'd beat up on him relentlessly the long hours their mother wasn't home.

"It's not uncommon," Charlie wrote. "Kids have nowhere to put their anger." He was still in touch with his brother, but it was hard to be close with him.

Anyway, he hoped it was okay to tell me that. He felt, for whatever reason, he should.

I was crashing with a coworker who was touchy about me using her computer, so I went to the public library to email Charlie back. There was a clock at the bottom of the screen that counted down the thirty minutes allowed for personal internet use. I reread Charlie's email slowly, then clicked reply.

"Dear Charlie," I typed. "I understand."

Then I stared at the screen until the clock ran out.

Charlie wrote to me once more after that, just checking in, he said. For months I planned to write back—Sorry it's taken so long!—and then too much time passed, and I thought if I wrote now, he'd tell me to fuck off, or that I didn't care about anyone but myself, or that I was too shallow to connect with anyone in a meaningful way. I thought all kinds of awful, true things he could say and about how I'd respond, whether I'd fight back or tell him he was right or just block him. I also knew none of this made any sense. If I'd written back, what was much more likely was Charlie would've be nice to me. Then a bunch of other things happened, and I stopped thinking about it.

About a year ago, I googled Charlie and saw he was coming to Chicago to give a reading. I'd moved back before I had my kid, wanting to be closer to family, but both my parents ended up moving out West when they retired.

Charlie had changed his author photo and was completely gray now, with new, boxy glasses that looked good on him. I planned to go to the reading but ended up getting in a huge fight with my husband and slamming out of the house without my purse. There was a fourth-step meeting we sometimes went to at the Unitarian church on Damen, so I walked over and caught the second half, got updated on everyone's shitty bosses and exes and health problems. When it was my turn, I just said I was grateful to be there, which is what you say when you're late and don't really deserve a turn.

Then I tried to walk to Charlie's reading. It was sixty blocks south and would have taken hours, but I walked that direction anyway, until I knew I was being stupid and turned around.

Maybe six months later, I googled him again and saw that he'd died. The funeral had been in Reno. He was sixty-three, survived by a brother. The obituary didn't give a cause of death.

I was home with my son, who was napping in my bed. Charlie died, I thought. He'd *died*. The fact of it filled me with a strange, bewildered lightness. If I met up with him now, over coffee instead of beer, the first thing I'd say is, "I can't believe you died!" and he'd laugh and say, "I know. What the fuck?" There was no one else I could tell, and I didn't mind knowing that. There are so many things you can't tell anyone, and that's just the truth, not a tragedy.

My son would be up soon. I was good with him. *Am* good with him. I did wish I could tell Charlie that, that I'd gotten my shit together to be good at that at least. My son wants me with him all the time. He's only three and can already write his name.

*Nominated by The Gettysburg Review*

# OBJECT LESSON

## by CLAIRE SCHWARTZ

from POETRY

You learn to recognize beauty by its frame.
In the gilded hall, in the gilded frame, her milky neck

extended as she peers over the drawn bath. A target,
a study, a lesson: she requires you

to be beautiful. You should save her, no matter the price.
No matter the price, the Collector will take it. His collection
　　makes him

good, when he lends the woman's image
to the museum, where schoolchildren stand

before it, anointed with lessons in color and feeling. *Pay
attention*, the teacher scolds the fidgeter in back. *Bad,*

the child whose movement calls to her own beauty, the child
whose wails insist his mother is most beautiful of all. *Eyes this way,*

the teacher syrups. All that grows, rots. Good little stillnesses,
guardians-to-be. If you are good, one day

an embossed invitation will arrive at the door of the house
you own. You will sit next to the Collector, light.

chattering along the chandeliers, your napkin shaped like a swan.
To protect your silk, you snap its neck with flourish. The blood,
   beautiful,

reddening your cheeks as you slip into the chair drawn just for you.
   *Sit*, the chair says
to the patron. *Stand*, to the guard. The guard shifts on blistered
   feet. *She loves you,*

*she loves you not.* The children pluck the daisy bald,
discard their little suns in the gutter.

*Nominated by Poetry*

# AUNT JOB

## fiction by NICKALUS RUPERT

from THE IDAHO REVIEW

From their exalted seats in the front of the car, Mom and Dad glare at me in a way that reminds me I'm one of *those* kids. Oversensitive. Scared of what shouldn't cause scare: grasshoppers, Spanish moss, clover honey. Dad likes to say my microphone's turned up too high—I'm picking up signals that aren't even there. He's been talking like this ever since he won his settlement against Norah Jones for allegedly stealing his lyrics.

"I'll give *church* another try," I say.

"You're such a baby," Megon, my younger sister tells me. She leans to my side of the back seat and swabs the inside of my ear with a wet finger.

"Dude," Dad says, "we've been over this." He uses a red light to give me a you've-made-me-take-my-eyes-off-the-road look."It's only a hand job. It's not like you have to sleep in Aunt Elyse's bed. It's not like you have to take her to dinner at Cracker Barrel and buy her a bag of fucking jellybeans from the gift shop."

I lean forward, so that my head enters the front-seat airspace. "Hand to God," I tell them, "I'll clean my room and Megon's for the next three months. I'll even clean Justice's terrarium. Just don't make me do it."

Next, it's Mom's turn to swivel and bitch. "So tired of hearing about this," she says. "You're worried about *receiving* a hand job? I have to jerk off all three of your cousins when they turn fourteen. Can you imagine—those three staph factories? I'll probably get warts." She's talking about her own side of the family—the ones we only see at Christmas because they're so woodsy.

Mom and Dad return to arguing over the lyrics of a Toto song on the radio. It's Sunday night, so we're heading out to eat with my aunt and

216

uncle, and lyrical disputes are part of the ritual. Mom and Dad were still teenagers when I was squirted into existence. Sometimes they seem more like roommates than parents. Dad says, "They're definitely saying, 'kiss.'"

Megon fires up *Peasant Slayer IV* on her phone. I watch as she raises a healthy, peaceful population of peasants on beets and sweet corn. Then, she spawns herself as the dragon that melts them down to skeletons—bone children wringing the hands of their bone parents. Sometimes I wonder about Megon.

"Why only the boys?" I ask Dad. "You going to let Unc Carl finger Megon when she turns fourteen next year? Have you thought about that?"

"Enough, you little perv," Dad says. "We didn't make the rules."

How am I the only one who finds the rules insane? Boys get one mandatory hand job from a maternal aunt to make sure their plumbing doesn't get backed up. Otherwise, they'll supposedly turn into violent, horny little maniacs.

"Do teenage boys need any help *expressing* themselves?" Mom asks no one in particular.

"Some do," Dad pipes in. "Think of it as a safety net."

And that's when I start slamming my head against the back of Dad's seat.

"Honey," Mom tells me, "you're being all dark and broody again. Remember when you tried to tell us that *Jaws* was really about communism?"

"How about the time he tried to calculate our annual carbon emissions?" Megon says.

Dad cuts off the Toto. "Be grateful," he says. "Your aunt's hands are small. Should've seen my Aunt Midge. Hands like lunchboxes. Looked like she was yanking on a tube of Chapstick."

"Let's not blame the poor woman's hands," Mom says. She clicks her green-sparkle nails against the radio's dial. "And it's definitely 'bless,' by the way."

The light changes. We lurch forward and no one cares. No one gets that the hand job is only Part A of the problem. Part B: tradition won't be enough for Aunt Elyse. My aunt plays to the balcony, no matter what. Every December she used to force Unc Carl to dress like Santa and crawl down the chimney pants-less so they could fuck beside the tree. It's Aunt Elyse's fault that he shattered his legs and pelvis so bad they now count each successful screw as a surprise victory. What worries me most is that Aunt Elyse might try to *kiss* me afterward. My birthday is

Tuesday, and God help me, I do not want my pantsuit-wearing aunt to be my first.

We land a table near the punk rock section of Hard Rock Café—Dad's favorite. He's been trying to get on the waitstaff for years, just for shits. The owners have thrown some new swag on the walls, and Dad can't stop mooning at Green Day's touring gear. Some drums, a few guitars, all items hung in a way that makes them seem like yard-sale trash.

"Couldn't they afford something from The Misfits?" I say.

"You sour little hipster," Dad says, standing to get a closer look at the suspended instruments. He checks to make sure no waiters are looking and then plucks a guitar string.

Before long, Aunt Elyse and Unc Carl show up. Unc recruits two mohawked waiters to help drag him and his prosthetic legs up the stairs, which move like actual piano keys, releasing the melody to Journey's "Faithfully." With each prosthetic step, my aunt winces. She's wearing her finest burgundy pantsuit—the one with the velvet buttons—and before she sits, she beelines for yours truly and bends down for some face-to-face.

"Two more days and I make you a man," she says, licking her painted lips. Then, she lets loose her patented explosive gasp, as if she can't believe what just flew from her mouth. She kisses her pointer finger and touches my nose, then she retires to the adult end of the table.

Megon takes a break from roasting peasants. "You're fucked," she whispers. "So glad I'm not a boy. If I had to get fingered by Unc I'd douche with kerosene and light a match." Megon still hasn't forgiven me for accidentally killing Siddhartha, Justice's cage mate.

Dad's feeling sporty tonight, so he orders a batch of Hot Hot Horsies for the table. They're part of a new and controversial line of appetizers designed using so much genetic modification that Dad has to sign a waiver. The discussion moves to my day of reckoning. Mom has ordered a cake in the shape of Aunt Elyse's hand. Aunt Elyse boasts that she's been practicing her twist-and-stroke to the point that Unc can take no more. She pats Unc's prosthetic thigh, which rings like bell bronze. Then, she bares her right arm and flexes. Despite Aunt Elyse's curvy figure, her arm is way more cut than mine.

"Your aunt's a goddamn maestro," Unc says, pointing at me for attention. "You're in for an adventure, little man, and I've got the friction burns to prove it."

Mom and Dad nearly fall from their chairs. Dad high-fives Unc just as the waiter arrives with our horsies. They're penned in a kind of wire basket, whinnying in terror. Our mohawked waiter pops open the little wire door and out they step. They're served raw, their heaving flanks crusty with dry rub. According to the waiter, their bones are mostly cartilage. Say what you will about Hard Rock, but their appetizers are unforgettable.

"They should've thrown these guys back," Dad says. "They're supposed to be rat-sized. These are hardly in the mouse range."

Unc's polishing his fork, no interest in Dad's complaint. He and Aunt Elyse can't afford to be picky eaters—not on her bank teller's pay. Unc grips the nearest horsie and dips it into a batch of Hot Rock Sauce, then he snaps off the head with his front teeth. There's something tacky about that saucepot, something that sinks my appetite. Spooked, the remaining horsies gallop toward my and Megon's end of the table. Adults make hasty grabs at the runaways. Dad's not the greatest musician, but he's quick-handed and manages to catch most of them, or at least knock them too senseless to flee. Two of the loosies end up near me and Megon. They tremble, seeking shelter. Megon grabs the nearest and chomps it unsauced without looking up. I stuff the remaining horsie into my shirt pocket. I'll eat it later, with ranch dressing.

Aunt Elyse makes a big show of getting her horsie's head neck deep into her throat before she chomps. Afterward, she does another comedic gasp and slaps the table. Her horsie's hindlegs are still kicking.

All dinner long, my aunt throws bawdy winks my way.


After the Blondie documentary finally wraps up, Dad knocks on my bedroom door. He wants to know if I'd like to play Legos, and, if not, would I mind if he played? I let him in and tell him where to find the bricks. Most of my finished sets are still intact, but Dad likes to dig through the slush boxes. He lies on his belly and builds, making laser noises with his mouth while the horsie in my pocket stirs and dozes. Dad ends up with a kind of cowboy space station—light swords and cacti and rancher-astronaut pilots.

*"Dad doesn't get it,"* Dad says, pitching his voice high. *"How could he possibly understand why I don't want my aunt to whack me off in front of the whole family?"* He winks. "Am I right?"

Dad hauls himself upright and moves to my bed. He holds an Old West spaceman between thumb and forefinger. For a moment it looks like he might carry it back to the box, but instead, he shoves it deep into the pocket of his jeans and sits beside me.

"Aunts have become a kind of sexual starter kit," he says. "It's the way of things."

"It's disgusting."

"Dude," he says, "I get it. You're in the right. I've been thinking about what you said, too. About Megon getting fingered by Unc Carl. It's fucking gross, which stands to reason why your aunt getting you off is almost equally terrible. *But*," he says, "Elyse needs this. She needs to feel like she's part of the family. She needs to know she's not a total fuck-up. We all deserve that,"

He notices the bulge in my shirt pocket, the tiny hoof shapes. We were out of ranch dressing.

"Son," he says, knuckling my shoulder with affection. "Did you pocket a Hot Hot Horsie?"

"I wasn't hungry for it," I say.

Dad's eyes swim. He smiles like a fiend.

"Let's put it in Justice's cage," he says. "See if they fight." Pocket-sized and bipedal, Justice and Siddhartha were supposed to be a joint venture between me and Megon—the latest in underground lizard breeding. One week, I fed Sid too many of the wrong kind of grub worm. Sid's bowels inflated and his skin grayed. After he went belly-up, the terrarium moved to Megon's room for good.

"Maybe later," I tell Dad.

"Come on. Let's do it."

"Not right now, Dad."

"Please?" Dad nudges my pocket, watches the horsie's shape stir and settle. I roll onto my back. In the dark of my pocket, a pair of glossy eyes. Fuck Justice. Justice can keep eating geckoes and crickets.

Dad lies on his back so he can toss and catch his Lego man. "I always wanted to be one of those cool rocker dads," he says, "but I guess what you really needed was a brainy dad. I know I can be pretty stupid, and I know life is a constant disappointment." Dad catches me rolling my eyes. "Point is," he says, "I do have some advice for you."

I pat my pocket to soothe the trembling horsie.

"Fake it," Dad says. "Let her work you over for a while and then fake a—" He coughs into his hand. "Fake an orgasm." First time he's said that word to me. We both blush.

"She'll notice, Dad. She'll be looking for evidence. She might even hold it up for the world to see. Proof of my manhood."

"She'll just assume your nuts haven't dropped all the way. Are you shooting the monkey juice already? Can't remember when that starts happening. Anyway, think it over. It worked for me. I couldn't have finished for Aunt Midge if I'd wanted to."

Dad leaves without picking up the Legos. I spend a few minutes sorting out his mess, then I pull my Amazonian Adventure playset from the closet, blow off the dust, and place the horsie inside. The horsie watches me from the faux jungle and shakes out its mane. Large eyes for such a tiny thing.

I head out front, past Mom and Dad's weedy lot. I pick some fresh grass from the finest, greenest patch on the neighbor's lawn. I fall asleep watching the horsie chew.


Monday morning, the horsie and I wake with runny noses. I arrange another plug of grass and a bottle-top full of fresh water in the terrarium. The little animal keeps rearing onto its hind legs and showing off its little horsie rod. I lie on my side and let him trot around the top of my bed, where wrinkled sheets become jumpable moguls. The horsie seems to enjoy showing off. When he gets tired, he climbs into my shirt pocket and falls asleep with his hooves hanging out. They'll never let me own another pet, but if they did I'd name him Earley.

At the breakfast table, Megon shoots me dirty looks over the screen of her phone.

"You stink like meat seasoning," she says.

"Sweating off last night's dinner," I say.

"But that's the thing," she says. "*You* never ate your horsie."

"I ate it last night. You were in your room, burning peasants."

Then, it's time for Dad to drop us off at school, and even Megon can't complain about how I smell over the pot fog that rides with him. For the entirety of the trip he grins, driving with one knee so that he can dance-drive to the latest shoe-gazer album. He keeps his right arm draped over Megon's shoulder. His left hand stays speared through the window, where it becomes an airplane wing.

"Love you fuckers," he says, just before our doors slam shut.

Mom and Dad haven't packed my or Megon's lunch in years. Dad usually gives us both a fiver for pizza under the stipulation that we don't tell Mom. Once he's gone, Mom sneaks into frame and gives us another five with the same stipulation.

Because I'm desperate, at lunch I invest in a slice of pepperoni and take a seat next to Arnie Fincter, who turned fourteen before the rest of us on account of getting held back. Arnie sits alone, near the vending machines. His incoming mustache and formidable nest of pubes should make him popular, but his social stock plummeted horribly in August when it came to light that he'd gotten himself off with the hand of a palsied kid at a weekend sleepover. Word 'round the campfire is that he's currently doing Mrs. Bellwether, the hunchbacked chemistry teacher.

"I'm not doing Mrs. Bellwether," Arnie says. "Let's go ahead and clear that up." He finishes the cheesy part of the slice in three bites, then he starts mopping up bright pepperoni grease with the crust. Arnie's not easy to look at. He doesn't tend to his acne as well as I do, and the artillery range on his chin appears ready to fire. "As for the hand job," he says, "there's no escaping it, but so what? Your aunt rubs your dick and you become a man. Eat some cake, have some laughs, maybe someone gives you a new sweater. Is your aunt diseased at all?"

I tell him no. I keep thinking about Earley, all by himself in the plastic forest.

"Well, mine was born without thumbs," he says. "Felt pretty wild." Arnie sneers, mustache grease-bright.

"What about Jerry's hand?" I say. "Did you use his thumb or did you want it to feel more like your aunt?" This is what I've seen people do in the wild—people with lots of friends. They create trust by mocking one another. Strange, but it works.

"Listen," he says, "I'm only talking to you because you bought me off. I'm not the one who bawled during *Lord of the Rings*. You're just wrong. Wrong all the way down."

"That was last year," I say. Even for Arnie this is low. My eyes may have watered but only because Gandalf's fall was so well shot. "Did your aunt try to kiss you afterward?" I ask.

Apparently bored, Arnie drags a finger through the waxed pizza paper and licks. "Maybe on the cheek." Then, he seems to remember his angle. "I might remember more if you buy me another slice. Why aren't you having one, anyway?"

It's not the money part that gives me pause. I could buy him an entire pie with all the lunch money I've squirreled away, but I can't stand to watch him, and I certainly can't stand to eat anything. My stomach's in turmoil. It's Arnie but really it's me. We're all too angular these days— our expanding bodies, our exploding faces, Arnie's mustache. Whatever this thing is, we can't seem to outrun it.

Behind us, in the part of the lunchroom where the elite gather, Katie Marcuso sits within a ring of admirers. Not that she's perfect. She still suffers the odd pimple (look closely, you'll see them piling up beneath a film of makeup). No doubt she's confused like me and Arnie, it's just that she seems to fit so well inside of her awkwardness. I watch as she plucks the vegetables—tomato, pickle, lettuce—from her home-made sandwich and stacks them on her lunch bag. Katie wears braces. You can tell what she had for lunch by what's netted in the wires. In the dark of her mouth, they flicker like star fields.

As usual, Megon beats me home. She's got a friend whose sister drives a Kia. I've got the bus. After confirming that Megon has eaten the last pack of Cheddar Puffs, I head to my room to find the plastic jungle graced with a pile of grassy droppings but no horsie. Only now do I think about how low the retaining wall actually is. I search under my bed, in the closet, in the laundry hamper, then under the bed again. My face is skimming dust bunnies when Mom reels through the door.

"You looking for your Fleshlight?" she says. "Don't forget to rinse that sucker off after you use it."

"Jesus, Mom. I don't have one of those."

I sit on the floor with my back to the bedframe. Once she's in, she'll stay till you've agreed to whatever she needs. Mom grabs the magnetic putty from my desk and falls backward onto the bed. She likes to knead out putty shapes while we talk. Last week, a giraffe whose head would swing when she ran the magnet past it. Through the wall, I can hear Megon calling Justice's name. Feeding time. Of course. *Justice.* I can't find Earley because Earley's not here. He's been abducted.

"Let's get down to brass tacks," Mom says. "If you let me live broadcast, I swear on your father's life we'll take you to Mariachi's next week instead of Hard Rock. We'll shoot you from the neck up, of course. Nothing indecent."

"I will burn this place to the ground and piss on the brass tacks."

"Honey, dial down the theatrics. Your Nana wants to watch, and you know how she is with road trips. Besides, yours is no special case. You think your guy friends won't get posted, too?"

Through the wall, Megon squeals with delight. Something spectacular's going on in there. To be rid of Mom, I say yes to all of it. Video, live Tweets, cat-face filters. The whole circus. When Mom's finally gone, I head to Megon's room and shoulder my way inside until the safety chain tears from her wall.

"Pervert!" she screams. She's got Justice's terrarium on her bed and she's lying on her pillow to peer inside. "What if I'd been masturbating?"

"You weren't," I say, "because you're even more repressed than me. You're also a dirty horse thief."

"Grow up," Megon says. "You're the pet killer."

And then I start to sort of pre-cry because it's unfair for Megon to call me that name now that she's fed Earley to her ungodly lizard. We've seen Justice disembowel field mice and eat them while they're still twitching. We've also seen her bite through their hamstrings and wait in the corner for the slow bleed.

"You should take a look," Megon whispers. She smiles and beckons, my heartless sister.

But when I peek in, Earley is still very much alive. In fact, the lizard has turned away from Earley, who has maneuvered around the lizard's tail and mounted up, so that he, too, stands upright. Earley's hips buck. His little horsie rod grows a pink extension that probes beneath the lizard's tail. When Earley notices me watching he lets out a high whinny. Justice flicks her tongue, same reptile scowl as always. Megon films it all in high definition. Afterward, the animals retire to opposite corners, Earley wobbly at the knees.

"This is pretty awful," Megon says, shaking her phone. "It'll get tons of views. Did I mention I'm being paid to film your little incest ritual tomorrow night?"

I brush Earley's mane with my fingers.

"I'll pay you to botch the shot," I say. "Name your price."

"Wish I could," she says, "but you can't hang with Mom and Dad's checkbook. They've got that Norah money."

"That Norah money won't last forever."

I head to my room, a new kind of betrayal boiling my heart. Megon has substituted spite for something more upsetting: cold practicality. Later that night, she delivers an exhausted Earley to my room and says I've learned my lesson.

After homework, I spend a few minutes whispering hate into Earley's jungle. *Traitor. Pervert. Lizard-fucker.* I tell him I should starve him. I tell him I should've drowned him in Hot Rock Sauce and eaten him hooves-first. Earley keeps pawing at the plastic loam, watching me with those unblinking eyes.

Awash in shame and sweat, I barely sleep. When I dream, it's visions of cackling cocktail-party heads and callous-fingered hand jobs gone viral.


I wake to Earley's glossy eyes, the soft rhythm of his chewing. There's some kind of goop running from the corner of his mouth, and I have to fight off a wave of nausea. Otherwise, he appears hopeful and refreshed, and I don't have it in me to hate him. I let him run laps around my bed. I brush his mane with my toothbrush until it's nice and glossy. Afterward, I put him back in his jungle, but he keeps clicking his hooves against the fence and staring at me with those doofy eyes.

"You can't come to *school*," I say, but Earley has already decided.

At breakfast, Dad eats a green apple instead of his usual bowl of Crunch Berry, and I know something's up.

"If I seem uptight," he says later, in the car, "it's because your mother's *serious* about coming home to a spotless house." He reaches into the back seat and frogs my knee. "Let's just say I lobbied pretty hard for you last night," he hisses. "Lobbied hard and *lost*. At least your end of the bargain's over in thirty seconds. *I* have to get a job."

Dad forgets to hand out our lunch money. We don't even get one of his affectionate curses.

Once I'm free of the car, I move Earley from my backpack to my shirt pocket, which makes both of us more comfortable. I don't give a damn who notices the bulge. With Earley, the world shifts into softer focus. I relax. No time left for anticipation, no more cowering in the shadow of the axe. For the first time in a long time, dread stands in a neutral corner. I tickle my shirt pocket until Earley stirs and whinnies. I am weak, but Earley is strong. He survived a hungry table at the Hard Rock Café. He seduced Justice, the murder-lizard. I can't avoid what's coming tonight, but there's still time to get my first kiss.

At lunch, I strut to the middle of the cafeteria and sit across from Katie Marcuso. My presence causes a few sneers and a great deal of eye rolling, but they don't tell me to leave. Before long, one of Katie's friends lets slip that today's my big day. Kids manage to sniff these things out, even when it concerns bottom-feeders like me.

"I bet you're nervous," Katie says. Food bits hang from her mouth wires. Strawberry seeds, apple skin.

"It's only a hand job," I say. "No biggie."

On the table, a pile of stripped-off sandwich debris. I pat my shirt pocket for luck, then I coolly pick up a discarded tomato slice and eat it without retching. Earley gives me a light kick for encouragement, so I wink at Katie. I'm going to be a *man*, after all. She can't help but be impressed.

"But it's your aunt," Katie says. "What if she wants you to shove it in her mouth? You're so weird you'd probably like that. What if you fall in love with her and you die a gross loser who no one wants to marry?"

My throat fills with hot glue, but my hands are steady as I pick up a discarded pickle.

"It's all perfectly normal," I say, pocket-patting. "I'm becoming a man. You can still be my first kiss if you want. There's still time."

And that gets them shrieking with laughter. One girl asks why I keep fondling my pocket.

"What's he got in there?" another asks. "Is that a turd?"

And that's when Earley pops his horsie head through the top of the pocket and barfs green stuff down the front of my shirt. Katie and her admirers scream and retch, and with good reason. Earley's mane is matted, and his eyes bug from their sockets. Apparently, these horsies are not bred to last. Plus, maybe I've patted too hard.

"What *is* that?" someone shrieks.

By this time, some of the teachers are starting to look in our direction. You can get suspended for bringing animals to school. Earley fires off a loud whinny, his eyes locked on Katie's. He wants to crawl from my pocket and go to her.

Katie and her posse flee to Arnie Fincter's table, where they can point me out and clue him in. Before long, Arnie's laughing harder than the rest.

"His only friend is an appetizer," Arnie calls.

Earley's hooves keep milling. He wants to ditch me, and the teachers are trying to get a better view of me and whatever wrong thing I'm doing. They were right all along. What's wrong with me is wrong down deep— all the way to the jelly inside my cells. I grin at Katie and her table. I wave. I'm ready now, ready for Aunt Elyse. I want it over with. I tell Earley I'm ready, even though he knows. Oh, he knows.


The adults gather in the kitchen, where, beside a hand-shaped cake, Mom has brewed up a punchbowl of red sangria that Megon and I aren't allowed to drink. Fine with me. Earley and I haven't felt great since lunch. He's still barfing green. My insides are sizzling, and I keep burping up the flavor of rot.

For the first time since I've known her, Aunt Elyse has chosen something other than a pantsuit. She wears cut-off shorts that put her creamy thighs on full display. Her shirt's some kind of low-cut white number, and at the neck there's a red felt target that makes a bullseye right be-

226

low her chest. She's also wearing a pair of novelty safety goggles like you see in science labs. I've never heard Mom laugh so hard.

"You believe this shit?" I ask Earley, but Earley's gone quiet. My stomach hisses. It makes the high keening noise of a doomed whale. I'm sweating again, and now there's dizziness.

Mom has fixed up a kind of fabric blind that rides at crotch level in front of our plastic-wrapped couch. The family will be able to see the legs and upper halves of me and Aunt Elyse but none of the dirty business. My aunt and I take our seats.

"You okay, handsome?" Aunt Elyse whispers. "You look a little green."

She invites me to pick one of the half-dozen bottles of lube she's brought along. I don't know the difference, so I grab the fruit-scented one with microbeads and some kind of self-warming feature.

"Same brand his father likes," Mom boasts.

"That's my boy!" Dad says. Unc begins to applaud. Behind them stands Megon, the world's saddest documentarian.

"I'm very proud of you," my aunt whispers. She tries her best to smile.

Aunt Elyse works open my fly and I help her slide down my shorts. There's something on her breath, something layered beneath the sangria fumes. A heavier liquor that I usually smell on Unc. Then, I notice her hands are shaking. Her pulse ticks rapidly in her neck. She's terrified. Not once did I imagine this through her end of the telescope—her desperation to please the family, her fear. She bends closer, ready to start the show, and that's when Earley springs from my shirt pocket, eyes grayed out, tongue dangling. This time, he barfs red and does a header between couch cushions.

There's a commotion among the adults about why I might be smuggling expired snacks, but I can't concentrate on anything beyond the howling pain in my guts. Gripping my belly, I tilt face-first into Aunt Elyse's lap. She holds her hands up to show that she hasn't hurt me—hasn't even *touched* me.

"That's not part of the ceremony." I can hear Unc struggling to his mechanical feet. "Get your face out of there."

"Earley!" I scream into my aunt's lap.

"It's *not* early," Mom says. "In fact, we'd be right on time if you'd straighten up."

I want to explain that Earley needs our help, but I don't have the air for it. Aunt Elyse rolls me onto my back and presses tenderly near my belly button. She asks where it hurts.

The ice cream at the hospital tastes like chalk, but the apple juice is good. My purple-haired doctor keeps bringing fresh cups. She seems disappointed to learn that I don't want to take home my exploded appendix in a little glass jar.

"*Never* order the horsies," she says. "They're perfect vectors for infection, just ask your little friend here." She shakes my jarred appendix, then turns to my dad. "They ought to make you sign a waiver."

The doctor's comment sends my teary-eyed Dad into the lobby. Apparently, he's been a wreck ever since he found out the horsie was to blame. The doctor follows him out, probably to talk some more about the wide spectrum of antibiotics I'll be taking. Mom follows them.

"Earley?" I ask.

Megon shakes her head. When I start to cry, she wipes away the first tear. "There's no video to post," Megon says. "That should make you happy."

But it doesn't, because you never really get what you want. You just delay the catastrophe a little while longer. When I get out of here, I'll give Earley a proper burial beneath the finest grass I can find.

"Tell them you want to eat at Hard Rock," I say to Megon. "Maybe it'll cheer him up. Just don't order any appetizers."

Megon tries to smile. It's like watching a dog mimic human expression.

When I wake, Aunt Elyse is sitting in the bedside chair. She's so close I can smell her perfume, and she's back in her pantsuit. She hugs me very gently and then she pulls back the fabric of my gown to see the long millipede of cut skin and stitches. She can only stand a momentary glance, then her eyes get red and shiny. No one else's eyes did that except Dad's. Aunt Elyse replaces the gown but leaves her hand near my hip, careful to avoid the wound.

"You'll be late for dinner," I say.

"Just between us, I hate that place. Your Unc and I only go to make your dad happy."

"Sorry my face went in your—" I grit my teeth against a flare of pain. "It just hurt is all. I wasn't afraid."

"Don't be sorry," she says, pouting her lips. "I know you're disappointed. I was supposed to make you a man."

"No big deal," I say. "There's a girl at school who's flirting with me big-time."

"But I *promised*," she says, moving her hand beneath the gown and downward, to my bare thigh.

'They'll be back soon," I say.

My aunt wrinkles her nose. "Your dad's pretty torn up, so your Mom's going to buy him Bahama Mamas till he can't see straight. It's what he needs right now." Her fingers slide across the top of my thigh and stall among the short hairs. We're stuck somewhere between scandalous and something worse. I think of her boozy breath, her need to be needed. It must mean a lot of pretending, this whole business of growing up.

"Are you going to kiss me or what?" I say.

My aunt gives me a look like she's deciding whether to reason with me or smother me with a pillow. "You don't kiss *family*," she says. "Not on the mouth."

With her free hand, she digs around in her purse, and out come the goggles.

*Nominated by The Idaho Review*

# FIFTY-EIGHT PERCENT IS CONCRETE ROAD, 12 PERCENT LOOSE SAND

by DAVID WOJAHN

from THE SOUTHERN REVIEW

Inside the iron gates of Sachsenhausen,
a dozen prisoners unloading shoes,

boxes littering the ground in teetering columns.
The Gypsies, the queers, the malingerers & Jews:

*The shoe-walking unit,* who now will test the soles
of a new synthetic rubber. Before them,

the shoe-testing track, winding to the horizon
& surfaced with Teutonic precision. Fifty-eight percent

is concrete road, 12 percent loose sand,
10 percent cinder path, 8 percent mud & meant

to stay continually underwater, 4 percent cobblestone
(looted from cities in West Pomerania);

4 percent coarse gravel, a cross section
of every surface where the Reich shall campaign.

The prisoners don the shoes; each has been fortified
by a mixture of cocaine & amphetamine.

Staring out toward the track, they are jittery, wild-eyed.
Today's quota: twenty-five miles. A freezing rain

& a camp doctor observing they are "marching machines,"
the machinery grinding past sunset, moonrise,

the cinder path raising small clouds of dust.
Predictably, the shoes prove more resilient than the men.

This one on his knees in gravel; that one facedown
in mud. A chain-smoking corporal stoops to examine

the drowned prisoner's upturned soles. Measurements
are taken. & thus David Wojahn has found some content,

another web search satisfied—prurient, calculated, cruel.
& now he retrofits these horrors into rime royal,

for this is a preferred device, though his skill at such forms
is doubtful. & thus he seeks the means to turn

this deficit to cunning. David Wojahn, who knows little shame,
though to utter this in couplets, to utter this in quatrains,

delighting as the pixels neatly stagger on a screen,
is seen by him as evidence of craft,

is seen by him as a plea for "social justice,"
a theme in his poems which has sometimes been praised.

I would ask David Wojahn to step closer, to gaze
upon the shoe-walking track anew. The shoe-walking dead:

Bend down, bend down & touch. Stroke this bloated face,
with the left hand first & then the right, a bookkeeper from Danzig,

open-eyed. A bookkeeper, like your mother. You have fashioned him
& have betrayed him utterly. & for this you will not be forgiven.

*Nominated by The Southern Review, Bruce Beasley, David Jauss, Tom Sleigh, Joni Tevis*

# WE AT *OLD BIRDS* WELCOME MESSAGES FROM GOD, EVEN IF UNVERIFIABLE

by ANNIE SHEPPARD

from FOURTH GENRE

Perhaps you are not aware that the United States are home to 35 lake monsters. Most are of the ordinary "Nessie" type, but we also have webbed hominids, giant eel-pigs, winged alligator-snakes, aquatic lynxes, and a goat man. If you were so inclined, you could probably make a career out of investigating lake monsters—or you might devote your retirement to it. It would make a nice focus for one's waning years, I think. It's good to have a purpose, after all, and gardening is not for everyone.

If lake monsters are not your bag, there are plenty of alternatives. You might find it more rewarding to seek out UFO landing sites—or lost gold mines, buried treasure, or sasquatches. If you prefer fact over conjecture, consider missing species. Worldwide, there are over 1,200 species of animals and plants considered not extinct but lost. Myanmar, for example, has a missing pink-headed duck. Rumor has it that a small flock of pink-headed ducks yet survives, paddling about in a remote swampy area. If you were to sell all your worldly belongings and move to Myanmar in order to devote your remaining years to finding the missing pink-headed duck, you would not be the first person to do so.

My retirement plan involves searching for the Lord God Bird, which has been more or less missing since 1940 or 1944, depending upon whose claims may be believed. This is one of the hallmarks—and charms—of missing things. No one can quite agree on the facts of the matter.

Another name for the Lord God Bird is the ivory-billed woodpecker, though of course it's more fun to say Lord God Bird. Its habitat is the hardwood swamps and pine forests of the southern U.S.—forests once so vast they blanketed entire states. Though conservation efforts are underway, only a few pockets of original forest remain. No one has taken a definitive photograph of the bird since 1938, but a few visitors to these forests in the intervening years have reported glimpses, usually fleeting, of a bird that appears to be *the* bird. Then, beginning in 2005, several reliable and otherwise trustworthy people—experienced birders, teams of ornithologists from universities like Cornell and Auburn, a solitary scientist from the Naval Research Laboratory—have reported with some certainty sightings of a bird that looks and sounds like the Lord God Bird. Unfortunately for science, none of these otherwise reliable people have managed to collect a feather or droppings that would make it possible to verify the bird's existence with DNA testing. None have taken a photograph that can be said without doubt to be of an ivory-billed woodpecker. One searcher did capture a short, blurry, indeterminate video of a bird that *might* be the bird. Others have made audio recordings featuring what may or may not be the Lord God Bird's signature double knock.

Other experts have expressed doubt. They question the lack of concrete evidence. The pileated woodpecker, they say, is easily mistaken for the ivory-billed, which, they add, is obviously extinct. Misidentifying a pileated woodpecker, these skeptics say, is an unfortunate but understandable mistake, made possible by hope—which, as any scientist knows, introduces an element of uncertainty into every rational inquiry.

Imagine being a member of one of those expert birding teams. Imagine that you yourself sighted the Lord God Bird, that you are almost certain of it. You can describe its white rump and distinctive white wing patches, visible only in flight. You know that the bird you saw was absolutely not a pileated woodpecker. You know your woodpeckers, and you would not have made such an amateurish error. You firmly believe that the bird you saw was an honest-to-God Lord God Bird. So are the others who sighted The Bird. One of them sat down, after he saw it, and cried.

But is it possible that you just really, really wanted to have seen it? This keeps you awake.

Though we tend to lose sight of the fact, it is not unheard of for the occasional missing species to be rediscovered. An entire taxonomy—the Lazarus taxon—has been created for species thought to be lost forever but found again. Some of these vanished species reappeared in the fossil record only to disappear once more, but others are living species. The Majorcan midwife toad, for example, was described from fossil remains in 1977; living animals were found in 1979. In the present, upwards of 1,500 breeding pairs of Majorcan midwife toads exist, putting them in the vulnerable but not critically endangered category.

Although it seems wrong to complain when a lost species is found, on the whole I think it preferable that our missing things stay missing. If we find these things definitively, we need no longer go looking for them, and we clearly need stuff to look for. This a view I inherited from my father, who always favored things that were missing over things that were found. He kept an extensive dossier on Bigfoot, for example, yet never once spotted so much as a largish footprint. He once wrote an article about the Port Orford Meteorite, which was discovered in 1856 in the hills of Oregon's south coast and immediately lost again. Dad looked for and failed to find the lost Port Orford Meteorite for many years. His article was a detailed, map-riddled deduction of where—in many square miles of steep, brushy, inhospitable forest—the meteorite would most likely be found, based on all the places it wasn't. Too bad the Port Orford Meteorite turned out to be a hoax and took all the fun out.

Dad was tenacious about looking for things and not finding them. He dragged my mother and us kids all over the Northwest in search of lost mines, prehistoric hunting sites, and ghost towns, which we almost never located with any certainty. The Lord God Bird was not on our radar, however. We lived in the wrong quadrant of the continent, for one thing, but we Sheppards were simply more inclined to look down than up. Were there any birds at all in the state of Oregon? Any sapsuckers, any warblers, any goddamned chickadees? Did we look up at all? We did not.

It is the duty of the younger generations to distinguish themselves from their parents. If one hasn't done so by midlife, it's time to get started. Accordingly, I began to look up in my 50s—and I discovered birds up there. Birds appear to be a fairly common midlife discovery. While one does come across a young birder now and then, as a pursuit birding seems to call almost preternaturally to the oldish. As time passes,

I reckon, we are increasingly dogged by our own lurking mortality and so need some kind of religion more than the young—and birding is one of those fields of inquiry that, no matter how rational its enthusiasts, manages to cross with some regularity into religious territory, even if unknowingly. Witness the awe, the uncertainty, the fleeting glimpses, the unverifiable sightings. Witness the name "Lord God Bird." According to anecdote, the name arose from a shout, or perhaps a whisper, uttered by a fortunate birder upon glimpsing the bird. The bird is also sometimes called the "Good God Bird" for the same reason, and while it is possible that these names arose from a startled outcry of discovery rather than one of religious awe, we should not overlook the universal human habit of joining surprise with divinity. From *Lord God* to *Good God* to *Holy Fuck*, we are unconsciously communicating with the divine whenever something awesome—or awful—catches us by surprise. Another way to say "communicating with the divine," of course, is "praying."

According to the writer Sam Keen, modern birders can be viewed as unwitting members of an ancient cult of bird worshipers, who believed that birds are messengers from God. Upon learning this, I immediately googled "ancient cult of bird worshipers," hoping it would be a real thing. It doesn't appear to be. The internet is aware of instances of bird worship in specific indigenous or historical populations—the worship of Crow by the Inuit, for example—but does not have any knowledge of a substantial and cross-cultural cult of bird worshipers currently or formerly active on the planet. This is both a disappointment and a relief. I have joined the cult in spirit, however. I like the simplicity of their dogma: birds are messengers from God, and you may do with that what you will. It's a religion I can tolerate.

The holy books of other religions are also gratifyingly full of birds: *I am like a pelican of the wilderness, I am like the owl of the desert*, etc. Not to mention angels, the ultimate messengers from God.

How an angel is like a bird: wings and feathers, a head, two feet, two eyes, messenger from God.

How an angel is not like a bird: everything else.

*　*　*

Wild birds don't age, as far as I can see. They are generally eaten before they have a chance to get old. The typical lifespan of a wild parrot is about 40 years, for example, whereas captive parrots regularly live 60 years or more—and a few live considerably longer. It is rumored that Winston Churchill's pet parrot is still alive at age 118, though it appears no one has tried very hard to confirm this. Like the Port Orford Meteorite and the Goat Man of Lake Worth, Texas, Winston Churchill's pet parrot is just more fun as a rumor.

For another view of aging, let's revisit my dad. I did this myself, just last week. I arrived at the care facility bearing gifts: a sandwich bag containing four ginger cookies, homemade by me. Kevin, a caregiver, saw me come in. "He's in his room," Kevin said. "He's revving up," he added, which is both a warning and a routine occurrence in this facility.

I knocked on Dad's door, which stood open. He was standing by his walker wearing a button-up shirt, adult diapers, and nothing else. He looked up. He did not say, "Hello, kid," as he once did. He said, "I need help." He had tried to pull a clean diaper on over a used one, but he didn't realize this. He said, "I can't pull them up for some reason."

I bent over, told him to lift a foot, okay, now the other foot. There was a time when I would have fetched Kevin and let him do the diaper work, but I've grown accustomed to helping Dad dress, undress, untangle. I'm used to his toothpick legs, his hairless pink testicles. Testicles hang low on old men. They sway. This is something I've learned.

I got Dad squared away: one clean diaper, one shirt, one pair of shorts, one pair of sandals. The ordeal tired him. He lowered himself slowly into his chair. "You can't trust anyone here," he said.

"What's happened now?" I asked.

"Someone's been in my room," he said. "They've taken things." I asked him what things have been taken. "My photos," he said.

The missing photos are in a blue binder. There are several dozen shots, black and white, arranged chronologically in plastic photo sleeves. The photos and the orderly arrangement are both Dad's work from an earlier, more organized time. He took them in the 1960s and developed them in his darkroom, which he had converted from a closet. The subject in every photo is my mother, nude. Seated demurely in an antique rocking chair, nude; reclined on a mid-century modern sofa nude, silhouetted against a curtained window, nude. She was twenty-something, willing, and beautiful the way the young are beautiful, which I now feel is mostly just unweathered. Mom and Dad were married to each other at the time and there is nothing inherently wrong with the photos, with Dad taking them, or with Mom posing for them.

Except this: Mom and Dad divorced in 1975. Dad has been married to his second wife for forty years. My stepmother takes her marriage seriously. She's not thrilled with these photos. And this: during a hospitalization last year, Dad invited four of his five daughters and stepdaughters on separate occasions to join him in bed. In the late 1970s, Dad made sexual overtures to a stepdaughter, age 13. He posed another daughter in a negligee and took pictures. To relax her inhibitions or maybe her scruples, he plied her with booze, which she dutifully drank. She was 16.

On one of my earlier visits, I had found the binder in Dad's dresser drawer in the care facility. I wasn't snooping; I was looking for hearing-aid batteries. When I next saw my mother, I asked her what she would like me to do, if anything, about the photos. "Please get them out of there," she said.

I am the thief. I remind Dad of this. I remind him of my sisters, and in case he has forgotten, I remind him of his transgressions against them.

Dad: "I don't know why I'm not being forgiven."

Me: "Because you haven't apologized."

Dad: "Other men have done worse things."

Dad will forget. He will continue looking for his photos and will continue not finding them. He will tell me someone has been in his room and has taken something. I will ask, what have they taken? and he will say, my photos.

Here's a little prayer for Dad: *God help you.*

❊    ❊    ❊

I am a birder. I am a member of the birding community. Sometimes, but not reliably, I report my bird sightings on eBird, a citizen science website run by Cornell, the same university whose expert birding team may or may not have sighted the Lord God Bird in 2005. On eBird I report that I traveled on foot for *one* hour. I agree that my primary purpose *was* birding. I report that I traveled 1.5 miles (birders cannot be expected to walk briskly) and saw: *15 American crows, 1 song sparrow, 6 common mergansers, 1 belted kingfisher, 40 tree swallows, 5 bush-tits,* and *4 cavorting ravens.* I am not actually allowed to insert the word "cavorting" with the ravens, but I can mention in the comments section that the ravens were cavorting so long as I am certain they were ravens and not crows. I am not allowed to report that I saw a flock of crows in a fir tree that may have numbered as few as 10 or as many as 25 individual birds. I must choose a number and declare it with certainty. I am not allowed to report that a hummingbird whizzed past my head but I don't know whether a rufous or Anna's—or even a calliope, which I have never identified with certainty but is uncommon in these parts and looks a lot like an Anna's, particularly if female. All I can report is the whizzing, and eBird does not find that helpful. It's a distinct sound, the whiz of a hummingbird, but it's not usually possible for a low-skills birder like me to identify the species based on the sound of whizzing alone.

eBird does not approve of uncertainty. It does not accept reports like *I saw a bird I believe was a wrentit but you know wrentits—they don't always let you get a good look at 'em*. eBird will gladly accept photographic evidence. eBird would love, for example, to see an unambiguous photo of an ivory-billed woodpecker. Recently, eBird introduced a feature that allows birders to rate each other's photos. Five stars is exceptional and rarely awarded. My best photo is of a hummingbird, a male rufous, who posed on the feeder and let me take his picture. In this shot he is sitting perfectly still, with the red buds of a Japanese maple blurred fetchingly behind him. It is his eye, however, that is the exceptional feature. It looks human. My hummingbird is a walnut-sized bird with a long black bill, an iridescent throat we birders call his gorget, and tiny clawed feet—and he looks back at us humans, in this one photo, with a human eye. Someone, an anonymous birder, has awarded my photo four stars. It is just slightly out of focus, just barely, almost imperceptibly not quite sharp. So, four stars instead of five.

While I agree that my photo deserves four stars and not five, the relevance is not in the stars. The relevance is in the eye. A human eye looking out from the face of a bird does not make the bird look human. It makes the bird look numinous. It looks holy, like a messenger from God.

I am a member of the birding community, but I am also a member of the ancient cult of bird worshipers. We bird worshipers are less concerned with correct species identification and sharp focus. We are more concerned with messages from God.

A citizen science website that someone should create but not me is *Old Birds*. This would be both a reporting site and a literary journal. Subjects sought by the editors of *Old Birds:* aging, dying, birds, and anything numinous. Artists please submit. Contributors may be of any age, but *Old Birds* is not the home for your academic work. Your MFA is neither helpful nor a hindrance, but your indignation is welcome, as are your sleeplessness, your impatience, your demented parents, and your lack of speed. Your long hindsight will find a home here, as will how dumb you still feel, even now, when you have been promised wisdom. We at *Old Birds* also welcome possible messages from God and any other sightings of a holy nature, even if unverifiable.

238

❧ ❧ ❧

One of the more endearing habits shared by birds and humans is the collecting of shiny objects—a thing crows and magpies are said to do. My own nest is lined with shiny objects—tarnished silver cups and odd little mirrors and small luminous paintings—things I've come across while out in the world and carried home as treasure. The internet tells me that the question of birds collecting shiny objects has been asked by science—and it has been answered. The answer from science is that birds emphatically do not collect shiny objects. Corvids—the family to which crows and magpies belong—collect food mostly, and are even somewhat alarmed by shiny objects. Science speculates that if these birds are sometimes seen with shiny objects it is because they want to be rid of them.

But the myth of crows and magpies collecting shiny objects is much loved by us bird worshipers. We point to news of a young girl in Seattle who has befriended a flock of crows. Her crow friends bring the girl gifts: charms and beads and fragments of sea glass. We are happy to learn the story is true—and we do not thank science for shooting holes in our favorite metaphors. Or for questioning the likelihood that lake monsters exist, or for telling us that our most poignant feelings are caused by brain chemicals, or that our blurry photos and fleeting glimpses are mere figments of irrational hope. We do not think science does humanity any favors when, in the name of rationality, it squashes all hope, especially the hope we need as we age that we will somehow continue, that we are not slipping inexorably toward our own extinction.

❧ ❧ ❧

So, I hear you asking, if your hummingbird is a messenger from God, then, um . . . what's the message?

The ancient cult of bird worshipers does not have a priesthood or hierarchy, or even a reliably argumentative cadre of theologians. It only has laity, most of whom do not even know they are members of the cult, much less capable of translating messages from God. Still, this one seems pretty obvious, even to us laity:

*I see you.*

❧ ❧ ❧

When Dad went looking for missing things, he took his family along— on trips to the mountains in search of Indian caves, to the high desert

239

on arrowhead-hunting expeditions, or into coastal forests, looking for the lost Port Orford Meteorite. He taught us how to navigate in the deep woods, how to read the cardinal directions on a cloudy day, and how to build a fire in the rain with only one match, in case we should ever be lost in the forest ourselves. He had fun: he drank Blitz beer though a silly straw, wore a rawhide hunting jacket with a fringe, and served up his mostly factual stories with a generous dollop of fiction. He did not have answers, as far as I can recall, for much of anything, but he had an admirable zest and enthusiasm for questions.

And he took liberties with his daughters. He took things from us—innocence, trust, confidence—that were not his to take, and he has been, so far, more defensive about this than repentant.

Dad's an old bird now, held in captivity well past his natural lifespan. He's tangled up in his diaper, he's weathered and hairless. He has, at best, a handful of rather grim years left to him. Science says that's all he has. One chance, you blew it, too bad.

But the Lazarus taxon says otherwise. The world itself says otherwise, in the roundness of the planet, in the infinite circularity of the water cycle, in the tides and the seasons. The world—the natural world—speaks a language more hopeful than the language of science. It says life is as resilient as it is beautiful. It says things come and they go and they come back again. They return. Some part of us knows this is true, or maybe we only hope it's true—that we return, that this one life is not our only chance. That we are seen. That, as the writer William Kenower says, "we are not here to just endure some meaningless crap until we're dead."

The ancient cult of bird worshipers does not have a holy book or creed. We are disorganized, credulous, irrational, and hopeful. We don't know much, but we know enough to be thankful for missing things—for the Lord God Bird and the pink-headed duck, for Bigfoot and innocence and all 35 American lake monsters, more or less, though no one can quite agree on a head count. We are thankful because missing things give us something to look for. If we had a prayer longer than *Holy Fuck*, it might go like this: *May our glimpses be fleeting and our photos blurry—and may we never prove a thing, one way or the other.*

We bird worshipers don't put much faith in answers, but we have a high regard for questions. We need questions because we need possibilities—that birds are indeed messengers from God. Or that they are God Itself, watching us through the eye of a hummingbird.

*Nominated by Fourth Genre*

# ALIVE

## by NATASHA SAJÉ

from POETRY

You and me, of course, and the animals
we feed and then slaughter. The boxelder
bug with its dot of red, yeast in the air
making bread and wine, bacteria
in yogurt, carrots, the apple tree,
each white blossom. And rock, which lives
so slowly it's hard to imagine it
as sand then glass. A sea called dead is one that
will not mirror us. We think as human
beings we deserve every last thing. Say
the element copper. Incandescence
glowing bright and soft like Venus.
Ductile as a shewolf's eyes pigmented red
or green, exposed to acid in the air.
Copper primes your liver, its mines leach lead
and arsenic. Smelting is to melting
the way smite is to mite. A violence
of extraction. What's lost when a language
dies? When its tropes oppose our own?
In the at-risk language Aymara
the past stretches out in front, the future
lags behind. Imagine being led
by knowing, imagine the end as clear.

*Nominated by Poetry, Elaine Terranova, Lee Upton, Nam Le*

# THE BOOK OF FLY

## by JOHN PHILIP JOHNSON

from RATTLE

*for* MIKE ALLEN

1:1
Feeding on the living is good,
   but feeding on the dead is better.

1:2
Nestle your offspring in the rancid.

1:3
The air is heavy; let it work for you,
   but fly only until you find beauty.

1:4
Shit is beautiful.

1:5
Rub your hands together before you eat.

1:6
If you land on the wrist that holds the swatter,
   consider yourself lucky, not clever.

1:7
Remain humble, if you think of anything.

1:8
You only have a few days;
   stay simple.

1:9
Breed when you are able.

2:1
And when you are licked
   by the frog's tongue,
or swallowed by a songbird,
or felled in a cloud of nerve gas
    and lie twitching, unconcerned,

2:2
know that it is the honor of a fly,
   it is its purpose,
      to die.

*Nominated by Rattle*

# ANATOMY OF A KOREAN INHERITANCE

## by ESTHER RA

from LIGEIA MAGAZINE

*an anagram*

*Inheritance*: an unchosen
housefire of years, a word
with the burden of fate.

I love and resent
my broken red jewels,
this *rite* to *enchain* me

in love. Love as a form
of slow violence, locking
my *heart* in an *ice inn*.

*Hence I train* myself
to offer welcome. Hence
I used to *incinerate* hope.

*Inheritance* is a dark gift:
both an *inner itch*
and a caress.

I fold myself into a kite,
fleeing to a borderless sky.
An *entire chain* ties

my feet to the past,
but my lips, at least,
brush against stars.

I run after the kingdom
of God. I *entice rain*
and drown in wild grace.

Only then can I live
as *heir* to these *ancient*
wounds. Only then

can I pass on this *ache*
that never grows *tinier*,
only then can I

*reincite han.*

*Nominated by Ligeia Magazine*

# THE MISSING ARE CONSIDERED DEAD

fiction by V.V. GANESHANANTHAN

from COPPER NICKEL

When my husband disappeared, my closest neighbor, Sarojini, hurried over from her house across our Batticaloa lane to tell me she had seen him being picked up and taken away. That is how we Tamil women talk about disappearing in my village, which is still my village after all this time, even though it has been stripped to its bones: we say *disappearing* when we mean kidnapped, and *being picked up and taken away* when we mean probably on the way to be killed. Sarojini had always liked to feel important, and although Ranjan was not standing next to me, smiling in the quiet way he had of letting me know he shared the joke of considering her a gossip, I saw no reason to stop her from telling me her version of the story. I didn't listen to her; I thought about Ranjan. Where was he? I was at the very beginning of a kind of wondering that would later become like breathing to me, if my own breathing could be not only necessary but also intolerable.

When Sarojini came in, shouting for me and shaking a rag in her fist, I was burning some things of his that he had left behind. She didn't say anything about the rubbish fire I had made in the courtyard behind my kitchen. Perhaps she didn't notice what was melting there, the acrid smell filling the air.

"I saw them!" she exclaimed. "The STF boys came and took him."

The army, which was not the Special Task Force, had come three times before taking Ranjan. I did not correct her.

"What did you see?" I asked her, because she wanted to be included in my loss.

246

"The one who likes to drink was the one who came to take Ranjan," Sarojini said.

That was true. The soldier who had come to take Ranjan had visited our house regularly, and my husband, who had once been with Karuna, who had once been with the Tigers, did drink now. Because he had been well liked and trusted in our neighborhood, after his return, our neighbors had kept him well supplied. The soldiers knew this and liked to invite themselves in to talk to Ranjan, who also spoke perfect Sinhala.

Hearing Sarojini but not listening to her, I went to the cupboard and poured myself a drink. The man who had taken my husband might come back, but I would no longer serve him whiskey. I had always known where Ranjan kept the liquor, so now that he was gone, what remained belonged to me.


To account for the gap of thirty days between the actual and official dates of disappearance, I can only tell you that even though I had seen Ranjan being taken away, even though Sarojini, too, had come to verify it, it took me a week to believe. And then I did not officially report that he was gone for another three weeks, because I could not bring myself to leave the house. My husband had left the house, and he had not come back. I wanted to plant my feet firmly in front of my household shrine and stay there. Later, the people on the lane asked how Ranjan could have been taken, why I had waited that long to tell anyone. The gossips whispered to each other, asking what was wrong with me. I heard them, and wondered too, which was what they wanted.

When at last I managed to file a claim, to walk out my own door without falling to my knees, the first person I told was Thushara, who had been at the Army sentry point set off from the corner of the lane for as long as Ranjan and I had been married. Thushara frowned when I told him, as though he were going through a mental phone book to see if he could guess who was responsible. But he didn't say anything; even when I cried a little bit, he pretended, kindly, not to notice, except for handing me the handkerchief he kept in his uniform pocket. After that, when he passed my house, he let his chin fall to his chest respectfully. A short while later he brought a colonel to my house to hear the details of the case. I invited them into our musty parlor and gave them tea as I related my story. The colonel took notes while Thushara stood behind him, looking both young and stern. Krishan was only a baby then, and cried behind me, and when the colonel heard his gulps and hiccups, he got up and went over and lifted him up, and Krishan was immediately quiet, as though Ranjan were there too, as though my child didn't know the difference between being held by one man or another.

And then, when I was done talking, when he was done listening, the colonel told me the rule. They had, he said, no record of my husband being taken in, so he was missing. He might turn up again at any moment. Three years would have to elapse before they would give me anything for losing him. I can only imagine that I looked stricken. Krishan was small and I hadn't worked outside my home since my confinement. I didn't have any money. What will you do? the colonel asked me, too solicitously, and then Thushara said, Sir, perhaps we can ask at the school if they have work for her.

That was how I began cleaning at the school where I had once been a student. There were so few other jobs in our town—nothing that I was qualified for, really, and I liked the walk to the building because it took me past the beautiful resort the soldiers were constructing on land that had once belonged to some of us. I could see where my father's old house had stood, and the well at which my grandmother had bathed. The well had not yet been completely destroyed and at first, if I went right up to the barrier wire, I could see the circle of broken cement. Thushara always waved to me as I went up the road with Krishan in my arms, and then later still, when he was old enough to walk himself, holding my hand. Hello, little man, the soldiers said, smiling at my fatherless boy, and I felt a little sick at the easy sweetness in their eyes, which reminded me of my husband. Of course I thought of their mothers, too, and held Krishan closer.

Three years seemed a long time to me, a woman without a husband, a mother without any money. I rubbed the floor in circles with a rag and washed the chalkboards. I reshelved the books that the students left on the desk; I wiped the tables where they ate their lunch, and remembered studying there myself. The students were kind to me, and the teachers ignored me, which was also a kindness; I think they knew that I was humiliated, working there, when I had once been good at maths, and even better at English, so good at English that some people thought I might go abroad, to the Middle East or even Europe. Now when there was a concert or special event at the school, I stood in the back with my broom, and everyone acted as though I were not there, so that I could also watch and feel that I was a part of the world, although I was less than a wife and less than a widow, and had never even been a Tiger. Even then, I imagined Ranjan next to me, his width and breadth,

248

the space his body would have taken up. His untidy mustache, his smile. Your son will study here someday, someone said to me generously, and I hated that I was supposed to be grateful.

During the first year, I went to talk to Thushara and the colonel once a week, to ask them what they had heard, if there was any news of Ranjan. I began in earnest. You know me, I said helplessly; you see me every day and you know me. I just want him back; if the army took him I won't tell anyone, I don't have to tell anyone, but he is not with the Tigers. He is just Krishan's father, and please, please, won't you tell me where he is? The colonel, who I think was not a bad man, and who was even farther from his village than Thushara was from his, stared at me and was silent. In the second year, when I had more work for less money than I could have dreamed possible, I went only once a month, even though every morning I woke up thinking Ranjan was next to me. Every once in a while Sarojini would wander across the road and tell me that she had heard a rumour about where he was being held. *Your husband.* I would have talked to her for any length of time to hear that phrase. But after some time even she stopped coming; perhaps my loneliness embarrassed her. Other neighbors who had visited me when my husband was home ignored me, averting their eyes when they saw me on the street. And then, at last, in the third year, my exchanges with the colonel became a formality. I asked him if there had been any progress, and showed him copies of letters I had written to various authorities, but when he nodded absently, I understood that there might never be any news. The only people who smiled at me, who could stand to smile at me, were Thushara and his friends, their faces bright with sweat as they poured concrete for the new military hotel, which rose like a growing child behind the barrier wire, in the place where some of our homes had been.

Every month on the seventh day I looked at the calendar and ticked the time away. I have told you that I was poor. By the end of the first year Krishan had no shoes; by the end of the second, his clothes no longer fit him; by the last days of the third year, my boy resembled Ranjan at the worst moments of his life, or at least his life as I had seen it, when his time with the Tigers had worn him thin and impatient. Krishan was still my sweet Ranjan-faced baby, still quiet, but every day he seemed to get smaller instead of bigger. He was only four.

Around that time, the new headmaster who had come to the school began asking me to stay late. He was also friends with the soldiers and knew how I had come to work there. You understand what I'm saying—he had his own things he needed cleaned and done and taken care of. Mending, sewing, filing, odd tasks—chores that other people wouldn't have been willing to do. What he wanted was a young and efficient woman who wouldn't complain, who wouldn't say anything, who needed the money. During the day Krishan went to a nursery run by the nuns, but in the evenings they had their own services and did not take care of children. I had no one to watch my child then, perhaps because the only people who visited my house now were the soldiers, checking on me. Could I take Krishan with me? He was unobtrusive; surely the headmaster wouldn't mind, and if he needed me to come somewhere that Krishan couldn't follow, my baby could wait quietly. He knew how to do that.

I had just decided to bring Krishan along when Thushara stopped by for a cup of tea, as he sometimes did. I could never refuse him, either. He, too, was starting to look older—his neck thicker, like a man's neck, his arms and shoulders filled out by the hard construction work the army did. I gave him the last biscuits I had, and told him that I would have to leave soon to go back to work. He had just come to see my son, he said, gazing at Krishan, who was playing with the dog that lived on our lane. You're going to work again? Thushara asked, confused. It's evening time, isn't it? I'll watch him.

I looked at Thushara, who even being a soldier was still a boy, and at my son, who would never be a Tiger like Ranjan, and I didn't wish that either of those facts were different. I left Krishan with Thushara, who, unlike some of the other soldiers I had met, thought he was my friend, and walked to work, where the headmaster was waiting for me in his office.

One month before my time—Ranjan's time—was up, a government man came to speak at the school where I worked. They hired more people to help clean the school for the special occasion, and the schoolchildren practiced singing the national anthem. I was given a new work uniform; as usual, I would be permitted to stand in the back. I was not too troubled about the visit, although I knew Thushara and the other soldiers in Batticaloa were excited to see this man, who was new and also old, having been in several earlier governments also. The soldiers came and stood near the front to receive him, as part of the military honor they usually performed for such visitors.

I watched the speech and thought of Ranjan, who had loved politics. I held my broom tight, my back against the wall at the back of the lecture hall. Even from that distance I could see the government man. He had a weak face, his jaw lost in the fleshy peace he had enjoyed for years while the husbands of my village left or were taken away, while the Thusharas and their colonel left their villages to occupy ours. The government man spoke in Sinhala, and I, who for so long had had no energy for anger, only sadness, tried to listen. I don't speak Sinhala well, even now. When he said the line that made people begin to murmur, I thought I hadn't heard properly. I didn't understand. I said, what? I wasn't sure. First I said it to myself and then again to the temporary worker next to me, but she also did not speak Sinhala, or had not heard properly, and the two of us craned our necks and stared at the government man as though he were going to repeat himself, as so many of the most important men do to emphasize how important they are.

But he did not.

I'll ask Thushara later, I told myself. Three years earlier, I would have asked Ranjan. The soldiers had liked to visit my husband in part because they could make him uncomfortable without translation.


What the government man said was that now, all the people who are missing are considered dead, Thushara said softly, and that we all know this. You could see from the fact that he was nearly crying—and that I was not—what a gentle young man he was. He had Krishan on his lap as he told me. I had given him whiskey instead of tea, and to hide his hurt from my son he turned Krishan around and made a horse of his knee. He let his own forelock fall over his forehead and into his eyes.

Amma, *horse*! Krishan said in Tamil. Horse, I said in English. And then, to Thushara: say it again. Say that sentence again in Sinhala.

On Thushara's lap, Krishan looked like a smaller version of him, and a smaller version of my husband, and a smaller version of the headmaster for whom I worked, and I couldn't tell any more which of the men I had known were real—whether I wanted time to pass, or rewind, or simply stop.

Three years after they take your husband they will pay you for him. They will give you a certificate that says you are entitled to certain monies. I waited for Ranjan, and one week before the third anniversary of my husband's disappearance they brought me another man.

He was in handcuffs, that man, his face so swollen that I didn't know what to do or how to talk to him. I could have fit his face into my palm, the way I had held Ranjan when it was just the two of us, and not known where his bones were under all that bruising. Thushara, beside him, turned his own eyes toward me with a hopeful look. I thought I heard the bound man mutter, *Tell them it's me, darling, tell them, sweetheart,* in the Tamil word we use for that endearment, but his mouth was not the mouth I had known, and the tongue was clumsy and fat with dehydration, the cheek ripe like old fruit. I thought of giving him a drink of water and whiskey and tea, and I didn't know if I was allowed to speak to him in Tamil, or if I should say to him in Sinhala the one sentence I had learned from the government man: *The missing are considered dead.*

This man is saying that he is your husband, the colonel said. You have been to see us every month. We wanted to bring him to you, so you would know that we are fair. If this is your husband, you should take him far from here. There is some land in the next village, which we can give you in exchange for yours.

*Should. Hare to Can.* These words translate differently. The missing *should be* considered dead. You *have to* consider them dead. You *can* consider them dead, the government man had meant. Had he thought he was freeing us? Should, have to, can—these words live everywhere. But no matter which words they used, I didn't want to leave my home with this stranger. I wished I could tell Ranjan about the burned LTTE ID card in its melted puddle in the courtyard. The plastic had hardened now into a different shape. I wished I could ask the stranger where he had been, what had been done to him, what would happen to him if I said no, what would happen if I took him in. If I walked out of my house with this beaten man, even to save him, my husband would never walk back in. The door would close behind me. But this strange man, too, was a man, and belonged to someone, and if I did not claim him now, it was possible that no one ever would, and that I would send him back only into the darkest kind of dark.

I don't know how long I stood there, wondering who I was and how much I had, before I heard Krishan's voice behind me. He put his little hand into mine.

Amma, is that my father? he asked.

The missing are considered dead, the government man had said, but he had for gotten to say: except by those who love them.

Is it? Krishan said. My father?

252

No, baby, I said. No. No, it's not, I said to the colonel, who nodded, slowly at first and then more firmly, as I said again, it's not him. Are you sure? Yes, I'm sure, I said, and although by then nothing could have made me change my mind, I also knew that I would never be sure that what I had done was right. I would have been afraid of looking at the stranger again, but he seemed just then to have no face, and they took him away.

When they were gone, I went once more to the calendar and thought not of rupees, but of the feeling around my chest someday loosening. They had told me the number of days left until the government would call me a widow, but no one could measure the many years stretching ahead of me still, the whole long life I could wait.

*Nominated by Copper Nickel*

# THE OUT-&-PROUD BOY PASSES THE BASEBALL BOY

by JOSH TVRDY

from COURT GREEN

& we look at each other heterosexually, which isn't
    a real kind of looking, a looking everywhere

besides his face, my face, O look at the sky, look
    at that nearly blooming magnolia, its heavy bulbs

needing one warm day to fully unbuckle,
    floppy white petals finally draped with sun.

Even at the club, where it was easy
    trying each other on—nervous fingers

sliding the spine's slick chute all the way
    down to sacrum, then lower—even there

he had to close his eyes, imagine me
    different. I don't blame him. I remember

that particular tint of shame, slipping it on
    like a rest stop Trojan fumbled from a pocket

& opened with teeth. Later that night he took
    my mouth to his starving places. Let me say that

less gay: I gave him a blowjob on a sinking
    air mattress in the corner of a cramped Air

BnB with somebody's foot flicking in sleep
    three feet away. He didn't kiss any part of

me, but it was good. It was. I'm trying to tell
    the truth. Trying to believe my body can pass

his on this cracked sidewalk without
    flinching into shadows because I'm nothing

like him. I've gnawed through every curtain
    to belong in this light. This gorgeous April light.

*Nominated by Court Green*

# LONGSHORE DRIFT

fiction by JULIA ARMFIELD

from GRANTA

There are basking sharks in the upper layers of the water—prehistoric things, nightmare-mouthed and harmless. Plankton-eaters, the way all seeming monsters are. They fill the coastal waters in the summertime, rising up to trawl the krill blooms. Puckered with barnacles, blasé as window-shoppers, they can grow over a lifetime to twenty feet in length.

There are warning flags along the wrack line: SHARKS—SWIM AT YOUR OWN RISK. The threat is actually minimal, basking sharks being liable to give you little more than a bump on the knee, but the effect of the signs is still an odd one. There are no barriers, the water is open, creating the sense of a curiously lackadaisical approach to public safety. *Danger, but do what you want, we're not the police.*

Around the rock pools, paddleboarders nudge the backs of sharks with oars and suffer no retaliation. Mackerel fishers follow the oily cut of dorsal fins, heading home with lockboxes full of tiddlers, waxing mythical about the one that got away. Tall tales abound, swimmers reimagine close calls and teeth where none existed. A story that seems to crop up every year sees a woman snorkelling for sea glass swimming right down into the open mouth of a basker, where she has a good look at the contents of its stomach before coming out again, unscathed. Ridiculous, of course, but in truth about as likely as anything else.

On the beach, Alice turns the truck at the wooden groyne which marks the end of the so-called *pleasure section* and idles the engine, considering the view. The afternoon has been bad, toothy with chill, no one buying much.

'Six Fabs and a Mint Cornetto,' Min recites, checking seven items off on her fingers. 'Slim pickings, Captain.'

'It's the weather,' Alice replies, gesturing at the window to encompass the wanness of the day. 'Who wants an ice cream in a funk like this?'

The afternoon is only an attempt at itself—fretful greyness, minnow stink of gutweed. Overhead, the vulture wheel of hunting gulls, a white-lipped, murderous sky. At the wheel, Alice squints towards the headland, the tidal band of beached sargassum running out before her like the rising of some long-backed creature from the sand. In the back, perched on some stacked boxes of Cadbury Flakes, Min kicks her leg reflexively against the wall. 'Bummer,' she nods, pulling a serious face but snorting when Alice glances back at her. 'Bummerama. What are you staring at? Don't act like you're not impressed by my urban vernacular.'

'You talk such shit.'

Alice finds she says this a lot, usually while smiling. Min laughs. Lit by the neon glow of the Polar slush machine, she is like something pulled from ice. Alice can imagine her, defrosted and on show in a museum— an artefact preserved for history, academics pointing to the places on her body where the cold has marked her, the diamond stud in her nose.

'*That girl is headed nowhere,*' Alice's mother likes to say. Going over the house with a Hoover after Min leaves, '*I don't know why she has to be here every hour of the day.*'

Her objections are routine: Min's tacky nylon glamour, the street where she lives, the father who won't get out of bed. Her hair is bleach-fried, wilting in natural light. In the presence of Alice's mother, she has a nervous habit of fluffing it out like a mammal inflating its fur.

'*You're such a clever girl,*' Alice's mother will say whenever Min has just departed. '*Can't you find a cleverer sort of friend?*'

At school Alice is streamed into all the hardest sets, and it seems that the friendships she is expected to cultivate are also the hardest and dullest, the ones that come with the most supplementary work. Last year, she had been involved in a punishing sort of best-friendship with a girl named Pam who had won several prizes for debating, and talked droningly about *their relationship* as though they were husband and wife. They had spent their Friday evenings locked in a revolve of interminable sleepovers, Pam insisting they watched movies of her choice and then talking over them. If Pam stayed over at Alice's, she would mention all the things it was a shame they couldn't do that evening: it was a shame Alice didn't have Sky or a real computer, it was a shame Alice's mother only made normal toast, unlike Pam's mother, who made it French. By the end of term, Alice had started hanging around with Min after art class, and it was only via a protracted period of passive cruelty that Pam, waiting doggedly for Alice outside the science laboratories or at the back gates at four o'clock, had finally been shaken off. These days, Alice only sees her occasionally, hanging around with another girl named Karen, who is apparently a big deal in choir.

In the back of the truck, Min pushes herself upright, clambering forwards over the gearstick and into the passenger seat, giving Alice a chuck to the head as she goes. Her silver hair is straggled back into a ponytail, acid bunch behind her ears.

'Cut our losses, I would,' she says, chewing gum and planting her feet on the dashboard. 'Take her on a victory lap and then get out of here.'

'Victory how?' Alice grumbles. 'Six Fabs and a Mint Cornetto does not a victory make.'

'Cheer up, honey pie,' Min rubs her hands vigorously on her polyester shorts before leaning over to touch Alice's cheek. A jolt of electricity. 'Magic finger.' Min laughs and Alice wriggles away from her, jerking the clutch into first.

The music starts automatically, the ice-cream jingle, 'Que Sera Sera' on imitation chimes. Gulls scatter as the truck eases forwards, trundling towards higher ground. The tourists, for the most part, tend to keep to the safety of the dunes, bracketed behind canvas windbreakers, hunkered grimly over sandwiches and picking sand from the spines of over-ambitious holiday books. Every year, the coastguard finds on average six copies of *Anna Karenina* abandoned on the flats between April and high summer. The council has plans for a small exhibition.

Alice aims the truck inland, a crunching movement rumbling through the fabric of her skirt. Plastic cups and discarded tennis balls everywhere, cigarette butts stamped down and forming shapes like lugworm burrows in the sand. Manoeuvring up towards the dunes, Alice notes a bright scrim of shiny paper—a crumpled Fab wrapper—and feels momentarily guilty. The back doors of the truck are panelled with warning signs, painted on by Min's uncle in thick black bitumen: LITTER MAKES THE FUTURE BITTER; KEEP IT NICE, DON'T DROP YOUR ICE.

Wondering whether she ought to stop and scoop up the wrapper, Alice glances at Min, only to find her bunching up her chewing gum in a paper napkin, preparing to throw it out of the window.

'Oh, don't,' Alice says, regretting it almost immediately—the mumsy tone. Min raises an eyebrow at her, though she does withdraw her hand from the open window, throwing the napkin instead in the cupholder beside the gearstick.

'Fair enough,' she nods, and while her tone is light Alice feels she can detect the faintest note of mockery. 'Mustn't be bitter with my litter.'

It can be like this, sometimes. A sudden quirk of the lip. Alice biting back the wrong words. Sitting together in History, passing notes until Alice writes something stupid or uncool, underlines the wrong thing, and Min crumples the note in her fist.

'Fair enough,' this stock phrase, its cringing detachment. The sudden removal of camaraderie and Alice clawing after it.


Alice opens her mouth to speak, but Min is now gesturing ahead to a group of teenaged boys who have wandered down from the slate flats that border the bank of seagrass. They are flagging down the truck. 'Thank fuck,' she exclaims. 'Passing trade. Pull up.'

Alice squints through the windscreen. The boys are their age or a little older. Of the group, three are in swimming trunks and two in wetsuits, all of them clutching preposterously at surfboards which collide as they approach the truck. The sea is still as pondwater.

'What are they going to do,' Alice grumbles as she brings the truck to a standstill. 'Build a fort with those things?'

'Who cares?' Min is already clambering back over the gearstick into the back section, sliding up the serving window and leaning almost all the way out. 'Well, aren't you boys a sight for sore eyes?'

The boys cluster like geese. One of them, wet-lipped with a tongue piercing, asks Min what she's doing selling ice cream on such a chilly day. *What's a nice girl like you doing in a truck like this.* Min's reply comes out static with the same electricity she discharged against Alice's cheek.

'Well, what are you doing *buying* ice cream on such a chilly day?' Over her shoulder, Alice sees her friend as though beheaded; green shorts and a silver thread in her sweater, leaning elbows on the serving ledge, resting her chest on her folded hands. Her legs are coarse as soap and chicken-skinned with a two-day growth of hair. At the back of one knee she has a small tattoo, a Russian doll with its top removed and another, smaller face peeking out. Alice was with her when she got it, held her hand and watched the anxious sweat soak into the back of her T-shirt. *I contain multitudes*—the tattoo seems to say—*or at least five or six*. Afterwards, the two of them had gone for burgers, Min with her bandaged leg elevated and her foot on Alice's knee. Smearing ketchup, sharing a lemonade, Min leaning over to lick a daub of mustard off Alice's wrist. They had wandered up to the arcade at the end of the pier and Alice had spent all her money buying them games on the *Mortal Kombat* machine until Min had decided she was sick of playing because none of the female characters ever won.

Alice doesn't realise she is scowling until she catches her expression in the rear-view mirror. The boy with the tongue piercing is talking, brassy glint of unprecious metal, and Min's laugh is the same upside-down thing it always seems. He is asking whether the truck belongs to her and she is weaving him a series of stories: *her family inheritance; driven it from one end of this country to the other; the things you see from a serving hatch, you wouldn't believe.*

'She can't drive,' Alice wants to call over her shoulder. 'Her uncle did his knee in playing five-a-side and she's roped me into driving his truck because I passed my test.'

'Because she knew I'd have nothing better to do,' she also wants to call over her shoulder.

'I don't know what I want,' the boy with the tongue piercing is saying now, in a voice which fairly communicates that what he wants is probably not included on the menu. The serving side of the truck is panelled with pictured offerings in frantic technicolor; Zooms and Magnums and Soleros, pre-packaged ice-cream sandwiches on which Alice has experimented, leaving them out on paper plates for hours, coming back slightly disconcerted to find that they have failed to melt.

At the window, Min hangs even more precariously outwards, shifting sideways in a way which suggests she might be pointing at some item on the menu.

'Take your pick—little bit of what you fancy,' she says in her Mae West leer.

'How about you surprise me,' the tongue-pierced boy replies, and his friends chortle in a weird tandem. There is a sudden, queasy rocking of the truck, as though several people have leant up against it at once.

260

'Earl Grey and sardine ice cream it is,' Min replies, and Alice grins despite herself. It is a sleepover game they play, dreaming up the most disgusting of possible flavour combinations: lemon curd and spare ribs, duck and Parma Violets, tinned pilchards and strawberry jam. A strange pretence at early teenhood, despite the fact that they are both nearly eighteen—nights spent sleeping top to tail in Alice's bedroom and playing stupid games, inking outlines of the constellations on one another's arms in biro, tweezing eyebrows and talking on and on about kissing, Min's little moonstone teeth in the dark.

At the serving hatch, Min hooks one bony ankle over the other and Alice wills her to retract her head and wink at her, give some sign that they still share ownership of the joke she has just hurled unthinkingly away from them. But Min remains where she is and the joke sails away over the head of the boy whose fingers now appear on the edge of the hatch.

'Whatever sounds good to you,' he says. 'What's your name, anyway?'

Min draws back a little, though only to open up the chest freezer and root around inside.

'Minerva.'

'You're sweet, Minerva.'

Min snorts, kicking back one leg as though the knee has just been swiped out from under her.

'Nah, you're just all hot at the thought of ice cream.'

She hands something over—bright red wrapper—and there is a renewed sound of butting surfboards.

'What's this?' the boy with the tongue piercing asks, an anticipatory tone which has no business being used for ice cream.

'Your heart's desire.'

'You reckon?'

Min laughs.

'Good going for two quid, yeah?'


Alice has no enthusiasm for boys, except as they appear in the abstract— the fictional approximations that people the books she reads, appealing only in silhouette and with the meat cut out of their middles. In reality, boys appear to her like plane trees in a photograph, sudden and ugly and always just in the centre of things, giving idiotic answers in class and telling boring stories about how drunk they got the night before. Exactly where this distaste springs from is unclear to her. She isn't gay—she's pretty sure. She's tested it, stared at the women in her brother's magazines. In truth, it is something she thinks about only seldom, usually as an afterthought to the late-night recollection of old humiliations—the time Toby Waters had been moved next to her as punishment for talking in English class and had told everybody afterwards that she smelled; the time she announced to a group of friends that her favourite character in *Grease* was Marty when everyone else was saying Danny; the way a girl in sixth form had once looked her over and told her, apropos of nothing, that she had a straight girl's way of doing her hair.

She has only been kissed once, by the stock boy at the cafe where she worked for most of the previous summer; a nineteen-year-old with a shining ham of a face, who ate egg-salad sandwiches on his lunch breaks and sweated dark crescents into the armpits of his shirts. He had trapped her on the galley steps that led down to the meat freezer one day when she was running back to fetch something, bracketing her head against the wall and telling her how cute she was. His smell like egg and perspiration, soft sour note of Glacier Mints and his teeth too big and scraping against her own. She had let him do it, and afterwards slid into the meat freezer and stood there wondering what it was she had come to fetch.

Min likes boys, although always the wrong ones, too loud, bad-smelling or encumbered with long-term girlfriends. She is the kind of girl stitched together by brief liaisons—'*Bad-news girl*,' Alice's mother says in her hands-up church voice, '*shakes herself out like sheets.*' In the wind-down days of the summer term just gone, Min had dragged Alice out almost every weekend to a seafront bar bizarrely named the Credenza, where they had flashed their fake IDs at an indifferent bouncer and danced until Min found a boy to kiss. On the dance floor, a chalk-smeared stretch of glittering malachite, they would shimmy to nineties music, Min's hair lit up like a chemical spill by the disco lights. Most of the time the boys came easily, sloping over the way one approaches a dangerous dog, wary but still irrationally keen to touch. Occasionally, when the music was sluggish and the attention not forthcoming, Min would loop her arms around Alice's shoulders and angle down through her hips, winking solemnly as she did so, a complicit little change of rhythm. This never failed. The boys were usually ones they knew from school, although sometimes there were tourists or boys from inland towns down for the weekend surf. Min would disappear with whoever approached first for half an hour to forty-five minutes, emerging always smeared and alone to find Alice drinking fizzy water, grabbing her hand and demanding that they leave. She would give these boys a phone number when they asked for it, though it would always be Alice's number rather than her own.

'*It's like you're my protector,*' she would say, after Alice had spent another Saturday morning fending off calls from boys with names like Gus and Sam and Timbo, '*fighting off the vagabonds who would do me wrong.*'

By the end of term, Alice had perfected a fair approximation of Min's voice, brushing off the boys who called her up less delicately than she would care to admit. *It was a kiss—move on. I have herpes. I'm in love with the girl you saw me dancing with before.*

At the serving hatch, Min is handing out Cornettos in a wide circle; clattering of surfboards like a racket of seagulls being fed.

'Calm down,' she says, clearly enjoying herself, 'plenty to go round.'

'Animals,' the boy with the tongue piercing agrees, prompting a grumble of insult from his companions. 'Grabbing at a girl like that.' 'Grabbing I can handle,' Min replies, and Alice finds herself rolling her eyes. The dispiriting sight of herself in the rear-view mirror, bad-tempered and raw with acne. She has never been very keen on the thought of herself as other people see her. The small lapine eyes, too far apart by several inches, the angry skin and colourless hair. Min likes to say she has a Georgian look to her, cutting black dots and stars out of sticky paper and patching her face with them. *There you go, blemish-free and oh-so-stylish.*

'Who else've you got back there?'

The question is sudden, the boy with the tongue piercing bracing his fingers against the serving hatch as though about to climb inside. Min glances back at Alice.

'Just my friend.'

'Just your friend?'

'Just my friend Alice.'

'Is Alice as sweet as you?'

A laugh. A boy comes round to the passenger-side window, pressing his face to the glass. Another boy joining him, and another. Gawping aquarium faces. Alice hooks her legs under her and looks over her shoulder at Min, who has turned back to the hatch.

'No, not as sweet as me.'

The boy with the tongue piercing laughs.

'So it's Sweet Mol—'

'Minerva.'

'Sweet Minerva and Savoury Alice.'

'That's what they call us.'


The day is darkening, growing soft about its edges. A rise in the wind has resulted in a minor improvement of the water, the waves now rolling at a choppy half-speed that has surfers picking their uncertain way down from the dunes. The boys around the truck seem collectively to notice this, sudden loosened pressure as they peel back from the windows to stare out to sea. A minor commotion. One of them has knocked against another and dropped his Cornetto. From the back of the truck, Min gives a high little laugh, but the attention trained on her moments before is distracted.

The boys are suddenly fractious, eager to be off. The one with the tongue piercing pulls his fingers from the hatch and Alice twists in her seat.

'He hasn't paid,' she says, not quite knowing if she means him to hear her. Min springs forwards through the hatch again.

'Wait a minute, this isn't a free dispensary—that's fifteen quid in total, thank you very much!' Her tone is irritatingly sweet, and the nonchalant reply only makes it worse.

'No money—nowhere to keep it in this get-up.'

Min retracts her head, white hair bristling at the nape of her neck, and Alice briefly envisages herself muscling up from the driver's seat and demanding the money.

'Tell you what though,' the boy with the tongue piercing continues, 'once we're done on the water we're going to get cleaned up and go into town. I'll have money then.'

'Not a lot of use to me now, is it?'

'No but it'll keep until I buy you a drink.'


The wind is coming in from the headland, pushing the ocean current sideways. Along the beach, Alice can see little tumbleweeds of silt and litter being blown across the sands, as though the beach has been tipped upwards at one corner and is leaking to the left. This gradual slip is one that has been going on for some years, a perpendicular drift of sediment caused by the swash and backwash of water on the beach. The wooden groynes that punctate the sands were set up only recently as a defence against this redistribution, though every year it still seems that a little more of the beach trickles gently off the surface of the map.

The boys move off in a pack, handprint smears of ice cream visible at the edges of their surfboards. Behind her, Alice hears Min slide the serving hatch shut. She puts the truck into gear without thinking about it and jerks the vehicle forwards, and Min stumbles against the freezer as she does.

'Hey, wait!'

The red flags along the wrack line beat out as if in semaphore, furling and unfurling in the breeze. Alice idles the van, waiting for Min to clamber up into the passenger seat, which she does with another chuck to Alice's chin. 'Safety first, Captain,' she says, ostentatiously drawing her seat belt across and grinning. She is happy again, though Alice's mood has darkened.

A hard sugar smell of freezer burn—dark smell, sweetness on the turn. Min kicks her feet up onto the dashboard and Alice finds herself irritated by her peeling toenail polish.

She looks at Min's arm, where the boy with the tongue piercing has scrawled a phone number. She wonders how he could have had a pen on him and claim to have nowhere to keep his change.

'He didn't pay,' she says again, squinting unnecessarily out of the front windscreen as she moves the truck forwards, as though trying to see her way through fog. The automatic chimes have started up again with the motion of the engine; 'Beautiful Dreamer' this time.

Min takes up the ball of paper in which she had previously wadded her gum and drops it out of the open window.

'We'll get it back.'

'What, when we go for a drink?'

Min leans her head forwards, fluffs out her hair.

'Exactly.'

'Pretty sure it was just you he was inviting.'

'Oh, Alice,' Min sighs, a voice that affects a weary maternal timbre; Alice's mother telling her to for God's sake stop picking her spots. *You're only making it worse.* 'If that's what you want to believe then I really can't help you. People don't issue exclusive invitations to drinks. He didn't call me up to the country club. Come or don't come, I don't know. Whatever you like. No one's going to care.'

The day is collapsing, soft deflation in the surface of the sky. Along the dunes, most of the tourists who have not already scuttled down to the sea are packing themselves away, hauling windbreakers inwards like sails to be stowed, throwing up the crusts of white-bread sandwiches to be caught mid-air by gulls.

'Best pack it in now, anyway,' Min is saying, and Alice finds herself scowling despite the logic of the statement. The ice-cream jingle has taken on a slightly unsettling tone with the threat of worsening weather—an eerie juxtaposition, the way wind chimes acquire a warning quality before a storm.

'Six Fabs and a Mint Cornetto.' Alice shrugs one shoulder, aiming the truck back up towards the concrete strip that leads into the upper car park. 'Your uncle's truck, your uncle's takings, not mine.'

'And fifteen quid's worth of ice cream just then!'

'Yes, well.'

'Yes, well to my unique powers of salesmanship!'

'Yes, well, all big business is run on the strength of IOUs.'

'All right, crabby.' Min leans back against the window, grinning slightly and moving one foot from the dashboard to prod at Alice's arm. Alice shrugs her off but Min persists, giggling as she moves her foot to again prod Alice's elbow, moving up in increments to tickle her shoulder, then her ear.

'*Stop it*,' Alice snaps without really expecting to, slapping at Min's foot until she removes it, her smile fading.

'Fair enough,' she shrugs, sitting back and slinking her feet beneath her.


Along the dunes that teeter from the upper car park, a blanket of glasswort creeps down towards the path. It is a samphire, of sorts, a prickled matting plant that grows in saline conditions and can, if burnt, yield soda and potash. Min's mother, on good days, sends her out to pull up handfuls of the stuff which she pickles in malted vinegar or renders into squat little soaps. These, in turn, she sells on Saturdays at coastal marketplaces, enlisting Min to lug them to and from the car, or to accost strangers and use her tight, acidic influence to persuade them to a purchase. Alice has accompanied Min once or twice on her harvesting trips, pulling up the sharp little branches more or less solo as Min sits higher up the flats and complains about her parents. '*Let her get an assistant,*' she'll say, watching Alice pulling weeds with little sense of irony. '*Let him get out of bed every once in a while and help her. What am I doing all this for, hey?*'

They had come down, once, at the very start of summer, tipsy after Min had got them forcibly ejected from the Credenza for yanking a bottle of Grolsch from behind the bar. They had managed to get away with the bottle and had skidded down the dunes in unsuitable shoes to drink it lying in the glasswort, each complaining at the spiny leaves creeping up beneath their skirts. Min, blue-lipsticked in a bluer twilight, had rambled on about a boy at the club who had ignored her, despite the fact that only two days previously she had allowed him to finger her behind the Hope and Anchor way out along the pier. Lying slightly side-ways, Alice had stared down at the wooden groyne stretching out towards the water and had registered a curious sensation of slippage, a drifting down of all the bits and pieces of her body like a sloughing off of sand. Beside her, Min had smelled of beer and peanut brittle, a squeeze of Dior Poison from the big bottle Alice knew her mother kept in her desk.

'Next week I'll take you to a *proper* club,' Min had said—something she was always saying. 'We'll go somewhere where the men are *adults*. I'll buy you a martini in a proper glass.'

Her teeth had been unnaturally white, like pieces of the moon, and Alice had rolled her shoulders and said nothing.

'I *will*,' Min had said, apparently goaded by her silence. 'We'll do all sort of things this summer. Find you a boy for once. World's our oyster.'

She had caught Alice's wrist between her fingers in the casual, trick-ling way she liked to touch—slotting her arms around Alice's neck or looping fingers over fingers, jewellery gestures, beading and bangling and always too loose.

'World's our oyster,' she had repeated, and her lips had been electric blue and too bizarre to kiss.


Min had dragged her down to the water that night, Alice's wrist still shackled between finger and thumb as they bolted down beyond the wrack line. At the edge of the water, Min kicked off her shoes but pulled Alice in without waiting for her to remove her own. She had lost them almost immediately, carried off with the first white heave of water the way so many things seemed subject to this endless sideways shift. In the dark the warning flags were grey, the clouds glassy and colour-blind. They had aimed for the headland, kicking, an unobtrusive blackened current. Alice had ducked her head and let her body rise, held up by clothes that tentacled around her ankles as Min dragged her further out.

There were sharks in the shallows—baskers, harmless. A few hundred feet from the shore, Alice had felt Min's fingers release her and, grasping after her, had tipped her head beneath the water, caught her legs in the tangle of her dress and very suddenly sunk. Alice had found one there, only feet beneath her. They are vast things, baskers, whale-mouthed—filtering their food through a cavernous yawn of jaw not unlike the drum of a washing machine. A wave passing over her head, Alice had sunk further than expected, scrambling with the sudden weight of her clothes as the shark filled her frame of vision. The great mouth had seemed toothless, ribbed with bone, a mouth that she momentarily looked down, feeling briefly convinced, in her drowning confusion, that she could see everything from its guts and gullet to the small internal secret of its heart. The shark, for its part, had seemed unbothered by her presence, only tilting slightly to avoid her as she struggled, bumping by her the way one small boat might pass another in the night. Twisting sideways and thrashing her legs away from her dress, she briefly panicked, until a hand again enclosed her wrist and dragged her upwards, Min laughing in her face as she crested the surface, flinging arms in blind confusion round her neck.

'I thought you'd gone,' Alice had choked, and Min only rolled her eyes, treading water, her hair a glowstick crackle in the dark.

'Where would I go?' Min had deadpanned. 'Pubs'll be shut by now.'

Beneath her, Alice had felt the bump of fins beneath her feet and drew her legs up, briefly allowing Min to keep them both afloat. Some way off, before the shadow of the headland, the pier, ghostly in the way that all piers are, shimmered unobtrusively in sea-light.

*Nominated by Granta*

# HOEING BEETS, 1964, SKAGIT VALLEY

## by SAMUEL GREEN

from PRAIRIE SCHOONER

*I think I will do nothing for a long time but listen . . .*
WHITMAN

What the farmer wants is plain.
He sharpened five hoes before dawn
on a wheel in the barn after fried oatmeal,
toast & eggs. He spends no time
with the names of weeds. Instead
he shows us what a beet leaf
looks like. Anything that isn't this,
he says, chop it out. Make it dead.
He hopes we wore practical shoes.

The four women run from nineteen
to thirty-five, three of them married.
What they want depends. Audrey hopes
to buy her daughter a bike. Linda's in love
with a sailor, owes her sister long
distance charges. Sheila hides vodka
away from her husband. Sue needs new
sheets for their bed, they're wearing
the bridal ones out.

What the gulls want is whatever we disturb
in this flood plain soil, beetles, grubs,

the wriggle & curl of worms. They follow
at our backs, a squalling storm of squawks & wing flaps.

Dust devils rise & spin beside us. A kitchen
screen door slams, then slams again. The farmer
bangs on something rusty with a wrench,
his arm halfway up before we hear the sound.
I am fifteen, standing in for my mother.
Anyone might guess what I think
I want: to watch the way these women
bend & reach, the slow stretch of fabric,
smell of their sweat, the way patches of skin

shine in the day's raunchy heat, how Audrey licks
the small fine hairs on her upper lip
after each swig from the red Kool-Aid jug,
how Linda plucks white threads from a rip
in her pink pedal pushers & winds them
round a thumb, how Sheila hums
a Patsy Cline tune chopping weeds
on each stressed syllable falling to pieces
all down the half-mile rows, how Sue washes
her feet when we stop for lunch, lets me
dry them with the loose tail

of my shirt. They work heads down, chittering
like starlings, these women who are tired
of pinochle, tired of perms, tired of opening
cans. They are a sisterhood of secrets, the uses
& failings of men. Their mothers are dealing
with night sweats, their grandmothers fret
about rest homes. They pretend to forget
I am here, a boy who plays cards with his mother
& friends, who behaves & keeps his mouth shut,
a boy they think of as shy. They know what I believe
I want, they know what I need, & they know why.

*Nominated by Prairie Schooner, David Jauss, Joni Tevis*

# MARCELINE WANTED
# A BIGGER ADVENTURE

by SHENA MCAULIFFE

from TRUE STORY

I would not have come across the grave of Marceline Baldwin Jones by chance. I like walking in the older, hillier section of Earlham Cemetery, where the crumbling graves are sometimes topped with the rain-softened shape of a lamb or praying hands, and the old Quaker names are in cursive scripts or simple block letters: Eliza and Caleb and Levi and Alice. Marceline's grave is in a newer section, an orderly corner far from the road, where the stones are organized like little villages, so their backs face each other and the heads of the dead rest together, sometimes arranged around the base of a tree. I looked up Marceline's grave on findagrave.com, and then located it on the cemetery map. I have visited deliberately, driven by twin habits of walking and curiosity. I do not know exactly what I am looking for.

It is a hot day in early spring, and I have sweated through my shirt. I have not brought water. I stand before the headstone. I see no evidence that anyone else has been here recently—no flowers or plants, no folded scraps of paper or envelopes. I hear the banging of a construction site somewhere far beyond the row of slender trees that marks the back edge of the cemetery. A few birds chirp.

Marceline Mae Baldwin was born in Richmond, Indiana, in 1927. She was a Methodist, a daughter and sister. She was, by all accounts, a generous and mild woman all her life. According to her cousin Avelyn Chilcoate, Marceline longed for a life outside the small town; the two young women, both nurses, had plans to move elsewhere together, maybe to somewhere in Kentucky. But then, in 1948, Marceline met a strange young man named Jim Jones, an orderly at the hospital where she worked, and together they stepped into the stream of history.

Jimmy Jones was born in 1931 and spent his earliest years living with his parents in a shack without plumbing in rural Indiana, not far from where Marceline is buried. They say he was a strange kid, and that he had a hard time making friends. They say he was very intelligent and obsessed with death and religion, that he occasionally performed funeral ceremonies for squirrels and rabbits, and that even as a teenager, he busied himself reading Stalin, Marx, Mao, Gandhi, and Hitler. Jimmy's father was a veteran of the First World War, his lungs severely damaged by mustard gas. He couldn't work because of his ragged breathing—there were times he could barely walk—but Jimmy's mother was ambitious and worked hard at whatever jobs she could get. For some reason, she did not allow her son in their house when she was out, so after school he wandered the streets, ducking into a store to "steal" a candy bar (which his mother would pay for on the weekend) or into the pool hall, where he might find his father, or he practiced dramatic sermons standing on a stump at the edge of the woods. Later, Jimmy coached younger boys at baseball, naming the local team after the Cincinnati Reds. When Jimmy was in high school, his mother left his father, and Jimmy moved with her to Richmond, Indiana, the small city on the border of Ohio where I have lived for the past three years. A serious young man, he sometimes preached on the streets in Richmond, a Bible tucked under his arm, and he graduated early from the public high school, which is still the city's only public high school and stands just across the river from my house. At sixteen, Jimmy got a job working nights at Reid Hospital, and it was there that he met the pretty, intelligent nurse with green eyes.

❧ ❧ ❧

*My first thought was that she was angelic, just glowing, shining, a will-of-the-wisp and obviously special. I wondered, "Whatever does she see in him?"*

—Jeanne Jones Luther, cousin of Jim Jones,
on the first time she met Marceline

*No smile, but a warm, worldly gaze that could hold you for-*
*ever. She is truly stunning, so sure and deep. She is exactly*
*what her young Jimmy Jones needs to become a man.*

Stephan Jones, son of Marceline and Jim Jones,
describing his parents as he sees them in a photo
taken during their courtship in the late 1940s

❀   ❀   ❀

When Marceline was twenty-two and Jim was nineteen, they married and moved across the state. In the years that followed, Jim was in and out of college, in Bloomington and Indianapolis, at IU and Butler. Marceline continued working as a nurse, and for a time, Jim worked for a monkey-importing business, selling pet monkeys door to door in Indianapolis.

Early in their marriage, Jim admitted to Marceline that he didn't believe in her God, but when the Methodist church committed to a new platform focused on racial integration and the alleviation of poverty, among other values that agreed with Jim's socialism, he decided to become a student pastor at a Methodist church. Marceline was thrilled, somehow seeming to forget that he wasn't actually Methodist, and maybe wasn't even Christian. Jim was a gifted preacher but soon became dissatisfied with the structures and routines of Methodism. He began preaching on the revival circuit, where he developed the kind of drama and charisma that drew crowds and donations. He began to perform healings, pulling "tumors" from people's mouths like coins from sleeves, like rabbits from hats. (In reality, they were rotten chicken livers he had learned how to palm.) Finally, he opened a small Indianapolis storefront church of his own. His parishioners were mostly African American women, and his services included helping them solve everyday problems, such as writing letters to the electric company to restore their power. His congregation outgrew the storefront, and in time, he bought a downtown building that had recently been vacated by a Jewish congregation. He named his church Peoples Temple, the apostrophe deliberately omitted because apostrophes indicate possession—ownership. The people of the temple were black and white, young and old, and Jim Jones was their leader, their reverend, and a socialist.

"Jim has used religion to try to get some people out of the opiate of religion," Marceline explained in a 1977 interview, many years after

273

she had come to terms with his lack of—and use of—Christian faith. Religion was a means to an end for him, a way to connect with the dispossessed. As for Marceline, she remained a faithful Methodist for a long time, but it isn't clear to me whether she still believed in a Christian God when she died.

Marceline gave birth to one son, whom they named Stephan, in 1959. Over the years, she and Jim adopted six other children: an eleven-year-old girl who may have been part Native American, three Korean orphans, a white American boy, and, in 1961, a black American boy they named Jim Jr. They were the first white couple in Indiana to legally adopt a black child, and they called their family a "rainbow family." Jim and Marceline were deeply committed to civil rights and egalitarianism, and Jim was appointed to the Human Rights Commission of Indianapolis. But all this, of course, was only the beginning of their story, and these things are mostly forgotten now.

❖     ❖     ❖

*In a deeply segregated city, [Peoples Temple] was one of the few places where black and white working-class congregants sat together in church on a Sunday morning. Its members provided various kinds of assistance to the poor—food, clothing, housing, legal advice—and the church and its pastor, Jim Jones, gained a reputation for fostering racial integration.*

Rebecca Moore, professor of religion and
sister of Carolyn Layton and Annie Moore,
devoted members of Peoples Temple who
both died at Jonestown

*His message was always very stark . . . brotherhood, all races together. You were accepted just as you were, you were not judged by the way you looked, or how much education you had, or how much money you had.*

—Rick Cordell, early member of Peoples Temple

❖     ❖     ❖

Jim Jones combed his black hair in a soft wave that dipped over his left eyebrow. His part was straight, and he kept his sideburns neatly trimmed. His nose was round and his cheeks were fleshy. He was a good-looking man—face full enough, eyes warm enough. He wore a sport coat and sunglasses, always the sunglasses.

Marceline shares a headstone with her parents. Walter and Charlotte Baldwin had visited their daughter in Jonestown in 1978, only weeks before she drank the poison, and then she was gone. I imagine them purchasing the plots and the stone, their own deaths still years in the future though their daughter's life was over at the age of fifty-one. Two of the Jones children—Lew Eric and Agnes Pauline—are buried beside their mother. Their stones are set slightly apart from hers, almost as if to protect their privacy in death. They were adults themselves—aged twenty-one and thirty-five—when they died in Jonestown, and they had children of their own who also died that night. Lew's son, Chaeoke Warren Jones, was a year and a half old when he died, which means he would be my age now, if he had lived. He is buried in a memorial site in Oakland, California, along with his mother, Terry Carter Jones, and many of the unclaimed or unidentified victims of the massacre.

As for Jim Jones himself, no one wanted his body buried in their cemetery, their town, their state. At first, the Baldwins and Jim's two surviving children planned to bury him in Earlham Cemetery, but the people of Richmond protested. His body was sure to draw an unsavory element, as well as possible violence at the funeral. Along with the rest of the bodies from Jonestown, his body was first flown from Guyana to Dover Air Force Base, in Delaware, but the people on the East Coast didn't want him buried in their states either. Some states devised sudden laws about whose bodies could and couldn't be interred within their bounds to ensure he would not be buried in their soil. In the end, his body was cremated, and his two surviving children scattered the ashes over the Atlantic.


In part, Marceline's grave is just a destination for a walk in a town where I have walked the same routes too many times, a town where I am sometimes bored by the walks, sometimes saddened by them—the boarded windows and potholes, the dogs that snarl and fling themselves at fences as I pass. I suppose I am walking here to meditate on Marceline, though I do not valorize her. She is mostly a mystery to me. Thinking about her makes me wonder about loyalty and love and how they can blind us, about agency and belief, about devotion and delusion. Perhaps I am only a lookie-loo, seeking her grave to stand safely near tragedy without truly experiencing it, to feel the buzz of some electrical darkness. It has been forty years since the deaths at Jonestown. There is nothing here but names on stones, bodies deep in the earth, invisible, still, and decayed.

When I was twelve, my dad took a new job and my family moved from a small town in Wisconsin to a Denver suburb, where the yards were fenced and treeless, the grass brown much of the year. The cost of living was higher than it had been in Wisconsin, and my sisters and I were old enough that it made sense for my mom to go back to work full-time. Our new home was, according to me and my sisters—and maybe my parents too, though they kept quiet about it—an ugly "suburban hell," and my sisters and I spent our unsupervised after-school hours indulging in MTV and other television we'd never been allowed to watch before. I still know well the songs and music videos that were popular in 1989, that first year in Colorado. Metallica's "One" tells the story of a World War I soldier who loses his limbs, sight, hearing, speech, and soul to a land mine. I was haunted by the image of a quadriplegic body draped in a sheet and isolated in darkness on its hospital bed. Skid Row's "Eighteen and Life" captured my imagination like a cheap novel, depicting a young life far more desperate and violent than my own middle-class existence. In these narratives, I recognized suffering, and I recognized my own safety and privilege.

Shortly after the move, my parents joined Amway, a pyramid scheme in which all members "own their own business" and earn a percentage of every product ordered by the business owners who join after them—beneath them on the pyramid. For a couple of years, my folks spent hours listening to cassette tapes that offered tips on how to approach friends, family, and strangers to get them to attend their meetings and join the business. At least one night a week they hosted a meeting in our living room, or attended one in the living room of their "sponsor," the person they'd joined under, or in the living room of one of the business owners near to them in the pyramid. The goal was always to bring a few "prospectives" to the meeting and get them to join. I spent many evenings babysitting for a one-year-old named Kelsey—a baby whose habits and expressions I grew to know well, a baby I grew to love—while her parents attended meetings with my parents. My dad shaved his beard during those years because Amway told him a clean-shaven face was a more successful and appealing business face.

One summer, my parents rented an RV and our family traveled to Spokane, where my parents attended the Amway Family Reunion, a convention where people like my parents listened to speakers meant to inspire them to get rich, and to teach them just how to do it. While my parents attended meetings, I babysat for Kelsey in the hotel. On the final morning, a Sunday, we attended a church service in the hall where the meetings had taken place. Amway had their own worship band, the Goads—even the band name was a spur, reminding you to get off your ass and sell and praise and live your best capitalist life. I think it was after the church service that we accepted an open invitation to visit the home of one of the top businessmen in the organization, who lived nearby. I had my picture taken in his garage beside his red Corvette.

Amway seemed a cocktail of capitalism, self-help, and religion. *Make money for your family. Be your best American self. Get rich while helping others get there too!* I don't hear much about Amway these days, but in the years after my parents let their branch of the business dwindle and die, I heard it mentioned now and then, usually as the punch line to a joke about rubes or sleazy businessmen.

I often wonder how my parents escaped the jokes and derision of Amway, why they were naive enough to join. They joined in the organization's heyday, but still: Wasn't it the sort of thing you stayed away from with a knee-jerk "no thank you," the same way you might hang up on a telemarketer? I think my parents did make a little extra money in those years, getting a percentage back on the products they bought that they would have bought anyway—the list of products was endless, everything from laundry detergent to cereal bars to plaque-fighting chewing gum—but how had they fallen for it? How had they so fully given themselves over, believing that they too could be millionaires, or at least a little wealthier, believing they'd earn college tuition for my sisters and me, or the sports car neither of them had ever desired?

When they quit, they argued about it. My mom wanted to keep their spot in the pyramid, making their small profit off products, but my dad wanted a clean break. Those in a pyramid scheme make no real friends; each person is using the others for financial benefit, and after they quit my parents spent a lot of time making formal apologies, calling friends and family they'd propositioned and then lost touch with, presumably because they'd offended them. My dad apologized to me and my sisters, too, for spending so much time on it, for letting those years pass too swiftly, with too much focus in the wrong places. It seemed there was something sticky in my parents' argument about quitting—some paradigm had lured them and shifted their vision, an illusion they now had to dismantle and release. Amway isn't a cult, and no one was going to ask them to drink poison, but it was a scheme that demanded they entangle their hopes for the future, their family, and even their faith, with their finances. It asked too much to be a safe venture.

For some months in the early 1960s, the Joneses lived in Brazil, one of the places Jim believed would survive nuclear holocaust, based on an article he had read on the topic in *Esquire.* And then there was the big move of Peoples Temple from Indiana to Ukiah, California, another safe area listed in the *Esquire* article. The people called Jim "Father," and Marceline was "Mother." Jim told Marceline—and his followers—that maybe he was God. Jim told his people to sign over their money and their goods, their social security checks. Sometimes, if they disobeyed, he beat them. There were drugs—lots of drugs—and Jim had sex with the men and the women of his temple. Some people left. Some people filed complaints. But the temple also helped people recover from addictions, and fed them, and helped them get jobs, and paid for them to go to college. It was an interracial, socialist family that shared what it had with every member, no matter their race or background.

Although Marceline couldn't bear any more children, she loved the ones she had, both adopted and biological. Her back ached with rheumatoid arthritis, and she couldn't have sex anymore, or not very often, but she stayed married to Jim even after he openly took a lover. Jim lived with Marceline for part of each week.

When I think about Marceline, I think about the strange avenues of our lives, the unexpected digressions, the ways, in retrospect, our paths can seem both fated and surprising, an impossible balance of magic and choice.

Never did I imagine I would live in Richmond, Indiana, a town to which I moved because there is a college here, where I am visiting assistant professor. I am forty-one years old, childless or—depending on how I spin it, depending on the day—child-free. I am standing in a cemetery at the grave of Marceline Baldwin Jones, a woman to whom I have no specific connection, but I would like to leave something here—flowers, a scrap of silk, a marble—some token that says *Rest in peace, my puzzle,* or *Someone was here. I remember you.*

Who else has stood here and marveled that they are standing at the grave of a woman they never knew, at the surprises of Marceline's life, the surprises of their own? And who has stood here who knew Marceline and wondered all the more at her unlikely path?

Stepping closer to Marceline's headstone, I now notice two pennies, heads up, resting on the back ledge, evidence that others wanted to leave something too. But my pockets are empty. No dandelions or violets grow here. I have only a small notebook, a pen, and my phone.


In 1977, an article in *New West* magazine made public some of the darker secrets of Peoples Temple. Former members reported that they had been harassed and coerced, that public humiliation and physical abuse of temple members were par for the course, that under threat of abuse and humiliation members were forced to donate belongings and property, including the deeds to their homes, that Jones faked healings of temple members, and that once he had feigned being shot so that he could also feign healing his own gunshot wounds. The temple ran a number of youth homes that received funding from the state, and a couple who had supervised one of the homes reported that state money meant for the care of boys who lived in the home was given instead to the temple.

Jones got wind of the article before its publication and, bracing for the fallout, he and hundreds of his followers moved to a settlement in Guyana, a newly independent socialist country where the people were mostly black and English was the official language. The relocation had been in the works since 1974, when the temple had leased more than three thousand acres of Guyanese land on which to build their communist utopia. A smaller group of Jones's people had been in Guyana for over a year, working to establish the settlement. The *New West* article raised doubts that everyone in Guyana was there of their own free will and questioned whether people would be able to leave should they decide Jonestown was not the life they wanted.

Deep in the jungle, the settlers built small frame houses and tried to grow food, and they named their village Jonestown after their leader. Jim Jones ruled over it, and ruled over them. He spoke to them for hours over a loudspeaker, late into the night after they had worked hard all day. He lived with Carolyn Layton and Maria Katsaris, his two long-term lovers.

For a time, Marceline stayed in California, leading Peoples Temple there and defending her husband to the press and the government. In October of that year, she moved to Jonestown, though she often flew to Washington, DC, to defend her husband before Congress or the courts. Sometimes, when Jones was feeling especially ill or drugged or had another commitment elsewhere, Marceline—Mother—spoke for him.

When I was twenty, in college, my parents came to visit me on a Sunday, and I took them to church with me. They had raised me Catholic, but I had been attending a nondenominational Christian church that gathered in the high school a few blocks from my house. We walked in the front doors of the school, past the taxidermied impala, a type of antelope that lives in southern Africa with long, thin legs and lyre-shaped antlers, for some unfathomable reason the school mascot.

We entered the auditorium. Spotlights lit the stage, where the worship band played songs with a lot of major chords. People waved their hands and closed their eyes and sang. I, too, closed my eyes and sang, and sometimes I raised my hands and imagined God's love as warm and yellow, like sunlight through my heart. The pastor, Johnny Square, was a compact, athletic man, always stylishly dressed in a suit, a passionate speaker. Johnny Square called on us to take some particular action that demonstrated our faith. He challenged us—and said that to disobey him would be to disobey God.

A few weeks later, my dad sent me a letter, though he lived only an hour away and I saw him regularly, and we sometimes also spoke on the phone. He wrote that he was worried for me, that he worried about my passion and idealism, that he knew how easy it was to follow powerful emotions, that he worried about obedience when it was demanded by a preacher, that he worried about cults.

I suppose a part of me was angry about the letter—at the lack of trust it exhibited, or at the challenge to my independence, as well as to my faith in Johnny Square, a man I had respected and considered a spiritual leader. But I don't remember the anger. I remember I thought my dad was sort of right.

For months before the letter arrived, my faith had been shaky. There were things about Christianity that I just didn't believe, and didn't like, and I had been trying out churches, riding my bike to a different one each week, seeking one that felt right, that really fit my idea of God and faith. My skirt would get tangled in the spokes as I rode, and I would arrive disheveled and feeling shy. I had started to skip a week now and then, and then I skipped more weeks than not. I shaved my head, something mildly symbolic of grief and newness. I took a lot of hikes and runs, and I spent countless hours behind my camera, photographing burnt trees and roadside firework stands and plastic baby dolls and orange peels. I spent entire nights, entire weekends, in the darkroom printing photographs. Gradually, in this way, art replaced my religious faith. I remember what it was like: not a sudden revelation, but a slow unwinding, a letting go.

Do I see in Marceline something of myself? Another path I could have taken, had I been born in a different time, had I found the perfect pastor, even—or especially—one whose faith was based on communism and not the Bible?

In the US, suspicion and worry about Jones and Peoples Temple gained steam. Family members of Jonestown residents formed a group, called the Concerned Relatives, and wrote letters to the Guyanese government and the US secretary of state, urging an investigation. In 1978, led by former temple lawyer Tim Stoen, the Concerned Relatives launched a human rights lawsuit against Jones, who quickly countersued for damages.

Complicating matters, Tim Stoen's five-year-old son, John, was in Jonestown and was at the center of a bitter custody battle. Jones claimed he was the child's father, and perhaps he was. Stoen had signed an affidavit stating that it was true, but perhaps he had done so under coercion—not an uncommon tactic for Jones. Stoen's wife, Grace, had left Peoples Temple in 1976, and her testimony against Jones was included in the *New West* article. Tim Stoen had remained a member of the temple and moved to Guyana with John. But in 1978, Tim Stoen, too, defected (or escaped), and joined Grace's custody battle. Courts ruled in their favor, but Jones refused to release the boy, even though the court ruling meant that he would be arrested if he returned to the US without surrendering the boy.

In the fall of 1978, California congressman Leo Ryan, heeding the requests of the Concerned Relatives, contacted Jones and expressed his wish to visit Jonestown. The request made Jones angry and nervous. It was Marceline who pleaded with him to be reasonable. They had nothing to hide, she said. Why shouldn't he visit? They would show the congressman what they were doing, and that people were not kept against their will. Eventually, Leo Ryan visited. The visit went horribly awry; on

November 18, 1978, one of the people of Jonestown shot the congressman dead on a runway in the jungle of Guyana.

Marceline Baldwin was born in Richmond, Indiana, and her body was returned to this place where I stand, a place that no one much knows or recognizes. Google immediately defaults to Virginia when you type "Richmond." But everything begins somewhere, and Jonestown began here, when Jim Jones met Marceline Baldwin, a woman with intelligence, compassion, social grace, and beauty. Her father was on the city council; she knew how to move among the educated classes and the politicians, and Jim learned from her. A typical Midwesterner, she was loyal to a fault. I think of Tammy Wynette's 1968 hit song, "Stand by Your Man," how Jim's good times paralleled Marceline's bad ones—until the times were bad for everyone. Afraid or miserable, betrayed or heartbroken, she had children with him, and she believed in his mission of equality and socialism. She stayed.

Is this part of what it means to be curious? I want to know about the pale bark of sycamores, a tree I don't remember seeing in the West, and about the ways people in different geographic regions slice their pizza (in Indiana: squares), and about the unknowable and surprising pathways of our lives. I live in here, in Richmond, Indiana, where Jim Jones once preached on street corners and Marceline Baldwin nursed people back to health. And so I read about Peoples Temple and about Jonestown. I look up the location of Marceline's grave and I walk to it. This is another way of knowing a place: I follow my curiosity with my feet. Marceline's stone and the strange path of her life are the shapes over which I drape my curiosity today.

I met the man who is now my husband at the wedding of our two best friends. After the wedding, we were at a pub with the bride and groom and other wedding guests, and in the din, he told me about his childhood in a commune, a "community" in which his parents still lived. He was delivered by a midwife in a cabin his dad had built on the shared community land in California, not far from the ocean. He was the first child born within the community, and when they knew he was a boy, his dad went out and waved a blue flag from the top of a hill to let the others know. My husband spent his first years in California among te-pees and hand-built shacks and gardens. Potty-training meant learning to use the outhouse, which scared him because it was full of spiders. He spent his days running naked with the other community children.

This was in the mid-1970s. In the early '80s—only a few years after the deaths at Jonestown—the community sold the California land, where they were stretched by bad financial decisions and harassed by fearful neighbors. They moved to rural Nevada, and after a year, most of them moved to Salt Lake City, where the community remained for the rest of my husband's childhood, supporting itself with a chain of natural food stores and other small businesses.

Sometime between California and Salt Lake City, my husband's mother became sick, and in prayer she promised that if she was healed of her illness, she would remain loyal to their spiritual leader, Norm, and to the community, where everyone meditated twice a day and put their faith in prophets and energy and love. She was eventually diag-nosed with Graves' disease. Her thyroid was irradiated, and she has reg-ulated her hormones with levothyroxine ever since. She remained committed to the community and her faith, even after Norm died, and even after her husband wanted to leave the community.

As my husband grew up, the community changed financial models many times, shifting from shared finances to more independent fi-nances, and with each new iteration, people left the group. When I met my husband, the community had moved back to California and owned a handful of stores there and in Arizona. There weren't many people still living on the land with the group, but many people visited them regularly for meditation or joined them for retreats. His parents stayed through it all, meditating twice a day, working for the stores or the church or the land.

When he told me part of this at the pub after our friends' wedding, I was intrigued. I'm a sucker for a good story, and as he spoke I imagined him as a suntanned baby in California, running among goats and flow-ers and guitars. But little of what I learned about the community in the months and years that followed, or when we visited his parents, aligned with my previous ideas about communes. The community members are teetotalers, for one, and Norm all but forbade extramarital or premari-tal sex. Their religion is an amalgamation of Eastern and Western be-liefs and practices. Over the years, there were many betrayals, both financial and personal. There were broken friendships and broken hearts. A couple of years after my husband and I married, his parents finally left the community. They still meditate every day, and they remain in touch with some of their old friends, but they live in Washington now, far from the people they worked, prayed, and lived with for more than forty years.

I note the similarities between my husband's family's community and Peoples Temple: The way that socialism shaped the members' lives and practices. The way they followed the directives of a single flawed and demanding man. The way some people stayed no matter the losses and betrayals and poor business decisions. The way their faith demanded everything from them. And I wonder at the differences. My husband's parents' faith demanded their lives, but not their deaths. How does one see this invisible line? Would they have refused? Would I?

After the congressman was murdered on the runway, the community of more than nine hundred people gathered at the center of Jonestown. There was a large pot filled with dark liquid resting on a table—grape Flavor Aid mixed with cyanide. Jim Jones told his people to drink the liquid from little cups, but first to use preloaded syringes to press the liquid into the mouths of their children so that their children would not be tortured by the capitalists and the government. He told them it was not suicide but a revolutionary act that would communicate their socialist ideals to the world. They could not go on living in such an unjust society. And they put the syringes to their children's mouths, and they drank from the cups, and they lay down in the dirt, and they died.

\*　\*　\*

*Marceline found solace in her children.*
　　　　　　　　　—Jeff Guinn, *The Road to Jonestown*

\*　\*　\*

All this, of course, is what we remember. Not socialism but "Kool-Aid." Not communism or public services or racial equality but fallen bodies, sneakers and dungarees and corduroys and T-shirts, so many bodies lined up and piled in the dirt. In photos taken from above, they appear like bags of garbage strewn across the land. The people of Jonestown dead together, facedown in the dirt.

On the recorded audiotapes from that night in Jonestown (they always recorded Jim Jones's speeches), Jim speaks to Marceline, saying, "Mother, Mother, Mother, Mother," asking her to stop crying and pleading. He asks her to obey, to drink the liquid, to die with the children, to die for The Cause. His voice is remarkably calm. After the children and the babies were dead—around three hundred of them—Marceline drank the liquid and died.

When I read about the tapes, I was surprised. I had always thought—though it was mystifying—that Marceline drank quickly and willingly, that everyone in Jonestown drank willingly, blindly, with devotion. I thought that to "drink the Kool-Aid" was to be a sheep, a gullible follower. But not everyone drank willingly. The group was surrounded by men with guns, and some of their bodies bore welts where they had been injected with cyanide when they refused to drink from the cups on their own. And the children died first, many of them at the hands of their own parents—an act more powerful than communism or socialism or God or Jim Jones. The children died first at the hands of the adults. How, after that, could the parents go on living?

Jim Jones died of a gunshot wound that he probably inflicted on himself. He did not press the syringe to his lips. He did not drink the juice from a little cup.

* * *

*I think my mom did the best that she could do with what she had because it was all that she could do . . . there were a lot of things that kept her there.*
                                                            —Stephan Jones

*Love of her children was foremost, as well as a sense of responsibility to all of Jones's followers, who she believed were good people, genuinely trying to change the world for the better.*
                                                            —Jeff Guinn, *The Road to Jonestown*

* * *

Marceline Baldwin Jones was once in love with a man, her husband. She was idealistic, committed to fighting racism and sharing resources and caring for children. She was loyal. But her life, her death, her loyalty, became a chilling warning against holding too tightly to ideals. *Be moderate; love reasonably,* her story whispers, opposing every message of love and idealism and generosity I have ever heard. This whisper is part of what draws me to her story and to her grave, part of what puzzles me. *Why did you do it, Marceline? What happened to you, Marceline? Why this blind spot? Why did you stay?*

Reid Hospital in Richmond, Indiana, where Marceline Baldwin met Jim Jones, was built in 1905 and served this small city for more than a hundred years. In 2008, the hospital sold the buildings on the original site to a group of developers and moved into a new facility up the road. Through a series of bad decisions, worse circumstances, and greedy betrayals, the old hospital was twice handed off from the original development group to other developers, but eventually all plans fell through; the last pair of investors stopped paying taxes and all but vanished from Indiana. The abandoned buildings have been rotting ever since. By the time I moved to Richmond in 2015, the old hospital was a hulking ruin, shameful, overgrown and broken, jagged and spray-painted. Thieves had stripped it of its valuable metals and set fire to the structure more than once. Even in a town with plenty of abandoned buildings, the hospital was a riveting eyesore of toxic decay, a testament to poor management and Rust Belt poverty.

But after a decade of vacancy, the building is finally, as I write this, being demolished. The place where Jim Jones met Marceline Baldwin—the woman who would become his wife, who would model for him effective political behavior, who would make possible his ascendancy as leader of Peoples Temple, and who would die at his side in a jungle settlement in Guyana—within another month or two, that place will no longer stand. But I will not see the demolition to its completion. My move is already planned, and I will be gone from Richmond before the building is gone. There are poisons locked within the old structure—asbestos certainly, and maybe mercury and lead. It is a scar that will not heal before I leave.

But I stand in this cemetery, by Marceline's stone. I have read too much about her, about Jonestown and Peoples Temple. I have let whole days dwindle to darkness as I read, questions swirling, wondering why I cannot look away. But today, the woods behind Marceline's grave are beautiful and straight and still against the sky, and the first leaves of spring are bright, tender green in the understory, and now I walk toward them, into the forest.

*Nominated by True Story, Melanie Rae Thon*

# SOMETHING STREET

fiction by CAROLYN FERRELL

from STORY

## I.

What is greatness? Funny dad sweaters, a sentimental nose, adorable crunkles in the corners of one's eyes. Hilarious tales of the old country, Somethingville, North Carolina, when men were men, women women, etc.—long-shouldered negresses being a special commodity, like lucky dice or a prize-winning calf. Fifty-four years ago, directly after our nuptials, Craw Daddy looked me dead in the eye and said, It's all mapped out, Parthenia, one foot after the other. Are you in or you out? Cause there ain't doing both.

We were honeymooning in a stately brick in the Irish part of Yonkers, and I was feeling too beautiful for my own good. Uppity, my mam would've said. Course I let him have his feet, one after the other. Up one street and down another. Upon one threshold and across another. Turn the other cheek, Mam advised me in a daydream. The women in those doors are not queens. They have nothing on you. They ain't even yellow.

## II.

Our marriage in 1956—with the understanding that some things get better and some worse but bottom line you ultimately float somewhere near the surface. *Yes* to the women fans, *yes* to the terribly late forays, *yes* to the pee smell of breath. *Yes* as long as he comes home by dawn and doesn't wake the children, *yes yes*. You float and float with affirmatives; you may not be kicking but you will be gulping.

287

Greatness is a cherished chestnut, humbly weaving its way out the co-median's mouth: *Did I ever tell you about the time Mama Love wh-upped my PARDON MY FRENCH?* We're in the auditorium of Ogden Hall, filled to capacity with hundreds here to see his Farewell Tour. The last time he will take us down Something Street.

And the comedian my husband glistens in the spotlight. Moments be-fore he took the stage, a lackluster girl student applied a hint of Ambi lightening cream under his eyes and over his cheeks, to promote his al-ready fulsome visage—Eboni, her name tag reads. The boy student next to her has a tag that merely says, HELLO MY NAME IS; both are otherwise nondescript save for the matching varsity scarves (neatly knot-ted) and Greek badges pinned on their breasts (gold, pearls and black enamel for Alpha Delta Pi). There is no hint of lotion on their volcanic-ash arms, and both heads are bone-withered with neglect. The eyes be-longing to this girl and boy seem overcast. One would think they had somewhere else to be.

But I know this type well. In all probability Eboni and HELLO MY NAME IS are kissing the ground Craw Daddy walks upon, grateful to have been granted the chance to tend to the comedian my husband dur-ing his annual visit to Hampton University (nee Institute, why in heav-ens did they change that glorious old name?). Before the performance HELLO MY NAME IS hauled a folding table center stage while Eboni poured a glass of water or gin into a tumbler. When Craw Daddy walked on and greeted the crowd, they stood back and looked up into the raf-ters, as if checking for dust mites in the beams of light. Likely their minds were like: *His air, Lord, how blessed we are to breathe in his air!*

It's a natural cycle; I know my head once worked that way.

The comedian my husband begins his set; the students are standing near me in the curtains, grimacing and scratching their coffee-colored necks with their hands. They notice the pram I'm rocking, perhaps they up here wondering whether the baby will be a potential disturbance? The girl and boy edge closer to me, sharpening their eyes in that sick-ening way the Sable-Tea Club ladies used to do (how I loved and dreaded their homilies on *The Progressive Colored Doyenne!*) and I can almost hear the prayer bursting forth from their reverent mouths: *Let the Good Lord do His work to preserve the peace so that The Almighty Come-dian may once again entertain us and lift us and teach us, etc. etc.*

I've heard that prayer before.

Eboni hisses at the boy, Where her chair at, Paul? You expecting her to stand the whole damn night? Paul scuttles away quietly, further back stage. Eboni's grimace does not leave her face. Your husband didn't mention his lady was gonna be here tonight, she said. Ain't that the shit?

## IV.

The floors of the ancient stage rattle as the comedian my husband wanders up and down in the ancient spotlight, beginning his stories. The audience hovers—I can tell there is nary a whiff of the Complaints anywhere at all. In this moment, nothing is lost. He is bright, he is shining. His teeth bare white into every soul in the house. *Mama Love, she made me who I am today. Y'all tell me if you heard this one before.*

## V.

In all other moments, we've lost damn near everything.

## VI.

Back in the day, the Sable-Tea Club ladies loved showing their Mahogany Maidens (yes, that was the word they used for us) the right way to act: how to set a table, to use silverware, to answer a telephone; they were against elbows, against overly-wide mouths and hands that did not obey; they absolutely loathed wagging tongues. We sat on a slip-covered couch in the home of a full-bodied New Rochelle matron, sipping sorrel tea, dreaming of biscuits and Shirley Temples, reciting the first few syllables of *Lysistrata*, stretching our pinkies in the air just like white girls, nodding tastefully to Perry Como and Nat King Cole—maybe someone would mention Dr. King, and like magic, the reverent swaying of heads and chests would commence. Our voices were orderly. *Did you know that at those marches, the wind can go and make one's hair most unflattering? Did you know you could wear out a good pair of nylons just by standing and holding a sign?* We were all for racial progress and whatnot, but honestly: none of us Mahogany Maidens *actually wanted* to use a public water fountain, colored or white.

289

## VII.

Who didn't think that being a part of the Sable-Tea Club Ladies wasn't greatness itself? After a customary lecture (perhaps on the place of classical Latin in the contemporary domicile), we made our way to the luncheon spread on a huge oak table covered in lemon wax and doilies. Meats, gelatin molds, cold European soups that tasted like resurrected earth. Watercress sandwiches, a charger of raspberry thumbprints. The Sable-Tea Club ladies thanked that very special matron for her hospitality, then made us hold hands for the Lord's Prayer. She whispered that if we messed up any of the words, we'd get our black behinds beat big time.

## VIII.

Your husband is a hell of a man, Eboni says to me. Paul brings the folding chair toward us and gently opens it. Your husband is a great man, Eboni repeats. All side-eye. Her voice is a stone of worship, and I shiver. What did you say your name was, I ask stupidly. A momentary blip. Everything is over her face.

## IX.

Greatness is the complete absorption of all surrounding good.

## X.

*Tell me if I'm repeating myself.* The comedian my husband actually stole this line from another funnyman, Canny Blackbottom at the Richmond Hippodrome 1963. Craw Daddy heard it, clapped his hands and announced: *That gold's mine.* He was fifth on the lineup after Canny, his belly hollowed out by the Hippodrome's hot-sauce chicken wings and rigorous barbecue pork. When it was his turn, Craw Daddy was hissed to shame. He looked back and saw Canny watermelon-grinning in the wings. My husband the comedian straightened his tie, tightened his belt. *You chitlin-circuit nigger, what the hell you got that I ain't?* My husband the comedian whispered the line a thousand times in case he might mispronounce it. *Tell me if I'm repeating myself.* Canny rose a fuss, but Craw Daddy ignored him. He made that line his own. He considered it merely borrowing.

## XI.

His career took off—money blew up like the Fourth of July. The 60s, 70s, 80s were a filament of cars, boats, houses, massive vacations. One time we took a riverboat down the Egyptian Nile, another we saw wild elephants tango-dance outside our hotel window in Nairobi. Occasionally there were diamonds and Russell Stover chocolate hearts and American Beauties in a Waterford vase—I didn't mind them at all. I remembered his words. At the start of the Complaints, people predicted his career would take a beating. Luckily the only aftershock I can recall was the loss of hearth home dignity courage and imagination. And it is scientifically proven you can rise back to the surface without any of those trappings.

## XII.

Paul grumbles something into Eboni's ear then takes off again, slue-footed as a Norfolk penguin. She is left to rummage through a patent leather purse draped across her chest, its strap hooking itself onto the varsity badge. I had not seen the purse earlier, and, for reasons I cannot ascertain in the moment, I smile. Sunday school, Easter parade, cotillion drag. Warmth fills my body. I want to share that warmth. I myself was Delta Sigma Theta through and through: *don't ask me bout my hair and I won't tell* (inside joke); I want to inquire about her days here at Hampton, to say something innocuous about how sororities must have changed since my time—but just as quick she snaps shut the purse and stares straight ahead. There is a key in her hands. It is pulled through her index and middle fingers, and it is something like a gun. That baby your grandkid, she asks. When I nod, she hoists the gun up to her lips.

## XIII.

Why you crying? What have I done to make you sad? Parthenia. Baby Girl. We've lived all over this great green country!

This is what he told me after the Beverly Hills house was auctioned.

No sense in crying, Parthenia. What matters most is the home in our heart.

This was said as a comfort. After the fourth Complaint, we had to give up Boca Raton and Savannah too, plus my Van Cleef and all the damn Christofle.

## XIV.

Historically he has always been a taker and a giver. Craw Daddy gave my parents just enough to ease their arms from around my shoulders. He took me when I wasn't looking. He gave a nearly sober speech at our wedding banquet, the one where some of the Sable-Tea Club ladies came to pay respects, handing over lavender sachets with ten-dollar bills sewn inside. He gave them his hand. *Yes I do swear to honor and obey this high society gal* (the Sable-Tea ladies may have detected a bit of sass in that vow), *Yes I am forever grateful she deigned look upon my face.* Craw Daddy rose from the ashes of poverty to claim me: I, who under normal circumstances would not have set foot on Something Street to save my life. What is greatness if not that?

## XV.

Outside, our driver waits for us in the parking lot off Shore Drive. His name is Clarence, a name the comedian my husband finds perfect in its old-fashioned darkyness (Craw Daddy's actual words were, *At least he ain't got one of these fake African bullshit monikers* though I've always dreamt of asking him what sort of name he considers *Marquita*— an appellation his mother—on her deathbed—forced upon our firstborn). Clarence the driver is likely on his cell phone, calling home, finding out supper; he couldn't be bothered with the Farewell Tour. He couldn't be bothered with the famed Ogden Hall of Hampton University (nee Institute) although he might pause and gaze balefully in our direction and think of millions of dollars lining his imaginary mattress, dollars he might could've had if he'd played his cards right (wasn't his cousin doing standup at the Newport News Laugheteria? Next month Las Vegas?)—Clarence might see in his mind's eye the way Craw Daddy strides up to the edge of the stage and begins his stories; he might see me propping myself in the curtains (the folding chair was too hard), the pram rocking under my hand, the grandson left to us by my third-born daughter as a wanton gift; he might not give a good goddamn. He might feel sorry for not acting the man earlier, when I was in his car.

Clarence will whip out a cigarette or joint, open his phone, scour personal ads, think up lottery numbers.

What's the baby's name, the girl Eboni asks me. Somehow I have learned that that she is a grown woman, all of thirty years old, and that the boy is her husband. Her exact words were: I should thank you for thinking me younger, but I'll just chalk it up to you being blind as a bat, Mrs. Craw Daddy. Why do you got your grandbaby here?

## XVI.

The boy comes up from behind suddenly with a large swivel desk chair which Eboni guides me into. My body is nearly too large for this seat but I do not say anything; I have grown old as gracefully as necessary. I hold out my hand to the boy but he does not take it—manners clearly elude this specimen. Never mind him, Eboni says. Why don't you sit, Mrs. Craw Daddy? Sitting will make it easier.

  She undoes the scarf around her neck. The area there is black as a banana peel: a hickey, a testament to youthful love. I have no idea where that key has got to.

## XVII.

Moses, I wanted to call him, the day I opened the front door of our present rental apartment in Aberdeen Gardens and found a baby swaddled in a basket—though the name our third-born daughter had given him in the attached note was different. Something in between Africa and Europe, a name meant to sound unique but that actually had the ring of homemade commons to it. *[..] will save you,* the note read, *Treat him better than you did your own girls.*

## XVIII.

Times past, Ogden Hall has been host to some of the finest black entertainers of the country; it is a killer diamond that's lived through the weight of history, all those marchers and protesters and mindblown soldiers of the 70s. I started out in 1955 but didn't actually finish my degree until I returned in 1974. Bit of a wait in the middle there, what with kids, house, houses, Craw Daddy's fame. The Complaints. Each time I was a student here, I was not a troublemaker. I did not wear an Afro nor did I burn my cotillion gowns. Ogden Hall counts itself lucky to invite the comedian my husband back every few years and have him actually come. They were saddened by the idea of a Farewell Tour but nonetheless welcomed him with outstretched arms. They have no idea we've lost everything, that the comedian my husband accepts every invite happily, including the retirement homes and dinner theaters. The Complaints are to blame, but what's a woman to do?

## XIX.

*Once upon a time there was dark-as-night wide-hipped sassy-lipped Mama Love and her famous flat iron. She was my mama, and she raised us all on Something Street.* Craw Daddy walks the stage as he narrates, gesticulating wildly, waving that flat iron in faces, sticking his hand round the waists of barrel-bodied women, pointing make-believe shot-guns at no-count lotharios, rubbing sleep from the eyes of drunks. Something Street is alive. Somehow Mama Love's flatiron—which had started out that day straightening his sister Flayla's nappy head—wants, in the end, to *smack some sense* into Craw (her only boy-child who'd innocently asked the meaning of the word *dyke*.) Loads of laughter. Before the first blow can be administered, the flatiron mys-teriously takes wing and sails into the sky, never to be seen again. All the while Flayla's eyes screw themselves deeper into her undone head. *Whatever could that child be guilty of?* Just then Butchy Barbara looms her head over the windowsill and smirks. *Wanna kiss, baby? We ain't got nothing to lose!* Where in tarnation did she come from? The crowd just about dies.

## XX.

In my second year as a coed at Hampton Institute, the great Maha-lia Jackson took this same stage. She sang only one song. But all around her: the hush of greatness, of legacy. Thoughts buzzing in grateful heads: How did we get here? How shall we remain? Are we witnessing the Negro's progress and legacy? All manner of monu-mental thoughts. I was already attached to Craw Daddy. I put my hands over my ears.

## XXI.

*Ya'll want to hear bout Mama Love and her twelve disobedient children and her ne'er-do-well mate, Drunky Poppy? Or do y'all want to hear about Mama Love and her thieving neighbor, Miss Hattie-No-Goody, who had a habit of tasting Mama's pies on the sill? Tell me, y'all, if you heard those ones before!*

The comedian my husband holds up his hand: *OK, OK, let's be serious for a moment. Without Mama Love and the kind of upbringing she instilled in me, I would not be standing before you today. Can I get an AMEN? I, a God-fearing man with a heart of pure gold and a lovely bride of fifty-four years—Hey Parthenia, whyn't you come out and meet my new friends? Praise God, but shouldn't we all have been raised by a woman like Mama Love?*

(A side whisper: *That is, if we remember to put the cast-iron pan inside our britches for protection seeing how Mama Love could swat you for days, and the lack of that pan meant certain death of the booty so can I get an AMEN?*)

The audience falls out their seats, bits and pieces of their limbs shattering on the tile floor. They don't wait for me to come out; I become an afterthought before I can even be. In 1956, the song Mahalia Jackson performed was "Move On Up a Little Higher." She walked past me as the applause enveloped her, slow and belligerent like an autumn cocoon. She did not lift her eyes.

## XXII.

First intermission: I leave the sleeping baby in the back and wander the aisles. The audience aren't finished slapping their knees, wiping away mirthful tears, coughing into wadded-up tissues. They slowly re-form themselves as the lights go up, turning toward one another and repeating the best bits. *Hey, you seen Craw Daddy's show in Atlanta? He had us rolling in the aisles with Mama Love and the wheelbarrow. Shit, yeah, Craw Daddy brung down the house there! Mama Love make me want to pee my drawers! Every. Damn. Time.*

In the midst of this, someone dares mention the Complaints—a woman, of course. Eyebrows are raised. Faces turned toward her with scorn. *Why you have to go and mention that, Gladys? Why even bring that shit up? Let the man have one night free and clear, now is not the time for that shit.*

The woman Gladys says something along the lines of *Well if it was my man out there doing that,* and they shut her down instantly. *Close your got-damn trap, Gladys. You bought a ticket same as us. He is our man, he will always be our man.*

## XXIII.

Back on stage, the comedian my husband is suddenly standing next to me, gulping down the glass of gin or water. Eboni stands in his shadow with his seersucker jacket over her left arm. With her right, she reaches down and scratches the back of her knee. I see that. I see her glance at her shoes, then straighten her jumper, then reach back down to that tender spot. She doesn't see me seeing her. But I do. The back of the knee can be the most telltale part of the body. There is the banana black of her neck but that means nothing to the soft mattress of her knee. I am frustrated to be completely out of tears.

## XXIV.

Girl, go get my wife something cold to drink, you see she about to faint, ain't you? Go to the fridge in my dressing room, hear? It's some refreshments there.

To me he winks. Child's an idjit, Parthenia. He waits a few heartbeats. Let me go find her and make sure she don't get the order wrong. I'm so sorry about before, Parthenia, you know it's not in me to hit a woman. Not even you. I have no idea what got into me back there in the car but I swear if I hurt you I got no reason to stand like a man. Forgive me?

I nod. He does not have a dressing room. There is no fridge.

You, you, you, you, you.

## XXV.

Ten minutes pass. The pair returns without my drink. Out of ancient habit I kiss Craw's cheek.

He hangs his big head into the pram. Be careful, little buddy, he says to the baby; then tells me he has to sail off to hair and make-up; he swears he needs more lightening cream. More Old Spice aftershave. Looks to Eboni and nods. I have seen many fans, many autograph-seekers, many groupies, if you will. I know the silence that overtakes them in the presence of greatness. She and him leave once more, and perhaps fifteen new minutes go by; when the comedian my husband returns—alone—his face is pure ravishment. Red pimples under graham cracker skin, the shine of battered delight. I know that look. A bargain is a bargain. But I know that look. Little Buddy, he whispers into the pram, This one day gonna be you. And I'm a lead the way.

## XXVI.

All her life, our third-born had been the sweetest of the three, hanging onto her father's every word, attaching herself to his leg as he walked, baking him cakes even when it wasn't his birthday. When she became a teenager, however, she took a different route. I would come home from a day of shopping and find Craw and Joanna at each other's throats; or else, late at night, we would find Joanna and her friends keying the cars in one of the driveways. The patio tables of every house were shattered with bottles of Ole Grandad and Lancers wine. Swear words galore. Drugs, powders, hypothermic needles, spoons. The comedian my husband said the girl was out her damn mind. His exact words. One time in Atlanta Joanna yelled up the stairs, *You want to screw Rochelle? Well, get this, old man: you ain't her type!* Her exact words.

Craw Daddy ran down and grabbed Joanna by the scruff. Everything about you abominates me to no end! You faster than a junkyard dog! Out here doing these drugs and out here to ruin my reputation. You and that slut Rochelle! What you thinking, girl?

(Rochelle, Joanna's best friend in Atlanta. A year younger in high school, pretty as a nectarine. Why in heavens would my daughter say such a thing? When things blew over, I told the girls I would take them shopping at Lenox Square, but Rochelle's parents would later tell me I was not appropriate.)

She mines and not yours, Joanne answered, to which she saw the back of Craw's hand. I did not like that one bit. I told my husband the comedian that he needed to stop hitting our third-born, that she was our flesh and bones, and after he landed another swop, he did.

(The Complaints were just a trickle on the horizon, nothing to get worked up about. Nevertheless I was left wondering: How does he know Rochelle is a slut?)

## XXVII.

During second intermission, Craw Daddy disappears into the aisles to sign early autographs. The baby wakes, and I bend to lift him into my arms. He is not our first grandparent rodeo, this boy. Marquita, our first-born, has a brood of boys almost large enough to fill the front row center. Several years ago, her (Howard University—*sigh*) husband literally whisked her off her Spelman feet and landed her not a mile from our alma mater in bare toes and bulging belly.

Now there are six grands that direction—oh, what the Sable-Tea Club ladies would have said! Back in the day, two was their perfect number. Two became the new one (one being a slavery number, as my mam used to observe); some years later, when my girls were grown, three became the new two. And shortly after that, five became the new three. Five is comfort, ambition, confidence. I believe that even my mam would not have frowned upon five. But six? Six is a descent back toward field days, God help us!

No matter. I loved those babies like I love myself until Marquita one day up and said: He's not allowed here anymore, Mom. I want different for my boys.

My mam no longer walks the earth. She's buried in Wartburg Cemetery, Mount Vernon, New York, right next to Daddy, who was lifted into his casket wearing his Pullman's uniform, God bless him.

Our second-born, Winifred, thought at first that the Complaints were a "racialist" attack of some sort. She wondered whether white comedians suffered the same sorts of condemnation. Winifred held her father's arm as we walked up and down the courthouse steps. After we lost the Atlanta house to a "fire" in 2000 (the police said they thought it was arson but had nothing real to go on) Winifred took a moment for herself, a timeout, she called it. She has not spoken to her father since.

I want to say *Her loss* in the way my husband says *Her loss* when he references Winifred—but the words stick in my throat. She and I began communicating on the q.t. A shopping mall here, a Baskin-Robbins there. Craw knew nothing. Winifred and I met at Buckroe Beach; she brought her three girls, whom I immediately doted upon with ice cream sandwiches and neon fizzle pop. Children can be such gems, I said. They are always the apple of their grandparents' eyes. Winifred wasn't having any of it. Mother, she said (in her usual two-pronged manner), It's only a matter of time. You're better than this.

The sun was magnificently high and away on that gray sand afternoon. I'm better than what, Winifred? Don't you know that it was *I* that got you here? Made you into a lady you are sitting before your little darlings?

Oh, Mother. We love you. But this is not you.

I finished my ice cream sandwich and tried to give my second-born the death stare. I couldn't, of course. I don't have some things within me.

Besides, a cadre of white people wandered past, all of them licking ice cream cones and admiring the glistening waters; it wouldn't do to show my colors in front of them. Old habits, I suppose. Winifred, I said, I've always tried to do my best. I don't abandon ship. I stand tall. I stand fast.

Oh Mother. No one is talking about a ship. It's the women he's had, some against their will. And you standing behind him.

Naturally I stand behind him. He is our rock.

Oh Mother. When will the world ever see your true face?

Hurtful words. Of course, home training has taught me to shield the world from my raging emotions, the overflowing cup of my indignations. Since that afternoon—two years ago now—I've sent Winifred weekly letters, but have yet to find an answer in my box. I sign my letters with, Warmly, or All My love, or Sincerely Yours, Mother Best.

This babe I currently swaddle, I have no idea when or where he was born, who the father. His tiny brown face is shaped like a heart, and his fingers are worse than vise grips. When she was not even out of elementary school, Joanna once told her father, I don't care what anybody say. You are my daddy and you are not bad.

*Time for you to make amends seeing as you didn't hear me the first time.* Such harsh words. They were written in the note pinned to the car seat, the one she parked on our front step in Aberdeen Gardens—complete with baby—five days ago. There was also a small Polaroid of Rochelle, whose face was against the camera. *Rochelle has been put away. I don't know if for good.*

Craw, I asked. Whatever does this mean?

## XXVIII.

In 1956 my beloved father took us into our parlor and loomed as the comedian my future husband sipped an Italian coffee—Mam had spent time on the Continent and was eager to show it. Now you listen, my father began. Parthenia, she is not like any regular gal off the street. She is a lady. She's had training. Me, I'm more like you—wrong side of the tracks and whatnot. Don't know which fork to use and whatnot. That is not Parthenia. Her mater and I done all we could to create her into a picture of feminine charms. And I command you to treat her as such. Am I making myself clear, son?

His broad brown hands, caked in oil; and when he spoke, he stooped. This was the voice he'd used with the young men at Union Station, the ones who needed the most Pullman training, the best guidance, my father misquoting Du Bois with nothing but love: *Work is the knob to uplift the people!* What I would give to hear that voice again. He would know what to do about the Complaints. He would know what to do with my soul.

## XXIX.

Craw's proposal under the Emancipation Oak was quick, mostly painless. There was hardly any blood. I hitched down my dress, thought about my Aunt Leah who'd married her first cousin despite her people's objections and then went around quoting Paul Dunbar: "This is the debt I pay, just for one riotous day." During Literary Hour in the New Rochelle parlor, we Mahogany Maidens found that line hilarious.

## XXX.

Craw and I had no major discussions, no mapping out of the future, no tender treading of intimate territories. When we came home from the Justice of the Peace, Mam served dandelion wine in tumblers bearing little umbrellas. Daddy made a show of wanting me to finish up school, but Mam said it was plenty of young colored ladies that started their families and went back later. In fact, she was even thinking of doing the same! (The liar!)

## XXXI.

Craw Daddy is back on stage, and next to me, Eboni's lips shine full blown in the darkness of the curtains, like freshly baked crescents rolls. Those lips have just been loved. Was it in her will or against it? She avoids my eyes and I'm understanding suddenly that I cannot possibly know the meaning of devotion and perhaps never could.

## XXXII.

Where were you all this time, I ask her. Have you been following the comedian my husband for an autograph? She looks away. Then says to me, I always pictured you different. Maybe it's the black eye.

## XXXIII.

*Did I ever tell you about the time Drunky Poppy nearly mowed our small house into the ground?*

Yes. The audience has heard Drunky Poppy many times before, even on televised appearances: Johnny Carson, the *Flip Wilson Show*. Dinah Shore had so many tears in her eyes from laughing it was rumored she passed gas on the set.

The crowd closes its eyes and envisions a raggedy, brown-skinned hunchback driving his summer tractor down the middle of Something Street. Forget the tobacco field, where his helpmeet and progeny stand under an unforgiving sun, covered in morning sweat. Mama Love and her twelve children will wait on that tractor unto eternity.

Tonight is a variant of the story: it so happens that Drunky Poppy woke up later than usual, and in an effort to avoid being castigated by Mr. Woodwardward (proprietor of the tobacco farm) jumps out the house without his spectacles. Mayhem ensues. He jumpstarts the tractor and makes a series of wrong turns, first passing the moonshine shack out back the farmhouse where he and his lady friend, a.k.a., Roomy Rhonda, secretly *rendezvous.* Laughter. He passes women hanging laundry, rustling children, and tending garden rows—don't even get him started on the various names of the garden tools (he will not bring himself to say *hoe*, that is a part of the contemporary vernacular he despises and claims will drag us colored folk straight to hell). Another moonshine shack nearby, then another. At the beginning of Something Street, Drunky Poppy nearly plows his tractor over some little old ladies. They are on their way to the Church of the Wooden Hand.

(Craw's actual mother had once tried to join the order of the White Ladies of Africa before they closed their door on her face.)

Drunky Poppy nearly flattens a group of deserving orphans playing stickball and, after that, practically kills the baker carrying the preacher's daughter's wedding cake—imagine the pandemonium!—before he careens into A. A.'s General Supply—the entire storefront has been crashed inward, there is clearly no saving anything, from the soda cracker barrels to the ladies' hysteria drops. *Sorry bout that,* Drunky Poppy calls out from the light fixture, which has crowned (but miraculously not hurt) him, *but mah oman done axed me to drive her car to church n pick huh up after preacher done got done.* By now everyone in the audience can smell the booze on the comedian's lips, feel it erupt from his pores like so many miniature volcanoes. I, on the other hand, can feel Mama Love's legs as she kicks away the biting flies in the tobacco field.

*Oh yeah?* This response comes from African Andy, the "blue-black" shop owner, who, from underneath a broken barrel of self-rising (!) flour, shouts, *Man, you gone pay wid yo life!*—(the audience goes wild!)—*and furthermore, you ain't driving no car! Your mama so dumb, Drunky Poppy, she done sold her car for gasoline!* Drunky Poppy puts the tractor in reverse before the good shopkeeper can collar him, then incredibly makes it to the church (pummeling over prize roses)—now there is the gang of deserving orphans in tow, all of whom vow to avenge themselves on the *"absinthetic ass."* They catch up to him, but not before Drunky Poppy runs over a fire hydrant—which spurts upwards like Niagara Falls—and washes just about everyone clear into the doors of the church (this part of the tale does take a while to wade through, no pun intended; it has never been my favorite, it defies every law of physics) and the water carries the man and his tractor right up to the pulpit, where a shocked (and portly) Pastor Breadlove falls into the arms of the choir women, one of whom is Miss *Poosy*, reformed lady-o-the-night (the audience screams). This literal turn of events horrifies the preacher's daughter, Velvet—the poor girl falls into the arms of her own betrothed, Stanley Morehousehead (in reality, Craw Daddy has hated every HBCU except Hampton)—and together the lovebirds are caught up in the raging waters; their choir gowns hook in the large left front wheel, forcing the pair to be dragged alongside the tractor as it heads up the aisle. Velvet must hold fast to the scraps that are her only covering; of course, Stanley Morehousehead is too stupid to try and rip his gown from his body and shield her.

(The audience roll from their seats into the aisles; it is too much, too much indeed!)

Velvet grabs her fiancé and together the (still unwed) couple allow themselves to be pulled along like a dog on a leash, her good cream-clotted skin turning red with humiliation, his dusky hue growing *nightier* by the minute. They flow out the church all the way to Buck River. There, the bridegroom catches hold of a tree (a weeping willow, of course) and frees himself from the flood, from Velvet. My mother always warned me about girls like you, he cries. Velvet is last seen washing along Buck River's tides toward the tobacco field, where the workers have long since elected to carry out their day.

(The audience is an utter paroxysm. Heads go rolling off the slippery slopes of shoulders, brassieres snap open, revealing breasts as deflated as summer pies. Pure unadulterated laughter. Madness, even. No one is remotely thinking about The Complaints.)

## XXXIV.

You know what he likes to do, don't you, the girl whispers. He's been doing it all week. I thought right up to now I liked it.

The look on her face. There were the regular places for the eyes, nose and mouth, and yet they been washed away, as in one of those old spiritualist photographs of the nineteenth century. Later in court I would learn that he was only *tryna show her a new way to please her husband.* Men can be fickle, Craw Daddy had assured her. With me what you see is what you get, baby.

## XXXV.

I'd been having thoughts.

## XXXVI.

More thoughts, new thoughts. Just this morning over breakfast I looked into the baby's eyes and then went over to Craw in the living room, fast asleep. We can't keep him, I say. We have no right. He is not yours. He is not mine.

Craw Daddy laughed in my face. I've always wanted a son, he said. What's wrong with that? Hell with Joanna and that other girl. They both gone crazy, you ask me.

They're not girls, I say. They haven't been girls for a long time.

Last I checked that Rochelle was nothing but a slut! Craw is silent after admitting this. I don't understand.

## XXXVII.

We can't keep this baby, I said again to Craw Daddy on the drive over here. Clarence the driver in the front seat. Craw raised his eyebrows. I put my hand on his shoulder. We just can't. We have no right.

My husband the comedian craned his neck toward our driver up front. You hear that, Clarence? You hear this fool woman? Thinking I'm not good enough to raise my own *so-called* flesh and blood?

Clarence remained driving. It was a light rain in the trees, a balminess settling over the windshield like a bassinet cover.

We have to do the right thing, I said. Remembering the sound of the word *so-called.*

303

A deal is a deal, he answered.

What if this baby is no deal, I asked. I was not even sure what I was meaning.

Silence. I don't know if he waited one or two minutes before slapping me. I do know the car swerved, that Clarence opened his door, jumped out, pulled Craw behind him. We just need some fresh air, Clarence said, wiping his forehead with an old-fashioned handkerchief. He looked into my eyes and turned away. I had no idea men still carried those sorts of things.

## XXXVIII.

Eboni says, You tell your husband when the show's done my husband'll be out back. We want to show him what he means to us.

## XXXIX.

The baby shifts in the pram, even tries to claw its way up to the hood. I quickly push it down, ignoring its cries, and head toward the stage door in back. I make noise as I clatter us out onto the neat cobbles of the pedestrian path just steps away from the river. The baby becomes more and more unruly, shirking at my touch. Can infants do such things, I wonder? I push that pram along from the cobbles to the rocky breaker blocking the rushing water; as I do, I long to pick up one of the cigarette butts at my feet. If I were a different kind of grandmother-type, I might stow this baby in a pie safe and run off looking for a tobacco field of my own.

## XL.

And here's Clarence clomping toward me, *sans* driving cap, his shirt partially undone, faux-tortoiseshell buttons; likely he'll think I'm mad at him from before—nobody likes a lady with a black eye. My mouth feels dry and my throat aches. You want me to push that for you, Ma'am? He asks, huffing beside me. Clarence had looked much slimmer from the back seat. Now I take in his large stomach, his saggy legs. I shake my head, unable to move my lips. He does not hear me choke for breath.

Don't do anything rash, Ma'am. You see, I could hear you all the way from the car. Come away from that river. I wouldn't want you to do anything rash.

## XLI.

As early as 1962, *Time Magazine* described my husband, Crawley Stevenson, as "The Only Wonder of the World That Will Make You Double Over . . . in Fits of Laughter!" In 1963, the *Amsterdam News* wrote, "The Negro Genius That Will Bring White Folks To Their Knees!" In 1967, the *Buffalo Challenger:* "Craw Stevenson Is More Than Meets the Eye!" The "reporters" of the September 1968 *Hampton Cotillion Broadside* called him "Our Favorite Mystery Date" and dared any woman on the planet to go up to my face and ask me what was my secret.

## XLII.

Los Angeles 2010. The Complaints did indeed vex me, but I raised my right hand to God and swore that the testimony I was about to give was the whole truth. For the courtroom I chose the Halston halter-neck Craw had bought in Beverly Hills just the month before; he'd told me he liked nothing better than seeing a strong black woman in a great dress turn all evil whites on their heads.

Complaint 1, August 1965: Craw was with me in Las Vegas, the Sands. We slept together in the same room. Craw went out briefly for smokes. How could he have done anything like that woman said he did—and in such a *short time?* Complaint 2, June 1979: Craw literally had to beat the fans off him—men and women alike—as he mounted that Little Rock stage. They wouldn't stop. Far as I'm concerned, you reap just what you sow. Complaint 3, April 1980: She stalked me, called the house more than once, even breathed heavy into the phone with her accusations. Craw had to put an end to those shenanigans. End of story. Complaint 4 (date unknown): Politically incorrect, yes, but it's the truth: she was not his type. Nothing could've happened. She was not even remotely yellow. Complaint 5 (date unknown): Can you blame him for placing five thousand dollars in an envelope and slipping it to the Atlanta concierge? How could he have known that cameras had been trained upon him? People will do anything to blackmail a good black man for a little extra cash. Complaint 6 (date unknown): Can he help it if he is so famous, so beloved? Complaint 7, November 1977: Things were rough, plus the girls all grown and hating me for no good reason. I spent time tending to my parents' home in Mount Vernon, and when I got back to Pensacola, Winifred is up here telling me about the two heifers that had moved in the moment I left, playing house in my kitchen, using my utensils, cooking his food. Marquita claimed she saw them suck his privates! And I slapped her—*He is still your father,* I said, *come hell or high water.* Joanna over in the corner: At least if we was in high water we could drown (to which I slapped her as well). <u>Complaint 8, December 1977</u>: This tramp in question was the daughter of someone at Links—do you know Links? They sent me a letter. *Please don't bother to ask, Mrs. Stevenson. We are a family-oriented organization, we only want credits to our race.* <u>Complaints 9 and 10, both in December 1991</u>: No comment, on advice of counsel. <u>Complaint 11, somewhere June or July 1999.</u> We all grew back together, branches on the proverbial family tree. Except without the branches. Never again answered the phone at night, never spoke to reporters. Never again raised my hand in protest, never again found anything missing from my kitchen.

## XLIII.

Clarence is steering the pram by my side. Smart Van Heusen shirt with hideous Haband trousers. I think he could be in love with men. *Why,* I want to ask him. *Why?*

## XLIV.

That is not the question, however. I ask Clarence if he could keep the baby overnight at his house, possibly longer, definitely longer, maybe forever? He looks at me crazy. What you mean, Mrs. Craw Daddy, he asks. I repeat myself: take the boy home. Your wife will know what to do. He can't belong to us anymore. He never has.

Heavens, I ain't married, Mrs. Craw Daddy! I couldn't take no child, it's just me and my cousin Junius.

I think for a moment. Mr. Clarence, I say. I'm not opposed to two men raising the tyke. I've never been opposed. Please excuse my husband the comedian for anything he might've said in the past that would indicate we are narrow-minded, Mr. Clarence. All God's children are free to love—

What you talking about, Mrs. Craw Daddy?

Just know that I want you and your cousin Junius to take this child. His mother has run out of steam. And Craw and I are a jeopardy.

This ain't right, Mrs. Daddy.

I bow my head: this will take longer than expected. And so—with the memory of those long ago Sable-Tea matrons that tried so very hard to instill in us a greater sense of truth, justice, and liberty for all—I begin.

Explaining to Clarence that the comedian my husband will likely go to prison for some time—we no longer live in an age of plentiful female-tampering—and that that incarceration will happen sooner rather than later. As for *moi:* I intend to go back to Mount Vernon and beg my dead mam's forgiveness; *Carpe noctum; you are our only hope.* I have no friends, no family other than my daughters and their young. But Marquita can barely handle the boys she has bred. And Winifred won't speak to me in a deeply known way. My youngest is likely gone forever, I say. Addled in some drug rehab or hospital for broken heads, or perhaps huddled under a bridge, exquisitely diaphanous—I have no clue. She is gone. This is my debt, I tell him. *One riotous day.*

Clarence shakes his head. Ma'am. Please calm yourself. I can call the cops.

You must please take the child, Mr. Clarence. Police are not a necessary ingredient here.

Please, ma'am. You are not yourself!

Around us, the rush of river surf hits the small cliffs of the path. God is somewhere, folded arms across His chest, angry toe tapping the tops of the clouds. I tell Clarence about Eboni. I tell him about the others. When he winces and touches my shoulder, I recoil: I tell him I belong in neither heaven nor hell, just in Mount Vernon, New York, where my elders lie. I am no one's forgiveness. Perhaps I'll buy a house in New Rochelle. Perhaps I'll run into someone I once knew and sit on another slipcovered couch and whisper the Lord's Prayer. I never did learn those words correctly, just faked my way through everything and did not once get my black butt beat.

Clarence listens. Just let me call home, he eventually says.

### XLV.

Do hours go by? I have no phone, no communication other than the moon that has been steadily grazing my shoulders and telling me to jump. I'm resting on a rock, like the girl on the can of White Rock soda. Baby finally asleep. If I don't learn to miss him I will hate myself forever.

Just then it's Clarence again, now with a man by his side. A man who, after brief introductions, grips my own elbow, all courtly. The Mahogany Maidens would have been all aswoon! They would have asked him to hold their *every* part. Are you Clarence's cousin, I ask. The man laughs. If that's who you want me to be, he says back.

307

Minutes later the men lead me to the car, the baby still fresh in their arms. Where is the pram, I wonder but do not ask aloud.

But then we do not go to the car. Instead, the men nod and then guide me fast toward Ogden Hall, eventually lighting at the bottom of a foot-hill leading up to the stage entrance. There is litter strewn everywhere, Coke bottles and crepe garlands and crumpled looseleaf paper. The stage door cracks open and a seam of light scissors the dark—it is then we see the outlines of two men fighting on the ground. One is pummel-ing the other, who is screaming, gibberish pleas. I have no desire to lis-ten. The door closes part way and I can make out the further outline of a knife, a key, a finger, a fist. Perhaps I smell blood from where I am standing. You stay here where you safe, Junius says, lowering me by the arms onto a grassy tuffet. I turn my head away, ignore the screeching, the laughter of young people, the old man on the ground, sunken like a Norfolk naval ship, the crush of young leaves all around—*You damn re-peated yourself one time too many, you black bastard!*—and I turn away, casting my eyes over treetops, toward the place I imagine the Emancipation Oak stands. I don't blame you for wanting to cut all ties, I tell it. But please look out for this baby. He has to matter.

Clarence and Junius scramble up the small hill to the fight but make no move, however, to break things up. They hold the infant between them as if it were a tiny gate to somewhere they'd never before considered.

When, all those years ago, Mahalia Jackson walked up the aisle toward the door, I reached out to touch her sleeve. Of course, I didn't get it; the wind of her walk sailed through me, like Velvet's wedding veil be-fore it hit the river. I knew enough not to beg Miss Jackson for another hymn, as the others in the auditorium were doing, stomping their feet under their seats. I knew enough, had understood briefly the importance of listening the first time. How had I lost that gift? We cannot exist by remaining greedy.

Eboni is stamping down the hill, backlit by moonlight. Her fists are tight by her side—she seems all greatness in her youthful march, her hair gone wild and free as it flutters in gangly strips atop her head—I want to find out if that is true. Are you great? Have you always been great? Hoisting myself from the grass, I stand and wave. Her silhouette inches closer to mine. My arms open, I start to cry. This girl is going to meet me for the first time, even if she doesn't yet know it.

*Nominated by Story*

# HOUSE OF PRAYER

## by ALYCIA PIRMOHAMED

from PALETTE

I walk into the beads of thirty-three *alhamdulillahs*,
I walk into my childhood mouth, repeat *alhamdulillah*.

Four decades ago. father too walked into this prayer,
his body nested in the oblong Boeing, his *alhamdulillah*

humming deep until it matched the scale of the engine.
It was during that first crossing from one *alhamdulillah*

to another home, that my father crushed open the chasm
he has since passed down to every poem I write: [   ]

the hollow, the forgotten Qur'an lodged deep in the night
of an unopened drawer. My quest to belong. *Alhamdulillah,*

forgive me, forgive me. I praise once again, I symmetry
like the wings of a migrating bird, I repeat *alhamdulillah*

and rinse and repeat and rinse and repeat, like the *rokrok*
of an egret. I hold this *tasbih* to count my *alhamdulillahs*

thirty-three times, ninety-nine times: the key is to walk
again and again into the holy, repeating *alhamdulillah*.

*alhamdulillah. alhamdullilah,* until the skyward calm. Father,
what did you hope for when you uttered *alhamdulillah.*

when you rinsed over the Atlantic in that giant bird?
When the egg cracked open and the yolk of *alhamdullilah*

spilled onto a new coast? Was it travelling homeward
or away from homeland? I have learned that *alhamdulillah*

does not resemble a border, but it is a house of its own.
*Alhamdulillah* glints beyond language: praise be to God.

My western tongue holds the syllables, unhooks the praise
in my own last name: *h-m-d.* Always, I recite *alhamdulillah.*

*Nominated by Palette*

# QASSIDA TO THE STATUE OF SAPPHO IN MYTILINI

## by KHALED MATTAWA

from THE KENYON REVIEW

Kyria, why do you stand askance, facing neither
                sea nor mountain,
not even toward your wildflower fields?

And the lyre on your shoulder, was it meant
                to be the size
of the plastic jugs shouldered by Moria's refugees?

I saw them in Sicily, too, home of your exile,
                where no rescue
could pause time grating at their memories.

Your island is empty of poets, Kyria. I came
                to meet them,
to recall the trembling earth under my feet.

Hangers-on reporting to newsletters
                throng the cafes, researchers
hacking at fieldwork, polishing CVs.

The migrants are all court poets now. At night
                they labor to translate
their traumas into EU legalese.

Or sit at your feet shouting into cell phones
             to scattered relatives,
trying to crack the code of the model asylee.

Kyria, there's no way for me to see you, no date,
             or sculptor's name,
only fascist graffiti below your knees.

Why do your eyes glare lifeless like apricot pits,
             your stone body dim,
a paper lamp trembling in the breeze?

Is that you now, Kyria, holding Cleis's hand
             wearing hijab,
glad to be home again, not quite at ease?

*Nominated by Carolyne Wright*

# LARAMIE TIME

## fiction by LYDIA CONKLIN

from AMERICAN SHORT FICTION

Matty and I had been living in Wyoming for three months when I agreed we could get pregnant. We were walking on a boulevard downtown over snow that was crunchy and slushy by turns, heading home from a disappointing lunch of lo mein made from white spaghetti. The air was so sharply freezing, the meal churning so unhappily in our stomachs, that I longed to brighten the afternoon. I'd decided the week before to give Matty what she wanted, but I hadn't found the right moment to tell her, when the air was clear enough for her to absorb the impact.

We were on foot as always–stubborn New Yorkers, despite the wild traffic and missing sidewalks–trudging through the uncleared snow in front of the former movie theater. The Christian who'd bought the place for nothing had arranged the plastic letters into rhetoric on the marquee: *GOD IS LISTENING GOD KNOWS YOURE ROTTEN.*

"Matty," I said, taking her hand. "I've decided." Last week's test results had exposed Matty's declining fertility. If we wanted to do this, it had to be now. I'd finally accepted this reality.

She aimed her freckled stub nose at me and studied my face. "Where to get dessert?" She spoke bluntly, the joke of what she really hoped in the deadness of her words.

"I want to have a kid with you." I meant the words to sound basic but invested with meaning–inflected emotion on "kid" and "you"–those two words the sum total of my future reality. But the sentence sped out like a sneeze.

"That's amazing." She spoke flatly, her unseasonable tennis shoes sinking into the slush. Why was she speaking flatly? "I'm glad you came around."

I expected the conversation to be joyful. Matty had begged me for a kid for years. She should've jumped into my arms when I agreed. She should've fucked me right there on the boulevard, even though it was winter in Laramie, and even though we're lesbians, so fucking wouldn't help with getting the kid.

"Aren't you happy?"

The bubble of a tear occluded one eye, but she squeezed it closed, squeezed both eyes closed. When she opened them, they were clear. "Thank you. I am happy." She sounded like a robot. But sometimes she was like that–a sweet little logic robot. She waited until we stepped onto the curb on Custer Street to clamp me in a cold hug.

That was it. After five years of debate. After crying and threatening to leave, after pointing out every child, even lumpy ones, after mentioning hormones and decreased viability and geriatric pregnancies whenever worry or resentment surged through her. And last week's freak out over the test results, Matty crying all evening that hope was lost. And now look at her, not even surprised. Maybe she figured I wouldn't have moved across the country to spend a year deciding not to have a child with her. But I was unpredictable and stubborn. She'd have known better than to count on me.

At thirty-seven, Matty was three years older than me and beyond ready. I'd wanted to develop my career before motherhood–for the last few years I'd drawn a comic strip about lesbian turtles. Material success with comics seemed an impossibly distant goal, safe because it would take forever. No one bought the Sunday paper anymore and alt-weeklies were dead. And when would a comic strip about lesbian turtles ever hit the big time? Turtles are the least popular type of animal, and lesbians are the least popular type of human. But the strip launched briskly from a shabby online platform, with interest ballooning on social media. People fell in love with the painted turtle with her red dots by each ear and the bigger softshell turtle. People liked their warm, squinted eyes, I guess, their pointy overbites and the way they tried their best–flippers out, balanced on stubby flat feet–to press their plated chests together. The strip got syndicated in the surviving indie magazines and mainstream newspapers in cities like Portland and Portland. The pilot for a TV show had been funded and shot by a hip studio, which was considering buying a whole season. If the studio picked up the show, the turtles would appear on the small screen as black-and-white, stiff-moving cutouts, each character voiced by me, identically deadpan, and we'd move to LA. Whenever I remembered this pending decision, my body trembled.

When the money for the pilot arrived, Matty had asked if we could try, and that's when deeper problems surfaced. For years I'd given the excuse of my career–noble, logical, inarguable, and in the service, ultimately, of family. We'd need money for a kid, of course, and Matty wouldn't want a co-parent who was harried and drawing in the shadows, sneaking away from milestone moments to ink in shell plates and beaky mouths. I was unhappy, and anxious, and I couldn't balance a kid with all that.

Once my career turned, with no more excuses, I had to face the fact that I had deeper issues, issues that were harder to articulate. My father claimed I'd cried when he first held me, and he took this as a permanent rejection of physical affection. He'd been clear with me, from age four, that he'd had me as a compromise, that he didn't want kids. He demonstrated this every day by declining to participate. I was so afraid my kid would feel like that–discarded, lonely, unwanted. I'd never trust myself to be ready enough, though I was afraid to explain all this to Matty, afraid she'd think I was loveless at my core. So when the official reason for my delay disappeared, her frustrations accelerated.

Sometimes, when I was in a certain mood–a dangerous mood maybe, or cruel–I'd speculate on scenarios where the drudgery of domestic life could appeal to some larger, weirder purpose, and I could almost justify the risk of making a child in my ambivalence. What if Matty bore twins, one with my egg and one with hers? Our kids would bond so hard in the womb that it would be like me and Matty combining in that popular, primal way. Matty's pinched-nosed kid stroking her lips like Matty did, smoothing her T-shirt like Matty did, laughing in a high keen like Matty did, falling in sibling love with my kid with dark messy hair and skinny wrists. Did sperm banks provide an anonymous grab-bag option? We could spend years gathering data on the father through the behavior of our child–he must have short eyebrows, he must like cantaloupe with pepper, he must be mean.

We'd moved to Wyoming at the end of the summer to "think about it" in a neutral zone while we lived off the rent from our subletter in New York. We nicknamed this period the Laramie Time. Matty had abandoned her career in academic publishing to finish a novel. Our close friend, Arun, a chatty professor, had spent years making the forgotten town with its wide streets and slouching wood-frame houses and

315

staring white men seem cool. He assured us cougars crossed the highway and food was cheap. He even secured us free housesitting for his colleague who'd left on sabbatical.

Arun insisted that the famous hate crime had unfairly stigmatized the town. Matty had been straight her whole life before me, and the idea of Laramie bothered me more than it bothered her. Arun looked at me when he explained that the whole town knew that Matthew Shepherd and his killer had been lovers. The crime wasn't political, but personal. As though that made it so much better.

The colorful clouds and mountains, the antelopes and antelope-crushing brackets mounted to truck fenders, the beef, the clingy community of intellectuals and creative semi-youths, they'd push us one way or the other. And they had. After three months working side-by-side on the flower-patterned secondhand sofa, Arun our only visitor, the tension of our future thickening the air, and the heartbreaking fertility test on top of it all, I came around to the idea of making a tiny third party to cheer us up. When Arun was over, Matty and I had fun like old times, setting bobcat skulls on our scalps and dancing for him, pretending we were the same cute girls as always. But Matty had only rare days when she was her old self alone with me, when we'd drive numbered country roads to Bamforth or Curt Gowdy or Hot Springs, wander the foothills seeking buffalo. She smoothed the wrinkles in her lip and spun stories: cows with warnings encoded in their spots or swingers sleepwalking on the prairie. That was before she gave up on her novel, when I was so absorbed by Matty that time disappeared in her presence. Anything was fun with her–the pharmacy, the dentist, stopped traffic behind a horse parade. Nowadays she gazed with reproductive lust at men in Safeway. A kid, I hoped, could bring her back.

✻   ✻   ✻

That evening, Matty and I ate buttered tangles of pasta around a mushroom-shaped ironwork table that was intended for outdoor use. Snow spattered the windows. Already in November it had snowed so often that we didn't point it out anymore.

"So what should we name it?" I asked, to prove I was serious. Matty had always taken care of me—financially, for years, and otherwise. I owed her this. I popped open my hands. "Let's discuss."

Matty laughed in her snorting way that made my heart lift. Her hand found mine under the table. She squeezed my fingers in a regular interval, like a heartbeat. "This is the right use for white spaghetti."

I blushed. I'd forgotten about lunch. "I'll make something else."

She gave me her weasel smile. "I like it. Theme days, right?"

We used to have themes, food-wise, back in New York, focusing a day's meals around a color, or a texture or a knobby vegetable pulled from the Chinatown market. The kind of premeditated silliness only Arun would appreciate. I stroked her hand so she'd relax her mechanical squeezing. Her face looked calm but her hand seized like a dying rodent.

"I'm serious, though," I said. "About the names. You must've thought of ideas, right? In all these years?" I was curious. I hadn't felt right asking before I'd agreed.

She glanced at me sharply, then her expression cleared. "Don't be silly," she said lightly. "You're getting ahead of yourself. It's not even conceived."

I shrugged. "It's fun to talk about though, right?"

"Jane," she said, anchoring her straw-colored hair behind her ear. "Or Michael. I'm sick of these pretentious names."

She returned to her pasta—over, decided. So what would we talk about for however long it took to conceive plus *nine months*? I'd thought jabbering about baby names, flapping through giant volumes, revisiting the hijinks of long-dead relatives, was how a couple worked up excitement over a forthcoming wrinkled intruder. What about Francine? What about Jiminy? What about Puck?

Maybe she'd reacted so glumly because of the lesbian turtles. Three weeks before, they'd agreed to adopt a ferret with much more fanfare than I'd offered her. They'd cried. They'd crinkled their papery skin and performed their shell-slapping embrace.

❋ ❋ ❋

The next morning, I found Matty pouring coffee to fuel her standard day of calling friends, donating tank-tops, and watching fake cowboys saunter outside. She freelanced, but that only filled a few hours a week, which she stretched out by typing slowly.

"I better keep up the hard work on my novel," she said, a bite in her voice already. "Wouldn't want to disappoint the reading public." She splashed coffee into her bowl until it overflowed.

Matty admitted to thinking about her novel while she lazed around, though she maintained there was no point pouring your life into some document no one would ever read. I understood that. What worried me was how she talked about it, unhappy, challenging, like she wanted me to quit my comic and mope with her. Her tone scared me, because my grip on my own work was shaky enough.

317

I snagged Matty's sleeve as she passed.

"Watch out." She brushed my hand away to protect her coffee. She looked like a mole, like she always did at this hour, which I'd found sweet. But today she was worse than usual. The skin at the corners of her eyes was blue, and her cheeks wore the rough texture they sprouted under stress. I hated to see her this way. I'd hoped so much that my agreement would be enough to cheer her. I thought of the softshell turtle fashioning a balloon from the hide of a turtle in the community who'd died, etching SON into the leather. Turtles and tortoises emerged from under lily pads and behind stones to fete the future moms.

Matty jiggled her coffee bowl. "Can I sit, please? Am I allowed?"

"Here." I pushed away my sketches. She scowled.

Most mornings I headed straight to my brush and dish of ink. Lately I had conference calls, too, and sometimes I was in LA. I had treatments to rewrite and producers to please and animators to supervise. Half of what I did for the show–which the producers had dumbed down to *Bisexual Turtles*–I did in a trance. Whenever Matty asked about moving to LA, wringing her hands and fretting about highways and actors and glad-handers talking shop, I told her not to worry. She was such a New York girl, striding through Manhattan in her black coat, snapping her way through editorial meetings while clinging to paper cups of coffee, acquiring her first-choice titles, always. Laramie was a way station, but LA was permanent, and the enemy.

I'd have to take my commitment one step further by discussing the sperm donor. The turtles only had to visit Ferret-O-Rama–the shop that appeared on the shore of their pond the moment they needed it. We had a process. And why not start? Matty had abandoned her career and writing and left herself with nothing. Maybe she wanted a kid to distract herself from losing her novel. That was fair. I wanted that for her.

I sat down with Matty and laced my fingers. "So," I said. "The journey begins."

She took a long sip of coffee, her eyes squinting in the steam. "Excuse me?"

"So," I said. "The journey begins."

She set her bowl down, but the heat still tightened her face. "I heard you. I just don't have any idea what you're talking about."

Had she forgotten what we'd decided? "Our journey to have a child."

Brightness flamed over her face, then extinguished. "What about it did you want to discuss?"

"We decided to do it," I reviewed. "We settled on names. What's left?"

318

"To get pregnant and have a baby and raise it to adulthood." She spared a smile for her own joke. "If something's on your mind, just say it." One eye checked me curiously.

"The *sperm*," I said proudly.

"Jesus, Leigh." She peered at me up and down. "You're really jumping right in, aren't you? You're really enthusiastic all of a sudden."

"Well, we have to select a man who embodies our values and love. We could have a fun ceremony where friends help us choose from the sperm bank." We'd be leagues more thorough than the turtles, who'd simply reached for the cutest ferret in the box. We'd invite our Laramie acquaintances to debate dad options. I saw myself lifting placards with photographs of little boys and statistics. Did we want a San Francisco engineer who's Boastful, Fun, and Curious? Or a math teacher who's Creative, Wry, and Caring? Did we want a soccer buff who enjoys Potatoes, Chats, and Items? Or an oak tree fan with a Meaningful Childhood I Long to Replicate in a Baby Version of Myself?

"But we have Arun," she said, studying my face.

"What?"

"Who else?" The top of her face shone with anticipation while her mouth stayed sour.

"Are you okay?" I asked. "You look off." I inched my chair closer to hers. I'd worried about her ever since she'd received her labs. I longed to embrace her, but she looked prickly.

"I'm fine." She kissed me, which sent a leak of molasses from my mouth to my core. If we weren't discussing such urgent matters, if she wasn't in her prickly mood, I'd have suggested she come upstairs and hide with me under the covers. "Don't worry about me."

I liked her hand on my shoulder, heating me in the cold static of the apartment. "Are you sure?"

"Certainly," she said, in her professional voice, her hand sliding free. "You've thought about it, haven't you?" Her eyes throbbed, watching.

I'd always pictured a sperm bank. But, of course, Arun would be better than anyone narcissistic or desperate enough to peddle their bodily fluids. He was a great critic, handsome and brilliant, and our best friend. We'd known him since he was in graduate school in New York, a precocious kid whose book Matty's press had seized before he even defended. We had endless fun in our group of three, and we were both close with him separately. Still, I was disappointed not to have a debate. "He's a start. But do you think he would? And wouldn't it be fun to throw around options?" I was desperate for her to talk to me about this decision, really comb through the details, so I could believe this was real. I was disturbed by how vague she'd been. "What about Rudyard?"

"Rudyard Beechpole? With the lank hair and aging rock-star face?" She didn't present these traits as entirely positive.

"He makes great chairs." His chairs were carved from blackwood with curlicues whittled into the seat like wormholes. We'd wanted one until we'd seen the price.

"I don't care if my baby makes chairs," Matty said.

"I wouldn't *mind* new chairs." I envisioned the apartment filling with increasingly elegant furniture as our baby developed as a craftsman.

Matty snorted. "I guess you can't have too many chairs. Especially fashioned by infants."

"See?" I nudged her with my elbow. She was cheering up. "We've got to weigh the options."

She checked me over. "So Beechpole is a contender for you?"

"Not really." I longed to keep discussing factors and eventualities, but the truth was, I loved the names Michael and Jane. And Arun was the perfect donor. "I'll call Arun now."

Matty looked up with a surprised frown. "Are you sure?"

I lay my hands flat on the table. "Matty. Seriously. What's going on?"

"I was just asking." Her coffee was nearly gone. She fingered the bowl, checking.

I pressed my palms into the ironwork lattices to steady myself. "I thought you wanted kids? I thought that was the whole theme of our relationship?"

She turned her bowl so the dregs swirled. "But I want to know what you think."

"I'm telling you I want to do this. I'm discussing the particulars." I felt my skin patterning with the table. "What more do you want."

Matty looked at me, her eyes pleading. I was terrified to question her further, afraid to find out what she was thinking. She got up and turned into the sink, rinsing her bowl for ages after it must've been clean.

Had she only wanted babies so intensely in the face of my resistance? I watched her until she looked away. Agreeing had been an act of faith, designed to please Matty and bring her back, but I wanted to fight about names and sperm donors until we pushed the process into the next century.

All night I sketched Matty in turtle form, appreciating my willingness to have a kid: kissing me with her beak, stroking me with her flat foot, dedicating to me the most intricate plate of her shell.

The weather turned the next week. Instead of dry slate skies confettied with snow, we were icy and windy and colder than ever. The hail was gunfire cutting at the glass. Even the cowboys stayed inside. We ate canned corn with rubbery ancient carrots on the days we couldn't bear to trudge through the snow to the convenience store and treat ourselves to sad packets of gummy fish and crumbly Wyoming pork rinds.

Matty requested that I ask Arun. He burst apart with happiness before I even got the words out, telling me he'd never wanted to raise his own kids, so he'd always hoped we'd ask. Without Matty's help, I arranged and paid for his genetic and STI tests at Ivinson and hired a lawyer to draft a contract regarding Arun's parental rights. I made her add a clause that we'd appreciate an informal involvement as all parties saw fit.

I wasn't ready for the kid itself, but each step was work I could handle, work that was productive. I felt competent consulting with the doctor over Arun's perfect genetic score, initialing the contract, cutting checks from my turtle earnings. I was giving someone I loved what she wanted, though Matty remained tepid, approving each step without engaging. I was acclimating to her coolness on the subject, though it worried me in spikes. She'd been through patches of depression before–after one of her pet books received poor reviews, and most recently after surrendering her novel. I figured nothing could be exciting when you've wanted it too long. Maybe she'd burned out her energy getting us to here. When the baby came, surely, she'd revive.

I bought her the thermometer and predictor sticks and vitamins and a logbook, and though she showed no initiative, she used them at my urging, keeping a faithful record by the bed. She didn't indicate when her body was ready. But I checked her journal, and when her hormones surged, I announced I was calling Arun.

Arun was the rare person who seemed too amazing for Laramie. Most people in Laramie are the opposite–they'd make no sense anywhere else. The quirkiest girl in Laramie, queen of the hipsters, would be a lame newbie in Brooklyn. Most Laramie men would appear creepy in other cities, and the ones that manage to appear creepy in Laramie would be arrested on contact with a New York City sidewalk. The craftsmen would look homeless, the business owners petty, the artists cheap. But Arun was beautiful. His hair lay flat and thick like cake and his face brightened for a stick of gum. He'd be a star wherever he landed.

Our first two months in Laramie, we saw Arun daily. He worked next to us on the couch after his classes and ate with us at the nineties-style vegetarian restaurant that leaned too heavily on bulgur. We climbed mountains on the weekends. We didn't find trails or pay for parks. We just picked a mountain and pulled over on the country highway and walked through sagebrush and over deer ribs until we achieved the top, Matty clinging to my arm, leaning her cheek against my shoulder and infusing me with love. She gathered treasures: a hiker's whistle, a snake head, a thorn as thick as a fang. I kept them all. At the peak, we'd look down at Laramie, squatting in the prairie. While Matty exclaimed over the landscape, I couldn't help picturing Matthew Shepherd out there on a fence, dying slowly. That his lover had killed him was worse, I realized, not better. Sometimes Matty asked what I was thinking and I'd say nothing; it was all so beautiful.

"I'm cold," Arun once said on a summit, and Matty threw him her tank top, spinning off like a naked animal into the aspens. He pulled the shirt over his head. The straps stretched across the drum of his chest, and he called Matty back, opening his arms. "Look—I'm finally a lesbian." His eyes sparkled. With Arun's admiration washing over us, we were easy with each other again.

The day after Matty's LH surge, I met Arun at the door to our apartment building, a mint green concrete block featuring Art Deco metalwork and block glass in the stairwell. His hand shook as he brushed ice off his shoulder. "Am I early?"

"You're perfect." I sounded like I was hissing, *Let me steal your genes.*

"Cool," Arun said. "I guess I should come in?"

I led him to the living room. Matty was waiting upstairs in the bedroom, because she was too nervous to socialize until the process was over, but it felt wrong to send Arun to masturbate instantly. Besides, I liked his company. Here was this thirty-five year old man, beautiful and brilliant with a perfect job, and he was fine without a baby or even a girlfriend. He saw a few girls in town and sometimes took trips to LA, returning sunny and fortified. But largely he was the picture of someone who could be satisfied alone.

"How's my Matty?" he asked.

"She's great." Arun loved Matty best. Everyone did. She was pretty like a fairytale girl lost in the woods, but brilliant. Everyone said she should go for a PhD before she got too old. "She's waiting upstairs."

"I forgot what she looks like, it's been so long." He scratched the stiff chin of the prairie dog we'd all bought on a joyride to Centennial. We'd pushed our old Civic to eighty, laughing when tumbleweed bounced over the hood, the misstuffed prairie dog goggling from the dash. "If it weren't for the paperwork, I wouldn't have seen you, either." He spoke lightly, as though his sorrow was distant now.

"Things have been rough," I said.

He looked up, his eyes big. "I know."

"Can I get you a drink?"

"Nice seduction technique," he said. "It's two p.m."

"How about some pork rinds?"

"I'll take a drink. This is the weirdest thing I've ever done."

I'd been headed to the kitchen and I turned to laugh–Arun always put me at ease, how could I have forgotten–and saw that he wasn't kidding. His face, forever photo-ready, had collapsed around the mouth. "You okay?"

"Just get me a drink." His tone was steely.

In the kitchen, I fretted over what to serve. I'd stocked his favorites–beer, Jack and Coke, single-serving cans of a spritzer called Naughty Fruits–but none felt tonally appropriate. I didn't want this baby conceived on an afternoon where we choked back bracing beverages, gripped couch cushions, and suffered. So I reached down a bottle of tangerine Schnapps leftover from a Christmas pudding and a bottle of bitters and a novelty soda called Cool Mint Surprise, and I whipped these with egg whites, blueberries, and coconut shavings. The colors refused to integrate and the drink was a bubbling rainbow.

I fit the glass into Arun's shivering claw. A question flashed across his face. He took a swig and grimaced. I wanted to tell him the drink was supposed to be funny, but the moment passed. When he swallowed, the liquid bulged down his throat like cotton. Perhaps he thought this was the best I could do and he didn't want to offend me. Or perhaps he suspected the drink was a joke and didn't want it taken away.

"Listen," I said. "You don't have to do this."

Arun gulped more rainbow. Egg white foamed on his chin. "You know I want to." He threw back another sip and the green portion of the drink splashed his shoulder. He didn't seem to notice.

"Then do you mind my asking why you're scared?"

He looked into the drink and blushed.

"You're worried you won't get off or something?"

He nodded slowly. "I don't masturbate that often."

I tried not to look shocked. "You don't?"

"I'm sure I'll squeeze one out."

"Yeah," I said. "Great."

I turned to face the wood paneling across from the couch. In my comic, Arun was a lanky, long-legged tortoise named AJ who stopped by with sour cream-and-onion snails and a goofy smile. As a Shakespearian, Arun found my comic unforgivably bizarre, though he treasured the small fame it afforded him with queer hipsters on campus. He'd been the most popular character since the beginning, according to the Twitterverse. *If AJ isn't on the show, I'll slit my wrist with a box cutter,* a tween had typed.

"You guys are good?" he asked, shifting his eyes to the ceiling.

"Of course." Since we'd moved to Laramie, I'd barely seen Arun alone, so we hadn't talked intimately in ages. "What do you mean?"

He shrugged at the ink on my wrist. I hadn't slept, so I'd drawn all night. "Your career."

This startled me. The issue with Matty had always been kids. Everything else was perfect–the sex, the conversation, we both loved hiking and rice and audiobooks and begging bakeries for fresh bread at 4 a.m. Neither of us cleaned refrigerators or harped on dusting. The lesbian turtles had the same, sole problem. In one strip, they looked into each other's beady eyes and whispered that they wished baby turtles didn't exist, that eggs couldn't gel in their ovaries, or that reproduction was automatic or mandatory, so they wouldn't have to decide. "There's just that one thing between me and Matty," I'd told friends. "That one thing."

Arun relaxed against the overstuffed cushions. "I mean, think about it. Your comic goes viral, it's bought by some hip feminist studio, you might get a bigshot writing gig in LA?"

"She's supportive."

"No kidding." Arun leaned forward, elbows on knees. "But think about it, Leigh. What's Matty doing?"

"Right now? Waiting." With no one to confide in, I hadn't faced a hard truth in months. I could tell he wanted to talk, but it wouldn't be that easy.

"No, honey. I mean, in general. She quit her job. She's editing, like, ten pages a week for some startup."

"But that's her choice." I remembered the last night of Matty's novel. She'd typed feverishly since predawn. She'd requested a stay on dinner, then another. As bedtime approached and we hadn't eaten, she shoved her laptop off the couch. "It's all made-up." Her fingers fluttered on the air. "Completely fake." There was panic in her eyes, but her body seemed to sag in relief. Matty's novel was a drug. She'd worked on it constantly, miserably. She was a great writer–you could tell even from her goofy road trip yarns–but writing made her unhappy.

Arun watched me. "Do you really believe she'd give up a project she sacrificed her career to write?"

"It was sad, yeah, but she said she wanted it." Guilt tugged at my brain. I should've tried to change her mind. I'd been too relieved to have my girlfriend back.

"Meanwhile, teen girls are coming over your turtles on Snapchat. And she's doing nothing. That's really what you think?"

I should've worked through the abandonment of her novel, ascertained she was all right. I should've offered to read her book, or at least assured her I believed in her. We hadn't talked in so long. The kid question had subsumed everything. If we talked about her novel, or LA, it would circle back to kids, so I'd avoided it all. But I knew, with Arun's disapproving gaze settling over me, that I should've forced the issue.

"That's why this is good." I gestured at Arun, accidentally aiming at his groin. We both grimaced. "Really. I've done what I wanted to do. And now I can do this." Instead of *this* I almost said *what Matty wants to do.*

Arun shook his head. "I shouldn't tell you this." His face softened like it would at a child. "But it might help you not to worry so much." He lowered his voice. "She's still working on her novel, Leigh. She has been all this time."

The skin on my face stiffened. "What do you mean."

"And it's going well," he whispered. "Really well. So you don't have to worry so much." He leaned back and nodded, as though expecting me to leap from my chair and dance.

"Oh." I was so shocked that my mouth stayed frozen in its little hole. The charade of giving up, all those disparaging comments, and Matty had been lying all the while? Sneaking off to write, when? While I was asleep? When she was pretending to freelance? When I was in LA? I saw her getting up at four, indulging in fifteen hours of writing, twenty, forsaking meals and snacks and the bathroom, her eyes burned dry at the end of the day, feeling thrilled and alive. That it was going well was worse, because why had she lied? I could understand if the work was going badly, if she wanted to wait to turn the corner before she shared the news. I felt the creeping realization: Matty couldn't write around me, couldn't celebrate. Maybe because of the turtles, or maybe it was something else. "I knew that," I said.

Arun leaned back, raising his eyebrows. "Did you?"

"Of course she told me," I said. "And I would've noticed anyway. You think she could hide that?" The words sent a crack of pain down my neck. We'd drifted further apart than I'd imagined. I couldn't believe I hadn't recognized the creative euphoria in my own partner, living beside me in the middle of nowhere for three months. What was wrong with me? I cleared my throat, trying to sound natural: "Can I ask you something?"

Arun nodded, watching me with concern.

"Why don't you want to raise kids?"

The egg white on his chin was an opalescent sheen. "You want to know?"

"Definitely." I needed him to talk for as long as possible while I gummed over this news about Matty. And besides, nothing he'd say would touch me. I'd heard all the arguments. I'd made them myself–global health, overpopulation, career surrender, drudgery. I hated chores. I hated shopping. I only liked one in a hundred kids–those were tricky odds. I'd hate pushing a doll through a castle door a hundred times–*Mommy, Mommy, again.* I didn't want kiddie barfing diseases. I didn't care about advancing my genes. I didn't want Matty's body to change. I didn't want to read a book about parenting. But everyone told you that, once the kid was born, you were happy.

"No one would admit they made a mistake," he said. "By having a kid, I mean. Not just because they wouldn't want to hurt the kid if he ever found out they'd said so, but because of the sacrifice. There's too much investment."

"Yeah, yeah." I'd thought of that when I'd tried to find testimonials from people who had and hadn't regretting reproducing, or had and hadn't regretted not.

"That's not why I'm scared, though," he said.

I knew I should end the conversation, that Matty was waiting upstairs, but I had to ask. "Then why?"

"My nephew," he said, "lives in Queens. When he was four he escaped his bed. He opened the front door and stood outside until a bus stopped. He got on the bus and rode into Manhattan."

"No," I said. Arun exaggerated all the time for laughs.

"He did." Arun set his empty glass on our steamer trunk. "My brother and his wife were asleep. They think the bus driver was high, but I bet everyone thought Sunil was with someone else. He rode over the Queensboro Bridge and into Midtown. He got off at Lincoln Center.

Seriously." Arun wore that hurt look he got when he feared we wouldn't believe him. "Later everyone said they wondered about the kid. But no one did anything." He rolled his eyes. "New Yorkers, man. No offense."

Arun was from New York, but he'd forsaken his past to live as a pure Westerner. "Hey," I said. "I'm in Wyoming now." If I'd found that kid I would've scooped him up and ferried him to safety. I would've made him laugh in my arms until his parents claimed him.

"Anyway," Arun said. "This lady found him."

"Phew," I said.

"No." His face darkened. "It's not good."

Arun never talked about his family. His parents were nasty to him and, I suspected, abusive. Part of his love for Laramie was that it was such a slog from New York. There were only two planes a day into town. You saw one in the sky and knew your visitor was on board.

"They went to a play." Arun frowned. "I guess it had some weird stuff. There was a man dressed as a wolf, there was a naked kid, there was a stone people handled. It was a festival entry–the script isn't published. I've looked. I'm sure you would've loved it."

"So they saw a play," I said. "So?" I liked the idea of a kid at a play: a head bobbing at knee level, following me to museums and parks and afternoon pubs. Just because I had a kid didn't mean we had to languish in pits of plastic balls.

"And we could figure out what he saw, right? We could find the script, interview audience members. But what gets me is the time around the play. Like what kind of person–and not to be sexist, but what kind of *woman*–sees a four-year-old lost in Midtown Manhattan and doesn't call the police? Instead she takes him to a goddamn play."

I looked at the ceiling. I wondered if Matty was angry we were taking so long. Stress impaired conception. I pictured the wrinkles around her mouth deepening. I was afraid to face her, afraid to look at the girl who'd lied about her brilliant novel.

"Something bad happened. Sunil wasn't the same after. He turned into this mini-adult. He didn't bounce around like he used to. You don't understand–he was a puppy before. Those questions and silly voices all the time–even in timeouts he'd dance in his corner–and then, suddenly, nothing. And it wasn't just the play. He didn't understand the play."

"You think she molested him?" My heart surged, I hadn't met Sunil, but I could picture him, his face tightly eager, his little hands grabbing the air, clowning as he bounced from foot to foot. "We'll never know." A moody look bled over Arun's face. "Because he doesn't know. He's forgotten, but it affected him. And he didn't have the resources to process whatever happened enough to tell us. Did she touch him? Did she say something? Did she show him a picture?" He gripped his knee. "Whenever I think of having kids, I think of that panic. I know it would never happen again, but a thousand things like it would. Little things, sure, but that day you let the kid loose, and it's seeing things you'll never know." He shook his head. "That spooks me."

"I get it," I said.

"I shouldn't say this crap to you." He raised his tumbler. "Your rainbow juice made me do it."

I lifted my water, and we clicked glasses.

"But you're not as paranoid," he said. "You haven't had my family." He gave a weak smile. He didn't know about my father, about how I'd felt as a kid. My story had always felt whiney in the face of the darkness he wouldn't name.

"You'll be a beautiful mother," he said, regret wet in his eyes, whether for his own childhood or his missed fatherhood, he couldn't tell.

I had a flash of wishing I'd been Arun's mother, and Sunil's. I saw a hairy, upright beast lurching across the stage, a little boy too shy to seize the sleeve of his chaperone. When it came down to assuming responsibility for a floppy body, loose in the world, I knew I could be flexible and resilient, that I could put a little person first. Not only that I could do it but that I wanted to, and not only that I wanted to, but that I had to.

❖   ❖   ❖

I sent Arun upstairs with my laptop and a glass vial. I should've checked on Matty, but the news about her novel, and Arun's story, had left me jittery. I lingered between my office, where Arun produced the ingredient, and our bedroom, where Matty lay. Both rooms radiated tense silence.

I could picture my child, finally, small and dark haired, strolling with me at the foot of the mountains. She was real to me, so real I was afraid to touch the air at my hip for fear of grazing her hair. But when I pictured life with her, Matty wasn't with us. I saw myself and the child, or the child alone, or another figure between us. Arun, even, but not Matty. I'd told myself our relationship was perfect, and I hadn't worried enough when the freeze set in. But she was happily writing in secret, while pretending to be depressed—or maybe she really was depressed. Maybe the novel was going well and she was sad she couldn't share that—because of my success, or because of competition between us, or maybe the novel was autobiographical and she didn't want me to know. Whatever the reason, it wasn't healthy. We couldn't survive like this. If we wanted to have kids, we needed to separate and have them apart, if we could manage. If there was time.

The thought of losing her and that dark-haired kid was a double punch in the chest. I loved Matty. And I loved the kid already so much, ridiculously much, and she'd never even breathe. Now I understood what I could've had: a girlfriend and a little person, in a jasmine-flavored yard in Los Feliz, pulling vines off the house and training them up jacaranda trees, writing with a sleeping baby's sunlit face pointing up at me from a cozy sling. The hot red loops of nostrils, the mouth sealed like it would never have reason to cry, the smell of sweet bread rising from that golden scalp.

I braced myself to tell her. But after I'd agreed to have kids, Matty had never raised the issue once. She must not have wanted a baby, or she'd come to the same realization that I had. She was afraid to tell me because she'd badgered for so long. So maybe we were on the same page. So this could be okay.

The door to the office opened. One of Arun's hands protected his crotch while the other extended the vial.

"Don't look at it," he said. "That's too weird."

"Thanks," I said. "You can go."

He looked at me, hurt. "Just like that?"

"I'm sorry." I wanted this whole sad attempt over. "Please, Arun."

"Okay, fine." He was disappointed. He'd hoped to be part of the family maybe, though he'd signed his rights away. "So long as you aren't mad. For the story or whatever."

Of course I was mad. "I'll call you."

❋   ❋   ❋

I held the vial with two hands as Arun thumped down the stairs and out the front door. The plan had been to keep the fluid warm and then draw it with the syringe. I opened the bedroom door with a shaking hand.

Matty was stretched naked on the bedspread. Her body was long, like a resting deer. Her sandy hair covered her shoulders and the tops of her breasts. There was this person who'd lied to me, who was happier than she could admit, who was thriving. My heart lifted for her, that she could have that joy, even if it was separate from me. Her deception was my fault. I hadn't made room for her, and I hadn't noticed in time that I hadn't.

329

"Hi," she whispered.

Warmth filled me despite the under-heated room. I hadn't seen Matty like this—lips melting, skin relaxed and smooth, breasts flushed pink–in weeks, not since I'd told her I wanted a kid. I'd forgotten her body ready for me.

"You okay?" I whispered.

"Can't you tell?"

She lifted her arms and I dropped into them, the vial still clutched in my fist, heating it with all my might though I didn't want it anymore. I felt right against Matty's velvet skin, her skinny limbs curving around me, the ache of her breath on my forehead. "What changed?" I asked.

She pulled her head back. She was glowing. "I had to know you're serious."

My heart clogged my throat. The vial went cold between my fingers. How had this sludge been so recently inside a body? She wanted a baby.

"You were testing me?" I flashed with fuzzy rage.

She tipped her head back. "Don't talk. Just touch me."

I was so grateful to be back with Matty that, even as a barb of anxiety drew through me, I hung above her, our bellies grazing. I thought of Sunil in the dark as a man-wolf stalked the stage, needing someone who knew him. I thought of the turtles' ferret, so sweet and easy he could never be real. I worried he'd be the only baby I'd ever create. But I couldn't do it with Matty. Not the silence and manipulation and lies. Not with a kid. Tomorrow I'd tell her what I was about to do. We'd fight, in a subdued, broken way, and we'd be over. The enormity of what I'd done wouldn't hit her for days, when she'd call, furious. I'd leave her without a job or girlfriend or a kid. I already knew exactly how our end would play out, and I was right.

I drew the semen into the syringe. But before I pushed it into Matty I aimed the tip down and pressed the plunger, freeing the sperm into the carpet under the bed. There was our baby, soaking into the floor, my only chance, as it would turn out, and hers, too. A shudder shook me, as though I knew this already. I dipped the syringe into her and then I lay on her body, focusing on her smell.

*Nominated by American Short Fiction, Tim Hedges, Barrett Swanson*

# METEOROLOGY IS THE SCIENCE OF REMEMBERING THE SKY STAYS RELATIVELY THE SAME

by INAM KANG

from GORDON SQUARE REVIEW

in poverty, the sky felt like
an unattainable parody. i say parody
like everyone reads stars and
my brothers and i just yell about good
shine on a black sheet. we grew
big in the after, made the sky a different
thing, nobody's home at the right
time, my mother there on the couch
with a telephone and du'a.
say bismillah a million times,
say hello to a new home. every single
morning, my family makes a run for
bigger wealth. still, there is the sky,
each shine set in place like a jewel in
ring. my mother held her own up close
to her eye and still kept an elbow
on the sill. she took a cheap glue

to it because somebody had to
commemorate the wedding with this.
me, bound against her fingers, too. my
brothers, late through the door. we
fish through a screen. again, there's the
sky. there's a reason to remember. this
time, not a war. this time, not a lost jewel
in the wrong place. this time, only a
small home where the people spoke
a single language from the tips of their
dry lips, this time, only the sky with
our bodies watching. crooning like
steam from a good meal in
a familiar country.

*Nominated by Gordon Square Review*

# THE SHAME EXCHANGE

by KAREN E. BENDER

from THE YALE REVIEW

No one knew who originally proposed it; the government would mandate an exchange of shame. Citizens who held too much shame, which interfered with their lives and productivity, would come to an official site where their shame would be handed to a government official who had none. Many people, in both the federal and technology sectors, were involved in organizing this exchange, and it had not been easy to agree on the terms. The government was, for years, not sufficiently responsive to the needs of its citizens and this was what a panel finally decided to do.

The citizens would be selected by lottery and interviewed, and those who were unduly burdened by their shame would be asked to participate. Psychologists had created a technique in which they could detect a person's shame and make it a physical, hulking thing. It was generally the size of a large pillow and resembled a raw steak. Before this exchange, selected citizens stored their shame in a refrigerator, carefully packaged by medical professionals, and would present it, in this controlled environment, to those who had none.

The meeting would take place in a large warehouse somewhere in the middle of the nation. Though there was much interest in the details of the exchange–who gave what to whom, etc.–no one outside of the participants would be allowed to watch. The event would be heavily guarded. No one was allowed to meet or speak to one other. Everyone was instructed to wear a mask—a simple plastic one, constructed in the shape of a lion, dog, rabbit, and other animals–to conceal their identity. They would all be told to dress professionally for the exchange, but in clothing suitable to an *office*.

The shame would be transferred between ordinary citizens and officials in the government. Elected officials would be required to undergo a test. Those officials whose shame did not reach a certain appropriate and decent level were ordered to the warehouse at the appointed time. Every member of the legislative, judicial and the executive branches would be required to take this test, and some would try, cleverly, to impersonate shame when they had none. But the test had questions that revealed these attempts at fake shame. Psychologists had worked very hard on these tests, and all attempts at false shame would be detected.

As word spread, more and more citizens signed up to hand over their shame. They could drive themselves or were provided a pleasant, air-conditioned bus from their homes to the warehouse. More buses were quickly added, as citizens, in buzzing, excited numbers, signed up.

As soon as certain elected officials were informed of their low scores of shame, they were escorted to locked vehicles that would transport them to the warehouse. No one quite knew what happened in the locked vehicles, though the rumors were that the politicians were, during that final ride, given anything they wanted. This had been negotiated, with much back and forth, in backroom deals. The vehicles sped across the country, not stopping until they reached the warehouse.

The ones with no shame entered a large, empty, light-filled building and stood across from the ones who were handing over their shame. The two rows of individuals stood across from each other, wearing masks, which made it appear that everyone was about to engage in a dance. Armed guards, screened for their capacity to resist bribery or threats, stood around all of them, watching. The ones with no shame moved slowly, coolly, but under their masks, appeared to be scanning the room, trying to detect who was here.

Those in Row 1 clutched their bags of shame, the bags heavy as though they contained broken, dripping melons. Some bags would be thick, double-bagged, as shame was both heavy and had a tendency to leak. There was a sharp and bitter odor of rot. They looked embarrassed, shoulders hunched, even if they were handing over this burden. They understood, all too clearly, what this entailed. They could not meet the eyes of the ones in Row 2. Some even seemed reluctant to hand over their shame at all, to burden another with it. But that was what they were here to do.

"Row 2, Hold out your hands," announced a voice.

The ones with no shame refused to follow instructions; they did not hold out their hands. The guards had to grab their hands and forcibly lift them up. The guards pried the fingers of the shameless ones and forced their palms open. No one said the recipients had to accept the shame willingly. A few of them screamed, and a couple large bodyguards stepped in to stop some from running away. A couple of individuals in Row 2 chuckled, as though not believing this would actually happen.

"Row 1, place your bag into the hand of Row 2."

Those in Row 1, some weeping or trembling, lifted their own bulky packages of shame, and placed each one in the hands of the person standing opposite them in Row 2.

There was a deadly quiet in the warehouse. The guards pressed the heavy packages of shame into the palms of those who had none. The ones in Row 1 stepped back.

They looked at each other and laughed. They were advised just to keep a handful of shame for themselves, not giving all of it up to the ones in Row 2. A handful of shame would help them get along with family, friends, work. A handful, that was all. Some had to be discouraged from keeping more, as the great majority of shame had to be given to the ones in Row 2. The warehouse was silent for a few moments, and then echoed with the sound of one person laughing, then another, then everyone in Row 1. The pure sound of being unburdened, relief. An ice cream truck was set up outside the warehouse, so that they could celebrate with free ice cream. Some of those in Row 1 literally skipped out the door.

The ones in Row 2 clutched the packages of shame, or, more accurately, the guards fit their hands around the packages. There was a deep silence, though some officials began to cry, in a choking, confusing way; it was the first time some of them had cried. Everyone in the warehouse watched them with interest, wondering what they would now be.

Everyone in Row 1 left the warehouse, zipped out to the rest of their lives.

Shame plinked onto the concrete floor. The ones in Row 2 now held shame in their hands, forever.

The warehouse was almost empty now. Outside, drivers stood by the vehicles that brought them here, waiting for the officials to come out. The drivers of the cars had been gathered in small groups, chattering with each other; when they saw the officials now burdened with shame, they quickly went to their respective cars and stood very still. In a few minutes, they would drive the officials back to the Capitol, where they would return to their work governing the nation.

Those who had organized this exchange had no further plan. They expected only that the ones in Row 2 would govern with sensitivity and in a kindly way. Would this happen? They checked that the locked vehicles held food that the officials had requested, though some might be so distraught they would not eat. Had the locked vehicles been cleaned? Were skilled therapists on board each vehicle? Were people knowledgeable about a variety of policies ready to ride back with them? Now that they were burdened with a great deal of shame, the officials needed to be treated with a bit of tenderness.

"This way," said one organizer. The ones in Row 2 filed out, slowly. The shame was now part of them and the packages could be taken to a sterilized and locked facility. Organizers in hazmat suits took the shame from their hands and set the packages into a special truck. The politicians moved slowly and with deliberation. They would not remove their masks until they were safely inside the cars; many people here were afraid to see their faces. So much work had gone into this exchange, so much planning. Was this, finally, the strategy that would help the nation? The organizers watched the officials get into their cars. The cars started, turned, and drove onto the highway. Those at the warehouse stood, watching the cars vanish into the distance, and then everyone—carefully—cheered.

*Nominated by The Yale Review, Robert Anthony Segal, Eric Wilson*

# ON THE OVERNIGHT TRAIN

by ALICE FRIMAN

from THE MASSACHUSETTS REVIEW

I remember an open window, my hair
blown apart by a hot wind, and me
itching to make love. We were headed
east through Poland on the old cattle-car
tracks glinting like teeth in the moonlight,
and there I was acting like a fifteen-
year-old boy, sexed up and oblivious.
The train hurtled through the dark,
shaking side to side past sleeping towns
where once in a while a spotlight from
a passing depot lit up our silhouette.
You were leery, the windows not
dirty enough to hide us, and me,
playing Alice down the rabbit hole,
*Let's see where this path goes,* tugging
at your belt and laughing, wanting nothing
but skin between us. That was the night
of repeated visits: passport control
banging on the door, guns drawn,
checking papers, or so they said. Thugs
headed by a dead-eyed woman with
bruised lips, a pen and a black book.

How to explain away that night, my body
operating on its own, divorced from

history: the country surrounding us
and the crimes committed there.
I tell myself it was the wind and balmy
velvet of the dark or the little green pills
the doctor gave me before we left home,
pills so good you can't get them anymore.
To be honest, there are many things
I'd like to change about my life.
Too much homework never finished,
too many lies to count, too many lovers
and too little love. But that night—
racing through the dark in a rattling
car filled with terror-stricken ghosts
and me, who, but for a trick of fate,
could have been, would have been
among them, one more yellow-starred
child pushed, shoved, jabbed and
jammed in with the whole doomed
lot—is not one of them.

Look, the body wants what it wants
when it wants it. But I do wish
we had found the courage to use
those purpled hours and put them
to work: defy decorum and undress.
Peel off, disrobe, strip down to the very
bones if necessary. Then, sternum to sternum,
femur to femur, click into place
for all those who couldn't, wouldn't
ever again.

*Nominated by Marianne Boruch, Andrea Hollander, Carolyne Wright*

# ON THE FOOTAGE OF MONET PAINTING

## by SAMUEL CHENEY

from SMARTISH PACE

Even if the projection
is quicker-than-life, he paints

fast and peeks faster,
as if afraid

that the light he spots
in each glance

will fade
if he takes too long

to capture it in oil—
or even dissolve

if it stays too long
fixed under his gaze—

that sight is best
sent sideways—

that water will never
be water alone—

that time cannot be taken
in a small enough dose

      —(infinity lays out
      in the knuckle-length ash
      he lets dangle from his cigarette)—

that the eye can be trusted
for just an instant—

that paint
is insufficient—

that to feel oneself
feeling something

is to feel
it fade away.

*Nominated by Smartish Pace*

# SYCAMORE

## by STANLEY PLUMLY

from AMERICAN POETRY REVIEW

If you couldn't have an elm-lined walk,
you might have one of these for show-and-tell,
with Mrs. Allen standing at the back end
of the class, who meant for us to hold up
one example of a leaf and talk the best
we could in front of every other stumbling
second-grader, whose usual was scarlet maple,
golden oak, or some hybrid color heart-shaped
half-spotted kind of thing, half-wet or fading
as the storyteller wandered through the history
of how he or she got here safely with it. Mine,
from the front lawn, was hardly any better,
since it covered more than twice my opened fingers,
palmate on my palm, and was turning toward
its dry and pockmarked end, like my now vein-heavy
hands, which, when the nurses try for blood,
are better than the arms. As I remember,
these thousand years ago, I held it from my body
as if while I was talking it had died and my story
was an elegy of time, the season passing, winter
coming on. Of course, this is a lie: I was silent
and stood there in my cylinder of silence like
the tree the leaf had fallen from, until the teacher,
in her mercy, told me to sit down, the way
I'm sitting now, typing. Nothing ever dies,

says the science of mortality—it's all chemistry
and change from one form to another. I was dying
holding on to dear life with a dead leaf that was
changing even further in the endless moment
that morning, curling, still alive, within my hand.

*Nominated by David Baker, Michael Collier, Sandra Lessley, Maxine Scates,
Jody Stewart, Richard Tayson*

# TURNER'S CLOUDS FOR PLUMLY

by DAVID BAKER

from AMERICAN POETRY REVIEW

—Cloud cold sky. He was speaking of Turner,
though we had just turned the corner on Well Walk
and down the last cobbles to the Keats house,
its gray-white stone walls gathered like ground fog.
He had talked all day—painting to painting—
through one long room in London's National.
He bit into his beard to quiet now.
Tight grass. Cankered catalpa in half-leaf.

In books he calls the paintings landscapes of
water, wild beyond human artifice.
They are what our feelings are without us.
They are, beyond us, peaceable masters—
in poem after poem on Keats, clouds,
then the talking essays, the cataloguing
student in him calling forth poetry
even in the later prose. Of *The Sun*

*of Venice Going to Sea*—dark oil. It
*is only a fishing boat, yet it casts*
*the larger spell of a vessel moving*
*in the direction of a destiny . . .*
—We'd crossed the entry room and started toward

the cellar. It's what he wanted to see,
a breath of cloud as coal smoke in shadow.
Mary first, then Margaret, Stanley, and me,

    descending. He touched her shoulder where
a wing would be, to steady her, or right
himself. He said he'd come to study soot
and size, the cellar smaller than the house,
the ways the old chute served the home. It was
like, he quieted again, a mother's
crawlway in a kitchen in Ohio.
Welded ductwork, a bucket of brushes.

    Nor had he needed to see the paintings.
It was companionship he wanted, like
confirming the coal service of the cellar,
and to hear himself mumble, just there, look,
the tree—his finger brushing air—and one
diminished figure in red, lost almost
in the landscape of the place. There he is.
Turner seemed to him like Keats must have felt.

    Yet it's Keats whose imagined every
step he traced, as though alongside the man
broaching "the thousand things"—Nightingales
and sleeplessness, dreams, poetry, whatnots . . .
One story goes, in his telling each time,
his melancholy knowingness, that Keats
was called by Dr.—over the heath
to speak with Coleridge, walking there as well.

    He was *a loose, slack, and not well dressed youth,*
the older poet would write, though they spoke
only a minute or so. *There is death
in that hand, I said to—, when Keats
was gone; yet this was, I believe, before
the consumption showed itself distinctly.*
From the first two specks of lung-blood coughed up,
Keats knew "the colour. I cannot be deceived . . .

that drop is my death warrant;—I must die."
Stanley said his started at a distance
five hundred and twenty light-years away
and fell as stardust into his sleeping mouth.
We live in one time but think in another.
When he saw the paintings again, the cloud
symbols, the impressionist's weightless swirls,
he must have felt the same something airy

and ominous coming down, the way each
canvas is an art of premonition.
In love we open our mouth. In dying
we open it wider, saying, he wrote,
in your voice, come forth. We came back up then
to the Keats room full of books and letters,
then out into the low front lawn and air
of a big tree's down-pitched breaking bough

sick with wilt. No one knew the bird singing
there, nipping berries from the bush broadside
to the gate. Constant the love song. Chatter
and trill. It gorged and sang, lifted to land
again on a subsequent twig. *Sweetheart*,
he said, and he might have meant a brown-gray bird.
Or any number of us in his flock
of friendships. He might have meant his mother

always with him, in sorrow, or another,
like others before her—the devotions,
adorations, the students at his feet . . .
Or he might have meant a song floating somewhere
else from a high silver-midnight plane tree
outside, calling all night long, in his voice,
*sweetheart*. He called to Margaret in the dark,
the last night of his mortal darkness—

it was his favorite time, after all, night's
black bird, starling, or startling redwing with its
wing-top slash of yellow from the midnight

branches of a tree, calling all night long
and ready now to leave among the leaves.
Turner paints the clouds as though they are thoughts,
he said, of what's to come. We see the end.
No one could see it brewing there but him.

*Nominated by American Poetry Review, Jane Hirschfield, Mark Irwin*

# GIVE MY LOVE TO THE SAVAGES

fiction by CHRIS STUCK

from BENNINGTON REVIEW

It was spring break, the riots had broken out, and I'd just flown into LA to visit my father. He picked me up from the airport in a new Porsche drop-top, and before I could even get my seat belt on he was yelling, "Status report, Junie" right in my ear. No "Hi, Junie," "I missed you, Junie," "Hey, how you been, Junie boy?" I hadn't seen him in months. All I got was, "That crackerjack jury just let the cops off. It's a goddamn uprising."

We were ripping east down the 105 by then, breaking away from traffic, and we could barely hear a thing. Pop refused to ride with the top up on any of his convertibles—it was California, for shit's sake—so whenever we got on the freeway we had to shout just to be heard over the wind.

He leaned in close, as he always did, and said, "Hey, dummy? You hear me?"

I leaned in close and said, "Yes, dummy. I heard you."

"Good. Because it's a goddamn rebellion, Junie. It's a fucking revolt."

I was twenty-one at the time and admittedly kind of a turd. When I was around my father, sarcasm was my mother tongue. "Really?" I said. "A revolt? You sure someone's not just having a really big barbecue, Pop?" I grinned at him, pleased with myself, but he never took kindly to my mouth. He looked at me like I was a mental patient. His face shriveled into a scowl. "No one likes a smartass, smartass. Watch yourself."

As we curled onto the 405 interchange and a new tangle of cars appeared up ahead, I told him to save the riot talk. The flight attendants told everyone on the plane before we landed. But he didn't want to hear it. He was still in a mood. A few of his businesses had screwed the pooch earlier that year, and he'd nearly lost his ass. The possibility of losing more in a riot probably had his sphincter knotted up good. He kept making the same face as when he'd broken his ankle two years before, when the painkillers he was on made him ferociously constipated.

"So the flight attendants told you about the riots, did they? Well, that's just fucking awesome. Did they tell you what it's really like down here, too? People looting and setting fires and shit?"

"No," I shouted. "But isn't that what people usually do when they riot, Pop? Loot and set fires and shit?"

He turned his head slowly and gave me the look, the icy gaze of ill intent he reserved just for me. He shouted, "Hey, smartass? What did I just tell you about being a smartass?" Naturally, when I opened my mouth to answer, he lifted his hand and said, "Shut it."

❋ ❋ ❋

He'd called me right before spring break, talking like a loan shark, as usual. Just under the wind, through the crackling connection of his car phone, I could barely hear him say, "You owe me a visit, Junie," "owe" being the operative word. Pop always liked his favors returned to him one way or another, and clearly he thought he'd done me a solid by "bumping pelvises" with my mother in the first place. I spent every spring break working as cheap labor at one of his car dealerships: answering phones, changing toner in the Xerox, and generally acting like I was working without actually doing any work, which, at that point in my life, was a talent of mine. He was always quick to remind me that he, not my mother, was paying for my East Coast education. In his mind, it made sense I repay him with the only valuable thing I had at the time: the best days of my youth.

Though I hadn't seen him in a year, much less talked to him, I didn't see any change in him whatsoever. He didn't look any older. He didn't look any wiser. He didn't look any less tan. If anything, he looked more like himself than he ever had. His hair was still long, bound into a glistening ponytail. He still preferred mercury-colored suits and white dress shirts open at the collar. And his jewelry—a pinky ring, a left earring, and a single gold chain—all sparkled as blindingly as ever, even in the haze-choked sun.

The only thing different about this visit was what Pop was now calling "the mutiny." It'd started around three that afternoon, a Wednesday, while I was flying somewhere over the Southwest. From the air, during my plane's descent, LA didn't look any different. It was the same sprawling mess I'd always known, the motherboard of downtown barely visible through the clouds. Everything seemed fine until we pierced the smog. I could see packs of tiny fire trucks and police cars in the streets, the odd blaze just beginning to grow. Something wasn't quite right, even for LA. And of course now Pop's sneaky ass was driving us right into it without any explanation.

* * *

He rocketed us onto the 405 North, zipping us in and out of traffic, cutting off practically every car on the highway. After the interchange, though, he miscalculated and got us stuck behind a bus of schoolkids. He cursed, swerved out onto the shoulder to MacGyver around them. Then he got neck and neck with the driver so he could give him the finger. Pop saluted the guy so long the kids on the bus laughed and waved their middle fingers back at us. He flipped them off too.

At the Manchester Avenue exit near Inglewood, he aimed the Porsche to the right and fired us off the freeway, saying, "Get ready," but mostly to himself.

Naturally, I asked what for.

He reached under his seat for his Walther PPK, checking the clip to see if it was full and then popping it back in. "Assailants," he said. "And before you ask, this is so they'll think twice about fucking with us."

I nodded, since getting fucked with in Inglewood was always a possibility, even without a riot going on.

We shot off the freeway and turned onto Manchester and ran straight into a wild mob. Every car in front of us immediately tried to pull a U-ey and get back on the freeway, but all they did was clog the street like cattle in a chute. "Geniuses," Pop said, as he kamikazed us into oncoming lanes until we reached Inglewood Avenue. There we were met by an even bigger hive of people.

Everyone was pissed off and confused, an odd mix of anger and exhilaration hot on their faces. Some ran from one side of the street to the other and then decided they didn't like it there and ran back. Some held bricks and rocks in their hands, just waiting for a worthy target, like us. As we weaved through, their white-people radar must've gone off, because they all stopped rioting, turned around, and watched Pop and me like we had horns growing out of our heads. I wanted to tell them we were the good guys, or at least that I was. Something like, "Hey, my mother's black. Like, really black. I'm one of you." But Pop took a different approach. "You don't have bumpers on your black asses. Get out of the street, numbnuts."

I elbowed him and said that probably wasn't the best thing to say right then.

"Yeah? Why not?"

"Because your ass isn't black. If your ass isn't black, you can't call their asses black. That's kind of the rule."

Pop shook his head as we threaded through another gang of looters. He laid on the horn, parting the crowd, and one of the harder-looking guys smiled at us. "Damn, white man. You got some nuts on you, know that? Don't you know where you are?"

"Yeah," Pop said. "I'm in America. Where are you?"

"Hell," someone shouted.

Given our present surroundings, right then seemed like a good time to ask what the fuck we were doing there.

"Oh, I don't know," Pop said. "How about driving around this town making sure none of my dealerships have been torched yet. Fine with you?"

After he picked me from the airport each spring, he usually took me to a bar or, if I was lucky, a strip club. By one or two in the morning, we'd end up at his house in Malibu, drunk and stewing away in his Jacuzzi. At that moment, however, flying down the road, I was in no position to complain, because, really, I never was. He was liable to say, "You want some cheese with that whine?" and then leave me there on the side of the road. He'd done it before.

✿  ✿  ✿

At the Inglewood car lot, we were greeted by Pop's fleshy face. It was pasted on a large billboard over a double-wide that served as the dealership office. His image was so gargantuan that his pores were as large as divots, his nose the size of a car door. Like most of his other lots, this one spanned an entire block, nothing but an asphalt parcel of clunkers, a neon price tag plastered on each windshield. Most of the inventory had been in accidents, fires, floods, or other cataclysmic events. Knowing Pop, there was always at least one that'd been sheared in half in a wreck and then welded back together.

We pulled inside the gates, and on the office roof, Burger, one of Pop's guys, was doing the cabbage patch to a soul song blasting from a boombox. Behind his lumbering silhouette, a helix of smoke twined in the air. "Look at him," Pop said. "The roof's on fire, and he's dancing up there like a circus bear."

The roof wasn't on fire. Burger was just grilling, albeit in an odd place. I pointed out the grill and the bag of charcoal, the pair of tongs in Burger's hand, but Pop still sprang out of the car like someone tossed a tarantula in his lap. "Hey, I'm paying you to make sure the place doesn't catch fire, not help it along."

"What you mean?" Burger said.

"Grilling on the roof doesn't seem like a fire hazard to you?"

"Maybe." Burger considered the situation now, apparently for the first time. "But everybody's on their roofs. Plus, I got hungry."

I checked the surrounding buildings, and, sure enough, there was a person atop each one, armed with a gun or a fire hose or both. Across a side street, a young Korean man patrolled the front of a small grocery with a pistol, while another watched from the roof like a tower guard, an AK-47 cradled in one arm and what could've been a rocket launcher in the other.

"We're turning bad rioters into good ones. Ain't that right?" Burger raised his fist in solidarity. The Koreans gave a salute and then returned to duty. "Y'all wanna get your stink on while you're here?" Burger held up two cans of Schlitz.

"Of course," I said. "When have I ever turned down a beer?"

He pointed at Pop with his tongs. "What about you, ballerina?"

Pop was still pissed, but he took one too. He'd never turned down a beer either.

We went back a long way with Burger, Pop's longest-serving employee. He was one of those black guys who always seemed at ease with his place in the world, even if deep down he really wasn't. I admired him for it. As a kid, when Pop wasn't around, I used to tell people that Burger was my real father. It was our little game. But for some reason no one ever believed me.

"Goddamn, youngblood," Burger said. "You sure picked a hell of a time to visit."

I cracked my beer. "Hey, I was cursed with bad timing and a rotten father. What am I gonna do?" I smiled at Pop as he guzzled his beer. In return, he gave me the finger.

"Well, what've you been up to?" Burger said.

"No good," Pop chimed in. "What do you think he's been up to? This is Junie you're talking to."

"Shit, I guess that makes two of us," Burger said. "I just got out of jail."

I asked what he was in for, and he gave his usual answer: "Various things."

Pop took a long pull and finished his beer, his eyes darting around as though he expected the lot to spontaneously combust. "Enough chit-chat. Burger, tell me nothing's happened yet."

"Nothing's happened yet."

"Nobody's tried to steal or burn anything down?"

Burger removed a revolver from his waistline and sat on the edge of the roof. He balanced the gun next to him and let his legs dangle as if he were sitting at the end of a dock. "Hell no. Ain't no niggas messing with this place. I told you. With me here, you can count on that." He shouted the last part loud enough for the gangbangers on Manchester to hear. They were my age, maybe a little younger, and veterans at mean-mugging. As I watched them, a light-skinned Blood with a red ban-danna around his neck waved at me. I nodded at him, and he mouthed, "Fuck you, white boy."

I wanted to walk over there and tell him I was only half-white, but I knew he'd just kick my ass. I slowly turned my attention back to Pop.

"We're counting on you, big man."

"I know," Burger said.

"Only shoot if you're absolutely threatened. You hear me? Absolutely." Pop always put extra emphasis on "absolutely." According to him, ex-cons couldn't understand instructions without this word, and ex-cons made up the majority of his workforce.

"Only if I'm absolutely threatened," Burger said. "I got it."

That was it. I told Burger to stay out of trouble. He said, "Ditto." Pop and I got back in the Porsche and sped off like criminals making a getaway.

❊ ❊ ❊

I was used to this. I'd been dividing time between Pop in LA and my mother in Boston since I was ten, when my parents went splitsville for good. I spent every spring break of my childhood with Pop, running endless errands around LA and the surrounding counties. Whatever he did, I did: lounging at the bar of Sam's Hofbrau while he flirted with dancers who fawned over me. Shooting at The LA Gun Club with my own Browning Hi-Power 9mm. Smoking Humboldt because Pop thought

I should choke on the good stuff with him in a controlled environment. How I hadn't been maimed or killed yet was beyond me.

From what I could glean as a child, my parents met during the height of their checkered pasts. Pop had connections to some crooked characters in Boston, owners of an establishment that my mother worked at called The Peephole. What her work actually entailed I never wanted to know. Regardless, my parents became a couple almost instantly. My white father had, at the time of meeting my mother, an exclusive thing for non-white women. My black mother, conversely, could never shake her attraction to moneyed men of the pale-faced variety. That being their only criteria for love, it was a wonder the marriage lasted long enough to produce light skinned, curly-haired, bony-assed me.

For as long as I could remember, every time my mother packed me off for my cross-country jaunts, she'd say, "You can't change the fact that you got some white in you, Junie, but it doesn't mean you gotta act like your father's white ass."

Sadly, up to that point in my life, I'd failed her.

Back at school, everyone called me June the Goon. Like my father, I'd cultivated a reputation as one of *those* guys. I was fairly smart, but I tended to do fairly dumb things. Not quite a trouble-maker. Not quite a fuckup. That fall and winter, though, I'd found myself sinking into trouble, having barely avoided jail time for an unfortunate incident. I was starting to look a lot like Pop, who'd found himself in the clink once or twice around my age. I knew if I kept it up, I'd quit school in a year, start selling cars, and, like him, date a series of shady women. I'd grow a ridiculous ponytail and start driving a Porsche. It was my biggest fear, one that produced a recurring nightmare: me not living my life but reliving his. Afterward, I'd always wake up in a sweat and reach for the jug of antacids I kept by my bed, crunching them as I tried to fall back asleep.

❊   ❊   ❊

By eight p.m., the entire proceedings were, in Pop's scholarly opinion, a shit circus. We were back on the 405, heading north again, and in the distance, more plumes of smoke snaked above the skyline. Even though the freeways, each an orgy of brake lights, were as still as paintings, Pop didn't let it stop us. He used every piece of pavement he could find— shoulders, medians, off-ramps—to zip us around the city. We'd checked on three more dealerships by then, Carson, Long Beach, and East LA.

353

Each lot was being guarded by new hires, guys I'd never met before. All three were black. All three had Jheri curls. And all three were named, oddly enough, Doozie. At each lot, it was the same as with Burger. Pop made sure they were armed. They were keeping the gates locked. Everything was tiptop. We moved on.

At the Huntington Park exit, he dumped us off the freeway and we trolled down Pacific Boulevard aimlessly. I asked where we were going, and he just patted his potbelly and grunted, "Food." I said, "Who gets hungry at a time like this?" But we both knew it was a stupid question. Pop's appetites could only be described as gluttonous. We passed a few restaurants, and they all seemed to be closing or getting plundered. So we skated a little farther down Pacific until we stumbled on an open but deserted In-N-Out. We pulled up to the drive-thru, and they took our order as if it were any old day. When we pulled around to pay, though, the Latina cashier didn't take our money. She just tossed the food at us, locked the window, and immediately put up the Closed sign. We pulled around and parked by a dumpster. Behind us, all the employees burst out of the restaurant like someone tossed a bomb in the place. Pop looked back, softly biting a Swisher Sweet with his teeth. "Well, that sure was interesting." Then he just stabbed a straw into his drink and started to eat.

We were the only bystanders out there, pushing our luck in a new Porsche among all that lawlessness. But, relatively speaking, things didn't seem that bad yet. No one was bothering us. No one seemed to even notice us. Across the street, a Payless shoe store was being ransacked, the parking lot littered with empty shoeboxes. Down the sidewalk, an interracial couple steered a new leather sofa dollied on two skateboards. Even some guy clutching an armful of bathrobes rambled by, touting, "Robe. Robe here," as though peddling peanuts at a Dodgers game. Who knew what would happen next.

On our left, a Humvee rumbled past Dick's Donuts. Not far behind, six National Guardsmen on horseback clopped by. A black dude who'd somehow climbed on top of Dick's and was now sitting inside the large donut on the roof yelled, "Hey, G.I. Joe. You hungry?" as he pelted them with donut holes. I turned back to Pop, but he was lost in thought, studying the smoke churning over downtown and feeding his face. He'd ordered two Double-Doubles Animal Style and had already dispatched both in ten flat. He was stuffing handfuls of fries into his mouth, while I only nibbled at my burger. I hadn't had an appetite for months. I didn't even bother with the bread, just ate the meat, which I was trying to choke down when Pop said, "You know why those flight attendants couldn't tell you nothing, Junie?"

"No," I said, "but I'm sure you're gonna tell me."

"Because they don't know nothing. I do. Cops in this town think their shit don't stink. But that don't make it cool for every black mope and his fat mother to turn the city into a goddamn ashtray, know what I'm saying?"

I just shook my head. "Black mope? Fat mother?"

"You see any white people out here other than us?"

"You mean other than you?" I scanned the street and spotted a scruffy white guy in two seconds. He maneuvered a shopping cart full of Budweiser with a perverse glee. "What about him?"

Pop blinked at him and then glanced at me. "An anomaly," he said.

"I'm just saying, Pop. You sound kind of Aryan right now."

"Do I? Well, I guess beating up a bunch of Indians makes you Martin Luther King."

My belly gurgled. I was pretty sure I had the beginnings of an ulcer. "It wasn't a bunch," I said. "Just one. And I didn't beat him up. I was only there."

He looked at me out of the side of his eye. "Only there, huh?"

I nodded and tried to take another bite of my burger but couldn't stomach it. I lobbed it into the nearest trashcan, took my pack of antacids from my duffel bag, and chewed a few.

"There or not, you're lucky I got you that lawyer. Otherwise, you'd be doing time right now."

"That lawyer was a horrible person."

"I know. Why do you think I hired him?"

"He made me sound like a sociopath."

"Yeah? What if you are one?"

I looked at him, wondering if he actually thought that. When he cracked a smile, I told him to eat me, and he slapped my thigh and laughed.

"Who cares what he said? You're free, aren't you?"

I was just about to say I shouldn't be when he turned to me with an indignant sneer.

"And how can you call *me* a racist? I married your mother, let's not forget. She's as black as they come."

I studied him for a moment. If I disagreed, he'd be mad at me for the rest of the night and probably punish me for it. I just said, "Yeah, you married her. And you had me."

He said, "Yeah, I did," as though that proved his point.

We sat there a little longer, being father and son in our own dysfunctional way, and for some reason everything stilled around us. The sirens ceased. The crashing glass and bleeping alarms stopped too. Looters froze mid-step and searched the sky curiously. Maybe it was over. In the distance, two helicopters clapped toward us from the south, their spotlights scanning Compton. I heard what sounded like a string of fireworks blocks away and watched as the helicopters split off from each other. One of them seemed to teeter, as if it would suddenly drop from the sky. Then, as if nothing happened, it righted itself, and the two of them moved back into formation. They quickly banked east in tandem, and I realized it'd been an evasive maneuver. Someone had shot at them from the ground.

"Damn. You see that?"

Pop swiveled his head, oblivious as always. "See what?"

Everything started back up, the sirens, the looting, the alarms, like a crazy merry-go-round cranking back to life.

"Nothing," I said. "Can we go now?"

He smirked and tossed his soda overboard. "Stop whining," he said. "We're going." He backed the car up and got us on the road. He pounded the Porsche into high gear. The whistling turbocharger went up an octave. The tires broke loose a bit.

"Where are we going now?"

He smiled. "You'll see."

※　※　※

That school year, I'd moved in with some white guys that I barely knew. We shared a crumbling Victorian near the UMass Boston campus, where our academic careers hung by a thread. Their families all had a lot more going for them than mine, but we'd all been given the same opportunities in life, good schools, summer camps, money. So, all of us living together didn't seem like such a bad idea. We were spoiled and took things for granted. We operated under the assumption that no matter what dumb shit we did, everything would somehow work out, the usual attitude of people who were high most of the time. We had so many pills and herbs and mind-altering powders in our house we didn't know what we were taking half the time. Speed or Ritalin for studying, K and E for screwing off. We were so out of hand that at parties we'd leave stray tablets of Correctol around and then make bets on which guest would be the first to mistakenly take one, hoping it was a Valium or Benzo, and get the squirts for a day and a half.

Our time would end badly. It was obvious. But stopping that freight train would've taken more willpower and sense than I had at the time. It was easier to just let it all go down in a ball of flame. At the trial for the thing with the Indian kid, I thought our guilt was pretty apparent. We'd be going away for a while. But not everyone thought so. Our families had money and lawyers. Young men like us couldn't have done such a thing. My mother blamed the white boys for it, not me. They corrupted me, she said. Anyone would end up in court after hanging around white kids named Tyler, Tucker, and Chase. They sounded like a law firm.

Her support was unquestioning at first, but once the trial started and our pictures were in *The Globe* every other day, she could barely look at me. She'd sit in the back of the court room, if she was there at all, wearing a wide-brimmed hat. When reporters rushed us as we left each day, she lowered her head, putting a gloved hand out at the sight of photographers. A couple weeks of that, and she stopped going altogether. From then on, I sat at the defense table, trying not to look over my shoulder every two seconds to see if she was there.

I couldn't blame her. The lawyer Pop hired painted me as some racially confused kid with neglectful parents. He even used an expert witness, a psychologist who testified to the emotional effects of being mixed race in this country, how it led to "antisocial behavior in the desperate quest to fit in." During the cross-examination, I turned to my lawyer and whispered, "You're making me sound like a freak." He said, "That's because you are a freak. This country made you that way. It's not your fault."

He insisted I believe it if I wanted to stay out of jail. In the end, he was right. I came home from sentencing and found my mother in her bedroom, whiling away her evening as she always did, at her vanity, nursing a glass of red wine and a roach clip. She didn't look at all surprised when she saw me there. "And?"

I loosened my tie. "Probation. Three months."

She took a sip of wine, set her glass down, and then turned away as though the sight of me burned her eyes. "And your friends? What about them?" She'd never called them my friends before.

"A year of jail time each."

She grunted as though it served them right. Then she got up and closed her door on me. I retreated to my room and hid there, chewing antacids till they stole all the moisture from my mouth.

357

*　*　*

By nightfall, Pop and I had to stick to the freeways, the 5, the 10, the 405, the 710. Driving the surface streets was no longer advised. Radio reports said whites traveling through black areas were being pulled from their cars and beaten. On Florence and Normandie, a white truck driver had been dragged from his semi and smashed in the head with a brick. At the same intersection, a Latino man, mistaken for Korean, had been wrenched from his car, stripped of his clothes, and spray-painted. And of course we were in a new Porsche, a fact Pop now regretted. "I should have my head examined for taking this car out on a day like this. Should've driven the Jeep. I finally had the bulletproof windows installed. I ever tell you that?"

"Why would you need bulletproof windows?"

He looked at me like I was stupid. "Because, Junie, this is LA."

There was no way we were going back to Malibu to switch cars. We just made do, ripping along, stopping to check on this dealership or that. Pop's mood gradually changed. He was back to his old self again and kept going on and on about the cops and the verdict and what he would've done had he been an elected official. None of it made a bit of sense. He took us down freeways and off-ramps so fast I could barely hear him over the wind, but I was trying to listen as best I could. If I didn't, I didn't know what he'd get me into.

We'd checked on all of his dealerships but the one in Koreatown. Pop was still talking a mile a minute, and I only caught a word or two. We slowed to take the 110 North exit, the wind dying down as we curved around the ramp, and I finally heard him clearly. "So I'm afraid I have to put you to work earlier than usual, Junie." His preface to any sort of bad news. "So I'm afraid your mother kicked me out, Junie. We're getting a divorce." "So I'm afraid you're going to rehab, Junie—again, you little shit" would come later in my life.

"Hey." He snapped his fingers. "You hear me?"

I nodded but didn't say anything. I looked farther up the highway at a white sheet draped over a fenced overpass. On it "No Justice 4 Rodney" was painted in a bloody maroon. I wanted to raise my fist in solidarity at the black kids standing next to the sign. But then I thought it might look weird coming from me: a mixed kid riding next to his white father in a new white Porsche.

Pop snapped his fingers again. "Hey, I asked you a question."

I rubbed my eyes. "Put me to work doing what?"

He actually grinned and patted my thigh again, his ponytail lashing his headrest. "Oh, you know. The usual."

I popped an antacid in my mouth.

"Keep eating those things, and you'll get kidney stones."

I waved him off and grabbed his pack of Swishers from the console. There was only one cigarillo left, hiding in the corner of the pack. I took it just to spite him. "Don't change the subject, dummy. You're getting me into some shit. Just say so."

He reached over and lit the cigarillo for me with his butane, a sly look on his face. "Don't doubt your pop." He gave me one of his special winks, the kind he used on ladies next to him at red lights. "Believe me, it won't be bad." He waited a moment, calculating as ever, and said, "Really," as though there was a chance of me believing him.

❖ ❖ ❖

The Koreatown lot was the dealership I'd worked at the most, and also the shittiest. Pop, the shrewd businessman, positioned his dealerships in some of LA's sketchier areas, places you'd see a good number of walls tattooed with graffiti, crackheads trying to sell you a broken VCR, or maybe a few women on the stroll. Whether he'd admit it or not, Pop capitalized on the low resources of the poor. Immigrants and black single mothers didn't have the money to sue if the hooptie they just bought took a crap a month later. It was how he made his money, how he buttered his bread, all of it owed to the inequity of the world. One day, my riches would be owed to it, too, as long as he didn't blow it all before he croaked. I was always pretty sure he would.

As we exited the 405, Pop took out the PPK again and held it in his lap. We crossed Venice and Olympia Boulevards, coasted down South Western Avenue. The surroundings worsened street by street. The tang of burning wood and rubber was heavy in the air. Crowds roared and security alarms sounded in the close distance. On Wilshire, hordes of people blocked the intersection, pushing each other around and throwing bricks at passing cars. A Toyota a block ahead got all its windows broken out. The glass had barely hit the ground, and looters were already reaching inside the car. The driver sped off with a couple of them hanging on for dear life.

We wove through the loose crowds as we approached Wilshire, Pop honking the horn for people to move. With the sun down and the fires more intense, Koreatown glowed a dangerous orange. I could feel the heat as we passed blazing storefronts. The ones that weren't on fire had looters gushing out of the shattered windows like water through a breached dam. They carried every kind of merchandise imaginable, random things like hair dryers and lamps and packs of lightbulbs. As we approached the mob, a small pocket of space opened, and Pop told me to hold on. He mashed the throttle, raised his gun, and waved it around like a wild man, parting the crowd.

We turned onto West Sixth and pulled up in front of the car lot. He gave me a ring of keys, and I got out and unlocked the gate. I got back in the Porsche as fast as I could, even though West Sixth was quiet and seemed to be untouched. Unlike Pop's other lots, this one was a small affair, a stamp of asphalt with a ten-foot fence surrounding it, only about fifteen clunkers on the premises. Once we'd pulled in and parked, I looked up at the roof to see if anyone was standing guard, but there was only Pop's huge face on the billboard. "WE FINANCE" in big block letters jumped out of his mouth.

"No one's here."

"I know." He scratched his nose.

"No fucking way."

He nodded. "We're gonna watch it till all this blows over." He shut off the engine and unlatched his seat belt. He opened his door halfway, and then he turned and looked back at me. "C'mon."

Without thinking, I got out of the car and closed my door. When I looked back, he was still behind the wheel. He closed his door and quickly hit the power locks. "Sorry to have to do this to you, Junie," he said, sitting back now.

I kept pulling at the door handle even though I'd just seen him lock it. "You're not sorry. You're never sorry."

"C'mon," he said. "Take it like a man. I need you here tonight. I got guys watching the other dealerships."

I hesitated and then asked if he was crazy. It seemed like an appropriate question.

"No," he said. "I'm as sane as ever."

"Pop, if you don't let me back in—"

He crossed his arms over his chest. "What? This'll all blow over by tomorrow. You'll forget all about this."

Sometimes, this was true. I could be bought off with drinks and a good time in the right context. It was how our relationship worked. He'd do something to piss me off, and then he'd buy me something or take me wherever I wanted to go. There'd be women and weed, and we'd be friends again.

"C'mon, Pop." I tried to climb back in, but his eyes went black.

"No, no, no." He took the gun from the dash and just held it. He chewed his lip and considered me for a long moment. Finally, he leaned over the seat. I thought he was going to unlock the door and let me back in. But his hand went to the glove box instead. He pulled out a PPK identical to his and held it out for me. "Here." When I refused, he shook the thing at me and then forced it into my hand. "And don't start whining. I'm tired of it. You sound like those bastards you call friends."

I was about to say they weren't my friends when he said, "Junie, don't kid yourself. You wanted to be just like those kids."

"I'm not like anyone."

"Sure you're not. You're unique." He fluttered his hands in the air. "A pretty little baby. That's what your mother wants you to believe."

As soon as he said it, something lit me up. I stood back and kicked the passenger door. "Say something else about my mother."

His eyes went blacker. "I swear, if you do that again, Junie—"

That was all it took. Heel to metal. "Look," I said. "I even took some paint this time."

A tense few seconds passed, and then a pack of looters ran near the lot. Some were silent and ashamed, the rest desperate and mechanical. They left quickly, and another small gang stopped at the entrance, at least ten deep. They were teenagers, black and Latino, in T-shirts or wifebeaters. They'd apparently never noticed the dealership before and now thought it suddenly looked like a good place to steal shit from.

Pop waved his gun. "Keep it moving, people." They didn't move so he aimed his gun and added, "Unless you feel like catching one in the ass." The pack paused for another second and then did as he said, shouting epithets as they left. Pop just rolled his eyes and waved, as if he knew them. "Yes, and give my love to the savages."

"Fuck you," they said.

He opened the car's console and removed a fresh pack of Swishers. "I don't care, Junie. Kick the car till your foot breaks. I can get another. You know how many insurance claims there are gonna be after all this?" He lit one of the cigarillos and sent smoke out his nostrils. For a long minute, he watched me, the smoke slithering up around his eyes.

"What?" I said. "The guilt finally getting to you?"

"No, not really." He slid the lighter into his breast pocket and put the car in reverse. "I don't have time for this. If I don't get off the streets now, that'll be the end of me."

"Yeah, that would be really unfortunate, wouldn't it, Pop?"

He looked at me and sighed. "Junie, it makes more sense for you to be here. No telling what they'd do to me, but you—they'll think you're one of them."

I shook my head, astonished at his stupidity. "How are you my father?"

He sighed again. "How are you my son?"

Both questions hung in the air. He'd been doing this to me since I was ten, leaving me places or with strangers, saying he'd be right back, and then not showing up for hours. Once, he tried to leave me at one of his girlfriend's houses when I was eleven. As he left, I beaned him in the face with a rock, splitting both his lips. He put me right on a plane back to Boston and didn't talk to me for a year after that.

I gripped the PPK. I hadn't held a gun in a few years, but I raised it and homed in on his tires as he pulled away. The PPK felt heavy, its trigger tight. It took a bit of finger power to pull it, but when it finally gave, the gun released a puny click.

Pop stopped the car and looked back at me with a smirk. "I knew you were gonna do that."

I tried to rack the slide to chamber a round, but I couldn't get it.

"You really are out of practice, aren't you?" After another moment, he pointed at the side of the gun. "It won't fire with the safety on, genius."

When I unlocked it, he sped off. I chased him into the street just to scare him, but he was already in third gear, heading down Sixth. I lowered the gun and reached in my pocket for my antacids. There weren't any left.

✴   ✴   ✴

Most nights, after my probation was up, I hid in my room with a towel under the door, smoking a bud or two I'd pinched from my mother's stash. I'd been forced to transfer to community college and was still just skating by. Somehow, I found myself back in my mother's good graces. My instructors were bigots, she said. They'd heard about my troubles and were punishing me for it. I'd look at the newspaper clippings I kept from the trial, studying that boy's name, Amarpreet, and his face, round and doughy, dark around the eyes. When I couldn't look at him anymore, I'd sneak out of our Back Bay condo and ride the T around the city. Some nights, I'd ride until they kicked me off. Other nights, I'd get off in Roxbury or Mattapan and wander the pitch-black streets. I hoped I'd get shot or robbed or beaten within an inch of my life. It only seemed fair.

The night everything happened, my roommates and I were making one last drug run for the night. We were trying to cop some coke from some black guys in the projects. As soon as they saw the money, they promptly robbed us, laughing as they pointed a gun in the car. I thought it was a sign we should go home, but my roommates wanted to hit a couple more spots. Every dealer was dry so we drove around, pissed off and drunk, passing around another bottle. One of the twins, Tyler or Tucker, said they felt like beating the shit out of someone. I thought it was just talk. We'd never gone looking for fights. We weren't even that tough, but because we had numbers, the feeling gained momentum. Pretty soon, they were assessing people we drove by, looking for some- one alone. I said, "Hold on, hold on," but they didn't hear me. When we rolled up in Chase's Mustang and saw Amarpreet, I knew they were going to pick him, even before Tucker said, "Look, a towelhead." With a screech, we parked. They jumped out of the car like SWAT, stopping the boy under a streetlight. When he looked up, he actually smiled. He couldn't have been more than eighteen, a chubby kid with pointy breasts pushing at the front of a Sox jersey, a tan turban around his head.

From the back seat I thought, Okay, a couple punches, a bloody nose, fine. They'll get it out of their systems. The kid could go home to his dorm room and cry himself to sleep. But after some pushing and shoving it was clear they weren't going easy on him. Tucker knocked him down with a brutal right. Amarpreet tried to get up, but Tyler promptly dropped him with an identical right. Chase grabbed him by the neck and unraveled the turban from his head like a bandage. They stood him up, the boy cry- ing now, whimpering. They pushed him against a wall. His hair cascaded over his face, black and shiny and stretching to his knees. It freaked them out enough to knock him down again and start kicking.

I didn't get out of the car. I just watched, the whole time wondering who that kid was. Someone's good son, an only child, a late arrival? Maybe his parents, older and gentler, were tirelessly devoted to him, blessed to be given a child at all. Maybe they kissed him on the cheek every morning at breakfast, a small ritual they performed all the way up to the morning he left for a far-off school. Even now, he would re- member to call them before bed, knowing the time difference would make it morning back home. They'd tell him not to call, to save his money, to buy himself something special, but he still called every night. Not just for them but for him. So he would feel like nothing had changed. He wasn't a lonely boy in a foreign country. He was there, next to them, at home, like a family. Because that was how most families worked.

When Chase said, "Junie, don't you want a piece of this little fucker?" I thought of all that, jealous of that poor kid. I almost got out of the car. A part of me wanted to hurt him, but I decided to stay put. Chase punched him and then looked back at me, laughing. "You sure?"

"Yeah," I said. "I think I'm good."

❊ ❊ ❊

It was well past one o'clock in the morning, and I hadn't heard anything from Pop. I called my mother, but the line just rang, so I wandered out to the parking lot and stood there, looking around. The rioting had quieted down for the night. Alarms were still going off, but I couldn't hear the crowds on Wilshire anymore, only an occasional whoop or shout. West Sixth was still empty, except for the Koreans who owned the convenience store across the street. Though there was no danger in sight, a younger Korean man barricaded the store by stacking metal shopping carts in front of the store's glass windows while an older man held a shotgun and patrolled the street. I watched them for a few minutes and realized they were father and son. Every now and then, the father would walk over and pat the son on the back, saying something encouraging in Korean. I looked over my shoulder, and there was Pop's billboard on the dealership's roof, his cartoon face smiling down at me. I aimed the gun at him, imagined a clean bullet hole in his head, but I couldn't pull the trigger.

I went inside the office and left the PPK on one of the desks. I rummaged through the lockbox till I found the keys for the sturdiest vehicle on the lot, a Chevy Suburban. Outside, I unlocked the gates and pulled the monster out into the street.

I left and drove down Sixth. I turned on Wilshire, passing buildings that had once stood three stories and now were charred rubble. Outside the buildings that still raged, people stood mesmerized by each fire. One man in particular tried to quench twenty-foot flames with a garden hose. Down alleys, I saw guys rocking cars that were lying on their sides. But I couldn't tell if the guys were trying to put them back on their wheels or flip them on their roofs. Every block was like that. Glass glittered the pavement, the specks glinting under the lights like a million tiny diamonds.

Traffic lights still worked. Abandoned cars still idled at intersections. I drove aimlessly, hoping I'd find someone to rescue, but no one needed my help. I navigated the streets, venturing deep into Compton and Watts, driving past shadowy figures gathered on porches and in yards.

Occasionally, as I'd pass, a rock would hit the side of the truck, and I'd hear them yelling for me to leave. I didn't know what I was looking for. I turned down dark streets, one after another. I honked the horn to let people know I was there.

\* \* \*

It wasn't until I went down a residential street near Slauson that I saw them: four black guys standing in the street next to an '80s Impala. They were leaning against the car, talking as if on their lunch break. Above them, a streetlight shone down in such a way that they looked like actors on a stage. I killed the Suburban's lights and rolled to a stop a half-block away. I put the truck in park across the street from them and ended up sitting there for a few minutes before they noticed me. They wore loose khakis, no shirts, and were passing around a couple forties of Olde English.

When I rolled down my window, one of them pointed me out to the others, and the tallest of the four stared at me, wary. He kept looking around and then squinting at me as if he thought I'd suddenly pull a drive-by. Finally, he walked over. An armor of muscles covered his body. His Jheri curl glimmered in the light. He came up near my window and looked at me for a minute before shouting, "What you doing?"

I didn't know, but I knew I couldn't say that. "Just driving around."

This didn't please him. "The fuck for? You crazy?" Even from five feet away, I could smell the liquor on his breath. He walked closer. "I asked you a question, white boy."

I must have smirked, because he was suddenly ready to kill me.

"I'm funny to you?" He looked back at his friends, who'd lost all interest in us.

"You called me 'white boy,'" I said.

"Yeah, I know. That's because you're white." He looked back at his friends, but they were shooting dice on the hood of the car, which upset him. His attitude seemed to be for their benefit. He yelled, "I know you ain't trying to cop some dope."

I shook my head no.

"What you want, then?"

I wanted to tell him to just hit me, to beat me into a coma, but I couldn't get the words out.

He spat on the truck and then started back to his friends. That's when I got out. I closed the door as hard as I could. He turned around, fists up. I needed to make it worth his while, so I took a clumsy swing from too far away. He sidestepped it and threw a punch that hit me on the chin. I saw a flash of white and then found myself on the ground.

"That all you came here for?" He seemed honestly disappointed.

Blood trickled from my mouth.

He kicked me in the side, and now I was lying face up. "You want some more?" He looked back at his friends, but they just shook their heads as though this kind of thing happened all the time. "You're crazy." He glanced at his friends. "He's crazy. Look at him." He started to walk off, but I grabbed his ankle.

"C'mon," I said.

He pulled his leg away and looked at me again, puzzled. He crouched down and stuck his face closer to mine. With his hot, beery breath on my skin, it felt as though we were sharing a moment. We could both see all the dumb things we'd ever done, all the dumb things we were ever going to do.

"I'm right here," I said.

He blinked and swallowed, and I realized just how young he was. He could've been my little brother. He could've been my little cousin. And in my mind, I said, You understand, don't you?

His hard look softened as he scanned my face. He seemed to hear me.

Sorry. I'm wrong to make you do this. I just need your help. I looked into his dark eyes and thought I could hear his voice now, gentler this time.

It's okay, white boy. I can help. But just this once. He looked back at his friends. You know this won't feel good, though, right?

I know.

Those boys over there will probably join in.

The more the merrier.

All right. He shrugged and took a step back.

I looked up at him. Thanks, by the way.

He chuckled. Don't thank me yet. And don't go thinking this a fair trade for what you did.

I said I wouldn't.

Our eyes locked. Our hearts beat as one. Somehow, through it all, we even managed to smile.

Ready whenever you are.

Good. He cocked his fist. You better be.

*Nominated by Bennington Review*

# CHILDISH THINGS

## by CHRIS FORHAN

from THE INDIANAPOLIS REVIEW

No more talk of them, no more thoughts
of that shambling summer, of the noons I stole

into the barn, gripped the knotted rope and hoisted
my bones toward the rafters. No more words

for the way, woozy in the pew, I squeezed past
grown-ups' knees, eased the weighty rear door open

and gulped with greed and relief the outside air.
Separateness was my sin, and it was continual—

the gerbil caged in my room whose teary bulging gray
infected eye made me turn from him, tell no one,

till he lay still and stiffened. No more of that
or of the shattered lamp and my subsequent silence,

the hiding, the hiding. Where has he gone,
that boy? He was not unlikeable, should not

have been scolded for what he did not know.
How would it hurt him now for me to tell him so?

*Nominated by The Indianapolis Review, Dana Roeser*

# ADAGIO

## by ROBERT PINSKY

from THIS BROKEN SHORE

More than midway along, the feeling changes.
The adagio traffic plunges, or else it rises,

From dolent meditation to vibrato chanting.
*Want-want*, and again, a punctuated longing.

After the stroke, his loss or deafness, or after
The bad election, the movement's harsher or sweeter.

Or one day vowels come out a little distorted
From the thwarted mouth. *Un poco deformato*,

"And yet if it doesn't seem a moment's thwart
Our *pizzicato* stitching and stitching fall short."

Ah *Ma non troppo:* in time the lines returned
For a reprieve, a refrain, the traffic sustained

On the right road, *molto espressivo* redeemed
Between the organ of expression and the mind.

But not so fast—*espressivo* of loss or redemption?
Punishment or joy? Or degrees of each, or neither?

*Want-want* the cello hums and the waters rise
And fall on the stars and break in years and days.

*Nominated by This Broken Shore, Tom Sleigh*

# RETURN OF THE BLUE NUN

## by MADELINE DEFREES

from *WHERE THE HORSE TAKES WING (TWO SYLVIAS)*

She comes at midnight, moon a thin wedge in
her window, when stars pulled from
old moorings, strike out against dark. She
glides the elliptical
track with the Book of the Dead pressed to
her forehead, raids the Sea of Tranquility
for cargo long since

                     pitched into the black
undertow. Serge of an outmoded
habit—disguise by the bolt—matches the ocean
surge over an undersea fault. Fabric
turns rust in the brine, turns green.
Framing the sun-starved face
white gauze corresponds

                   to the serial white
of breakers shattered on rock. Awake,
she will need a hand, if only
her own, into the lifeboat. The deep sea
recedes, robbed of its nightly prey.
She will climb aboard on a jolt of caffeine
and set her course—steady—to the shark-
shadowed cruise of another day.

*Nominated by Two Sylvias*

# "A BELOVED DUCK GETS COOKED"

by LYDIA DAVIS

from THE VIRGINIA QUARTERLY REVIEW

## ON FORMS AND INFLUENCES

The traditional literary forms—the novel, the short story, the poem—although they evolve, do not disappear. But there is a wealth of less traditional forms that writers have adopted over the centuries, forms that are harder to define and less often encountered, either variations on the more familiar, such as the short-short story, or inter-generic—sitting on a line between poetry and prose, or fable and realistic narrative, or essay and fiction, and so on.

I think of myself as a writer of fiction, but my first books were slim small-press books often shelved in the poetry section, and I am still sometimes called a poet and included in poetry anthologies. It is understandable that there may be some confusion. For instance, my collection of stories titled *Samuel Johnson Is Indignant* contains fifty-six pieces, including what could roughly be described as meditations, parables, or fables; an oral history with hiccups; an interrogation about jury duty; a more conventional, though brief, story about a family trip; a diary about thyroid disease; excerpts from a bad translation of a poorly written biography of Marie Curie; a fairly straightforward narrative about my father and his furnace (though ending in an accidental poem); and, scattered throughout the book, brief prose pieces of just one or two lines as well as one or two pieces with broken lines.

When I began writing "seriously" and steadily in college, I thought my only choice was the traditional narrative short story. Both my parents had been writers of short stories, and my mother still was. Both of them had had stories published in the *New Yorker*, which loomed large in our life, as some sort of icon, though an icon of exactly what I'm not sure— good writing and editing, urban wit and sophistication? By age twelve, I already felt I was bound to be a writer, and if you were going to be a writer, the choices were limited: first, either poet or prose writer; then, if prose writer, either novelist or short-story writer. I never thought of being a novelist. I wrote poems, early on, but to be a poet was somehow not an option. So if, eventually, some of my work comes right up to the line (if there is one) that separates a piece of prose from a poem, and even crosses it, the approach to that line is through the realm of short fiction.

In college, when I told one intelligent friend of mine, with confidence and exuberance, that my ambition was to write short stories, and specifically, to write a short story that would be accepted by the *New Yorker*, he was startled by my certainty. He was also somewhat scornful, and suggested that maybe this should not be the full extent of my ambition. I was so surprised by his reaction that the Manhattan street corner where we were talking is engraved on my memory: Broadway at 114th Street. My fixed ideas had been shaken.

Although I now did not have quite the same confidence in the *New Yorker*, I did not immediately see an obvious alternative to writing short stories, so I continued to work in that form and develop in that direction for the next several years, though the subject matter of the stories gradually moved away from the most conventional. I found the writing difficult; it was pleasurable or exciting only at moments. I worked on one short story for months and months; I spent about two years on another one. I followed the oft-repeated advice, which was to combine invented material with material from my own experience.

My reading might have shown me other possibilities. In addition to a healthy diet of the classic short-story writers, such as Katherine Mansfield, D. H. Lawrence, John Cheever, Hemingway, Updike, and Flannery O'Connor, I was already reading writers who were more unusual formally and imaginatively, such as Beckett, Kafka, Borges, and Isaac Babel.

I was in my early teens when I first laid eyes on a page of Beckett. I was startled. I had come to it from books that included the steamy novels of Mazo de la Roche—though not too steamy to be included in a very proper girls'-school library—and the more classic romances of *Jane Eyre* and *Wuthering Heights*, as well as the social panoramas of John Dos Passos, the first writer whose style I consciously noticed and relished. Now here was a book—*Malone Dies*—in which the narrator spent

371

a page describing his pencil, and the first plot development was that he had dropped his pencil. I had never imagined anything like it.

When I look at Beckett now, to try to identify more exactly the qualities that continued to excite my interest as I read his work over the years and did my best to learn from him, I find at least the following: There was his precise and sonorous use of the Anglo-Saxon vocabulary—especially, in this example, the way he gives a familiar word like "dint" a fresh life by using it in an unfamiliar way: ". . . the flagstone before her door that by dint by dint her little weight has grooved . . ." There was his use of Anglo-Saxon and alliteration to produce what were almost pieces of Old English verse: "worthy those worn by certain newly dead."

There was his use of complex, almost impossibly tangled, yet correct, syntax for the pleasure of it, though perhaps also as a commentary on composition itself: "were it not of him to whom it is speaking speaking but of another it would not speak."

There was his deft handling of image and his humor, almost certainly poking fun at more traditional romantic or lyrical writing that I myself quite enjoyed: "the little summer house. A rustic hexahedron."

There was the way he balanced the sonority of rhythm and alliteration with the unexpectedly compassionate depiction of character: "so with what reason remains he reasons and reasons ill."

And lastly, there was his acute psychological analysis, so closely accurate that it became absurd and yet moving at the same time: "Not that Watt felt calm and free and glad, for he did not, and had never done so. But he thought that perhaps he felt calm and free and glad, or if not calm and free and glad, at least calm and free, or free and glad, or glad and calm, or if not calm and free, or free and glad, or glad and calm, at least calm, or free, or glad, without knowing it."

(Here he is no doubt again poking fun at conventional sentimental writing.)

If Beckett interested me more for the way he handled language—the close attention to words, the mining of the richness of English, the ironic distance from prose style, the self-consciousness—and less for the forms in which he wrote, still, as with Joyce, Beckett's example provided a pattern of development through different forms over a lifetime of writing: Both these writers started by writing poetry and went on to write short stories, and then novels, and then, in Joyce's case, the most intricately inventive, nearly impenetrable novel, *Finnegans Wake*, in Beckett's case the plays and the briefer and increasingly eccentric fictions. Both evolved to a point where they seemed to leave more and more readers behind and write more and more for their own pleasure and interest.

I had the example of writers within the traditional form but abbreviated, as, for instance, Babel with his condensation, emotional intensity, and richness of imagery, especially in Walter Morison's translation of the *Red Cavalry* stories. One of these, "Crossing into Poland," ends with the thin pregnant woman standing over her dead old father:

> "Good sir," said the Jewess, shaking up the feather bed, "the Poles cut his throat, and he begging them: 'Kill me in the yard so that my daughter shan't see me die.' But they did as suited them. He passed away in this room, thinking of me.—And now I should wish to know," cried the woman with sudden and terrible violence, "I should wish to know where in the whole world you could find another father like my father?"

The ending is abrupt; the story, for all its power, is only a little over two pages long.

I had the example of Grace Paley, who defied conventional pacing and packed every sentence with so much wit, richness of character, and worldly wisdom that the lines were often explosive. Her story "Wants" is, again, all of two pages long. Here is the opening page:

> I saw my ex-husband in the street. I was sitting on the steps of the new library.
>
> Hello, my life, I said. We had once been married for twenty-seven years, so I felt justified.
>
> He said, What? What life? No life of mine.
>
> I said, O.K. I don't argue when there's real disagreement. I got up and went into the library to see how much I owed them.
>
> The librarian said $32 even and you've owed it for eighteen years. I didn't deny anything. Because I don't understand how time passes. I have had those books. I have often thought of them. The library is only two blocks away.
>
> My ex-husband followed me to the Books Returned desk. He interrupted the librarian, who had more to tell. In many ways, he said, as I look back, I attribute the dissolution of our marriage to the fact that you never invited the Bertrams to dinner.

That's possible, I said. But really, if you remember: first, my
father was sick that Friday, then the children were born, then
I had those Tuesday-night meetings, then the war began. Then
we didn't seem to know them anymore. But you're right. I
should have had them to dinner.

(Notice, by the way, in this excerpt, how fond she is of short sentences,
often following the same pattern, which is the simplest one: subject,
verb.)

Yet I was apparently not ready to try the sort of story she was writ-
ing. And it took me another decade to see that you could take the ma-
terial of a story very largely from your own life, as I suspect she did, or
even, though in a selected version, almost entirely from your own life,
as I later did.

I also had the example of Kafka's very brief *Parables and Paradoxes*,
some of which were not so much stories, of course, as they were medi-
tations or logical problems. I studied them closely. Yet I seemed to think
that only Kafka, not I or anyone else, could write such odd things.

They all work in slightly different ways. One, for instance, "The Si-
rens," might be a reinterpretation of a familiar legend:

These are the seductive voices of the night; the Sirens, too,
sang that way. It would be doing them an injustice to think that
they wanted to seduce; they knew they had claws and sterile
wombs, and they lamented this aloud. They could not help it
if their laments sounded so beautiful.

Another, "Leopards in the Temple," might be the creation of, and com-
mentary upon, a ritual:

Leopards break into the temple and drink to the dregs what
is in the sacrificial pitchers; this is repeated over and over
again; finally it can be calculated in advance, and it becomes
a part of the ceremony.

Another might be the reinterpretation of a moment of history ("Alex-
ander the Great"):

It is conceivable that Alexander the Great, in spite of the mar-
tial successes of his early days, in spite of the excellent army

that he had trained, in spite of the power he felt within him to change the world, might have remained standing on the bank of the Hellespont and never have crossed it, and not out of fear, not out of indecision, not out of infirmity of will, but because of the mere weight of his own body.

(Kafka himself, apparently, was inspired by two of his contemporaries or predecessors who wrote in the very short form: the Swiss Robert Walser, also a novelist, whose late writings, almost illegibly tiny, were recently deciphered; and the Viennese coffeehouse bohemian Peter Altenberg, writing at the turn of the twentieth century.)

For a long time, I did not see Kafka as a model to be emulated, nor other more eccentric or unconventional writers. I did not yet know the work of many writers who later, over the years, became interesting to me or influential: the strange narrative voices and bizarre sensibilities in the stories of the American Jane Bowles or the Brazilian Clarice Lispector or the Swiss Regina Ullmann (whose 1921 collection of stories was not translated into English until 2015, nearly a hundred years after it appeared in German); or the startling and calmly violent, syntactically complex single-paragraph stories of the Austrian Thomas Bernhard's collection *The Voice Imitator*, which I discovered by chance in an airport bookstore; or the tiny chapters of the Brazilian Machado de Assis's novel *Epitaph of a Small Winner*; or the autobiographical paragraph stories of the Spaniard Luis Cernuda; or the many, many small, whimsical tales written in the 1940s, '50s, and '60s, of the Cuban Virgilio Piñera; or, finally, the meditative, semi-autobiographical, very brief stories of the Dutchman A. L. Snijders or the Swiss Peter Bichsel, so appealing to me that I have been translating them for the past five years or so.

But those discoveries were still to come.

At the age of about twenty-six, after having ignored the model of Kafka for so long, I was jolted into taking a new direction, at last, after reading a collection of stories by the contemporary American prose poet Russell Edson.

I had been slogging away at a stubborn story. I had been fighting off my inertia and apathy. I would read, go for a walk, eat. In the midst of this inertia, a friend who had been witnessing it said, "You just sit around all day doing nothing." (I wasn't doing nothing—I was agonizing!) Then I read Edson's book called *The Very Thing That Happens*.

Edson is a very unusual writer: You could characterize many of his stories as brief, fantastic, and often funny tales of domestic mayhem involving family members but also, sometimes, their pots and pans, animals, buildings, parts of buildings, and so forth. But some of the pieces are lyrical meditations, or sunnier moral tales. Russell Edson himself calls them poems, sometimes fables. Here is one on the idea of generations ("Waiting for the Signal Man"):

> A woman said to her mother, where is my daughter?
>
> Her mother said, up you and through me and out of grandmother; coming all the way down through all women like a railway train, trailing her brunette hair, which streams back grey into white; waiting for the signal man to raise his light so she can come through.
>
> What is she waiting for? said the woman.
>
> For the signal man to raise his light, so she can see to come through.

Here, in "Dead Daughter," is a rather brutal family interaction:

> Wake up, I heard something die, said a woman to something else.
>
> Something else was her father. Do not call me something else, he said.
>
> Will it be something dead for breakfast? said the woman.
>
> It is always something dead given by your mother to her husband, said her father, like my dead daughter, dead inside herself; there is nothing living there, no heart, no child.
>
> That is not true, said the daughter, I am in here trying to live, but afraid to come out.
>
> If you're in there oh do come out, we're having a special treat, dead daughter for breakfast, dead daughter for lunch, and dead daughter for supper, in fact dead daughter for the rest of our lives.

And here is a drama involving inanimate objects as well as human beings ("When Things Go Wrong"):

> A woman had just made her bed. A wall leaned down and went to sleep on her bed. So the ceiling decided to go to bed too. The wall and the ceiling began to shove each other. But it was decided that the ceiling had best sleep on the floor. But the

floor said, get off of me because I am annoyed with you. And the floor went outside to lie in the grass.

Will you stop it all of you, screamed the woman.

But the rest of the walls yawned and said, we're tired too.

Stop stop stop, she screamed, it is all going wrong, all is wrong wrong wrong.

When her father returned he said, why is my house destroyed?

Because everything went wrong suddenly, screamed the woman.

Why are you screaming and why is my house destroyed? said the father.

I don't know, I don't know, and I am screaming because I am very upset, father, said the woman.

This is very strange, said the father, perhaps I'll walk away and when I return things will be different.

Father, screamed the woman, why do you leave me every time this happens?

Because when I return things will be different, said the father.

Edson opened a path for me for several reasons. One reason was that not every one of his stories succeeded. Some were merely silly. Maybe this had to do with the way Edson went about writing them. As Natalie Goldberg describes it in her book *Writing Down the Bones:*

> He said that he sits down at his typewriter and writes about ten different short pieces at one session. He then comes back later to reread them. Maybe one out of the ten is successful and he keeps that one. He said that if a good first line comes to him, the rest of the piece usually works. Here are some of his first lines:
>
> "A man wants an aeroplane to like him."
> [. . .]
> "A beloved duck gets cooked by mistake."
> [. . .]
> "A husband and wife discover that their children are fakes."
> "Identical twin old men take turns at being alive."

Some of the stories I found brilliant, but others faltered. Yet the stories that did not quite succeed showed me two things that were helpful to a young writer: They showed more clearly how the stories were put together; and they showed how a writer could try something, fail, try again, partially succeed, and try again. A third thing the stories showed me, both the brilliant ones and the faltering ones, was how you could tap some very difficult emotions and let them burst out in an unexpected, raw, sometimes absurd form—that perhaps, in fact, setting oneself absurd or impossible subjects made it easier for difficult emotions to come forth.

I read this book, and I began writing paragraph-long stories, sometimes just one story on one day, sometimes more.

They, too, arose from different sources and worked in different ways. One, "In a House Besieged," used the landscape where I was living at the time, taking real features of it but putting them together in such a way that the piece sounded like a fable or a fairy tale:

> In a house besieged lived a man and a woman. From where they cowered in the kitchen the man and woman heard small explosions. "The wind," said the woman. "Hunters," said the man. "The rain," said the woman. "The army," said the man. The woman wanted to go home, but she was already home, there in the middle of the country in a house besieged.

Another, "The Mother," was entirely made up, but was based on an emotional reality:

> The girl wrote a story. "But how much better it would be if you wrote a novel," said her mother. The girl built a dollhouse. "But how much better if it were a real house," her mother said. The girl made a small pillow for her father. "But wouldn't a quilt be more practical," said her mother. The girl dug a small hole in the garden. "But how much better if you dug a large hole," said her mother. The girl dug a large hole and went to sleep in it. "But how much better if you slept forever," said her mother.

Some of the stories remained unfinished, rough. Some grew to be a page or two long, or longer. These short-short stories, as a group, had a different feel to them from what I had done before—they were bolder, more confident, and more adventurous; they were more of a pleasure to write, and they came more easily. Whereas until this point writing had often felt like hard work, now I began to enjoy it.

One of the longer stories was "Mr. Knockly," which begins: "Last fall my aunt burned to death." It was only much later that I realized that this story had very likely been influenced by an Edgar Allan Poe story, "The Man in the Crowd": The main plotline of both stories is the narrator's obsessive pursuit of a man through the streets of a town. And over time I have seen how certain forms, even the forms of nursery rhymes, may impress themselves on us when we hear or read them, and that some of our later work may slip right into these preestablished matrices.

I did not go on to buy and read every one of Russell Edson's books over the years since then. One book was enough—as, often, even a single page of a piece of writing may be enough—to cause a change of direction. I no longer felt that I had to write in accordance with an established, traditional form. After that, although I remained loyal to the traditional narrative short story and revisited it from time to time, I also kept departing from it to try other forms. Sometimes the forms simply occurred to me, and sometimes they were directly inspired by another writer's piece of writing.

About twelve years after I first read Edson, for instance, I was reading a poem by the American poet Bob Perelman on a train going down the coast of California. I was startled—he was incorporating a grammar lesson in this poem! Could one really do that?

Here is the lesson in Perelman's poem, called "Seduced by Analogy," from his collection *To the Reader*:

> With afford, agree, and arrange, use the infinitive.
> I can't agree to die. With practice,
> Imagine, and resist, use the gerund. I practice to live
> Is wrong.

A train, or in fact any public transportation, is often a very good place to think and write. After I read this poem, I realized: You could teach French in a story. You could write the story in English but incorporate French words and ideas about language. I began writing "French Lesson I: Le Meurtre" right there on the train, without any more plan than that:

> See the *vaches* ambling up the hill, head to rump, head to rump. Learn what a *vache* is. A *vache* is milked in the morning, and milked again in the evening, twitching her dung-soaked tail, her head in a stanchion. Always start learning

your foreign language with the names of farm animals. Remember that one animal is an *animal*, but more than one are *animaux*, ending in *a u x*. Do not pronounce the *x*. These *animaux* live on a *ferme*.

And the lesson continues, with a short vocabulary list at the end.

All of which is to say that a good poem is bound to offer you something surprising in the way of language and thinking, even if some of its meaning eludes you.

The American contemporary Charles Bernstein is another interesting poet and one of the originators of the so-called Language School of poetry. Bernstein ventures into all sorts of new formal territories—he has even written the libretto of an opera based on the work and life of the critic Walter Benjamin.

One of Bernstein's long sectional poems, "Safe Methods of Business," includes a letter protesting a parking ticket.

> The summons charges me with parking at a crosswalk on the northeast corner of 82nd street and Broadway on the evening of August 17, 1984. The space in question is east of the crosswalk on 82nd street as indicated by the yellow lines painted across the street. This space has been a legal parking space during the over ten years I have lived on the block. Cars are always parked in this space and have continued to (unticketed in several observations I made yesterday and today). Apparently, new crosswalk markings are currently being painted in white on both 82nd street and 83rd street. At this time, the process is not complete. When these new lines are finished, several spaces may be eliminated. However, as they looked at the time I received the ticket, they did not appear to override the yellow lines according to which I was clearly in my right to park in the space.

I read Bernstein's poem as a poem, de facto, partly because it has line breaks, partly because it is one section (twenty-six lines long) of a more obviously poem-like long poem, and partly because it is included in a collection of poems and is surrounded by other poems. Yet how does it work as a poem? Certainly not by the same rules as the poem by Perel-

380

man above. What it does show is how other factors besides the style, form, and language of a poem, particularly the context in which we read it, may determine how we receive it—and this in itself can open up new possibilities for a writer.

Perhaps this unusual form of "poem" lodged in my brain somewhere, so that years later a letter of complaint seemed a good form for a story, and I wrote "Letter to a Funeral Parlor," objecting to the use of the word *cremains*. This letter started out as an actual, sincere piece of correspondence and then got carried away by its own language and turned into something too literary to send.

After I wrote it, I realized how many other things I had to complain about and wrote three more: "Letter to a Hotel Manager," in which I objected to the misspelling, on the menu, of "scrod," the famous Boston fish; "Letter to a Peppermint Candy Company," in which I reported that in the expensive tin of peppermints I had just bought, there were only two-thirds the number of peppermints the company claimed to have put in it; and "Letter to a Frozen Peas Manufacturer," objecting to the artwork on the package.

Some influences reveal themselves only long after the fact, but some are quite conscious. Once, many years ago, I was reading David Foster Wallace's "Brief Interviews with Hideous Men." It was difficult to read, because the men were truly hideous. But the form was a powerful one—in each interview, we were given the answers at length, but the questions were left blank. I did not finish reading it, but the form stayed with me. And some time later, after I had had the interesting experience of being on call for jury duty and wanted to write about it, this form felt like the perfect one to use. The content of the story, which was titled "Jury Duty," was taken nearly completely from my own experience, but the story was transformed into fiction by the illusion of the questioner, or examiner.

*I was in my early teens when I first laid eyes on a page of Beckett. Here was a book, Malone Dies, in which the narrator spent a page describing his pencil, and the first plot development was that he had dropped his pencil. I had never imagined anything like it.*

Here is the opening of the story:

Q.

A. Jury duty.

Q.

A. The night before, we had been quarreling.

Q.

A. The family.

Q.

A. Four of us. Well, one doesn't live at home anymore. But he was home that night. He was leaving the next morning—the same morning I had to go in to the courtroom.

Q.

A. We were all four of us quarreling. Every which way. I was just now trying to figure it out. There are so many different combinations in which four people can quarrel: one on one, two against one, three against one, two against two, etc. I'm sure we were quarreling in just about every combination.

Q.

A. I don't remember now. Funny. Considering how heated it was.

The form is enjoyable because of what you can do with the unspoken questions. Sometimes it's obvious what the question has been. For instance, we know the questioner has had trouble understanding the name Sojourner Truth—the former slave and women's rights activist—because it has to be repeated several times; but at other points in the story we cannot guess what the questioner has asked: I end the story with the answer "Yes!"—and you will never know what the question was.

Some years ago, during the extended period in which I was working on my translation of Proust's *Swann's Way*, not wanting to stop writing altogether and yet having no time, I tried another form that intrigued me: Perhaps because I was spending the days translating such long, complex sentences—though I found this activity engrossing and even exciting—I wanted to see just how brief I could make a piece of writing and still have it mean something.

Perhaps I had also been influenced by a postcard I had kept up on my bulletin board for years. It contained a three-line poem—a translation from the Cheremiss—by the American poet Anselm Hollo:

i shouldn't have started these red wool mittens.
they're done now,
but my life is over

Even though it's so short, it surprises me each time I read it—which is something I think a good piece of writing should do.

Perhaps, too, the idea for this very brief form was planted in me years ago by some of the entries in Kafka's *Diaries*, which I read very closely when I was in my twenties. For instance, here is one entry, in its entirety:

The picture of dissatisfaction presented by a street, where everyone is perpetually lifting his feet to escape from the place on which he stands.

In just a few words, he offers a different way of seeing a commonplace thing. I wondered if I could write a piece that short—a title and a line or two—that would still have the power to move, or at least startle, or distract, in a way that was not entirely frivolous. I also wanted the piece to stay firmly in the realm of prose.

Here is one, "Lonely," that has some of the rhythms of the Hollo poem:

No one is calling me. I can't check the answering machine because I have been here all this time. If I go out someone may call while I'm out. Then I can check the answering machine when I come back in.

Here are two that are shorter:

"Hand"

Beyond the hand holding this book that I'm reading, I see another hand lying idle and slightly out of focus—my extra hand.

"Index Entry"

Christian, I'm not a

Legend has it that Hemingway once wrote what he called a one-line short story: "For sale: baby shoes, never worn"—misquoted ephemerally by someone on the internet as: "For sale: baby crib, never used." But writers working in very short forms are usually poets. There is Samuel Menashe, who often wrote in four short lines and whose interesting work is too often overlooked (untitled):

Pity us
by the sea
on the sands
so briefly

Another poet who is a master of brevity and the concrete is Lorine Niedecker, one of the less well-known poets in the so-called Objectivist group that followed a generation or so after Ezra Pound. Here is one of her short, pithy poems, this one untitled, about a thing that comes back, or might come back, to haunt the poet, having a life and will of its own.

The museum man!
I wish he'd take Pa's spitbox!
I'm going to take that spitbox out
and bury it in the ground
and put a stone on top.
Because without that stone on top
it would come back.

Then there is an interesting, anarchic poet near Woodstock, New York, known only as Sparrow. Some years ago he became famous—in small circles, anyway—for staging a one-man protest in the reception area of the *New Yorker* for several days, objecting that the magazine published only bland, predictable poetry, rather than offbeat, eccentric poetry such as, in particular, his own. Eventually, in fact, the magazine bought three of his poems and published at least one of them. (Sometimes it pays to be persistent, and to protest.)

Sparrow has written many very small poems, such as the following ("Poem"):

This poem replaces
all my previous poems.

The poems of his that interest me are not lyrical. I like the ones in which he sees things in a different way—as Kafka does in some of his diary entries, as I do in my piece "Hand."

Here's another small poem, "Perfection Wasted":

The problem with dying
is you can't be funny anymore,
or charming.

When I read this, I thought it was an original poem of his, but in fact it is a "translation" of a sonnet by John Updike that appeared in the *New Yorker*. I found it in a group of poems by Sparrow called "Translations from the *New Yorker*." This was in a book of his called *America, A Prophecy: A Sparrow Reader*.

Another translation of his is "Garter Snake." I'll quote Sparrow's translation first, then a little of the original:

A snake moved through grass
and I watched.
It looked like an S.

When it stopped, it was very still.

The grass shook slightly when it moved.

The original, by Eric Ormsby, has a lot more words in it, which is one thing I suppose Sparrow is trying to get away from. Here is the first verse of the original:

The stately ripple of the garter snake
in sinuous procession through the grass
compelled my eye. It stopped and held its head
high above the lawn, and the delicate curve
of its slender body formed a letter "S"
for "serpent," I presume, as though
diminutive majesty obliged embodiment.

Further along in the poem, where Sparrow's translation reads "The grass shook slightly when it moved," the original reads:

> . . . it gave the rubbled grass
> and the dull hollows where its ripple ran
> lithe scintillas of exuberance
> moving the way a chance felicity
> silvers the whole attention of the mind.

That's the end of the poem. Sparrow's plainer version may not quite succeed as a poem, and some readers will prefer the richer original. But Sparrow's translations raise several interesting questions about writing, and about form in particular—which is what I've been exploring here.

The most pressing question, of course, is one that would take us, if we pursued it, straight into the realm of translation theory and all its intriguing conundrums: Can you say the same thing in radically different ways? If you write it so differently, are you, in fact, saying the same thing?

*Nominated by The Virginia Quartery Review, Ben Stroud*

# LETTERS

by ILYA KAMINSKY

from ORION

Snow has eaten ¼ of me

yet I believe
against all evidence

these snowflakes
are my letters of recommendation

here is a man worth falling on.

*Nominated by Jane Hirschfield, Aimee Nezhukumatathil, Michael Waters*

# FREAK CORNER

fiction by JOHN ROLFE GARDINER

from ONE STORY

The new Margaret Kipps made her switch without going under the knife. This in mid-twentieth century when an operation for the full change might have been offered in Scandinavia, but not to Alfie Kipps of Arlington, Virginia, who became Margaret in dress and address in the summer of 1953. No loss or gain of genitalia.

I don't remember how that detail was brought to light, whether by my parents' investigations or the reports of shaken neighbors in the Meadow Brook development. We could only imagine the inward clap that must have concussed his household before outward reverberation shook our community to its furthest reaches, where a maiden sister in a surviving Victorian would lower her voice to begin, "My dear!"

Alfie, in his late twenties, still living at home, had been working, he told us, in the city, in the circulation office of a trade magazine as a punch card operator, that once pervasive data management job, long extinct. The change was more shocking because Alfie had never shown us a feminine inclination. In fact, there were young women who used to drive into our development to wave at the Kipps porch, coming and going. We assumed it was a mark of Alfie's popularity, not a sign of social reticence or sexual confusion.

Now Alfie—Margaret, please—began to follow the era's fashion of soft wool sweaters, presumably padded, and skirts that fell demurely to just above her ankles. My parents' reaction was pity: "poor boy." My concern for him was mixed with skepticism at such a sudden transformation. Memory says he affected a brunette wig that fell to his shoulders until his own hair should catch up with its dutiful length. His voice seemed stretched to a higher note, something he might be trying on, like the new clothes.

My mother asked me to ignore the changes. As if it were a social duty to accept the remarkable alteration, even as she and my father discussed the "situation" across the street. Meanwhile, Meadow Brook at large was not opening its arms to our newcomer. Small children were warned away, teens felt predictably threatened in their emerging sexuality, and adults were troubled by the notoriety coming our way.

Gregory and Harmon Knox, who lived a few doors away from us, members of my senior high class, were openly hostile to Margaret. They made sure we were all aware of their disgust. Gregory, a year older than Harmon, had got himself held back in junior high, I think to become his brother's closer ally in life's progression, making a disruptive team in our shared classroom. They existed, it seemed, to threaten Meadow Brook and our schoolyard with their black hair in duck's ass dos fixed in place with Vitalis, that grease-and-alcohol tonic, since gone the way of the punch cards.

Enabled in arrogance by a proud father, the brothers drove a Chevrolet heap with ear-blasting, glasspack mufflers. The rest of us, standing mute at our school bus corner, waited in impotent irritation for the daily insult of their racket and their obscene gestures, sometimes a vileness directed my way:

"Has your retard sister's thing got hair on it yet?"

How could we know in our adolescent dismay that these would not be the lasting enemies of our lives, that our real trials would be more subtle and born of our own deficiencies, or that the destiny of the Knox boys was already fixed? No match for the Provost Marshall in the brig at Fort Dix, New Jersey, where they eventually spent the second year of Army tours before dishonorable discharges and lives beyond our ken on some other unlucky street.

Freak Corner was the brothers' name for the end of the block where our brick rambler stood across from Alfie's house, identical but for some glass-brick courses in the Kipps front wall, too cloudy to see anything but shadows moving behind them. Our house, the other piece of their "freak corner," being home to my sister Gayle, whose limited vocabulary and floating inflections left a constant question on her face: *Is this the way it should sound?*

Gayle, pre-lingually deaf, never heard a word our parents said, though it took them nearly two years to understand that placing herself in front of them when they spoke was not a child's remarkable politeness but her need to see the movement of their lips. Accepting the diagnosis, they were determined, with little debate, that Gayle would be an "oralist," a mainstreamed member of the hearing world.

Her early years must have been a time of dim confusion and bewildered anxiety. As she grew older, the indignities were felt if not heard: "Call her dummy. She can't hear you." Worse came later—subjection to a community pique at what it took to be her conceited diffidence, then to pity for her presumed cognitive deficit. I grieved with Gayle, which only gave fuel to her frustration.

Retard? I hadn't the ready wit to counter the Knoxs' uninformed cruelty. I was too angry to be afraid of them but couldn't offer a reasoned defense of my sister's quavering voice and pleading eyes, the contortions of her mouth, the disturbing approximate sounds of speech. She was quite beautiful when her face was relaxed in its normal symmetries.

But what was retarded if not a daily ride to special classes in a bus with the handicap symbol announced on its back door, hours spent with a remedial teacher and a speaking vocabulary at age ten of perhaps a hundred words? I loved her and accepted that her deafness must be loved as well. She turned fourteen in the summer of 1953. I was almost seventeen, a rising senior, her regular chaperone and protector.

I shouldn't say our street was ruled by bullies. Nor was it some benighted middle-American cul-de-sac spending its days in ignorant goodwill and nights tied by rabbit ears to television's big-bosomed Dagmar. Across the way, Mr. Kipps, Margaret's father, was an officer of the region's electric company. Other near neighbors—a real estate agent, a high school principal, a clerk in the Government Printing Office, a pharmacist, a stock broker, a title attorney, the manager of a vacuum-cleaner store—were men and the occasional woman who had achieved comfortable middle-class lives.

The Knox boys' father was a bail bondsman with an office next to the county courthouse. My father was manager of men's clothing at Woodward & Lothrop, that staid Washington department store where you could still check the fit of new shoes through a fluoroscope, see your skeletal toes squirming in a sea of electric green.

When TV antennas began to alter Meadow Brook's roofscape, radio was still our home's prime medium. The radio, once a humming of vacuum tubes nesting in oversized living room furniture, had shrunk to fit in streamlined, bedside plastic. It might seem a transparent feint at authenticity to seed my sister's story with yet another of that decade's commercial markers, but her story was no fiction. And to the brother of deafness, radio, as nothing else, signified her missing American childhood—comedians, singers, and serial heroes.

This was long before signing for the deaf became a duty at public events. The words *rock* and *roll* had not been twinned as musical genre, so no band called Lather, Rinse, Repeat. Still in the atom's tomb, punk and rock had not yet combined, so that musicians still unborn had not thought of Laudable Pus as a name that would travel so well from Brighton to Blackpool and across the Atlantic.

When the pioneering Christine Jorgensen went under the knife to become a woman, the shocking story did not fly across the ocean in an internet instant but reached us a week or so later on the cover of *LIFE* Magazine. Who but the bravest would dare such extreme deviation in that decade when "commie" and "queer" were thrown so carelessly at the least aberration? To us it might have seemed Alfie had turned into a woman so that the distant Christine wouldn't be so lonely and despised in the world's eyes.

It shouldn't have surprised me in that time when so few of us knew how insidious and ripe were our own prejudices that my sister Gayle would be the one most intrigued by Alfie's transformation, the least threatened, the most eager to seek his company, our family's goodwill ambassador. With a fortitude we lacked, she crossed the street to wait on the Kipps' stoop each afternoon for Margaret to come out and sit beside her.

From our house I could see Gayle entertaining her new friend with hand signals—I supposed of her own devising—until my mother would send me across the street to fetch her home for supper. That was Gayle's only homework. We thought of it as a daily good deed, a window scene that could wet our cheeks. I watched beside my mother as sentiment, at first, overcame our fears for my sister.

In the fall of her thirteenth year, she'd begun to move with a lighter step, and her face was lit with a new enthusiasm. In her mumbling way, Gayle was attempting words we could not make out because it didn't seem possible she could know them, even abstract ideas—"reason," "eternity." For some time her speech had been left behind her reading level.

Her handicap had disguised a phenomenal intelligence, far beyond the norm of hearing peers, and polar opposite of the impression she made in our neighborhood where she was presumed to be an empty vessel, a sphinx without a secret. But now, for a child in her predicament, she was a miracle to her teachers. By rights she might have had the vocabulary of a pre-kindergartener by then, and commensurate developmental delay.

For a time our parents' pride in their prodigy pushed aside questions of what lay behind the transformation. There was Gayle, grinning at a Salinger story in a magazine beyond my interest or comprehension. Had it all been unwitting trickery? Had she actually been hearing words and processing grammar while barred from response by some neurological anomaly? Was she a mute we were forcing to speak?

From age seven, she had a private tutor, Aimee Chapin, fresh from post-graduate audio study and a charming presence in our lives. Shy, with a saintly devotion, Aimee had been hired to make Gayle a speaking member of the hearing world. Nothing less—or more—period, a firm command. Aimee sat beside Gayle in school, and spent hours alone with her in our home, with endless patience for her deaf charge.

How clever Aimee was in her grand deception of my parents. How stealthy, using me as intermediary to cover her betrayal of their no-signing order. Sometimes when she left the house she would pull me outside with her to chat about Gayle's progress. One evening she stopped beyond our front door, her eyes pleading for understanding, her face so close to mine I thought she might be waiting for me to take her in my arms.

"Your sister *is* a freak," she said, "an intellectual phenomenon. Were you aware that people can have ideas before they have the words to express them?" If she was walking here on the edge of philosophical debate, so, it seemed, was her student. "Do you know what Gayle asked me this afternoon? 'Is eternity on both sides of us?' Where do you think that came from?"

Aimee knew a family struggle lay ahead, and she wanted me in Gayle's corner when the battle began. And my sister, breaking through chains of ignorance, though well aware of Aimee's danger, could not withhold the truth any longer. Her grand transformation had been thanks to Aimee's instruction in total disregard of our parents' commands.

"Columbia Institution," Gayle wrote on a scrap of paper, a preparation for my own tutorial. Next time Aimee had me alone she held nothing back. Did I know that if I could not name things, I'd remain a stranger in the world, even in my own home? Did I know that the native deaf, if taught speech alone, were lucky to speak at a fourth-grade level when they left high school, that this could have been Gayle's fate? Had I noticed that my remarkable sister now had a grammar and critical mass of vocabulary that was growing in all directions as a context of visual symbols began to teach her what she could not hear and scarcely pronounce? That she had a phenomenal plasticity of mind that might one day study elusive dimensions of mathematics, if that was her passion? It wasn't. Though letters stumped her lips and tongue, they were already flying through her mind in connected patterns that a hearing child might envy.

In short, did I know what had happened?

By then, perhaps, I did, but I didn't want to admit it.

For almost two years Aimee had been teaching Gayle sign language, flouting our parents' edict, and Gayle, knowing she was in danger of losing her confidant, her treasured Aimee, had kept it a secret between them. Signing—anathema—that pit of grimacing pantomime my parents could not bear to have their daughter fall into. Gayle, Aimee lectured me, should not be held in a conceptual prison, even if with the best intentions. There was a world of joyous communion waiting for her. In fact, she said, my sister had come too far for any of us to prevent it.

Aimee had no right to solicit my part in her work with my sister. It was unprofessional, unethical. At the time, I had to side with my parents in this, but their firing Aimee, their effort to have her barred from all deaf instruction, brought a swift reaction in the house—locked doors, sobbing, a shelf of old stuffed animals with legs removed. The tantrum was not an infantile meltdown but a forerunner to Gayle's passive-aggressive attack, her refusal to speak at all, turning away from the movement of our lips.

Yet every afternoon she walked out of the house, across the street to join Margaret Kipps on her stoop, where, from our living room window, we could witness another performance—arms and hands plying the air, head cocked inquisitively from side to side. It was tormenting to know that neighbors would be taking this for chaotic neurological disorder, or imagining her a lesser organism stirred by satisfaction of an instinctive need. Not Margaret. If she was baffled, she responded with complete absorption and hand-clapping admiration.

Gayle was showing us all a latent animation, stifled so long, now free to stab not just at the names of things—smells, tastes, sensations—but her emotional appreciation of the whole perceived world. And as Aimee predicted, her radical whirl of symbol was ready to become a feast of sharing, regardless of our fears or any efforts to restrain her.

If Gayle was an emotional mess after Aimee's firing, my parents wept in private. I was the dry-eyed pivot they swung on or grabbed at for support. Not a good time for them to be reading the conventional texts on deafness: "Signing foments the passions, while speech elevates the mind." This, along with "Signing feminizes the male and makes the female masculine," while our brave Gayle crossed the street each afternoon to visit her ambiguous "sister." These warnings were uppermost in my mother's mind. And there was Gayle, teaching the sign for transvestite, a loose-wristed twist of the hand in front of her chest for the admiring Margaret, who reached for the hand in gratitude.

I was glad the Knox brothers were not out on queer patrol. I've tried to think of something that would redeem these two from stock players as one-dimensional fools in Gayle's history. I could as easily convince myself that Nature had a purpose for two more wasps. Nothing to admire; only their likeness to a Biblical plague, testing our faith, or teaching us to appreciate decency by showing us the opposite.

Another afternoon when I crossed the street to bring her home, Gayle was sitting with Margaret on the front steps, a hand on her knee, as if her friend needed comforting. Annoyed by the familiarity, I sat down beside them to coax my sister. I was met with a twist of her shoulder and head turned away. At that moment the Knox boys came around the corner in their noisy heap. Seeing us, they braked suddenly and rolled down their windows.

"Freaks!"

"Fairy!"

"Queer bait!" was the last phrase as they gunned away.

Margaret stiffened. "I'd chase the bastards if it wasn't for this damned skirt." Remembering herself, she softened and asked, "Do you like my new outfit? Garfinkle's."

If Gayle had missed Margaret's actual disgust for women's clothes so tastefully purchased, she could not have missed the disarming change of mood. The same day, our mother had learned more about Margaret, something heard at market. Her parents were moving to their retirement in South Carolina. She'd be living alone. "And she isn't a trans-sexual, she's a transvestite."

Both new words to us. No matter their definitions, I knew something was twisted. But Gayle was far too invested to find fault in Margaret's sisterhood. She had her own dilemma—our parents' loving intention pitted against her struggle for freedom. Persistent in turning her head away from every movement of their lips, she was slowly forcing them to relent, undeterred in her resolve to be part of a signing community.

Twice a week I drove her to the Columbia Institution campus in Washington. Then it was every day. A revelation. Gayle and I reintroducing ourselves in a way that made us happier in each other's company. My signing proficiency would never catch up with hers, but this whole-self language left the hearing world somewhere outside our reborn mutual love.

She and a dozen other teenagers were transformed that summer into a brother-and-sisterhood of hand actors in a drama of laughter with the relaxed brows of dawning comprehension. Not in the Columbia class-rooms, but in the cafeteria and other gathering places where two older students were introducing them to the full informal signing system of their peers, what is now called American Sign Language along with the hand alphabet, already fixed in Gayle's muscle memory. She was timed at twenty seconds, A to Z. I watched her hands rising, swooping, pointing, in feints too fast for me, then a sudden switch to letters with her fingers in prestidigital dazzle. The muscles of her face shifting in shades of pleasure, in harmony with her hands' performance.

Gayle captivated those peers; her physical beauty only half the attraction. She was always in front of someone, ready to inform or be informed. At the end of the informal classes one of the mentors took the group under the shade of the "swearing tree," a live oak, where he led a rump tutorial in cursing, a wide-ranging hand and finger medley of street vulgarity. The young initiates were freed once over, arming themselves with a code of theatrical defiance, and Gayle absorbed the whole of it. Though, as one of her newly discovered authors had written, there could be no final glossary of words whose intentions were fugitive, especially not in the expanding world of signing. The shared mischief was a further liberation.

For all that, Gayle came home each day to Freak Corner, to a community that had little comprehension of her new world, to neighbors who still patronized and pitied, and to her own fearful parents, fore-warned by the oralists about the perverse dangers in signing. My father was not so worried that Gayle might acquire masculine traits but was prey to any father's fear of a daughter's new alertness to the ubiquity of sex in the world. He thought the signing made her look cheap. Freak-ish, if he'd dared to say the word.

I supposed the fired Aimee's intentions must have been the same as the Columbia Institution's—a struggle for the acceptance of signing against the ruling orthodoxy of deaf education—oralism. Not so. And Colum-bia had been warned about Aimee. She was barred from their class-rooms, where not even the deaf believed their signing was a legitimate language, unaware that change was afoot.

A new member of the faculty, a man name Stokoe who had come to teach Chaucer, was about to rile the campus with his assertion that sign-ing, dismissed as "picture writing in the air," was actually a complete language with a grammar beyond shapes and gesture, hidden in the fourth dimension of timing.

The Knox brothers had been stalking Margaret Kipps, following her in their car into the District. They brought back a story for over-the-fence exchange. There was a night club in the city's southeast where men who dressed as women looked for friendships. The brothers had seen Mar-garet give a doorman money before disappearing inside. Another time, they had followed him to work, not into Washington as he'd said, but somewhere on the Virginia side of the Potomac, where his car dis-appeared down a restricted roadway.

Alarmed, Mother told Gayle she'd have to give up visiting Margaret or else forfeit her lessons at Columbia Institution. Gayle pulled me to her room and declared, part pantomime, part in writing, that she wasn't giv-ing up her friendship with Margaret, who'd been eager to learn signs herself; nor would she be kept from Columbia. Was I on her side, or not?

She told me the new professor had chosen her for a demonstration that would prove what he'd been saying, that signing was a full language. She circled her palms over the tips of her still-growing breasts—*I'm excited*—and we shared a grin at our parents' expense.

"But what about—?" My hands moved over my own chest, down my sides, and over my hips, signifying dress, meaning *what about Margaret?*

Gayle didn't care how Margaret dressed or what her clothes signified. She was defying our mother, walking out of the house that very afternoon, crossing the street to see her friend again. She knew we'd have a curtain pulled aside, watching her every move. Margaret opened the door but didn't come out to sit with Gayle on the stoop. Instead the two of them disappeared into the house.

Mother started for the front door, then turned back for the telephone. To call my father? The police? But what would she say? *My daughter is visiting our neighbor who wears women's clothes?*

"Give them a few minutes," I begged her.

A few minutes became five. There was no holding my mother back. We crossed the street together and knocked on the door. Two of our neighbors were watching from their stoops as we pushed through the unlocked front door of Margaret's house.

"Gayle! Gayle!" my mother called through an empty hallway as if fear for her daughter could restore her hearing. We went searching through rooms, upstairs and down, before we saw the two of them facing each other in the backyard, playing a sterile game of pat-a-cake, their hands never even touching. Actually, another signing lesson under a dogwood tree.

"Gayle was teaching me how to say 'charade,'" Margaret told us before asking Mother, "Have you come to rescue me?"

Toward the end of summer came the defrocking. Margaret was Alfie again! Rushing across the street to us in a T-shirt and trousers now, bosom gone, in full throat as Alfie Kipps. "What happened here today?" he wanted to know, turning first to Gayle as if she'd betrayed him. There was no explanation for the masculine renewal.

Someone had broken into his house, ransacked rooms, emptied drawers, rifled through the closets. There was broken glass and china on his kitchen floor, and a lipsticked message on the wall too foul for repetition. Well, then, had any of us seen the Knox boys entering his house? We must have seen something.

Gayle was close to tears as she watched him drive away, thinking he was renouncing their friendship for good, never mind that he'd deceived all of us—not a woman in any sense, it seemed. Gayle was thinking she might never see him again. I walked across the way for a look through his windows. Over the kitchen counter was the lipstick message on the tile and a crude phallus flying toward the sink.

That evening there were police cars in the street, officers at the Knoxs' door, and more county police the next afternoon, with warrants this time, pushing past Mrs. Knox. Later we saw the brothers come out their door to show the departing police cruisers the well-practiced finger salute.

No lights that night in the Kipps house; Alfie hadn't come home. Later in the week, still no trace of him. Dark sedans with tinted windows parked in front of his house, a federal posse there for a closer look at the vandalized residence. Alfie was gone. Gayle's hands flopped over, palms down, as she gave a shrug for question mark. Was he dead, she was asking. Out of our mother's sight, she confessed to me she'd known for some time that Alfie's emergence as Margaret had not been the transformation he'd pretended. He was frightened, she said. His makeup had become sloppy, black stubble showing through a moist layer of white powder.

Gayle didn't tell me what to expect at Columbia, which recently had changed its name to Gallaudet. She wasn't sure herself. We had just gotten out of our car on the campus, and were met by a dean. "Professor Stokoe's demonstration isn't going to happen," he told me. Why tell me instead of her?

Because he doesn't know how to sign, Gayle explained. Students gathered around my celebrated sister, begging her to stay. She got back in the car and made me drive her home. She wasn't jeopardizing her chance of enrollment there.

Turning into Meadow Brook, we saw Gregory Knox wantonly banging his push mower into the curbstone at the edge of his lawn. He stopped long enough to call out, "Where's your fairy?" Not chastened by the police investigation, more likely embarrassed to have his house searched for evidence he'd been with his brother on a panty raid in the Kipps place.

That week the evening paper carried the story of a police search for a missing man, Alfred Kipps of Arlington's Meadow Brook development, lately employed by *Broadcasting*, a trade magazine with offices in the city. The morning news brought another report of the disappearance, with a denial by the magazine that Mr. Kipps had ever been employed there. His story stayed news with the revelation that Kipps was a transvestite, leading another group of reporters to our street. We told them we were as mystified as our neighbors.

Weeks, months, a full year with no word of him before journalists were back on the missing man's trail. Alfred Kipps (was that even his real name?) had been an employee of the Central Intelligence Agency, a "Company man," far off the Company's reservation, spying on an American citizen, they reported—and not just any citizen. This was political tinder.

Meanwhile Gayle had been accepted at Gallaudet while I enrolled at Georgetown University across town, my signing proficiency jumping ahead with every vacation we spent together. We spent a lot of time on old wounds. Gayle had never believed Alfie was gone for a palms-down certainty. I asked her if she missed Aimee. "Yes, but I miss Alfie too," she told me. While Aimee had taught her signing, it was Alfie who, before others, had delighted in her mysterious signals. And she'd been intrigued by his indifference to the world's opinion of him at a time when she'd almost ceded her own independence to "oralist prison."

We were better equipped to sort fact from fiction than most reporters on the story. Alfie had been a powerless queen in the CIA's rules-shifting chess game with the FBI, training in female impersonation for a part in the grand American comedy, that fear of sexuality and its attendant hypocrisies. He'd been charged to spy on the FBI chief, a night-sporting cross-dresser himself, whose files tagged our Ambassador to Russia as a security risk for the way his tongue slid over his lips "in a feminine manner."

To think our Freak Corner had touched that wider world of national intrigue in those months when fear ran through our own house. I can see my father, watching Gayle practice signing in front of her mirror. For him it was as if she were advertising her availability. He'd recently been pushed aside on the men's floor of his department store. He traced the demotion to his failure to specify "no pleat up to the belt line" in a large order for dress pants. The pants, "too effeminate," had languished on the racks, unsold at half-off.

Gayle has gone on to fame in the tradition of Professor Stokoe who taught her Chaucer while proclaiming the completeness of American Sign Language and creating a notation for its first dictionary. My sister dedicated her life to the welfare of the profoundly deaf, spreading the news of her own transformation. She became a world traveler for signing, even lecturing at the campus that had once denied her an informal platform, Gallaudet University.

In spite of her efforts, it took Gallaudet, premier center of Deaf education, another decade before accepting the truth of Stokoe's assertion that American Sign Language had its own grammar. And a decade more before a campus uprising established the principle of Deaf leadership.

Her PhD thesis asserted the administrators of a monumental institution like Gallaudet were not masters but caretakers, and in 1988, on an arthritic hip, she marched with a thousand others from the campus to the university's board meeting across town, then to the White House, the Capitol, and back to campus, signing all the way, "Deaf President Now."

Gayle's best-known work, *The Handicap of the Hearing*, through multiple editions and translations, circled the globe with a jolt for the world's majority, "sadly poorer, for the limitations of their spoken languages." It holds no recrimination for her parents, and no criticism for those whose fulfillment is immersion in the hearing world, but a warning: "Let no life be undiscovered, lost, or stolen by an aversion to signing, or to the joy in emotive, kinetic kinship it offers."

It seems a short way back to the afternoon Gregory Knox found my sister and me on our sidewalk. It was the day after we learned of Alfie's disappearance. Gayle signing her sorrow, and my own hands moving around my head signaling confusion, had set Gregory off. He walked up staring at our hand dance, calling me a tool and my sister a cretin. He began to move his own hands around his head, twisting his mouth this way and that, mocking our silent conversation. Gayle's hands began to move faster.

"You having some kind of fit?" he asked her. She was repeating everything he said, turning mockery back on him in a dazzle of arms and hands, his bluster no match for its kinetic translation. She even signed his head-to-toe appraisal of her:

"You wouldn't be so bad if your voice didn't squeak."

I circled a forefinger over the pursed ring made by the top of my fist (*anus*), then pulled a thumb from the bottom of the same clenched hand, signing's way of calling him excrement. Gayle pushed my hands aside. He wasn't worth our anger.

A few weeks later we watched the brothers drive off to ill-fated Army enlistments with raised middle fingers, their unfailing salute to the neighborhood. Gayle shook her head, not in disgust so much as pity for their impoverished vocabulary.

*Nominated by One Story*

# UNTITLED

## by TC TOLBERT

from FOGLIFTER

What I want is not
from the Greek
*light*—seeing
begin to relax—
repeating
cut flowers drinking
something other than
my body—

to be full of his body—
*phantazesthai to picture to oneself*
bones all over the yard
a hole is all I hope to own—
the shape of my mother
water drawn on cut glass—
insistence—I should have died—
she didn't have to—*I wish you*

my father's hardness—fantasy
related to *phainein, to show, bring*
the dogs with their empty mouths
the hunger of an hour—
in the window—the hunger of
I want to know love—
she didn't say what we all lost to
*had never been*—what was born

*Nominated by Foglifter*

# RIVERS

## by JO McDOUGALL

from ARKANSAS REVIEW

Rivers are born unlucky.
They bloat. They freeze.
They curate dead bodies nibbled to lace.

You may think them postcard picturesque,
calm as storks,
winding through aspens.

What do you know?
This is not their warp. They rankle, they plot.
They have the soul of a snake.

And yet, they seduce.
You stand on the banks of a majestic one, gawking.
It sends a rat to your ankles.

*Nominated by Arkansas Review, Alice Friman, William Trowbridge*

# THE FIFTH HOUR OF
# THE NIGHT

## BY FRANK BIDART

from THE PARIS REVIEW

*The sun allows you to see only what the sun*
*falls*
*upon: the surface. What we wanted was what was elsewhere: cause.*

❋

Or some books say that's what we once wanted. Prophets of
cause
never, of course, agreed about cause, the *uncaused* cause: or they

❋

terribly did. Asleep, I struggle to stay inside sleep, unravaged by
heart-
piercing dreams—craving, wish, desire to remain inside, if briefly,

❋

obliteration. I cleave to the voice of Poppea's nurse:
*oblivion*
*soave.*

❋

Not frightening, the word
*oblivion*
as Oralia Dominguez, hauntingly clinging to the sound, in 1964 sings it.

❋

Eating today, however
satisfying, frees no creature from having to eat tomorrow. *Sun*

*cycle*
*built into us. It's because you are an animal with a body.*

However
filling.

As soon as adolescent sex ended this hunger
that you had not known was yours until the moment you

satisfied it, at the moment you satisfied it
the hunger returned.

It would never be satisfied. It would
never not return.

*Cycle*
*built into us, returning each day like the sun's diurnal*

*round: in adolescence, more than once each*
*round. It's because you are an animal with a body.*

The night we found we were starving, what
larks! With what

relish we devoured dish upon dish placed in front of us.

&#10038;

Cycle of the sun that each day.

Cycle of the sun that each day wipes the slate.

Promises to wipe the slate.

Deep wrongness between the two that somehow nothing can wipe
clean.

They love each other more than anything and their child knows that.

404

They love each other more than anything but the well is poisoned.

Thirst no well can satisfy.

The well of affection that bloods the house is poisoned.

Love that bloods the house is poisoned.

He was smart and good-looking and charmed everyone.

She was beautiful and smart and charmed everyone.

Deep wrongness between the two that somehow no fury can wipe
   clean.

Thirst no wife and child can slake or satisfy.

The well is poisoned.

*The well that allows you to think the earth your hand touches is good.*

                                          ❖

*Gone, except within anyone who had lived there.*

                                          ❖

Unforgotten hour. Permanent
horizon-line

you cannot rip from your eye. Permanent
under-taste

you cannot
untaste. *Hour that stains, unerasable, unforgotten.*

II
Sun that, each day, promises. Cycle of the sun that each day
reconciles
creatures that flinch at pain, sentience reconciled to the predations of

                                          ❖

405

ordinary existence. After food, after
satiation,
shit. Poppea? We know her name because she risked becoming

*

Empress. Nero, who made her, as she wanted, Empress, later
kicked
her to death. She had few, had no illusions about what would

*

follow getting what she wanted. Monteverdi's ruthless
librettist
imagines a Poppea who believes in nothing—and tries everything.

*

After one, exhausted by the attempt, has tasted each thing the sun
offers,
erasure

*

more than half-
desired.
What is too little, mysteriously tips into—too much. Surfeit

*

breeds loathing. *Oh sun-worshippers, sun-*
*treaders:—*
*creatures*

*

*endowed with what they have learned are mouths and teeth*
*dream*
*not repetition, ease of unendingly getting whatever you must eat, but*

*

*sudden*
*vision—*
*after twisting fogbound dizzying hairpin mountain turns in darkness for*

*

*hours, the vehicle in which you are riding, are trapped, is abruptly above*
*the clouds, you*

❋

*see, for the first time, the ancient*
*G L A C I E R*
*whose gigantic face rises past sleeping farmhouses in eerily calm*
  *moonlight.*

❋

In 1961, at the Simplon Pass, a remnant of the Ice Age
thrust
upon me the sublime. Now it is melting. I read that it is melting, for

❋

miles has melted. By the child's fifth year, the poisoned house was
gone,
except within anyone who had lived there. The crack that replaced it

❋

went down and down, went through everything
bottomlessly.
I thought it had to have an end but could see no end. Or the crack

❋

was not a crack, but an invisible
indivisible
living seam—joining love and hate

❋

seamlessly, *this* and what seemed *not-this*
savagely
suddenly melting into each other.

❋

*It was the sun-filled, seamless surface of glare-filled*
*reality,*
*full of cracks.* I was trapped in a small dark house, my grandmother's

*

house, full of cracks. After the divorce, my grandmother and I loved
watching wrestling together, lost before the screen of our first TV.

*

One day I told her (I must have been
seven,
eight) that, after school that afternoon, I had eaten

*

at the house of a new friend. The family lived
two
blocks away. They were black.

*

Fury. Her sudden fury made
clear
that as long as I lived in her house, I must not

*

enter or eat at his house again. Must
not
remain his friend.

*

The rage I felt at what she demanded did not
preclude
my furious but supine eventual acquiescence.

*

I was a coward. I *was a coward*. I never
forgave
her. I never forgave her for showing

*

me
me.
For years I drew thousands of floorplans for the perfect

❀

house, but what remained unerasable, without solution were
her
and me. Small dark labyrinthine

❀

house without end. One day I swung at her. The half-door window I
smashed
cut my wrist close to the artery.

❀

What did she see outside the open third-floor hospital
window
one night from her room she climbed into?—

❀

*For years, his half-expectant, then*
*indifferent*
*eyes as I walked past. I told myself we had nothing in common. He*
   *was a jock.*

❀

In the years that followed, impossible to
heal
what my coward hand had severed.

❀

After centuries, at last my father's only son, the maw more and more
ravenous
within him, discovered that what he could

❀

make (the mania somehow was to
make,
he discovered that he must make—) was

❀

poetry. Dark anti-matter matter whose matter is
words

in which the seam and the crack *(what Emerson*

*

*called the crack in everything God made)* are in
fury
fused, annealed, ONE.

III

His circumspection hides, but does not quite hide, thirst too-like
    his father's.
His mother's constant admonishment that what he must not be is
    his father.
*What as a kid I loathed in my father, now I understand.*
Aging men want to live inside sharp desire again before they die.
The terrible law of desire is that what quickens desire is what is
    DIFFERENT.
Thirst for the mirror on which is written: *Fuck me like the whore I am.*
Thirst for erasing the pretense of love.
Thirst for the end of endless negotiation.
Thirst for the glamour and magic that cost too much.
Thirst, hidden but not quite hidden, for buying submission to your will.
They will see that what you have bought is compliance.
Thirst for fuck the cost.

*

No one formula for the incompatibilities
that
are existence.

*

Sleeping in a motel with my father, when he, in anguish and crying,
implored
me to try to get my mother to return to him,

*

I said I
would,—
   . . . and knew I wouldn't.

*

At the bottom of existence, contradictory necessary
demands
unsolvable, a dilemma.

                                        ✿

Both my parents ended their lives—lives as flesh—seemingly
without
catharsis. Amid trivia and resentment and incompletion, the end.

                                        ✿

My mother's anguish at walls onto which, as a child, I had flung
shit.
No scrubbing can clean them. If, somewhere in death, my mother

                                        ✿

has her will, she is still scrubbing. Again and again I return to
drink
from the poisoned well, but she cannot see this. Ineradicable

                                        ✿

disgust at
existence
that, to my terror, intermittently rises in me, she

                                        ✿

senses—but cannot name. She is bewildered by such
anger
in her child. She wonders when, tonight, he will sleep, what

                                        ✿

he will in time love. Now, she sees that he is
writing,
writing. She is afraid of what he writes: *Sun-worshipper,*

                                        ✿

*your fellow sun-treaders*
*run*
*the world. Watch as they kneel to the sun.*

*Nominated by The Paris Review, Lloyd Schwartz*

# MY FATHER RECYCLES

by NAIRA KUZMICH

from THE PINCH

For nine years the glass, the aluminum, the plastic we drink from in the house we live in, have purchased, finally, after fifteen years in America. By purchase I mean, of course, have mortgaged, but no matter, no matter, he recycles, like a real American, honest to God. He places the cans, the bottles, in one of the three blue containers the homeless Mexican man has given him over the years, tied with string to my father's gate, first one box, then one more, then once again. Law of supply and demand. My father: greencard holder, watching his breadwinner wife leave early in the morning, return late in the evening; my father, once a dreamer dreaming of his own shoe repair shop in East Hollywood, California, but soon a cynic, embarrassed of his accent, of who he has become, made to be, in this new country, in the America of Americas, the always bigger and better, new city of Los Angeles. My father does not care about the environment, about green grass, about ozone layer and smog. He recycles only for the homeless who roam the alley behind his house with their grocery carts. At first, he collects the bottles in a plastic bag, just holds it out for any man or woman he sees rifling through other people's trash, waits for them to come to him. But sometimes, he does not wait. He is not a patient man, my father, his patience having run out waiting for the prices of houses to drop in Los Angeles, years lost, thousands of dollars saved and lost, waiting, waiting, hoping for the market to turn, and turn his way. Never does. Never ever does. Watching the men and women in the alley, he quickly finds a favorite, likes best the discipline of one man, a man of routine, the homeless Mexican who comes by every week, loyal to his route. My father begins to collect, then, the glass, the aluminum, the plastic, in a cardboard box, gives the cardboard box to the Mexican as he would his daughter a precious gift, gently, both

412

hands outstretched, as if he was the one begging, but one day this box gives under the weight of his labor. The homeless Mexican—sorry, wait, I must stop. Who am I to say he is homeless? I'm a nobody, an immigrant, too, once a five-year old staring at her feet as she wandered the streets of her new neighborhood, collecting cigarette cartons, mama and daddy cutting out the paper barcodes to send in an envelope to a Marlboro catalogue. A family exercise in getting by, getting what you can in America: a red duffel bag, an air mattress, a small portable grill. A family of nonsmokers, never-smokers, never-ever-smokers, advertising a tobacco company during Sunday trips to the beach. Me, a nobody immigrant, it seems, always and forever, at 22, 23, 24, 25, 26, 27, taking the red duffel bag to countless cities and countries after I've left home, this house, left only a year after my parents sign on the dotted line, buy it, mortgage it, finally, finally, after fifteen years in America. The red duffel a handy carryon, the perfect size, all this before my diagnosis, all this before 28, this year, this faithful year, now—where was I? I was with the Mexican man who's with my father as the cardboard box gives under the weight of his labor. A week later, my father finds a blue container tied with string to the gate that separates his backyard from the alley where the homeless roam, and the poor, too, and the immigrant. My father knows it's from the Mexican man, a gift. How could you know, I ask him, remembering that first month we slept in this house when some racist graffitied wetbacks on our garage door. My father and the Mexican have never exchanged names, pleasantries. Only one word, only one from each of them over nine years. "Come," my father, standing in his wifebeater and tracksuit pants, hearing the telling grocery cart wheels turning, struggling down the gravely path of the alley. The Mexican in his white baseball cap and ungloved hands: "Tomorrow"—his cart full that time, a lucky, lucky day, indeed. Maybe a party down our street, or a wake, the start of something new or the very end. I just knew, my father explained. Gut feeling it wasn't a threat, not even a message, not even a thank you, just a simple gesture: You give me something, and I return it. A favor, immigrant to immigrant. I'm trying to explain what I feel so heavy in my chest, what I just know, too. Yesterday, my father was helping me to the couch when he heard the wheels turning again. He continued his work, lifted my feet to the coffee table, placed a pillow underneath them. For months now, I need the help. Sitting, standing, sleeping. Can't even cry without someone holding onto me, can't even lie back and wallow because the cancer is in the spine, too. Go, I told him, Go or you'll miss him. You're comfortable, he asked, his eyes darting from my face to the window and back again. Behind the window, the backyard, behind the backyard, the man with his recycled grocery cart, wheels turning, turning. Are you sure, he asked, almost embarrassed. No, not for this, daddy, no. Of course, of course, I told him with a smile, waving my good arm. Everything on the right side of my body is dying. I watched him run, this sixty-two year old man, my father, the remote control to the gate suddenly in his fist, the gate opening like I imagine a gate will open for me in heaven, slowly but surely, imagine more and more frequently these days, and I tell you I remembered then the Marlboro cartons, how grateful we all were back then to live in this country where someone else's trash turned to our treasure. My father only collected bottles once, in 1993, the year we arrived in this country from that country, Armenia, to take to the recycling center for some extra cash like the Mexican does now, like so many do now, and more have done, will do, again and again, forever. My father collecting bottles to supplement the three dollars an hour he got paid under the table to make rich women jewelry downtown, make them feel beautiful. Embarrassed again, made to feel embarrassed, when he saw men much worse off than him at the center, and with less bottles to show for it. But one envelope of cigarette carton barcodes and magically we had a bed, a red duffel bag, a novel way to cook our hot dogs—not on our cheap apartment stove in our rusted pot of boiling water, no. Grilled, grilled on the beach, on a grill, like real Americans. Can you imagine us? Because I remember. The Mexican man appears only a few years older than my father, but both are healthier than I. I can't help but think this sometimes, especially at night: luckier. You can google the statistics for lung cancer, you can take the time. I will take your pity. I will take anything you give me. Tell me: what can you give me that I can exchange for more time? I've already taken what the universe has given me and I've taken from the universe what I can. I've tried to make something beautiful happen here. But how can I say in words that I have never smoked, and where did that get me? How can I say it without suggesting others deserve my fate? Because they don't. Still, which lyric turn holds my bitterness, the terrible surprise? What immigrant language can explain irony without resorting to coincidence, mere cliché? But I can say I've watched my father run, that I've watched him recycle. I can say I've come back home, to this house, to this city, the America of Americas, to be healed and to die. I can say it, I'm saying it. I've tried to make something beautiful happen here.

*Nominated by The Pinch*

# IN A GOOD WAY

## fiction by POLLY DUFF KERTIS

from HYSTERICAL RAG

Barreling east on the Long Island Rail Road toward the wedding, I felt uneasy.

My date was a guy who was just my roommate Jacob. He had dated only guys, until we split a bottle of red wine and had sex, after which he left for his room on the other side of the wall, and I stared at the ceiling until deciding to take an Ambien. The next morning our platonic roommate friendship—according to the way he was acting, which was as if nothing had happened—returned to normal (but not). He sat on the couch engaging with his interests on his laptop. Usually, I'd cuddle up next to him and see what there was to see—most often memes about memes—but that morning I just felt bad for not having an enthusiasm of my own to intimately research over coffee.

The groom was a guy I'd had a one-night-something with about a year ago that didn't involve any actual penetration but did involve me jerking him off and him saying it was "humiliating in a good way" and him spanking me so hard it left a dark and disturbing bruise, which I didn't see until an aesthetician gasped, held up a mirror, asked me a question in a judgmental and unintelligible Scandinavian language, and waxed more of my pubes than I thought I'd asked her to, which was humiliating in a humiliating way.

The bride was my childhood friend who'd been dating the groom when said one-night "hand" occurred.

My outfit consisted of crepey floral pants I stubbornly thought of as fashion-forward even though my date insisted they reminded him of his MeeMaw.

The thing with the groom happened while my childhood friend was out of town. Though drunkenness at the time seemed like a passable excuse, our hangovers created a putrid cocktail of shame and deceit that neither of us could stomach. Still, we decided over fancy coffee that it was best not to tell her. I thought, *Of course not, and you'll be out of the picture soon because you're clearly a bad boyfriend, and I'll never have to worry about it again.* It was my turn to take an overly simplistic justification system for a spin: I muscled the transgression into a frame of ho's before bro's. But then they kept not breaking up, and I kept knowing that he was uncircumcised, and then they invited me to their wedding, and I had to think about what it would feel like to know that as they kissed and walked up the aisle together hand in hand. I was single at the time, and inviting my gay roommate (who was still 100%, uncomplicatedly gay back then, as far as I knew) seemed like a way to make the best of an awkward situation and set myself up to get laid—maybe even meet someone to eventually marry.

On the train, Jacob looked up from his phone and noticed me picking at my cuticles. He told me to stop. *You're right,* I thought. *I'm a cesspool of a human.* Then he conceded, "What's wrong?"

Lots of things were wrong, and I didn't know which won the contest of least uncomfortable to be stuck on a train unpacking until I started telling him about the thing that happened between me and the groom.

"You have to say something," he said, his good person eyes earnest behind his buy-a-pair-give-a-pair glasses. "I mean, you kinda *have* to. You're a *brides*maid." He had a point, but there were *six* bridesmaids, and it's not like I was the *maid of honor.*

"I don't *want* to," I whined. I was a child. I was a bad person, really a 35-year-old toddler. My inner conflict had the strange effect of making me a bit horny for Jacob. I looked to see if there was a bathroom on our car. Was I thinking that we could join some sort of train version of the "Mile High Club"? The "Mile Long" club? The "Slow Train to the Hamptons" club? I was. The heavy sliding door banged loosely as the train clattered along. I realized that's where the stink on our car was coming from.

"What am I supposed to do? Really. *Ruin* their wedding? Because of one little *thing*?" I considered making a penis joke about it actually being a good-sized thing when Jacob saved me from doing that by clearing his throat like he was about to say something.

But he didn't say anything right away. He looked out the window at the dingy backyards, with their unsanitary above-ground pools and rusty swing-sets, rushing by. He scrunched up his nose and looked back to me. "You're right I guess. In the grand scheme of things, it *is* small, but—are you *ever* going to tell her? Don't you think *he'll* probably tell her? Do married people *tell* things like that to each other?"

I thought about heteronormativity, and the fact that lots of husbands-to-be probably cheated on their wives-to-be before they even knew they'd marry each other. For that matter, lots of husbands cheated on their wives (and vice versa). Not that any of this made infidelity OK. And it didn't make me feel any better about what *I'd* done to my *friend*. I wondered about the *normal* thing to do. I often asked myself, *What would a normal person do?* when I was trying to think of the right thing to do. It rarely worked, though, because I always ended up feeling like one had to be normal for even *one* possible answer to that question to present itself. I took a deep breath. The bathroom door banged. My vagina pounded along with my heartbeat at the thought of being pounded by Jacob. I desperately wanted to be part of a club; I didn't care which one.

"I don't know."

Jacob smiled, "You're a *slut*." He said it in a teasing voice. Maybe he was flirting.

"I know." I buried my stupid smile in my hands and groaned. "I'm the *worst*." I liked his attention, but I felt unattractive—sluttiness could go either way, but it always seemed to go the wrong way for me. I peeked over my fingers at him and did my best impression of getting serious for a second, "Would *you* want to know?"

Jacob sighed. He sucked his teeth, thinking and squinting. I wanted to nuzzle my face into his neck. I knew what he smelled like there.

"I don't think I would?" He scrunched his nose and raised his eyebrows like he knew that wasn't the exact right thing to say, but he didn't care because it was how he felt and he owned it. It occurred to me that owning anything was hot, even if it was the wrong thing.

"That settles it then. I won't say anything." I pressed my lips together and locked them with an invisible key that I then swallowed.

His eyes crinkled up, and they were so dewey and comforting that I thought we should have our own wedding. He shoved me playfully. "How can you swallow the key if your lips were already locked?" It would have been the perfect time for us to kiss, but he looked back down at his phone, done with me.

After the rehearsal dinner that night, Jacob flirted with the only other clearly queer wedding guest—the groom's brother—which, I cut him slack for, because I'm a good person, and: gay rights. Realizing I would not be having sex with Jacob again, I pouted, as is my wont, by leaving the bride at the VIP table, taking an Ativan, sidling up to the free bar, and drinking a lot and staying put because mixing Ativan and alcohol tended to make regular drunk walking look like stroke-victim drunk walking. As always, these counterproductive choices left me feeling alienated, but this was a rehearsal dinner, and everyone over-medicated to feel less awkward, so I had plenty of company. My first visitor was the groom's college friend.

"A terrible thing, a wedding," is how he started the conversation.

I frowned at him. He looked like a brown-haired version of the blond groom, dressed like a stereotype of a young bachelor: chocolate corduroy blazer, shirt with no tie, nice jeans, nice sneakers. He smelled like brown booze.

"I know, I know. It's supposed to be joyous, right? But, come on, at this point, we all know humans are not meant to be mo-*nah*-gamous." He leered around the room, then his gaze landed back on me, stopping briefly at my cleavage on its way to my eyes. "Y'should have seen this guy in college."

I wondered if he wanted to fuck me.

"Always had tons of girls. None of them ever knew about each other. He was never caught. It was amazing, actually." He frowned into the distance as if contemplating quantum physics or chaos theory. "Anyway, th'poor bride is crazy to think being hitched," he stifled a burp, bringing a gentlemanly fist to his mouth, "will change anything. Rick Brogan," he held the burp hand towards me to shake. "You? Whose side are you on?"

I squinted at him.

"Oh, neither. I'm a plus one," I said strategically, but it didn't matter. He assumed—because I'm a woman I guess—that I was a bride person, and continued.

"Oh, well, it's better that you know now rather than later, or, better that you're prepared now so that when your friend comes crying to you later, or, maybe she'll never know, but either way, it's better you know now."

"Right. Thanks?"

With a salute and a bow, he staggered off towards the restroom.

Next to approach was an elderly woman with a stately bosom who was draped in loose-fitting linen in varying shades of gray, which matched the cloud of hair haloing her round face.

"You must be a bridesmaid," she trilled in an accent I could not place—British? Or maybe just rich?

Accordingly, I arranged my face into an expression of kindness. I decided to rustle up some patience for this old broad, thinking it might earn me some much needed karma points. "Yep. We've been friends since we were kids."

"Just as I thought," she brought her head back, taking me in. "You have the look of one—maybe not as *ripe* as the typical bridesmaid, but certainly as single."

"Oh, I'm definitely single." I tried not to sound offended and kept smiling. "But I like the freedom," I lied.

"Mm." She saw right through me. "In my day, any single woman at a wedding was a bridesmaid, and any single man was a groomsman and everyone just," she crinkled her eyes at me naughtily, "*Matched up!*" Now her accent seemed southern.

I turned away from her, pretending to itch the back of my head, to hide my wince. Humoring her was getting boring, so I tried again to wrinkle her linen. "But what if no one liked each other? Doesn't that seem like a set-up for an unhappy marriage? Don't you think we know better now?"

"You're calling me old-fashioned." She said it in a tone that expressed a real resistance to offense. "Since when is it old-fashioned to be impulsive?" She winked. "What you don't know yet, young lady, is that all marriages are unhappy and happy and," she waved her hand dreamily as she sipped her clear drink and swallowed, "everything in between, as they say." She shrugged, and looked for a moment like a moon faced visionary or monk or something. "Sounds nice, doesn't it?" She sipped her drink again and sighed wistfully. "Well, I still think weddings are beautiful." She was back to being filled with dull, bovine *wist*. She looked around. "There's my husband there." She gestured with her glass at a disheveled man sitting and talking emphatically with a baby-faced over-dressed teenage boy who seemed to have stopped listening a long time ago. "We met at a friend's wedding forty two years ago," her tone changed and she leaned in closer, "not that he ever remembers our anniversary, the useless *slob*." Then she cackled maniacally, ending with a sing-song sigh. "No matter. Some people enjoy humiliation, you know. Maybe I used to be one of those people, but I don't feel humiliation anymore." She gestured at herself with her drink then brought it to her mouth for a sip. "What's left to feel humiliated?" She heaved yet another sigh. "Still, aren't weddings beautiful? Everything's still so *fresh*." Her attention shifted to a bouquet on the bar, which she reached out to caress. "Aren't these flowers *ju*bilant? I told her just where to go for the best wedding flowers, and she resisted at first, but in the end she took my advice, and just *look* at these. *Ju*bilant."

"Is that kid yours?" I gestured back to where her husband was sitting beside a young man.

"Oh, Justin? He's my sister-in-law's. Justin! Come!"

The kid snapped to, and stood without a word to the lady's husband. As he neared the bar, I saw that he was very, very high on weed.

"Hey. Sup, Aunt May?"

She pulled him into a tight side hug. "Tell us what you make of all this. What does the next generation think of marriage?"

He freed himself from her embrace and treated us to a digressive, but richly researched lecture, concluding, ". . . but bo*no*bos, they don't even *have* a patriarchal system of hierarchy. They honor the females. The ladies are totally in charge. And they have all kinds of sex for pleasure, and not just with the dude bonobos. They, like, lez out on each other. It's a total matriarchy, complete with cunnilingus, polyamory, like the summer of love all the time. And sexual favors can lead to an individual's increased rank in the troop; like, if the chief lady bonobo likes your work down there, she'll promote you to executive geisha or some shit. I dunno. I did a report on it for AP bio." He took his aunt's drink from her hand and before she could protest gulped from it. He winced a little and handed it back empty, held in a belch, and added, "What does 'normal' even *mean* anymore, Aunt May?" Then he sauntered off.

Neither of us knew what to make of it, so we both raised our glasses "to youth!" and awkwardly went our separate ways, which for me just meant swiveling away from her on my stool.

I struck up a conversation with a dude who turned out to be too young and sober and smart for me, but fun to talk to. A PhD candidate working on a dissertation about gender fluidity in 18th, 19th, and 20th century America, he made me feel like a total square, but in a good way—in a way that rounded my edges a bit, made me think about the groom and infidelity and moral and normal and amoral and anormal and anomaly and how all those words seemed suddenly *of a piece*.


After making her obligatory bride rounds, my friend found her way to me at the bar. At this point, she had really hunkered into her state of schnockeredness and was downright ugly with drink. I smirked to myself. *Taking pleasure in an ugly bride—a new low, even for me.* She leaned into me with all of her unsteady weight, told me I was her best friend, thanked me for being with her on the night before the most important day of her life, and, belching shamelessly, asked if she could make a confession. I nodded, looking around. Most people had left, and those that remained were old friends huddled in drunken confessionals of their own, or new friends, names slipped from memory, making out with each other. I didn't see Jacob.

She stage-whispered, leaning in even closer. "I fucked with Jacob." She snickered, self-deprecating. "No. I mean—I'm sorry, I'm a liddle drunk. Are you maddat me? He's your *date* to the wedding?"

I shook my head, totally confused about why it was such a big deal that she pranked Jacob.

"I mean, I got *fucked* with Jacob." She furrowed her brows, concentrating. "No. I mean, Jacob and me and—*fuck*." Unable to speak in clear sentences, she resorted to playground sign language and made a sloppy sex motion with the index finger of one hand and a circle made with the thumb and fingers of her other. "I'm so *stupid*. It was that time when you went to visit your grandma or grand-aunt or something. Do you think it's really bad? Even though I wasn't married yet and Jacob is mostly gay? Do you hate me for being such a bad person?" She made a horrible puppy dog face at me, her lips pickly and smeared.

"No." I didn't. I felt stupid. I hated me. It was the perfect time for me to hug her, so I did, because ho's before bro's.

In a voice muffled by our hug, she asked, "Didju know he's not all the way gay?"

Eventually her maid of honor—a work friend and compulsive exerciser with an infuriatingly perfect ass who'd sent so many gratuitous emoji-filled emails to me and the other bridesmaids that I stopped reading them months ago—came to escort/carry the bride to bed, leaving me alone. I felt fucking pissed. Both the sick-sweet guilt lollipop I'd been sucking *and* my maybe gay wedding date had been stolen from me by the person I'd traveled an uncomfortable three hours to perform with in a show I'd seen a billion times already.

But then I felt someone step on my foot, and it was a dude, and he was touching my arm to apologize, and he was not exactly my type, but not exactly not my type, and when he smiled at me, I didn't worry about whether he wanted to fuck me because I just wanted him to keep smiling at me with his kind of crooked teeth and half-sweet half-unpredictable eyes, and so I smiled back. Emboldened by the Ativan and the glasses of free wine I'd stopped counting after three, I asked if he'd do an experiment with me. He nodded, I was perfectly intoxicated now, and I said, "I'll tell you how I'm fucked up, and you'll tell me how you're fucked up, and then, if things work out, we won't be shocked or resentful or whatever years from now when we're married and all our other married friends are in couples therapy being told to tell each other why they love each other while a smug androgynous woman with an MSW tries not to fall asleep."

He maintained an impressive poker face, but I could see I'd amused him.

"How am I fucked up?" he stroked his chin and narrowed his eyes.

"And this isn't like a job interview. You can't say that you're a *perfectionist* or some shit."

"Is *that* how you're supposed to answer that question? I always just told the truth and told them I resist authority and punctuality."

"What HR person is asking you how you're fucked up?"

"I've been on some *rough* job interviews . . ."

"OK OK. But really. Let's get to the juicy stuff."

He sipped his drink. "Like . . . that I hate my dad?"

"That's pretty good!"

"And I have to be right all the time?"

"Great!"

"And I sometimes think Ted Kaczynski had some really interesting ideas," he took another sip, seeming to delight in my raised eyebrows, "But I don't really consider that a way that I'm fucked up, more just an example of my open-mindedness."

I nodded and pretended to look around the room for someone else to talk to.

"Seriously," he said. "Have you read his manifesto?"

This schtick was working on me.

"Can't say I've had the pleasure."

"Well, it comes highly recommended. It's a tragically overlooked text."

"That's one way of putting it." I smiled.

"Well? How are *you* fucked up then?"

I took a deep breath, squinted at him, and decided he could handle the truth, so I told him about my thing with the groom and my thing with Jacob and the bride's thing with Jacob, and took another deep breath, and resisted pointing out what a depraved sex-addict I must seem like, and looked up to gauge his reaction.

"That's it?"

"That's a *lot*, isn't it?"

He drank from his drink. "Something's *always* going down." He patted my knee in a way that wasn't paternalistic but actually comforting. "It sounds to me like you're just closer to the center of the storm than you've ever been before."

He told me about his sister's wedding—how his cousin confessed his love for her at the part when the priest asks for people to speak or forever hold their peace. We laughed. We talked about other things. We touched each other's arms, we touched each other's hands, and then he walked me to my room, which I hoped to god Jacob wasn't butt-fucking in. I unlocked it and, finding it blessedly empty, walked in, assuming my new friend would follow me and that we'd have a good old fashioned drunken roll in the hay. He pulled me by the hand back towards where he stood at the threshold, and leaned in to kiss me goodnight like mother-fucking *Hugh Grant* in a movie with a holiday for a title and a Nora Jones theme song. This gesture blind-sided me so extremely that I actually laughed out loud instead of kissing him back. And with a look of someone whose ego was bruised but astonishingly still intact, he patted me on the shoulder and said, "OK, then. That was awkward, but also lovely. See you tomorrow."

The bride wanted to be alone with the groom at the altar (which I was totally fine with), so I sat in the audience with the other bridesmaids and our dates and all the other guests on hay bales covered in brightly colored blankets, my ass still sore from its long night on the hard barstool, my head dull and useless from all the wine and Ativan and new information and not getting fucked and not letting a guy I actually liked kiss me and eventually taking an Ambien to quiet it all, but with a look on my face that I hoped was at least mildly pleasant.

Tasteful classical music by a composer someone with an education as expensive as mine should know the name of was piped in, and the familiar pageant began to unfold. The wedding was at the groom's parents' Montauk home, and while people seated near me sniffed and wiped their eyes, the smell of rotting fish settled into my nostrils. I heard faint catering sounds in the distance and hoped there'd be mini lobster rolls and corn soup sips at the reception. My stomach made grouchy sounds.

I looked around. Rick Brogan was lock-jawed and clammy behind Ray Bans, a monument to masculinity of yesteryear. Aunt May cooled herself with a paper fan, languid as a Buddha. Justin slumped and stared, an idiot savant. With a subtle glance over my shoulder, I was scanning the faces behind me for the PhD when I met eyes with my favorite Ted Kaczynski fan. He acknowledged me with a wink, and before I could figure out the least humiliating way to respond, Jacob leaned over whispered to me that the groom's brother was uncircumcised.

*After SH.*

*Nominated by Hysterical Rag*

# AND I THOUGHT OF GLASS FLOWERS

## by A. V. CHRISTIE

from *MORE HERE THAN LIGHT* (ASHLAND POETRY PRESS)


Some say superior people disdain the glass flowers at Harvard,
and so I sought the flowers out.
Arrayed they were, in low light, in glass cases.

I cried unexpectedly at their glass roots, cried
at the beauty of the task:
transverse section, frond, pod, stamen, thousands
of botanical specimens made to hold still.

And I felt there was, too, something unlawful about it.
        Where there was first an iris, an iris to the touch,
        there was now a glass iris—.
Now loss. Now triumph.

And I saw that
laid open, every song is a love song.

*Nominated by Genie Chipps*

# CHASTITY

by SIQI LIU

from THE HARVARD ADVOCATE

In the early 1970s, several construction workers uncovered three ancient tombs on the side of a hill in Mawangdui, Changsha while building an air raid shelter for a nearby hospital. The construction halted, archeologists were summoned, and an excavation proceeded that revealed what was to become the crown jewel of our hometown: Xin Zhui. We called her Lady Dai, the wife of Li Chang, the Marquise of Dai, the Ancient Hag. We saw the 2,100-year-old woman in a makeshift museum exhibit later. Her breasts, chalky white and full of craters, reminded us of the moon. Her tiny nose hairs—still intact thanks to the acidic, magnesium-rich preservation liquid that soaked her body— looked like either the legs of the flies that we regularly caught or the hairs that were beginning to sprout from our own armpits. Her face was the shape of a sunflower seed and her mouth, gaping open with the tongue protruding like a tiny white fish, suggested that she was laughing in her moment of death.

The archeologists said Xin Zhui was a noble woman who enjoyed fine musical performances and had a taste for imperial foods. They had found 138 melon seeds in her stomach, from which they deduced that she had eaten a melon two hours before her death, and that she died during the summer when the fruits were ripe. She was buried with over 1,000 pieces of vessels, tapestries, and figurines. Her tomb was adjacent to the tombs of her husband and her son, who had died years before her and whose bodies were fully decomposed.

When the museum opened the makeshift mummy exhibit for locals (the actual exhibit, the one the whole world would come to know, wasn't

426

completed until we were in our twenties), we went every afternoon. We pressed our noses against the glass case and fogged it up with our breaths. We agreed that the Ancient Hag must have been, once upon a time, very beautiful. How could they have wanted to wrap her dead body with twenty layers of silk cloth otherwise? Her skin must have been luminous and pale, her eyes double-lidded like those of a true Chinese beauty, her cheek charmingly sunken with dimples, or *wine nests,* as we called them.

In public, we made sure to pair these compliments with derision, for we knew that it was improper to praise pretty things. It was an era in which we scoffed at skirts and cut our hair short like boys, a place in which the ugliest peasants were lauded. We had burnt our silk handkerchiefs and jade jewelry in a great fire that lasted for three days and three nights. Our books, too: translated copies of *A Midsumer Night's Dream, Pride and Prejudice, Uncle Tom's Cabin, The Complete Sherlock Holmes* wilted in the flames. The fire had kept away mosquitoes as we danced around it, chanting songs praising Our Great Leader. So, even as we admired the mummy's silk wrapping and richly colored robes, we denounced her as a capitalist. Even as we fantasized about her alabaster skin and soft pink lips, we called her the Ancient Hag.

On the walk back from the museum, we'd stop by a street stall and get popsicles. We licked and sucked on them until the cold sweetness broke into small pieces that we tucked under our tongues. Sometimes we held competitions to see who could insert the greatest length of popsicle into their throats while neither choking on nor breaking it. The trick was to tip our faces toward the sky and pretend that we didn't have gag reflexes, that our bodies were no different from those of long, brown eels that had a straight tunnel from mouth to anus. In fact, we pretty much were eels. Our limbs were always covered with fine brown dust. We only wore earth-toned clothes. Whatever accumulated under our fingernails was the color of shit. The only bright hue that disrupted our brownness was the red scarf we wore around our necks. Yet despite our eel-ness, whenever we held our popsicle-eating competitions in the humid Changsha afternoons, men smiled at us in the streets and called us *tongzhi,* comrades.

Because there had not been school in years, because our older siblings had left to work in communes in remote parts of the country, because our parents had been reassigned from their college professorships or editorial jobs to faraway factories where they made matchboxes or envelopes by hand, we did whatever we wanted that summer. One day we walked eight kilometers to the only pond in Changsha that still had wild frogs and speared them with sticks. We were too young to remember starvation in the way our older siblings did, but we craved meat. We roasted their bloody little legs over a fire and ate the charred pieces with our dusty fingers. One day we wrote *dazibao* denouncing our old English teacher as a Rightist and pelted him with stones until he died. He had once humiliated two of us in front of the whole class for mispronouncing the word *sandwich*. One day we met up with boys who used to be our classmates and went swimming in the Yangtze River. When we emerged from the brown water, our shirts soaking wet, our hardened nipples pointed at them like fingers.

Every day we went to visit the Ancient Hag in her glass case. Every day she seemed to grow younger, her cratered skin smoother than it had been the day before, her sinewy arms leaner and stronger. At that point the museum had been open long enough that most locals had already seen her, so we had the room to ourselves. What a disgusting member of the bourgeoisie, we'd say, loud enough for the guard to hear. But silently we compared her to the beautiful Chang'e, the goddess of the moon who achieved immortality when her husband did not and lived for an eternity in her chilly palace, accompanied only by her white rabbit. Such must have been the case for the Ancient Hag, too. The plaque by her body explained how she had died years after her husband and remained widowed, never remarrying. She was the emblem of a virtuous woman, a loyal wife. Now her body, touched by no one besides her husband until its unearthing, was alone behind this glass while his had long returned to the soil. On our walk back, sliding the popsicles up and down our hot throats, we concluded that she was buried with such riches not only because she was beautiful, but also because she was chaste. Didn't our fathers tell us about our great-grandmothers who were honored with tall stone arches for refusing to remarry, keeping their bodies untouched for thirty years? Didn't they build wide white bridges over rivers in the countryside for the women who had killed themselves to follow their husbands into the afterlife? Surely the Ancient Hag was rewarded, too, for her chastity.

We didn't think of chastity in terms of sex, of course. Sex was bourgeois, individualistic, dirty. We never thought about sex (we only thought about sex when we saw dogs doing it in the streets, but that was before they were all eaten along with the cats and rats). We believed chastity was like loyalty. Devoting your body to a person and a cause. Our Great Leader told us that a revolutionary should be loyal to the Party and free of vulgar desires, so we strove to be chaste. We purged ourselves of all but the most necessary wants. Aside from the popsicles—the only thing that stood between us and heat strokes—we ate one meal a day. We allowed ourselves to smile only when we discussed revolutionary activities. We never wanted the boys with whom we went to the river; the only man we found handsome was Our Great Leader. Although he was in his seventies by then, most pictures of him showed a man with slick black hair who looked younger than our fathers. Didn't our mothers tell us that the big yellow star on the Chinese flag represented Our Great Leader, and the four little stars surrounding it represented the flock of women who wanted to marry him? Wouldn't it be an honor to keep our bodies pure so that one day, we might be worthy to bear for Our Great Leader the foremost spawn of the revolution?

With that logic, we assuaged the guilt we had once felt for admiring the Ancient Hag. After all, she was a role model in her own way: an embodiment of chastity and loyalty, even if she was a capitalist. We began to adore her openly. We admired out loud her snow-white burial robe and the cloud-shaped designs on her red lacquer dinnerware. We argued boisterously about which one of us might one day be as beautiful and chaste as she, our voices shrill and insistent in the empty museum chamber. By August we had ceased to be afraid of the guard, a stooped old man who stood still as a Buddha statue while eyeing our brown limbs.

Inspired by the Ancient Hag, one of us suggested a vow of chastity. It seemed like the logical next step for our aspiration toward complete purification, a process in which our brown bodies would be scrubbed and made precious. It was the year in between years when we had no school, when our parents had stopped speaking to us out of fear, when our siblings had disappeared. We belonged to no one and strove for nothing (we were told that we must lay down our lives like bricks in the building of our Great Socialist Society). But we'd rather be vases, emptied and refilled with crystal-clear water. Or even better, arrows. How lovely it would be to shrink into skinny lines with sharp points, possessed by someone and held tenderly at the bow, something that can never deviate from the path dictated by its owner.

We enthusiastically agreed, but we asked, chastity for whom? There was no boy whom we loved, no one whom we waited for.

For Our Great Leader, of course, she said. You dumb eggs.

Suddenly it became clear what we must do. Yes, we would keep our bodies chaste for Our Great Leader. Wasn't that what we were all supposed to secretly want? We loved him more than our parents, more than our siblings, and certainly more than the smelly boys we played with. We vowed to save ourselves for Our Great Leader and never to touch another man. Sometimes we saw the years of our lives stretching before us like an eternity, so we imagined ourselves wearing flowing white dresses and living alone in a chilly palace, like the immortal Chang'e. Other times we craved the day of our death, for on that day we would sure to be buried with great fanfare, like the Ancient Hag, or have stone memorials erected in our honor, like our great-grandmothers. The only difference was, we would not want to be buried with anything except our little red books. We would accept nothing other than the simple wooden coffin of a peasant.

We should reiterate, though, that we did not think of any of this chastity stuff in terms of sex. Sex was bourgeois, individualistic, dirty. We believed chastity was like loyalty. We were devoting our bodies to Our Great Leader and the Revolution. So, imagine our horror when we discovered erotic excerpts from one of our comrades' diary published in an anonymous *dazibao*, taped to the front door of her home! Someone had stolen her diary (her younger sister, we suspected) and copied the very yellow scenes elaborated over pages and pages in big black characters on white paper: *I opened to him like a soft red peony and a drop of blood stained the white sheets . . . His hands roamed over my body, those small hills and streams . . . Our Great Leader's seeds flooded me at last . . .*

After we recovered from our initial shock and shrieks, alternating between feeling scandalized and giggling behind our hands, we realized that we had been surrounded by a group of our former classmates. Some were the boys we saw at the river every week, some were boys and girls we had not seen for years. Like us, their necks were collared with red scarves, but there was not a trace of amusement on their faces. The author of the diary, a mousy girl who wore her hair in pigtails and ate her popsicles so slowly they'd often melt into thin white paths along her fingers, was nowhere to be seen.

"How dare she write about Our Great Leader using such disgusting language!"

"Who does she think she is?"

"That unclean bitch!"

We stayed quiet even though our hearts felt like ants crawling atop a hot stove. What should we say? What should we do? If we agreed with the others, our friend would surely get into trouble. At best she might

430

be dispatched to do hard farm labor in some rural region, permanently losing her city *hukou* and never able to return. At worst she might die right there. But if we tried to defend her, we might be seen as counter-revolutionary. After all, weren't her words denigrating to the Party? Wasn't it akin to smearing a big pile of shit on Our Great Leader's name? Didn't he teach us that we should place Party righteousness above even our families? As we caught the faltering in each other's eyes, the boys in the crowd spat angrily on the ground, each *splat* landing like a bullet.

Fortunately, we did not have to make a decision. At that moment, the mousy girl pushed her way through the burgeoning crowd and anchored herself next to the *dazibao* like a dog guarding her bone. Her pigtails were lopsided, and strands of wet black hair matted to her forehead. It was hard to tell whether she had just cleansed herself in the river or whether she was sweating profusely.

"Comrades!" She shouted to the crowd, raising her arm like a general. The dreamy look she usually wore on her pimply face was contorted into an inscrutable mask. "You are all making a mistake. These words are proof of my untainted and unsurpassable love for Our Great Leader. I am willing to devote my whole body and my whole soul to him. I am willing to bear his child and carry the seeds of the revolution—metaphorically or literally! I am willing to not look at a single man for the rest of my life out of my enduring love for him! I am willing to throw myself onto his funeral pyre because my loyalty to him lasts beyond this lifetime! Which one of you can say that? Which one of you can say you love Our Great Leader more than I? Which one?"

We all fell silent. The ants within us crawled at a more frantic speed. Could she be right that she loved Our Great Leader more than any of us? We had never encountered this strange situation before, so we could not fathom how we should react. If we accused her of being counter-revolutionary, we might have to prove that we loved Our Great Leader more than she claimed she did. It was one thing to take a secret chastity vow; it was an entirely different thing to publicly proclaim that we desired to have sex with Our Great Leader. Plus, if she was indeed a loyal revolutionary, it would be a crime to punish her.

The crowd's collective hesitation gave the mousy girl more strength. With her chin tipped toward the sky, she peeled the *dazibao* from the door in a single, swift motion and folded it eight times into a small square. Transformed into that compact size, it suddenly seemed precious, like a love letter. "Whoever posted this is clearly a counter-revolutionary," she yelled, waving the square in her hand. "I will find them and report them to the Party."

With these words, the mousy girl turned and entered her house, slamming the door behind her so hard one of the hinges dislodged like a broken tooth. We shuffled in uncomfortable silence for a few seconds. Someone said they were thirsty. Someone said it was too hot. We were all relieved to have an excuse to disperse.

While we were glad we did not have to pelt her with stones, we also never spoke to her again. It would have been too dangerous to be associated with such an individual. Who knew what else she had written in her diary that could get her in trouble? And why was she writing, anyway? None of us had written a single word in our diaries for years. Even though we thought only revolutionary thoughts and said only revolutionary words, we were afraid of what might happen if we pried too deep into our consciousness.

She seemed to deliberately avoid us, too. After that day, she never set foot in front of Old Chen's popsicle stall again. Nor did she show up to look at the Ancient Hag in the afternoons, or catch flies with us in the dried-up reservoir. That fall, rumors circulated: Some said she volunteered to do farm labor up north in the wintery region of Heilongjiang, where the ground froze solid by November. Some said that, after having heard about her supreme loyalty to Our Great Leader, the local Party committee had nominated her as an exemplary youth. Out of curiosity, we changed our route so we could pass by her family's home every day, hoping to either catch a glimpse of her or confirm her disappearance. From a certain angle, crouching behind the willow tree across the street, we could see through a tiny opening in the newspapers crudely patched over a makeshift window. Only once, during a thunderstorm, did we see a swath of soft white gown flit past the opening. We were shocked—where had she obtained such a gown? Or had we seen a ghost?

We never walked past her home again. It was old-fashioned—perhaps even counter-revolutionary—to be superstitious, so we pushed thoughts of the mousy girl out of our minds. In the middle of that winter, sometime after the first snowfall we had seen in eight years, we heard from an old woman in our neighborhood that she had indeed been approached by high-ranking members of the regional Party Committee. They thought she had demonstrated exemplary devotion to Our Great Leader during the *dazibao* incident. Because of their nomination, she was now attending the prestigious school for revolutionary thought in Wuhan, training to become a full-fledged cadre. Outwardly, we applauded her meteoric rise; inwardly, we applauded ourselves for having the foresight to not pelt her with stones.

To everyone's relief, we, too, went back to school the following autumn. By that time, we found ourselves eager to receive homework, for even the Ancient Hag and all the lore she had inspired had ceased to entertain us. We heard that without us, the exhibit sat empty day after day. In fact, it was not until years later—after they had finished excavating the site and added a number of additional artifacts to the original exhibit—that foreigners from all over the world started coming to see it.

When we started classes again, we noticed how the boys we had swam with were taller and darker, how the place where their t-shirt sleeves ended and their upper arms began bulged. We passed them notes folded into tiny squares and sometimes tasted their mouths in the twilight-lit alleyway between the school and the field. Eventually, enough seasons had passed that when the mousy girl did come up in conversation—as she did when we reminisced about that unusually hot summer—we no longer spoke about her in hushed tones. We agreed that in hindsight, what she had done was an ingenious political maneuver. She had escaped from the tiger's jaws so effortlessly that we could not help but admire her cleverness. In fact, we began to think that she had devised the whole scheme from the beginning, knowing that it would help her accrue revolutionary credentials. A few of us seemed to remember that it was she who had proposed the vow of chastity in the first place.

By the time Our Great Leader passed away, she was the last thing on our minds. With the announcement of his death, we cried until our voices went hoarse, and tear streaks etched our cheeks like claw marks. Every street stall was draped with black strips of cloth. We felt directionless in this world without Our Great Leader, a heap of sand suddenly blown loose, arrows with their heads chopped off. In school, we turned in nothing but eulogies for Our Great Leader and skipped class to take turns reciting them on the field.

The third morning after we learned the horrible news, we saw a woman with gray hair running through the street, beating her chest with her fist and weeping. She wore black cloth slacks that hung to her ankles and a black shirt with only three of the dozen buttons fastened. As she approached, we could see the lumps of her breasts occasionally jump through the shirt like unruly animals. We assumed that like everyone else, she was mourning Our Great Leader, so we paused to admire how sincere her self-beating appeared, how heart-wrenching her shrieks sounded. Suddenly, as she passed by Old Chen's stall, she began crying, "My daughter! My daughter!"

It was September, but we suddenly felt faint. We ran after the woman, pushing past the walls of black cloth that brushed coldly across our faces like rain. When we reached the one-room house, we saw the mousy girl we had once known dangling from a ceiling beam, wearing a soft white gown. A piece of paper resting on the fallen chair beneath her contained big characters written in black ink that read, "Bury me with Our Great Leader."

We stared at the words as the wails of her mother and father shook our bones. The woman blubbered about how her daughter had returned home the previous night for the first time in years. Burying his wet face between his wife's breasts, the man emitted a howl-like sound, one that echoed throughout a room that was empty except for two small beds in the corner, a coal stove, and three metal pans hanging by the newspaper-covered window we had once peeked through. Something about the acoustics of the room—perhaps an attribute of its emptiness—amplified each noise they made as if we were in a museum. At last we brought ourselves to look at her face. Even though her cheeks were the color of eggplant and her tongue stuck out from her swollen jaws, we couldn't help but notice that the white dress made her look beautiful and timeless—just like Chang'e, just like the Ancient Hag.

We tried our best to honor our friend, we really did. We wrote letter after letter to the Party about her devotion to Our Great Leader. We beseeched them to bury her next him, or even near him—anywhere within a three-kilometer radius will do, please, it was her dying wish. We recounted her untainted revolutionary spirit, her bravery, her unflinching loyalty to the Cause. Even as the leaves began to fall, we continued writing with a passion that we hoped was fiery enough to burn away the vines of our own guilt. But sending off those letters was like dropping paper into a deep well; there was not even an echo to be heard. By then her body had begun to rot in the makeshift coffin. We told her parents that maybe we didn't have the right address.

In the spring, a few months after the mousy girl had finally been buried, one of us returned from a trip to our nation's capital bearing incredible news. She had seen the body of Our Great Leader in a glass case, perfectly preserved for the next thousand years as if in a deep sleep. The line of visitors who wanted to grieve him was so long it wrapped three circles around the mausoleum. He looked so serene that he must have been smiling in his moment of death, she said, and his skin was smooth, like he had died a young man. We shook our heads at this news, remembering the mousy girl and how beautiful she had looked in her white dress. This time, rather than imagining her in a simple wooden coffin next to Our Great Leader, we imagined that it was she, not he, who lay in the glass case.

*Nominated by The Harvard Advocate*

# IT'S NOT YOU

fiction by ELIZABETH MCCRACKEN

from ZOETROPE: ALL-STORY

Hotels were different in those days. You could smoke in them. The rooms had bathtubs, where you could also smoke. You didn't need a credit card or identification, though you might be made to sign the register, so later the private detective—just like that, we're in a black-and-white movie, though I speak only of the long-ago days of 1993—could track you down. Maybe you anticipated the private detective, and used an assumed name.

Nobody was looking for me. I didn't use an assumed name, though I wasn't myself. I'd had my heart broken, or so I thought, I'd been shattered in a collision with a man, or so I thought, and I went to the fabled pink hotel just outside the Midwestern town where I lived. The Narcissus Hotel: it sat on the edge of a lake and admired its own reflection. Behind, a pantomime lake, an amoebic swimming pool, now drained, empty lounge chairs all around. January 1: cold, but not yet debilitating. In my suitcase, I'd brought one change of clothing, a cosmetic bag, a bottle of Jim Beam, a plastic sack of Granny Smith apples. I thought this was all I needed. My plan was to drink bourbon and take baths and feel sorry for myself. Paint my toenails, maybe. Shave my legs. My apartment had a small fiberglass shower I had to fit myself into, as though it were a science fiction pod that transported me to nowhere, but cleaner.

I would watch television, too. In those days, I didn't own one, and there was a certain level of weeping that could be achieved only while watching TV, I'd discovered—self-excoriating, with a distant laugh track. I wanted to obliterate myself, but I intended to survive the obliteration.

It wasn't the collision that had hurt me. It was that the other party, who'd apologized and explained enormous deficiencies, self-loathing, an unsuitability for any kind of extended human contact, had three weeks later fallen spectacularly and visibly in love with a woman, and they could be seen—seen by me—necking in the public spaces of the small town. The coffee shop, the bar, the movie theater before the movie started. I was young then, we all were, but not so young that public necking was an ordinary thing to do. We weren't teenagers but grown-ups, late twenties in my case, early thirties in theirs.

New Year's Day in the Narcissus Hotel. The lobby was filled with departing hangovers and their owners. Paper hats fell with hollow pops to the ground. Everyone winced. You couldn't tell whose grip had failed. Nothing looked auspicious. That was good. My New Year's resolution was to feel as bad as fast as I could in highfalutin privacy, then leave the tatters of my sadness behind, along with the empty bottle and six apple cores.

"How long will you be with us?" asked the spoon-faced, redheaded woman behind the desk. She wore a little white name tag that read *Eileen*.

"It will only seem like forever," I promised. "One night."

She handed me a brass key on a brass fob. Hotels had keys, in those days.


I had packed the bottle of bourbon, the apples, my cosmetic bag, but forgotten a nightgown. Who was looking, anyhow? I built my drunkenness like a fire, patiently, enough space so it might blaze.


You shall know a rich man by his shirt, and so I did. Breakfast time in the breakfast room. The decor was old but kept up. Space-age, with stiff, Sputnikoid chandeliers. Dark-pink leather banquettes, rosy-pink carpets. Preposterous but wonderful. I'd eaten here in the past: they had a dessert cart, upon which they wheeled examples of their desserts to your table—a slice of cake, a crème brûlée, a flat apple tart that looked like a mademoiselle's hat.

I had my own hangover now, not terrible, a wobbling threat that might yet be kept at bay. I had taken three baths; my toenails were vampy red. I had watched television till the end of broadcast hours, which was a thing that happened then: footage of the American flag waving in the breeze, then here be monsters. In my other life, the one that happened outside the Narcissus Hotel, I worked in the HR department of a radio station. I lived with voices overhead. That was why I didn't have a television. It would have been disloyal. I'd found a rerun on a VHF station of squabbling siblings and then wept for hours, in the tub, on one double bed, then the other. Even at the time, I knew I wasn't weeping over anything actual that I'd lost, but because I'd wanted love and did not deserve it. My soul was deformed. It couldn't bear weight. It would never fit together with another person's.

The rich man sat at the back of the breakfast room in one of the large horseshoe booths built for public canoodling. His pale-green shirt, starched, flawless, seemed to have been not ironed but forged, his mustache tended by money and a specialist. His glasses might have cost a lot, but twenty years before. In his fifties, I thought. In those days, *fifties* was the age I assigned people undeniably older than me. I never looked at anyone and guessed they were in their forties. You were a teenager, or my age, or middle-aged, or old.

The waiter went to the man's table and murmured. The man answered. At faces, I am terrible, but I always recognize a voice.

"Dr. Benjamin," I said, once the waiter had left. He looked disappointed, with an expression that said, *here, of all places*. With a nod, he recognized my recognition. "I listen to you," I told him.

He had an overnight advice show, 11 p.m. to 2 a.m., on another AM channel, not mine. He had a beef-bourguignon voice and regular callers. Stewart from Omaha. Allison from Asbury Park. Linda from Chattanooga.

"Thank you," he said. Then added, "If that's the appropriate response."

"I'm in radio, too," I said. "Not talent. HR."

The waiter stood by my table, a tall, young man with an old-fashioned, Cesar Romero mustache. When I looked at him, he smiled and revealed a full set of metal braces.

"I will have the fruit plate," I said. Then, as though it meant nothing to me, an afterthought, "and a Bloody Mary."

It is the fear of judgment that keeps me behaving, most of the time, like the religious. Not of God, but of strangers.

"Hair of the dog," the radio shrink said to me.

"Hair of the werewolf," I answered.

"You could be. On air. You have a lovely voice."

In my head, I kept a little box of compliments I'd heard more than once: I had nice hair (wavy, strawberry blonde), and nice skin, and a lovely voice. I didn't believe the compliments, particularly at such times in my life, but I liked to save them for review, as my mother saved the scrapbooks from her childhood in a small town, where her every unusual move—going on a trip to England, performing in a play in the next town over—made the local paper.

Who in this story do I love? Nobody. Myself, a little. Oh, the waiter, with his diacritical mustache above his armored teeth. I love the waiter. I always love the waiter.

The Bloody Mary had some spice in it that sent a tickle through my palate into my nose. A prickle, a yearning, an itch: a gathering sneezish sensation. One in ten Bloody Marys did this to me. I always forgot. I took another drink, and the feeling intensified. Beneath the pressure of the spice was a layer of leftover intoxication, which the vodka perked up. I thought, not for the first time, that I had a sixth sense and it was called drunkenness.

"No good?" the radio shrink asked me.

"What?"

"You're making a terrible face."

"It's good," I said, but the sensation was more complicated than that. "What are you doing in this neck of the woods?"

"Is it a *neck*?" He touched his own with the tips of his fingers. "I like the rooms here."

"You probably have a nicer room than I do. The presidential suite. Honeymoon?"

"I'm neither the president nor a honey-mooner."

"Those're the only suites I know," I said. It was possible to be somebody else in a hotel; I was slipping into a stranger's way of speaking. "Still, far from Chicago."

"Far from Chicago," he agreed. He picked up his coffee cup in both hands, as though it were a precious thing, but it was thick china, the kind you'd have to hurl at a wall to break. "Business," he said at last. "You?"

"I live here."

"You live in the hotel?"

"In town."

"Oh, you're merely breakfasting, not staying."

"I'm staying." I started to long for a second Bloody Mary, like an old friend who might rescue me from the conversation. "Somebody was mean to me," I said to the radio shrink. "I decided to be kind to myself."

He palmed the cup and drank from it, then settled it back in the saucer. The green shirt was a terrible color against the pink leather. "It's a good hotel for heartache. Join me," he said, in his commercial-break voice, deeply intimate, meant for thousands, maybe millions.

There were other radio hosts in those days, also called "Doctor," who would yell at you. A woman who said to penitent husbands, *You better straighten up and fly right*. A testy man—*No, no, no, no: Listener*—he called his listeners "Listener"—*Listener, this is your wake-up call*.

But Dr. Benjamin practiced compassion, with that deep voice and his big feelings. *Once you forgive yourself, you can forgive your mother*, he would say. Or perhaps it was the other way around: your mother first, then you. He told stories of his own terrible decisions. Unlike some voices, his had ballast and breadth. For some reason, I'd always pictured him as bald, in a bow tie. I pictured all male radio hosts as bald and bow-tied, until presented with evidence to the contrary. Instead, he had a thatch of silver hair. The expensive shirt. Cowboy boots.

I listened to his show all the time, because I hated him. I thought he gave terrible advice. He believed in God and tried to convince other people to do likewise. Sheila from Hoboken, Ann from Nashville, Patrick from Daly City. On the radio, it didn't matter where you lived, small town or suburb or New York City (though nobody from New York City ever called Dr. Benjamin): You had the same access to phone lines and radio waves. You could broadcast your loneliness to the world. Every now and then, a caller started to say something that promised absolute humiliation, and I'd have to fly across the room to snap the dial off. *My husband cannot satisfy me, Doc—*.

So long ago! I can't remember faces, but I can remember voices. I can't remember smells, but I can remember in all its dimensions the way I felt in those days. The worst thing about not being loved, I thought then, was how vivid I was to myself.

Now I am loved and in black and white.

Up close, he seemed altogether vast. Paul Bunyan-y, as though he'd drunk up the contents of that swimming pool to slake his thirst, but he didn't look slaked. Those outdated glasses had just a tinge of purple to the lenses. Impossible to tell whether this was fashion or prescription, something to protect his eyes. His retinas, I told myself. He'd slumped to the bottom of the hoop of the horseshoe, his body at an angle. I sat at the edge to give him room.

He said, "Better?"

"Maybe," I said. "Are you a real doctor?"

He stretched then, the tomcat, his arms over his head. His big steel watch slipped down his wrist. "Sure."

"You're not."

"I'm not a medical doctor," he allowed.

"I know that," I said.

"Then, yes. Yes, I'm a doctor."

The table had an air of vacancy: he'd eaten his breakfast, which had been mostly tidied away, except for the vest-pocket bottles of ketchup and Tabasco sauce, and a basket filled with tiny muffins. I took one, blueberry, and held it in the palm of my hand. The waiter delivered a Bloody Mary I hadn't ordered, unless by telepathy. "You have a PhD," I said.

"Yes."

"It's strange."

"That I have a PhD?"

"That we call people who study English literature for too long the same thing we call people who perform brain surgery."

"Oh *dear*," he said. "Psychology, not English literature."

"I'd like to see your suite."

He shook his head.

"Why not?"

"I'm married," he said. "You know that."

Of course, I did. Her name was Evaline. He mentioned her all the time: he called her *Evaline Robinson the Love of My Life*.

"That's not what I mean," I said, and I tore the little muffin in half, because maybe it *was* what I'd meant. No, I told myself. Every time I walked down a hotel hallway, I peered into open doors. Was there a better room behind *this* one? A better view out the window of the room? Out of all these dozens of rooms, where would I be happiest—by which I meant, least like myself? I only wanted to see all the hotel rooms of the world, all the other places I might be.

I was waiting to be diagnosed.

He said, "You're a nice young woman, but you won't cut yourself a break." He said, "All right. OK. We can go to my suite. They've probably finished making it up."

441

Even the hallways were pink and red, the gore and frill of a Victorian valentine: one of those mysterious valentines, with a pretty girl holding a guitar-size fish. The suite was less garish, less whorehouse, less rubescent, with a crystal chandelier, that timeless symbol of One's Money's Worth. The two sofas were as blue and buttoned as honor guards. A mint-green stuffed rabbit sat in a pale-salmon armchair.

"What's that?" I asked.

He looked at it as though it were a girl who'd snuck into his room and undressed, and here came the question: throw her out, or . . . not.

"A present," he said.

"Who from?"

"Not *from*. *For*. Somebody else. Somebody who failed to show up."

"A child."

He shook his big head. "Not a child. She must have lost her nerve. She was supposed to be here yesterday."

"Maybe she realized you were the kind of man who'd give a stuffed bunny to a grown woman."

He regarded me through the purple glasses. Amethyst, I thought. My birthstone. Soon I would be twenty-eight. "You are young to be so unkind," he observed. "She collects stuffed animals." He turned again to the rabbit and seemed to lose heart. "This is supposed to be a good one."

"What makes a good one?"

"Collectible. But also, it's pleasant." He plucked it from the chair and hugged it. "Pleasant to hug."

"Careful. It's probably worth more uncuddled." I put myself on the chair where the rabbit had been. I don't know why I'd thought the chair might still be warm. He sat on the sofa, in the corner closest to me.

"I thought you might be her," he told me. "But you're not old enough. How old are you?"

"Twenty-seven."

"Not nearly old enough."

"Do I look like her?"

"Oh. I mean, I'm not sure." He made the rabbit look out the window, and so I looked, too, but the sheers were closed and all I perceived was light.

"A listener," I said. "A caller. You're meeting somebody. Linda from Chattanooga!"

"Not *Linda* from *Chattanooga*," he said contemptuously. He put the rabbit beside him, as though aware of how silly he appeared.

After a while, he said, "Dawn from Baton Rouge."

I couldn't remember Dawn from Baton Rouge. "What does she look like?"

"I only know what she tells me."

"Should've asked for a picture."

He shrugged. "But: cold feet. So it doesn't matter."

"And now you've invited me instead," I said, and crossed my legs.

"Oh god, no," he said. "No, darling—"

The endearment undid me. I was aware then of what I was wearing, a pair of old blue jeans but good ones, a thin, black sweater that showed my black bra beneath. Alluring, maybe, to the right demographic, slovenly to the wrong one.

"Sweetheart," he said. He got up from the sofa. It was a complicated job: hands to knees and a careful raising of the whole impressive structure of him. "No, let's have a drink." He went to the minibar, which was hidden in a cherry cabinet and had already been unlocked, already plundered, already refreshed. Imagine a life in which you could approach a minibar with no trepidation or guilt whatsoever.

He lifted a midget bottle of vodka and a pygmy can of Bloody Mary mix; he didn't know I'd ordered a Bloody Mary because it was one of the only acceptable drinks before 10 a.m. He was a man who drank and ate what he wanted at any time of day.

"We'll toast to our betrayers," he said.

Because it was something he might say to a midnight caller, I said, "I thought we only ever betrayed ourselves."

"Sometimes we look for accomplices. No ice," he said, turning to me. "To get through this, we're gonna need some ice."

For a moment, it felt as though we were in a jail instead of a reasonably nice hotel, sentenced to live out our days—*live out our days* being another way to say *hurtle toward death*.


In those days, it was easy to disappear from view. All the people who caused you pain: you might never know what happened to them, unless they were famous, as the radio shrink was, and so I did know, it happened soon afterward, before the snow had melted. He died of a heart attack at another hotel, and Evaline Robinson the Love of His Life flew from Chicago to be with him, and a guest host took over until the guest host was the actual host, and the show slid from call-in advice to unexplained phenomena: UFOs. Bigfoot. I suppose it had been about the unexplained all along. All the best advice is on the internet these days, anyhow. That person who broke my heart might be a priest by now, or happily gay, or finally living openly as a woman, or married twenty-five years, or all of these things at once, or 65 percent of them, as is possible in today's world. It's good that it's possible. A common name plus my bad memory for faces: I wouldn't know how to start looking or when to stop.

The minibar wasn't equal to our thirsts. He sat so long, staring out the window, that I wondered whether something had gone wrong. A stroke. The start of ossification. Then, in a spasm of fussiness, he untucked his shirt.

He said, "In another life—"

"Yeah?"

"I would have been a better man. How long?"

"How long what?"

"Was your relationship with whoever broke your heart."

"He didn't break my heart."

"'Was mean' to you," he said, with a play-acting look on his face.

I did the math in my head, and rounded up. "A month."

"You," he said, in his own voice, which I understood I was hearing for the first time, "have got to be fucking kidding me."

It had actually been two-and-a-half weeks. "Don't say I'm young," I told him.

"I wouldn't," he said. "But someday something terrible will happen to you and you'll hate this version of yourself."

"I don't plan on coming in versions."

"Jesus, you *are* young." Then his voice shifted back to its radio frequency, a fancy chocolate in its little matching, rustling crenellated wrapper. "How mean was he?"

"He was nice, right up until the moment he wasn't."

"Well," he said. "So. You're making progress. Wish him well."

"I wish him well but not *that* well."

But that wasn't true. I wanted them both dead.

"The only way forward is to wish peace for those who have wronged you. Otherwise, it eats you up."

I wished him peace when I thought he was doomed.

How can it be that I felt like this, over so little? It was as though I'd rubbed two sticks together and they'd detonated in my lap.

"I bet you have a nice bathtub," I said.

"You should go look."

I got myself a dollhouse bottle of bourbon. At some point, he'd had ice delivered, in a silver bucket, with tongs. I'd never used tongs before. I've never used them since. The serrations bit into the ice, one, two, five cubes, and I poured the bourbon over, a paltry amount that mostly didn't make its way to the bottom of the glass, it just clung to the ice, so I got another. The bathroom was marble—marble, crystal, velvet, it would be some years before hotels stopped modeling opulence on Versailles. There was a phone on the wall by the toilet. I ran a bath and got in. This was what I needed, not advice or contradiction, not the return of the person who'd broken my heart, because I would not be able to trust any love that might have been offered. It took me a long time, years, to trust anyone's.

The door opened, and another tiny bottle of whiskey came spinning across the floor.

"Irish is what's left," said the radio shrink through the crack of the door.

"You're a good man," I said. "You are one. If you're worried that you're not."

Then he came in. He was wearing his cowboy boots and slid a little on the marble. Now he looked entirely undone. In another version of this story, I'd be made modest by a little cocktail dress of bubbles, but no person who really loves baths loves bubble baths, nobody over seven, because bubbles are a form of protection. They keep you below the surface. They hide you from your own view. He looked at me in his bathtub with that same disappointed expression: *just like you to bathe in your birthday suit.*

"I have some advice for you," I said to him.

"Lay it on me," he said.

"*Lay it on me.* How old are you?"

He shook his head. "What's your advice?"

"You should call your callers 'Caller.' Like, 'Are you there, Caller?'"

"They like to be called by name."

"Overly familiar," I said.

"That's your advice."

"Yes," I said.

He was sitting on the edge of the tub. The ice in his glass, if there'd ever been any, had melted. I had no idea what he might do. Kiss me.

Put a hand in the water. His eyebrows had peaks. Up close, his mustache was even more impressive. I'd never kissed a man with a mustache. I still haven't. It's not that I'm not attracted to men with mustaches, but that men with mustaches aren't attracted to me.

"Can I have your maraschino cherry?" I asked.

"No maraschino cherry."

"I love maraschino cherries. All kinds. Sundae kinds, drink kinds, fruit cocktail. Tell me to change my life," I said to him, and put a damp hand on his knee.

"I won't tell you that."

"But I *need* someone to tell me."

He put down his glass beside the little bottle of shampoo. Such a big hotel. So many minuscule bottles. "You must change your life," he said.

"Good, but I'm going to need some details."

"I keep sitting here, I'm going to fall into the water." He stood up. "You know where to find me."



There isn't a moral to the story. Neither of us is in the right. Nothing was resolved. Decades later, it still bothers me.



No way to tell how much later I awoke, facedown in the bath, and came up gasping. I'd fallen asleep or I'd blacked out. It was though the water itself had woken me up, not the water on the surface of me, which wasn't enough, not even the water over my face, like a hotel pillow, up my nose, in my lungs, but the water that soaked through my bodily tissues, running along fissures and ruining the texture of things, till it finally reached my heart and all my autonomic systems said, *Enough, you're awake now, you're alive, get out.*

That was one of the few times in my life I might have died and knew it. I fell asleep in a bathtub at twenty-seven. I was dragged out to sea as a small child; I spun on an icy road at eighteen, into a break in oncoming traffic on Route 1 north of Rockland, Maine, and astonishingly stayed out of the ditch; I did not have breast cancer at twenty-nine, when it was explained to me that it was highly unlikely I would, but if I did, *it was unlikely*, it would be fatal, *almost never at your age*, but when at your age, rapid and deadly.

Those are the fake times I almost died. The real ones, neither you nor I ever know about.

The radio shrink would have said, *I guess she died of a broken heart*, and I would have ended my life and ruined his, for no reason, just a naked, drunk, dead woman in his room who'd got herself naked, and drunk, and dead.

But I wouldn't see the radio shrink again. I was gasping and out of the tub, and somebody was knocking on the bathroom door. I don't know why knocking—the door was unlocked—but the water was sloshing onto the floor, the tap was on, it couldn't have been on all this time, and I'd soon learn that it was raining into the bathroom below, I had caused *weather*, and the radio shrink had packed up and left and hung the *Do Not Disturb* sign outside his room and paid for mine. Dawn from Baton Rouge was a disembodied voice again, but the redheaded woman, Eileen, she was here, slipping across the marble, tossing me a robe, turning off the tap, tidying up my life.

"You're all right," she said. I could feel her name tag against my cheek. "You should be ashamed of yourself, but you're all right now."


I would like to say that this was when my life changed. No. That came pretty quick, within weeks, but not yet. I would like to say that the suggestion of kindness took. That I went home and wished everyone well. That I forgave myself and found that my self-loathing was the curse: forgiveness transformed me, and I became lovely. But all that would wait.

He was wrong, the shrink: nothing truly terrible ever happened to me, nothing that would make me cry more than I did in those weeks of aftermath. I'm one of the lucky ones. I know that. I became kinder the way anybody does, because it costs less and is, nine times out of ten, more effective.


At some point, it had snowed. The night prior, that morning. It had been hours since I'd been outside. The snow was still white, still falling, the roads marked by the ruts of tires. Soon the plows would be out, scraping down to the pavement. My clothing, left behind by the side of the tub, sopping wet, had been replaced with a stranger's sweat suit, abandoned by some other guest at the Narcissus Hotel and found by Eileen, a stranger's socks, too, my own shoes and winter coat. I had to walk by the house of the couple who'd been necking everywhere, a story that seemed already in the past. By *past*, I mean I regretted it, I was already

447

telling the story in my head. The woman I hadn't been left for drove a little red Honda. There it sat in her driveway, draped in snow. That was all right. It was a common car in those days, and I saw it and its doppelgängers everywhere. Even now, a little red Honda seems to have a message for me, though they look nothing like they used to. *When will this be over*, I wondered as I pushed through the drifts. The *humiliation* is what I meant. Everything else is over, and all that's left are the little red Hondas.

You would recognize my voice, too. People do, in the grocery store, the airport, over the phone when I call to complain about my gas bill. *Your voice*, they say, *are you—?*

*I have one of those voices*, I always say. I don't mind if they recognize me, but I'm not going to help them.

He kept telling me I had to be kind. Why? Why on earth? When life itself was not.

*Nominated by Zoetrope: All Story*

# REMEMBERING
# JOHN L'HEUREUX

## By MOLLY ANTOPOL

From SEWANEE REVIEW

John L'Heureux, who died this past April, was an exquisite writer—to the very end; a master teacher; a deeply thoughtful man of faith; and a mentor, in the most profound sense of the word. He carried himself with more innate dignity than any person I have ever known—in his manner of speech, the ideas he imparted, even the way he dressed: always in newly shined shoes and an elegant sports coat. When he taught my workshop at Stanford, I'm pretty sure he was the only one in the classroom wearing gold cuff links.

John also read more, knew more about, and better understood American Jewish literature than almost any other former Jesuit priest I know. I remember countless lunches with him, talking about Paley and Ozick and Pearlman and being awed by the depth of his understanding not only of their technical skills but of their experiences—for good and bad—as Americans and as Jews. Before I encountered Grace Paley's stories as an undergraduate, I had never before seen the older generations of my family depicted on the page. She captured it all: the role of women in supposedly progressive movements, the way politics could seamlessly slide from the kitchen table to the playground and out into the world. Paley had utter compassion for every one of her characters. She was deeply funny without ever resorting to meanness. She wrote political stories, but they were never didactic. John intuited all that, but rather than simply praising her, he wanted to talk about *how* she accomplished these things. Prior to talking Paley with John, I felt I understood her because her characters were the closest I'd come to finding my relatives in literature. The more we talked, the clearer it became that John understood her work on a different level—he was engaging with it through a thorough exploration of what was happening on the page. And through our discussions I came to appreciate Paley less because her characters were recognizable to me and more for her impeccable craft—which John could parse with Talmudic nuance.

At some point it occurred to me that if John could talk this way with me about my favorite writers, he could probably do the same with anyone else in the workshop about theirs. And he could. John spoke with erudition about Southern literature, Japanese fiction, European experimentalists, but especially, it turned out, about *The Sopranos*, a show he analyzed in minute—and brilliant—detail, and which he considered on par with Dostoyevsky and Tolstoy.

John was my very first teacher when I arrived for the Stegner Fellowship in 2006, and I was incredibly nervous. When the director called with the news of my fellowship, my first thought was: this must be a mistake. She must have meant to call the *other* Molly Antopol. I was convinced everyone belonged in that room but me, that I was the one impostor there. But the moment I walked into that first workshop with John, the moment I understood how he ran the class—well, it would be a lie to say those impostor feelings melted away; even now, thirteen years later, I still have them every day when I sit at my computer, but suffice to say they were quieted. John, of course, had a unique aesthetic in his own writing. Take, for example, the opening to his extraordinary story, "The Long Black Line," published last year in *The New Yorker*.

> Finn said an awkward goodbye to his parents and watched them drive off in the new Buick they had bought in case he changed his mind. They were pleased, of course, at Finn's decision to study for the priesthood, but they were wary, too. It was 1954, and priests were still thought to be holy, and Finn . . . well . . . Finn knew that he wasn't holy, but during a retreat in college he had succumbed to a fit of piety and, dizzied by the idea of sacrifice, applied to join the Jesuits. They had put him through a series of interviews, and let him know that he seemed altogether too caught up in theatre, but in the end they had accepted him. So now here he was, almost a Jesuit, and this annoying Brother Reilly kept calling him Brother.
>
> Brother Reilly had given him a short tour of the public areas—the chapel, the guest parlor, the dining hall—and then escorted him to the front veranda, where the other postulants

had gathered to admire the grounds. A green lawn cascaded down the hill to a small wilderness of trees, with a lake beyond. Everyone agreed that it was beautiful. They stood in little groups, sweating in their jackets and ties, while the novices—the real Jesuits—made awkward attempts at conversation. Finn introduced himself to the group around Brother Reilly, and, after the expected handshaking, silence descended. Finn was not good with silence, so he cleared his throat and wondered aloud if they all felt as strange as he did in his jacket and tie. There was eager agreement and a little self-conscious laughter that encouraged him to wonder further when they would get to wear a cassock, "if it's O.K. to ask," he said.

"A habit, Brother Finn, not a cassock," Brother Reilly said quietly, a gentle rebuke.

"Sorry. A habit," Finn said. "But when?"

"In good time, Brother Finn."

Finn realized that he should shut up, but he couldn't help himself and, attempting friendliness, he said, "Just call me Finn. Brother Finn creeps me out."

When he died, John had been publishing books consistently for more than fifty years. He wrote more than twenty of them, as well as dozens of individual stories and poems. Much of the work—like this story— revolved around questions of faith and guilt, and he imbued all of it with his characteristic self-deprecation, compassion, and humor. His work was always sardonic, it was always witty, and it always managed to be at once deeply pious and hilariously irreverent, like John himself. What strikes me about "The Long Black Line" is John's evident skill for finding the perfect word, one that not only accurately described what it was supposed to describe but also—and as importantly—implied a judgment: Finn didn't experience a moment of piety, he had a "fit" of it. He didn't love sacrifice, he loved "the idea" of sacrifice—which is very different. John chose his words carefully, on the page and in life, and all of this made up his inimitable aesthetic.

But in workshop, John never imposed his aesthetic on anyone else. And he didn't play favorites. All he cared about was the writer's intent, and whether the words on the page were furthering that intent. His greatest talent as a teacher was his imagination: his ability to look at an early draft of a story, imagine what it might one day become, and offer guidance on how to get there—guidance that was always rigorous, some-times tough, and invariably right.

He had the unique ability to look at each piece of writing as both a writer and as an editor—which he was. Before arriving at Stanford, John was an editor at the *Atlantic* for eleven years. The way he edited sub-missions in our workshop insisted that we put every word on trial, that we ask of every sentence: Is it doing the work it needs to do to propel the story forward?

I remember sitting around Antonio's Nut House after workshop and marveling with my fellow fellows about the fact that John seemed to have a definitive answer to any question we could throw at him—grand and global, tiny and technical. I once asked him a question I had been struggling with for months: I said, "John, I'm writing a story in the pre-sent tense that then moves into back story—how many times do I have to say the world "now" to let the reader know when I've jumped back to the present?"

John, without blinking, said: "Three."

That was it. Definitive. End of answer.

There was a comforting certainty in his approach—a certainty that made anxious young writers feel there were, in fact, objective answers, if only you asked. A certainty that bordered on the religious.

Which brings me back to John's love of American Jewish literature. I've always believed it derived from his immense respect for other faiths. From his curiosity about people of different backgrounds. From his de-sire to understand what other people think and feel and believe. To comprehend their narratives. From the wells of their specific stories, John strove to extract that which was universal.

All of which, of course, is another way of describing what the very best writers do.

It's by now cliché to tell a writing student to "show, don't tell." But John couldn't help but show his students what they might become. In this way, John was a true mentor. He was also one of the quickest, fun-niest, warmest people I have ever been privileged to know. He showed me, in every interaction, how to be a better teacher, a better editor, and a better person.

Life is quieter without him in it.

*Nominated by Edward Hirsch*

# THE NIGHT DRINKER

Fiction by LUIS ALBERTO URREA

From McSWEENEY'S

A CHRONICLE OF THE LAST DAYS OF TENOCHTITLAN,
BUILT ON LAKE TEXCOCO, KNOWN NOW AS MEXICO CITY,
HOME OF THE ANCIENT GODS. 2040 A.D.

(FROM THE NOTEBOOKS OF JOAQUIN HERNANDEZ III,
HISTORIAN. FOUND IN THE RUINS OF IZTAPALAPA, 2045.)

In those years, the one world, Ce Anahuac as the Aztecs called it, was dying of fever. The world was so hot that monarch butterflies easily caught fire in our mountains. Once the whales died, the oceans crawled onto the shore faster than the scientists had predicted. They came ashore like insidious, living beings, filling the lowlands and drowning the ports. Many crops perished down below; the Mexican plateau around us was safe from ocean flood, but not from drought. The sea was a taunt from the earth–those thirsty people and animals were given water that could not be drunk, and in that tide came garbage and dead creatures and black waves. Mazatlán and Vallarta and Cozumel and Acapulco grew beards of bleached seaweed and battlements of ghostly fishing boats and sideways cruise ships now populated by shrieking coastal birds and starving sea lions. The agua negra poisoned aquifers, as if punishing the land for its sins. Soon, the salted tides corrupted hydroelectric plants and caused blackouts all over the country. Here in La Capital, as my generation still called it, we had wind generators, solar panels, and smart roofs that used greenery, filters, and rain collection to try to clear the air.

The catastrophes in the lowlands panicked the refugees into moving farther and faster than they had moved before, but they were greeted in every territory by walkers fleeing toward the places they'd left. We could not help but be amused when the throngs of gringos rushed the border heading for Chihuahua and Sonora. But who could judge them? The far American West was in ruins. Earthquakes fractured the land, drought killed the crops and turned the hills into tinder, the unexpected monsoons eroded the denuded hills onto the ruins. The Sea of Cortez crept up the dry bed of the Colorado River, then jumped its banks and made a swollen dead sea that poisoned Yuma and Mexicali and Calexico. Those of us with dark senses of humor, and what Mexican does not have a dark sense of humor, found it amusing that the parts of the great border wall still above water were used to tie off the boats of floating scavengers and the undocumented.

Canada finally closed its own borders and used its military to keep Americans from invading. They could not stop the heat, though, or the subsequent spread of tree borer beetles, and the great pine forest fires of 2030 gave them a gray desert north of Minnesota.

The refugees turned to the highlands. San Miguel de Allende, that great Disneylandia of art and crystals and movie stars and peace, already gentrified long ago by expats to the point of pushing local people to the outskirts, began to see walkers from Brazil and Haiti and Honduras and Salvador and even Eritrea, who were climbing up through Guanajuato and Guadalajara on their long journeys to find higher ground. Drought and tides and despair pushed the people. And the refugees rose up the mountains, searching for sanctuary. People thought they were safe in San Miguel, but they weren't.

I, like my grandfather before me, have long been a lover of North American literature, and the writers were always there in San Miguel. I enjoyed San Miguel for many reasons, but Jack Kerouac and Neal Cassady were my chosen ghosts, as I liked to say. I knew which wooden stools in the La Cucaracha bar they had sat on in 1969. I knew the exact bend in the rail line where Cassady lay down and died on a cold night. When San Miguel was overrun, those barstools were burned by refugees to cook meat and the rail line was where they slept. How "beat"–is that not the word? All those expats who had not fled in time–though where would they have gone?– could not drive, since the gasoline had already run out. And they couldn't stay put, for the human wave was rising, and fire came behind it. So they joined their new brothers and sisters and began the painful long climb to Mexico City, the high plateau at the heart of our land.

So many had come to us already, we were bedeviled by our own popularity. We are generous people, and we did our best. I believe we would have managed the crisis if not for the cataclysms to come. But none among us could see the future.

You might recall the greatness of our city, the magnetic draw of our nights. We were the New World City, bigger than New York. More beautiful, more dangerous, more stylish. We were near twenty-five million in the valley, and daily more came. What other city was also the nation itself? There is no Argentina City. No Nigeria City. No USA City. Ce Anahuac, One World—One Mexico.

Outsiders' cars were banned. The moneyed Africans came to my neighborhood of Iztapalapa. Cubans and Chinese took penthouses in the center of the city. Undocumented gringos sucked up real estate and apartments and great homes in Lomas de Chapultepec. In the 2020s, we had managed to clear the air by cutting coal emissions, limiting auto exhaust, and launching the famous government program that set out to plant some million trees in the city and on the outskirts and on the slopes of El Popo, the great father-volcano. It looked like the American state of Colorado up there when the pines and aspens grew, though a haze of yellow smog still wafted across those slopes. Trees and solar and wind. We were mending, we believed. But what we lacked was water. The theory held that trees would inhale carbon and clear the air and cool our skies, and they would exhale water vapor to bring us rain. But the walkers kept coming. And the parks filled with bodies. And the old empty buildings were filled. And the barrios and alleys. With their fires and their smoke and their shit and their bodies. We had nowhere to go.

Still, we were not beaten. Over and again, we have claimed our patrimony as the center of the world, the greatest civilization, the most resilient and creative people. Only the northern country failed to see it. And we rose, as best we could, to every challenge. For example, this: along with heat, and the droughts that assailed us, there came rageful downpours. Drenching tropical assaults from the hot-seeming clouds. We suffered these, but we are ironists. We appreciated the wicked wit of the earth, drowning us in a time of thirst. Every Mexican child knows that Great Tenochtitlan, the capital of the Aztec world, was built upon a lake. The waters vanished and the buildings appeared and the earthquakes we survived were vicious because the lake bed was clay and mud and the city shook itself apart when the earth moved. And then the water was all sucked from the ground, and the clay beneath our feet hardened and crumbled and the city began its slow entombment as the edifices sank, and the tallest buildings wanted nothing so much as to tip sideways and lie down in exhaustion.

These aguaceros, as we called the drenching rains, were fodder for our computer analyses, and by 2035 the government and the scientists of UNAM assaulted our thirst with Proyecto Tlaloc, perhaps the largest drought amelioration project in history. I was there to see it–I was Tlaloc's contracted historian. Rain seemed at first a further punishing apocalypse–yes it flooded us, yes it brought down mudslides and avalanches, yes the refugees and the poor suffered the most, though we all suffered. But we soon saw it was a reprieve if we had the will to take creative action. The kilometers of standing buildings were perfect water-collecting sites. Like the solar-panel and wind-turbine platforms they had become, we repurposed them. We created vast networks of flumes and reservoirs to slake our valley's thirst. The army, the Red Cross, and hordes of volunteers–many of them, it pains me to say, gringos–evolved instantly into a disorganized but miraculous bureaucracy of hope. Of course, we named this epic movement of assets (you can't imagine the vast array of engineers and laborers and technicians and vehicles) Tlaloc, after the ancient god of rain. The irony of drowning in a universal drought was the subject of many editorials and cartoons when the newspapers still appeared in our city. In 1805, we published the first daily newspaper in Nueva España, and in 2040, ours were among the last.

By any measure, you can see how heroic was our battle.

I am not a superstitious man. If you are reading this, you must understand. In light *of what I* am about to relate, I must assure you I am a man of letters, a man of reason, a man who rarely even enters a church. But this was Mexico. There came a day when I wondered if Tlaloc the god had actually heard us. I believed he was not impressed. (Indigenous people who still followed the Nahuatl way told us these entities were not gods, but embodiments of the energies of nature, embodiments of elements of our own souls. Westerners did not understand and called them gods. I am a Westerner.)

Tlaloc, too, is an ironist. For the dried lakebed of Texcoco was also a rainfall reclamation area. And the lake, in mockery of our heat plague and of our thirst, began to refill. But the water in the lake was so full now of sewage and chemicals that none could drink it.

I had come to Mexico City from the lush breadbasket of Sinaloa. It was, of course, infamous for drugs and cartels when I was a boy. But the decriminalization of drugs in 2025 gutted their businesses and sent sicarios looking for work as soldiers of fortune and crime enforcers. The days of billions of dollars of illicit profits were over. The crops began to fail anyway, even the lucrative marijuana plantations that rivaled bananas and coffee as Central America's greatest export. Bananas went extinct in the wild, and coffee was losing ground as well. Even the great tobacco corporations of El Norte couldn't rescue the vast marijuana fields, although their research into reclaimed sewage for irrigation saved some communities in the greenbelt states. Water, even stale and badly used water, was the drug of choice by then.

We often looked to the sleeping lovers, Popo and Ixta. Our mountain guardians. Our sentinels. The only place of snows, now bare. Our volcanoes.

I remember saying to my lover, "What is next? Locusts? Rains of blood? Or the volcanoes erupting."

I actually laughed. She put her hand over my mouth.


When the volcanoes erupted, the Little Brother arose and brought with him the old religion of the Night Drinker. Hermanito Jorge. Oh, he was here before. He had many followers on social media. He had all those things that seem absurd now, that seem like legends of a distant past, things our children will doubt in school, will sleep through and get wrong on exams. I have much to say about him, but we must wait just a moment before we become exegetes of the religion of the Hermanito.

When it became clear that the eruptions would not finish us off, that we would continue, as we had continued through every cataclysmic event that ever tried to destroy the heart of Mexico, Jorge told me, "I am the eruption, Joaquin. I am the horseman."

I thought he was part of the history of my country. I thought I'd write books about this era. And this self-made shaman, he thought he was the entire history.

"You are a demagogue," I replied.

We had developed that relationship that Mexican men so enjoy with each other. An intimacy of bluster. A romance of insults.

"You will see, cabrón," he replied.

Anyone who speaks Mexican Spanish will know that *vas a ver* is also a threat. You'll get your comeuppance soon enough.

But I get ahead of myself. The fevers confuse me. To the volcanoes.

What did that old racist Lovecraft call it? "Eldritch horror," I believe. Before I relate the rest of this narrative, our own visit to the mountains of madness, I feel compelled to insist upon my theory as it relates to catastrophe. The human mind, in distress, cannot hold onto reason. And the degradation of the planet is not simply a scientific or ecological conflagration, but also an eroding of the human mind. Reason itself catches fire and burns. The fevers make men see the dead, hear voices, make them think they can fly beside lovers unseen for twenty years. Even the hills and lakes went mad. The earth itself had typhoid. The hallucination of history broke loose among us.

Popocatepetl (Mountain That Smokes) has always been our sentinel, the volcano both loved and feared throughout time. The place where Mexicans could look to see snow–that most unlikely Mexican vista. Father of pines and deer. Maker of clouds. Even the epicenter of the UFO crazes in Mexico City during the 1990s and early 2000s. The very volcano Malcolm Lowry wrote about in *Under the Volcano*. And Popo was stern with us. He erupted in sequences that inspired Chilangos to mount Popo-cams that celebrated its paroxysms on such old platforms as Twitter. They called themselves Twiteadores.

Like the creeping heat and the rising seas, its eruptions became regular to us. We shrugged one shoulder in old-school Mexican fashion and drank toasts to him in our bars. Never believing the worst could happen, for this was mere gringo paranoia, or the fretfulness of the rich and the bourgeoisie. Disruption was not what they wanted, and they were moving to Aspen and Nueva York–one of which flooded and began to rot as soon as they got there. This amused us.

When Popo erupted, truly erupted, it was an explosion that shattered the top third of the mountain and bombarded the city with missiles of burning rock. His being seventy kilometers from Mexico City was a true blessing. We believed the lava and gases would never reach us.

Then his bride, the great Iztaccihuatl (The White Woman) chose to die with her lover and erupted shortly thereafter. Scientists spoke of crustal torsion, an agony of the earth's surface wrenched by forces like the weight of the water, triggering fault lines. But the Mexicans knew better. Izta's suicide was the stuff of ranchera ballads.

She scolded us like a mother gone mad. The earth heaved as the pyroclastic flows of boiling ash asphyxiated and burned whole communities, and lava raised tsunamis of fire, and the ground beneath our feet became waves that toppled even the cathedral of the Virgen de Guadalupe. Our towers fell. The national cathedral on the Zocalo, built by the

Aztec slaves of Cortez's Inquisition forces, constructed of the shattered stones of the Temple of the Sun and the great temples of the old city, came apart and spilled across the wrenching earth. The figurines of old gods freed at last from between the Catholic stones, placed there by devout pagans who could pray to their sleeping lords rather than the invader Christ. Looters dared the toppling walls to crush them while stealing the gold still in the rubble.

Hermanito organized armies of heroes through his network: social media, if one could raise a signal. Shortwave radio for others. Runners in the old Aztec style as well, making their ways across the crumbling earth. His followers dug through the ruin with their bare hands and rescued the famous image of the Virgen, thrown to the floor but–of course, it was a miracle!–undamaged. They carried it to the top of Tepeyac, the lovely little hill where she had once appeared to the Indian Juan. There, they guarded her day and night.

If I may offer you one thought about Mexico, it is this: the past is not in the past. Even if the pagan spirits do not exist, we summon them into being. And this we did.

No reasonable people took the Little Brother seriously before the eruptions. Hermanito Jorge, his nom de guerre, was borrowed from both the native healer communities and the evangelical missionaries. The Little Brother rose from the millennial UFO cults that flourished on Mexican social media. The Christ-was-an-astronaut crowd. He also served as an astrologer on one of the Telemundo afternoon talk shows, where he donned golden robes and frolicked with dyed-blonde actresses and dapper Eurotrash-fashioned male hosts. He quickly traded on his minor fame to host a series of very popular vlogs about the narco world that was still flourishing in that era. Interestingly, the narcos themselves seemed to appreciate his reporting. He was not harmed, at any rate. And he was clearly becoming wealthy–there was a vibe (is that the word? una vibra?) about him reminiscent of the old televangelists. For Hermanito Jorge had a specific theme: that narcos and sicarios, without knowing it, had begun reenacting Aztec human sacrifice rituals. Their worsening depredations, lovingly chronicled on video, fed the gruesome interests of working-class Mexico. The people who read the weekly tabloid *Alarma!*, with its infamous photographs of murder, torture, dismemberment, accidents, suicides, read it right till the end. *Alarma!* never went out of print.

Hermanito Jorge maintained that the reenactment of sacrifice would awaken the old gods, who would come to the portals between worlds, thinking that we had returned to their true religion. But that sooner or later, their joy would collapse into rage. These sacrifices were not loving gestures, were not ceremonies beseeching them for mercy and increase, but irreligious acts of greed and commerce. He had to keep the most heinous images off of broadcast television.

But Hermanito was a sensation on his vlog, avidly and breathlessly reporting on the horror. Yes. Conrad: "The horror. The horror." He posted everything he found. A pornography of death and suffering. So much so that the torturers sent him clips seemingly shot for his use. He was decried and denounced, but his followers were legion. And their numbers grew. Amidst this abattoir, he also floated more sedate paranoias: he chased conspiracies and "proved" over and over the imminent return *of Planet X*, the fabled Nibiru. For decades, this cosmic invader had been mere miles behind our sun, Hermanito warned, about to appear and disgorge alien overlords, The Nephilim, the Watched Angels who would impregnate Earth women. He was so obsessed with invasion that we intellectuals named him Hermanito Trump. What did he care? He had three million followers, and his podcast had an international audience–they said he was especially popular in Colombia, a land with its own burden of magical thinking and upheaval.

Twitter, by then, had already collapsed and been abandoned, and Hermanito Jorge was quick to plant his flag upon the new "Latinx" messaging community, known as Chayo. The Chayonauts were especially active in Mexico City. We elders didn't understand their newspeak. Mexico City, for example, had gone on Chayo from being known as CDMX to merely X. If you were connected to the apocalypse culture, the evolution was clear. If you hadn't followed, you really didn't understand what Hermanito Jorge meant when he launched the meme: XT.

XT HAS RETURNED.
XT REAPS HIS HARVEST.
XT FOR THE NEW SKIN.
XT IS THE SACRED NIGHT DRINKER.

❊   ❊   ❊

Hermanito Jorge found me for a monstrous reason.

I state this now: he was not a monster. In spite of the horror he brought, in spite of the gruesome death, he was without horns or a tail. In the beginning, his followers fed the refugees. They led the weary to shelter. They used their communication devices (plastic walkie-talkies from La Target) to send civilian guards to protect the Museum of

Anthropology—armed men stood watch before the great Aztec calendar that had not even cracked in the tumults. The Little Brother himself had made a camp on one of the ancient chinampas in Xochimilco. He ruled from there. Those old floating islands made by the native people of the lake, still vibrant, still afloat, still rich with chiles and frijoles and what corn was left. The Little Brother's doctrine was proven by these spring-fed watercourses: the past is alive, forever. The spirit of the old ones will forever flow.

Jorge Makasehua (the invented Mexican name Hermanito fancied) was a small man, quick to laugh. Generous and loving with children and the poor. Like me, he was a kind of historian. As the climate shifted, so did the podcasts and the Chayo feed. In the growing vacuum of political leadership, people were seeking guidance. Hermanito Jorge offered solutions that fed their emotions.

I risk the reader's impatience by stepping back, just for a moment. When I first began my studies and writings in Mexico City, it was the end of the 1990s. It seems Edenic now. I had arrived from Culiacan with my history degree and my training in writing historical books from my grandfather.

My area of expertise was the roots of our culture, specifically the ancient gods. I state here, although my countrymen will take offense: the Mexican gods were terrifying. For example, Tlaloc, our beloved rain god, was satiated only by the tears of the innocent. So before they were sacrificed, children were tortured until they cried. And their tears were collected. And then they were publicly sacrificed. Perhaps the reader will forgive me this immodesty, but I had a reputation as a popularizer of history and myth. I could tell the stories. Which is why Jorge came to me, to talk about Ehecatl, the god of wind.

I confess to a fondness for Ehecatl. I don't know why—being the god of the winds somehow made him seem like a rock star. I suppose wind equaled song in my mind. I imagined him as some Jim Morrison figure. You might meet him at a crossroads north of the city, in the shadows of the great pyramid of Teotihuacan. In my mind, Ehecatl wore a zoot suit and had a raven feather in his brim.

You may recall the discovery in 1999 of "Aztec death whistles." I happen to have been with the anthropologists when they uncovered sacrificial victims clutching these carved stone skulls in their skeletal hands. The size of an infant's skull, these carvings had hideously open mouths and looks of utter anguish on their semi-fleshed faces. These were in the hands of people sacrificed to Ehecatl. My old rock god. I

461

chronicled the find in a series of articles. But none of us was prepared for the one researcher with enough imagination to wonder, much later, why these skulls had holes in the tops of their heads, and open mouths. He blew through a skull one day, and we broke and ran when we heard what emanated: the skull shrieked with the voice of a human being slowly slaughtered. Utter terror overtook us. This was the sound of sacrificial Tenochtitlan.

Even at the very end, one could buy replicas on websites, and the replicas screamed like dying women under the knife.

I was presented with one of these ghastly skulls in thanks for my chronicle of the find. Feeling a shudder of irrational fear upon taking this accursed artifact home, I locked it inside a cabinet where it would be safe and out of sight.

But somehow Hermanito Jorge knew I had the whistle. And he wanted it.


He startled me over our first dinner, off the Zocalo in that wonderful café where the waiters floated Malbec wine atop a small sea of pinot grigio, and the roasted corn exploded in the mouth. Gone now. But the gods were capricious, and in the middle of devastation one would find entire blocks unscathed. And so this café, which for a time survived without even one window cracked, one day vanished when the flooded underground metro opened a sinkhole.

After enjoying a robust jousting session of me mocking his beliefs and him jovially dismissing my "false scientific/historical reason," we sat back and basked in the glow of a fine cognac and a dessert of small camote empanadas. We, among the last western degenerates of the gone world before the lava made its way from the outskirts, wise people heading north, all the pilgrims climbing into the ruins thinking they might escape. We were connoisseurs of the end of days.

"It's all illusion," Jorge said.

"It is what we have."

"We have nothing. The president has fled," he said. "The army has fled. Neighborhoods are small empires now. It is like the 1500s. Before Cortez. Do you see? We are tribes again."

"Help will come," I said.

He laughed.

"Help? Who will help?"

I thought about it.

"I have no fucking idea."

He laughed again.

"I need your screaming skull," he said abruptly.

"Hell no."

"You hate it. It frightens you."

"Indeed."

"Do you know why?"

"If you heard it, you'd know why."

"It is summoning the spirits. You don't want to be there when they arrive."

"No mames, guey," I said. I took a drink. "The whistles were to frighten enemies in battle."

"Oh really. Is that your theory?" He nodded and shrugged. "This is why it was clutched in a sacrifice's hand?" He leaned into me. "That is his voice in the skull. His voice. His soul is captured inside the skull. And what you can't hear in the subsonic note, only the spirits hear. They are answering your dead friend's call."

"He's not my friend," I muttered, suddenly not at all amused.

He gestured out the window. Shuffling people like hunched wraiths could be seen against the wavering red light in the sky. How had we found a way to live amidst this chaos? Intermittently, the windows rattled.

"They love you," he said. "They are coming for you. You cannot escape, amigo."

I took him home with me and unlocked my cabinet and thrust the skull into his hands and saw him out. I locked the doors and pulled out an old bottle of Yaqui Bacanora and drank until I could sleep. My dreams were of screaming.


"What Mexico City needs now is a cacique," he said to me at our next and last dinner meeting. "And a high priest."

"And which are you, cabrón?" I asked.

He laughed. He was unnervingly charming. He'd had a craftsman fashion a small gold replica of the screaming skull, which he wore on a black choker around his neck.

"Oh, I am not a politician," he said. "I was hoping, once XT returns, you might be a leader. Joaquin the Cacique."

"And you–"

"The high priest."

I raised a toast to his egomania.

"Do you regret inviting me into your house the other night? If you do, well, so be it."

"I think I do, yes."

He smiled warmly.

"I am the capital now. I am Mexico. My flowers will do my bidding. I can ensure your safety if you but ask."

"Your flowers?"

"Yes. My harvest of millions."

Harvest. Good God. He had gone mad, I thought.

"Well," he said. "You invited me by your own free will." He whispered: "Be careful what you summon."

"I'm leaving."

Lighting a black French cigarette, he said, "Wait. Dear Joaquin, you misunderstand the fate of the world."

"How so? We face extinction."

"Claro, amigo." He leaned forward, breathing smoke into my face. "What you don't understand is that extinction is love."

"Bullshit."

"The gods are hungry."

"Angry?"

"That, too," he said. "But hungry."

"What gods?"

"The true gods."

"And what are they hungry for?"

"They desire revenge. They are hungry for hearts. Flesh. Blood."

"Jesus Christ," I responded.

He smiled almost shyly.

"Not exactly."

Honestly, Hermanito Jorge slipped easily from my mind. I was never interested in the cultish activities or superstitious manias that were springing up everywhere in this world, struggling to understand the apocalypse. Jorge's obsessions seemed to echo every other millennial upheaval through the ages. But this time, they were almost fifty years too late. The millennium had come and gone. I was more interested in hard fact, science and history.

Then, one day in Garibaldi, I saw it. A billboard with the letters XT and the visage of an Aztec god. I knew with the rationality of a bad dream that Jorge truly believed he could resurrect the ancient and terrible gods.

I knew to the depth of my soul that he believed the ferocity of the old religions was a form of ghastly future grace. I backed away from the billboard. I knew that for Jorge, our only hope would be in the gift of blood.

It suddenly made chilling sense to me: XT was not a place or a thing, but a being. An old god. The one god of all our mythologies that terrified me. Xipe Totec. If you who find this chronicle do not know how to say such a name, try saying this: *Sheep eh Toltec*. Leave out the *L*. But I beseech you, do not say it out loud.

The God of the Harvest. Also known as the Flayed One. The Skinned God. Father of Suffering. And the Night Drinker. I took that last to be his most poetic name, for does not the harvest drink the night rain? Xipe, who brought our food from the ground. Xipe, who cared for the corn, the sacred grain of the New World, the holy food debased into corn chips and whiskey and syrups that added fresh poison to manmade drinks engineered to taste like the fruits and berries Xipe brought us in bright fields and shady valleys. Xipe, who knew that the bounty of the earth, the easy inspiration of poets and lovers, seemed gentle but was not. The birth of the plant from the seed was violent and torturous. The earth had to break to allow life free rein. And the exhausted earth required the corpses not only of expired plants, but of the rotting creatures who walked upon the plants, who fed on them and on each other. The earth and the flowers were eaters of the dead. Drinkers of their blood. Death, then life; agony, then relief; resurrection, then harvest.

My fear was visceral. Statues of the god always show a grimacing deity seemingly in pain. And hanging from his wrists, extra hands. From his ankles, extra feet. Flat empty breasts flap upon his chest. Over his penis, drooping reproductive organs. For Xipe Totec has been flayed. He lives without skin, his nerves bared and raw. Like the seeds, he needs to be covered. And our flesh is his personal soil. He loves you as he peels away your soil with his obsidian knife.

As a boy, I read that his priests flayed human sacrifices alive, and wore their pestilential skins until they rotted away and new ones were collected.

I had nightmares of these priests dancing in the plaza with their lips singing from between the lips of the dead.

And then one night, my satellite phone buzzed. All cell lines were down after the eruptions. Landlines were long forgotten.

"We are coming to your house," Hermanito Jorge said.

"Who is?"

"We priests."

"Why?"

"You are the historian. You must witness."

"Witness what, cabrón!"

"The ceremony. It is time. The Lord has come."

"Time for what?" I yelled.

"The first sacrifice. You are my witness."

"Go to hell!"

"Hell is outside your door."

They kicked it open and rushed in.

They were in loincloths and feathers. They were painted in grotesque caricature of what they imagined Aztec warriors might have looked like. They had bound my arms to my sides and my ankles tight to each other. "Am I to be a sacrifice?" I cried. They ignored me. "Please. Please, Jorge." He gently patted my head as they carried me.

The sky was bright red as the mountains continued to melt. These priests were burned all over their bodies, for cinders and sparks fell around us. Some of them had ribbons of blistered skin blowing behind them as if they themselves had been flayed. I passed out when they threw me into the back of a flatbed truck.

I awoke to the screams and moans. The smell came to me as I opened my eyes in the dark. Why be coy? I smelled blood. Enough blood that the air was moist, humid. I was bound upright to a pole, and the red glow far behind us lit the strange scene. I could tell from the position of the light, and the silence aside from the cries, that we had gone north. Into farming territory. In the distance, I saw houses burning.

As my eyes adjusted, I saw Jorge's minions walking under a vast framework, a kind of long trellis, and thrusting spears up through its roof which I realized was made of human beings. They were tied, men, women, and children, facedown across the wooden slats. The spear carriers stabbed those sacrifices until they stopped writhing and crying out. But their blood pattered like a small rainstorm.

Jorge appeared beside me.

"Behold," he said. "The Night Drinker ceremony."

"What have you done?" I think I said. In spite of my bindings, I was shivering in fear.

"The Flayed One, amigo." Jorge was smiling. "The rain brings life to the fields, the harvest. Our beautiful little brothers, the seedlings beneath the soil are drinking our love."

"You're fucking crazy."

"And the god," he continued, as if he hadn't heard me, "comes to drink his fill as well."

"There is no god here."

He put his hands on either side of my head and gently turned my face. I squinted. There, in the darkest shadows beneath the human trellis, I saw a figure. There are no words for this creature. I, the man of words, fail utterly before the alienness of this apparition. For there was no etheric dark angel there. It was a human figure, but one taller than any man I'd seen. The feathers he had tied to himself seemed, in that darkness, almost to be tentacles.

"I thought he'd be smaller," I blurted, stupidly.

"Dios!" Hermanito Jorge called out, then fell to his knees and put his face in the dirt.

The figure turned and looked us over. I began to twist against the ropes, harder, more desperately. And he came forward. I watched him walk. The blood on his face and chest caught glimmers from the volcanoes. He moved lightly, like some bloodied deer. Like some god.

He paused before me, tied helplessly to this pyre.

His face was covered by the face of another.

His eyes pondered me through the leathery eyeholes of the sacrifice he wore.

His partially covered lips grinned.

He spoke. His breath was cool. It smelled of honey, and poppies, and sweetgrass, and agave. He knew my language.

"Is it not beautiful, my child?" He looked over his shoulder at the writhing bodies dying above him. "You must see beyond what you see," he said. "You must see the world as it gives birth."

I was openly weeping now.

"You must break for me, as I am flayed for you. Tell my story."

Then his hot, raw palm, sticky and pestilential, rose, cupped my cheek, and held it still as his two sets of lips descended to kiss my own.

*Nominated by McSweeney's*

# A REFUSAL TO MOURN THE DEATHS, BY GUNFIRE, OF THREE MEN IN BROOKLYN

## By JOHN MURILLO

From AMERICAN POETRY REVIEW and KONTEMPORARY AMERICAN POETRY
(FOUR WAY BOOKS)

> *And at times, didn't the whole country try to break his skin?*
> —*Tim Seibles*

You strike your one good match to watch its bloom
and jook, a swan song just before a night
wind comes to snuff it. That's the kind of day
it's been. Your Black & Mild, now, useless as
a prayer pressed between your lips. God damn
the wind. And everything it brings. You hit
the corner store to cop a light, and spy
the trouble rising in the cashier's eyes.
TV reports some whack job shot two cops
then popped himself, here, in the borough, just
one mile away. You've heard this one before.
In which there's blood. In which a black man snaps.
In which things burn. You buy your matches. Christ
is watching from the wall art, swathed in fire.

> *This country is mine as much as an orphan's house is his.*
> —*Terrance Hayes*

To breathe it in, this boulevard perfume
of beauty shops and roti shacks, to take
in all its funk, calypso, reggaeton,

and soul, to watch school kids and elders go
about their days, their living, is, if not
to fall in love, at least to wonder why
some want us dead. Again this week, they killed
another child who looked like me. A child
we'll march about, who'll grace our placards, say,
then be forgotten like a trampled pamphlet. What
I want, I'm not supposed to. Payback. Woe
and plenty trouble for the gunman's clan.
I'm not supposed to. But I want a brick,
a window. One good match, to watch it bloom.

> *America, I forgive you. . . . I forgive you eating black children, I know your hunger.*
> *— Bob Kaufman*

You dream of stockpiles—bottles filled with gas
and wicks stripped from a dead cop's slacks—a row
of paddy wagons parked, a pitcher's arm.
You dream of roses, time-lapse blossoms from
the breasts of sheriffs, singing Calico
and casings' rain. You dream of scattered stars,
dream panthers at the precinct, dream a black-
out, planned and put to use. You dream your crew
a getaway van, engine running. Or,
no thought to run at all. You dream a flare
sent up too late against the sky, the coup
come hard and fast. You dream of pistol smoke
and bacon, folded flags—and why feel shame?
Is it the dream? Or that it's only dream?

> *& still when I sing this awful tale, there is more than a dead black man at the center.*
> *—Reginald Dwayne Betts*

You change the channel, and it's him again.
Or not him. Him, but younger. Him, but old.
Or him with skullcap. Kufi. Hoodied down.
It's him at fifteen. Him at forty. Bald,
or dreadlocked. Fat, or chiseled. Six foot three,
or three foot six. Coal black or Ralph Bunche bright.
Again, it's him. Again, he reached. Today,
behind his back, his waist, beneath the seat,

his socks, to pull an Uzi, morning star,
or Molotov. They said don't move, they said
get down, they said to walk back toward their car.
He, so to speak, got down . . . Three to the head,
six to the heart. A mother kneels and prays—
Not peace, but pipe bombs, hands to light the fuse.

> Fuck the whole muthafucking thing.
> —Etheridge Knight

A black man, dancing for the nightly news,
grins wide and white, all thirty-two aglow
and glad to be invited. Makes a show
of laying out, of laundry airing. Throws
the burden back on boys, their baggy wear
and boisterous voices. Tells good folk at home
how streets run bloody, riffraff take to crime
like mice to mayhem, and how lawmen, more
than ever, need us all to back them. Fuck
this chump, the channel, and the check they cut
to get him. Fuck the nodding blonde, the fat
man hosting. Fuck the story. Fuck the quick
acquittals. Fuck the crowds and camera van.
You change the channel. Fuck, it's him again.

> I enter this story by the same door each time.
> —Julian Randall

At Normandy and Florence, brick in hand,
one afternoon in '92, with half
the city razed and turned against itself,
a young boy beat a man to meat, and signed,
thereby, the Ledger of the Damned. Big Book
of Bad Decisions. Black Boy's Almanac
of Shit You Can't Take Back. We watched, in shock.
The fury, sure. But more so that it took
this long to set it. All these matchstick years . . .
He beat him with a brick, then danced a jig
around his almost-carcass. Cameras caught
him live and ran that loop for weeks, all night,

470

all day, to prove us all, I think, one thug,
one black beast prancing on the nightly news.

*And when it comes to those hard deeds*
*done by righteous people and martyrs,*
*isn't it about time for that to be you?*
—*Gary Copeland Lilley*


Not Huey on his high-back wicker throne,
beret cocked cooler than an Oaktown pimp.
Or young Guevara marching into camp,
all swagger, mane, and slung M-1. But one
less suited, you could say, for picture books
and posters, slouching on a northbound Bolt,
caressing steel and posting plans to shoot.
He means, for once, to be of use. Small axe
to massive branches, tree where hangs the noose.
He says he's "putting wings on pigs today,"
wants two for each of us they've blown away.
Wants gun salutes and caskets. Dirges, tears,
and wreaths. Wants widows on the witness stand,
or near the riot's flashpoint, brick in hand.

*I itch for my turn.*
—*Indigo Moor*


Like Malcolm at the window, rifle raised
and ready for whatever—classic black
and white we pinned above our dorm room desks—
we knew a storm brewed, spinning weathervanes
and hustling flocks from sky to sky. We dozed,
most nights, nose deep in paperback
prognoses. *Wretched* and *Black Skin, White Masks,*
our books of revelation. Clarions
to would-be warriors, if only we
might rise up from our armchairs, lecture halls,
or blunt smoke cyphers. Talking all that gun
and glory, not a Nat among us. Free
to wax heroic. Deep. As bullet holes
through Panther posters, Huey's shattered throne.

*Poems are bullshit unless they are teeth . . .*
—*Amiri Baraka*

It ain't enough to rabble rouse. To run
off at the mouth. To speechify and sing.
Just ain't enough to preach it, Poet, kin
to kin, pulpit to choir, as if song
were anything like Panther work. It ain't.
This morning when the poets took the park
to poet at each other, rage and rant,
the goon squad watched and smiled, watched us shake
our fists and fret. No doubt amused. As when
a mastiff meets a yapping lapdog, or
the way a king might watch a circus clown
produce a pistol from a passing car.
Our wrath the flag that reads *kaboom!* Our art,
a Malcolm poster rolled up, raised to swat.

> every once in a while
> i see the winged spirits of niggas past
>    raise out the rubble
>                    —Paul Beatty

Could be he meant to set the world right.
One bullet at a time. One well-placed slug,
one dancing shell case at a time. One hot
projectile pushing through, one body bag
zipped shut and shipped to cold store, at a time.
Could be he meant to make us proud, to fill
Nat Turner's shoes. Could be he meant to aim
at each acquittal, scot-free cop, each trigger pull
or chokehold left unchecked, and blast daylight
straight through. Could be he meant, for once, to do.
We chat. We chant. We theorize and write.
We clasp our hands, spark frankincense, and pray.
Our gods, though, have no ears. And yet, his gun
sang loud. Enough to make them all lean in.

> Paradise is a world where everything
> is sanctuary & nothing is a gun.
>                    —Danez Smith

A pipebomb hurled through a wig shop's glass—
nine melting mannequins, nine crowns of flame.

Hair singe miasma, black smoke braided. Scream
of squad cars blocks away. Burnt out Caprice
and overturned Toyota. Strip mall stripped.
And gutted. Gift shop, pet shop, liquor store,
old stationery wholesale. Home décor,
cheap dinnerware. An old man sprinting, draped
in handbags, loaded down with wedding gowns.
Three Bloods and two Crips tying, end-to-end,
one red, one blue, bandana. Freebase fiend
with grocery bags, new kicks, and name brand jeans.
Spilled jug of milk against the curb, black cat
bent low to lap it. This, your world, burnt bright.

> *I love the world, but my heart's been cheated.*
> *—Cornelius Eady*

He thought a prayer and a pistol grip
enough to get it done. Enough to get
him free. Get free or, dying, try. To stop
the bleeding. *Blood on leaves, blood at the root.*
I didn't root, exactly, when I heard
word spread. Word that he crept up, panther like,
*and let loose lead. A lot. Before he fled*
the spot, then somewhere underground, let kick
his cannon one last time. "One Time," our name
for cops back at the crib. It had to do,
I think, with chance. Or lack of. Chickens come
to roost? Perhaps. I didn't root. Per se.
But almost cracked a smile that day. The news
like wind chimes on the breeze. Or shattered glass.

> *We beg your pardon, America. We beg*
> *your pardon, once again.*
> *— Gil Scott-Heron*

To preach forgiveness in a burning church.
To nevermind the noose. To nurse one cheek
then turn the next. To run and fetch the switch.
To switch up, weary of it all. Then cock
the hammer back and let it fall . . . But they

were men, you say, with children. And so close
to Christmas. But their wives, you say. Today
so close to Christmas . . . Memory as noose,
and history as burning church, who'd come
across the two cops parked and not think, *Go
time? One time for Tamir time?* Not think *Fire
this time?* To say as much is savage. Blame
the times, and what they've made of us. We know
now, which, and where—the pistol or the prayer.

> . . . . *like sparklers tracing an old alphabet in the night sky*
> —*Amaud Jamaul Johnson*

It's natural, no, to put your faith in fire?
The way it makes new all it touches. How
a city, let's say, might become, by way
of time and riot, pure. In '92,
we thought to gather ashes where before
loomed all that meant to kill us. Rubble now
and lovely. Worked into, as if from clay,
some sort of monument. To what? No clue.
Scorched earth, and then . . . ? Suppose a man sets out,
with gun and half a plan, to be of use.
To hunt police. Insane, we'd say. Not long
for life. In this, we'd miss the point. A lit
match put to gas-soaked rag, the bottle flung,
may die, but dying, leaves a burning house.

> *Afro angels, black saints, balanced upon
> the switchblades of that air and sang.*
> —*Robert Hayden*

But that was when you still believed in fire,
the gospel of the purge, the burning house.
You used to think a rifle and a prayer,
a pipebomb hurled through a shopkeep's glass,
enough, at last, to set the world right.
Enough, at least, to galvanize some kin.
Think Malcolm at the window, set to shoot,
or Huey on his high-back wicker throne.

Think Normandy and Florence, brick in hand,
a Black man dancing for the camera crews.
You change the channel, there he is again,
and begging: Find some bottles, fill with gas.
Begs breathe in deep the Molotov's perfume.
Says strike your one good match, then watch it bloom.


*Nominated by American Poetry Review, Beth Ann Fennelly, Shelley Wong*

---

**A Note on the Poem**

"A Refusal to Mourn the Deaths, by Gunfire, of Three Men in Brooklyn": The title is a nod to Dylan Thomas' famous poem, "A Refusal to Mourn the Death, by Fire, of a Child in London." The poem itself was written in part as a reflection on police-community relations since the 1992 uprisings, and partly as a response to the killing of two NYPD officers and subsequent suicide of twenty-eight-year-old Ishmael Brinsley. On December 20, 2014, Brinsley shot and killed Brooklyn officers Rafael Ramos and Wenjian Liu, before fleeing the scene and ultimately shooting himself dead on a subway platform. Brinsley also shot and wounded his ex-girlfriend before boarding a bus that morning from Baltimore to New York City. His attack on the officers was reportedly motivated by the rash of police killings of unarmed Black people nationwide. Coincidentally, while Brinsley was carrying out his attack, poets were gathered in New York's Washington Square Park to read poems in protest of said killings.

# GOVERNING BODIES

By SANGAMITHRA IYER

From THE KENYON REVIEW

The Irrawaddy River in Burma is named after the mythical, multi-trunked, white elephant, Airavata, whose name is derived from the Sanskrit word *Iravat*, "one who is produced from water."

My family history is a story produced from water. If I were to trace my grandfather's engineering career, I'd follow it along the Irrawaddy River. If I were to trace mine, I'd follow it from streams in the Catskill Mountains through aqueducts and tunnels to New York City's pipes and faucets. My experience is also in the Yosemite Valley—Sierra Nevada snowmelt that gravity carries to San Francisco. It is on rooftops and in rain barrels in Cameroon; in buckets in the Sanaga River.

When I was accepted into engineering school, a local newspaper in New York wrote a story on me saying that I was tracing the footsteps of my paternal grandfather, a civil engineer turned water diviner who was a follower of Mohandas K. Gandhi. I did not know much about this man to whom I was often compared but never met.

These lines of Alfred Lord Tennyson were passed down in my family from my grandfather to my father to me:

> And out again, I curve and flow
> to join the brimming river,
> for men may come and men may go,
> but I go on forever.

Thatha, my paternal grandfather, had worked for the British in Burma before moving his family back to southern India in the 1930s. "I do not want my house to be walled in on all sides and my windows to be stuffed. I want the cultures of all lands to be blown about my house as freely as possible," Gandhi said in a speech in 1921. Back in Tamil Nadu, Thatha built the family's Kallakurichi house on these principles, to have no interior partition walls or rooms, just common spaces, with no locks on doors or windows—an experiment in trust. Kallakurichi was my grandfather's attempt to practice nonviolence while the society around him was teeming with oppression, both from colonialism and the caste system.

My father—the youngest of Thatha's thirteen children—was born in Kallakurichi, where he grew up learning Sanskrit and English in addition to speaking Tamil at home. Each day, my father copied a page of the dictionary by hand and memorized Shakespeare, Tennyson, Goldsmith, and others. My father had given me his beat-up copy of *Memory Work and Appreciation*, a collection of poems that I could also recite "by heart." His father had given it to him; this book of British verse was the only physical artifact passed on among our three generations.

I now find it curious that Thatha, who quit his civil engineering post with the British in Burma to join the freedom movement in India, showered his children with the oppressor's literature. But relationships are complicated, and noncooperation need not apply to poetry.

When I was twenty-five years old, I recited those lines of Tennyson to my father at Good Samaritan Hospital in Suffern, New York—the hospital where I was born. My father left the world from the same place I entered it.


There is a sepia-toned photograph of my father at Jones Beach from 1971. He is standing on his head with his legs bent in the lotus position. East meets West, and the world is upside down.

As a new arrival in the US, he befriended and taught yoga to hippies in New York City. His body in this picture is slender and nimble, unlike his body in the hospital in 2003, the one that later was burned to ash and immersed into the coliform-infested waters of the Ganga while foreign tourists watched from a distance as families like mine grieved.

My body does not remember the yoga my father taught me. After his death, I entered a Vinyasa yoga class at a YMCA in Brooklyn. "Flow," was what my acupuncturist told me my grief-ridden body needed—to restore my flow. The yoga instructor, a young white male, clasped his hands and bowed at me. "Namaste," he said.

He read to the class a passage from Yoga.com from his iPhone. He told us that if we were unable to keep up, "just go back to child's pose." I was too embarrassed to ask which one is child's pose. My body eventually remembered. I collapsed my torso over my bent knees.

At the time of the Jones Beach photograph, my father had been in this country for two years. He arrived with only seventy-five cents in his pocket. Back in India, he studied social work, wrote poetry, and dreamed of being a journalist or working in foreign service. He had a sales job and moonlighted tutoring English to the wife of the Congolese Ambassador to India. In New York, my father was a social worker at Manhattan Psychiatric Center on Wards Island.

A colleague from work told me about the time she was stationed at the Sewage Treatment Plant on Wards Island in the 1980s. "After a while, you got used to the smell," she said. "You didn't even notice it anymore." She also told me back then, there were wild dogs all over the island. "You had to run to your car at night to avoid them. Then one year, they were all gone."

I began to wonder what my father smelled back then. The Clean Water Act was only enacted in 1972, and it would take years before this plant would come into compliance. What was the thinking behind placing a mental hospital and a wastewater treatment plant in close vicinity to one another?

Did my father think about the connections between sanitation and social justice on Wards Island like his father did about the poor and access to water in India? Did it bother him the proximity to the sewage treatment plant? I never had the opportunity to ask him.

I now imagined my father on his lunch break feeding the stray dogs and looking out onto the East River.

"I thought you followed the elephant," my mother told me.

She was recounting a story from when we moved back to India for two years after I was born while she pursued her master's degree. My first language was Tamil, one I largely lost when we returned to America. One day during this time, I disappeared. It was January, and an elephant adorned with garlands of marigolds and graffitied with sandalwood paste marched through the streets as part of a temple procession. The elephant's human handlers guided her to each house. Families offered bananas to the auspicious pachyderm believed to be a stand-in for a god. She was trained to place her moist snout on the devotees' heads—a tickle perceived as a blessing. She left behind a trail of droppings the size of coconuts.

After the elephant reached my maternal grandparents' home in Bangalore—where we were living at the time—I vanished. My mother assumed that since I, like my father, had a fondness for animals, I must have followed the elephant. She and my uncle ran around the neighborhood trailing the procession, asking if anyone had seen a small girl wearing a striped T-shirt and a pair of jeans with short hair closely cropped to her head.

They eventually found me at a neighbor's house. After observing the largest creature I had ever seen in my life, I went over there to tell them that there was an elephant in the street decorated just like the elephant statue they had displayed on their shelf in their home. The miniature suddenly seemed insufficient and could not move her ears, trunk, and tail in the same manner as the live one.

I don't remember this event. But I try to imagine my toddler self. My little arms extend wide, approximating the size of the elephant, and then I point to the small replica. A discovery. A story I had told in a tongue I no longer command except for a few words like Thatha—grandpa, Patti—grandma, and Yanai—elephant.

I grew up worshipping the elephant-headed god, Ganesha. I was taught to cross my arms over my chest, pull on my ear lobes, and squat-bow to the half-pachyderm deity, the remover of obstacles. I learned the story of how Ganesha got his face: After Lord Shiva accidentally beheaded the goddesses Parvati's son, he ran into the forest and took the head of the first creature he encountered, a baby elephant, to bring the boy back to life. I soon began to lose my faith. I couldn't imagine wanting to worship a god who would behead two beings. The boy was resuscitated as Ganesha, but I asked, "What happened to the baby elephant?" Still, I was curious about this elephant-headed boy—comprised of two beings deprived of their whole.

In the suburbs of New York City, the aroma of cumin and coriander permeated our home, seeped into my clothes and backpack, and was transported into my locker at school.

"What's that smell?" a schoolmate asked one day as we grabbed our books between classes.

"I don't know," I said, embarrassed, as I shut my locker door and rushed off to class.

One day in elementary school, I forgot my packed lunch, and my teacher decided to buy me food in the cafeteria. They were serving hamburgers that day.

While waiting in the cafeteria line, I motioned to my teacher to bend down so that I could tell her something. I whispered to her that I didn't eat meat.

"What do you want on your bread then?" she yelped.

"Lettuce." Another whisper.

"What else besides lettuce?" she asked.

"Nothing," I said.

"You can't eat just that. That's rabbit food!" The little kids on line erupted with laughter.

Despite my desire to be perceived as "American" at this age, I never wished to eat meat, but I didn't have the words to describe why not when bombarded with questions.

"Don't you want to know what it tastes like?" kids would ask me.

"You never ate meat in your life?"

"Not even by accident?"

Back then, there were many things about myself I was discovering, many things I was uncertain about. As a child of immigrants, I was reconciling my identity between two worlds, neither to which I felt I fully belonged. But not eating animals was one thing I was sure of even if it alienated me further from my peers.

It was sometime in middle school when I made it clear that this was my choice, not a family or religious obligation. A sense of justice expressed in a shift in diction. A change in two letters.

"You can't eat meat?"

"I *won't* eat meat."

I think back to this time, and I see a child having to reconcile violence commonly accepted and rarely questioned. She refuses to participate.


On a trip to India as an adult I accompanied my aunt and uncle to a temple in Tamil Nadu. Adjacent to the temple hall was a medium-sized room with a separate entrance. The gates to this area opened, and I was surprised to see an elephant—just barely smaller than the room she was enclosed in—walk out. Devotees paid money to feed the elephant—a business scheme for the religious enterprise. No one suspected a Hindu temple to be guilty of animal cruelty.

A man with a stick stood next to the elephant to control her. I attempted to use my native Tamil to interrogate the handler but could bark only a few basic questions. *Eat? Sleep where? Children?*

I wanted to channel that younger me with her near-shaven head, Tamil fluency, and astute observations. I could see her again extend her arms wide and then point to the elephant's enclosure. She could say all that I could not. How can you restrict this wild animal to this small space? Why must you control her body?


My aunts and uncles noticed that my father and I shared more than a physical resemblance. They described my father as *rumba* sensitive. Very sensitive. As a child, he'd disappear to the bend in the Gaumuki River to find calm when his twelve older siblings would fight. He despised the firecrackers his brothers and sisters lighted during Diwali. He knew the sounds upset the monkeys in the trees.

As an adult, my father was always taking care of injured wildlife in the American suburbs. When we were young, my parents took my brother and me to see *Return of the Jedi* in the movie theater. My father was so disturbed by the sight of Jabba the Hutt eating a live frog that he walked out of the theater.

My father's death certificate said cardiac arrest. But his heart had long suffered from extraordinary empathy.


After my father's death, I realized there were so many things I didn't know about his past, which suddenly felt so relevant as I was figuring out how to move forward with my own life. What did I want to contribute to this world? I needed to better understand where I came from, which was intimately tied to my grandfather's life. I was interested in how people defied what was expected of them to pursue something meaningful.

I knew my grandfather became a water diviner in India after leaving Burma.

I loved that word—*divining.* "Water dowsing" and "witching" are other names for it. *If I can locate water*, I thought, *I can trace it back to my grandfather. It will tell me a story.* A Y- or L-shaped branch is all I would need, and someone to teach me.

I studied groundwater hydrology in graduate school and have overseen the drilling of several wells. It sounds strange, even to me, that I would resort to a tree branch to locate water or uncover family history. But my grandfather was a civil engineer turned water diviner, too. I pictured myself holding the tips of a Y-shaped branch and feeling the force of water pulling me in one direction. Where could it take me?

Could the divining rod guide me to all of my grandfather's engineering posts in Burma from the Irrawaddy's source at the confluence in Myitsone down to the small lighthouse island near Tavoy where the river emptied into the Andaman Sea? Could I channel his decision to leave?

Without my father to tell me stories, I had only fragments of family anecdotes, fuzzy dates, and stories that contradicted themselves. It took me years to begin to piece together my family history. Ten years after my father's death, I received a grant to go to the British Library in London to review the India Office Records. There was a chance I might find records of my grandfather's life as an engineer in Burma.

The vastness of the collections housed there—the legacy of colonialism—was both impressive and unsettling. History was controlled as colonized bodies were controlled—through a rigid bureaucracy.

It was February, and I kept thinking of the claymation zoo gorilla from *Creature Comforts* in her British accent: "I don't like being cold and I don't like being rained on, and I find that here I'm often cold and I'm often rained on."

I bought an umbrella in the library gift shop and registered for a reader pass. I had to check my coat and umbrella in the cloakroom before entering the Asian and African Studies reading room with my permitted items—a pencil and laptop contained in a clear plastic bag to be inspected upon arrival and departure.

And so I began navigating the archives of an empire. One librarian wrote me before my trip: *"If your grandfather was employed as an engineer in Burma by the British Government he 'may' appear in either the Burma V/12 (Histories of service) or V/13 (yearly civil lists) series. These can be researched when you visit us in person."*

I was able to make up to ten requests for records a day, and each request took about seventy minutes to fill. I pored through volumes of names until I saw the words Manakkal Sundaralingam Narayanan—M. S. Narayanan, my Thatha. He was here! I made my way through his entire service record in the Public Works Department, compiling notes in a massive spreadsheet, tracking changes over time. I learned all places he was posted, sometimes what project he was working on (i.e., lighthouses, roads, bridges), changes in his salary, when he passed his Hindustani and Burmese language exams.

I, too, have a civil service record in New York City. It could tell you I worked for the Department of Environmental Protection for more than ten years on water supply projects, but it wouldn't tell you my hopes and fears, with whom I shared my home, or what made me feel alive. You wouldn't see the hours on the subway I spent writing, the stringbean and tofu dish I ordered at my vegan lunch spot in Queens, how I mimicked the sway of the trees in Forest Park when I ran in the mornings, and how my rescued pit bull would lick the sweat off my face when I came home.

Can you re-create a life—*re-member* a body—from the knowns and the unknowns?


I learned that in 1919 at the age of twenty-three, my grandfather, M. S. Narayanan, received his first job as a civil engineer for the British Public Works Department in Burma, then part of British India. Thatha was the first in his family to leave their South India home. According to the Yearly Civil Lists, in October of 1919, M. S. Narayanan served as a temporary engineer in Toungoo, a sleepy logging town in the middle of the country, making 250 rupees a month. By February of 1920 he was promoted to assistant engineer, with a salary bump up to three hundred rupees. According to revenue reports from this time, the Public Works Department in Toungoo was charged with the replacement of timber road bridges and construction work along the road to Mandalay.

Over ninety years later, I biked around this small town, stopping along the road bridges. I was in search of memories that have been buried, washed away, or built over. Giant trucks hauling tree trunks extracted from the forests passed me on the road. Logging was a huge industry in my grandfather's time, too.

Like my grandfather, elephants were charged with bridge and road building. One compilation of elephant stories in Burma is a book called *Elephant Bill: The Best Selling Account of the 1920s Life in the Jungles of Burma* by Lt. Col. J. H. Williams. Williams, or "Elephant Bill," as he was called, worked as a forestry assistant for the Bombay Burmah Trading Corporation, a logging outfit, which was partly responsible for the British annexation of Burma in 1886. (The British viewed a conflict between the company and Burmese King Thebaw as an excuse to invade and drive the monarchy out of Burma.)

Williams was tasked with working with elephants in the forested regions up north to carry and drag teak timber logs to the river, where they would float on wooden rafts that would slowly make their way down to Rangoon. Depending on the density of the tree and the flow and height of the river, it could take a year or eight years for the logs to travel downstream to arrive at their destination. At the time, three-quarters of all of the world's teak came from Burma. Colonialism and logging in Burma were linked and all part of a long game in service of the growing empire. A British veteran of WWI, Elephant Bill arrived in Burma in 1920 around the same time my grandfather did. He observed everything about the elephants—their health, relationships, communications, and how they thought. "The elephant knows the margin of safety to a foot, and when the log is ten feet from the edge, she refuses to haul it any closer," Elephant Bill wrote in his memoir.

I liked thinking of elephants as engineers who understood the land and its limits. But what was more important to me was learning about these rare moments of agency, when their bodies refused the commands of men and listened to other cues.

Williams's elephants worked during the day but were left to roam and feed themselves at night. Their less-fortunate kin, held captive in the timber mills in Rangoon, never had access to the forests, were kept in chains, and were rarely able to reproduce from the stress.

The working jungle elephants had an illusion of freedom at night. Their *oozies* or *mahouts* came to fetch them in the morning to serve the empire for another day. During their evenings off, the elephants were free to mate. Sometimes these logging elephants wandered off to mate with their wild counterparts. I tried to picture what those encounters were like. The free elephant might place his trunk on the working elephant and smell the scent of man. He could divine her loss. When the working elephant saw the free elephant, memories of childhood might come back. Each day she would toggle back and forth between two selves.

Thatha was soon toggling between being a British civil servant and an Indian family man. In July of 1921, my grandfather took his first leave from work—one-month long. His wife, Lakshmi, had come to join him. They were married ten years prior, when he was fifteen years old, and she was only eight.

Being only eight years old, Lakshmi didn't fully understand what was happening on her wedding day. It is tradition in my family that the bride

484

and soon-to-be wife wear a nine-yard saree, as opposed to the typical six yards. How many times did these nine yards go around her eight-year-old body?

During the ceremony, my grandmother started to cry. Someone gave her a banana. She stopped crying. This is the only story I have heard about their wedding day.

When I was eight, I declared I would never have an arranged marriage. No one had suggested I would. But I imagined how terrified I would be if I were in that situation—one that all of my forbearers endured—how trapped I would feel. A banana alone could not remedy the situation.

At the age of eighteen, Lakshmi left her parents' home to finally live with her husband of ten years. Her father accompanied her on a ship to Chittagong, in what is now Bangladesh. From there she made the journey to Burma. What do my grandparents do in that first month together? Perhaps he takes her walking along the Kaladan River in Sittwe. They would observe the fruit bats hanging upside down in the trees during the day, dark sacks adorning the branches. Just nearing sunset, in that golden hour, the bats would wake and fill the sky.

My grandfather might tell her things he's learned about Burma, what is similar and different from home. The essential Burmese phrases like *thek that lut* to indicate vegetarian, but its actual translation is closer to "free from killing life."

My grandmother, or Patti, might admire the sandalwood paste, *thanaka*, that the women apply to their faces to keep them cool in the heat. Though they have been married for ten years, my grandparents are strangers. Over the next twenty-two years, they will have thirteen children together. But in those first three years, it was just the two of them in Burma. Is she scared, excited, or both? How do their bodies come together? Does it seem natural or forced?

In Rangoon, they lived where Forty-second Street met the Rangoon River. My grandfather built a cantilever deck that looked out over the river where he and Patti played cards and watched the ships go by. It was there, along the Rangoon River, where the treasures of Burma—like the teak extracted by Williams's elephants—passed, before being shipped out to the rest of the world.

In his memoir, Elephant Bill detailed what an elephant birth is like in the wild. An elephant mother chooses a safe place for birth, usually somewhere low on the ground "where a river has suddenly changed its course and taken a hair-pin bend." Bounded on three sides by banks and river, the female elephants bellow to protect the new mother and calf from intruders. These "aunty" elephants—*twai sin*, as the Burmese called them—protected the newest member of the herd.

In 1924, Patti had returned to a safe place, her parents' home, to have their first child, a daughter, Parvati. Thatha took three months' leave to go back to India, and Patti's aunt helped care for her and the baby during this time. This aunty was once a child bride, too, one who was widowed before ever living with her husband, and never remarried. She was a *twai sin* and came to protect Patti's family as her own.


In 1926, Thatha was posted for a year to Myitkyina in the northern reaches of Burma in Kachin State. Myitkyina means "near the big river," referring to the Irrawaddy. The following year, Thatha was stationed a little farther south along the Irrawaddy in Katha. What I know of Katha I learned from George Orwell. Eric Blair, the young British police officer, worked in Katha from 1926 to the middle of 1927, until he contracted dengue fever and returned to England. Emma Larkin, in her book, *Finding George Orwell in Burma*, argues that what Blair witnessed in Burma led to the creation of George Orwell, a writer of conscience. In his short story "Shooting an Elephant," Orwell writes, "As for the job I was doing, I hated it more bitterly than I can perhaps make clear. In a job like that you see the dirty work of Empire at close quarters."

In his novel *Burmese Days*, based on his time in Katha, Orwell describes the racism of the British officers as they debate whether to allow an "Oriental" into their elite gentlemen's club. Orwell alludes to the fact that the Indians and Chinese public servants did all the hard work, while the Europeans were paid more to supervise them. Through *Burmese Days*, I caught a glimpse of a troubled young man no longer wanting to serve his state. It is still from the vantage point of the colonizer, reluctant as he may be. How did the racism of empire affect my grandparents, stationed at the same time in the same small town as Eric Blair? My father and his siblings all refer to my grandfather's title in Burma as "Chief Civil Engineer." The civil service records list him only as assistant engineer, never rising above this post. I wondered if he did the work of chief and was paid as assistant.

I try to imagine the things said and left unsaid between my grandparents at night in this remote post. I wondered if there was the language to talk about race.

486

Although I was a US citizen, I was never perceived as American with my brown skin and name no one could pronounce. There were the tiny things that were said to make me feel other.

"Where are you from?" they all asked.

"New York," I'd say.

"But what is your nationality?"

"American, I was born here," I told them all.

"But where are you really from?"

I wondered if the British treated my grandfather as they did the "Orientals" in Orwell's novel? Did he tell Patti about these encounters or hide them, as I did from my parents? Assimilation is a form of survival, but so much is lost in the process.

When wild elephants were first caught to work in the logging industry, they were subjected to a brutal process called "kheddaring" to break them in. Their *oozies* trapped, frightened, and beat them into submission. A kheddared elephant "can be immediately recognized by the training scars on its legs," Elephant Bill wrote. He had a disdain for this process and preferred to train the offspring of captive elephants that were easier to control.

Williams worked with the young calves, but they, too, at first objected. In her biography of Williams, *Elephant Company*, Vicki Croke writes: "The little elephant would be showered with treats and praise from the handlers. Despite that, the calf protested—often too upset to even collect a morsel. 'For about 2 hours it struggles and kicks, then sulks and eventually takes a banana out of sheer boredom and disgust—the expression on its face can only be compared to that of a child who eventually has to accept a sweet from a bag,' Williams noted."

Still, Williams claimed his elephants were "far nearer to the wild state than any other domesticated animal." He believed they were domesticated only for eight out of the twenty-four hours in the day. Each morning the elephant and her *oozie* went through a ritual. The *oozie* first had to track her down in the jungle where she would travel about eight miles in the course of the night. The *oozie* then sang to her. "He gives her time to accept the grim fact that another day of hard work has begun for her. If he hurried her, she might rebel," Williams wrote. It was a cruel compassion to understand an elephant's desires, yet steer her away from them.

What is it like for an elephant to be part wild belonging to nature and part subject belonging to empire? When does she submit and when does she choose to rebel?

I wondered how my grandfather's rebellion was slowly simmering during those years in Burma. He was earning a good living, was able to support his family, and sent his siblings to college on his salary. British colonialism was successful because it tricked its subjects into believing that they were better off under its rule. But seeing the work of empire up close had an effect on my grandfather, too, that could not be justified by material wealth. His kheddaring scars were present even if not visible. How did he as a vegetarian cope with being stationed in the forest with the Europeans who hunted for sport? How did it feel to help make the roads and bridges in a country only to have that infrastructure be used to remove the riches from this land?

In 1928, Thatha was in Rangoon working as an engineer at the new lunatic asylum in Tagadale. What I could find about Rangoon's first lunatic asylum from British archival records was this: "As might be expected, coolies, cultivators, and petty traders supply the greatest number of patients." How much of the madness was caused by the state? The institutional reports also indicated specific details about the siting of this institution: "Rangoon lunatic asylum situated at the north western corner of central jail, on open space, with good natural slope, affording excellent means of conveying the surface water from grounds during the rains." These bureaucratic reports spoke more beautifully about the drainage of the asylum site than they did of its inhabitants.

In 1929, Thatha was posted in Rangoon on foreign service under the governing body of the University of Rangoon, where student protests were gaining momentum over the past decade. In March of that year, a frail-looking man, draped in homespun cotton and subsisting primarily on fruits, arrived in Burma to raise funds for his causes—the revitalization of rural villages, the boycott of foreign cloth and spinning cotton, or *khadi*, as means toward self-sufficiency. He appealed to the Indians living in Burma. "I know there are still many who laugh at this little wheel and regard this particular activity of mine as an aberration," the lawyer-turned-*khadi* activist shared with the crowd in Rangoon. But Mohandas Gandhi encouraged his listeners to study more deeply "the immense bearing of the spinning," not only upon their own lives, but upon those of "the starving millions of India" as well. My grandfather was in the audience and heard this appeal and met the famed *satya-grahi*.

I picture my grandfather listening to Gandhi's speech, like he is listening to a familiar song. Initially, he moves his body only in ways prescribed to him. Suddenly, the music changes, and the song morphs into a different sound. It is startling at first, but he is more surprised that his body knows what to do. He finds himself moving in ways no one said he could. No one taught him. It was as if he always knew. Dancing was a way of remembering who he was.

I pour through the transcripts on Gandhi's speeches in Burma from 1929 to find the change in the music, to pick out the surprise that made the unfamiliar familiar again.

What was it about this spinning wheel that captivated my grandfather?

And then I read this: "If you import foreign cloth you deny yourselves the privilege and duty of working with your hands and preparing your own cloth. This is like cutting off both your hands."

I could picture my grandfather in India after quitting his job, as he was described to me, wearing nothing but the white cotton loincloth he wove himself, making oil by crushing sesame seeds in the fists of his own hands, and carrying his divining rod from village to village to locate water wells. His hands were never idle.

The abbreviation PR (Permitted to Resign) appears next to my grandfather's name on the yearly civil list in 1934. Because the records of my grandfather's service are found only in colonial archives, the British control the narrative. Thatha was permitted to resign.

But I wonder what his resignation letter—this document that signified his shift from engineer to activist, from civil servant to freedom fighter, from subject to rebel—said. Thatha, like all of us, was produced mostly of water. It wasn't about resigning but rather about restoring flow—like water desiring to be undammed.

*I will not worship your god. I will not follow your rules. I will not eat your banana. I will not drag your log. I do not need your permission.*

I imagine Thatha, like a large tusker no longer willing to submit to empire, dropping his final log on a bridge, and then simply walking away.

*Nominated by The Kenyon Review*

# SPECIAL MENTION

(The editors also wish to mention the following important works published by small presses last year. Listings are in no particular order.)

## FICTION

Jessica Hollander — The Stickiness of Air (Gettysburg Review)
Erin Somers — Waltz (Ecotone)
Julianna Baggott — Cubby Safe (Cincinnati Review)
Richard Bausch — The Fate of Others (Narrative)
Jem Calder — Good Progress (Granta)
Lisa Taddeo — Singapore (Missouri Review)
Samantha Edmonds — Earthgirl & Starboy (Ninth Letter)
Joyce Carol Oates — Damned Little Dog (Exile)
Hilary Leichter — In The Mist of Everything (Conjunctions)
Cynthia Ozick — Sin (American Scholar)
Alex McElroy — The Cruise (Ninth Letter)
Erika Krouse — North of Dodge (Glimmer Train)
Stephen Dixon — Tomorrow (Agni)
Molly Quinn — The Crenoplossis (Epiphany)
Sarah Blackman — The Key to the Fields (Cincinnati Review)
Steve Stern — Last Laugh (Jewish Fiction)
Amy Neswald — Forty-Six (The Rumpus)
Emily Greenberg — Houston, We've Had a Problem (Chicago Review)
Yu-Mei Balasingamchow — The Prisoner (Mississippi Review)
Rick Moody — One-Eyed Jack (Conjunctions)
Sharon Solwitz — Six Lectures in Normal (New England Review)
Ayse Papatya Bucak — The Dead (Bomb)

Samuel Kolawole — Sweet Sweet Strawberry Taste (Agni)

Mario Alberto Zambrano — Some of You (Ploughshares)

Weston Cutter — Midwest Rules of Sales (Gettysburg Review)

Emma Duffy-Comparone — The Package Deal (New England Review)

Rebecca Makkai — Webster's Last Stand (American Short Fiction)

Tony Tulathimutte — The Feminist (n+1)

Jennifer Anne Moses — The Holy Messiah (Another Chicago Magazine)

Alex Lumans — There and There . . . (Electric Lit.)

Stefanie Wortman — Never Shake A Baby (Worcester Review)

Jonathan Wei — Capybara (Nimrod)

Brooke Champagne — Bugginess (Chattahoochee Review)

Chee Brossy — Movin' It (Prism)

Terri Leker — Coyotes (New Ohio Review)

Luke Dani Blue — Dogs of America (Crab Orchard Review)

Elizabeth Mosier — The Pit and the Page (New Rivers Press)

Stephanie Allen — Come On Up—(*Tonic and Balm*, Shade Mountain Press)

Brenna Lemieux — We Were Happy (Meridan)

Keith Rosson — Ben Benske and the Hand of Light (Outlook)

Kelle Groom — The Year Without Summer (About Place Journal)

Jessie Van Eerden — Meet You At the Dollar General . . . (Blackbird)

Danielle Dutton — Nocturnals (Conjunctions)

Anu Kandikuppa — The Red Bump (Prism)

## NONFICTION

Roy Scranton — We Broke The World (The Baffler)

Joaquin Fernandez — The Scorpion (Pidgeonholes)

Fabienne Josaphat — The Birds Sang Tyranny (Hong Kong Review)

Fred Bahnson — On The Road With Thomas Merton (Emergence Magazine)

Michael Fischer — Pleese (Nowhere Magazine)

Houman Harouni — Three Notes On John Berger (Arrowsmith)

Natasha Stovall — Whiteness On the Couch (Longreads)

B. D. McClay — The Ills That Flesh is Heir To (Hedgehog Review)

Martha Petersen — Remnants (Witness)

Jeremy Lybarger — Walt Whitman's Boys (Boston Review)

Jan Shoemaker — Grace (River Teeth)

Jill Logan — The People's Exhibit (Colorado Review)

James Riach — Reservation Dogs (Creative Nonfiction)

Peter C. Baker — This, Too, Was History (The Point)

Jessica Jacobs — The History Before Us (Guernica)

Ceridwen Hall — Network (TriQuarterly)

Shena McAuliffe — Of Glass, Light & Electricity (Coppernickel)

Alice Mattison — Eye Of The Beholder (Paris Review)

Katherine Seligman — Someone To Listen (The Sun)

Vu Tran — Origins (Ploughshares)

David Zoby — Fish Poison (The Sun)

Brian Trapp — Twelve Words (Kenyon Review)

Kevin Schaeffer — First World Problems (*As I Hear Rain*, PEN
    America)

Emily Fox Gordon — How I Learned To Talk (American Scholar)

Richard Adams Carey — Icon (Alaska Quarterly Review)

Aysegul Savas — The Cost Of Reading (Longreads)

Herbert Gold — Oatmeal Raisin Cookies And The Jewish Problem
    (Hudson Review)

Alberto Chimal — The Grand Experiment (World Literature Today)

Ann Pancake — Take, Eat (Williow Springs)

Charlie Geer — Pistol In A Drawer (The Sun)

Ge Gao — A Survey Of My Right Arm (Threepenny Review)

Alisa Koyrakh — Tomorrow We Travel (New England Review)

Logan Scherer — Bedfellows Forever (Oxford American)

Leah Hampton — Parkway (Ecotone)

Rachel Heng — The Rememberers (McSweeney's)

Rick Bass — Fifteen Dogs (Narrative)

Alicia Mountain — The Gay Horizon (Georgia Review)

Rob Nixon — Fallen Martyrs, Felled Trees (Conjunctions)

Tracy Daugherty — So Much Straw (Ploughshares)


POETRY


Victoria Chang — Obit (Poetry)

Alison Hazle — If I Could Paint Some Surreal Image (Grub Street)

Al Maginnes — Stern (Rattle)

Angel Nafis — Ode To Dalya's Bald Spot (Poetry)

Naomi Shihab Nye — Every Day Was Your Birthday (Mizna)

Jamila Osman — Folklore (Adirondack Review)

John Poch — God In the Shape Of Texas (WordFarm)

Alicia Jo Rabins — A Passover Story (Los Angeles Jewish Journal)

Cody Smith — Just Music (Delta Poetry Review)

Charles Harper Webb — Forgetful God (Four Way Review)

Ericka Brumett — Cunnilingus (Halcyone)

Hajjar Baban — If My Father Gave Me The Words In His Language (Glass)

Jane Huffman — The Waves (Columbia Review)

Marianne Boruch — Pieces On The Ground (Poetry)

Arisa White — My Dead (The Quarry)

Dilawar Karadaghi — Like Perfume, We Will Wear You (Consequence)

Paul Tran — The Cave (Poetry)

Maggie Smith — Confessions (Image)

Jeff Buckley — The Last Thoughts of Jeff Buckley in Memphis (Poets.org)

Natania Rosenfeld — Beret (Yale Review)

Nathan McClain — Excerpts from the Compendium of the Fig Wasp and the Fig (Matter)

Ama Cadjoe — Burying Seeds (The Common)

James Richardson — Epilogue in Stone (American Poetry Review)

Kate Farrell — The Costume (The Manhattan Review)

Timothy Donnelly — The Stars Down to Earth (A Public Space)

Carl Phillips — Little Shields . . . (Zyzzyva)

Valzhyna Mort — Ars Poetica (Poetry)

Lloyd Schwartz — Titian's Marsyus (*The Eloquent Poem*, Persea Press)

R.T. Smith — Pigeons, Pears, Hush (*Summoning Shades*, Mercer University Press)

Daniel Tobin — With the Gift of a Feather at Coole Park (Hudson Review)

M. Soledad Caballero — Gravity Haunted (Tahoma Literary Review)

Donald Platt—Black Prince (Tin House)

# PRESSES FEATURED IN THE PUSHCART PRIZE EDITIONS SINCE 1976

A-Minor
About Place Journal
Abstract Magazine TV
The Account
Adroit Journal
Agni
Ahsahta Press
Ailanthus Press
Alaska Quarterly Review
Alcheringa/Ethnopoetics
Alice James Books
Ambergris
Amelia
American Circus
American Journal of Poetry
American Letters and Commentary
American Literature
American PEN
American Poetry Review
American Scholar
American Short Fiction
The American Voice
Amicus Journal
Amnesty International
Anaesthesia Review
Anhinga Press
Another Chicago Magazine

Antaeus
Antietam Review
Antioch Review
Apalachee Quarterly
Aphra
Aralia Press
The Ark
Arkansas Review
Arroyo
Art and Understanding
Arts and Letters
Artword Quarterly
Ascensius Press
Ascent
Ashland Poetry Press
Aspen Leaves
Aspen Poetry Anthology
Assaracus
Assembling
Atlanta Review
Autonomedia
Avocet Press
The Awl
The Baffler
Bakunin
Bare Life
Bat City Review

Bamboo Ridge
Barlenmir House
Barnwood Press
Barrow Street
Bellevue Literary Review
The Bellingham Review
Bellowing Ark
Beloit Poetry Journal
Bennington Review
Bettering America Poetry
Bilingual Review
Birmingham Poetry Review
Black American Literature Forum
Blackbird
Black Renaissance Noire
Black Rooster
Black Scholar
Black Sparrow
Black Warrior Review
Blackwells Press
The Believer
Bloom
Bloomsbury Review
Blue Cloud Quarterly
Blueline
Blue Unicorn
Blue Wind Press
Bluefish
BOA Editions
Bomb
Bookslinger Editions
Boston Review
Boulevard
Boxspring
Brevity
Briar Cliff Review
Brick
Bridge
Bridges
Brown Journal of Arts
Burning Deck Press
Butcher's Dog
Cafe Review
Caliban

California Quarterly
Callaloo
Calliope
Calliopea Press
Calyx
The Canary
Canto
Capra Press
Carcanet Editions
Caribbean Writer
Carolina Quarterly
Catapult
Cave Wall
Cedar Rock
Center
Chariton Review
Charnel House
Chattahoochee Review
Chautauqua Literary Journal
Chelsea
Chicago Quarterly Review
Chouteau Review
Chowder Review
Cimarron Review
Cincinnati Review
Cincinnati Poetry Review
City Lights Books
Cleveland State Univ. Poetry Ctr.
Clover
Clown War
Codex Journal
CoEvolution Quarterly
Cold Mountain Press
The Collagist
Colorado Review
Columbia: A Magazine of Poetry and Prose
Columbia Poetry Review
The Common
Conduit
Confluence Press
Confrontation
Conjunctions
Connecticut Review
Constellations

Copper Canyon Press
Copper Nickel
Cosmic Information Agency
Countermeasures
Counterpoint
Court Green
Crab Orchard Review
Crawl Out Your Window
Crazyhorse
Creative Nonfiction
Crescent Review
Cross Cultural Communications
Cross Currents
Crosstown Books
Crowd
Cue
Cumberland Poetry Review
Curbstone Press
Cutbank
Cypher Books
Dacotah Territory
Daedalus
Dalkey Archive Press
Decatur House
December
Denver Quarterly
Desperation Press
Dogwood
Domestic Crude
Doubletake
Dragon Gate Inc.
Dreamworks
Dryad Press
Duck Down Press
Dunes Review
Durak
East River Anthology
Eastern Washington University Press
Ecotone
Egress
El Malpensante
Electric Literature
Eleven Eleven
Ellis Press

Empty Bowl
Ep;phany
Epoch
Ergol
Evansville Review
Exquisite Corpse
Faultline
Fence
Fiction
Fiction Collective
Fiction International
Field
Fifth Wednesday Journal
Fine Madness
Firebrand Books
Firelands Art Review
First Intensity
5 A.M.
Five Fingers Review
Five Points Press
Fjords Review
Florida Review
Foglifter
Forklift
The Formalist
Foundry
Four Way Books
Fourth Genre
Fourth River
Frontiers: A Journal of Women Studies
Fugue
Gallimaufry
Genre
The Georgia Review
Gettysburg Review
Ghost Dance
Gibbs-Smith
Glimmer Train
Goddard Journal
David Godine, Publisher
Gordon Square
Graham House Press
Grand Street
Granta

Graywolf Press
Great River Review
Green Mountains Review
Greenfield Review
Greensboro Review
Guardian Press
Gulf Coast
Hanging Loose
Harbour Publishing
Hard Pressed
Harvard Advocate
Harvard Review
Hawaii Pacific Review
Hayden's Ferry Review
Hermitage Press
Heyday
Hills
Hollyridge Press
Holmgangers Press
Holy Cow!
Home Planet News
Hopkins Review
Hudson Review
Hunger Mountain
Hungry Mind Review
Hysterical Rag
Ibbetson Street Press
Icarus
Icon
Idaho Review
Iguana Press
Image
In Character
Indiana Review
Indiana Writes
Indianapolis Review
Intermedia
Intro
Invisible City
Inwood Press
Iowa Review
Ironwood
I-70 Review
Jam To-day

J Journal
The Journal
Jubilat
The Kanchenjunga Press
Kansas Quarterly
Kayak
Kelsey Street Press
Kenyon Review
Kestrel
Kweli Journal
Lake Effect
Lana Turner
Latitudes Press
Laughing Waters Press
Laurel Poetry Collective
Laurel Review
L'Epervier Press
Liberation
Ligeia
Linquis
Literal Latté
Literary Imagination
The Literary Review
The Little Magazine
Little Patuxent Review
Little Star
Living Hand Press
Living Poets Press
Logbridge-Rhodes
Louisville Review
Love's Executive Order
Lowlands Review
LSU Press
Lucille
Lynx House Press
Lyric
The MacGuffin
Magic Circle Press
Malahat Review
Manoa
Manroot
Many Mountains Moving
Marlboro Review
Massachusetts Review

McSweeney's

Meridian

Mho & Mho Works

Micah Publications

Michigan Quarterly

Mid-American Review

Milkweed Editions

Milkweed Quarterly

The Minnesota Review

Mississippi Review

Mississippi Valley Review

Missouri Review

Montana Gothic

Montana Review

Montemora

Moon Pie Press

Moon Pony Press

Mount Voices

Mr. Cogito Press

MSS

Mudfish

Mulch Press

Muzzle Magazine

n + 1

Nada Press

Narrative

National Poetry Review

Nebraska Poets Calendar

Nebraska Review

Nepantla

Nerve Cowboy

New America

New American Review

New American Writing

The New Criterion

New Delta Review

New Directions

New England Review

New England Review and Bread Loaf Quarterly

New Issues

New Letters

New Madrid

New Ohio Review

New Orleans Review

New South Books

New Verse News

New Virginia Review

New York Quarterly

New York University Press

Nimrod

9×9 Industries

Ninth Letter

Noon

North American Review

North Atlantic Books

North Dakota Quarterly

North Point Press

Northeastern University Press

Northern Lights

Northwest Review

Notre Dame Review

O. ARS

O. Blk

Obsidian

Obsidian II

Ocho

Oconee Review

October

Ohio Review

Old Crow Review

Ontario Review

Open City

Open Places

Orca Press

Orchises Press

Oregon Humanities

Orion

Other Voices

Oxford American

Oxford Press

Oyez Press

Oyster Boy Review

Painted Bride Quarterly

Painted Hills Review

Palette

Palo Alto Review

Paper Darts

Paris Press

Paris Review

Parkett

Parnassus: Poetry in Review

Partisan Review

Passages North

Paterson Literary Review

Pebble Lake Review

Penca Books

Pentagram

Penumbra Press

Pequod

Persea: An International Review

Perugia Press

Per Contra

Pilot Light

The Pinch

Pipedream Press

Pirene's Fountain

Pitcairn Press

Pitt Magazine

Pleasure Boat Studio

Pleiades

Ploughshares

Plume

Poem-A-Day

Poems & Plays

Poet and Critic

Poet Lore

Poetry

Poetry Atlanta Press

Poetry East

Poetry International

Poetry Ireland Review

Poetry Northwest

Poetry Now

The Point

Post Road

Prairie Schooner

Prelude

Prescott Street Press

Press

Prime Number

Prism

Promise of Learnings

Provincetown Arts

A Public Space

Puerto Del Sol

Purple Passion Press

Quaderni Di Yip

Quarry West

The Quarterly

Quarterly West

Quiddity

Radio Silence

Rainbow Press

Raritan: A Quarterly Review

Rattle

Red Cedar Review

Red Clay Books

Red Dust Press

Red Earth Press

Red Hen Press

Release Press

Republic of Letters

Review of Contemporary Fiction

Revista Chicano-Riqueña

Rhetoric Review

Rhino

Rivendell

River Styx

River Teeth

Rowan Tree Press

Ruminate

Runes

Russian *Samizdat*

Salamander

Salmagundi

San Marcos Press

Santa Monica Review

Sarabande Books

Saturnalia

Sea Pen Press and Paper Mill

Seal Press

Seamark Press

Seattle Review

Second Coming Press

Semiotext(e)

Seneca Review

Seven Days

The Seventies Press

Sewanee Review

The Shade Journal

Shankpainter

Shantih

Shearsman

Sheep Meadow Press

Shenandoah

A Shout In the Street

Sibyl-Child Press

Side Show

Sixth Finch

Small Moon

Smartish Pace

The Smith

Snake Nation Review

Solo

Solo 2

Some

The Sonora Review

Southeast Review

Southern Indiana Review

Southern Poetry Review

Southern Review

Southampton Review

Southwest Review

Speakeasy

Spectrum

Spillway

Spork

The Spirit That Moves Us

St. Andrews Press

Stillhouse Press

Storm Cellar

Story

Story Quarterly

Streetfare Journal

Stuart Wright, Publisher

Subtropics

Sugar House Review

Sulfur

Summerset Review

The Sun

Sun & Moon Press

Sun Press

Sunstone

Sweet

Sycamore Review

Tab

Tamagawa

Tar River Poetry

Teal Press

Telephone Books

Telescope

Temblor

The Temple

Tendril

Terrapin Books

Texas Slough

Think

Third Coast

13th Moon

THIS

This Broken Shore

Thorp Springs Press

Three Rivers Press

Threepenny Review

Thrush

Thunder City Press

Thunder's Mouth Press

Tia Chucha Press

Tiger Bark Press

Tikkun

Tin House

Tipton Review

Tombouctou Books

Toothpaste Press

Transatlantic Review

Treelight

Triplopia

TriQuarterly

Truck Press

True Story

Tule Review

Tupelo Review

Turnrow

Tusculum Review
Two Sylvias
Twyckenham Notes
Undine
Unicorn Press
University of Chicago Press
University of Georgia Press
University of Illinois Press
University of Iowa Press
University of Massachusetts Press
University of North Texas Press
University of Pittsburgh Press
University of Wisconsin Press
University Press of New England
Unmuzzled Ox
Unspeakable Visions of the Individual
Vagabond
Vallum
Verse
Verse Wisconsin
Vignette
Virginia Quarterly Review
Volt
The Volta
Wampeter Press
War, Literature & The Arts
Washington Square Review
Washington Writer's Workshop
Water-Stone

Water Table
Wave Books
Waxwing
West Branch
Western Humanities Review
Westigan Review
White Pine Press
Wickwire Press
Wigleaf
Willow Springs
Wilmore City
Witness
Word Beat Press
Wordsmith
World Literature Today
WordTemple Press
Wormwood Review
Writers' Forum
Xanadu
Yale Review
Yardbird Reader
Yarrow
Y-Bird
Yes Yes Books
Zeitgeist Press
Zoetrope: All-Story
Zone 3
ZYZZYVA

# THE PUSHCART PRIZE

# FELLOWSHIPS

*The Pushcart Prize Fellowships Inc., a 501 (c) (3) nonprofit corporation, is the endow-*
*ment for The Pushcart Prize. "Members" donated up to $249 each. "Sponsors" gave be-*
*tween $250 and $999. "Benefactors" donated from $1000 to $4,999. "Patrons" donated*
*$5,000 and more. We are very grateful for these donations. Gifts of any amount are*
*welcome. For information write to the Fellowships at PO Box 380, Wainscott, NY 11975.*

### FOUNDING PATRONS

The Katherine Anne Porter Literary Trust
Michael and Elizabeth R. Rea

### PATRONS

Anonymous
Margaret Ajemian Ahnert
Daniel L. Dolgin & Loraine F. Gardner
James Patterson Foundation
Neltje
Charline Spektor
Ellen M. Violett

### BENEFACTORS

Anonymous
Russell Allen
Hilaria & Alec Baldwin
David Caldwell
Ted Conklin
Bernard F. Conners
Catherine and C. Bryan Daniels
Maureen Mahon Egen
Dallas Ernst
Cedering Fox
H.E. Francis
Mary Ann Goodman & Bruno Quinson Foundation

Bill & Genie Henderson
Bob Henderson
Marina & Stephen E. Kaufman
Wally & Christine Lamb
Dorothy Lichtenstein
Joyce Carol Oates
Warren & Barbara Phillips
Stacey Richter
Glyn Vincent
Kirby E. Williams
Margaret V. B. Wurtele

## SUSTAINING MEMBERS

Anonymous
Agni
Margaret A. Ahnert
Jim Barnes
Ellen Bass
Ann Beattie
Rosellen Brown
David Caldwell
Christian Jara
Dan Chaon
Lucinda Clark
Suzanne Cleary
Martha Collins
Linda Coleman
Ted Colm
Stephen Corey
Pam Cothey
Lisa Couturier
Josephine David
Dan Dolgin & Loraine Gardner
Jack Driscoll
Penny Dunning
Nancy Ebert
Maureen Mahon Egen
Elizabeth Ellen
Entrekin Foundation
Alan Furst
Ben & Sharon Fountain
Robert Giron
Jeffrey Harrison
Alex Henderson
Bob Henderson
Helen Houghton
Mark Irwin

Christian Jara
Don and Renee Kaplan
Peter Krass
Edmund Keeley
Wally & Christine Lamb
Linda Lancione
Stephen O. Lesser
William Lychack
Maria Matthiessen
Alice Mattison
Rick Moody
John Mullen
Neltje
Joyce Carol Oates
Barbara & Warren Phillips
Horatio Potter
C.E. Poverman
Elizabeth R. Rea
Stacey Richter
Schaffner Family Fdn.
Alice Schell
Dennis Schmitz
Sharasheff-Johnson Fund
Sybil Steinberg
Sun Publishing
Elaine Terranova
Upstreet
Glyn Vincent
Michael Waters
Susan Wheeler
Diane Williams
Kirby E. Williams
Eleanor Wilner

## SPONSORS

Altman / Kazickas Fdn.
Jacob Appel
Jean M. Auel
Jim Barnes
Charles Baxter
Joe David Bellamy
Laura & Pinckney Benedict
Wendell Berry
Laure-Anne Bosselaar
Kate Braverman
Barbara Bristol
Kurt Brown
Richard Burgin
Alan Catlin
Mary Casey

Siv Cedering
Dan Chaon
James Charlton
Andrei Codrescu
Linda Coleman
Ted Colm
Stephen Corey
Tracy Crow
Dana Literary Society
Carol de Gramont
Nelson DeMille
E. L. Doctorow
Penny Dunning
Karl Elder
Donald Finkel

Ben and Sharon Fountain
Alan and Karen Furst
John Gill
Robert Giron
Beth Gutcheon
Doris Grumbach & Sybil Pike
Gwen Head
The Healing Muse
Robin Hemley
Bob Hicok
Jane Hirshfield
Helen & Frank Houghton
Joseph Hurka
Christian Jara
Diane Johnson
Janklow & Nesbit Asso.
Edmund Keeley
Thomas E. Kennedy
Sydney Lea
Stephen Lesser
Gerald Locklin
Thomas Lux

Markowitz, Fenelon and Bank
Elizabeth McKenzie
McSweeney's
Rick Moody
John Mullen
Joan Murray
Barbara and Warren Phillips
Hilda Raz
Stacey Richter
Schaffner Family Foundation
Sharasheff—Johnson Fund
Cindy Sherman
Joyce Carol Smith
May Carlton Swope
Glyn Vincent
Julia Wendell
Philip White
Diane Williams
Kirby E. Williams
Eleanor Wilner
David Wittman
Richard Wyatt & Irene Eilers

## MEMBERS

Anonymous (3)
Stephen Adams
Betty Adcock
Agni
Carolyn Alessio
Dick Allen
Henry H. Allen
John Allman
Lisa Alvarez
Jan Lee Ande
Dr. Russell Anderson
Ralph Angel
Antietam Review
Susan Antolin
Ruth Appelhof
Philip and Marjorie Appleman
Linda Aschbrenner
Renee Ashley
Ausable Press
David Baker
Catherine Barnett
Dorothy Barresi
Barlow Street Press
Jill Bart
Ellen Bass
Judith Baumel
Ann Beattie
Madison Smartt Bell
Beloit Poetry Journal

Pinckney Benedict
Karen Bender
Andre Bernard
Christopher Bernard
Wendell Berry
Linda Bierds
Stacy Bierlein
Big Fiction
Bitter Oleander Press
Mark Blaeuer
John Blondel
Blue Light Press
Carol Bly
BOA Editions
Deborah Bogen
Bomb
Susan Bono
Brain Child
Anthony Brandt
James Breeden
Rosellen Brown
Jane Brox
Andrea Hollander Budy
E. S. Bumas
Richard Burgin
Skylar H. Burris
David Caligiuri
Kathy Callaway
Bonnie Jo Campbell

Janine Canan
Henry Carlile
Carrick Publishing
Fran Castan
Mary Casey
Chelsea Associates
Marianne Cherry
Phillis M. Choyke
Lucinda Clark
Suzanne Cleary
Linda Coleman
Martha Collins
Ted Conklin
Joan Connor
J. Cooper
John Copenhaver
Dan Corrie
Pam Cothey
Lisa Couturier
Tricia Currans-Sheehan
Jim Daniels
Daniel & Daniel
Jerry Danielson
Ed David
Josephine David
Thadious Davis
Michael Denison
Maija Devine
Sharon Dilworth
Edward DiMaio
Kent Dixon
A.C. Dorset
Jack Driscoll
Wendy Druce
Penny Dunning
John Duncklee
Nancy Ebert
Elaine Edelman
Renee Edison & Don Kaplan
Nancy Edwards
Ekphrasis Press
M.D. Elevitch
Elizabeth Ellen
Entrekin Foundation
Failbetter.com
Irvin Faust
Elliot Figman
Tom Filer
Carol and Laueme Firth
Finishing Line Press
Susan Firer
Nick Flynn
Starkey Flythe Jr.
Peter Fogo

Linda Foster
Fourth Genre
Alice Friman
John Fulton
Fugue
Alice Fulton
Alan Furst
Eugene Garber
Frank X. Gaspar
A Gathering of the Tribes
Reginald Gibbons
Emily Fox Gordon
Philip Graham
Eamon Grennan
Myma Goodman
Ginko Tree Press
Jessica Graustain
Lee Meitzen Grue
Habit of Rainy Nights
Rachel Hadas
Susan Hahn
Meredith Hall
Harp Strings
Jeffrey Harrison
Clarinda Harriss
Lois Marie Harrod
Healing Muse
Tim Hedges
Michele Helm
Alex Henderson
Lily Henderson
Daniel Henry
Neva Herington
Lou Hertz
Stephen Herz
William Heyen
Bob Hicok
R. C. Hildebrandt
Kathleen Hill
Lee Hinton
Jane Hirshfield
Hippocampus Magazin
Edward Hoagland
Daniel Hoffman
Doug Holder
Richard Holinger
Rochelle L. Holt
Richard M. Huber
Brigid Hughes
Lynne Hugo
Karla Huston
1–70 Review
Iliya's Honey
Susan Indigo

Mark Irwin

Beverly A. Jackson

Richard Jackson

Christian Jara

David Jauss

Marilyn Johnston

Alice Jones

Journal of New Jersey Poets

Robert Kalich

Sophia Kartsonis

Julia Kasdorf

Miriam Polli Katsikis

Meg Kearney

Celine Keating

Brigit Kelly

John Kistner

Judith Kitchen

Ron Koertge

Stephen Kopel

Peter Krass

David Kresh

Maxine Kumin

Valerie Laken

Babs Lakey

Linda Lancione

Maxine Landis

Lane Larson

Dorianne Laux & Joseph Millar

Sydney Lea

Stephen Lesser

Donald Lev

Dana Levin

Live Mag!

Gerald Locklin

Rachel Loden

Radomir Luza, Jr.

William Lychack

Annette Lynch

Elzabeth MacKieman

Elizabeth Macklin

Leah Maines

Mark Manalang

Norma Marder

Jack Marshall

Michael Martone

Tara L. Masih

Dan Masterson

Peter Matthiessen

Maria Matthiessen

Alice Mattison

Tracy Mayor

Robert McBrearty

Jane McCafferty

Rebecca McClanahan

Bob McCrane

Jo McDougall

Sandy McIntosh

James McKean

Roberta Mendel

Didi Menendez

Barbara Milton

Alexander Mindt

Mississippi Review

Nancy Mitchell

Martin Mitchell

Roger Mitchell

Jewell Mogan

Patricia Monaghan

Jim Moore

James Morse

William Mulvihill

Nami Mun

Joan Murray

Carol Muske-Dukes

Edward Mycue

Deirdre Neilen

W. Dale Nelson

New Michigan Press

Jean Nordhaus

Celeste Ng

Christiana Norcross

Ontario Review Foundation

Daniel Orozco

Other Voices

Paris Review

Alan Michael Parker

Ellen Parker

Veronica Patterson

David Pearce, M.D.

Robert Phillips

Donald Platt

Plain View Press

Valerie Polichar

Pool

Horatio Potter

Jeffrey & Priscilla Potter

C.E. Poverman

Marcia Preston

Eric Puchner

Osiris

Tony Quagliano

Quill & Parchment

Barbara Quinn

Randy Rader

Juliana Rew

Belle Randall

Martha Rhodes

Nancy Richard

William Strachan
James Charlton
Lily Henderson
Paul Bresnick

Philip Schultz
Daniel Dolgin
Kirby E. Williams

# CONTRIBUTING SMALL PRESSES FOR PUSHCART PRIZE XLV

*(These presses made or received nominations for this edition.)*

The A 3 Review, Calle Jacinto Verdaguer 2, 8C, Madrid 28019, Spain
A&U: America's AIDS Magazine, 21-17 41st St.,, #3, Astoria, NY 11105
AbstractMagazineTV.com, 1305 E. Boyd St, Norman, OK 73071
Abstruse Press, Higgins, 41 Edward Rd., Bristol, BS4 3ET, UK
Abyss & Apex, 1574 County Road 250, Niota, TN 37826
Academy of American Poets, 75 Maiden Ln, #901, New York, NY 10038
Accents Publishing, PO Box 910456, Lexington, KY 40591-0456
Active Muse, c/o Kadapa, Flat #3, Abhiman Apts, Left Bhusari Colony opp
    Spring Orchid School, Paud Road, Kothrud 411038, Pune, India
Ad Hoc Fiction, 6 Old Tarnwell, Stanton Drew, Bristol, BS39 4EA, UK
Adelaide Books, 244 Fifth Ave., Ste. D-27, New York, NY 10001
Adirondack Review, 11 Smith Terrace, Highland, NY 12528
The Adroit Journal, LaBerge, 1223 Westover Rd., Stamford, CT 06902
Agni Magazine, Boston Univ., 236 Bay State Rd., Boston, MA 02215
Alabama Literary Review, English, Troy University, Troy, AL 36082
Alice James Books, 114 Prescott St, Farmington, ME 04938
Altered Reality, 1403 Iron Springs Rd., #36, Prescott, AZ 86305
Always Crashing, 1401 N. St Clair, #3A, Pittsburgh, PA 15206
American Aesthetic, 624 East Pleasant St, Amherst, MA 01002
American Chordata, 2102 Beverly Rd., #1C, Brooklyn, NY 11226
American Journal of Poetry, 14969 Chateau Village Dr., Chesterfield, MO
    63017
American Literary Review, 1155 Union Cir, #311307, Denton, TX 76203
The American Scholar, 1606 New Hampshire Ave. NW, Washington, DC
    20009
American Short Fiction, P.O. Box 4152, Austin, TX 78765
American-Turkish Assoc., PO Box 3035, Cary, NC 27519

Ancient Paths, 3316 Arbor Creek Lane, Flower Mound, TX 75022
Anomaly, 28150 Chief Rd., Millsboro, DE 19966
Another Chicago Magazine, 1301 W. Byron St, Chicago, IL 60613
Apogee, 359 St Mark's Ave., #2, Brooklyn, NY 11238
Appalachia Journal, Woodside, 41 Bridge St., Deep River, CT 06417
Appalachian Heritage, PO Box 5000, Shepherdstown, WV 25443
Apple Valley Review, 88 South 3$^{rd}$ St., #336, San José, CA 95113
Aquifer, PO Box 161346, Orlando, FL 32816-1346
Arachne Press, 100 Grierson Rd., London SE23 1NX, UK
The Ardent Writer Press, 1014 Stone Dr., Brownsboro, AL 35741
Arizona Authors, 1119 E. LeMarche Ave., Phoenix, AZ 85022
Arkana, Thompson Hall 324, 201 Donaghey Ave., Conway, AR 72035
Arkansas International, UAR, Kimpel Hall 333, Fayetteville, AR 72701
Arrowsmith Press, 11 Chestnut St, Medford, MA 02155
Artemis Journal, PO Box 505, Floyd, VA 24091-0505
Arts & Letters Journal, Box 89, Georgia Coll., Milledgeville, GA 31061
Ashland Poetry Press, 401 College Ave., Ashland, OH 44805
Asian American Writers Workshop, 112 W. 27$^{th}$ St., 6$^{th}$ Fl., New York, NY
    10001
Atlantic Review, 686 Cherry St NW, #333, Atlanta, GA 30332-0161
Atticus Review, 1201N 3$^{rd}$ St, #308, Philadelphia, PA 19122
Aurora Poetry, 1918 S. Harvard Blvd., #10, Los Angeles, CA 90018
Autumn House Press, 5530 Penn Ave., Pittsburgh, PA 15206
Azure, 104 Adelphi Sr., #422, Brooklyn, NY 11205

Back Patio Press, 305 Alewife Brook Pkwy, Somerville, MA 02144
Bacopa Literary Review, 4000 NW 51$^{st}$ St., F-119, Gainesville, FL 32606
Baffler, 19 West 21at St, Ste. 101, New York, NY 10010
Bamboo Ridge Press, PO Box 61781, Honolulu, HI 96839-1781
Baobab, 121 California Ave., Reno, NV 89509
Bare Life Review, PO Box 352, Lagunitas, CA 94938
Barrelhouse, Gonzalez, 532 Lefferts Ave., #3H, Brooklyn, NY 11225
Basset Hound Press, 2327 F St., Sacramento, CA 95816
Bat City Review, English, 1 University STA B 5000, Austin, TX 78712
Bayou Magazine, UNO, 2000 Lake Shore Dr., New Orleans, LA 70148
Bear Review, 4211 Holmes St, Kansas City, MO 64110
beestung, 28150 Chief Rd., Millsboro, DE 19966
Belletrist Magazine, 3000 Landerholm Circle SE, Bellevue, WA 98007
Bellevue Literary Review, NYU Medicine, 550 First Ave, OBV-A612, New
    York, NY 10016
Bellingham Review, MS-9053, WWU, Bellingham, WA 98225
Beloit Poetry Journal, PO Box 1450, Windham, ME 04062
Beltway Poetry Quarterly, 626 Quebec Pl NW, Washington, DC 20010

Bennington Review, 1 College Dr., Bennington, VT 05201

Berlinica Publishing, 255 W. 43rd St., #1012, New York, NY 10036

Better Than Starbucks, 146 Lake Constance Dr., West Palm Beach, FL 33411

Bettering American Poetry, 28150 Chief Rd., Millsboro, DE 19966

Between the Lines, 8456 Indian Hills D., Nashville, TN 37221

BHC Press, 885 Penniman #5505, Plymouth, MI 48170

Big Other, 1840 W. 3rd St, Brooklyn, NY 11223

Big Table Publishing, 747 Leavenworth St., #4, San Francisco, CA 94109

Big Windows, 2012 Marra Dr., Ann Arbor, MI 48103-6186

bioStories, 225 Log Yard Ct., Bigfork, MT 59911

Bird Brain Publishing, 7640 Ridgeway Ave., Evansville, IN 47715

Bird Dog Publishing, PO Box 425, Huron, OH 44839

Birmingham Poetry Review, English, UAB, Birmingham, AL 35294-0110

BkMk Press, UMKC, 5101 Rockhill Rd., Kansas City, MO 64110-2446

Black Earth Institute, P.O. Box 424, Black Earth, WI 53515

Black Mountain Press, PO Box 9907, Asheville, NC 28815

Black Warrior, Univ. of Alabama, Box 870244, Tuscaloosa, AL 35487

Blackbird, VCU, English, PO Box 843082, Richmond, VA 23284-3082

Blank Spaces, 282906 Normanby/Bentinck Townline, Durham ON N0G 1R0, Canada

Blanket Sea Magazine, 516 ½ N. Ainsworth Ave., Tacoma, WA 98403

BlazeVOX, 131 Euclid Ave., Kenmore, NY 14217

Blink Ink, P.O. Box 5, North Branford, CT 06471

Bloomsday Literary, 1039 Orchard Hill St., Houston, TX 77077

Blue Unicorn, 13 Jefferson Ave., San Rafael, CA 94903

Bluegrass Writers Studio, Eastern Kentucky Univ., Mattox 101, 521 Lancaster Ave., Richmond, KY 40475

Bluestem, English, 600 Lincoln Ave., Charleston, IL 61920

BOA Editions, 250 N. Goodman St., Ste. 306, Rochester, NY 14607

Bodega Magazine, 451 Court St., #3R, Brooklyn, NY 11231

Body Without Organs, PO Box 1332, Gambier, OH 43022

The Boiler, 311 Jagoe St., #7, Denton, TX 76201

Bone & Ink Press, PO Box 85278, Racine, WI 53408

Boom Project Book, 4850 Brownsboro Rd., Louisville, KY 40207

Booth, 4600 Sunset Ave., Indianapolis, IN 46208

Border Crossing, 650 W. Easterday Ave., Sault Ste. Marie, MI 49783

Bosque Press, 508 Chamiso Lane, NW, Los Ranchos, NM 87107

Boston Review, PO Box 425786, Cambridge, MA 02142

Bottom Dog Press, PO Box 425, Huron, OH 44839

Brain Mill Press, 2359 Sunrise Crt, Green Bay, WI 54303

Brevity, c/o Moore, 265 E State St., Athens, OH 45701

Briar Cliff Review, 3303 Rebecca St, Sioux City, IA 51104-2100

Brick, Box 609, Stn P, Toronto, ON M5S 2Y4, Canada

Brick Road Poetry Press, 341 Lee Rd. 553, Phenix City, AL 36867
Bridport Prize, PO Box 6910, Bridport, Dorset, DT6 9BQ, UK
Brilliant Flash Fiction, 4201 Corbett Dr., #343, Fort Collins, CO 80525
Bristol Short Story Prize, Unit 5.16, Paintworks, Bath Rd., Bristol BS4 3EH, UK
Broad Street, 4214 Southampton Rd., Richmond, VA 23235
Broadkill Review, PO Box 63, Milton, DE 19968
Broadstone Books, 418 Ann St, Frankfort, KY 40601-1929
Brooklyn Poets, 135 Jackson St., #2A, Brooklyn, NY 11211
Brooklyn Review, Boylan Hall, 2502 Campus Rd., Brooklyn, NY 11250
BTS Books, 22 Bramwith Rd., Sheffield, S11 7EZ, UK

Café Abyss, 2050 Kingsborough Dr., Painesville, OH 44077
Cagibi, 801 Avenue C, #4C, Brooklyn, NY 11218
Cajun Mutt Press, PO Box 572, Newark, IL 60541
California State Poetry Society, PO Box 2672, Del Mar, CA 92014
Calliope, 2506 SE Bitterbrush Dr., Madras, OR 97741-9452
Cape Cod Poetry Review, 61 Lily Pond Dr., S. Yarmouth, MA 02664
Capsule Stories, 6008-A Kingsbury Ave., St Louis, MO 63112
Capturing Fire Press, 1240 4th St NE, #239, Washington, DC 20002
Carousel, PO Box 141, Stn P, Toronto, ON M5S 2S6, Canada
carte blanche, 1200 Atwater Ave., #3, Montreal, QC H3Z 1×4, Canada
Carve Magazine, PO Box 701510, Dallas, TX 75370
Catamaran, 1050 River St, #118, Santa Cruz, CA 95060
Catapult, 1140 Broadway, Ste. 704, New York, NY 10001
Cateret Writers, PO Box 2284, Morehead City, NC 28557
Cathexis Northwest Press, 5524 NE 12th Ave., Portland, OR 97211
Cave Wall Press, PO Box 29546, Greensboro, NC 27429-9546
Centered, 150 Berle Rd., South Windsor, CT 06074
Central Avenue Publishing, 254-1582 Gulf Rd., Point Roberts, WA 98281
Červená Barva Press, PO Box 440357, W. Somerville, MA 02144
Chaffey Review, Chaffey College, Rancho Cucamonga, CA 91737-3002
Chaffin Journal, Mattox 103, 521 Lancaster Ave., Richmond, KY 40475
Charles River Journal, PO Box 15274, Boston, MA 02215
Chattahoochee Review, 555 N. Indian Creek Dr., Clarkston, GA 30021
Cheap Pop, 110 S. Canopy St, #B316, Lincoln, NE 68508
Chestnut Review, 213 N. Tioga St., #6751, Ithaca, NY 14850
Chinese Poetry Association, 5923 N. Artesian Ave., #2, Chicago, IL 60659
Chiron Review, 522 E. South Ave., St. John, KS 67576-2212
Cholla Needles, 6732 Conejo Ave., Joshua Tree, CA 92252
Cimarron Review, English, OSU, Stillwater, OK 74078
Cincinnati Review, English, PO Box 210069, Cincinnati, OH 45221
Cinco Puntos Press, 701 Texas Ave., El Paso, TX 79901

Cinnamon Press, Ty Meirion, Glan yr afon, Tanygrisiau, Blaenau Ffestiniog, Gwynedd LL41 3SU, Wales

Circling Rivers, PO Box 8291, Richmond, VA 23226

Cirque Press, 3978 Defiance St., Anchorage, AK 99504

Citron Review, 291 Walnut Village Lane, Henderson, NV 89012

Cladach Publishing, PO Box 336144, Greeley, CO 80633-0603

Clash, PO Box 487, Claremont, NH 03743

Clockhouse, PO Box 784, Middleburg, VA 20118

Cloudbank, PO Box 610, Corvallis, OR 97339-0610

Coal City, English Dept, University of Kansas, Lawrence, KS 66045

Coal Hill Review, 5530 Penn Ave., Pittsburgh, PA 15206

Collective Unrest, 4960 Coronado Ave., San Diego, CA 92107

Colorado Review, CSU, English, Fort Collins, CO 80523-9105

Columbia Poetry Review, 600 So. Michigan Ave., Chicago, IL 60605

Columbia Review, 70 Morningside Dr., 1836 Wien, New York, NY 10027

Common Foundation, Amherst College, PO Box 5000, Amherst, MA 01002

The Comstock Review, 4956 St John Dr., Syracuse, NY 13215

Concho River Review, Angelo State Univ., San Angelo, TX 76909-0894

Concrete Wolf, PO Box 445, Tillamook, OR 97141-0445

Conjunctions, Bard College, Annandale, NY 12504-5000

Connecticut River Review, 9 Edmund Pl, West Hartford, CT 06119

Consequence, PO Box 323, Cohasset, MA 02025-0323

Constellations, 127 Lake View Ave., Cambridge, MA 02138-3366

Copper Nickel, UC-D, Campus Box 175, Denver, CO 80217-3364

Court Green, Columbia College, 600 S. Michigan Ave., Chicago, IL 60605

Cowboy Jamboree, 605 Wright's Crossing, Cobden, IL 62920

Crab Creek Review, P.O. Box 1682, Kingston, WA 98346

Crab Fat Magazine, 1128 Hermitage Rd., #303, Richmond, VA 23220

Craft, 70 SW Century Dr., Ste. 100442, Bend, OR 97702

Crazyhorse, College of Charleston, 66 George St, Charleston, SC 29424

Cream City Review, UW-M, PO Box 413, Milwaukee, WI 53201

Creative Nonfiction, 5119 Coral St., Pittsburgh, PA 15224

Cross & Hammer, 354 Consuelo Ave., San Antonio, TX 78228

Cultural Weekly, 3330 S. Peck Ave., #14, San Pedro, CA 90731

Cumberland River Review, English, TNU, Nashville, TN 37210-2877

Cutbank Magazine, 2803 Camino del Bosque, Santa Fe, NM 87507

Cutthroat, A Journal of the Arts, PO Box 2414, Durango, CO 81302

Cyberwit.net HIG 45 Kaushambi Kunj, Kalindipuram, Allahabad-211011 (U.P.) India


D. M. Kreg Publishing, 3985 Wonderland Hill Ave., #201, Boulder, CO 80304

Dash, Cal State Fullerton, English, PO Box 6848, Fullerton, CA 92834

december, P.O. Box 16130, St Louis, MO 63105

decomP, Jordan, 3002 Grey Wolf Cove, New Albany, IN 47150
Deep Overstock, 612 NE Brazee St, Portland, OR 97212
Deep Wild, 504 Walnut Rock Springs, WY 82901
Delacorte Review, Columbia U., 2950 Broadway, New York, NY 10027
Delmarva Review, PO Box 544, St. Michaels, MD 21663
Delta Poetry Review, 523 Guthrie Rd., Sterlington, LA 71280
Deluge, Cunningham, 260 Davis Estates Rd., Athens, GA 30606
Diode Editions, PO Box 5585, Richmond, VA 23220
Dionysia Press, 1205 E. 13th St., Lawrence, KS 66044-3609
The DMQ Review, 16393 Bonnie Lane, Los Gatos, CA 95032
Dream Pop Press, PO Box 2924, Taos, NM 87571
Driftwood Press, 14737 Montoro Dr., Austin, TX 78728
Drunk Monkeys, 252 N Cordova St, Burbank, CA 91505
Dryland, 4437 Radium Dr., Los Angeles, CA 90032

Eastern Iowa Review, 6332 33rd Avenue Dr., Shellsburg, IA 52332
Ecotone, UNCW, 601 S. College Rd., Wilmington, NC 28403-5938
805 Lit + Art, 1301 Barcarrota Blvd W, Brandenton, FL 34205
Ekphrasis, PO Box 161236, Sacramento, CA 95816-1236
Ekphrastic Review, 602-49 St. Clair Ave West, Toronto, ON M4V 1K6, Canada
Electric Literature, Ste. 26, 147 Prince St., Brooklyn, NY 11201
Elephants Never, 241-B Crafton Ave., Staten Island, NY 10314
Elm Leaves, English, Ketchum 301A, 1300 Elmwood Ave., Buffalo, NY 14222
The Emrys Journal, PO Box 8813, Greenville, SC 29604
Encircle Publications, P.O. Box 187, Farmington, ME 04938
Epiphany, 133 7th Ave., #4, Brooklyn, NY 11215
Epoch, 251 Goldwin Smith Hall, Cornell University, Ithaca NY 14853
Ethel, 1001 Willow Pl., Lafayette, CO 80026
Evansville Review, UE, 1800 Lincoln Ave., Evansville, IN 47722
Event, PO Box 2503, New Westminster, BC, V3L 5B2, Canada
Evening Street Press & Review, 2881 Wright St, Sacramento, CA 95821
Exile Editions, 901–1175 Broadview Ave., Toronto, ON M4K 2S9, Canada
Exit 13, PO Box 423, Fanwood, NJ 07023
Eye to the Telescope, SFPA, UNI, Gotera, Cedar Falls, IA 50701-0502

F. Y. D. Media, 5 Morgan Rd., Bell Canyon, CA 91307
failbetter, 2022 Grove Ave., Richmond, VA 23220
Fairy Tale Review, English Dept, Univ. of Arizona, Tucson, AZ 85721
Falling Star, McGee, 487 Encino Vista Dr., Thousand Oaks, CA 91362
Fiction, College of NY, English, Convent Ave & 138th St, NY, NY 10031
Fiction International, SDSU, English, 5500 Campanile Dr., San Diego, CA 92182-6060
Fiction on the Web, 12 Leigham Vale, London SW2 3JH, UK

Fiction Week Literary Review, 887 South Rice Rd., Ojai, CA 93023

Fiddlehead, Box 4400, Univ. New Brunswick, Fredericton NB E3B 5A3, Canada

Field, 50 North Professor St, Oberlin, OH 44074-1091

Figure 1, 286 Union Ave., #4A, Brooklyn, NY 11211

Fine Print Press, PO Box 49102, Austin, TX 78765

Finishing Line Press, PO Box 1626, Georgetown, KY 40324

Five Points, Georgia State University, Box 3999, Atlanta, GA 30302

Fixing Island, 1125 Brookside Ave., #B25, Indianapolis, IN 46202

Flash Back Fiction, Jendrzejewski, 2 Pearce Close, Cambridge, CB3 9LY, UK

Flash Fiction, Balboa, 3448 Colonial Ave., Los Angeles, CA 90066

Flash Flood, Jendrzejewski, 2 Pearce Close, Cambridge CB3 9LY UK

Floating Bridge, 909 NE 43rd St, #205, Seattle, WA 98105

Flock, 6001 Thomaston Rd., Macon, GA 31220

Florida Review, PO Box 161346, Orlando, FL 32816-1346

Flowersong Books, 1218 N. 15th St., McAllen, TX 78501

Flying South, Lindahl, 546 Birch Creek Rd., McLeansville, NC 27301

Foglifter, 1200 Clay St., #4, San Francisco, CA 94108

Folio, American University, Literature, Washington, DC 20016

Fomite, 58 Peru St., Burlington, VT 05401-8606

Foothill Poetry Journal, 160 E. 10th St, Claremont, CA 91711-6186

Forge, 4018 Bayview Ave., San Mateo, CA 94403-4310

Four Way Books, 11 Jay St, 4th Fl., New York, NY 10013

Four Way Review, 1217 Odyssey Dr., Durham, NC 27713

Fourth Genre, 434 Farm Lane, Rm 235, MSU, East Lansing, MI 48824

Free Inquiry, PO Box 664, Amherst, NY 14226-0664

Free State Review, 3222 Rocking Horse Lane, Aiken, SC 29801

Freshwater Literary Journal, ACC, 170 Elm St, Enfield, CT 06082

Frontier Poetry, PO Box 700, Joshua Tree, CA 92252

Funicular Magazine, 16720 111 St, Edmonton, AB T5X 2R4, Canada

Funny Looking Dog, 918 N. Glenwood Ave., #15, Chicago, IL 60640


Galleywinter Poetry, 2778 Elizabeth PL, Lebanon, OR 97355

Garden Oak Press, 1953 Huffstatler St, Ste. A, Rainbow, CA 92028

Gargoyle Magazine, 3819 13th St No,, Arlington, VA 22201-4922

Gelles-Cole Literary Enterprises, PMB 01-408, 2163 Lima Loop, Laredo, TX 78045

Gemini Magazine, PO Box 1485, Onset, MA 02558

The Georgia Review, University of Georgia, Athens, GA 30602-9009

The Gettysburg Review, Gettysburg College, Box 2446, Gettysburg, PA 17325

GHLL, Green Hills Literary Lantern, Baldwin Hall 209, 100 East Normal St, Kirksville, MO 63501-4221

Ghost Parachute, 2262 Tall Oak Ct., Sarasota, FL 34232

Gigantic Sequins, 209 Avon St, Breaux Bridge, LA 70517

Gival Press, PO Box 3812, Arlington, VA 22203

Glass Lyre Press, PO Box 2693, Glenview, IL 60025

Glass Poetry Press, PO Box 6654, Toledo, OH 43612

Glassworks, 201 Mullica Hill Rd., Glassboro, NJ 08028-1701

Gobshite Quarterly, 338 NE Roth St, Portland, OR 97211-1082

Gold Man Review, 4626 Nantucket Dr., Redding, CA 96001

Gordon Square Review, 10429 Baltic Rd., Cleveland, OH 44102

Grain Magazine, PO Box 3986, Regina, SK S4P 3R9, Canada

Granta, 12 Addison Ave., Holland Park, London W11 4QR, UK

The Gravity of the Thing, 17028 SE Rhone St, Portland, OR 97236

Grayson Books, PO Box 270549, West Hartford, CT 06127

great weather for MEDIA, 515 Broadway, #2B, New York, NY 10012

Greate Idiot, 2421 10th St, Irving, TX 75060

Green Hills Literary Lantern, TSU, English, Kirksville, MO 63501-4221

Green Linden Press, 208 Broad St South, Grinnell, IA 50112

Green Mountains Review, Johnson State College, 337 College Hill, Johnson, VT 05656

Green Writers Press, 139 Main St., #501, Brattleboro, VT 05301

Greensboro Review, MFA Writing, UNC, Greensboro, NC 27402-6170

Grid Books/Off the Grid Press, 118 Wilson St, Beacon, NY 12508

Grist, 301 McClung Tower, Univ. of Tennessee, Knoxville, TN 37996

Grub Street, English, TU, 8000 York Rd., Towson, MD 21252-0001

Guernica, Ste. 424, 157 Columbus Ave., New York, NY 10023

Guesthouse, Huffman, 219 N. Linn St, #210, Iowa City, IA 52245

Gunpowder Press, 1336 Camino Manadero, Santa Barbara, CA 93111

Gyroscope Review, 1 Declaration Lane, Gillette, WY 82716


Habitat, 150 West 30th St, Ste. 902, New York, NY 10001

Halfway Down the Stairs, Nigam, 200 S. Linden Ave., Pittsburgh, PA 15208

Hand Type Press, P.O. Box 3941, Minneapolis, MN 55403-0941

Harbour Publishing, PO Box 219, Madeira Park, BC V0N 2H0, Canada

Harmonia Press, 295 Willow St, #104, Stratford, ON N5A 3B8, Canada

The Harvard Advocate, 22 South St., Cambridge, MA 02138

Harvard Review, Lamont Library, Harvard Univ., Cambridge, MA 02138

Hayden's Ferry Review, P.O. Box 871401, Tempe, AZ 85287-1401

Headmistress Press, 60 Shipview Lane, Sequim, WA 98382

Healing Muse, SUNY Med. Univ., 618 Irving Ave., Syracuse, NY 13210

Heartland Review Press, 600 College St. Rd., Elizabethtown, KY 42701

Hedgehog Review, UV, PO Box 400816, Charlottesville, VA 22904

High Shelf Press, 5524 NE 12th Ave., Portland, OR 97211

Highland Park Poetry, 376 Park Ave., Highland Park, IL 60035

Hip Pocket Press, 5 Del Mar Court, Orinda, CA 94563

Hippocampus Magazine, 210 W. Grant St, #108, Lancaster, PA 17603

Hobart, PO Box 1658, Ann Arbor, MI 48106

The Hollins Critic, Hollins University Box 9538, 7916 Williamson Rd., Roanoke, VA 24020

Hong Kong Review, Delgado, 4700 SW 94 Ct Miami, FL 33165

Hoot Review, 4534 Osage Ave., Philadelphia, PA, 19143

The Hopper, 4935 Twin Lakes Rd., #36, Boulder, CO 80301

Hot Metal Bridge, English, Univ. of Pittsburgh, 4200 Fifth Ave., Pittsburgh, PA 15260

Howl, English Dept, Copper Mountain College, 6162 Rotary Way, PO Box 1398, Joshua Tree, CA 92252-0879

Hoxie Gorge Review, SUNY, English, PO Box 2000, Cortland, NY 13045

The Hudson Review, 33 West 67th St, New York, NY 10023

Human/Kind Journal, 4 Taylors Mill Ln, Wilmington, DE 19808

Hypertext, c/o Rice, 1821 W. Melrose St., Chicago, IL 60657

Hysterical Literary, 485 7th Ave., #2, Brooklyn, NY 11215


I-70 Review, 5021 S. Tierney Dr., Independence, MO 64055

Ibbetson Street Press, 25 School Street, Somerville, MA 02143

The Idaho Review, Boise State, 1910 University Dr., Boise, ID 83725

Ilanot Review, English, Bar-Ilan Univ., 52 900 Ramat-Gan, Israel

Illuminations, College of Charleston, 66 George St, Charleston, SC 29424

Image, 3307 Third Avenue West, Seattle, WA 98119

Indianapolis Review, 5906 W. 25th St, Apt. B, Speedway, IN 46224

Inner Child Press, 202 Wiltree Court, State College, PA 16801

Into the Void, 801-200 Jameson Ave., Toronto, ON M6K 2Z6, Canada

Inverted Syntax, PO Box 2044, Longmont CO 80502

The Iowa Review, 308 EPB, University of Iowa, Iowa City, IA 52242

Iris G. Press, 1838 Edenwald Ln, Lancaster, PA 17601


J Journal, 524 West 59th St, 7th Fl, New York, NY 10019

Jabberwock Review, MSU., P.O. Box E, Mississippi State, MS 39762

Jacar Press, 6617 Deerview Trail, Durham, NC 27712

Jaded Ibis Press, 4392 Trias St, San Diego, CA 92103

Jellyfish Review, Medit 1, D26KF, TJD, 11470 Jakarta Barat, Indonesia

Jersey Devil Press, Sweeney, 813 Waverly Ave., Neptune, NJ 07753

jmww, 2306 Altisma Way, #116, Carlsbad, CA 92009

The Journal, Ohio State Univ., 164 Annie & John Glenn Ave., Columbus, OH 43210

jubilat, South College, U. Mass, Amherst, MA 01003

Juked, 108 New Mark Esplanade, Rockville, MD 20850

Juniper, 47 Robina Ave., Toronto, ON M6C 3Y5, Canada

JuxtaProse, 4430 Aster St, Springfield, OR 97478

Kallisto Gaia Press, 1801 E. 51st St, Ste. 365-246, Austin, TX 78723

Kaya Press, (c/o USC ASE), 3620 South Vermont Ave., KAP 462, Los Angeles, CA 90089

Kelsay Books, 502 S. 1040 E, #A119, American Fork, UT 84003

Kelsey Review, MCCC, 1200 Old Trenton Rd., West Windsor, NJ 08550

Kenyon Review, Finn House, 102 W. Wiggin St, Gambier, OH 43022

Kerf, COR, 883 W. Washington Blvd., Crescent City, CA 95531-8361

Kestrel, Fairmont State Univ., 1201 Locust Ave., Fairmont, WV 26554

Kitty Wang, PO Box 5, North Branford, CT 06471

Knights Library Magazine, 7460 Drew Circle, #9, Westland, MI 48185

Ko(A) Media, 92 Parkview Loop, Staten Island, NY 10314

Kyoto Journal, 76-1 Tenno-cho, Okazaki, Sakyo-ku Kyoto-shi Kyoto-shi, 606-8334, Japan

KYSO Flash, PO Box 28386, Bellingham, WA 98228


L'Éphémère, 253 College St, #1312-D, Toronto, ON M5T 1R5, Canada

Lady/Liberty/Lit, 667 Country Club Dr., Incline Village, NV 89451

Lake Effect Humanities, 4951 College Drive, Erie, PA 16563-1501

Lascaux Review, 3155 Pebble Beach Dr., #10, Conway, AR 72034

Latin American Literature Today, University of Oklahoma, Kaufman Hall #106, 780 Van Vleet Oval, Norman, OK 73019

Laurel Review, NWMSU, 800 University Dr., Marysville, MO 64468

Lavender Review, P.O. Box 275, Eagle Rock, MO 65641-0275

Light, 500 Joseph C. Wilson Blvd., CPU Box 271051, Rochester, NY 14627

Lilipoh Publishing, 317 Church St, Phoenixville, PA 19460

Lily Poetry Review, 223 Winter Street Whitman, MA 02382

Liminal Books, 8456 Indian Hills Dr., Nashville, TN 37221

Liminal Residency, 47c Anerley Rd., London, SE14 2AS, UK

Lips, P.O. Box 616, Florham Park, NJ 07932

Liquid Imagination, 7800 Loma Del Norte Rd. NE, Albuquerque, NM 87109

The Literary Hatchet, 345 Charlotte White Rd., West Port, MA 02790

Literary House Press, Washington College, 300 Washington Ave., Chesterton, MD 21620

Literary Review, Fairleigh Dickinson U., M-GH2-01, 285 Madison Ave., Madison, NJ 07940

LitMag, Greeley Square Station, PO Box 20091, New York, NY 10001

Little Blue Marble, 37-1015 Ironwork Passage, Vancouver, BC V6H 3R4 Canada

Little Fiction/Big Truths, 1608-1910 Lake Shore Blvd. W., Toronto, ON M6S 1A2, Canada

Live Mag!, P.O, Box 1215, Cooper Station, New York, NY 10276

Livingston Press, Stn 22, Univ. West Alabama, Livingston, AL 35470

Loch Raven Review, 1306 Providence Rd., Towson, MD 21286

Longreads, 189 Smith Ave., Kingston, NY 12401

Longridge Review, 325 W. Colonial Hwy, Hamilton, VA 20158

Longship Press, 1122 4th St., San Rafael, CA 94901

Lost Balloon, 1402 Highland Ave., Berwyn, IL 60402

Louisville Review, Spalding U., 851 South 4th St., Louisville, KY 40203

Loving Healing Press, 5145 Pontiac Trail, Ann Arbor, MI 48105-9238

Lucent Dreaming, 122 Woodlands Rd., Barry, Vale of Glamorgan CF62 8EE, UK

Lumina, Sarah Lawrence College, 1 Mead Way, Bronxville, NY 10708


The MacGuffin, 18600 Haggerty Rd., Livonia, MI 48152

Madcap Review, 245 Wallace Rd., Goffstown, NH 03045

Madville Publishing, PO Box 358, Lake Dallas, TX 75065

Manhattan Review, 440 Riverside Dr., #38, New York, NY 10027

Mānoa, UH, 1733 Donaghho Rd., #626, Honolulu, HI 96822

The Mantle, 21-33 36th St, Astoria, NY 11105

Marsh Hawk Press, PO Box 206, East Rockaway, NY 11518-0206

Matchbook, 333 Harvard St, #5, Cambridge, MA 02139

Matter, 212-30 23rd Ave., #1K, Bayside, NY 11360

Mayapple Press, 362 Chestnut Hill Rd., Woodstock, NY 12498-2419

McSweeney's, 849 Valencia St, San Francisco, CA 94110

The Meadow, VISTA B300, 7000 Dandini Blvd., Reno, NV 89512

Medusa's Laugh, 340 Quinnipiac St, Bldg. 40, Wallingford, CT 06492

Menacing Hedge, 424 SW Kenyon St, Seattle, WA 98106

Mercer University Press, 1501 Mercer University Dr., Macon, GA 31207

Meridian, Univ. of VA, PO Box 400145, Charlottesville, VA 22904-4145

Michigan Quarterly Review, 0576 Rackham Bldg., 915 E. Washington St, Ann Arbor, MI 48109

Michigan State University Press, 1405 S. Harrison Rd., Ste. 25, Manly Miles Bldg., East Lansing, MI 48823

Micro Press, 1001 Willow PL, Lafayette, CO 80026

Mid-American Review, BGSU, English, Bowling Green, OH 43403

Midway Journal, 216 Banks St, #2, Cambridge, MA 02138

Midwest Fastener, 9031 Shaver Rd., Kalamazoo, MI 49024

Mikrokosmos, Lindquist 620, 1845 Fairmount St, Wichita, KS 67260

Milk & Cake Press, PO Box 13177, Hamilton, OH 45013

The Minnesota Review, Virginia Tech, 202 Major Williams Hall, Blacksburg, VA 24061

Minola Review, 669-A Crawford St, Toronto, ON M6G 3K1, Canada

Misfit Magazine, 143 Furman St, Schenectady, NY 12304-1113

Mississippi Review, USM, 118 College Dr., #5144, Hattiesburg, MS 39406-0001

Missouri Review, 357 McReynolds Hall, UMO, Columbia MO 65211

Mizna, 2446 University Ave. West, #115, Saint Paul, MN 55114

Mobius, Journal of Social Change, 149 Talmadge, Madison, WI 53704

MockingHeart Review, 2783 Iowa St, #2, Baton Rouge, LA 70802

Modern Haiku, PO Box 930, Portsmouth RI 02871-0930

Modern Language Studies, Susquehanna Univ., English, 514 University Ave., Selinsgrove, PA 17870-1164

Moon City, English, MSU, 901 So National Ave., Springfield, MO 65897

Moon Park Review, PO Box 87, Dundee, NY 14837

Moonpath Press, PO Box 445, Tillamook, OR 97141-0445

Moon Pie Press, 16 Walton St, Westbrook, ME 04092

Moria, Woodbury U., 7500 N. Glenoaks Blvd., Burbank, CA 91504

Mount Hope, RWU, 1 Old Ferry Rd., GHH Bldg., Bristol, RI 02809

Mountain State Press, PO Box 1281, Scott Depot, WV 25560

Mud Season Review, Post, 80 Austin Dr., #94, Burlington, VT 05401

Muddy River Poetry Review, 15 Eliot St, Chestnut Hill, MA 02467

Muse-Pie Press, 73 Pennington Ave., Passaic, NJ 07055

Muzzle, S. Edwards, 107 Shaftsbury Rd., Clemson, SC 29631

Mythic Delirium, 3514 Signal Hill Ave. NW, Roanoke, VA 24017-5148


Narrative, 2443 Fillmore St, #214, San Francisco, CA 94115

Nashville Review, English, VU, 331 Benson Hall, Nashville, TN 37235

Nat Brut, 1509 W. Davis St, Burlington, NC 27215

National Flash Fiction Day, 2 Pearce Close, Cambridge, Cambridgeshire CB3 9LY, UK

Natural Bridge, English, UMSL, 1 University Blvd., St Louis, MO 63121

Naugatuck River Review, PO Box 368, Westfield, MA 01086

Negative Capability Press, USA, English, Mobile, AL 36688-0002

Neon Books, 15/2 Gordon St, Edinburgh, EH6 8NW, UK

New Delta Review, LSU, Allen Hall 15, Baton Rouge, LA 70803

New England Review, Middlebury College, Middlebury, VT 05753

New Flash Fiction, 210 W. Lincoln Ave., Indianola, IA 50125

The New Guard, PO Box 472, Brunswick, ME 04011

New Internationalist, 106–108 Cowley Rd., Oxford OX4 1JE, UK

New Limestone Review, English, 1249 Patterson Office Tower, Lexington, KY 40506

New Ohio Review, OU, English, 360 Ellis Hall, Athens, OH 45701

New Pop Lit, 2074 17th St, Wyandotte, MI 48192

New Quarterly, 290 Westmount Rd. N., Waterloo, ON N2L 3G3, Canada

New Rivers Press, 1104 7th Ave. S., Moorhead, MN 56563

The New Territory Magazine, Foster, 2002 6th Ave., Canyon, TX 79015

New Verse News, Les Belles H-11, Serpong Utara, Tang Sel 15310, Indonesia

New World Writing, 85 Hardwood Rd., Glenwood, NY 14069

New York Quarterly, PO Box 470, Beacon, NY 12508

Newfound Journal, 6428 Alamo Ave., St. Louis, MO 63105

NewSeason Books, PO Box 1403, Havertown, PA 19083

Newtown Literary, 61-15 97th St, #11C, Rego Park, NY 11374

Night Ballet Press, Borsenik, 123 Glendale Ct, Elyria, OH 44035

Night Picnic Press, PO Box 3819, New York, NY 10163-3819

Nightboat Books, 310 Nassau Ave., Unit 202, Brooklyn, NY 11222-3813

Nimrod, Univ. of Tulsa, 800 South Tucker Dr., Tulsa, OK 74104

Nine Muses Poetry, 'Y Dderwen' 17 Snowdon St, Y Felinheli, Gwynedd LL56 4HQ, Wales

Ninth Letter, 608 S. Wright St, Urbana, IL 61801

No Rest Press, 2724 S. Crowell St, Chicago, IL 60608

Noon, 1392 Madison Ave., PMB 298, New York, NY 10029

North Carolina Literary Review, ECU Mailstop 555 English, Greenville, NC 27858-4353

Northern California Writers, 2580 E. Harmony Rd., #201, Fort Collins, CO 80528

Nowhere Magazine, 1582 Atlantic Ave., Brooklyn, NY 11213


Offcourse, 6 Oak Dr., Albany, NY 12203

The Offing, PO Box 220020, Brooklyn, NY 11211

Ogham Stone, University of Limerick, Limerick, Ireland

Okay Donkey, 3756 Bagley Ave., Unit 206, Los Angeles, CA 90401

One Story, 232 3rd St., #A108, Brooklyn, NY 11215

Orbis, 17 Greenhow Ave., West Kirby, Wirral, CH48 5EL, UK

Orca, 6516 112th Street Ct., Gig Harbor, WA 98332

Origami Poems Project, 1948 Shore View Dr., Indialantic, FL 32903

Orion, 187 Main St, Great Barrington, MA 01230

Osiris, 106 Meadow Lane, Greenfield, MA 01301

Outlook Springs, 193 Leighton St, Bangor, M 04401

Oversound, 1202 Woodrow St, Columbia, SC 29205

Ovunque Siamo, 17 Douglas St, Ambler, PA 19002

Oyster River Pages, 1 Greenwood Ave., Glen Burnie, MO 21061


P. R. A. Publishing, PO Box 211701, Martinez, GA 30917

PS Publishing, Grosvenor House, 1 New Rd., Hornsea, East Yorkshire, HU18 1PG, UK

Paddock Review, 452 Gen. John Wayne Blvd., Georgetown, KY 40324

Painted Bride Quarterly, Fitts, 2222 S. 13th St, Philadelphia, PA 19148

Palette Poetry, PO Box 700, Joshua Tree, CA 92252

Paloma Press, 110 28th Ave., San Mateo, CA 94403

Pank, 2347 Hollywood Dr., Pittsburgh, PA 15235

Paper Crown Press, 6903 Jackson St., Guttenberg, NJ 07093

Paper Darts, 1310 West 28th St., #3, Minneapolis, MN 55408

Parhelion, 13142 Hampton Meadows Place, Chesterfield, VA 23832

Paris Morning Publications, PO Box 16023, Saint Paul, MN 55116

The Paris Review, 544 West 27th St, New York, NY 10001

Parks and Points, 707 Beverley Rd., #2K, Brooklyn, NY 11218

Pasque Petals, PO Box 294, Kyle, SD 57752

Passages North, English, NMU, 1401 Presque Isle Ave., Marquette, MI 49855-5363

Paul Dry Books, 1700 Sansom St, Ste. 700, Philadelphia, PA 19103

Paycock Press, 3819 13th St. No., Arlington, VA 22201

Peach Mag, 138 Harvard Pl., #2, Syracuse, NY 13210

Peach Velvet Mag, 101 N. Five Points Rd., #I-3, West Chester, PA 19380

Peauxdunque Review, 4609 Page Dr., Metairie, LA 70003

Pelekinesis, 112 N. Harvard Ave., #65, Claremont, CA 91711

Pembroke Magazine, P.O. Box 1510, Pembroke, NC 28372-1510

Pen & Anvil Press, PO Box 15274, Boston, MA 02215

Pen + Brush, 29 East 22nd St, New York, NY 10010

Penn Review, 3805 Locust Walk, Philadelphia, PA 19104

Permafrost, Univ. of Alaska, P.O. Box 755720, Fairbanks, AK 99775

Perugia Press, PO Box 60364, Florence, MA 01062

Phoebe, GMU., MSN 2C5, 4400 University Place, Fairfax, VA 22030

Pigeon Pages, 443 Park Ave. S., #1004, New York, NY 10016

Pigeonholes, 5329 9 Avenue, Delta, BC V4M 1V8, Canada

The Pinch, English Dept., 467 Patterson Hall, Memphis, TN 38111

Pinesong, Griffin, 131 Bon Aire Rd., Elkin, NC 28621

Pink Plastic House, PO Box 1491, Pensacola, FL 32591

Pinyon, 23847 V66 Trail, Montrose, CO 81403

Pithead Chapel, 110 Montgomery St, #403, Syracuse, NY 13202

Pleiades, UCM, English, Warrensburg, MO 64093-5214

Ploughshares, Emerson College, 120 Boylston St, Boston, MA 02116

Poet Lore, 4508 Walsh St, Bethesda, MD 20815

Poetic Justice, 1774 SE Port St Lucie Blvd, Port Saint Lucie, FL 34952

poeticdiversity, 6028 Comey Ave., Los Angeles, CA 90034

Poetry Box, 2228 NW 159th Place, Beaverton, OR 97006-7612

Poetry, 61 West Superior St, Chicago, IL 60654

Poetry Northwest, 2000 Tower St, Everett, WA 98201-1390

Poetry Society of Texas, 556 Royal Glade Dr., Keller, TX 76248-9735

Poetry South, 1100 College St, MUW-1634, Columbus, MS 39701

Poets' Hall Press, Brown, 433 Beachgrove Dr., Erie, PA 16505

Poets Wear Prada, 533 Bloomfield St., #2, Hoboken, NJ 07030

The Point, 2 N. LaSalle St., Ste. 2300, Chicago, IL 60602

Poise and Pen, 11323 126th St, Edmonton, AB T5M 0R5, Canada

Pole to Pole Publishing, PO Box 85, Woodbine, MD 21771

Ponder Review, 1100 College St, MUW-1634, Columbus, MS 39701

Popnoir Editions, 1851 Oneida Court, Windsor, ON N8Y 1S9, Canada

Porter House Review, 601 University Dr., #365, San Marcos, TX 78666

Posit, 237 Thompson St, #8A, New York, NY 10012

Potato Soup Journal, 13303 W. Engelmann Dr., Boise, ID 83713

Potomac Review, 51 Mannakee St, MT/212, Rockville, MD 20850

Prairie Journal, 28 Crowfoot Terr. NW, PO Box 68073, Calgary, AB, T3G 3N8, Canada

Prairie Schooner, PO Box 880334, Univ. Nebraska, Lincoln, NE 68588

Prelude, 589 Flushing Ave., #3E, Brooklyn, NY 11206

Presence, Caldwell U., English, 120 Bloomfield Ave., Caldwell, NJ 07006

Press 53, PO Box 30314, Winston-Salem, NC 27130

Pretty Owl, Andrews, 423 Cedarville St, Pittsburgh, PA 15224

Printed Words, Steel, 11 Seymour Rd., Flat, Manchester, M8 5BQ, UK

Prism International, UBC, Buch E462, 1866 Main Mall, Vancouver BC V6T 1Z1, Canada

Prism Review, Univ. of La Verne, 1950 Third St, La Verne, CA 91750

Progenitor, ACC, Box 9002, 5900 S. Santa Fe Dr., Littleton, CO 80160

Prospect Park Books, 2359 Lincoln Ave., Altadena, CA 91001

Provincetown Arts, 650 Commercial St., Provincetown, MA 02657

Psaltery & Lyre, 4917 E. Oregon St, Bellingham, WA 98226

A Public Space, 323 Dean St, Brooklyn, NY 11217

Pulp Literature Press, 21955 16th Ave., Langley, BC, V2Z 1K5, Canada

Puna Press, PO Box 7790, Ocean Beach, CA 92107

Punctuate, English, 600 South Michigan Ave., Chicago, IL 60605


Qu Magazine, Queens Univ., 1900 Selwyn Ave., Charlotte, NC 28274

Quarterly West, Univ. of Utah, English/LNCO 3500, 255 S. Central Campus Dr., Salt Lake City, UT 84112-9109

Quiet Lightning, 3921-A Webster St, Oakland, CA 94609

Quill and Parchment, 467 W. Cedar Lake Rd., Greenbush, MI 48738

Quip, Bailey, 1920 SE Madison St., Portland, OR 97214


Rabbit Catastrophe Press, 411 N Upper St, #2, Lexington, KY 40508

Rabid Oak, 8916 Duncanson Dr., Bakersfield, CA 93311

Radar Poetry, 19 Coniston Ct, Princeton, NJ 08540

Radix Media, 522 Bergen St, Brooklyn, NY 11217

Raleigh Review, Box 6725, Raleigh, NC 27628

Raconteur, 2261 Lakeshore Blvd. W., Toronto, ON M8V 3×1, Canada

Raritan, Rutgers, 31 Mine St., New Brunswick, NJ 08901

Rattle, 12411 Ventura Blvd., Studio City, CA 91604

Raven Chronicles, 15528 12th Ave. NE, Shoreline, WA 98155

The Raw Art Review, 8320 Main St., Ellicott City, MD 21043

Read Furiously, 555 Grand Ave., #77078, West Trenton, NJ 08628

Red Bridge Press, PO Box 591104, San Francisco, CA 94159

Red Fez, 3811 Northeast Third Court, #G-208, Renton, WA 98056-8510

Redactions, 182 Nantucket Dr., Apt U, Clarksville, TN 37040

Redivider, Emerson College, 120 Boylston St, Boston, MA 02116

Reed Magazine, SJSU, English, 1 Washington Sq., San José, CA 95192

Resolute Bear Press, PO Box 14, 1175 US Rte 1, Robbinston, ME 04671

Reunion: The Dallas Review, PO Box 830688, Richardson, TX 75080

Rhythm & Bones Press, 2099 Cocalico Rd., Birdsboro, PA 19508-8566

Riddled with Arrows, 117 McCann Rd., Newark, DE 19711

Ristau: A Journal of Being, 1935 Gardiner Ln, #A-8, Louisville, KY 40205

River Heron Review, PO Box 543, New Hope, PA 18938

River Teeth, English, Ball State Univ., 2000 W. University Ave., Muncie, IN 47306

Roadrunner, Fordham, 4500 Riverwalk Pkwy, Riverwalk, CA 92515

Rockford Writers Guild, PO Box 858, Rockford, IL 61105

Rogue Agent Journal, 5441 Covode Place, Pittsburgh, PA 15217

Rogue Phoenix Press, 7442 Lofty Loop SE, Salem, OR 97317

Round Table Literary Journal, Hopkinsville Community College, Hopkinsville, KY 42240

Rumble Fish Quarterly, 2020 Park Ave., Richmond, VA 23220

Ruminate, 2723 SE 115th Ave., Portland, OR 97266

The Rupture, 2206 W. Broadway Ave., Spokane, WA 99201

Rust + Moth, 4470 S. Lemay Ave., #1108, Fort Collins, CO 80525


Sagging Meniscus Press, 115 Claremont Ave., Montclair, NJ 07042

Salamander, Suffolk U., English, 8 Ashburton Pl., Boston, MA 02108

Salina Bookshelf, 1120 W. University Ave., Ste. 102, Flagstaff, AZ 86001

Salmon Creek Journal, 14204 NE Salmon Creek Blvd., Vancouver, WA 98686

Salt Hill Journal, English, Syracuse Univ., Syracuse, NY 13244

San Pedro River Review, 5403 Sunnyview St, Torrance, CA 90505

Sand Journal, c/o O'Donovan, Sonnenallee 54, 12045 Berlin, Germany

Santa Barbara Literary Journal, Borda, 19 E. Islay St, Santa Barbara, CA 93101

Santa Fe Literary Review, 6401 Richards Ave., Santa Fe, NM 87508

Santa Monica Review, 1900 Pico Blvd., Santa Monica, CA 90405

Saranac Review, SUNY, English, 101 Broad St, Plattsburgh, NY 12901

Saturnalia Books, 105 Woodside Rd., Ardmore, PA 19003

Saw Palm, 4202 East Fowler Ave., CPR 107, Tampa, FL 33620

Scattering Skies Press, 3950 Kalai Waa St, D-103, Wailea, HI 96753

Scribble, 7137 Cedar Hollow Circle, Bradenton, FL 34203

Scribendi, MSC06-3890, 1 University of New Mexico, Albuquerque, NM 87131-0001

Seems, Lakeland Univ., W3718 South Drive, Plymouth, WI 53073-4878

Seventh Station Publishing, 27362 Tossamer, Mission Viejo, CA 92692

Sewanee Review, 735 University Ave., Sewanee, TN 37383

Shabda Press, 3343 E. Del Mar Blvd., Pasadena, CA 91107

Shade & Sellers, 3536 79th St, #53, Jackson Heights, NY 11372

Shade Mountain Press, PO Box 11393, Albany, NY 12211

Shallow Books, 8 Beach St, #7, New York, NY 10013

Shark Reef, Hammer, 90 Buck Way, Coupeville, WA 98239

Sheila-Na-Gig, 203 Meadowlark Rd., Russell, KY 41169

Shenandoah, Washington & Lee Univ., English, 204 W. Washington St, Lexington, KY 24450-2116

Shrew, 142 Mineola Blvd., #1, Mineola, NY 11501-3918

Sibling Rivalry Press, P.O. Box 26147, Little Rock, AR 72221

Silver Blade, 1574 County Road 250, Niota, TN 37826

Sinister Wisdom, 2333 McIntosh Rd., Dover, FL 33527-5980

Sinking City, 5975 SW 59th St, South Miami, FL 33143

Sixfold, 10 Concord Ridge Rd., Newtown, 06470

Sixteen Rivers Press, PO Box 640663, San Francisco, CA 94164-0663

Sky Island Journal, 1434 Sherwin Ave., Eau Claire, WI 54701

Slag Glass City, English, 2315 No. Kenmore Ave., Chicago, IL 60614

Sleet Magazine, 1846 Bohland Ave., St. Paul, MN 55116

Slice Literary, 150 Oak Lane, Dayton, ME 04005

Slippery Elm, University of Findlay, 1000 N. Main St, Box 1615, Findlay, OH 45840

Slipstream, Box 2071, Niagara Falls, NY 14301

Smartish Pace, 2221 Lake Ave., Baltimore, MD 21213

Snap Screen Press, 6 Dwinell Dr., Concord, NH 03301

So to Speak, MS 2C5, 4400 University Dr., Fairfax, VA 22030

The Southampton Review, 239 Montauk Hwy., Southampton, NY 11968

Southeast Review, English, Florida State U., Williams Bldg. 205, Tallahassee, FL 32306

Southern Humanities Review, 9088 Haley Center, Auburn Univ., Auburn, AL 36849-5202

The Southern Review, LSU, 338 Johnston Hall, Baton Rouge, LA 70803

Southwest Review, PO Box 750374, Dallas, TX 75275-0374

Space & Time, PO Box 214, Independence, MO 64051

Spadina Literary Review, 307-155 Kendal Av., Toronto, ON M5R 3S8, Canada

Sparks of Calliope, 716 N. Sheppard St, Ironton, MO 63650

Spelk, 20 Bell Rd., Belford Northumberland, NE70 7NY, UK

Spillway, 1296 Placid Ave., Ventura, CA 93004

Split Lip Magazine, 112 East 74th St, Apt 5N, New York, NY 10021

Split Rock Review, 30330 Engoe Rd., Washburn, WI 54891-5855

Split This Rock, 1301 Connecticut Ave. NW, #600, Washington, DC 20036

Splonk, 10 Mountpleasant Ave., Old Mountpleasant, Ballinasloe H53 R970, Co, Galway, Ireland

Spoon River, ISU, Campus Box 4241, Normal, IL 61790-4241

St Ōde Press, 171 Main St, Eastsound, WA 98245

Stairwell Books, 161 Lowther St, York, YO31 7LZ, UK

Star 82 Review, PO Box 8106, Berkeley, CA 94707

Still, 89 W. Chestnut St, Williamsburg, KY 40769

Still Point Arts, 193 Hillside Rd., Brunswick, ME 04011

Stockholm Review, 157 Eastern Rd., BN2 0AG, Brighton, UK

Story, 312 E. Kelso Rd., Columbus, OH 43202

Story Quarterly, English, Rutgers, 311 N. Fifth St, Camden, NJ 08102

Sugar House Review, PO Box 13, Cedar City, UT 84721

The Summerset Review, 25 Summerset Dr., Smithtown, NY 11787

The Sun, 107 North Roberson St, Chapel Hill, NC 27516

Sunbeam, 756 N 100th Ave., Hart, MI 49420

Sunlight Press, 3924 G Quail Ave., Phoenix, AZ 85050

Sunspot Literary Journal, PO Box 122, Hillsborough, NC 27278-0122

Sweet, 83 Carolyn Lane, Delaware, OH 43015

Sweet Tree Review, 423 E. North St, Bellingham, WA 98225

SWWIM Every Day, 301 NE 86th St, El Portal, FL 33138

Sybaritic Press, 12530 Culver Blvd., #3, Los Angeles, CA 90066

Sycamore Review, Purdue Univ., 500 Oval Dr., West Lafayette, IN 47907-2038


Tadorna Press, 306 N. Cayuga St, Ithaca, NY 18450

Tahoma Literary Review, PO Box 924, Mercer Island, WA 98040

Tar River Poetry, ECU, MS 159, Greenville, NC 27858-4353

Temz Review, 845 Dufferin Ave., London, ON, N5W 3J9, Canada

Terrain.org, P.O. Box 41484, Tucson, AZ 85717

Terrapin Books, 4 Midvale Ave., West Caldwell, NJ 07006

Territory, 3414 Meadowbrook Blvd., Cleveland Heights, OH 44118

Test Literary Series, 4918 N. Glenwood Ave., #15, Chicago, IL 60640

Texas Review Press, SHSU, Box 2146, Huntsville, TX 77341-2146

Thimble, 6399 Drexel Rd., Philadelphia, PA 19151

Third Flatiron, 4101 S. Hampton Cir., Boulder, CO 80301

32 Poems, English Dept, 60 South Lincoln St, Washington, PA 15301

Thirty West Publishing, 2622 Swede Rd., #C8, Norristown, PA 19401

This Broken Shore, 15 Sandspring Dr., Eatontown, NJ 07724

Thomas-Jacob Publishing, P.O. Box 390524, Deltona, FL 32739

3: A Taos Press, P.O. Box 370627, Denver, CO 80237

3 Elements Review, 198 Valley View Rd., Manchester, CT 06040

Theee Mile Harbor Press, PO Box 1, Stuyvesant, NY 12173

Three Rooms Press, 561 Hudson St, #33, New York, NY 10014

Threepenny Review, PO Box 9131, Berkeley, CA 94709

Thrush Poetry Journal, 889 Lower Mountain Dr., Effort, PA 18330

Tiger Bark Press, 202 Mildorf St., Rochester, NY 14609

Tipton Poetry Journal, 642 Jackson St., Brownsburg, IN 46112

Toho Journal, 2001 Hamilton St, #619, Philadelphia, PA 19130

Tortoise Books, 1415 W. Jonquil Ter. #3, Chicago, IL 60626-1211

Trio House Press, 2191 High Rigger PL, Fernandina Beach, FL 32034

TriQuarterly, English, University Hall 215, 1897 Sheridan Rd., Evanston, IL 60208

True Story, Creative Nonfiction Fdn., 5119 Coral St, Pittsburgh, PA 15224

Tule Review, Grellas, 1719 25th St, Sacramento, CA 95816

TulipTree Review, PO Box 723, Cañon City, CO 81215

Twist in Time, 132 Statesman Rd., Chalfont, PA 18914-3581

Two Sylvias Press, PO Box 1524, Kingston, WA 98346

Twyckenham Notes, 14223 Worthington Dr., Granger, IN 46530

Typehouse Magazine, PO Box 68721, Portland, OR 97268


Umbrella Factory, Winters, 227 Cattail Ct, Longmont, CA 80501

Unchaste Readers, PO Box 19102, Boulder, CO 80308

Under the Gum Tree, PO Box 5394, Sacramento, CA 95817

Under the Sun, 2121 Hidden Cove Rd., Cookeville, TN 38506

Undertow, 1905 Faylee Crescent, Pickering, ON L1V 2T3, Canada

University of North Texas Press, 1155 Union Circle #311336, Denton, TX 76203-5017

University of Oklahoma Press, 2800 Venture Dr., Norman, OK 73069

University of Wisconsin Press, 728 State St, #443, Madison, WI 53706-1428

Utopia Science Fiction, 145 N. Pearl St., Meriden, CT 06450


V Press LC, 36 Dover Dr., Taylors, SC 29687

Vagabond, 4342 Elenda St, Culver City, CA 90230

Valley Voices, MVSU 7242, 14000 Hwy 82 W., Itta Bena, MS 38941

Vallum, 5038 Sherbrooke St. W., PO Box 20377 CP Vendome, Montreal, QC H4A 1T0, Canada

Vamp Cat, 16 South Rd., Saffron Walden, Essex, CB11 3DH, UK

Véhicule Press, PO Box 42094 BP ROY, Montréal, Québec H2W 2T3, Canada

Veliz Books, PO Box 920243, El Paso, TX 79912

A Velvet Giant, 951 Carroll St., #3A, Brooklyn, NY 11225

Vestal Review, PO Box 35369, Brighton, MA 02135

Virginia Quarterly, 5 Boar's Head Lane, PO Box 400223, Charlottesville, VA 22904-4223

Virtual Zine Magazine, 101-B Junction Rd., TS20 1PX, UK

Vox Viola, 79 Gorham Rd., Fairfield, CT 06824


Waccamaw Journal, 100 Chanticleer Drive East, Conway, SC 29528

Wandering Aengus, 1459 North Beach, Box 334, Eastsound, WA 98245

War, Literature & the Arts, 2354 Fairchild Dr., Ste. 6D-149, USAF Academy, CO 80840-6242

Wards Lit Mag, 3212 E. Hillery Dr., Phoenix, AZ 85032

Washington Square Review, 58 W. 10th St., New York, NY 10011

Water~Stone Review, MS A1730, 1536 Hewitt Ave., St Paul, MN 55104

Wax Paper, 2906 Kenwood Ave., Los Angeles, CA 90007

Waxwing, 242 Orchard Hill, St. SE, Grand Rapids, MI 49506

Wayne State University Press, 4809 Woodward Ave., Detroit, MI 48201

Wesleyan University Press, 215 Long Lane, Middletown, CT 06459

West Coast Weird, 27362 Tossamer, Mission Viejo, CA 92692

Whale Road Review, 3900 Lomaland Dr., San Diego, CA 92106

Whistling Shade, 1495 Midway Pkwy, St Paul, MN 55108

Wigleaf, Univ. of Missouri, 114 Tate Hall, Columbia, MO 65211

The Wild Word, Zimmermannstrasse 6, 12163 Berlin, Germany

Willow Springs, 668 N. Riverpoint Blvd., #259, Spokane, WA 99202

Windmilk, Hofstra Univ., 109 Mason Hall, Hempstead, NY 11549

Wising Up Press, PO Box 2122, Decatur, GA 30031-2122

Witness, Black Mountain Inst, PO Box 455085, Las Vegas, NV 89154

Witty Partition, 136 Muriel St, Ithaca, NY 14850

WMG Publishing, 1845 SW Hwy 101, Ste. 2, Lincoln City, OR 97367

Wolf Ridge Press, 350 Parnassus Ave., #900, San Francisco, CA 94117

WomanSpeak, PO Box 90475, Anchorage, AK 99509

Woodhall Press, 81 Old Saugatuck Rd., Norwalk, CT 06855

The Worcester Review, PO Box 804, Worcester, MA 01613

WordFarm, 140 Lakeside Ave., A-303, Seattle, WA 98144-2633

Wordrunner eChapbooks, PO Box 613, Petaluma, CA 94953-0613

Words On The Street, 6 San Antonio Park, Salthill, Galway, Ireland

World Editions, 159 20th St, #1B, Office 1, Brooklyn, NY 11232

World Literature Today, 630 Parrington Oval, Ste. 110, Norman, OK 73019-4033

World Weaver Press, PO Box 21924, Albuquerque, NM 87154

Woven Tale Press, PO Box 2533, Setauket, NY 11733

Wraparound South, PO Box 8026, Statesboro, GA 30460

Wrath-Bearing Tree, 8550 Cirrus Ct, Colorado Springs, CO 80920

Writing Maps, Ap. De Correos 7050, Madrid 28080, Spain


Yellow Medicine Review, SMSU, 1501 State St, Marshall, MN 56258

Your Impossible Voice, 4972 Fairview Rd., Columbus, OH 43231


Zephyr Press, 400 Bason Dr., Las Cruces, NM 88005

Zoetrope: All Story, Sentinel Bldg., 916 Kearny St, San Francisco, CA 94133

Zone 3 Press, P.O. Box 4565, Clarksville, TN 37044

ZYZZYVA, 57 Post St, Ste. 604, San Francisco, CA 94104

# CONTRIBUTORS' NOTES

AAMINA AHMAD'S first novel is out soon from Riverhead Books. She holds an MFA from Iowa Writers' Workshop.

MOLLY ANTOPOL is author of *The Un-Americans*, a story collection published in 2014. She teaches at Stanford.

JULIA ARMFIELD is author of the story collection *Salt Slow*. She lives in London.

DAVID BAKER'S most recent book is *Swift: New and Selected Poems* (W. W. Norton, 2019).

KAREN E. BENDER is the author of two story collections and two novels. This is her third Pushcart Prize.

FRANK BIDART won the Pulitzer Prize for poetry in 2018.

LEILA CHATTI is author most recently of *Deluxe* (Copper Canyon, 2020).

SAMUEL CHENEY'S poems have appeared in *Meridian*, *Forklift Ohio*, *The Literary Review*, *Whiskey Island* and elswhere. He lives in Baltimore.

A. V. CHRISTIE (1963–2016) was the author of *Nine Skies*, winner of the National Poetry Series, and other books.

LYDIA CONKLIN was a Stegner Fellow and has published in *Tin House*, *Southern Review* and elsewhere.

LYDIA DAVIS is winner of the Man Booker International Prize. She is a short story writer, a novelist and translator.

MADELINE DEFREES was a Catholic Nun until 1973. She published two memoirs and eight poetry collections. She died in 2015 at age 95.

ANTHONY DOERR has appeared in four previous Pushcart Prize collections. His *All The Light We Cannot See* was a *New York Times* bestseller.

CAROLYN FERRELL teaches at Sarah Lawrence College. Her story collection is *Don't Erase Me*.

CHRIS FORHAN teaches at Butler University and is the author of three books of poetry and a memoir.

ALICE FRIMAN was poet-in-residence at Georgia College. Her *Blood Weather* was published by LSU Press.

V. V. GANESHANANTHAN'S novel is *Love Marriage* (Random House).

JOHN ROLFE GARDINER is an honorary member of the Mark Twain Society and is the author of several novels, most recently *The Magellan House* (2004).

KARL TARO GREENFELD'S books include the novel *Triburbia* and the memoir *Boy Alone*. He has appeared in many "best" collections.

T. R. HUMMER most recent book is *Afterlife* (Acre Books). He lives in Cold Spring, New York.

SANGAMITHRA IYER is the author of *The Lines We Drew* (2014, Hen Press). Her work has appeared in *N & J*, *Open City*, *One Green Planet* and elsewhere.

KRISTOPHER JANSMA is director of Creative Writing Studies at SUNY, New Paltz, New York.

MENG JIN is the author of *Little Gods*. She lives in San Francisco.

JOHN PHILIP JOHNSON'S two comic books of graphic poetry can be found at www.johnphilipjohnson.com.

ILYA KAMINSKY holds the Bourne Chair in Poetry at Georgia Institute of Technology.

INAM KANG is a Pakistani-born poet and curator. He directs the winter Tangerine Workshop.

POLLY DUFF KERTIS co-founded the Moby Dick Marathon in New York City. Her writing has appeared in *Tin House*, *No Tokens*, *Brooklyn Rail*, *Literary Mama* and elsewhere.

DARRELL KINSEY'S short fiction pieces have been featured in *Noon*, *Gettysburg Review* and Literary Hub.

TED KOOSER lives in Garland, Nebraska and has appeared in five Pushcart Prizes.

NAIRA KUZMICH was born in Armenia and lived in Los Angeles. She published nonfiction in *Ecotone*, *Threepenny Review*, *Guernica* and elsewhere before her death at age 29 in 2017.

KHALED MATTAWA'S *Fugitive Atlas* is just out from Graywolf Press. He edits *Michigan Quarterly Review*.

SHENA MCAULIFF teaches at Union College. Her novel is *The Good Echo* and essay collection is *Glass, Light Electricity*.

ELIZABETH MCCRACKEN'S most recent book is *Bowlaway*. A new collection of stories is due in 2021.

JO MCDOUGALL is the Poet Laureate of Arkansas.

JOYELLE MCSWEENEY is the author of ten books. She teaches at Notre Dame University.

DAVID MEANS has authored five story collection, and a novel, *Hystopia*, long listed for the 2016 Man Booker Prize.

JOHN MURILLO'S work is published by Four Way Books in New York.

LEIGH NEWMAN'S memoir is *Still Points North*. She is an editor at Catapult.

COLLEEN O'BRIEN'S chapbook is *Spool in The Maze*. Her work has appeared in *Fence, Kenyon Review* and *Antioch Review*.

PETER ORNER has published six books, most recently *Maggie Brown and Others*.

MATTHEW OLZMANN teaches at Dartmouth College and has published three poetry collections.

DUSTIN PEARSON'S 2019 book is *A Family Is A House* (C & R Press) He lives in Pittsburgh, Pennsylvania.

CATHERINE PIERCE teaches at Mississippi State University. She has published three poetry collections.

ROBERT PINSKY'S most recent book is *At The Foundling Hospital*. He lives in Cambridge, Massachusetts.

ALYCIA PIRMOHAMED is a doctoral candidate at the University of Edinburgh. She has published two chapbooks.

STANLEY PLUMLY died in April, 2019. His posthumous collection, *Middle Distance*, was published by W. W. Norton.

ESTNER RA works in Seoul, South Korea and helps provide mental and medical care for North Korean refugees. She is editor of *The Underwater Railroad*.

JANISSE RAY is author of five volumes of literary nonfiction and two books of eco-poetry.

NATASHA SAJÉ lives in Salt Lake City, Utah.

CLAIRE SCHWARTZ won the 2016 Button Poetry Contest. She edits poetry for *Jewish Currents*.

POPPY SEBAG-MONTEFIORE teaches modern Chinese fiction at King's College, London, and is at work of a novel.

AUSTIN SMITH'S two poetry collections are published by Princeton University Press. He teaches at Stanford.

CHRIS STUCK'S story collection, *Give My Love To The Savages*, is due soon from Amistad/HarperCollins.

BRIAN SWANN'S latest poetry collection, is *Sunday Out of Nowhere* (Sheep Meadow Press, 2018).

ANNIE SHEPPARD'S work has appeared in *Phoebe*, *McSweeney's* and *The Writer*.

TC TOLBERT is Tucson's Poet Laureate and author of *Gephyrmania* (Ahsahta Press).

JOSH TVRDY'S poems can be found in *Gulf Coast*, *Hobart* and elsewhere. He holds an MFA from North Carolina State University.

LUIS ALBERTO URREA'S volumes include *The House of Broken Angels*, a 2018 finalist for the NBCC award in fiction.

SHAWN VESTAL'S literary debut, *Godforsaken* (2014), won the PEN/Bingham Prize.

DAVID WOJAHN has published nine volumes of verse and two books of essays.

# INDEX

The following is a listing in alphabetical order by author's last name of works reprinted in the *Pushcart Prize* editions since 1976.

536

538

542

547

551

560